DECIPHER

DECIPHER

STEL PAVLOU

SIMON & SCHUSTER
A VIACOM COMPANY

First published in Great Britain by Simon & Schuster UK Ltd, 2001
A Viacom company

1 3 5 7 9 10 8 6 4 2

Simon & Schuster UK Ltd
Africa House
64–78 Kingsway
London WC2B 6AH

Simon & Schuster Australia
Sydney

A CIP catalogue record for this book is available from the British Library

ISBN Hardback 0–743–20857–9
ISBN Trade Paperback 0–743–20858–7

This book is a work of fiction. Names, characters, places and incidents are
either a product of the author's imagination or are used fictitiously. Any
resemblance to actual people living or dead, events or locales is entirely
coincidental.

The artwork on p143 is credited to Hannah Moseley.

Typeset by Palimpsest Book Production Limited,
Polmont, Stirlingshire
Printed and bound in Great Britain by Butler & Tanner Ltd, Frome and London

For Camille

TEP ZEPI

THE FIRST TIME

AVESTIC ARYANS — PRE-ISLAMIC IRAN — MIDDLE EAST

Ahura Mazda created Airyana Vaejo, the original paradise and birth-place of the Aryan race. There were seven months of summer and five of winter. But after Angra Mainyu, the Evil One, was finished, there were only two months of summer and ten of winter. A mighty serpent, intense cold, thick ice and snow is all that haunts the land now. It is so cold that nothing can survive there. Yima, instead of building an Ark, was ordered to make a *Var*, an underground place linking the four corners so that specimens of every living thing could be brought there and saved.

Excerpt from: *Tales of the Deluge: A Global Report on Cultural Self-Replicating Genesis Myths* Dr Richard Scott, 2008

EVIDENCE BEFORE THE UNITED STATES SENATE
WASHINGTON D.C.

June 14, 1960

(Based on actual transcripts)

'If this agreement is approved,' Senator Aiken said as he tapped out his ash from behind a thick veil of blue cigarette smoke, 'Antarctica becomes a country without a government. Of course, it doesn't have too much government now, but no government is provided for Antarctica under any conditions in the future?'

Herman Phleger shuffled through his papers and coughed, hoping to cash in on some spit. He failed. It was a hot, humid day. The brass and maple ceiling fans worked overtime. A whiff of freshly cut grass wafted in from the lawn outside. Manicured, the way mankind intended. And Herman Phleger was forced to cough again.

'Is there a problem, Mr Phleger?'

'Uh, yes, sir—' Phleger croaked. He looked around for a clerk. Stood.

'Please use the microphone in front of you, Mr Phleger. I think we're all agreed we can't quite hear you.' The Senator's smile to his colleagues was a craggy one. There was a ripple of humorless laughter from the rest of the committee. It echoed off the wood paneling and around the sparsely populated Congressional hearing room.

Phleger leaned down close to the gadget. The squeal of feedback was painful. 'Uh, I could use some more water, Senator.' He straightened his tie and re-took his seat.

Aiken waved at a clerk to take some water over to the State Department's legal advisor. After all, Herman Phleger was the man who had headed the US delegation at the Conference on Antarctica. He at least deserved a glass of water.

Phleger leaned in close to the microphone again as he adjusted his chair and thanked the Senator. He could almost hear the old bastard's cogs whirring from across the room. The Red scare. Grab some territory now while we still can. What with Khrushchev still fuming over that U-2 spyplane business back in May and Eisenhower on the defensive, sending 120 planes out to South-East Asia last Thursday. Yeah, okay, so China and Russia aren't exactly on speaking terms but that's playing with fire. Of course Francis Gary Powers was working for the military: everyone in the State Department knew that. Although it wasn't exactly a lie when the government had tried to say he was flying a 'weather' plane. They simply wanted to know 'whether' or not the Russians had any missiles in the area.

The clerk set a pitcher of ice water down on the desk. The legal advisor ignored the hissing and popping of exploding ice cubes as he poured himself a glass and gulped down a mouthful.

'Senator,' he said, sighing with relief and mopping at his brow, 'the Treaty specifically provides that no one surrenders its claim. There are seven claims which cover eighty percent of Antarctica: the United Kingdom, France, Argentina, Chile, New Zealand, Australia, and South Africa. You take the sector Argentina and Chile have – they've incorporated it into their metropolitan territories and have criminal codes which they claim apply to them, and the same is true with respect to New Zealand. So they do have government in those territories.' *So tough shit, Senator, we just weren't quick enough when it was time to stake a claim. Just be glad the Russkies don't have a plot either.* Phleger coughed again. 'So, Senator, there may only be fifty people in the area but they do have governments.'

Aiken was clearly uncomfortable with that thought. He shifted in his chair, like his ass spoke his mind for him. 'But after the adoption of this Treaty, would the laws of a dozen countries apply?'

Phleger didn't need to check his notes. He shook his head. 'The Treaty says that the signatories do not give up their claims, but the other signatories like the United States that do not recognize their claims do not by the Treaty recognize the claims and their position of non-recognition.' There, that ought to confuse the old buzzard. It did. He watched him shift on his ass again.

Phleger pretended to be impatient. 'For instance,' he added, 'if there was a commercial man – the Treaty deals with scientists and it deals with military matters . . .' It was clear Aiken wanted a re-cap on that area. Phleger took another breath.

'Okay,' he said, 'if we send a scientist or an inspector into the section claimed by Chile, he can't be arrested by Chile. Our juris-diction applies to him no matter where he is in Antarctica – because we made the decision not to recognize other claims to the territory, and because those other claimants made the concession that they would allow our scientists and unarmed military personnel to work within their territory on Antarctica. But, if there should be a mining engineer who went down into the sector claimed by Chile and he got into some trouble, Chile would claim that its laws governed.'

Aiken frowned.

Phleger shifted this time. Was Aiken really that low on short-term memory? 'And in that case, Senator,' he explained, 'we would claim that Chile's law did not govern because we do not recognize Chile's claim, and there would then be an international controversy as to who had jurisdiction over the individual.'

It was double-Dutch. Phleger knew it was double-Dutch. Aiken didn't appear to know it was double-Dutch, but he didn't appear not to know either. Which was fine. So long as they were all in agree-ment. Since in essence, they were merely playing out what the Antarctic Treaty stated, which was: no matter what the claims of a single country over the region known as Antarctica, those claims could be freely ignored by everyone else. Except, and this was an important proviso, except in the case of a military build-up, which, it was agreed, was to be banned by everyone. Totally. Unless, of course, someone infringed upon the rights of the others as set out by the Treaty, in which case—

'We don't even recognize any claim of our own, do we?' Aiken reiterated.

Phleger almost nodded. He rubbed his chin. This was their 'legal' reasoning. 'By recognizing that there is no sovereignty over Antarctica we retain jurisdiction over our citizens who go down there and we would deny the right of the other claimants to try that citizen. Yes.'

Aiken sat back in his chair, a crooked grin on his craggy face. That pleased him enormously. He stubbed out his cigarette and immediately reached for another. 'Boys, I think we just found one more virtue of the bomb!' There was another ripple of laughter. He was right. Aside from the Soviet Union, who the hell was going to argue with them? You didn't need to be the first. You needed to be the toughest.

Aiken lit the fresh cigarette and inhaled. He had a curious look on his face. Somber. 'Suppose, Mr Phleger,' he pondered, 'that there was a sudden and tremendous demand for emperor penguins?'

'Sir? I'm not sure I'm follow—'

'Penguins, Mr Phleger. There are serious conservation issues here. What if people went down there and started killing all the emperor penguins. Who could prevent that?'

'The people in each of the geographical areas covered by the seven claimant nations would claim they had a right to protect those penguins.'

'Then suppose one of our boys went into the Chilean area and stole a snow cat. What law would he violate?'

A snow cat?! What on earth was this old buzzard talking about? Snow cats didn't come from Antarctica. Phleger bit the bullet. 'The Chileans apply Chilean law,' he said.

'And we would deny it?'

'We would apply US law and we would have an international controversy.'

'I see.'

'Senator, it doesn't matter, the reason for the crime. Yes, the environment down there is an issue in the Treaty, but the situations you describe just aren't covered. We would have to go to mediation over the issue, if it ever arose. We are dealing with an area where we have no territorial claims and this Treaty deals with matters in the international field exclusively. That's why it's important that Antarctica remain demilitarized.'

Aiken's face adopted another grimace. 'That's all well and good, Mr Phleger, but supposing natural resources of great value were discovered in Antarctica, of value enough so that it would justify an immense cost to exploit them. It might be a vein of diamonds a foot thick.'

Phleger let a sneer cross his face. He was no fan of Aiken, but he was a patriot. 'There is no provision in this Treaty which would deal with that situation, Senator. If there was a discovery of value in a sector which was claimed by one of the claimant nations it would naturally claim sovereignty and the right to dictate the manner of exploitation. The United States on the other hand, never having recognized the validity of that claim, is in a position to assert that it has rights in respect thereto. And of course, should someone break the Treaty on demilitarization to protect its claim, the United States may use whatever force is necessary in order to protect the Treaty.'

Aiken smiled. 'At least, that's what we can say.'

'Yes, Senator. We can.'

The Antarctic Treaty was ratified by the US Senate by 66 votes to 21 on August 10, 1960. And that was how the world left it until 1993, when it was agreed that everyone should plow through this shoddy mess one more time. And again it was agreed that apart from the banning of the military and banning the exploitation of mineral wealth in respect to the environment, no country could lay claim to Antarctica.

Which was a dangerous conclusion to reach for a number of reasons, one of which had yet even to be addressed. For it proved that the Antarctic Treaty's vague double-talk had achieved exactly what it had set out to do: that should it stand as law in the face of overwhelming social change, its basic tenet would remain: that if anything of value were discovered in Antarctica, anarchy would reign supreme.

The Antarctic Treaty guaranteed that even if mankind had any desire to rid itself of the Seven Deadly Sins, Greed had been assured of a place in our hearts by virtue of time. By writing it down on a piece of paper and parading it as law and belief, Greed could be resurrected at a moment's notice.

That was the beauty of the written word. It was invariably taken at face value and granted permit to be spoken as the truth. It lived longer than the man.

And wreaked havoc in the process.

ANTARCTICA

The sacred symbols of the cosmic elements, the secrets of Osiris, had been hidden carefully. Hermes, before his return to the heavens, invoked a spell on them and said, 'O holy books which have been made by my immortal hands, by incorruption's magic spell, remain free from decay throughout eternity and incorrupt by time. Become unseeable, undefinable, from everyone whose foot shall tread the plains of this land, until old Heaven shall bring instruments for you, whom the Creator shall call his souls.' Thus spake he, and laying the spells on them by means of his works, he shut them safe away in their rooms. And long has been the time since they were hid away . . .

The Virgin of the World
Taken from the *Corpus Hermeticum* circa AD 100

Return-Path: latest@reuters.newsserv.com
Received:mirage.rola.com(dispatch.services) 205.174.222.1001.407839.70])byemin08.mail.col.com
(8.6.12/8.6.12/4.9078.96)with ESMTP id SAA8933 for: >ralph.matheson@rola.com<; RCINS
March 8, 2012 09:53:38-0400 / PAGE 7 of 32

Washington D.C. — 1PM EST

With reports surfacing of unusual activity in the region of *Jung Chang*, a Chinese Research Station based 130km west of Mount McKelvey in central Antarctica, Secretary of State Irwin Washler has refused to confirm or deny that the United States placed a counter-offensive task force on standby in the South Pacific this morning. This despite confirmed sightings of 6 US warships heading for the Ross Sea. Reports also indicate over 6000 US troops encamped on the Falkland Islands, a British colony in the South Atlantic.

Chinese activity has been under intense scrutiny since NASA's confirmation of high-quality mineral deposits in the upper Antarctic basin last month and their announcement this week of radiation emissions in the vicinity of the Chinese base. 'A vast amount of heat is being generated down there,' said Dr Charles Taylor, head of the Antarctic Scientific Committee. 'We know Antarctica has a lot of volcanic activity, but this is distinct from any geology we know of.' To generate that much heat would require nuclear power, which is banned under the Antarctic Treaty. As one source remarked, 'According to these numbers, either they've cracked nuclear fusion, or they've found a power source of even greater magnitude.'

The US, having sworn to defend the principles of the Antarctic Treaty banning military entrenchment, was outraged by the recent publication of satellite photographs clearly showing a Chinese military convoy landing at *Belgrano II*, the Argentine base camp on the Weddell Sea. But with its oil industry lobbying to establish offshore platforms in the region, the US position is weak. The Chinese have refused to comment.

> **SPORTS AND WEATHER NEWS FOLLOWS . . . >>>**

WEATHER HEADLINES:

SEVERE WEATHER PLAGUES WHOLE CONTINENTS

ICELAND – 2 PM GMT

Reports are emerging of an imminent flood in the southern coastal region. Glacial ice has started melting from within for some weeks now and whole reservoirs of melt water have built up to disturbing levels. Preliminary indications also show sea temperatures have risen by five degrees in the last three weeks and are on a steady increase. The fear is that the warm seawater will rapidly erode the glacier walls, which are holding back the melt water. Similar reports of a sudden global rise in sea temperatures are emerging from all over the world. Scientists are at a loss to explain it, other than as another manifestation of Global Warming.

[click for more information on these environmental hotspots]

Madras, India – Typhoons continue. 1500 dead.
Tokyo, Japan – Multiple Tsunami warnings issued.
California, USA – 200 dead in massive earthquake.
London, England – pre-tremors detected.
Mid-West, USA – storms and severe weather freeze potato belt.
Transfer interrupted! <<<
Communications Error 343571 <<<

USERS ARE ADVISED. If error message 343571 appears – DO NOT ADJUST YOUR SYSTEM. An error has occurred in the communications system. A satellite has stopped responding to messages and may not be relaying information. This is usually caused by solar flare activity and is nothing to be alarmed about. Normal service will be resumed shortly. We apologize for any inconvenience this has caused . . .

LAT. 67°20'S, LONG. 180°16'W

ROSS SEA – OFF THE ROSS ICE SHELF

NEW ZEALAND ROSS DEPENDENCY

Ralph Matheson felt nauseous. So much so, he'd just lost his breakfast, which was now a glistening yellow tiger-stripe frozen solid down the side of *Red Osprey*'s iron-oxide-colored hull.

He had the shakes bad. Always did when he felt sick. He quickly wiped his mouth on his coat sleeve before gripping the rail tightly and heaving again. Frozen chunks hit the swell below, but the sound was lost in the roar of the storm.

'Hey, dickhead!' a crusty voice commented. 'There's a ten-thousand-dollar pollution fine for puking in the ocean.'

Jack Bulger was a craggy old bastard. Fifty and solidly built. His voice sounded like throat cancer was paying a visit, while he wore his gray hair in a buzz-cut like a marine's. A sharp contrast to Matheson's curly nut-brown mop which he kept firmly tucked inside his hood. Matheson was sure Bulger had his head bare just for machismo. Not that Matheson could care less. He just wanted to stay warm. That was why he'd grown the beard to begin with.

Bulger be damned. Matheson didn't want to be out here anyway, checking main derrick up-links. He'd avoided it all morning. Hid in the galley for a half hour, reading a print-out of Reuters news reports off the web and nursing a coffee and doughnut.

As far as he could tell, the sensors attached to the base of the huge, battered drilling tower were fine. The intermittent signal drop-out was down to a faulty connection which he'd fixed in seconds.

There was no way that his equipment was going to jeopardize the drilling process. The weather, on the other hand, he had absolutely no control over.

He eyed the mass of nine-foot sectioned steel drill pipe as it shot up and down, caged inside the derrick. Bad idea. He gripped the hand-rail again. Clenched his stomach.

Bulger swiped his co-worker on the back. It seemed playful to outsiders, but Matheson knew better. Bulger was trying to make him spew his guts again.

Matheson watched the smoke from Bulger's cigar mix with his breath and drift his way. He shivered. Trying to keep his voice slow and even so he could hold his temper and the rest of his breakfast down all in one go, he said, 'There are *seven* lows gathering – all within a fifty-mile radius. This is *not* typical Antarctic weather. I was told to expect four, maybe even five lows – ferocious weather conditions by anyone's standards. But seven is unheard of! I do not relish the idea of being part of weather formation history!'

Bulger puffed on his cigar. 'Bracing, isn't it?'

'Bracing is not a word I'd choose to use!' Matheson shrieked. 'Hell on earth, maybe. Or the final Canto in Dante's *Inferno*, if you knew what the hell that was! If you read anything other than *Penthouse!*'

The weather fronts were moving in fast and deadly. Coming out of nowhere. Matheson was acutely aware that out here there was a good chance it might get him killed. And listening in on the scientific chatter from McMurdo Station hadn't helped matters. The scientists had absolutely no explanation for such severe weather.

Antarctic weather. The only certainty was, it was going to be bad. At approximately 60 degrees of latitude south, the winds thundered in from every major ocean with nothing to stop them. Not one island. Not one mountain. A ship could set a course to follow precisely LAT. 58°S, in effect circumnavigate the globe, and never once run into dry land. The Antarctic was the most forbidding place on earth and Matheson was certain of one thing: he wanted to go home.

'What do you want, anyway?' he asked Bulger shakily, wiping at his mouth again. Bulger didn't bother replying. Just braced himself as a small wall of water crashed across the bow and sprayed the crew. He watched with a satisfied air as it caught Matheson off-guard.

Matheson wiped his face down.

They were both engineers. Matheson was usually a desk man, designing set-ups on a workstation and never going anywhere near the field. Bulger was the exact opposite. A real hands-on kind of guy who spent most days elbow deep in grease, fixing problems with common sense, guile and a wrench. They both knew their stuff, of course. Pressures per square millimeter, per square inch. How to cause a stress fracture, and how not to. They both knew textbook stuff and more. But Bulger knew construction workers and roughnecks. He knew how their minds worked and how they liked to work. As far as he was concerned, Matheson knew shit. And Matheson knew this.

Bulger climbed up to the upper deck, announcing. 'There's a problem with your node.'

Matheson's face fell. 'What kind of problem?'

The drill ship lurched, bucking on another ferocious wave. They were getting bigger, Matheson thought. That one had to be at least 30 feet high. He felt his knees tremble as he watched the turquoise ocean race up to meet him then dip away again. A thunderous blast of freezing blue water and ice crashed over the bow and swept up deck in a tidal wave. In the time it took him to turn his head to see, the vast yellow derrick, the mighty drilling tower, had already borne the brunt of the impact and the 50-knot winds were whipping the water back into a frenzy. Before he even knew what hit him, Matheson was knocked on his ass and smacked backwards.

He jerked to a stop, his nylon safety line creaking with the strain. There was little he could do but stay put until the bitter salt water washed over him. He choked when he could finally take a breath, and shuddered from the cold despite the protection of his rubbery Day-Glo orange survival suit and layers of thermal underwear.

Thank God he'd remembered to clip himself on. It wasn't the sort of routine he was used to. After all, there wasn't much chance of being swept overboard on the way to work in San Francisco. Trams were like that.

Staggering to his feet, Matheson went to pull his cold and wet balaclava back into place but it stank of bile, so despite it being minus 80°C with the wind-chill factor, he removed it instead. As a result, he could feel his nose hairs freezing. Breathing through his mouth made him cough. Breathing through his nose wasn't much better, but it was vital. He had to warm the air up despite his sinuses. People were known to die of shock breathing air that was too frigid.

He had to get out of the cold. He could feel the seawater freezing on his face. What kind of a welcome would he get if he went home to Wendy and asked her to marry him with his skin hanging from his face?

Bulger was watching him from the upper deck. 'What sort of problem?' Matheson demanded, well aware that his voice was turning hoarse and feeble. 'What's wrong with the node?'

'Check it out for yourself,' Bulger snapped. 'You couldn't design a fucking vending machine for a parking lot.'

Matheson wanted to yell after him, but Bulger was gone. Ralph was only out here in Antarctica because Bulger had insisted he come out and field test the thing. The man was going to make his ulcer worse, keep plugging away at him like this.

He made a grab for the ladder then changed direction. He jerked his head to the side-rail again and hung over it. He could feel the freezing cold of wet metal through the thermal gloves. Already the seawater was starting to freeze around his hand and he had trouble pulling his fingers away. He retched, but there was nothing left to bring up.

The roughnecks were watching. That was the most embarrassing part. Matheson tried to compose himself; he had his pride. He wanted to look them in the eye and exit gracefully, but of course he knew if he took his eye off the horizon he'd throw up again. So instead he clung to anything he could find that was solid enough and inched his way to the ladder.

He clipped his safety-line to a rung and had just about plucked up enough courage to climb when a delicate ungloved hand thrust a small silver hipflask into his hand. He glanced around surprised to find the cool blue eyes of Ilana Petrova, one of the Russian rough-necks. He couldn't see her straw-blonde hair. Like him, she kept her hair hidden away in the warmth of her survival suit hood. They all wore them on deck. He could see her tight smile though. Her thin, pink lips. 'Thank you,' he said meekly. 'What is it?'

'It's good,' she said in her thick Muscovite accent. 'Rum. And

eat dry bread. When you throw up again, you need something to –
to –'

'To throw up,' Matheson smiled, embarrassed. 'Yeah.' Ilana nodded
at the flask encouragingly. Matheson took a swig. Wiped the top and
handed it back. 'Thanks,' he said.

She tucked the flask away, slipped a glove back on and nodded
in that curious Russian way. They eyed each other, and for just a
brief moment Matheson actually didn't feel quite so ill. It didn't last
long.

'What's the problem with the node?' he asked tentatively.

Ilana frowned. 'Nothing,' she said.

'Nothing?' Matheson mused. He watched her walk away, her
familiar wiggle on display as she negotiated the rusty metal deck
plates. He watched her climb the crane, get a slap on the ass and
kick the guy in the face as another wave hit the bow and crystal
droplets scraped against his skin. His stomach twisted in knots again
as he climbed up out of the bitter cold. Questions formed in a torrid
swirl in his mind. Why weren't his sea-sickness pills working? What
was the point of wearing a survival suit in a place where you were
unlikely to survive?

And what was Bulger playing at?

The control room was dark, bathed in a deep red glow. Banks of
monitors blinked reams of data at hunched engineers. The room
stank of cigarette smoke and every so often he could smell Bulger's
cigar. He was lurking in here somewhere. The murmuring was active
as information traded hands and the drill's progress was tracked. He
glanced at a bank of screens showing the rig outside and watched
for a moment as the pipe appeared to ram up and down inside the
tower like a piston, as the ship bucked on the waves. It was impressive. There had been trials up in Alaska, of course, but this was the
first true exploratory oil drill in a polar region. Problem was, this was
Antarctica. Where it was illegal.

But then illegal was not an alien concept to the big oil companies.
Matheson never forgot his college days when a ship by the name of
the *Exxon Valdez* poured over ten million gallons of oil straight into
the eco-system. That may have been an accident, but *Exxon's* poor
attempt at wriggling out of cleaning up its own mess was not.

But there was no National Oceanic and Atmospheric Administration in Antarctica to bring Rola Corp. into line if it screwed up. The company could effectively do what it liked. Yes, a permit was required to be here, but unofficially if *Red Osprey* struck oil in the meantime, the company was sure it could all be worked out. That was the trouble – Rola Corp. had plans on Antarctic oil, with or without Ralph Matheson. So he figured it might as well be with him and by default with somebody who would make sure the *Exxon Valdez* never happened out here.

Trouble was, they'd pulled the rug out from under him. They weren't supposed to be out here for another six months. They just weren't ready.

'What's going on? Bulger said something about a problem with the node.' Matheson unzipped the parka part of his suit and made a bee-line for Charlie Harper, a black systems specialist from Wisconsin. They were friends, and had worked together before out in Saudi Arabia a few years back. He was about the only person Matheson trusted on this ship. He could feel his teeth chattering as he lowered himself into a comfortable chair.

Charlie replied almost too lethargically: 'Nothin' much. Just the same ole same ole.' Which was Charlie-speak for: Shit's hit the fan.

Charlie was focused on his monitors. Clicked the mouse a couple of times. When his gaze met Matheson's it was worried. 'We got a warship. Chinese.'

Charlie had the Global Positioning System, or GPS, on line and was busy monitoring air and sea traffic. GPS kept track of the position of every vehicle linked into its network of satellites. Those vehicles could access all kinds of navigational data, including pinpointing all the other vehicles plugged into it, anywhere on earth, at any given time. It had been developed by the US military sometime in the last century. Now it was an everyday part of civilian life.

Clearly a Chinese warship was bad news. There was every chance now they would have to dump the pipeline and move on quickly. *Red Osprey* had a distinct advantage over the warship in that, thanks to some bright young computer programmer, it didn't actually register on any GPS system. At a distance, *Red Osprey* was to all intents and purposes invisible. But if they were found, they would be boarded.

Matheson had seen the news. He knew what was going on and it wasn't good. *Red Osprey* was flying the US flag. To the Chinese right now that was a red rag to a bull. 'Is this what Bulger came down to see me about?' Matheson snapped, agitated. He didn't need this right now.

'Yeah. He thought maybe they could hear what we're doing in the water.'

'And can they? Charlie, I need to know. My ass is on the line here.'

'No, man! No way they could hear us. You did good.'

'I did good? I did *good*? I did a goddamn miracle, Charlie. Next to loaves and fishes, bringing this project forward six months was a goddamn, honest to goodness miracle. How do you *know* they can't hear us?' Matheson was working himself into a sweat.

'I know they can't hear us, coz I've been listenin' to *them* on the radio for a half hour. Man, they too busy partying to be bothered snooping around for us. They've been hanging around all morning watching our guys over at McMurdo preparing a new landing strip. They're too distracted. Shit, I can hear somebody over there singin' Abba – in Chinese.'

Matheson frowned in surprise.

'What can I say,' Charlie shrugged. 'The node's got great ears.'

'What song?'

'"Supertrooper".'

If *Red Osprey* were discovered it would blow the whole situation. They'd already had one close encounter with a wing of Chinese fighters out on patrol. They hadn't been discovered, but with Chinese and US forces facing off over mineral rights, in a world where dwindling fossil fuels were sending prices skyward, *Red Osprey*'s surreptitious oil tapping could spark a war.

Bulger had been bugging him about friction vibration for weeks. It was what they had been most concerned about. Screw whether it actually worked. Just make sure the damn thing didn't make any noise.

The 'damn thing' was the heart of Matheson's design, a device called the Depth Node. It had been transported out to the Ross Sea under cover of darkness last winter and dumped directly beneath them. Then, controlled remotely, it had dug in on the sea floor. It was the main point for capping the well and heating the buried pipe-work. The node was what made polar oil exploration possible and the company intended to set up nodes all over the Antarctic coast. Drill, strike oil, then cap off, only returning to a node when they wanted to fill a tanker. Refining was done aboard ship. The node would take care of everything else. Its power unit ran on hydrogen and oxygen – essentially water – and was designed to last twenty years. But the prototype had only been in the ground for nine months. It was supposed to run silently. What if it *had* failed?

Water power was a new technology which Rola Corp. had acquired the patent to about fifteen years previously and sat on. So far, the rival water-powered generators that had emerged onto the market were so extremely expensive only western nations could afford them. Which was good because it meant it would be decades before the Third World could scrape together enough cash to buy the technology. Until then, they would need oil. The problem was, there had been no mass testing of this new technology. What if there was a problem with the water-powered section of the node, something beyond Matheson's predicting capabilities and the Chinese had detected this? They were a sitting duck.

Charlie handed Matheson a mug of coffee as he watched the screens. Absorbed, as if he were playing a game. 'What's that?' Matheson asked, pointing to a series of blips.

'That red one's the Chinese sub. The other's a US carrier. And that there, see that blue one? That's a plane on its way from Chile to Pirrit Hills, in the Chilean sector. And I can tell you right now, they's up shit creek without a paddle.'

'What's happening?'

'It's a small aircraft,' Charlie explained. 'That storm we got moving in just fucked up their day. They're past the point of no return. They're going to have to find somewhere to land and refuel if they're going to get back. And between you and me, I don't think they're even gonna make it to their fuel dump.'

'What do we do? Charlie, we can't just let them crash! What if it was us out there?'

'We can't just get on a radio, either. We're not supposed to be here, Ralph.'

'I know, but – look, see? The two closest research stations to Pirrit Hills are both American. Siple, and Sky-Hi – y'know, Eights Station. They're both manned. Charlie, you gotta send out an emergency message – on the Internet at least. Just make sure they're anonymous.'

'If I send out *any* message, they'll know somebody's out here,' Charlie said defensively.

'You gotta do something,' Matheson argued, distressed.

'I'm sorry, but they're on their own.'

Matheson watched the scope. Watched the plane head off into oblivion.

'What's that?' He gestured at a red blip about twelve miles off their port bow and sipped his coffee. It was bitter. Shittiest coffee he'd ever tasted.

'That's our carrier I was tellin' ya about. Been doin' maneuvers or something. They're too busy worryin' about each other to give a damn about us. But hey, fuck 'em. So Frankie ran a simulation test on a dump. We can be outta here before they get close enough to sniff around.'

Matheson nodded and had more coffee. On his computer screen a graphic cut-away view showed the drill in progress. A string of steel-alloy pipe extended down from *Red Osprey* to the node. The node then ran its own length of pipe vertically down a further 500 meters. The pipeline then changed direction dramatically and had been steered around difficult strata of rock. It was approaching the estimated site of the oil field at a gentle downward sloping angle.

Directional drilling had been pioneered by the Norwegian National Oil Company in the early 1990s when they sank a well nearly 24,000 feet horizontally from a starting point 9,000 feet under the North Sea. It was so successful there was a rush to adopt the technology since it allowed for more oil drainage than conventional means.

'Thorne was on the sat. again,' Charlie dropped in casually.

Matheson almost choked on his coffee. 'What did he want?'

'Test results. Come on, Ralph, he wants to know how your baby's holding up. Just thank God he's not on a plane out here.'

Matheson gulped more coffee. Tried not to taste it, just enjoy its warmth. But his hands were shaking and this time it had nothing to do with sea-sickness.

Rip Thorne, President of Rola Corp. Exploration. Asshole. Just a mention of the guy's name was enough to give Matheson the willies. Thorne was the one who had caused his ulcer in the first place. Rip Thorne and Bulger. Between them, they were responsible for him winding up out here. Six whole months. How the hell could Thorne expect to bring this project forward by six whole months and expect it to work? And what was with Bulger anyway? Thorne's personal little Rottweiller. He'd already overruled the first test drill site, said he wanted to drill someplace else. Someplace he'd personally picked out.

Matheson checked the data. 'Charlie, please tell me you didn't give him an answer.'

Charlie glared at his friend. 'Without checking with you first? Are you shittin' me? Of course not! I told him he'd have to wait for your damn report.'

Matheson nodded. Tried to shake off his mood. He checked the data again. 'Remote drill-bit's operating fine,' he relayed warily. 'Geo-steering sensor . . . Hmm. Interesting rock composition . . . crystalline? Huh . . . MWD, MWD, where are you? Uh, got it.' He clicked on the Measurement-While-Drilling icon and checked the torque and forward force on the drill-bit. It was high. Within operating limits, but still high.

They had hit a tough strata of rock earlier in the day and were trying to break through, so the order had been given to go to full power. It would wear the drill-bit out at twice the rate, but since this drill-bit had been going for a day and it wasn't unusual to change the bit every twenty-four to forty-eight hours, they might as well just let it burn itself out.

Geology was a funny business though. No one was quite sure what kind of rock they had encountered. And in the past six hours they had only advanced enough to attach one more nine-foot section of drilling pipe. So just in case the drill broke through to an underground cavern or soft, particulate matter, like sand, a clamp harness had been attached to the pipe their end to stop the bit running off with the entire pipe-line if there was a sudden lurch forward. It would scupper the whole job if that happened and nobody wanted that, since retrieving miles of pipe from the ocean floor just wasn't an option. They would be forced to start again from scratch.

Glancing at the secondary monitor, Matheson hesitated over the three data icons. One meant a remote data dump via satellite to his workstation back home. A second meant an immediate digital download onto the ship's system core. And the third one – was yellow. *Yellow?* What did that mean?

'This is my ship! What did you think you were doing?'

He turned from the screen as the door flew open and the captain of *Red Osprey* stormed in. Jaffna was a small man with Indian features and a western temper. He flipped the lights on and everyone screwed up their eyes for a second. Abuse was hurled, but he didn't give a damn. He zeroed in on Bulger.

Bulger was on his feet. 'You're a fucking idiot!'

'I gave direct orders and you overrode them. Try it again and I'll take your head off!'

'Are you an idiot, Jaffna? Is that it?' Bulger met him center-stage. Everyone else knew better, and got out the way. 'What kind of a fucking idiot displays the signal? Anyone with a good pair of fucking glasses could see it, goddamnit!'

Matheson leaned in quick and whispered, 'What signal?'

'Jaffna turned the lights on,' Charlie explained quickly and quietly. 'Flew the signal that we're doing sub-aqua work to passing traffic. Bulger told a deckhand to switch 'em off.'

Matheson shook his head in surprise. 'Well, by international law he's supposed to.' He grimaced and sat back. Watched the two men go at it and was even enjoying the entertainment until suddenly it hit him.

Yellow meant block resistance. Recoil forces and internal pumping pressure.

Matheson spun around fast. 'Shit!' He grabbed the mouse, clicked on the yellow icon, called up the data. 'Shit!' Shit! Shit!' He spun back around. The recoil was massive. It hadn't struck oil at all. 'Who's on forward resistance?'

As Bulger and Jaffna stuck at it, Jaffna screaming something about not wanting to lose his license and planning on captaining another ship some day, Matheson scrambled to his feet. Screw them. Screw the Chinese navy. This was more serious. The shit had already hit the fan and none of them knew it.

He scanned the room fast. Jabbed a finger at Frankie, a fat, young, nervous-looking guy. 'You!' he growled. 'You were monitoring forward resistance. Why didn't you pick up on it!'

'I – I went for a piss,' Frankie stuttered.

Matheson shoved him out the way, dived for his monitor. 'The bit's broken through. It's pumping pressurized seawater!' This was unprecedented. He wheeled round and bellowed at everyone in the room. 'Dump the pipe now! We got a Code Zero!'

Everyone knew what that meant. There was a terrified silence. Code Zero was a theoretical situation they'd computer simulated back in the States. They had broken through to an underwater sink-hole. At this temperature the water should have been solid ice, but the pressures exerted from the sheer weight of the glacier ice shelves above meant the water was under extreme pressure and remained liquid. Give it a means of escape and of course it was going to take the path of least resistance. Recoil effects would be buckling the pipe. In this cold, the pipe should have snapped, but it couldn't because it was a steel alloy designed to remain elastic. For the node to work, the pipe-line was a pipe within a pipe. It was the central-core pipe that was going haywire, and it was the core pipe that *Red Osprey* was directly connected to. The recoil would be speeding up the pipe in waves. At some point it was going to reach the ship. In calm weather they'd clear decks until all the fun was over. But in this storm – it could sink them.

Everyone dived for the controls. Bulger hit the alarm and was on the intercom in a blink. Klaxons whirred. Hazard lights flashed. 'This is an emergency! Everyone below decks, now! Get off deck! Leave everything! This is not a drill! Go! Go! *Go!*'

No one stuck around to ask questions. But it was already too late. The first buckle hit *Red Osprey* when it was already in the throes of another thirty-foot icy wave. The roughnecks all lurched in one direc-tion as they started to unclip safety-lines and transfer over to the main deck-rails. But the pipe whiplashed with such force that it righted the ship on the crest of the wave, and when *Red Osprey* finally lurched to port, three roughnecks were catapulted into the ocean. They were dead inside a minute.

*   *   *

Matheson watched the monitors when he should have been concen-
trating on his readings. He watched Ilana climb down from the
crane as a brace from the derrick sheered off and shot straight
through her abdomen. It blasted out her back and took her guts
with it. Blood sprayed red across the sky like lightning and was
gone in the crash of another wave. Her body clung to the ladder
for a moment – then broke away. She never had time to change
her expression.

Matheson heard Charlie's breath catch in his throat. Glancing at
him quickly he saw his friend was glued to the monitor too. He had
the look of a man who'd just lost his lover. When had those two
gotten together? The ship lurched and swung back. Screw Charlie's
love-life. Matheson dived across the room. Everyone was panicking.
He flipped up the Plexiglas sheath on the central console and
hammered the bright red abort switch.

More sirens added to the din. The computer confirmed that the
node had capped off and had jettisoned the ship's umbilical. But the
internal pressure readings didn't change. Something had been
pumped and was rocketing up the inside of the pipe-line. If they
didn't dump the umbilical now it might catch on the sea-bed and
they'd never get out of there.

Matheson whirled around looking for the dump controls. He
found Captain Jaffna already on the intercom, yelling at the bridge
for full ahead. His fingers flew across the keys. The umbilical would
be gone in seconds.

Matheson checked the monitor again, checked Jaffna. Watched
the pipe begin to fall through the deck-hole into the water below.

The remaining roughnecks scrambled for cover. Some made it,
but some didn't.

Dumping the umbilical was becoming impossible. As it slid into
the ocean it caught on more sheering braces. Hanging limply from
the towering derrick it was 3000 feet of dead weight pipe under no
control, at the mercy of the undercurrents.

The creaking got louder. The derrick buckled, came crashing
down and crushed another roughneck. Matheson could see the guy's
thick bushy moustache. His name was Pete. He was still alive, but
he was trapped, Matheson realized, under a pipe-line that was now

pointing directly at the bridge and living quarters. Directly at them. Like a cannon.

Matheson braced himself, watching Pete struggle under tons of battered steel until the nozzle inevitably exploded. Freezing mud blasted out, smashing everything in its path. Fists of rock tore through portholes like bullets. The smell of sulfur was overwhelming. And the cold . . .

Jaffna never wavered. Always thinking, always looking for an option. He keyed more controls and the ship rocked as a blast ripped through the deck-hole. Jaffna had instigated an emergency dump. The pipe-line was gone and they were free. But the devastation was immense.

Red Osprey tossed back and forth several times before Jaffna's orders finally kicked in and the ship steamed full ahead. But she was limping badly, smoke pouring from her engine room.

Bulger thumbed the klaxons off. Everyone stood motionless, trying to take it all in. Charlie, his dark skin stained with tears, rubbed his cheeks angrily and tried to focus on the GPS systems.

'The sub?' Matheson demanded.

Charlie shook his head and shot a look at Jaffna. 'We got a destroyer coming at us. North-north-west. Full speed. Sending out registry *USS Ingersoll DD-990* . . . it's the Marines.'

Jaffna nodded. It was time to get out of here. He yanked the door open and let a slew of mud and rock slide into the room as he beat a retreat to the bridge. The large picture porthole beyond was smashed and the wind and ice gusted in, driving it all across the floor. A large knot of muddy rock skidded up to Matheson's boot.

Matheson turned to Charlie. They eyed each other for a moment before he tentatively stepped out onto the upper deck, ignoring the squalls that blasted his face with ice. The drilling tower was buckled the length of the deck. Bodies lay strewn about. Huge boxes of equipment were broken and junked from stem to stern.

'Clip yourself on,' Bulger ordered quietly. He was looking distastefully at his cigar. He tossed it overboard as he clipped his own safety-line to the main rail and made his way down the ladder. All Matheson could hear him keep saying was: 'Christ, what a fucking mess. Oh, Jesus, this is terrible.'

Stunned, Matheson went down to the main deck to give a hand with the clearing up. He'd have preferred to go back to bed and give the day a shot from another angle. Even a sunset would have given him the sense of closure he wanted. But this was Antarctica and sunset wasn't due for another six weeks.

He had set to work making a note of the victims. There were thirteen dead in all. As he ticked them off on a clipboard, trying his best not to be sick again, a roughneck by the name of Pico interrupted. He had a large chunk of something in his hands. It looked heavy. 'Hey, I think this must be yours. What kinda stuff did you guys have on deck? This looks pretty expensive.' He handed it over.

'I don't remember us having anything on deck,' Matheson commented. He frowned and examined the object, turning it over in his hands. He wasn't the only one. Bulger had a piece and Frankie made a grab for a chunk. Now he came to think of it, there were lumps of the stuff all over the deck. 'This isn't from any of our equipment.'

Matheson took the rock-like object over to a puddle and started washing the dirt away. It was crystal, and picked up the light so effectively that it appeared to be glowing pale blue. Almost clear. He shared a wary look with Bulger and for that brief moment they both forgot their differences. 'It's a piece of rock . . .'

'What kind of rock?' Frankie asked furtively. His skin was peeling. He hadn't used his balaclava either and looked terrible.

Matheson turned it over again. 'Looks like diamond.'

'Doesn't look like any diamond I ever saw,' Frankie mused. 'It's heavy, but it ain't nearly heavy enough. Did this come through the pipe-line?'

Charlie stepped up to them. Exchanged sympathetic glances. 'Must have,' he said.

Slowly, very slowly, Bulger smiled, bearing his teeth like a shark. 'I knew it,' was all he said.

Matheson suddenly held his piece up to the light. 'Well, I'll be damned.' He positioned himself so they could all see. 'Look,' he said, disbelievingly. 'It's got writing on it.'

Glinting in the light were finely etched, perfectly formed glyphs – ancient-looking symbols whose meaning was lost on them. So clear were the hieroglyphs that it looked like the diamond itself had incorporated the writing into its natural structure.

It was astounding.

'I wonder what it says?' someone was asking.

'Looks Egyptian.'

'Egyptian?' Matheson jerked a thumb at a distant iceberg. 'Out here? Come on, man!'

Frankie set about picking up every piece he could find. 'We gotta get more of this stuff,' he said. 'Someone needs to take a look at this. We're gonna be rich!' But his hand was quickly squashed under the sole of Bulger's thick heavy boot.

'This shit right here is company property, Fat Boy. You collect it all up for the company.'

Matheson warily ran his fingers over the etchings on the stone. Thirteen people had just died because of this stuff. He gripped it tightly. They were going to be rich? Somehow, he wasn't so sure. He held the stone up to the light again. Took another good look. And that was when he noticed the black smudge on the horizon closing in rapidly. A black smudge of storm clouds against a green sky . . . a *green* sky?

Klaxons erupted on deck again before he could say anything. As cliff-sized waves crashed across the bow, and the destroyer circled in from the North, Matheson watched a sleek gray military Sea-Hawk helicopter swoop in from the sky, its screaming engines barely making a dent in the noise from the storm. Hovering low over the center deck where *Red Osprey* moved least and the derrick lay crumpled, its doors slid back abruptly. Ropes were tossed out. And as a dozen marines swung down from above, a loud-hailer fixed next to missiles on the stub wings of the chopper suddenly sprang to life.

'This is the United States Marine Corps! Stay where you are on deck! You are being boarded!'

Machine guns were cocked. Hands held high. A braided officer took center-stage. With a scowl firmly fixed to his young face he assessed the crew with one definitive sweep before finally locking his gaze on Matheson and making a bee-line for him.

Still gripping the rock, Ralph Matheson had a manic grin smeared across his face.

The Marines were here.

They had been caught at last. Thank God, he thought.

THE EIGHTH DAY

It is a curious thing that God learned Greek when he wished to turn author – and that he did not learn it better.

Friedrich Nietzsche, Philosopher, 1844–1900

FULTON CONFERENCE CENTER

MAGNOLIA UNIVERSITY, NORTH MISSISSIPPI

March 16, 2012

'In the beginning was the word,' Dr Richard Scott announced, fumbling with the switch and pressing it twice by mistake. The digital projector raced through a sequence of images so fast it was impossible to pick out the detail. Scott muffled a groan and tried in vain to cue the slide up once more, but couldn't find the number to punch in. He looked to the audience. Letting his shoulders sag. 'And that word is currently not repeatable in public,' he said.

The audience gave a louder than expected note of amusement but somehow Scott couldn't trust their motives. They were academics for the most part, with a sprinkling of students. They had come to listen to the man whose little tour had caused quite a stir in some circles. Even the President, a devout and notable Baptist, had felt the urge to come out and actively question his work. One tiny professor from U-Dub. It was ridiculous. Where was the religious freedom in this country anymore? Had it all been a myth to begin with?

Scott glanced down exasperated at the equipment and caught a glimpse of his own reflection. Neatly trimmed hair. Square jaw. He fiddled with switches, but it was no use. Forlornly, he glanced over to the student research assistant they had assigned to him for just this kind of emergency. 'Uh, could you – uh? Hello?'

A guy from *Federal Express* was getting her to sign for a package. Scott was amazed. 'Uh, excuse me, sir? I'm trying to lecture here.'

'When we promise ten-thirty, sir, we mean it.'

Scott couldn't help it. He broke into a smile and burst out laughing to a squeal of feedback off the PA system. The audience laughed with him.

'A round of applause for our friends at *FedEx*,' Scott chuckled.

The delivery guy took off his cap and gave a bow on his way out, to the delight of the audience. Meanwhile, Scott's assistant had dumped the package and was vaulting onto the stage.

Scott cupped his hand over the microphone. 'Thanks.'

She was a bright girl, November Dryden, very bright. Very attractive. But more importantly – very patient. 'Knock 'em dead,' she said, returning to her seat with a smile.

With his lecture back on track, Scott shared an amused jibe with the audience. 'I think, on balance, ancient manuscripts are a lot easier to handle,' he said.

Another ripple of laughter bounced around the auditorium as the audience settled down and the first slide popped up onto the screen.

Scott was a linguistic and cultural anthropologist by trade. He studied social structures, law, politics, religion and technology, but his specialty was language. He was an epigraphist who spent years deciphering ancient inscriptions. Yet despite the confidence he had in his own work, he'd worried about this lecture more than any other. It might be dangerous to his health, because this was the Bible Belt. A lecture on newly discovered ancient manuscripts that called the Bible into question, wasn't going to cause lively debate, so much as explosive disagreement. And then there was the other issue –

'To begin again,' Scott continued. 'In the beginning was the word. And that word is "unbeliever". Let me start my lecture today by being very honest about my beliefs.' He took a deep breath. 'I don't believe in Jesus Christ.'

There were stunned expressions in the audience. Scott shuffled his papers.

'The Gospels,' he explained, 'were written in Greek. Where we have "word" the Greeks have *logos*. But *logos* means more than just "word". It means thought, deed, action. It means "word in action". It's the same in Hebrew and in Aramaic. Some have recognized this dilemma and opted for the word "act". In the beginning, there was the act.

But that still doesn't convey the full meaning of *logos*. Christians wanted to attract Jews to their faith; Jesus was, after all, a Jew. So Christianity – like all great religions – borrowed from its predecessors both the language and imagery of what had gone before. Hence, in the beginning was *logos* because to the Hebrews, this was nothing new. In Proverbs it's the wisdom motif.

'To entice Pagans, all they did was move into a bunch of old churches and not bother redecorating. All those vast mosaics of Christ, the bearded savior – those are portraits of Zeus and Jupiter. Those churches are Greco-Roman. So Christianity then, is the earliest known example of religious re-cycling. However, how *much* it borrowed has always been a source of debate. But today I brought the answer with me. And, if I may, I'd like to share it with you.'

Scott sipped his water. Partly to quench his thirst, but mostly to gauge his audience.

Ancient texts. They had been calling Christianity into question now for decades. The first had turned up in 1947. A shephered boy by the name of Muhammad adh-Dhib, or Muhammad the Wolf, of the Ta'amireh tribe of Bedouin, had passed by the ancient settlement of Qumran, by the Dead Sea, and stumbled upon ancient scrolls in some clay jars in a cave. The most recent, the *Istanbul Genezah*, had been found in a chest in the roof of a mosque. A *genezah* was a collection of prayer scripture – stored but no longer used, usually because they were worn out. These things hadn't seen the light of day in at least 1,500 years.

Throughout this time the Christian establishment had suppressed any information that questioned its religion. But since the mid-1980s a small academic fringe had seen it as their duty to reveal Christ as merely a man. It was a viewpoint Scott hadn't entirely shared to begin with, but things had changed.

'So,' he continued now, 'if we've got problems with just one word, think about the sort of problems we have when we consider that the Bible contains hundreds of thousands of words, and all of them from mostly dead languages. We have to admit that our interpretations, from any point of view, are going to be open to error. For example, how many of you know somebody who speaks fluent Aramaic and uses it in everyday speech?' He let slip a smile. Time for an anecdote.

'Okay how many of you here speak German?'

There was a flutter of hushed conversation from the assorted nervous academics.

'Don't worry, I'm not going to call you up on stage and saw you in half. Just give me a round figure. One, two? Six?' He could see a few hands slowly go up. He nodded. 'Six. Right. Okay – out of an audience of maybe two hundred. In Europe, maybe a hundred million people speak German. Maybe more, I don't know. To tell you the truth, I don't care. The point is, if you wanted to know how to speak German you'd ask a German, right? I mean, they use it every day.'

Sounds of agreement.

'Which is ironic, because people still get it wrong. Even when it comes to the simplest phraseology. Like President Kennedy when he went to Berlin back in the middle of the last century. What did he do? He got up and addressed thousands of Germans, intent on telling them that he was willing to embrace Germany after all the ill-will of the Second World War. Intent on telling them he was one of them. He wanted to say that he understood them. That he too was a Berliner, you know, as opposed to a New Yorker or a Londoner. He wanted to say: I am a Berliner. So right off the cuff he announced: *Ich bin ein Berliner!*'

He paused. 'For those of you who don't know, *ich* means "I". *Bin* means "am". You know, *ein, zwei, drei* – one, two, three. Well, *ein* also means "a". And "Berliner" does indeed mean "coming from Berlin". So on the surface of it Kennedy said exactly what he wanted to say, right?' There was murmuring, but these were academics. They knew they had been led into a trap. And some of them were old enough to remember the trap the first time around. But for the gullible in the audience, Scott carried it through. He let his face fall. Let his voice go very quiet.

'Except that it doesn't quite take into account the nuance of German grammar. By placing *ein* in front of *Berliner*, President Kennedy turned *Berliner* into a noun instead of an adjective. He'd already said "A Berliner" by using *bin*. But by using the word *ein* it turned *Berliner* into a thing, not a place. And a Berliner is a very different "thing" to the capital of Germany.

'What President Kennedy actually proclaimed, when he stood

up in front of the world's media that day, was: *I am a doughnut.*

'I leave it to you to decide which of the two statements was more accurate.'

The slide up on the screen was of a small fragment of papyrus.

'This was found in 1920 in Nag Hammadi, Egypt,' Scott told his audience. 'It dates from 100–150 of the Common Era, or CE. I use CE instead of AD and BCE in place of BC. I don't think dates should hinge on the birth of Christ.' The audience definitely did not like that. 'So what does this papyrus tell us? In short, that John's Gospel was written at least fifty years *after* the death of Jesus. It's therefore not an eyewitness account, and must be suspect.

'Think about it . . . all that. From one tiny piece of papyrus.'

For Scott it also confirmed that John was written at a time when the Roman Empire was considering adopting Christianity to maintain its grip on power by representing the masses. John, therefore, was probably written by a Roman, since it was fundamental in describing Jesus's role, and the rules governing Catholicism – a Rome-orientated institution. As a religion it looked to Scott like it had very little to do with God and a lot to do with politics.

'The Nag Hammadi scrolls are interesting because among them was found a complete Gospel of Thomas consisting of one hundred sayings of Jesus – a Gnostic text that pre-dates the Gospels yet the Catholic Church has branded it heretical. Historical fact is *heretical?*

'Okay, since there are freshmen in the auditorium today, you'll forgive me if I over-explain terminology. "Gnostic" is Greek and means "hidden knowledge" – usually, hidden knowledge of the divine. Why do we know there's hidden knowledge? Because the language of the text has quite clearly been manipulated. It uses imagery as its weapon. After all, this was a new religion. In order to lure in new worshippers they needed to make them feel comfortable. So when, for example, Jesus Christ – Christ simply being Greek for "Messiah" and Jesus being Greek for the name Joshua – when *Joshua* walks in the wilderness or walks on water . . . there's only one other guy who ever did stuff like that, and he too was a prophet. He was never played up to be supernatural although he *was* played by Charlton Heston. I am, of course, referring to Moses. So what better way to enhance your power than by being likened to the best – that went *before* you.'

Scott took another sip of water and eyed the audience. A couple of people were walking out. He wasn't surprised. He was, however, surprised that there hadn't been more. He waited for the door to close gently behind them. People had a peculiar habit of conveniently forgetting even the most widely accepted facts. After all, hadn't the Egyptian goddess Isis promised an afterlife that was better than this life, thousands of years before Christ?

Scott smiled, warmly. This was where the fun began. 'The Nag Hammadi scrolls are also interesting because they're Coptic – written in the later form of Egyptian which used a Greek alphabet. But Joshua and his contemporaries spoke Aramaic, so was it unusual for people who spoke Aramaic to write everything down in Greek? Well, actually no. If we think about present-day Belgium, no one writes in Dutch or Flemish, they write in German or French, or more often than not, English.

'Although none of the Gospels are written in Aramaic, we know the writers spoke that language because Aramaic language structures are hidden within the text. Remember my point about German grammar?'

He keyed the machine and another slide popped up into view – an ancient scroll covered neatly in ordered brown script. 'But, that,' he said, 'is the opening page of a lost book. One I think you'll all find quite fascinating.

'For years there's been speculation about a lost book of Q, or Quelle, which was extensively researched by John Kloppenborg in the mid 1980s. Kloppenborg believed that somewhere, there must be the original first-hand account of Jesus before the writers of the Gospels had their say. The consensus was that *The Book of Q*, which has shaped our culture, was a *verbal* history, which may initially have been written in Aramaic.

'But that page,' he pointed to the screen, 'proves something else entirely. It is not, and I stress *not The Book of Q*. It's much older, as indicated by Chlorine 36 isotope tests. The genetic deterioration shows it was written on the skin of a very old goat. And it proves for the very first time that Christ borrowed his ideas *from the cult of Mithras*. This book dates from four to five hundred years before any such Jesus Christ was ever born. Yet the New Testament shares its imagery and its symbolism almost perfectly, almost word for word.

It is *not* a Mithraic text, and it is *not* Christian. It's a combination of the two. It's the proverbial missing link. And it was written in Aramaic.'

Scott grinned, a touch smugly. He finished off his lecture with a simple, quiet question to the audience. 'Anyone here still want to be Christian?'

It was sometime later that Scott found himself inside a wooden box. Clean and white, the whole approach was airy, instead of the dark and murky confessionals of Old Europe. Barely masking a schoolboy chortle, he announced: 'Bless me Fergus, for I have sinned.'

The hatch behind the grating slid back with a vicious clap. 'Yes, yes. Cut the crap.'

There was a sigh, followed by a dull tapping sound. It stopped for a moment, then continued. Scott sat forward and peered through the grill at the priest beyond. He could see him rolling his eyes, while fishing around inside his black cassock for a Zippo. He was mumbling some sort of an apology to the heavens as he tapped out a cigarette.

'What're you doing?' Scott asked. The first puff of smoke drifted over. He could smell it was a good brand of cigarette. Almost certainly European.

'Calming my nerves. I can't believe the sort of hornet's nest you've managed to stir up, Richie, my boy.' He tried to spit out a shred of tobacco but it was sticking to the tip of his tongue. He brushed at his cassock. 'A real big fucking mess.'

They eyed each other. 'Let's eat,' Scott said.

They strolled across the neatly cut glade in the center of the Grove, heading for the Associated Student Body building where there were better cafeterias and a livelier atmosphere.

The Grove was a magnificent piece of parkland at the heart of Magnolia University. It may have been March, but it felt like summer in Mississippi. The sun shone brightly through the trees and left beautiful dappled spots of shade on the ground. For the most part, the students wore shorts and T-shirts. In his priestly guise Fergus seemed to be taking it all in with the serene air of a good Catholic gentleman. Which for the most part he was.

But Scott knew him better than that; they'd grown up together, after all. Scott knew the date, time and telephone number of the girl Fergus had lost his virginity to. Fifteen years later and Scott still couldn't accept that his best friend had become a man of the cloth. And as for that girl jogging down sorority row, was she wearing any underwear?

'You're a married man, Richard, stop embarrassing yourself.'

'Separated,' Scott grunted, kicking the grass in lazy strides and digging his hands in his khaki pants. 'What happened to us, Fergus?'

'You and me? Or you and Jessica?'

Scott winced at the mention of his estranged wife's name. His friend really did have this priest thing down to a fine art. Fergus had flown in from the Vatican City especially for his lecture and would be going back in the morning, but somehow Scott got the impression their friendship had nothing to do with Fergus's decision to come here.

Fergus reached for another cigarette and scratched his head. 'Look, Richie, that was an interesting lecture you gave, but are you honestly trying to say that the Catholic Church was involved in a sixty-year conspiracy to keep the Dead Sea Scrolls suppressed?'

'And others.'

'Absurd. We can't even keep our own clergy in order, so who the hell was supposed to be trustworthy enough to sit on that particular time-bomb? Ireland's government fell in 1994 because some priests turned out to be pedophiles. I *know* the Church is fallible.' He paused, then: 'Yes, there was a conspiracy, but an academic one. I agree, it's indefensible. A gang of pompous old asses refusing to release the documents until they'd had first crack at translating them. But what you came out with today . . . well, I can't see the Church crumbling over that one. You know what people are like when they hear a new crackpot theory – they ignore it. Like the one about Jesus going to Britain and starting a school, or the one where he married Mary Magdalene and moved to France—'

'I happen to like that one.'

'And then there was that half-assed theory about how he'd been trained in the mystical arts of Egyptian magic. People will believe what they want to believe. And they believe in Jesus Christ, Our Lord. *I* believe. Richie, you're throwing your career away on bullshit!'

'You're changing the subject.'

'The Church obviously means a lot to you, or you wouldn't put in this much effort.'

They faced off on the lawn. Scott still had his fists planted firmly in his pockets. His tie flapped lightly against his crisp pale-blue shirt in the breeze. He smirked. 'Religion, Fergus, is like a disease of the human mind. It's like rabies. You get bitten and suddenly there's this great foaming at the mouth, all sense and reason thrown to the wind. There's a lot of shouting and then you bite someone else in all the madness and it gets passed on down the line across generations, and national boundaries. Forget AIDS. This stuff kills millions.'

Fergus simply took a long drag on his cigarette.

Scott said: 'Ever heard of the Church of Simon Kimbangu?' The priest shook his head. 'It's on the west coast of Africa. Simon Kimbangu was a militant who believed in democracy. The government considered him a revolutionary and arrested him, but his followers, believing he'd gone to heaven, set up a church in his honor. Prayed to him for salvation. They did any damn idiotic thing except bother to take the twenty-minute walk down to the local jailhouse where Kimbangu was starving to death. And even more insane – the church still exists today! Think about it! Why did the Crusaders lay siege to a castle at Hosen Al Akre for three days before realizing it was populated by sheep?' Scott suddenly asked innocently. 'Religion, that's why.'

Fergus glowered. 'Religion,' he corrected, 'is the closest we can get to the beginning. To knowing where we come from as a species. And why we're here.'

'Why are *you* here?'

It was as pointed as it was grim. And Fergus's mood altered to accommodate. 'I came to let you know that as of this morning, the Vatican is the major benefactor for the Anthropology Department at Washington State. In order to conclude the deal certain prerequisites were required. One of which was to shake up the Epigraphy wing.'

Scott's face drained.

Fergus gulped. 'They let you go. There's a letter already waiting for you in your hotel room. I'm sorry.' He took a final drag on his cigarette before stubbing it out with his foot.

* * *

They let him go. It wasn't entirely unexpected, but the manner in which they delivered the message was a jolt. Sending Fergus was a stroke of genius.

'Dr Scott! Dr Scott!'

Scott spun on his heel to see November Dryden racing across the lawn toward them. The sun made her skin look like fine porcelain, and her body moved with a rhythm all of its own. He tried to focus on that and shift his mood into another gear but it wasn't happening. 'November,' Scott said in a daze. 'What can I do for you?'

Her chest heaved as she got her breath back. She glanced nervously at Fergus, who was busy enjoying the air, and tried to smile but she was a southern girl through and through. This was a man of the cloth and deserved respect. Scott made a mental note to himself. November was a smart young woman. He had to make sure that when the tour was over, he would set aside some money and sponsor her to get a place in college, well out of state. She'd been mentioning she wanted a shot at a research assistantship. Maybe he could swing something.

'You forgot your package,' she said breathlessly. 'You know – the one from your lecture?'

November handed over a large brown paper package which Scott immediately ripped open. It contained a set of documents, photographs, articles – a whole geological report on global flooding by a women named Sarah Kelsey. But then he found the covering letter.

'What is it?' Fergus asked warily when he saw the expression on Scott's face.

But Scott wasn't about to tell him. His mind was racing as he took out the slip of paper from inside. It was an itinerary. Hotel and flight details. But the really important feature was the handwritten note on the back. To the average Joe it didn't mean a thing, but to Richard Scott it meant the world. And that the world itself was about to have a very rude awakening.

He started across the lawn, lost in thought before he realized he'd left Fergus standing there. He turned and met the priest's gaze. 'Tell the Board they didn't fire me,' he called out steadily. 'I quit.'

Then he picked up the pace. Re-reading the note.

Civilization was said to have begun in the third millennium Before the Common Era, or Before Christ, with the advent of a writing system called cuneiform. Before that point, writing was thought to consist of crude scratchings and ill-thought-out pictographic symbols. Any evidence of a complex language and writing system *pre-dating* cuneiform would therefore mean a major re-think of the dawn of civilization. Every history book would have to be thrown out the window.

It would be earthshattering.

All the note said was: *Am in possession of pre-cuneiform text. Request your immediate assessment. Yours truly, Ralph Matheson.*

Scott beckoned to November as he backed up across the lawn. 'Still want that assistantship?'

'Yeah!' she replied enthusiastically. 'Why?'

Scott reached into the package and plucked out two airline tickets. 'Pack your bags. We're going to Geneva.'

THE BERESOVKA RIVER

FEDERAL REPUBLIC OF SIBERIA

7:32 AM

It was still dark when she got the call. She swung herself out of bed about fifteen minutes later and had a piping hot shower. She downed a shot of *kvass* for breakfast and pulled on two layers of underwear. Her sweater was thick and heavy and her parka went taut when she zipped it up.

She caught a glimpse of herself in the mirror. Long dark hair. Dark eyes. Signs of a tan and a dimple in her chin. She felt drained; this assignment was killing her. 'God, you look like shit, Sarah,' she spat at herself. 'Why, thank you, Sarah,' she grumbled. She tried to make the coat look a little baggier. A little less full. It was stupid, she knew. Under all that there wasn't a lot of her anyway. But it helped to show it off. 'Come on, Sarah. Smile, you bitch.' She forced a grin. It hurt. How the hell had she wound up in Siberia? This hadn't been in the grand plan of her youth.

She slammed the draughty wooden hotel door shut as she went.

The 4×4 they'd loaned her for the job had seen better days, but the lights were good and the suspension held up to the mud-track roads. It took forty minutes to get from the hotel and upriver out to the site. When she did get there she found a hive of inaction. Around the periphery, trucks were still being loaded up with rubble and hauling out. But in the center, work had stopped. The cranes were idle. Floodlights lit up the equipment but she couldn't see any workers. As she climbed out of the 4×4 she could hear voices shouting

instructions in Russian dialects and human whistles screeching out
as the workforce tried to co-ordinate their efforts.

She had to trudge on foot over the mud rise, past the *Rola Corp.*
sign and down to the main construction site. More lights had hastily
been erected. From a distance it looked like a UFO had landed –
but Sarah hoped for the Martians' sake that they hadn't. This project
was so far behind that she was liable to march straight up to them
and smash in their little green faces. She did not want to hear about
any more delays. She just wanted to get her job done and get back
to the States.

There was a bulldozer down in the pit, past steel and concrete
foundations. It had stopped, but the engine was still ticking over.
Slapping a plastic yellow hard hat on, she pushed past a couple of
workmen and made her way to the front where all the attention had
gathered. Her mouth hung open when she finally got there.

'Hey, Sarah. How ya doin'?' came the big, grinning welcome of
Steve Lustgarten, the foreman. He was struggling to loop a steel cable
around a thick trunk of frozen fur.

The whole scene was starting to take on primordial qualities as
the steam from everybody's breath clung to the air. They were all
gathered around a huge, magnificent creature that had walked the
tundra long ago. At least fourteen feet high, it was staring straight at
her, its eyes black and glassy, as though it was close to tears. The
creature was in a sitting position, reared up on its front legs. It had
an elegant, dignified expression on its face. Its matted fur was long
and shaggy. It looked almost regal, frozen solid. Its ivory tusks
extended out like the last vestiges of a cry for help. Its trunk was
curled and it had decayed buttercups hanging from its mouth. It had
been eating buttercups when it had died.

'That's a mammoth,' Sarah announced, surprised. She moved to
the left and could see where part of the body was missing. It looked
ripped away rather than rotted. It was hollow now, except for the
remnants of a fetus. She had been pregnant. There was no smell,
except for the mud and the river.

Steve grinned again, with a nod. 'Yeah. Isn't she a beauty?'

Sarah was furious. This was all completely lost on her. She dug
her fists into her pockets, and screwed them up into balls. 'No. There
is absolutely nothing beautiful about a twelve-thousand-year-old

frozen elephant! You called me out here, in the middle of the fucking night to see a goddamn woolly mammoth? You gotta be shittin' me! That's precisely why I didn't want to come to fucking Siberia in the first place. I hate Siberia. I hate Alaska. I hate the Canadian north. You can't dig a fucking hole to piss in without running across a thousand fucking extinct, fucking frozen animals. If it's not mammoths it's saber-toothed tigers. You know, last year I found a fucking mastodon? I'm sick of this!'

The Russian workers couldn't speak English, but they could sense she was upset. The murmuring ceased abruptly and they all stared at the half-crazed American lady. Steve left the loop to dangle and straightened up. He was frowning now, annoyed. '*I* didn't call you, Sarah. Someone else did. Go piss *them* off. I don't get to see too many of these things.' He delved into his pocket for a camera and handed it to a Russian. 'Now if you don't mind, I wanna take a picture for my kid before the museum people drag it away.' He posed like a big game hunter next to the massive creature.

Sarah suddenly felt very sorry for it. She turned her back.

She could hear her name being called, but she couldn't figure out from where. Seconds later two guys in hard-hats and big green rubber boots were waving their arms about trying to remain upright while they slid and stumbled down the black mud bank. As they drew closer she could see that the smaller, thinner one of the two was dressed in a suit and a gray crombie. The other one was dressed sensibly. 'Sarah Kelsey? Ms Kelsey, is that you?' the man in the suit was calling out, trying to keep his hat on.

'Yes, it's me,' Sarah said frostily.

'The geologist, right?'

'Yeah.' She whirled around when she heard a chainsaw spark into life. She glanced at two of the Russians ripping into the carcass, then turned back to the men. 'Are you the people who called me?'

'Yes,' he smiled. 'Yes, we are.' He stuck out his hand, but she eyed it distastefully. 'Jay Houghton.' He rubbed his hand absently on his coat. Perhaps it had been dirty. His eye caught something peculiar. He was like a child. 'Wow, is that a mammoth?'

'I dunno. What do you think?' she asked sardonically.

'It sure looks like a mammoth.'

'Well, then I guess it must be one.'

There was more shouting as a few more Russians came tearing over the hill with an oil-drum on wheels, a fire raging inside it. Someone else carried the ketchup and the barbecue sauce. The guy with the chainsaw started cutting up steaks and slapped them on the grill mesh they had fastened to the top of the drum. Lustgarten was horrified.

'What're they doing?'

Houghton looked visibly sick. He put a gloved hand over his nose as the smell and the smoke wafted over. 'Good God!'

'I thought they were museum people!' Lustgarten yelped. 'They can't eat it!'

'Oh, come off it,' Sarah snapped at him with a scowl. 'That's more steak than these people have ever seen. Of course they're going to eat it!'

The guy next to Houghton was laughing. He puffed on his cigar and watched with some amusement. Lustgarten tried to stop the Russians, but they just elbowed him out the way. Offered him some barbecued mammoth, but he wasn't having any of it. They ignored him from then on. He might be their boss, but the guy obviously had no appreciation of the finer delicacies.

Houghton coughed on the smoke. 'How long has that thing been in the ground?'

Sarah was climbing the bank. She turned back. 'Twelve, maybe fourteen thousand years. At the very least.'

'And they're gonna eat it? They must be crazy. It'll kill 'em.'

Sarah just shook her head. This guy Houghton was an idiot; she could tell that much already. 'I doubt it,' she said. She took another step but they weren't following. Hadn't they read the report on this place? Mammoths were turning up all over this region. There was a famous case from 1902 when one had been found in a bank just down the river from here. The same river. 'It was super-frozen,' she explained.

'Huh? It was what?'

'The Arctic isn't cold enough to freeze something the size of a mammoth without ice crystals forming in the blood and spoiling the meat. That mammoth was supercooled. The temperature had to be around minus 100°C. It was dead inside thirty minutes, and encased in permafrosted silt about the same time. Perfect preservation. The meat's fine. It's just . . . very old.'

Houghton was stunned. 'How's that possible? What could cause that kind of destruction?'

'And before the advent of the refrigerator . . .' the guy with the cigar chipped in.

'How the hell should I know?' Sarah shrugged.

'Well, uh, you're a geologist, you must have some idea.'

Sarah wasn't listening. She was climbing the bank. Houghton eyed the mammoth again. 'I wonder what it tastes like,' he mused.

'Chicken,' the other guy smirked, and puffed on his cigar.

Houghton shot him a glance. He didn't seem to know if he was being played with or not. He looked for Sarah. She was heading away from them, back to her 4×4. They climbed up out of the pit behind her. But Houghton couldn't help but pause briefly and take another lingering look at the mammoth. Dignified even in death. 'Wow.'

Lustgarten was raising his fist, directing the driver in the cab of the bulldozer to shift into reverse. There was a mechanical roar as they started to drag the animal out of their foundations. Houghton did a doubletake and realized they were losing Sarah. He chased after her.

'Ms Kelsey! Wait up, please! This is important. This is company business.' He slipped on the mud. Tried not to land on his ass. 'Ms Kelsey!'

Ripping the driver's side door open, she said: 'I'm just getting my purse, is that okay with you?' She slammed it shut again. Reached for a cigarette. The other guy accommodated with a light. She eyed him suspiciously. No wonder she didn't recognize him – he was wearing a ski mask. She couldn't see him. 'Who're you?' she demanded.

'Bulger,' he said. 'Jack Bulger. Chief Field Engineer with Rola Corp. We're practically family.'

She sucked down some smoke. Nodded. 'Oh.'

'Gee, Ms Kelsey, I'd really appreciate it if you could explain more about this super-freezing business,' Houghton said. He was acting like a real nerd, but he was far from actually being one. He was too slimy. She was only just starting to realize that about him. He eyed her stonily. 'I'd be *real* appreciative. After all, you're supposed to be the star of the company, but just how much geology do you really know? Only the company's thinking of downsizing and I'm here on orders from the highest regard.'

She blew smoke. That had caught her attention. 'How high?' she asked.

'The highest.'

A cheap test. Maybe he wasn't so stupid after all. What the hell. 'Okay,' she said, leaning against the car, 'all over the arctic tundra, from Siberia to Alaska, people have been finding frozen animals, hundreds of thousands of them, all caught in the middle of something, taken completely by surprise. They were running, or eating, or whatever. In any event, their deaths were not slow. They were sudden, within minutes. They're encased in silt, not ice. They were not swept down rivers, they were entangled in masses of trees, vegetation, boulders. Real Wrath of God-type stuff. You ever read your Bible?' Houghton nodded. 'Well, the only thing that could do that, about the only thing that fits the description, is Noah's Flood.

'But it had to have been more than just a flood, because most of the mammoths in this region were found eating buttercups, grasses – stuff you can only find in temperate areas. Not arctic tundra, which suggests that Siberia has moved, shifted its entire position. But we know that's impossible. However, we also know there are ashes in the silt, so there was burning. Possibly volcanoes, which would explain the extreme cold if enough dust was hurled into the upper atmosphere and obscured the sun on a large enough global scale. That, Mr Houghton, is what my geology tells me.' She puffed again on her cigarette. 'It's all in my report,' she said. 'You should call up Head Office and order a copy.'

It had taken her six years on and off. Collecting statistics and working on a coherent synthesis.

In 1940, in the Tanana River, in the Yukon, Alaska, hundreds of thousands of mammoths, mastodons and bison were found in twisted, torn heaps. Piled with splintered trees and four layers of thick volcanic ash. But no mere volcanic explosion could have caused such massive destruction.

In one particular century, 120,000 years ago, findings imprinted in limestone just off the Bahamas showed that the ocean rose twenty feet above today's sea levels. Then plunged thirty feet below that soon afterwards. Considering average sea levels rose between one and five millimeters a year, the recorded fluctuation was massive. And the only solution – put forward by Texas A & M University – was a sudden melt and refreeze of the Poles. But by what mechanism?

Jacques Cousteau found a series of underwater caves in the same area with huge stalagmites and stalactites – proof they were once above water. The unusual structure of the stalactites showed that a geological upheaval had occurred around 10,000BC. As a result, the earth's crust in that region became tilted at an angle of fifteen degrees. The caverns were now hundreds of feet below water, and one was almost spherical in shape – an indication of one of two things: volcanic activity, or manmade underground explosions.

Other statistics showed the earth's sea level and climate historically oscillated in keeping with solar radiation. One peak of solar radiation, in 15,000BC, coincided directly with a rise of world sea levels of 350 feet. The final peak in the constant fluctuation was in 4,000BC – fitting in with the same time that Babylonian, Egyptian and Hebrew cultures first spun their Flood stories. Sarah didn't know much about ancient scripture, but she did know the final upsurge was a sea-level rise of 9.5 meters in 250 years; 9.5 meters equaled 30 feet, and 30 feet, in ancient measurements, was 15 cubits. Exactly the same as the depth of Flood mentioned in *Genesis* when Noah boarded the Ark.

Indeed, other geological evidence had uncovered the fact that around 5,000 years ago, vast sections of the earth were flooded suddenly when the huge volcanic fracture down the center of the Atlantic gave way and blasted billions of tons of water into the atmosphere.

And in 1996, scientists at the Lamont-Doherty Earth Observatory in Palisades, New York, drilled cores of rock in the North Atlantic sea floor only to discover that the earth's climate changed abruptly every 1,000 to 3,000 years.

In short, Sarah had done her homework. And they knew it, or they wouldn't be here. But why were they interested? It was a novelty item. Interesting, but hardly useful.

Houghton eyed Bulger briefly and shrugged. 'She'll do,' he said. 'Let's get inside. Bring your equipment.' He headed for the temporary cabin on the far side of the construction site.

Bulger made a slight bow and indicated the way. 'After you,' he said.

Inside the cabin there was a bottled gas fire and some lighting. Houghton flipped the whole lot on and rubbed his hands in the heat. There were maps and plans tacked to all the walls, and sets of papers spread out over the tables. It may have been the twenty-first century, but nothing much had changed. Rola Corp. was in the middle of building a new oil refinery and the mammoth had been directly in the path of where the outflow pipe-line was due to go. The whole project so far had been one geological headache after another.

Sarah dumped her case on one of the desks and stood on the other side of the room. They might all work for the same happy company, but they were still two strange men, and she was still a lone female. Why the hell should she trust them?

'Sorry,' Sarah said now. 'I can't quite remember what it is you said you do for the company?'

'I didn't say,' Houghton told her. 'But, for your information, I'm a lawyer.'

'*Lawyer*? Then what the hell are you doing out here?'

Houghton glanced at Bulger, but inclined his head toward Sarah. Bulger dug into his pocket, pulled out a clear plastic bag and emptied a small crystal into his hand. He tossed it to Sarah. She caught it with one hand and turned it over in the light. There was writing on it.

'What is it?'

Houghton tutted and generally looked disappointed.

Sarah heaved a sigh and sat at the desk. 'Okay,' she grumbled. She flipped her case open and went to work. There was a laptop computer built into the upper section, some small electronic probes that measured resistance and other properties, a set of electronic scales and the usual tools, like a small gem pick, a file and some tweezers. A microscope was packed away in its box. Opting for the age-old method, she picked up her eyepiece and took a good look.

The two men seemed more interested in other things, their minds elsewhere as they agitatedly conferred. More than likely, they already knew what it was. Which irritated her even more.

She turned the stone over and over, was about to announce her conclusion and then thought better of it. What kind of lattice structure *was* that? She switched the computer on and called up some files. She raced through every structure she thought it matched and drew a dead end. So she did a couple of quick tests with the other equipment, before calling up theoretical models. She'd seen this structure somewhere before.

'This is some kind of diamond,' she announced.

Houghton took in a deep breath. He straightened. 'We know,' he replied flatly, as if to imply, 'Is that all you can come up with?'

'But it's not like any diamond I've ever seen,' she went on. 'It's not natural. This was manmade. Its molecular structure's a bucky-ball. You know what a bucky-ball is, right?' This was staggering news. Her eyes never wavered from the back of Houghton's head. Finally he turned to face her. Grim.

'Yes,' he said, 'I know what a bucky-ball is. Our people at the research center back in Dallas were kind enough to explain it to me. It's a theoretical molecular arrangement of carbon atoms. We have three in nature – basic carbon, which gives us coal and to which we all owe our lives. The other two are graphite and diamond. Buckminster Fuller's Buckminsterfullerene, or bucky-ball, shouldn't exist. It's stronger, more resilient; if you could find any, you could build an elevator to the moon.'

'Right,' she said. 'But it's just . . . well. Kroto and Smalley won a Nobel Prize for making enough to fit on a pin-head. Other than that it's supposed to be just a theory.'

'Not anymore.'

'I take it you didn't create it or you wouldn't be coming to me.' She glanced at Bulger. Asked pointedly: 'Where did you find this?'

'Antarctica.'

That was not what she had expected to hear. She balked. 'Excuse me?'

Houghton reached into his pocket and pulled out another stone. He tossed it to her. 'Next surprise,' he said.

She compared it to the other one. Same writing. Same structure. 'This from Antarctica too?' She asked.

Houghton shook his head. 'No,' he said. 'Another site. You have two hours to get packed.'

* * *

'Another site?' A second site? What site? Where?'

'Somewhere warmer than here.'

Sarah was on her feet, closing her case. The men were already halfway out the door. She mulled it over. Warmer than here? This was good. Anywhere hot was better than here.

She looked at the stone. It was Carbon 60. And from what she could determine, it was integrated with another type of diamond that was even tougher, conceived of in the mid-1990s by some Harvard professors and christened Diamonite. It was a compound of carbon and nitrogen atoms. β-C_3N_4. The bucky-ball chunk of diamond was made up of molecules that consisted of sixty carbon atoms in a spherical geodesic formation. Known as $C60$, it was tough. And Diamonite was theoretically even tougher. Together, they made a formidable compound – ten, maybe a hundred times stronger than ordinary diamond. This definitely couldn't be naturally occurring. Since the mid-1950s, when General Electric had a stab at it, people had been trying to synthesize diamond. The best anyone had come up with was an inferior film that could be coated onto the tip of tools. This was evidence of a far more advanced technology.

'You'd need powerful lasers to cut this stuff,' Sarah said, shaking with excitement. Diamonite *and* $C60$? Not only was this the find of the century but it was her ticket out of here. Finally a shot at pure research, maybe even some exploration. 'There need to be more tests,' she stated, handing the samples back.

'We're doing more tests,' Houghton replied. 'In Geneva.'

'That's where you're going?'

Houghton simply nodded as he held the door open and let the wind whistle around the room as Bulger laid out the plan. 'The most powerful lasers in the world are in Geneva. Ever since that thing in the Ross Sea, Rola Corp.'s been under scrutiny. Thorne's been in the White House more times this week than the Vice President. We have full government and military backing, provided the tests in Geneva are good. We'll wind up as the sole suppliers of $C60$ to the entire western world.'

Houghton pulled the collar of his coat up around his neck. 'No need to remind you, Ms Kelsey, the Chinese may already be ahead in the race. We want you to head up the geologic survey at the second site. Learn everything you can. When we're done in Geneva we'll pick you up on the way through. You have days, not weeks, to complete your assignment.'

Sarah was stunned. She shivered with the bitter winds. 'Through to where?' she asked apprehensively.

'We're going back to Antarctica,' he added.

But the door had already banged shut behind him.

CONNECTIONS

The Universe may not only be queerer than we imagine; it may be queerer than we *can* imagine.

J.B.S. Haldane, Geneticist and Biometrician, 1892–1964

42,000 FT

SOMEWHERE OVER THE NORTH ATLANTIC

CLUB CLASS

The storm below was ferocious. Heavy rain driving in squalls. Vast freezing sheets lit up brilliant white against a grim black sky as lightning coursed through thick angry cloud.

When the plane shuddered this time, it caught November Dryden, who had been staggering up the aisle, completely off-guard. She gripped the nearest head-rest, which forced Richard Scott to snatch his drink off the tray before it shot across the cabin.

He glanced up at the student. 'Are you okay?' he asked gravely.

November wiped her mouth. Her face was pale; sweat beaded across her forehead. 'Professor, do I look okay to you?' she mumbled.

'No. You look like shit.'

'Then stop asking stupid questions,' she growled, resuming her struggle for the nearest bathroom.

The man sitting next to Scott nodded his approval. 'I like her.'

Scott smiled briefly by way of a polite response and returned to reading Sarah Kelsey's extraordinary geology report. It made for disturbing reading, and for a while Scott hadn't even figured out why he'd been sent it in the first place. But then he had remembered that the oldest known piece of literature was the Sumerian *Epic of Gilgamesh*. It was the story that formed the basis for the Bible's tale of Noah's Ark, and was written in cuneiform. Perhaps this Ralph Matheson person was anticipating that this new *pre*-cuneiform text was an even earlier version of that same story. Sarah's report may have been sent to get him in the mood. Now *that* would be something special . . .

'Tell me, Dr Scott, how do you really feel about the possibility of doing archeology in Antarctica?'

Scott snapped his head up from reading. 'Excuse me?'

The plane shuddered again as the guy indicated an identical set of documents on his own tray, right down to Sarah's geology report. 'It's all right here,' he replied.

Scott studied the man next to him with some suspicion. He had tanned Hispanic features, thick black hair, and was leaning against the window, looking bored but he had an enigmatic hint of amusement tugging at his lips.

'I, uh, I didn't get to that part yet. I'm sorry. How do you know who I am?' Scott demanded.

The man held up a copy of the thesis he was reading. *Tales of the Deluge: A Global Report on Cultural Self-Replicating Genesis Myths* by Dr Richard Scott. It even had his photo on the back.

'I pay attention to the details, don't you?' the man responded. 'I'm reading yours; you're reading hers.' He sighed. 'But no one seems to be reading mine . . . In any event,' he added, 'I think this is all a crazy notion. Have you seen how cold it is down in Antarctica? First of all I'd have to ask who the hell lived there? And second of all I'd have to ask who has that kind of stamina that they could actually do archeology in those temperatures.' The guy smiled. Quietly punched a button on his arm rest, closed his eyes, and reclined.

'There must be some mistake. I didn't agree to go on any dig. Someone wanted my opinion on some texts, that's all. Who *are* you, anyway?' Scott insisted.

The guy snapped his eyes open suddenly as the plane dipped wildly. He stuck his hand out but Scott was in no mood to shake it. 'I'm sorry,' he said. 'How rude of me. Here we are about to crash into the ocean and we haven't been properly introduced. I'm Jon Hackett. I believe we're going to be working together in Geneva.'

Scott was confused. 'In what capacity? And what makes you think we're about to drop into the ocean?'

The main cabin lights suddenly dimmed. The whole plane

shuddered as the lights flickered off then on. There were screams from somewhere in the rear. Call bleeps rang out throughout the cabin. Seatbelt signs blazed.

Scott and Hackett squirmed in their chairs as they hurried to comply with the directive. Those who were standing had already dived for the nearest available seats. Hackett eyed his own belt disdainfully as he buckled up. 'Oh, this'll help,' he said dryly.

Scott eyed him warily, trying to ignore the fact that the buffeting was getting worse. 'So tell me, how did you know this was about to happen? I don't believe in chance.'

Hackett did not respond immediately. Neither did he make eye-contact when he did. Instead his eyes were sharp, focused on the rest of the plane panicking around him. Still with that same curious smile attached to his mouth, he answered: 'Educated guess.'

Scott knew that expression. It was the look of a pure academic: someone who had spotted a chance to observe his own work in action. Hackett was studying these people as though they were research for a thesis. It made Scott angry. 'I hardly think this is time for experiment.'

'On the contrary, this is very much part of a grand experiment,' Hackett replied. 'Y'know, I knew a girl who studied which way up a slice of buttered toast would land. Dropped it over and over for a month. Found it was pure chance. Fifty-fifty.' He sat back in his chair. 'Of course, her methodology was flawed. She didn't take into account nearly enough variables. Dropping toast, I told her, is not a random event. Everybody knows it'll land buttered side down.'

'This is no time for statistics either!'

'I'm a physicist,' Hackett explained as if that excused everything. 'I warned these people on the ground we shouldn't be flying in these conditions but they wouldn't listen. Practically accused me of aero-phobia.'

'You're afraid of flying?'

Now Hackett opted for eye-contact. 'Oh, dear me no. Flying's not a problem,' he said decidedly. 'Falling . . .' He thought about it for another moment. 'Now *that's* a problem.'

'Well, if you knew there'd be trouble, why did you take this flight?'

Scott felt his stomach drop out from under him again. He tried to remain calm, but it was difficult to control the rush of adrenaline that came with every lurch.

Hackett turned to him. 'It was the only connecting flight to Geneva. And I do have to get to Geneva.'

'What *is* in Geneva?' Scott demanded.

'The Swiss?' Hackett winked.

'It's called CERN,' Hackett explained. 'Europe's biggest nuclear research facility. That's where they're sending us.'

'I don't get it,' Scott replied absently. Right now, he was more concerned for November's safety. He hoped she was okay in the bathroom.

'You don't have to "get it". Come on, what are the odds? Two heavyweight professors in different fields sitting next to each other on a plane going to CERN. You just said so yourself, you don't believe in chance. We both know the world's far more complex than that. Complexity . . . It's the key to everything.

'We're the military's show boys, Dr Scott. The government's excuse to go marching into that Chinese base in Antarctica and find out what's going on down there. Under the terms of the Antarctic Treaty, that has to be a scientific team. That's us. I used to work at CERN, so I called an old friend. The US military are crawling all over. A Colonel personally booked both our tickets.'

'The military? I've heard nothing about the military. What are you talking about? I've been invited to Geneva to work on an ancient text. I did not—'

'Oh, what did they do? Appeal to your better nature? Cute. I don't happen to have a better nature so they paid me lots of money. Don't you watch the news? Haven't you been following what's going on? Chinese scientists are seen sunbathing in Antarctica. Now you don't light the touch paper to a power source as powerful as a mini-sun unless you invented it or found it. If you invented it – get the hell off Antarctica. If you found it, then we want it. At all costs. We're the excuse to start a war.'

Richard Scott suddenly had that dawning feeling that, in all the euphoria of putting one over on Fergus and the University, he had failed to consider just what kind of a situation he was putting himself into. How bad could it be?

The cabin lights flickered on and off disconcertingly.

'What's with this plane?' Scott exclaimed.

Hackett sketched out complex mathematics on a tatty page of his notebook. 'Roughly every twenty-two years, the sun goes ballistic, with sunspot activity. Solar flares.' He waved his hands melodramatically. 'Radiation – *that's* what's wrong with this plane.'

Scott clamped his eyes shut as the plane shuddered furiously. 'We're caught in a storm,' he said thinly.

'Yes, but what causes the storm?'

'I don't care,' Scott told him.

'The sun, Dr Scott, causes the storm. The sun is causing all this. We're not actually in a storm, we're thousands of feet above it. But the sun is disrupting the computer that flies this plane. The earth's magnetosphere is dragging all these highly charged particles down into the atmosphere. You've seen pictures of the Aurora Borealis, the Northern lights. All those colors moving in stripes across the sky are the earth's magnetic field-lines lit up because all this sun "stuff" is trapped in them, and is being burnt up.'

'And your point would be?'

'My *point* is, it all just hit the earth's atmosphere. And if my calculations are correct, it's a prelude to something bigger. Much bigger.'

Scott tried to keep his breathing shallow and steady.

'You don't seem to be taking in the enormity of the situation,' Hackett nagged.

Scott didn't answer.

'Want to know what sunspot cycles can do? When your TV goes nuts, it's because of the sun. When your radio won't tune into a station, it's because of the sun. In March 1989, sun-spot activity was so violent, the voltage in Quebec's power-grid fluctuated. Lights went out. Microwaves refused to wave. Six *million* people were left without electricity for *nine* hours. NASA lost track of spacecraft. The Aurora was spotted in Key West. Telecommunications and computers went haywire. Sophisticated planes dropped from the sky. Sound familiar to you?'

Scott simply glared as *bang*! the bathroom door up the aisle was snapped back and November emerged with the most hateful look on her face.

'Nobody go in there,' she announced as she fell into her seat.

All stability collapsed around them at that point. They could hear the whine of the engines and feel them vibrate as they struggled to provide enough power. Hackett grabbed his drink before it spilled all over his lap. The main intercom bleeped sporadically as the captain cut in to explain the situation. But it didn't take a genius to figure out: they were going down.

Prayer erupted in the cabin. There was a pounding noise in the background. A fat lady across the aisle had shut her eyes and was making a cross over her heart. There was a pounding noise in the background. She was doing it backwards and Scott reasoned she must not have done that sort of thing in a long time, if at all, before now. Others had already started bracing themselves for impact. There was a pounding noise in the background.

Hackett edged forward in his seat. Curious. 'Where's that noise coming from?'

A young guy was standing up, banging the overhead compartment, trying to get at his oxygen mask.

Hackett leaned in close. Pointed with his drink before taking another sip. 'Now that's just plain silly.' A flight attendant rushed in and started forcing the passenger back into his seat. 'I don't recall us losing air pressure, do you? Why on earth would he think he needs oxygen?'

'He's panicking,' Scott snapped. 'He doesn't know what he's doing.'

Hackett glanced out the window, then back at his watch. 'I'd say we've got about three, maybe four minutes.'

Finally Scott lost all patience. 'Will you shut up!' he barked.

Hackett didn't seem willing to listen. 'The problem with society today,' he went on placidly, 'is its singular lack of communication. We live in the information age. We talk to each other all the time – on the net, on the phone. We have TV, HV, VR. But we're *not* communicating. We seem to be amassing so much garbage, but we're not conveying what's really important.'

Scott faced front and tried to ignore Hackett. He would have preferred to listen instead to some music or watch TV, but the equipment had been switched off and wasn't working anyway. His skull bounced off the head-rest as the plane took another pounding. He could sense their angle of descent getting steeper.

'And the problem's even more acute in academia.' Hackett finished his drink, wondered what to do with the empty glass before opting to hang on to it. 'You're a Professor of something or other and I'm a Professor of Physics. How much are you willing to bet our two departments have never communicated with each other?' Hackett didn't seem to notice that Scott had other things on his mind.

'Exactly!' Hackett nodded, as though Scott had replied. 'Never. Like that ancient Chinese proverb where three wise men are blindfolded and told to identify the mystery guest just by their sense of touch. The first insists it's a snake because it's long and muscular. The second thinks it's a tree trunk. Finally, the third guy says it's a bird. It has to be a bird – its wings are flapping.' He stuffed the glass into the seat pocket in front. Licked his lips. 'Well, didn't they feel like fools when they ripped off their masks to find an elephant.' He smiled pragmatically.

'My point is, that's what it's like working in modern science today. Everything's so compartmentalized. Nobody shares information. Three different sciences could study the same thing and never know it. For all we know, the ancients were right – the Earth *is* being carried through the universe on the back of a giant turtle. But the turtle's so big and we're only studying such microscopic parts that we haven't noticed.'

Very slowly, Scott turned his head toward Hackett. He was sweating heavily and it was all he could do not to throw up on him. 'What – are – you – talking about?'

Suddenly the seat in front tipped backwards revealing a couple spontaneously making out. Scott didn't recall them having known each other previously.

Hackett reinforced the point with the thrust of a hand. 'Put *that* in a movie and no one would believe you. 'He glanced at the gold Rolex strapped to his wrist. 'Thirty seconds,' he announced.

'Thirty seconds from what?!'

'We're gonna die! Oh my God, we're gonna die!' the man seated right next to November started to shriek. His breathing was ferocious. Labored.

November snatched the sick bag up from the pocket in front and tossed it in his face. 'You're hyperventilating,' she growled. 'Breathe into the damn thing and shut up!'

Hackett methodically counted out the seconds, each number growing progressively louder until confidently he announced: 'And we should bank to the left, right about . . . now.'

The plane started banking to the left.

The shuddering subsided. The engines sounded a little healthier. After a moment or two Scott could feel the whole cabin leveling out. The sigh of relief was palpable and for most of the passengers it was about the right time to let the tears flow.

Hackett sat back, looking smug. 'Pilots,' he pontificated, 'only really like talking to other pilots. When someone from an unrelated field tells him that a phenomenon from an equally unrelated source is going to play very real havoc with his marvelously integrated transportation system, the chances of him paying any attention at all are nil. Until, of course, all hell breaks loose. In which case the pilot's going to make damn sure he's explored every available option. Including reading the message the unrelated someone insisted he keep in his jacket pocket. You see, what we've just experienced is a Complex Adaptive System in action. Complexity. Order, in a seeming myriad of chaos.'

Despite Hackett's amused chuckle, Scott remained silent. Stone-faced.

'In other words, Dr Scott: ain't sun-spot activity a bitch? Who knew we'd get weather like this?' Hackett stood, unconsciously smoothing out the creases in his pants. 'Excuse me, I need to use the bathroom.' He stepped out into the aisle, much to November's irritation.

'I said, nobody go in—'

Scott shot her a look and flapped his hand. Let the idiot find out for himself.

Hackett pulled the cubicle door open, allowing Scott a brief glimpse inside. Putrid yellow slime was sprayed everywhere. Chunks of stomach lining clung to the aluminum bulkhead, in massed lumps. Despite his best efforts, Hackett couldn't help but reel at the smell. And slowly, very slowly, Scott smiled.

'It was Buddha, by the way,' he said casually.

Hackett seemed distressed. 'What was Buddha?' he snapped, as he was forced to take in a breath and gagged in the process.

'Who told the parable of the wise men and the elephant. And it was *four* wise men.'

'Oh . . . thanks,' Hackett replied distantly as he gingerly stepped into the cubicle.

Scott idly thumbed through the illegible figurework in Hackett's notebook, but immediately wished he hadn't because to illustrate his points Hackett had drawn little pictures next to his calculations. The sun exploding. The earth in dire trouble. And underlined at the bottom of the page Hackett had written: *It's begun.*

Scott set the notebook down. 'No shit,' he said.

CERN

AZTEC − ANDES MOUNTAINS − CENTRAL AMERICA

During the time of the Fourth Sun (Epoch), to save one man, Coxcoxtli, and one woman, Xochiquetzal, from the crashing floods of heaven, the god Tezcatilpoca instructed them to build a boat. They landed atop a mountain where they settled and had many children. But their children remained dumb until a dove in a tree gave them the gift of languages. But the languages differed so much they could not understand each other.

Excerpt from: *Tales of the Deluge: A Global Report on Cultural Self-Replicating Genesis Myths* Dr Richard Scott, 2008

SECURITY CLEARANCE LEVEL 3

It was cold in Switzerland in March. That was the first thing November Dryden noticed. Then there were all the different languages being spoken – French, Italian, German, as well as English. And Switzerland was so small, sandwiched in between France, Italy, Lichtenstein, Germany and Austria. Mississippi it wasn't.

CERN was situated just outside Geneva, on the shores of Lac Léman, directly on the French border close to Mont Blanc. It was a city dedicated to cutting-edge science with no walls or gates but rather, main roads and highways. They'd been driving through the place for ten minutes before she realized they'd already arrived.

As they entered the main reception area she read the daunting blue signs ahead:

SUBGROUPS:
    PHYSICS ANALYSIS
    SMD
    TEC
    ECAL & HCAL
LEP 11 PHYSICS:
    SCINTILLATORS
    MUON CHAMBERS

'Welcome to the large Hadron accelerator,' Hackett announced proudly, as he guided Scott and November through the security check and into the lobby. 'The main ring is twenty-seven kilometers in diameter, housed one hundred meters underground. Each electromagnet is twice the size of a big-rig and accelerates a particle to almost the speed of light. That's fifty-*thousand* times around the entire length of the ring – *per* second. Welcome to the largest wonder of the modern world.'

'I thought they were building a bigger one in Arizona?' November remarked.

Hackett eyed her up and down before leaning in close. 'Particle envy,' he said dryly, over-pronouncing the 'p' sound to obvious effect.

'I don't see the relevance. Particle physics?' Scott queried.

'Relevance? Sub-atomic particles, quantum mechanics, the building blocks of the universe. It's dangerous, exciting stuff. It's not like studying botany: elementary particles are not normal.'

'Kinda like you,' November noted.

Hackett feigned a smile. 'Cute,' he said. Then got alarmingly serious. 'When you smash elementary particles together you don't destroy them, you just create more particles. It's like nothing you've ever known. Imagine you have a strawberry, and you decided to smash it into another strawberry. You don't get squished strawberries, you get a whole fruit salad, and sometimes the pieces of fruit are *larger* than the strawberry you started out with. Fruits like electrons with no dimension, but can be sensed. Whole bunches of non-sized particles. Gluons, Mesons, Anti-up Quarks, Anti-down Quarks, Beauty Quarks. Reality is *far* stranger than fiction.'

November appraised him 'Anything in particular you're looking for? Like an apple?'

'The graviton,' he explained. 'Find the graviton and you master gravity. Master gravity and you master the universe. Master the universe and . . .'

'You'd be God,' Scott finished.

Hackett shrugged. 'It's the only big field left to explore. I think *that's* pretty relevant.'

'I meant relevant to why we're here.' Scott glanced at his watch. 'Didn't they say they'd be meeting us here at seven o'clock?'

'Doctors Scott and Hackett, I presume.'

They all turned to see three men striding towards them. Two were civilians, but the third was not. Sure enough the military were involved, just as Hackett had warned. Indeed, he couldn't resist sidling up next to Scott and whispering, 'I told you so.'

Of the two civilians, one had a beard while the other had long, scraggy mid-brown hair and a pair of small, round, gold-rimmed glasses. His gray sweatshirt was two sizes too big and he looked like he did an awful lot of thinking, and forgot about things like a hair-cut and a social life. He dashed forward with his hand outstretched, grinning from ear to ear, and gripped their hands tightly in turn, managing to shake for much longer than was necessary. When he got to Scott he used his other hand to reinforce his thanks and completely forgot to let go.

'Bob Pearce. I'm so *very* pleased to meet you, Dr Scott. I've followed your work for a long time.'

'Thank you,' Scott replied, finding it difficult to get his hand back. 'May I?' He literally yanked it free.

Pearce's face dropped suddenly and he released his grip in a flash. 'Oh, I'm sorry. I'm so sorry. Here, uh, let me, uh . . .'

The others stepped forward. 'Major Lawrence Gant, Marine Expeditionary Force,' the braided officer announced by way of intro-duction, 'and Ralph Matheson from Rola Corp.'

Scott's ear pricked up at that. 'I got your note,' he said redun-dantly.

Gant made a gesture to all of them that they should get going. 'Shall we? This way.'

They took a left. The walls were white and antiseptic throughout, the windows few and far between, the lighting bright and constant. It could be any time of day or night and no one would know. The scientists working here probably liked it that way, November figured as she watched some of them go about their business, unhurried, faces pressed against hard copy read-outs. The corridors were wide and longer than any she had ever seen.

Taking in every detail quietly, she noted anything that might be important including Major Gant's perfect butt marching up ahead inside a perfectly pressed blue marine uniform.

Matheson decided to strike up conversation first and turned to Hackett. 'I hear you saved everyone's asses last night.'

'Oh, it was nothing, really. Just a minor quirk of physics,' Hackett replied modestly, but November couldn't decide if it was conceited or not. Hackett . . . Now she had time to think about it, that name was ringing some bells. 'The solar flare activity was playing havoc with the plane's electrical equipment,' he went on. 'The storm just acted as a buffer area into which we could escape.'

Then it hit her. 'Hackett? Dr Jon Hackett? Of the Santa Fe Institute?'

'I'm a visiting professor at Santa Fe. Currently, as you can see – not, uh, visiting.'

Scott was surprised. 'You know him?' he asked November.

'I know *of* him. He's brilliant – one of the foremost minds on complexity theory in modern physics. I read about him in science class.'

'You're very kind.' Hackett shrugged in mock humility.

'How did you know to turn into the storm?' she asked earnestly, aware that Scott was watching Hackett closely as his inevitable twinkle gave November its fullest attention.

Scott seemed to feel obliged to put the record straight though, which was cute of him. 'She's only nineteen,' he explained.

Hackett smiled as he eyed November up and down without even realizing it. 'Yes, yes,' he agreed. She smiled back. 'It's really quite complex. It has to do with charged particles, electrical potentials across a moving body. Ionization. Solar winds, friction and . . . more friction.'

Scott raised his voice. 'Hello?' Hackett looked round, sharply. 'She's nineteen.'

Hackett glanced back at the wide-eyed teenager and said with as much charm as he could muster, 'I think he thinks I'm deaf.'

November gazed back. Then asked innocently, 'Are you on drugs?'

The laughter was loud, and Hackett's expression was hurt. But the grin and the wink she got from Major Gant suddenly made it seem worthwhile. What was it about men in uniform?

Finally they arrived at their destination where the sign on the door read: **MOLECULAR PHYSICS. QUANTUM TUNNELING, JFOT & NMRS.**

The room served as an observation deck overlooking the main lab below. An onyx table stood in front of the vast, thick overhang windows that were tilted out at 45-degree angles. Through them could be seen scientists over a hundred feet below working with pieces of machinery so large that the technicians had to climb up ladders to adjust and calibrate the polished steel components.

At the end of the room Matheson set out stacks of papers on the table and rolled out maps with excruciating efficiency, as if he had rehearsed this moment for weeks. A screen was hung on the wall and digital pictures were already being displayed.

Pearce guided them over to the table and pulled out chairs like an over-zealous waiter. He leaned in close to Scott. 'Sorry about your hand. I, uh . . .' His voice trailed off like his brain had just shifted gear into another subject. His eyes darted frantically but never focused on Scott. He turned and walked off to his papers.

Scott turned to talk to November, only to find her sitting so close they were in kissing distance. He sat back with a start and tried to smile. 'Sorry,' he muttered. She flashed him a smile in return, but he wasn't quite sure what she meant by it.

There were layers and layers of paper on the table now. Much more than was probably needed. Pearce beamed at Scott. 'This is *so* exciting.'

But Hackett's gaze was squarely onto Matheson. He glanced at the picture of some icebergs on the screen. Back to Matheson. Then it clicked.

'You were on that ship,' Hackett said – and the way he said it made the others sit up and listen. Scott and November knew just what he meant. It had saturated the news all week. America was on the verge of war with China over mineral rights in Antarctica. Their position had been weakened when an American oil-ship was spotted trying to sneak out of the area. The government had claimed no knowledge. Rola Corp.'s corporate headquarters in New York had been under constant media bombardment ever since the story broke last week.

That was why they recognized him. Ralph Matheson had been unlucky enough to get caught on film, disembarking at the docks. He had been on that ship.

Matheson nodded silently.

'What were you doing out there?' Scott asked directly.

Pearce stepped in to rescue his colleague. 'I enjoy your work, Dr

Scott,' he interjected. 'I myself have done some extensive research on Zoroastrianism. If I remember my studies accurately, wasn't Zoroaster thought to have instructed Pythagoras?'

'Yes,' Scott agreed. 'Zoroaster had a great influence on ancient Greece.'

'I'm sorry,' November nervously butted in, 'but what does this – Zoroaster? Is that right? – what does he have to do with Dr Scott's work?'

'Mithras,' Pearce explained impatiently, but cheerfully.

Gant and Hackett shared a look. They too seemed none the wiser.

'Shall I explain?' Scott offered.

Pearce grinned again and shrugged sheepishly. 'Oh, yeah. Sure. Go ahead.' He ran his fingers through his hair and sat back in his chair. He tried to look studious as he gripped a pen between his thumb and forefinger and nodded agreeably to everything Scott said.

'Zoroaster came from what we now call Iran.'

'So he was Muslim?'

'No. This is way before then. At least a thousand years. The whole Middle-Eastern region has had a myriad of cultures. Babylon. The Chaldeans. The first culture ever to settle there, in fact, the earliest known civilization in the world, were the Sumerians—'

'Who wrote in a language we call cuneiform,' Pearce chipped in pleasantly.

'Right. The ancient Greeks considered the center of knowledge to originate from Babylon and the Egyptians. It's a myth that the Greeks invented mathematics. It was the Babylonians and the Egyptians who *taught* the Greeks. And alongside math, they also taught them philosophy, astrology, alchemy. Plato himself acknowledges it, but some academics out of sheer arrogance like to ignore that.'

'Zoroaster's teaching revolved around a god called Ormazd,' Pearce added. 'And it wasn't until the Jewish exodus from Egypt that all sorts of Zoroastrian traditions started turning up in their own religion as they traveled further east back towards Israel. That's probably what got Moses so mad. The idea of guardian angels was Zoroastrian.'

Scott eyed him sharply. 'Yes. As was the resurrection, which they believed in for hundreds of years before the Jews *or* the Christians.'

Hackett wanted to know: 'Who was this Mithras person?'

'Mithras was a branch of Zoroastrianism. You know, like Baptist is a branch of Christianity. But Mithras was also the main god they worshipped. He was closely connected with the sun. The fall and rise of the sun related to the death and resurrection of life. And the symbol they used for the sun was a cross. Actually, in their writing it was a halo. But for architectural simplicity it was a cross.'

'They weren't alone, either,' Pearce added. 'A lot of cultures around the world use the symbol of a cross to represent the sun.'

Hackett raised an eyebrow. 'The sun?'

November glared accusingly. 'Is that true?'

Pearce was confounded by her reaction. He shifted in his chair. 'Yes,' he said defensively.

'A real crucifixion scaffold,' Scott added, 'isn't shaped like a cross. It literally is a scaffold. Lots of cross-beams. There was no cross. At least, not until early artists got hold of the idea and added a glowing sun-like halo around Christ's head—'

'Which came directly from statues of the Greek sun god Helios,' Pearce nodded.

'Which leads us all back to the Sumerians,' Scott concluded. He was met with silence in the room as they all picked over the implications.

'I read the geology report,' Scott said excitedly. The cult of Mithras provided the vision of Heaven and Hell, The Last Supper, a sacrifice and an ascension. Mithras had its roots in Sumerian tradition. For them, ancient whisperings told tales of an entire people sacrificing themselves to save the world. 'The first ever story about a global flood and Noah came from Sumeria. Is that what you think you have here? An earlier Epic of Gilgamesh?'

'Uh, not quite, Dr Scott,' Gant replied.

'Sorry to be a pain, but . . .' November had been raised a strict Christian and it was obvious she was having difficulty assimilating these concepts, though to her credit she did not simply dismiss them out of hand. 'Dr Scott – you said that every major religion in history borrowed from what went before them. Well, if that's so, where did the Sumerians get *their* ideas? And where did they come from?'

Scott hesitated, but Pearce was more than willing to step in. He sat forward and waved his pen around. 'Nobody knows!' he grinned, then his face fell serious. 'Until now.' He keyed the remote control to the digital screen, making sure the sound was turned low.

'Yeah, this is where I come in,' Matheson told them all. 'You might recognize the pictures from the news. What you're seeing is the drill ship *Red Osprey*. I'm an engineer by trade. We were out in the Antarctic, doing an exploratory drill when we hit a problem . . .'

The screen showed all hell breaking loose. The pipe buckling. The deaths and the eventual blast of mud into the bridge. Everyone in the room winced instinctively. Whereupon the footage changed suddenly to show white-coated scientists cleaning large diamonds in a lab and analyzing them. A close-up of one of the diamonds appeared next, at which point Matheson froze the film. The diamond was unusual, quite clearly. For a start – there was writing on it.

Scott sat forward sharply.

'On the face of it,' Gant remarked, 'what language would you say that is, Dr Scott?'

Scott turned to the officer. 'It looks . . . well, initially, it looks cuneiform. But it can't be!'

'Why can't it be?'

'Well, it's loaded full of symbols I've never seen before. The markings are too precise. It looks like a more complex, modern language. At least, that's how it appears from a photograph.'

Cuneiform from the Latin *cuneus*, meaning wedge. Cuneiform writing simply meant that the style was wedge-shaped. It was used by the ancient Persians, Assyrians, Chaldeans, Akkadians, Baby-lonians and of course, Sumerians. It dated back to 3,000–3,500 BCE. The language was difficult to translate because the symbols stood for entire words as well as syllables, and each symbol was made up of collections of wedges, sometimes up to thirty of them.

'Is it possible I could look at the real thing?' Scott ventured. To say that he was dying to take a look was an understatement. 'I'd get a better feel for it, you understand?'

Pearce and Gant eyed each other closely. 'Can you read it?'

'I wouldn't like to say,' Scott said frankly. 'Bits of it, maybe. But this kinda job needs work, and a lot of time.'

Major Gant looked pensive. 'That's a problem. Time is something we don't have.'

'What do you mean?'

Pearce interjected, 'I suppose the big question is: do you agree that it's *pre*-cuneiform and not *post*-cuneiform?'

Scott knew what Pearce was getting at and frankly it made him uncomfortable. Cuneiform was the first ever example of the human written word, but the curious thing about it was that the earlier forms were the more complex. The Sumerian and Babylonian alphabets started out with at least 600 characters. Later ones dropped to about 100, and by the time of the Egyptians, the written word had changed to hieroglyphic pictograms before writing evolved into letters again and took the form that was current. The theory was that Sumerian writing evolved from pictograms, but there was very little evidence for this. There were clay tokens and so on, but they were more like early coinage.

In fact, there was more evidence for the reverse – that cuneiform started out complex and got simpler over time by a process of cultural amnesia. It suggested an advanced *pre*-Sumerian civilization. And Scott was more inclined to side with that camp. Put simply, no one knew where the Sumerians had come from. There was every reason to suppose that they brought their writing with them.

Scott gave a nod. This was earth-shattering. A *pre*-cuneiform text, at last. Pearce seemed pleased with the response, but the big question remained. What on earth was that text doing in the Antarctic? That defied all logic. It had to be a hoax. There were theories that many of the ancient civilizations had had navies that were far more powerful than had at first been assumed. There was increasing evidence that many, like the Phoenicians, Minoans and the Egyptians, had sailed as far as the Americas.

In Brazil there was a bay known as the Bay of Jars because Roman jars and other pottery kept turning up at intervals, presumably from a sunken Roman ship. Also in Brazil an unknown Mediterranean language was discovered on clay inscriptions. A picture of a pineapple, an American fruit, was found in Pompeii. Bearded figurines had been found in Mexico when facial and body hair is alien to native Americans. The sweet potato and peanuts over 2,000 years old had been unearthed in China – more American foods. And in India there were drawings of women holding ears of maize.

Tests on the hair of Egyptian Mummies had shown that they

smoked cannabis, tobacco and cocaine. Trouble is, cocaine and tobacco only come from one place – South America. Chinese silk from 1,000 BCE also found in Mummy hair meant certain trade with China. This was coupled with the fact that dragon's head lode stones, the stones used to weight down ancient sailing ships, had been found in the Pacific off the coast of Chile. Ancient South American cultures used dragons in their mythology, so it was more than likely they traded with China.

Curiously, before Columbus, European legend had it that a land known as Hy Brazil existed west of the Atlantic. So when new settlers arrived in South America they named the land Brazil after the legend. The curiosity being that *brzl* was a Hebrew and Aramaic word meaning 'iron'. Sometime later it was discovered that Brazil had one of the richest iron-ore deposits to be found anywhere on earth.

But as Scott saw it, all this evidence pointed to a global system of trading blocks. Ancient ingenuity meant these blocks traded goods over many thousands of miles. The Chinese might buy cocaine from South America and sell it on to Egypt or an intermediary without ever having used the stuff. It did not necessarily mean Egyptians ever went to South America. But could some have sailed as far south as the Antarctic? He wasn't so sure.

Pearce and Matheson started spreading out their sheets of paper. It was a big job and Scott, November and Hackett had no other choice but to watch for a moment. Spread out across the table were maps – primarily maps of Antarctica – and geological surveys from Rola Corp. Some were copies from ancient sources, but others were military surveys from satellites.

Scott had to know. He eyed everyone around the table. This was more than just a translating job. Much more.

'Excuse me,' he asked quietly, 'but just what is it you think you've found?'

Gant was candid. 'Atlantis,' he said.

CHARTS

Scott's shoulders tensed. He looked to Hackett and November in turn. Yes, he *had* just heard that right.

Atlantis be damned! Hare-brained theories over the existence of Atlantis had been floating around since Plato first told of Solon's meeting with the mystical Egyptian high priests. It had been ripped apart in the Atlantic Ocean. It was in the Bahamas. The Mediterranean. It was in South America. It was all over the damn place and it couldn't be proven one way or the other. Atlantis was in the purview of the fruitloops, the astrologers and the crystal-ball gazers. But these were the military. They were not fools. What did they know that he didn't?

Matheson pointed at the table. 'Antarctica was discovered in 1818, right?'

Scott took a moment to remember, but when he did, he nodded. 'Yes.'

'Here's a copy of a map drawn up for a Turkish Admiral named Piri Reis in 1513. On the map, he expressly says it was based on an original that was kept elsewhere. Said his sailors had never authenticated the map because the others he used were based on the same older sources which always proved to be accurate. This map shows the coastlines of West Africa, South America *and* more importantly, Queen Maud Land and other parts of Antarctica. They're so accurate the USAF authenticated the detail using satellite imagery, because the map shows the actual coastline of Antarctica – not ice floes. Have you ever been to Antarctica, Dr Scott?'

'No.'

'No? Well, since I just got back I'll tell you why that's so incredible. Because it's only been sixty years since we've had the technology available to see through the ice and take a look at the real coastline. And that particular stretch of beach hasn't been free of ice for at least six thousand years. So how was somebody supposed to draw a map of it, unless they had a ship capable of taking them there – which automatically means civilization, and considering the accuracy, automatically means an advanced civilization?'

Pearce nodded vehemently. 'Piri Reis's maps were based on originals that were sacked from the great Library of Alexandria, in Egypt, and brought to Constantinople,' he said. 'But he wasn't alone. Oronteus Finaeus drew one in 1531, based on ancient charts, that showed the whole of Antarctica with mountains and rivers. That means you needed to know the interior, not just the coast, and it had to be free of ice.'

'Do you know how big Antarctica is, Dr Scott?' Matheson asked. Scott shook his head. 'It's big. It's twice the size of the United States. You can't just go chart rivers and mountains, and get them exact in a couple of days on the back of a raft. I design stuff for a living, so people can go to far-off places and work, and mine and drill for oil. I'm screwed without a map and a geological report. But these old maps – they got everything!'

'In the mid-1500s,' Pearce continued, 'we got a guy called Mercator, real name Gerard Kremer. Supremo map-maker, who draws an exact map of Antarctica from ancient sources and develops a sudden need to run off and visit the Great Pyramid in Cairo. And then in 1737, French geographer Philippe Buache comes up with a map that is so accurate, it shows what Antarctica would have looked like with no ice on it – *at all*. Which would have been around fifteen thousand years ago! This is a hundred years before it was even supposed to have been discovered, Dr Scott! Then we got Hadji Ahmed's map of the world from 1559. He was another Turk, and his chart also shows a land bridge between Siberia and Alaska.

'I got on the phone to Sarah Kelsey, our company's best geologist.

You read her report. She said there used to be a land bridge there about twelve to fourteen thousand years ago. There's tons of scientific evidence for it. Copies of all those maps are on the table too, if you care to look.'

Scott stood firm. He was not so easily swayed. 'I've heard of most of those maps, Mr Matheson. They're not new to me. But – and it's a very big but – they do not prove the existence of Atlantis. They simply prove that our ancient ancestors were damn good map-makers and that we as a species are very forgetful. I won't dispute with you on that count. But think about what you're asking me to do. You're asking for a leap of faith of such magnitude that it defies all reason.' Scott looked at him sadly. 'I'm sorry.'

Pearce was shaking his head. 'Aren't you the same guy who collected the myths and legends of over five hundred cultures from around the world which speak of an ancient flood – the deluge myth? Isn't that you? You *are* Dr Richard Scott, aren't you?'

'Tales of the Deluge. Yes. But those are *myths*. Legends. Stories that make great bedtime reading. The Sumerian *Epic of Gilgamesh* dates from around 5,000BCE. It has the same flood story as the Bible's – matches Noah's story exactly. But it's just literature . . . A story.'

'Schliemann followed a story and found the lost city of Troy.'

Pearce rounded the desk. Snatched up the remote again and keyed the play button. The picture was a little fuzzy and was of far lower quality than before, but it was clear what was happening. A tiny camera was descending down the inside of a long dark pipe-line. There was another, smaller pipe about five inches in diameter going down the center through which the oil would have been funneled. It was clear that the camera was lodged in between.

'It's a service camera,' Matheson explained, 'designed to check the pipe-line from the drill node on the sea floor, down to the bore site. Visual was really irrelevant, but it was a prototype, so I stuck a camera on the thing. Didn't think we'd ever need it.'

The camera got lower and lower. Some of the damaged pipe was visible, and there were tears in the steel-alloy. Finally, through a mist of debris in the water, the destination became visible.

'These weren't rocks we found on the sea-bed, Dr Scott. We hadn't hit a buried shipwreck. This is two miles down. Half a mile into the sea floor. We hit a wall. A real, honest to goodness wall. Like you build houses out of. A *wall*. Are you following me?'

'Yes,' came the clipped response.

'Only this wall wasn't made out of bricks and mortar, it was made out of diamond. One, huge, solid chunk of diamond. And there's no telling how vast it really is.'

Through the darkness, lit up by the onboard flashlight, a field of blue crystal was visible. At the bottom of the picture sat the destroyed drill-bit. In the wall was an impact crater where chunks of the diamond had sheered off and a hole was punctured straight through the wall. It was obvious that beyond there must have been water under intense pressure from the weight of the ice-pack above which blasted up the pipeline when it broke. Overall, however, it seemed the wall fared better than the machinery.

The wall was faultless otherwise, and was covered in fine, delicate-looking lettering. It was the proof that was needed.

'Now you tell me, Dr Scott. Who the hell went out and built a wall two miles down in sub-zero temperatures – in a subterranean cavern? In all my experience as an engineer, drilling for oil all over the world, I've never seen anything like it. I don't know of any country, and I mean *any* country, that has the current technology to be able to do that. And that amount of diamond? Hell, you'd destroy half the entire world's financial base overnight. The King of England might as well have acorns stuck in his crown, they'd probably be worth more.'

Scott could not believe what he was being presented with. 'You want me to translate all that?'

November pored quickly over the maps. Tried to make sense of it all. 'Dr Scott,' she said huskily. 'I think this is for real.'

Hackett remained insouciant and unreadable.

'D'you know how long it takes to translate archaic texts?' Scott tossed out.

'Yes.'

'No, I don't think you do. It took the collective minds of a good chunk of academia over a hundred years to translate the Mayan codex, and that language still existed in the Yucatan Peninsula of Eastern Mexico. Pre-cuneiform is a dead language. It's forgotten. I wouldn't know where to begin.'

'Then you'd better figure out a way pretty sharply, Dr Scott,' announced the Admiral, marching in through the far door. 'Because lives depend on it.'

The name on his tag read: *Dower*. The look on his face said: *Read my name tag*. Admiral Dower was an imposing figure. Tall, slim and black. He kept his head shaved under his hat.

Anyone who knew military matters would have noticed he had the Legion of Merit, with one gold star, pinned to his chest. They would have noticed the Defense Meritous Service Medal, the Meritous Service Medal, the Strikeflight Air Medal (with eight subsequent awards), the Navy Commendation Medal with combat 'V', the Presidential Unit Citation, and the Gulf War Cross of Gallantry, and these were but a few of his numerous campaign medals. Rear Admiral Thomas C. Dower, USN, had seen some action in his time. He had a right to live up to his name.

Following on behind him was a civilian and a whole host of other military personnel. But only Dower and the civilian took seats. Matheson introduced the other man as Jay Houghton from Rola Corp. legal.

Houghton flicked his eyes across the yellow legal pad and couldn't help but growl like some kind of courtroom trick he'd picked up at Law School. Make it seem all the worse so that when you did pull the rabbit out of the hat, you got to look like a genius. Though Scott doubted the man ever went anywhere near a courtroom these days. Corporate lawyers never did. Just got their secretaries to mail out death threats before lunch every Monday.

'We just met with the Chinese officials at the UN's Palais des Nations,' he explained. 'There is no way in hell the Chinese are gonna let just anyone walk onto their base in Antarctica.'

'Unfortunate,' muttered Gant.

'It's what we expected,' Dower reminded him.

'It's still unfortunate,' Gant replied heavily. 'I don't want to take in a civilian search-party. They're not trained for it, mentally or physically, sir.'

'The Chinese have no objections to a UN inspection team in principle,' Houghton added cheerfully. 'But they will be vetting for any kind of military connection.'

'I bet they will,' Gant spat harshly, only adding a final 'sir' in deference to the Rear Admiral, at the last moment.

Scott and November exchanged anxious glances. Inspection teams? What did they have planned?

'Is that spectroscopy equipment down there?' Hackett asked wistfully. He'd gotten to his feet when Dower entered and now stood by the window assessing the surroundings. He faced the assembled body with his familiar faint smile. 'Nuclear Magnetic Resonance, if I'm not mistaken. Tut, tut, Admiral. I'm sure the physics boys really appreciated a chemistry toy being wheeled into their precious laboratory.'

'They whined, as usual. Hello, Jon. How was your trip?'

'Bumpy.'

Dower pursed his lips before responding. 'It's getting worse, isn't it?'

Hackett didn't seem like he wanted to answer, but Pearce did. 'Much worse,' he intervened. 'I think this planet is being subjected to levels of solar radiation the like of which haven't been seen for over twelve thousand years. Twelve thousand and twelve – to be exact.'

Papers were shuffled. Two officers conferred with Dower and passed over notes as Hackett commented: 'Well, that was a little melodramatic, maybe. But off the mark? No.'

Scott sat apprehensively, catching Hackett's eye momentarily.

Another one of those infuriatingly enigmatic smiles tugged at the physicist's lips. Slouching against the window he chewed a thumbnail briefly. 'You're looking at the assembled heads of the United States Space Command, Dr Scott,' he said gently. 'I've briefed Tom Dower on physics more times than I care to remember. Los Alamos as a grad student was the first time, wasn't it, Tom?'

Scott was none the wiser. 'Space what?'

'Space Command,' Dower said gruffly. 'We're advising the government over policy, while they negotiate with the Chinese. We are the last line of defense between peace and World War Three.'

Buried under 18,000 feet of granite, deep within the Cheyenne Mountains of Colorado, Dower told them, stands a door twenty feet wide and four feet thick, designed to withstand a nuclear attack. Behind it lies the military intelligence nerve center known as NORAD.

And part of that nerve center is given over to the United States Space Command, whose remit is two-fold.

'We track space debris, Dr Scott. We estimate over nineteen thousand objects are in orbit at any one time, from flecks of paint to defunct satellites. Over eight thousand of these objects are larger than a baseball and are tracked twenty-four hours a day, seven days a week. But when the sun goes into spasm and ejects plasma during a sun storm, it can knock out our tracking system from anywhere up to ninety-six hours – four full days and nights.'

'And that's bad?'

'Oh, that's pretty bad,' Hackett stepped in. 'When sun-storm plasma hits the earth, it causes the atmosphere to expand. The increased drag slows orbiting objects down. Some re-enter the earth. And the signature of that re-entry tends to mimic an incoming warhead.'

It was Gant's turn again. 'In any event, a sun storm is a good time during which to launch an attack undetected. The sun is about to spasm again, and the Chinese know this.'

'I'm sorry, but didn't the sun already just do that?' Scott was shaking his head. 'And how can you be so certain the sun is about to flare up again? It's chaotic, isn't it? Unpredictable?'

'It's complex, not chaotic,' Hackett said irritably.

'We can predict the sun,' Pearce added. 'It goes around in mini-cycles every eleven years.'

Hackett grabbed a magic marker from the table and sketched out a circle on the wipe board at one end of the room.

'I'm not going to insult your intelligence by giving you all a lecture on solar and magnetic physics, but there are a couple of important points you need to remember. The sun is not, contrary to popular belief, much like the earth. It's massive. It's so vast that the average size of one sunspot on its surface would envelope the earth two or three times over. It's a continual mass of shifting nuclear explosions, held together in a ball due to its mass. It's big. It's heavy. It's violent. It also – and here's the most important point of all – has more than two magnetic poles.

'We have north and south. The sun has *six* poles. Call them whatever you want – North, South, Tim and Clarence. It really doesn't matter. What matters is that it has highly complicated magnetic structures which we're only just beginning to understand. It has a North and South Pole like we would understand it, but because it is a ball of superheated plasma, it has four other poles spaced equally around its equator. And *because* it's a ball of plasma, it doesn't rotate evenly. You get a shorter day at the equator than if you were further north or south.'

There were three Admirals, Scott realized. No, scratch that. Two Admirals and a General. There was a Major, Gant. There were five Lieutenants who acted as aides. Two much older than the rest and obviously important. Introductions had not been made. Their minds were sharp and they seemed to grasp what Hackett was saying with relative ease, which was disconcerting at best. Downright embarrassing, at worst. Either way, the questions that were filling his head were likely to remain there for some time. Hackett wasn't finished.

The physicist tapped the marker on the board. 'In its smallest fraction, the cycle repeats itself on a tiny scale every eighty-seven and a half days. An event cycle, the timing between similar intense events, is every twenty-two years. What you were describing, Bob, I'm sorry to disagree, was only half a cycle, but statistically similar events have occurred at the eleven-year point. A full sun-spot cycle – when sunspot activity appears to start from square one again – is actually once every one hundred and eighty-seven years. And the cycle Bob was referring to is highly theoretical, but it's based on the movements of what we call the sun's warped neutral sheet. Which theoretically cycles once every three thousand years or so.'

'What happens when the neutral sheet cycles round?' Scott asked.

'According to theory, it's so devastating you want to be someplace else.'

'Which means what?' November jumped in. 'I'm not a physics major.'

Scott folded his arms and said, 'Look, I didn't major in physics either. I'm a linguist. What the hell does this have to do with me? I came to visit some rocks. There *are* rocks, aren't there?'

'All you need to know is that bad things happen on the sun every eleven years,' Pearce said succinctly, shooting a look at Hackett who scrawled the number 22 on the board and underlined it emphatically. 'Just keep adding eleven and eleven and eleven together until you reach three thousand. Geological records show clearly that the earth's climate changes drastically every three thousand years. Six thousand years ago, the period of climatic change was so severe many ancient civilizations set their calendar by it. The Mayans called it Year One; in our terms it was 3113BC, August twelve to be exact when a whitebearded man descended from the sun. The Egyptian Year One was around 3141BC, called the Age of Horus. Horus was the son of Ra – who in turn was the sun. The Hebrew calendar says the earth was created in September of 3761BC. They were so influenced by lunar and solar cycles they put a sun on their flag in the shape of a six-pointed star. The fact is, every fourth cycle something *really* bad happens. Then you've got a legitimate reason to panic. The geological record shows four cycles ago – or twelve thousand years ago – there was a flood. And guess what? Time's up again.'

'We think the sun is about to reverse its magnetic poles, Dr Scott,' Rear Admiral Dower said solemnly. 'We think it just reached the high point in a twelve-thousand-year cycle, and that it is about to set off a chain reaction of events that puts this planet in very real danger.'

'Wait a minute!' Scott cried. 'Are we talking about the end of the world here?'

Hackett shrugged. 'Oh, no, no, no,' he said. The others sighed with relief. 'Just everything on it. Tell me, Admiral, what's the end of the world going to feel like?'

Gant moved to the far end of the room and stood by a large digital screen mounted on the wall. 'Admiral. With your permission?'

Dower gave a quick nod of approval.

The lights dimmed. Up on the screen a photo-real representation of the earth spun effortlessly through space. With a constantly shifting perspective, its orbit around the sun was depicted, followed sharply by close-ups of countries that were best placed to serve as monitors.

'There are six main observatories on earth given over exclusively to monitoring solar activity twenty-four hours a day,' Gant explained steadily. 'The normal procedure is that once an event has been witnessed, we are notified immediately, and the effects are felt back here approximately forty-eight to seventy-two hours later.'

Scott and November instinctively looked to Hackett for confirmation. He nodded, saying: 'The sun is made up, primarily, of hydrogen that's in a continual state of nuclear fusion, keeping its surface temperature at over two million degrees Celsius. When a coronal mass ejection occurs, highly charged particles are thrown out and wrapped into a ball with its own magnetic field – called a plasma. About the size of Jupiter, this plasma cloud contains enough energy to boil the Mediterranean Sea dry. It travels at about two million miles an hour, so . . .' Hackett totted up the calculations briefly. 'Yeah, I'd say it takes about three days to get here.'

November gulped. 'And this is about to happen?'

Hackett smirked. 'Oh, that happens every week. What Major Gant is about to explain, I assume, is much worse.'

'On March eight, exactly nine days ago, an unprecedented number of sun spots were observed on the surface of the sun. Solar-storm activity was intense and the release of plasma was both rapid and vast. The magnetic turmoil within the sun was such that at precisely seven-oh-nine that morning, exactly eight minutes after several ejecta events simultaneously exploded around the equator of the sun, the effects were detected here at CERN.'

Hackett was suddenly very alert. 'How?' he asked simply. 'You're talking about an effect that we could feel, that traveled just as fast as light.'

'There are five experiments currently set up around the earth to do the kind of physics we're talking about. One in Japan, at ISAS. One in Russia. Two in the States, at Caltech and Stanford. And one here in Switzerland. The other four were undergoing recalibration and were off-line, while the one here at CERN was the only one operational at the time, and was the only one that detected – *a gravity wave.*'

Now was the time to sit down, Hackett decided. He ran his fingers over the cold black onyx table-top. 'Good God . . . they finally did it.' No one else seemed quite that overjoyed. 'The graviton,' Hackett said, smug in his own certainty, 'is the key to everything.'

Scott shifted in his chair and murmured, 'Sorry to disappoint, but it wasn't the key to the breakdown of my marriage.'

'How long did it last?'

Scott had to think for a moment before he realized Hackett wasn't talking about his marriage while Gant announced: 'Four point three micro-seconds. Congratulations, Dr Hackett. Physics proved another theory.'

Hackett scratched his neck. 'I'm not sure I should be glad about that.'

Gant took a long, deep breath. 'The laser-light interferometer equipment used in ELIGO was not the only thing to react to the gravity wave.'

Scott shook his head for a re-cap. 'ELIGO?'

'Explanations later,' Rear Admiral Dower insisted gruffly, eager to get to the point.

Gant pressed another button. Images of ice floes and the Antarctic basin were suddenly visible. Details spewed down one side of the screen. Complex and nonsensical to the layman.

SPACEBORNE IMAGING RADAR-C/X-BAND SYNTHETIC APERTURE RADAR (SIR-C/X-SAR)

GROUND PENETRATING RADAR (GPR)

CONJUNCTIONALITY EXTRAPOLATION FROM NEMESIS.

MICROWAVE LENGTHS:

L-BAND (24 CM)

C-BAND (6CM)

X-BAND (3CM)

MULTI-FREQUENCY ENHANCEMENT: ON

GPR DIGITAL WASH FILTERS: ON

GPR WAVE-LENGTH FEATURES: [WITHHELD — AUTHORIZATION FAILED. **ACCESS DENIED.**]

Suddenly, close-up images of Chinese armored columns came into focus, slowly making their way across the ice. Black specks against pure white, like ants on icecream. Buildings appeared. Fortifications were being erected. The Chinese base, *Jung Chang*, was well equipped.

'Needless to say, ladies and gentlemen, this is classified information—'

'But hardly secret,' November interrupted cheekily. Gant shot her a look. 'You flicked on CNN lately?'

'Believe me, Ms Dryden,' the major intoned, 'CNN does not have its hands on this particular tape.' He turned to the others. 'We've had the Chinese under surveillance for some time. Their recent pursuit of fossil fuels and mineral ores has been relentless, as has their experimentation on hightech weaponry. Approximately three months ago, at their base in Antarctica, they sunk a well and started complex drilling procedures.

'Two weeks ago we detected a signal indicating that an enormous power source had been activated. As this hidden power source's output began to increase, so too did sun-spot and solar-flare activity. Naturally we want to know what they've found. If we switch to Ground Penetrating Radar . . .' the image on the screen turned psychedelic '. . . what you're seeing is a false color image of what the human eye cannot see.'

Scott squinted. 'What exactly *are* we seeing?'

Hackett stepped up for a closer look. 'We did the scan you asked us to perform, Jon,' Dower explained.

'And?'

'And you were right.'

'Shit.'

'Right? Right about what?' Scott wanted to know.

Gant nodded at the screen. 'Just wait.'

A clock cycled down. The date read March 8, 2012. Suddenly purple waves blasted out in tremendous ripples and dissipated some distance on.

Pearce had already seen the footage but was still impressed. 'Woah!'

Hackett craned forward. 'Can we see that again – from a wider view?'

Gant keyed in the request. Again, huge false color waves spread out across the ice as if a pebble had been dropped into a pond.

'The area of land you're seeing is roughly the size of Manhattan.'

Scott was confused. 'What the hell was that?'

'What you're looking at is some kind of energy wave,' Dower offered by way of an explanation. 'Traveling well over two miles beneath the ice, through what appears to have the same geological signature as a material called Carbon 60.'

Hackett was resting his chin on his fingers, studying the image intently, when he asked quietly, 'Can you slow the film down for me – a lot.'

Gant and Dower exchanged knowing looks. Dower seemed pleased. 'We thought you might notice that.'

'Notice what?' Matheson demanded. It was clear he was out of the loop on this one.

Hackett never took his eyes off the screen. 'There's structure within the wave pattern.'

'What are you talking about? Structure? I don't understand.'

'Major Gant, can you separate out each individual frame where the energy waves have expanded out from the epicenter?' Hackett requested. 'And then, overlay them on top of one another.' Gant said he could and went to work as Hackett addressed the others. 'Every time the wave gets bigger I'm getting him to take a snapshot of it. Then by overlaying each shot, like a stack of pancakes, the overall image of what I think I can see should, uh . . . should present itself.'

Like a jigsaw puzzle of concentric purple circles the image slowly built up until the screen turned more and more purple with each overlay. And what was becoming clearer to everybody was that structure had indeed been revealed within the energy waves. With the exception of the military, a mood of excitement and incredulity filled the room. Cubes. Oblongs. Curved surfaces. All the hallmarks of construction stood out as glitches in the purple. It was intricate. Vast and dense. Like the layout of –

'That's a city,' Scott whispered. 'Under the goddamn ice . . . A lost city!'

'And somehow,' Dower said gravely, 'it appears to be linked to the sun.'

Pearce was mesmerized. 'Not *a* lost city. *The* lost city. Ladies and gentlemen – welcome to Atlantis!'

'My God . . . we're talking about a complex adaptive system on a scale I've only ever theorized about,' Hackett murmured darkly.

Gant flipped text up onto the screen in a separate sub-box. *Tales of the Deluge: A Global Report on Cultural Self-Replicating Genesis Myths* by Dr Richard Scott. In his hand he had a hard copy. He scratched his cheek in between thumbing through the hefty document.

'Dr Scott,' he said, 'according to your research, in Central Colombia, South America, and I quote: "Bochica, a bearded man of another race, brought law, agriculture and religion to the Chibcas savages. But one day his evil wife, Chia, appeared to thwart his plans and flooded the lands killing almost everyone. Bochica exiled his wife to the sky where she is now the moon, and brought the survivors down from the mountains to start over".'

Scott was excited. Felt that rush of adrenaline coursing through his veins. He knew what the Major was driving at as Gant turned another page.

'Or what about this? In China, the water god, Gong Gong, caused a twenty-two-year flood. People escaped to the mountains and the trees. While according to the Chickasaw Indians, the world was destroyed by water and all except one family and two animals of every kind survived.'

'You want to try another letter?' Scott suggested excitedly. 'How about "I"? The Incas reported that torrential rains fell and volcanoes erupted, flooding the earth and burning it. When the sky went to war with the earth, they believed the Andes were split apart. Whereas the Inuit thought there was a terrible flood followed by an earthquake that happened so fast that only the quick-witted were fast enough to flee to the mountains or take refuge in their boats.

'There are more than five hundred deluge legends around the world,' Scott summarized. 'I built on the work of Richard Abdree who studied eighty-six of the legends back in the mid-1980s. Three were European, seven African, twenty Asian, forty-six American and ten were from Australia or the Pacific Rim. He found out that sixty-two of these cultures had never come into contact with the Hebrew or Mesopotamian legend – the one from which we derive Noah. That means they sprang up independently. They are distinct – and separate.'

When Scott started work on the project he found a wealth of information he frankly hadn't expected. He'd discovered flood stories that were Roman and Scandinavian, German and Assyrian, Hebrew, Christian and Islamic. There were Sumerian flood stories and Babylonian. Chaldean, Zoroastrian, Pygmy, Kikuyu and Yoruba. There were tales of an ancient deluge from the Basonge, Mandingo, on the Ivory Coast, Bakongo, western Zaire and Cameroon. The Kwaya of Lake Victoria shared a similar tale, as did the Hindus and the Chinese. In Thailand it was the Kammu, and in the Philippines the Ifugaos. There were the Batak in Sumatra who also saw the earth resting on a giant snake. Curiously, the symbol of the snake cropped up time and time again. The list of flood myths went on and on. From New Zealand to Arkansas.

Everywhere Scott looked he had found an ancient culture that believed the earth had at one time or another been devastated by a vast torrent of water.

But there was a problem, and Scott was already starting to see the connection between Atlantis and the sun. Hesitantly he said: 'Many of these same ancient myths also refer to the cyclical nature of the destruction of the earth.'

'How many myths are we talking about, Dr Scott?' the Admiral inquired.

'If I had to hazard a guess,' Scott replied, rubbing his hands together nervously, 'I'd say over a hundred. Our own Christian beliefs see the turn of the millennium as something to fear. The Age of Aquarius began in 2010 – the symbol for water. The Mayans predicted a cataclysm would befall the earth on December 24, 2011. That was just three or four months ago.'

The linguistic anthropologist eyed everyone around the table. Deeply concerned.

'The Dusan tribe of western Borneo, or Kalimantan, have the idea that the sky retreated when six of the original seven suns were killed,' he explained. 'The pre-Hispanic Mexicans believed various past ages were each brought to an end by violent upheavals. In the old Mayan *Annals of Cuauhtitlan*, written in 1570 but based on texts thousands of years old, these past ages were called "suns". They were epochs, or in Mayan: *Chicon-Tonatiuh*. Even Amerind people, and remote tribes of the Amazon have beliefs that many times over the earth has been destroyed by fire, prolonged darkness and a deluge.

'The Voguls of Siberia believed recurrent devastation was accompanied by terrible thunder. The Welsh Triads refer to three cataclysms as a deluge, a fire and a drought. Anaximenes and Anaximander of the sixth century BCE, and Diogenes of Allollonia in the fifth century BCE speak of the world being periodically destroyed and reborn. Aristarchus of Samos, two hundred years later, said the earth underwent destruction by fire and water every two thousand, four hundred and eighty-nine years. The people of Hawaii, the Bengal Sea, the early Icelanders and the Hebrew traditions all share similar myths. The *Visuddi-Magga*, the ancient book of the Buddhists, mentions an older book called the *Discourse on the Seven Suns,* and speaks of the same periodic destruction.

'The Chwong people of Malaysia say this earth is Earth Seven and that everything is turned upside down and destroyed at intervals. Egyptians believed in *Tep Zepi*, the first time, before the present age when the gods walked the earth. The Greeks and Romans had this notion too. Under Hinduism it gets a little more specific. Their belief is there are four ages that span five thousand years for our existence. The Golden Age, which was unpolluted. The Silver Age, where the scattered people no longer remembered their roots or lineage and perceived themselves as different tribes and families. They say this was followed by the Copper Age, when trading began. Followed by our Age, the Iron Age – the Age of Kali, when sinning developed. The rich became richer, marriages broke down, people stole. War, technology and science became the evil of the day, until a cosmic renewal known as the Confluence Age briefly destroyed the earth by fire and flood.'

'Sounds great,' Hackett mused.

Scott added, 'The Hindus say that time is now.'

'Did you also know,' Pearce added, 'that the Chinese were the first people ever to chart sunspot activity?'

'No, I didn't know that.'

'Oh yeah. They've been doing it for more than two thousand years. They were the first people to scientifically recognize the cycle. They have twelve astrological years. Y'know, the Year of the Rooster and so on? That's very close to sunspot cycles.'

Silence clung to the air as Gant keyed the screen. Dramatically, multiple images from the international news channels played side by side. Ferocious images. Frightening.

'At the same time the gravity wave hit Malaysia. Fifteen hundred dead in a series of typhoons. Tokyo was hit by a tsunami. Two hundred dead in earthquakes in California. And snow storms in the Mid-West. Pre-tremors felt in London . . .'

'London?' Scott queried. 'London's not on a fault-line, is it?'

'The British Geological Survey say it is. And they just started measuring activity from some unusually deep fault-lines that stretch all the way across to France. Earthquakes hit London on a large scale once every two or three hundred years. The last one was in 1776. So the next one's past due,' Gant told them. 'And London, like a lot of Europe, isn't built with earthquakes in mind. So when the big one does hit . . .' He didn't need to elaborate.

'We've also charted for some time sunspot cycle activity which matches *El Nino*, and the indications are not good.'

El Nino was a weather phenomenon where an area of the Pacific Ocean the size of Europe warmed to a greater degree than usual every decade or so. The result was that the Trade Winds reversed and went East. The heat flowing with it raised temperatures several degrees farther. It meant flooding in the Americas and droughts in the Western Pacific and Africa.

'1983 was an *El Nino* year. It caused dust storms to hit Melbourne with ten thousand tons of dust at fifty miles an hour, creating a wall of dust five miles across. It was a hundred and ten degrees Fahrenheit in the city, a hundred and thirty in the desert. By the time of the next *El Nino* in 1998, most of the Pacific Basin was on fire due to massive droughts, while America and China were hit with the worst floods ever recorded. Three month's worth of rains fell in some places in six hours. July of 1998 went down as the hottest global month ever recorded. A few years on and 2012 is shaping up to be the worst recorded year for climatic change and natural disasters in history.'

Hackett was on the edge of his seat. He raised a finger like a schoolboy. 'And this is linked to the city under the ice . . . How?'

Gant exchanged a hesitant, uneasy look with Dower before continuing. The Admiral nodded for him to proceed. Gant pressed the button and the images on the screen were replaced with video feed from the Arctic. The image on the screen was alive with a mass of bright pink gases undulating in huge swathes across a dark sky and disappearing over the horizon.

'This is the Aurora Borealis at the North Pole – the Northern lights, created by the plasma that's ejected by the sun – hitting the earth's atmosphere. Pink is good. Pink says there's little activity. Pink says that the earth's magnetic field is deflecting the plasma. Green . . . Green is bad. Green tells us that the plasma is penetrating the earth's magnetic field and is bombarding the atmosphere. But we *know* the activity is bad – so bad that we're on high alert. So where's all the green gone?'

Hackett was cautious. 'You're suggesting Antarctica?'

'I'm not suggesting,' Gant advised. 'I'm telling you. Look.'

Vast ribbons of green energy swirled above a sparkling city that sat in the darkness below.

'Melbourne, Australia. That's how far north it's stretching,' he said. The screen changed again. To daylight and ice. Antarctica. The caption read: *Live Feed from McMurdo Station.* Despite the daylight, the sky was still alive with the green phenomenon.

'That's not unusual,' Hackett chipped in. 'That happens from time to time. A plasma cloud has its own magnetic field. It'll react to the earth's field. When the plasma storm is positive, it gets attracted to the earth's negative. Gets sucked right on in, and it's *going* to go to the South Pole. Opposites attract.'

'Except *this* plasma cloud is also negative,' said Gant.

Hackett almost choked. 'That . . . th-that *is* unusual.'

'Unusual? You know it's impossible, Professor. Like does *not* attract like.' Figures and charts spewed onto the screen. 'By our calculations, all it takes to cause a global environmental disaster is just three successive plasma storms to hit and be absorbed by the atmosphere. We're talking storms of such magnitude that entire continents will be engulfed. Seas really will boil. Increased atmospheric pressure and ionization will trigger earthquakes and in turn will create tidal waves in the oceans. But to suck in a plasma cloud takes a power source of unimaginable proportions. Something currently beyond our own technical capabilities. Something, somewhere in what we believe to be Atlantis is the only likely candidate responsible for what's happening. Some kind of device that the Chinese may have uncovered, and are manipulating.'

'Legend states,' Dower interjected, 'that Atlantis would rise again of its own accord. For the past fifty years, despite environmental protection measure, the ozone layer in Antarctica has depleted, creating a hole that has allowed cosmic rays and other radiation to bombard it like no other place on earth. The ice has begun to retreat. So we cannot rule out the possibility that something in Atlantis is waking *itself* up – is reacting to what's going on around it. London didn't wake up. New York sure as hell didn't react to a gravity wave. But Atlantis . . . did.

'We cannot prevent what's happening to the sun. It would be ridiculous to even suggest such a thing. But make no mistake: mankind's back is against the wall. A device that just lit up the security net of an entire Superpower is something to take very seriously. There is every indication that it is speeding up the changes that are taking place within our atmosphere. It is helping – whether by design or flaw – to destroy us.'

Matheson was incredulous. 'We're looking at one hell of a machine,' he remarked, 'to show up on satellite and do what it's doing. We're talking about a machine maybe the size of Atlantis itself.'

'We don't know that. But we will not sit back and do nothing while our planet is climatically destroyed. Whatever's beneath the ice does not appear to be our friend. We want it shut off. And we want it shut off – now.'

'And exactly how do you propose to do that?' Scott asked innocently.

All eyes fell on him.

'The writing's on the wall,' Dower commented.

'Pardon me?'

'There is ancient writing – on its walls, Dr Scott. The fact that Atlantis now exists is testament to all those ancient myths and legends you're so familiar with. Whoever built Atlantis left a lot of incomprehensible writing scrawled all over it. They must have done that for a reason. We're proposing that they left us some clue, some indication as to what it was they were trying to achieve. Some indication on how to switch the damn thing off.'

'Admiral, with all due respect,' Scott said, startled, 'if what you say is true it's hardly going to be like programming a fucking VCR.'

Dower took a breath. 'If everything that's taking place is down purely to Mother Nature, then we surrender. There is absolutely nothing we as a species can do about it. Just like the dinosaurs, we can kiss our asses goodbye because God's about to wipe the slate clean. But . . . and it's an uncertain but . . . if there is any chance at all that the structure in Antarctica is the cause of this environmental nightmare that's unfolding, then our only option is to enter the city and turn it off. And we can do that by one of two ways. You can figure out what they wrote. Or we can install a thermo-nuclear device – and blow the shit out of it.

'Ladies and gentlemen, God may play dice, but we do not. We will look for any means of raising our chances of survival. And if humankind depends on it – *we will destroy Atlantis.*'

There were stunned expressions on the faces of the scientists sat around the table. No one knew quite how to react. Taking a thermonuclear warhead to Antarctica was problematic for two reasons. One: it was illegal under the Antarctica Treaty. And two: the Chinese had a base sitting right above where Atlantis appeared on the map.

Dower drummed his fingers on the table. 'There is one other thing,' he added quietly. 'We may be able to get a dry run at this. There is the slim possibility that we may have found a second device of similar magnitude.'

Scott's ears pricked up. 'What do you mean?'

'Our use of the search parameters suggested by Dr Hackett led to the discovery of Atlantis. And with the help of Bob Pearce's abilities, and other at Rola Corp. we have detected a second site on this planet that appears to be giving off similar readings to Atlantis. If we can gain access, we might be able to get some insight into what to expect in Antarctica.'

Scott shot forward. 'So where is it?'

EL-QAHIRA

History is a set of lies agreed upon.

Napoleon Bonaparte,
Emperor of Europe, 1769–1821

THE GIZA PLATEAU

CAIRO

'For me? Aw, how sweet. I hope that thing's got coffee in it!' Sarah Kelsey yelled, holding tightly onto her navy-colored baseball cap. The battered old EH-101 helicopter veered back up into the air behind her, whipping up a sandstorm as it went.

The company guy in the gray boiler suit and the red company cap stood clutching a gray stone long-necked jug. He exclaimed: 'Afraid not! But this *is* for you to take a look at. What do you make of it?' He coughed up sand as he handed over the artifact. Seemed reluctant to straighten up after ducking out the way of the rotors. Introduced himself. 'Name's Eric. Eric Clemmens.' He tried to shake hands and hold on to his own hat all at the same time. His face was caked in dust. 'We gotta short walk,' he explained. 'They won't let us land choppers near the monuments. Sand damage, you know?' Sarah understood as Clemmens pointed her in the right direction. 'So what do you think?'

'Granite,' she said, turning the jug over in her hand. 'Half-inch diameter neck at the top, opening out to about six inches. No striated markings, as you'd expect. This is stone, not clay, so it wasn't on a potter's wheel. It was turned on a lathe, and the internal volume drilled out.'

Clemmens was elated. 'That's *exactly* what *I* said!'

'Any geologist or engineer could tell you that. Why? What's the problem?'

'The problem? I don't think the Egyptologists here have had any real engineers or geologists take a close look at any of the artifacts and monuments before.'

'What makes you say that?'

'Because they've been busy dismissing anything that challenges their view of ancient Egypt. Like this jug.'

'We're not archeologists, Eric.'

'But they say we're wrong because there's no evidence ancient Egypt ever had lathe technology.'

Sarah was concerned. 'You can't make a jug like this without a lathe.'

'Precisely, but I guess hard evidence just ain't good enough for 'em.' They crossed through a minor outer complex and headed down a long gravel track. 'If it was a single jug, maybe they'd have a point. But it's not. We've got eleven more of these things. Plus sixteen diorite bowls, eight quartz bowls and a feldspar and quartz bowl. And they all show the same signs. Wanna know the screwy thing?'

Sarah said she did as she peered into the camp and familiarized herself with the layout as they went. The last thing she needed was to get lost.

'How fast does a modern drill work?' Clemmens asked with a shrug. 'Tungsten carbide.'

That was easy. They worked for an oil company, after all. 'For fine work on stone? Say around 900 rpm. Cuts into stone about one ten-thousandth of an inch per revolution.'

'Close enough. But the inner surface of this jug shows all the signs that it was drilled a *tenth* of an inch per revolution. At that rate it would have to have had a metric ton of pressure behind it. And on a jug this small? That kind of pressure would have blasted it apart. By my reckoning, whoever made this jug used a drill that operated five hundred times faster than the ones we use in this company.'

'Are you serious?'

'Sarah, it gets screwier with the feldspar and quartz bowl. The drill seems to have cut through the quartz portion faster than the feldspar.'

'That doesn't make any sense,' she protested. 'Quartz is harder than feldspar.'

'We use a lot of vibration in drill bits to get them to cut quicker,'

Clemmens said. 'For the Egyptians to have cut through a denser, harder type of rock faster, I'm guessing they used vibration like an art form. Some kind of oscillation technique's my guess. Maybe even sonic.'

'Sound waves?'

Clemmens shrugged. He knew it was conjecture. 'We got a specialist in, to give a preliminary date to the bowls. The guy studied the ground strata where they were found. It was a grave-robber tunnel. And he wound up giving us a date of over 4,000BC.'

'And that's a problem, how?'

'The grave-robber tunnel appears to wend its way over to the pyramids, though it's filled in now. But if a grave-robber tunnel was constructed in 4,000BC, just what were they robbing? The Pyramids didn't exist until 2,500BC.'

In some areas, Arab workmen in long white cotton galebeyas were already hard at work shifting chunks of concrete without even breaking a sweat. Heavy machinery was busy clearing away rubble. Generators and night-lights were housed next to steel chain-link fences and store houses. Portakabins and trailers marked the nerve center. And then there were the Pyramids.

'Tell me about the Carbon 60,' Sarah said. 'What's the story on that?'

'We found a few smashed pieces in a little cloth sack, along with the pots. There's evidence of a fire down there, and some kind of close-quarter battle. Scorchmarks. Extremely violent. But so far – no bodies.'

'Maybe the grave robbers were discovered?'

'The fire indicates it started somewhere further down the tunnel – from the *pyramid* end. Whoever caught them had to be in one of the monuments, and went after them as they were on their way out.'

They arrived near the front gate. Sarah was about to respond when she shortened her stride.

A crowd had gathered. Military police were guarding the entrance to the site, and were unhappy with the situation. One of them was a little too eager in raising the butt of his rifle.

Sarah felt her heart miss a beat as they approached. 'What's going on?'

'Never mind,' Clemmens muttered as they headed in.

She could hear machinery. Heavy and loud just behind the sheer cliffs of devastation that marked the demolition zones within the camp. Plumes of oily blue smoke were shooting up into the sky marking their tracks in the distance. But that was nothing compared to the shouts of the crowd. There were about a hundred of them, Sarah guessed, mostly westerners. Some even had placards. About one third were media types with cameras and microphones. There was no choice but to bite the bullet and jostle their way through.

'Hey, do you mind? I'm trying to get to work, here!' Sarah shoved the large guy in front out the way. But the mere mention of work caused the crowd to turn like a shoal of fish. She exchanged a brief look with Clemmens.

'That was a really bad move,' he mouthed.

'We demand access!' the protesters were shouting. 'We have a right to know!'

Sarah struggled with more bodies. It was like an Eco-battle with a bunch of students, but for the life of her she couldn't figure out what they were complaining about. Reporters hurled questions at her about Thorne. When did they expect him? Was Rola Corp. facing a board of inquiry at the Senate? But Sarah didn't know what they were talking about. She ignored them all until a middle-aged woman with long silvery hair, tied back in a pony-tail, emerged from the mass to confront her. She wasn't a ringleader as such, but she certainly had influence. The crowd eased back, but they remained loud. Her eyes were deep and penetrating. Sarah had never seen eyes like them before.

'You will help us,' she said. Her voice cut through the din like a knife.

Sarah tried to ignore her but found that she couldn't.

The woman added: 'Cayce was right.'

Sarah frowned. She tried to respond, but didn't know how.

'You'll see,' the woman concluded. Her face was engaging, enigmatic.

Sarah remained transfixed but in a flash she was being herded off. The soldiers had cut a path through the crowd and Clemmens was bundling her into the camp. 'Come on!' he was yelling, and within seconds they were through.

Sarah kept trying to look back. Thought she'd caught a glimpse of the woman again, but Clemmens had a hold of her arm and was marching her up the path, deep into Rola Corp. territory. Moments later he let her free. 'Who's Cayce?' she asked.

Clemmens shrugged.

'What do they want?'

'I don't know,' he grumbled. 'What d'you care? They're nut-balls. Conspiracy theorists. End of the world freaks. They're insane. A pain in the ass.'

Sarah eyed him closely. 'So do they have anything to worry about, Eric?'

Clemmens seemed to grimace. Steered her onwards by pointing to a series of pits and leveled areas across from the Sphinx. They were foundations to a series of buildings that had been ripped from the ground. Twisted pipe-work still protruded in places. Chunks of concrete were piled to the sides.

'That's where we found the grave-robber tunnel. It's empty now, of course.' He whipped out a postcard. Passed it over. 'Used to be a whole bunch of restaurants and tourist shit. We leveled it. That's roughly where they want to build the museum. Hey, have you seen pictures of what it's gonna look like?'

'Yeah. It's pretty. It's like that one they built at the foot of the Parthenon in Athens.'

'It's gonna be more than pretty. It's gonna be awesome – sunk into the ground, looking up at the Sphinx and the Pyramids. Anyways, we've been running a geo-physics survey over this entire area, like you asked when you called last night. Monuments an' all.'

Sarah eyed the postcard casually. A grimy Arab stood by a rusted sign for Coke and a Seven-up vending machine. She handed it back. 'Good. What did you find?'

Clemmens took a breath. 'Granite under the Sphinx.'

Sarah faltered. She glanced over to the crowd still attached to the front gate before facing Clemmens again. They exchanged a look and they both knew. All bullshit aside, something strange was going on. Sarah set it down in her mind for a moment. It required focused thought, not some half-assed theory. A couple of Arab workmen saun-tered past. They were chatting away cheerfully until they came across Sarah. They looked vaguely shocked when they spotted her and gabbled to themselves with a scowl. Clemmens waved them on while Sarah tried to shrug it off.

She said: 'They don't get out much around here, huh?' Clemmens was silent. And then she heard it – the call to prayer. The muezzins were wailing high up in their minarets.

'Welcome to Cairo,' Clemmens chipped in glibly.

Sarah had been to Egypt before when she was twelve. It was winter, she remembered, and she'd arrived in Alexandria on a cruise ship. People herded sheep and goats in and out of filthy, dilapidated British colonial apartment blocks. It was a shock to learn those people also lived with the animals.

The other memory she had was animal-related too and equally squalid. She'd watched some kids play soccer on a patch of scrubland. It was near a mosque and she could still recall the faint scent of rosewater wafting across from the cart of a leathery old vendor. She'd strayed from her parents. They were bartering over a piece of cheap tourist papyrus, she remembered, when the boys noticed her. They'd grinned and kicked the ball over, hoping she might join in. Being a westerner they must have figured she could play soccer. Being American, of course she could not. She'd grinned in return, and glanced down to kick the ball back. But it didn't take long for her to realize what she was looking at. They were playing soccer with the decapitated head of a Labrador puppy. Its gums had rotted, and the teeth that remained were white. Snarling. Obviously she screamed. The mud was thick too, she remembered. Black. Yes, Sarah had lots of memories about Egypt.

She could feel perspiration starting to build up on the back of her neck. Already it was 30°C, and it wasn't even 8 o'clock yet. This wasn't right. It was only March.

They crossed out into the open, passed more demolition areas and moved on into the arena of the Pyramids. The huge, jagged-edged megaliths seemed to cut into the very sky itself. The desert beyond them stretched on to infinity while the Sphinx, ever enigmatic, sat passively waiting in a vast and relentless mass of shifting amber sands, each grain accompanied by a whiff of palpable history.

Sarah had to admit, she was impressed. She chewed her gum. 'Cool.'

They reached the geo-physics team, which was already hard at work.

Two operators methodically humped a set of meter-high electrodes around the site a yard at a time. Sarah recognized it immediately as an electrical resistivity survey, the type developed a couple of years ago that was able to peer through sand. Before then, sand showed up as solid rock and the ground had to be damp for the probes to function properly. It worked by passing a current directly into the ground and measuring the electrical potentials across the electrodes. In this way they built up a picture of the subsurface geology resulting in an underground map of the area without anyone lifting a shovel.

Sarah could see the operators were already struggling in the heat and dust. 'You didn't opt for a seismic survey then?' she asked.

'Are you kidding?' Clemmens did a double-take before realizing he was being had. He shook his head. 'Yeah, right. Blasting holes in everything with dynamite and listening to the echoes on geo-phones is really gonna go down well in this neighborhood.'

'I take it the archaeologists round here want access to the data. You know how they love to save money.'

'That's, uh, well . . .' Clemmens scratched his head. 'You'd better just talk to Douglas about that.'

Sarah eyed him coolly, unsurprised. Douglas was a company drone in charge of Rola Corp.'s construction arm. It was a small wing set up to accommodate favors for Third World governments, based on the notion that if they built a few things like a palace and a hotel, immediate tangible things, then they could dig or drill all they liked.

She found Douglas in the makeshift survey tent. Under the shade of some dusty green canvas and surrounded by a myriad of trailing cables and wires, he was the picture of organization. Hair slicked back, he wore a thin cotton shirt and dark glasses. He drank orange juice from a disposable plastic carton and jotted notes down on a yellow legal pad. Next to him on a rickety desk were stacks of papers in neat, tidy piles. He was standing, leaning over his notes when he glanced up. He did not look pleased.

'Wear longer sleeves next time, please,' he remarked.

Sarah gave a cursory glance at her bare arms. She was wearing khakis and a plain white cotton T-shirt. The humidity was low. The breeze coming in off the Sahara was dusty and harsh on her skin, but it was better than frostbite. And besides, she was damned if she was going to wrap up for these people.

'Fuck that,' she said angrily, throwing her purse down on the table.

Clemmens winced and ducked out of the firing line by taking up a position at one of the monitors. Douglas looked around sharply to see if any locals were in range. He let out a sigh of relief when he was certain there were not.

'Listen, Doug. Is this Islam thing gonna affect my entire stay?' Sarah glared. 'Gee, well at least I missed Ramadan. People going scatterbrain, starving themselves half to death from dawn till dusk for a month and dropping like flies because of it. Are you gonna ask me to abstain from sex too? Is that it?'

Douglas tried to let it roll over him. Failed. He slapped down the document he was working on. 'Just try to stay out of trouble. I haven't gotten your visas all cleared yet.'

'It may have escaped your attention, but I'm not a Muslim and I've no intention of becoming one. So you can stick your dress code up your—'

'I get the point. I'm just passing on information. It'll make working here a damn sight easier. Since the extremists started taking over, this is a changed country, you know.'

Sarah kept her gaze level. 'No shit,' she said. 'They're screaming for your blood at the gate.' Douglas inclined his head and let her win that one.

Clemmens eyed Douglas derisively as he handed Sarah a sprawling print-out with a set of gray-scale graph lines running down the entire length of paper. She thanked him under her breath. Clutching the data tightly, she speed-read the first sweep geo-physics survey sheet. It was a torrent of numbers.

Clemmens said, 'It's to a depth range of around fifteen meters.'

'They got the sub-structure readings for this entire area?'

Clemmens confirmed that they had, but Sarah was shaking her head. 'This can't be right.' She held up the scan for all to see. 'This is a perfect heptagon. There's a seven-sided structure – *directly beneath the Sphinx.*'

* * *

It was clear Douglas and Clemmens were well aware of this revelation.

Clemmens jerked a thumb in the direction of the two operators. 'Sally's out there now doing another sweep.'

Sarah tossed the print-out aside and went to one of the computers. She glanced down at the bearded, chunky guy sitting at the terminal and waved him away. He didn't look like he wanted to move.

'Frankie, this is Sarah Kelsey. She's the geology—'

'Oh, the geology chick.'

Sarah ignored them both as she tapped away on the keyboard. Clemmens had taken his cap off and was scratching his head again, embarrassed. 'Yeah, the chick.'

'You're sure about these figures?' Sarah demanded. She keyed in reference points and analyzed the test results.

Clemmens dug into his shirt pocket and thumbed through his notebook. 'Yeah. On the, uh, the fifth we took a core sample, authorized by the EDA at section G-one-eighty-seven.'

A core sample was taken by literally drilling a long hollow pipe into the ground and pulling it out again. The pipe would fill up with soil and rock and the resulting core was a cross-section of the ground. From that, each stratum could be measured and analyzed. A history of the entire area could be charted. If there was ash then chances were there'd been a fire. If there was a lot of ash, chances were a volcano had been nearby. If there was any organic matter it could be carbon dated. And even though it was an unreliable method it still gave a relative age, which could be assigned to that stratum, the logic being that if a fly was fifteen hundred years old and five feet down the core, then five feet represented fifteen hundred years ago. Any flies found further down the core sample had to be older.

Sarah scrolled through pages of the project specs before she found the information she was looking for. 'What did the core reveal?' she demanded, tapping the screen and jotting down the figures she needed.

'A big ole chunk of Aswan granite,' Clemmens confirmed. 'Just like the survey said we'd find.'

Sarah looked up sharply. 'Aswan granite?'

Clemmens shrugged. 'Yeah, you and me both know – Aswan's five hundred miles south of here.'

'You and me both know there isn't any natural granite anywhere in the Nile Delta, especially not here at Giza. It's a sandstone out-cropping.' She confirmed and tapped the geo-physics survey. 'And there's no way in hell that this seven-sided granite . . . thing was created by Mother Nature.' Her gaze rested on Douglas. They locked eyes for a moment.

'So what d'you think?' Clemmens prompted.

Sarah was cautious. But firm. She looked from man to man. 'I think someone leaked this to the crowd outside.'

'No way,' Douglas growled. 'Forget about them, they don't know anything. That's not why they're here.'

'Why are they here?'

Douglas wasn't biting. 'What is your opinion on the granite?'

'I think,' Sarah said tentatively, keeping a fixed gaze on the foreman, 'a good archeologist will tell you that the ancient Egyptians shipped all the granite they needed, downriver. Who's to say they didn't just build something under the Giza plateau?'

Clemmens was stunned. 'How?'

Sarah looked pensive. 'Who knows. Who cares. It's not our concern.'

'It's a natural formation,' Douglas insisted.

'Oh, come on!' Sarah scoffed.

'It's natural.'

'Who's the geologist here?'

Douglas glared, causing Sarah to fall silent. So that was it. Cooperation with the Egyptian Department of Antiquities was not what was going on here. Like her other trips to Egypt, the greasing of government palms was what was important here. To begin with, Rola Corp. had drawn up a strategy on how to tap oil in the Northern Desert west of the Nile, and had assessed the potential of the water reserves on the southern borders with Sudan. Both of these major resources, discovered in the late twentieth century, were vital to Egypt. Being the second largest international, and US, aid recipient in the world, a large proportion of her 70 million-strong populace needed immediate relief. And having just flown over Cairo this morning Sarah was in agreement. The Bulaq district was a slum. The Nile stretched off into the distance, a vast glistening life-line broken up by the Sixth of October Bridge and the island of Zamalek. But even now, well into the twenty-first century, the best public housing Egypt had to offer was still made from mud brick. The people were desperate. The nation was on the verge of turning fundamentalist and the government had its back to the wall. And Rola Corp. knew how to manipulate that to its advantage.

The computer beeped as it popped up another window of data. 'Gotcha,' she said, as a steady stream of spikes appeared all over the geo-survey.

Egypt had mineral deposits. But nothing as exotic as the readings she was seeing. Gold was more her thing, found mostly to the east, in the Nile valley and the Sinai Mountains. Granite under the Sphinx was interesting but completely irrelevant to Rola Corp.

What *was* of prime relevance were the tiny spikes of data forming a pattern beneath the surface across the entire Giza site map. Sure enough they'd found more Carbon 60, just as Houghton had said.

Sarah eyed Douglas again. 'Exactly what kind of a museum are we building here?'

Douglas said: 'Rola Corp.'s been out here almost ten years now, Sarah. Made a lot of people a lot of money. Won a lot of friends.' He finished off the last of his juice. 'The government likes the work you did when you were out here last. And you of all people know how they like to reward loyalty.' He let the words sink in. 'But there are only two certainties in this country. Poverty and sunstroke. So what do you do? Your education system sucks. Your industry – well, forget your industry. You got a few offshore rigs in the Red Sea, but that's about it. Half your population works for other countries and sends home next to nothing. But you got minerals, and you know minerals are power.'

'Egypt's a real target for this company,' Sarah quipped with fake enthusiasm.

'Think about it. You suddenly find a solution. Carbon 60. Heaps of the stuff. All the experts tell you it's the future in computing, in precision engineering. It'll change the face of the world overnight. Trouble is, somebody made a pretty little statue from the stuff. So what do you do? If the moralists find out they'll be screaming for display cases. So do you really put it on show and hope enough fat Americans waddle past in their plaid pants, waving their five bucks? Do you opt for tourism – again? Or do you blow it all to pieces and sell off the chunks? Do you get rich quick and give your people a life? What do you do, Sarah? What do you do?'

Sarah did what she always did. She went for her purse and grabbed a pack of cigarettes. Camel lights. Her heart was sinking fast and she was starting to feel sick. She'd been ambushed. This wasn't what she'd been expecting, or hoping for. She wanted a little adventure, a chance at pure research and exploration again. But this wasn't it. She was building herself a great reputation as a first-class geologist, even if she was stuck in a shit-heap company, but she knew that this wasn't research *or* exploration. She was being used. To the company, she was a commodity, an official line they could tack onto their pet projects.

She blew smoke rings. They were intended to irritate but Douglas acted like he hadn't noticed. Clemmens and Frankie watched in quiet trepidation.

'I'm excited,' she said finally with a hint of a smile. She was doing her best to hide her anger but she had a feeling she couldn't mask the betrayal in her eyes. Douglas did not respond. 'I've never been to the Pyramids. When I came as a kid the bus broke down and we never got out the harbor.'

Douglas's expression was unreadable.

'What you're proposing is totally unethical. Not to mention illegal, most probably. I couldn't possibly associate myself with—'

Douglas started grabbing his paperwork and shoving it into a well-worn leather briefcase. He eyed her again. 'Your opinions are not required. You work for the company – remember that. So where's this little ethical streak suddenly springing from, Sarah? You getting broody in your old age? You want a better future for your theoretical kids?' Suddenly his tone was loudly aggressive. 'Well, forget it! The company didn't pay your way through college for nothing! They probably got enough stuff pegged on you so that you'll never work again. You've okayed enough shitty shit for this company – you'll be finished. But right now you've got a good reputation.'

Sarah's face was ashen. She said: 'So what's the plan?'

Douglas stepped over to the monitor and pointed to the images on the screen. 'It's simple. You dig. Eric here's working on the nuts and bolts strategy on how to get down there. When you reach the site you've got a few hours to decide. Is it Carbon 60 – or isn't it? If it is, you smuggle it out – fast. The official line is we found a small mineral deposit and are deciding if it's worth mining. If it isn't, then tomorrow morning on CNN Live, I announce to the world that Rola Corp. is, quote: "Proud to announce the discovery of a major new archeological find." It's that simple.'

Sarah was skeptical. Things were never that simple.

Douglas glanced at his watch. 'I've got to get to the Department of Trade by noon.' He handed Sarah a pen and pointed to the desk. 'If you'd be so kind. Sign that temporary work permit and you're all clear.'

Bewildered, Sarah did so. But it was as she glanced at the other papers still on the desk that she noticed the front page of the *Egyptian Gazette*. She picked it up and scanned the headlines, which gave her yet another jolt. Here was the reason why the crowd had gathered outside.

'Thorne's coming here?' She was talking to herself.

'Yes,' Douglas replied warily. 'Is that going to cause a problem?'

'No.'

Douglas hesitated. 'Have you met Thorne before?'

'Not much of a company stooge, are you? Who does your research?' Sarah puffed on her cigarette and smiled. She remembered when she first came to Egypt as an employee of Rola Corp. 'Yeah, I've met him before. I used to fuck him.' She blew smoke. 'How the hell d'you think I got this job?'

Douglas rocked on his heels and rubbed his chin. A rueful smile was emerging.

There was the sound of a snigger or two, then muffled laughter. Clemmens was scratching his head again. Frankie was sporting a lopsided grin. 'I'm starting to like this chick,' he said. Almost immediately he wished he hadn't said a word as Sarah clouted him up side the head.

'Cut the sexist bullshit, Fatboy,' she scowled, and walked out to supervise the next set of measurements. It was a good feint because she actually felt like crying. Thorne was coming. Finally, everything had come full circle. Things couldn't get any worse.

She crossed the sand. Watching the geo-physicists, she realized they had stopped to huddle around some readings. For geo-physicists that was tantamount to a riot. She was about to cross over to them and see what all the fuss was about when suddenly they all started whooping and hollering. Sarah broke into a run as their cries echoed across the site. 'We got another tunnel! A goddamn tunnel!'

Sarah was amazed as she took a look at their readings. 'Where is it?' she demanded.

'Right beneath our feet!'

'But these readings,' Sarah remarked, confused, 'are these live? Are you still hooked up?'

'Uh-huh.'

'They're spiking. They keep changing. What's going on down there?'

'Exactly what they told us to expect.'

'They? They who?'

'The people in Geneva. That's power you're seeing on those readings. Electricity, flowing underground. If we didn't know to look for it, we'd never have known it was there. It's like looking at some kind of machine.'

CERN

EXPEDITION PLANS

'I'm – I'm shocked, is what I'm saying,' Hackett said numbly. 'I'm stunned. That the complexity of the situation hasn't been totally grasped.'

'What are we overlooking?' Dower wanted to know as Scott and Matheson pored over a map of the pyramids at Giza.

'Gravity. It's not something to be taken lightly. It's the basic rule of thumb for all life. Before something can reproduce, it has to withstand gravity.' Hackett was banging his balled fist into the palm of his other hand. 'It's what keeps us *glued* to this planet. It's what keeps us whizzing around the sun. It's what smacked an apple into Newton's head. We can defy it temporarily. We can *escape* it, momentarily. But we can't ever hide from it. It affects everything, the entire universe. And that's big.

'Here we are, talking about the effects of an actual gravity wave, and you're not even considering the full complexity of the implications. Instead, we, we, sit here, *discussing* a city that not more than twenty or thirty minutes ago no one knew even existed. And your first thought is to march halfway across a frozen continent and blow it up. All I'm saying is, there might be other ways in which we could be applying our minds. Important ways. But instead, with all due respect to Dr Scott, you have a linguist here to translate the writing on a bunch of rocks. You have strategists carping on about how best to avoid a war – and still be able to blow things up. I think I wouldn't be the first to suggest this. But even as a complexity theorist, whose job it is to discover the hidden connections to things that apparently have no connection – I just don't see the connection. It all sounds like so much panic-driven nonsense.'

Everyone around the table seemed to be shifting uneasily in their chairs. 'Jon, what are you saying?' asked Dower.

'What I'm saying is, I don't think this is the time to act like a bunch of ostriches and bury your heads in the snow. Do you realize what a gravity wave could do? It could shift the orbit of this planet at a whim, add a few extra days, or take a few days away – if we managed to stay in orbit at all.'

Jon Hackett eyed the faces around the table and was met by a wall of unblinking eyes. It was as if he'd asked for a medium-rare steak at a vegetarian luncheon, and that wasn't good. Didn't they see?

'My question is, what are you going to do about *that*?' he persevered. 'Are you going to build an Ark and save mankind? Do you have contingencies?'

'There's nothing we *can* do about the Sun,' Dower said flatly.

'Can we contact Egypt now?' Scott insisted.

Hackett drew a finger to his lips for silence as if he were talking to a child. 'Dr Scott, uh, if I may. Admiral, did it ever occur to you that the resurrection of Atlantis may be a good thing?' Dower frowned. 'Aside from the absolute latest ground-breaking technology here at CERN, the only thing to react to the sun, and on a spectacularly massive scale, is Atlantis. Did you ever stop to consider that it might have more of an idea of what's going on than we do?'

'You sound like you think it's alive,' Pearce reacted.

'It's survived twelve thousand years under the ice, and come out the other end of its slumber. It might be an automatic response, but it's still a response. Yes.'

'It didn't do any good during the last flood,' Scott pointed out.

'That's why it's under all that ice.'

'The resurrection of Atlantis as a good thing?' Dower mused briefly. Then: 'No.'

'This is McMurdo Station. Lieutenant Roebuck reporting.'

The voice was tinny. Hollow, like it was coming out of a long metal tube. A burst of interference cut deep across the screen. He wasn't in uniform, this Lieutenant Roebuck. With a sheet of paper in one hand, he wore a gray T-shirt bearing his unit crest. He had a towel slung over one shoulder, like he'd just gotten back from the gym. And in the background, next to the charts and monitors, hung the insignia of the Marine Expeditionary Force, Antarctica Unit. Penguins hugging an anchor.

Scott was puzzled. T-shirts in Antarctica? Well, at least it wasn't thin nylon tents and frostbite. If this was a foretaste of what to expect then Scott reckoned he could handle it.

The US station at McMurdo Sound was the largest permanently manned base anywhere on Antarctica. With over 1200 men and women in residence at any one time, Gant had described a village containing scientists, military personnel and civilians all living and working side by side. As Gant explained, there were private quarters and research facilities all ready and waiting for them.

Roebuck was ready to debrief and Gant stood by the screen adjusting the system to try and clear out the static. Houghton chose that moment to re-enter the room, casually slotting his phone back into his pen and slipping it inside his jacket pocket. 'Just the UN,' he said as he retook his seat at the table, completely unaware that Pearce was watching him closely.

'And?' Dower asked.

'It's all set for tomorrow morning at ten,' Houghton said. 'We meet with the commission at the Palais des Nations to discuss an inspection team going onto the Chinese base.'

'Took long enough,' Dower growled.

'Proper channels, Admiral. Proper channels, and proper procedure, or the UN will smell a rat.'

Dower flicked a finger at Roebuck on the screen, indicating to the soldier that he could continue.

'Yes, sir. Thank you, sir.' Roebuck cleared his throat as Matheson continued to paw over the set of schematics that had been placed on the table for him. Several military specialists had joined him to exchange notes as Roebuck spoke up.

'At fourteen hundred hours, GMT, we sent a warning signal to the fleet, Admiral,' he explained hesitantly. 'The British Antarctic Survey issued a statement to all shipping in the area off the Larsen

Ice Shelf to watch out for a fifty-mile-wide iceberg that has calved off and is heading out to the open sea.'

Houghton was aghast. 'Fifty miles! Is that possible?' But he was ignored.

'Where is the Seventh Carrier Group now?' Dower asked.

Roebuck was apprehensive. 'The *Nimitz* is further out. But the *Sacramento* and the *Ingersoll* have been hunting down a Chinese sub all week.'

Matheson looked up to see Gant tense. He knew about the *Ingersoll*. That was Gant's ship, the one he'd been assigned to when he led the boarding party onto *Red Osprey*. It was a Marine Expeditionary Force Destroyer attached to the Seventh Carrier Group of the Pacific Fleet. It was as fast and dangerous as it was beautiful.

Dower demanded: 'Which sub?'

'We think the *Qingdao*.'

'*Qingdao*? Han Class attack sub. Type 92. That's big.'

'The size of two football fields, sir. Should we warn the Chinese?'

Dower was firm. 'No,' he said. 'To hell with the Chinese.'

'The Chinese,' Matheson commented, standing back from the diagrams with a mystified air, 'have got some real specialist drilling equipment here. If I didn't know better I'd say they got a head start in all this. It makes me think they already know about the C60.'

Still looking at the diagrams, he was completely unaware of the curious expression on Houghton's face.

'Interesting hypothesis,' Hackett ventured. 'But how would the Chinese already know there's a city down there?'

'They wouldn't,' Dower blasted. But Houghton remained quiet.

'They *may* do, sir,' Gant disagreed. 'The Chinese have been on a technology kick for over a decade and show no signs of slowing down. You can never tell what the Chinese know . . . sir.'

'Then we're in for the race of our lives, Major. You ready for that?' the Admiral queried.

'Sir, yes, *sir*!' Gant barked.

Matheson rubbed his beard. Embarrassed. 'Oh, please . . .'

Roebuck fidgeted on the screen. 'Amundsen-Scott Station at the South Pole report no increased activity at *Jung Chang*,' he said, 'but we've sent out a couple of SaRGE probes, sir. I really think you should take a look at what we got.'

'Are the vehicles online now?'

'One is, sir. I can transfer control of the signal if you'd prefer.'

'I prefer,' Dower confirmed. 'But before we sign off, Lieutenant, I'd like you to take a look at some of the faces sat around this table. They're our inspection team. Doctors Hackett and Scott. Engineer Ralph Matheson. Specialist Robert Pearce—'

'I understood you were sending a geologist as well,' Roebuck said. 'Sarah Kelsey.'

Houghton sat up in his chair. 'Uh, we will be,' he confirmed as Hackett and Scott exchanged anxious glances. 'She's on another assignment right now. Preparatory work.'

Roebuck said, 'Understood. Admiral, it's just accommodation space is tight. I need to know supply details. Does anybody have any special dietary requirements?'

There were meek looks all around the table.

November leaned in close to Scott. 'They'll have burgers, won't they?'

'I think you can just transfer SaRGE over to us now, thank you, Lieutenant.'

'Just being thorough, sir.'

A steady stream of data swept across the screen. Gant punched in commands and a grid unfolded followed by live video feed.

He announced: 'Here's the view from SaRGE.'

Matheson shot him a look.

'Stands for Surveillance and Reconnaissance Ground Equipment.'

Matheson tried to look knowledgable, failed. Said: 'Which is what?'

'Now if we told you that,' Dower said dryly, 'we'd have to take you outside and shoot you.'

'So who's on the end of that camera?'

'Right now? Just Major Gant. We dropped SaRGE behind enemy lines, so to speak.'

'So it's a robot?'

'Of sorts.' He looked to Gant. 'Position?'

'Elevation: five thousand seven hundred and fifty-nine feet above sea level. Approximately forty-two miles from Blue One runway and the coastline of Queen Maud Land.'

They were looking at a vista of ice and snow with huge fingers of dark granite jutting out like the frozen digits of a long dead giant. Without any familiar objects in the picture it was difficult to judge any real perspective. Dower pointed to one of the formations.

'What's that?' It looked like a vast granite skyscraper.

Gant checked the details on the readout next to the picture first. The quality was good, though there was intermittent signal break-up. Probably due to the fact that it wasn't coming direct from Antarctica, but via a myriad of military spy satellites.

'That's Rakenkniven,' he said. 'The Razor. It's half as tall again as the World Trade Center. First point of contact with the Filchner Mountains and controls the access to two main valleys that lead directly into the continental interior: the Kubusdalen and the Djupedalen Passes.'

'Who named these damn things?'

'The Norwegians, sir.'

Dower studied the picture carefully. Small red cross-hairs were flashing on the screen where SaRGE had detected enemy activity.

'Focus in on that,' he said. 'At the base of the Razor.'

The magnification was increased several times before the targets came into full view. There were heavy vehicles on caterpillar tracks. Armored Personnel Carriers. Troops on Skidoos kicking up plumes of snow in their wake, and what looked like supplies. Their presence suddenly brought the sheer scale of the Razor into sharp relief. Human activity in Antarctica was clearly insignificant.

Gant shook his head respectfully. 'Goddamnit, Mr Pearce. You were right again.'

'That's what we pay him for,' the Admiral said quietly.

It was not a comment that went unnoticed by everyone else in the room. Scott zeroed in on him, while Hackett raised an eyebrow. Just what did Bob Pearce do for these people?

Pearce didn't bother answering.

There were thirty vehicles in all, painted black with bright orange markings. It didn't take long for Gant to inspect them and give a brief though subdued summary.

'That's three, no wait . . . four UNIPOWER, 20,000-liter combat refuellers, on modified old-style M-series eight-by-eight chassis. Hmm . . . They put 'em on tracks. Everything's on tracks. They're not fooling around. They've adapted everything for long-term use in the cold.'

Scott asked: 'Otherwise, what would happen?'

'At minus fifty degrees C,' Matheson explained, 'rubber tires would shatter like glass. A non-adapted metal chassis would snap like a twig. When you get down to those sorts of temperatures, all the rules change. Materials start to act very differently. An ordinary gun would explode if you tried firing. At minus fifty degrees C,' he added darkly, 'it's impossible to run. The ground is frozen solid to a depth of eight feet. At minus sixty degrees C unless you cover your face it's impossible to breathe. And when your breath does hit the air it turns instantly to ice crystals – what Siberians call "the whispering of the stars".'

Scott eyed Dower anxiously. 'You're covered for this, right?'

'The Marine Expeditionary Force has all the right gear, Professor. With long-range naval support and air superiority, it shouldn't be a problem.'

Gant ran a finger across the vehicles on the screen again. The sky was sharp powder blue, the sun strong and vibrant.

Hackett sat upright. 'The sky – it's blue. The Aurora must be in a stable period.'

But Gant was interested in something else on the screen. Something much more immediate. 'There's five Swedish-made BV 206 all-terrain vehicles. One of 'em, look, that's obviously radar. The rest are troop-carriers. And there's a couple of British-made Leyland Medium Mobility Carrier DROPS vehicles.' He caught another curious look from Matheson. 'Demountable Rack Off-loading and Pick-up System. Add a coupla Russian BMP-3 infantry fighting vehicles and a Bofors/Hägglunds CV9040 combat vehicle. Christ, there's gotta be more stuff on the way. I think they're still building up.'

'What makes you say that?' the Admiral probed.

'There's too much variety in their vehicle choice. Something goes wrong on one of those things you're gonna need spare parts. If it's a small operation you opt for uniformity.'

'Makes sense.'

Scott was awestruck. 'My God,' he said. 'It really is a war zone over there.'

'That's what you're facing when you get there, Dr Scott, yes,' the Admiral confirmed.

Scott shifted uncomfortably in his seat as an insistent tiny red arrow flashed on the screen. It had been intriguing Matheson, but he'd said nothing until Gant finally was in a mood to respond to it.

He ordered SaRGE to zero in on the target in question, which turned out to be 2,000 feet up. The Chinese had placed a command station on the top of the Razor.

'They clearly don't want anyone coming through that pass after them,' Matheson commented. 'Jesus, they have 360-degree visibility.'

'Move in closer,' Dower rapped out. 'Let's see what kind of radar and EW systems they got.'

The clearer image was an eye-opener. There were satellite communications dishes. Radar masts. An array of antenna – anti-aircraft guns and long-range artillery all anchored by carbon-fiber cables and hooked up to solar panels. There was a hut. Windbreaks. And there were two Chinese soldiers, Commandos or some kind of special forces, one of whom was operating his equipment a little too well, because he had his eye firmly on SaRGE, and was smiling and waving to camera.

Dower blinked in rage and frustration. 'Motherfucker,' he said.

It wasn't what anyone had expected to hear from an Admiral.

PAPERWORK

2:01PM

Dower was on his feet. Being passed around the table were indi-vidually labeled documents. They bore the names of the people who had to sign them. They were release forms, temporarily signing over their services to the United States government, as stark-looking as the white continent itself.

'Ladies and gentlemen,' Dower announced, 'I urge you to be very sure about what it is you are doing. You are about to embark on a journey that will take you to the most ferocious and inhospitable landscape on Planet Earth. It will not be like any part of this planet you've ever been to before. There will not be a single tree or shrub. Nor a blade of grass. There certainly will not be a Seven-Eleven just around the corner because there *are* no corners. You will be expected to adhere to the strictest guidelines. And your actions will have profound consequences. We do not wish to provoke a war with the Chinese, despite what you may think, but we will be prepared to fight one. And war in Antarctica would just about be the most hellish thing imaginable.

'You were all selected because of your experience, knowledge and expertise in your fields. And so I ask you, as a servant of the United States of America, to think very carefully before putting pen to paper. For the task ahead is not an easy one.'

No one hesitated.

Everyone signed.

FIRST ORDER OF BUSINESS

2:17 PM

It was a polished steel container. Square, with very few markings or embellishments. It hissed as the locks were popped and the pressure equalized within. Bringing the case over to the table, Gant carefully lifted the lid and displayed the neatly arranged shards of Carbon 60. The stones glowed with an iridescence that seemed to feed off the ambient lighting in the room. Scott peered in at them, and could clearly see the writing etched across their surfaces.

'This,' Dower explained, 'is what all the fuss is about.'

Scott almost giggled like a child as he gently lifted one of the rocks from the container. 'My fingers – they're tingling. This stuff feels weird.'

'Mankind's greatest and newest invention over the past decade has been the production of the Carbon 60 fullerene. It's financed by the Defense Department, but our best minds can only produce it by the gram. The piece you have in your hand is worth a quarter of a million US dollars. Atlantis represents billions upon billions of tons of the stuff.'

'So should you have to blow the crap out of the most eagerly sought archeological site known to man, the fact that the debris will be worth millions must be a comfort?' Hackett prodded indelicately.

Dower ignored him. 'So you see, Dr Scott, you find yourself in a unique position. Your knowledge of flood mythology and your ability to decode ancient languages is unparalleled. Combined with the fact that our best twenty-first-century minds have difficulty doing what our ancestors could do standing on their twelve-thousand-year-old heads – manufacture and manipulate Carbon 60, you might say we have an unusual situation. One where science, language and history are forced to work together.'

A buzzer interrupted. Gant thumbed a wall switch next to the screen, and gave a terse: 'What?'

'Gentlemen, we're ready to repeat the test,' a tinny voice announced. 'If you'd care to come to the windows and don't forget to put on your goggles.'

Tinted safety goggles were hurriedly passed around as everyone did as they were told and moved to the windows for a good view of the experiment below. Scott took the chunk of C60 with him and Matheson watched as he ran his fingers over the etchings, almost like a blind man reading Braille.

'What's going on?' November asked quietly, edging closer to Major Gant.

'Pure Carbon 60 is a yellowish-brown color. This stuff is bright blue, so it has to have something else in with it,' Gant told her. 'Maybe pure diamond – that's blue.'

'So what're they gonna do?' She was struggling with her goggles. Gant took them out of her hands, made the elastic headband wider and fitted them in place.

'Okay?' he asked gently. November nodded.

'What they're gonna do,' Hackett said, digging his hands into his pockets and having absolutely no trouble at all with his own goggles, 'is put a piece of that rock into a chamber, fire up the most powerful laser in the world, blast that sucker to atoms, and study the residue. Then they'll know what it's made of.'

Bright yellow warning lights suddenly flashed. Klaxons whirred and the countdown began. But Scott wasn't concerned with what was outside the window. He was concerned with what was in his hand. Could it really be? He turned back to the screen. The city under the ice. The overall layout could be simplified down to two distinct images. A series of concentric circles cut into quarters by a large cross. It was an ancient symbol, which Scott knew well. And as he held the crystal up to compare it, he couldn't deny the exact same symbol was also etched onto the crystal. Concentric circles and a cross.

His gut told him he was right. But could it be? This was an unknown language. Was it really that simple? He realized he was being watched and glanced over to share a nervous smile with Matheson, who fidgeted with anticipation, like he was waiting for the results of a blood test.

'This is the symbol,' Scott said, 'for the sun.'

Awed, Ralph repeated: 'The symbol for the sun?'

The klaxons whirred once more. And the entire room was flooded with light.

AMAZON

[Out] of 6 million years, only 100,000 [fossilized species] may be represented by surviving strata. In the unrecorded 5.9 million years there is time for even advanced civilizations to have come and gone, leaving hardly a trace.

Michael A. Cremo and Richard L. Thompson,
Forbidden Archaeaology, 1996

THE PINI PINI RIVER

PERU

'What the fuck is this?' Maple spat as he jumped down from the prow of the dilapidated shallow-bottomed scow they'd hired back in Iquitos, its blue paintwork chipped and faded. He was up to his ankles in muddy water and floating debris – leaves and shit from the jungle floor, so thick and tangled that he couldn't for a moment figure out if the twisted knots of tubing up ahead were snakes or vines. Partially submerged, they bobbed in the water at the base of some huge tree.

He shook out one lizardskin boot and adjusted his Panama hat. The tail of a yellow, red and blue woolen twirl hung down the back of it and swung back and forth by his neck. He pulled out his Beretta and slammed in a clip. Over his shoulder Carver emerged from the filthy tarp that clung to the aluminum and cane frame, under which the others sat guarding supplies.

Carver thumbed through the digital map on his GPS notepad and waved it as evidence. 'According to this,' he said, 'we should be two miles inland.'

Maple chewed his tobacco, spat a lump out and fished for some more. 'It's flooded then. The whole goddamn basin's flooded.'

'We can't pull out now. We ordered the drop three hours ago.'

'The drop can be moved,' said a voice from inside the boat. Clambering out and blowing thick blue cigar smoke was Jack Bulger, wearing a camouflage jacket and tapping an old-fashioned paper map. 'Radio the plane,' he instructed. 'Tell them to drop the gear two miles farther north.'

Carver didn't move. Waited for the okay from Maple, who chewed thoughtfully for a moment. 'Yeah, radio the plane,' he said.

Carver did what he was told without comment, checking the density of the deep green overhead leafy canopy before thumbing the transceiver and broadcasting the message. There were complaints from the pilots. Pilots always complained, but Carver didn't give a fuck about their fuel load. They could land somewhere else on the way back home.

Maple jammed his fingers into his mouth and let out an ear-splitting whistle. 'We walk from here!'

His team numbered eight. And they weren't hot on conversation – which was good. He'd hired them across the border. They were western mercenaries working in Colombia, each with a good reputation and few ties to permanent work. And for once the pay from an oil company was better than the drug cartels.

Yes, Rola Corp. was paying handsomely for this little trip.

The two *madeireiros*, or lumberjacks, who'd hired them the boat and served as guides upriver, whispered to each other anxiously. Pointing to the water, pointing to the sky. The color of the vegetation. Since Maple could speak neither Aymara nor Quechua their comments were incomprehensible. Spanish he could deal with, but they rarely spoke Spanish.

'They're nervous,' Carver said with a little understatement. 'They think the spirits are against us. They think maybe the Jaguar has returned to destroy the earth.'

'The Jaguar?'

Carver shrugged. 'That's what they say.'

'It's not the Jaguar,' Maple scoffed.

The *madeireiros* helped with the packs and loaded the men up, which was foolish really, because in the end, their first instinct to just set the boat in reverse and go would have been the best move.

Instead, Maple grinned like a shark. He patted one of the guides on the back of the neck in a friendly manner and made like he was fishing for money. But the grip around the man's neck quickly tightened, and the money was actually his Beretta.

'Thank you, Possuelo,' Maple said with some affection before leveling the barrel between the man's eyes and blowing his brains out.

The stunned expression on Possuelo's face sank beneath the muddy water.

His friend screamed and bolted into the jungle, but was brought down by a second bullet.

'No need to worry about the Jaguar now, my friends,' Maple added. 'But I'm afraid we cannot be followed.'

'I'm not sure that was wise,' Carver said.

'Let me worry about how wise it was.'

'The Machiguenga Indians,' Carver insisted. 'They'll know we're here.'

'Good,' Maple snarled arrogantly. 'I hate the element of surprise. It takes all the fun out of the slaughter.' He thumbed at a junior to take point along the trail. Pulled his collar up, searched the sky through the branches of the trees and said: 'Looks like rain.'

They moved on, hacking their way through the undergrowth. Within thirty minutes the hairs on the back of every man's neck stood on end. Shadows were glimpsed, movement spotted. And the hunt was on. For a fraction of a moment or two it wasn't quite clear just who was being hunted. But as they all took up a defensive ring posture and shot their first attacker, right through his hairless red chest, it was clear Maple was going to get his way.

He pulled out a GPS device, black and oblong, like a book. Raised the aerial and zeroed in on something on the horizon of more concern to him than the rapid gunfire being loosed all around. As the battle cries of the Machiguenga doubled in number and arrows started whizzing past, Maple remained unphased, continuing to track the signal until the target came into view.

Through the trees in the distance, rising up out of the horizon was a jungle-covered rise. Kind of like a mountain, but too regular in shape. Triangular maybe. Or pyramid-shaped.

'Bingo.' He handed the device to Bulger, who was crouching by his heel and wincing every time a shot was squeezed off. 'Here,' he said. 'You can call home now.'

Bulger keyed the sat-phone on the side of the device. Waited for the ringing and hit speakerphone at the pick-up.

'Hello?'

'Rip, is that you?'

'No,' came the measured response. 'This is Houghton. Rip's gone to Cairo.'

'Afternoon, Jay. This is Bulger. We're in position.'

'Situation secure?'

Bulger jammed a finger in his ear as Maple leveled the gun over his head and picked off another target. He watched with some satisfaction as the Indian's guts spewed out his back.

'Yes, I believe so,' he replied. 'What about you? Did the military buy it?'

There was a chortle on the line. 'Hell yeah, they bought it. In fact, we're just discussing strategy right now. We'll have to persuade them not to go nuclear though. Morons. Radioactive Carbon 60 isn't worth shit.'

'Be careful,' Bulger warned. 'They may be dumb, but they're not stupid.'

'Don't worry,' Houghton said. 'There will only be one company that controls the world's supply of Carbon 60. And one way or another, it *will* be Rola Corp.'

AS ABOVE SO BELOW

And King Cheops said: 'It has been said that you know the number of the secret chambers in the sanctuary of Thoth.' And Djedi said: 'So it please you, O sovereign my lord, I know not the number thereof, but I know the place where it is.'

Excerpt from: *King Cheops and the Magicians*, c. 1700BCE, from an earlier text *c.* 2500BCE. Translated in: *The Wisdom of Ancient Egypt*, Joseph Kaster, 1968. Revised from: *The Literature of the Ancient Egyptians*, Adolf Erman, 1927

SYMBOLS

'The cross and the circle representing the sun is the oldest piece of symbolism known to mankind,' Scott explained hurriedly as the team donned white boiler-suits for their sojourn down to where the Carbon 60 crystals sat, surrounded by highly sensitive research equipment.

He grabbed a pen and started scrawling. 'They occur all over the world. These are Stone Age glyphs from India: ⊕⊕. This is the Rongorongo script sun symbol from Easter Island: ⋇. This symbol pops up in Venezuela: ✴. This Mayan symbol for the sun was also the phonetic sound 'kin': ⊠. In South America the quincunx or cross was also the symbol indicating mankind's existence at the intersection of the physical world represented by the horizontal plane, and the eternal world represented by the vertical plane. If you think about it, the Egyptian ankh represents eternal life and that's a cross and a circle just in a slightly different form: ⸸. At the Temple of Paintings, at Bonampak near Palenque in Mexico, they even have pictures of fishmen visitors bearing crosses in circles.'

November frowned. 'Fishmen?'

'Foreign visitors with beards and fish on their heads. Go figure.'

'So it all comes down to a big cosmic game of tic-tac-toe – noughts and crosses, huh?' Hackett smirked.

Scott ignored him. Tapped the drawings again. 'Palenque is the site of the Temple of the Sun and the Foliated Cross.' Suddenly clicking to what he'd just said, he grabbed Gant's attention. 'Hey, did anyone point a satellite at that site and look for C60?'

'Mm-hmm. Rola Corp. did a sweep. Came up negative.'

Scott seemed deflated. 'Oh well. Cross symbolism was real big in South American culture. Quetzalcoatl, the tall white-bearded savior who brought civilization to the Incas wore a robe fringed with white crosses. Okay, he wasn't Mayan, but—'

'It still came up negative.'

Pearce zipped his boiler-suit up to his neck as he came over to inspect Scott's doodled glyphs. 'I think I remember reading somewhere that Linear B, the distant cousin to ancient Greek, had a cross and circle symbol too.'

'Oh, you mean this one? ⊕ Yeah. Now that's interesting because Linear B and the other Greek cousin, the Phaistos Disk, which used this symbol: ✤ were both phonetic. These signs didn't mean the sun, but stood for the sound "ka".'

'Ka?' Pearce questioned. 'In ancient Egypt the Ka was divine essence. When you were born, your double, or your Ka was created and remained in the divine world. Guiding you and protecting you until you died and rejoined it.'

'Well, I wouldn't get too excited,' Scott warned. 'This symbol ⊕ is also used in early cuneiform, in Sumeria, and it means sheep.'

'Sheep . . .?'

Now November was intrigued. 'Dr Scott, you said Jesus was given the symbol of the cross and the halo after his death from other religions. What about the sheep? They called him a lamb all the time. I thought it was to do with Passover. Y'know, a symbol for sacrifice?'

Scott mulled it over as Hackett retorted, 'Come on, are you saying the resurrection of Atlantis is actually the Second Coming?'

'No, that's not what I'm saying at all,' November bridled, defensive and angry. 'We're talking about symbols. Mythology—'

Scott held up a hand. 'Shut up!' he barked. 'Y'see? Y'see what religion does to people?' He turned his attention back to his doodle pad. Scrawled another glyph. Beckoned everyone to stand around and join him. 'Now look,' he said, 'this symbol is ancient Egyptian too. But this one doesn't mean any of those things.'

'That's the closest symbol so far to the layout of Atlantis,' Matheson commented. 'That and the Indian one. What does it mean?'

'It's Hieroglyphic Egyptian,' Scott explained. 'Denoting a city.'

All eyes turned to the screen where the sub-ice images of Atlantis were being displayed. 'Plato said his story of Atlantis originated in Egypt,' Scott told them. 'His description of the city was of concentric circles of land and water, divided into quarters by land bridges. From the air it would seem like a series of circles and a cross.'

'So the Egyptians knew about Atlantis?' Matheson asked.

'Possibly. Either that, or they knew about ancient Mexico City.'

Pearce blinked. 'Okay, now I'm confused. What's the connection?'

'Aztec legend has it that after the flood, Coxcoxtli and his wife landed at Antlan and journeyed eventually to Mexico, where they set about reclaiming land and built the city of Tenochitlan. When the Europeans arrived it was still in existence and was larger and more impressive than anything back home. It had temples, pyramids, canals, aqueducts, markets. It matched the layout Plato gave for Atlantis, but was referred to by the Aztecs as a replica built in honor of their own lost "Aztlan", the birthplace of their own civilization, which was washed away in a flood. Today, Mexico City stands on that site.'

'Did they say where this Aztland was?'

'Somewhere to the South.'

Major Gant finished suiting himself up and was about to lead them all to the door where they would make their way down to the research lab's main floor when he turned back. 'Out of interest,' he said, 'do you happen to know the Chinese symbol for the sun?'

'This is the earliest one from the Shang Dynasty,' Scott said as he drew it. 'Eventually it evolved into a square shape, for reasons only the Chinese know. As you can see, it's the odd man out. It's not a cross.'

They all eyed the symbol.

'Curious,' Hackett responded. 'It's the only one that's scientifically accurate.'

Scott frowned. 'What do you mean?'

'Positive and negative,' Hackett explained. 'The basics you learn about magnetism in school. North is positive, represented by a cross. The South is negative, represented by a minus sign. Atlantis is situated at the *South* Pole. The Chinese aren't just telling us that the sun is important – they're telling us where to go to find the answers.'

All suited up in their white coveralls, they followed Gant through the door and out onto a metal gantry overlooking the vast research facilities below where bundles and bundles of wires were hanging in looms above the pipe-work of liquid gas coolant systems, banks of computers, dials and switches.

As they clanked their way down the flights of steps they could smell the plastic and metal odors of scientific research. The clinical aroma of technology. When they reached the bottom they could see a table stretched before them. And piled on top of it across its entire length were rows and rows of blue crystals. The Carbon 60 shards brought back from Antarctica.

'This is your research, Dr Scott,' Gant announced, as the epigraphist gasped and ran his eyes the length of the display.

Scott was about to field more questions when an excited scientist wearing similar gear came rushing over and handed Houghton a piece of paper. 'This fax just came in for you,' he said. 'It's fantastic!'

Houghton read it quickly before passing it around.

The buzz of excitement it generated was matched only by the buzz of high-voltage electricity coursing through the equipment and around the room.

ROLA CORP. *Making Energy Work*

FAX

TO: JAY HOUGHTON, CERN, GENEVA

FROM: SARAH KELSEY, CHIEF FIELD GEOLOGIST, EGYPT

DATE: MARCH 18, 2012

REF & SPEC: 410B/C/24794AH-409

Be advised. At 11.03:AM today, ground was broken to sink a well down to a cavity detected 30 feet underground in the region of the Sphinx. A number of similar cavities have also been detected in and around the pyramid site.

Please be advised also: Carbon 60 *has* been positively identified. Will keep you briefed as and when.

Interesting fact number 2: Erosion damage to the Sphinx shows vertical channels through the horizontal layers of sandstone. Indications of classic flood damage. Subsurface weathering analysis shows deep penetration erosion at a microscopic scale. Stress caused by heat, cold and moisture which takes 1–2,000 years per foot to advance. 4 feet deep on the rear half, 8 feet on the front half suggesting the Sphinx was built in two halves separated by 4,000 years. Makes the Sphinx at least 8,000 years old! When I mentioned this to the archeologists here they got real pissed. Insisted the Sphinx was built in 2,500BC by Pharaoh Kafra. I seriously think they're wrong.

ABUL-HOL

FATHER OF TERROR

ROSETAU

'*Yallah! Yallah!*' came the surrounding calls. Hurry! Hurry!
'*Shuuftibi! Bisuurah!*' Look! Quick!

The earsplitting whistle that ripped through the dry air to accompany the shouts was a workman's. He whistled again, jamming his grimy fingers tightly into his parched mouth.

They had found something.

Sarah and Eric eyed each other before breaking into a run.

At the well, where steel-mesh collars had been lowered into the hole to support the particulate sandstone sides from collapsing in on the workers, there were signs of digging still taking place at the bottom. Sarah picked her way past trays loaded with bagged artifacts, took up a perch near the edge of the well and peered down.

More assorted bowls and pottery were carefully being passed up, followed by bucketloads of sand, and one agitated Arab worker. A couple of Egyptian Antiquities Police Officers had moved in too. Black greasy Kalashnikovs slung at their shoulders. One was on the radio.

Professor De la Hoy shook his head. He was Chief Archeologist in the Egyptian Department of Antiquities. And was busy to one side of the well, using his own set of dental tools on one particular pot. He was visibly moved. Kept mumbling about some archeological dig in 1893 when the great Flinders Petrie dug at Naqada, 300 miles south of Cairo, and found exactly the same type of pots that he couldn't place in the standard archeological timeline. He ended up attributing them to a 'New Race' and they had since been academically ignored. De la Hoy added that 30,000 similar pieces of pottery were discovered beneath the step Pyramid of Zozer at Saqqara. But somehow, Sarah knew that wasn't what was getting to the man. It was the fact that he had spent thirty years of his life on a flawed science.

The dust was thick, taking its time to settle. The grit-caked galebeya of the sole remaining Egyptian at the bottom of the well was ripped and soaked in sweat. But the excited, wide-eyed expression on the man's deeply tanned face said it all, which was useful, because Sarah couldn't understand a word he was actually saying: '*Hiya daraja! Ajid Daraja!*'

He was twenty-five to thirty feet down. Too shallow a depth to have hit the Carbon 60 yet. Scanning the faces above, he reached for his crude hand-brush made from desert broom, when he spotted Sarah. He set about sweeping off sand from a plinth of stone that crossed the width of the well at one end.

Scurrying about on all fours, ignoring the sharp stones that cut into his knees, the busy Egyptian proudly picked out the edge of the stone with his bare fingers. Brushed away more stones and looked up, patting the ground with the flat of his hand, trying to bridge the language barrier with simple signing and body language.

One, he seemed to be saying with a pat. One stone. And under here – a second. Then three, four, lower and lower—

'He's found a step,' Sarah realized. 'He's found a set of steps.'

Clemmens pointed at each end of the uncovered step. 'It goes about one or two feet deeper into the side of the well's my guess.'

'That answers one question,' Sarah added under her breath so only Clemmens could hear. 'These are manmade *ceremonial* tunnels. No way we can pass these off as a natural phenomenon.'

Clemmens smirked. 'Boy, is Douglas gonna be pissed if the media get a hold of this.'

Sarah looked to the other diggers questioningly. 'Can we get more workers down there?' she asked. 'Dig those steps out?'

The Egyptians sprang into action, lowering one of the smaller men down, although it was clear the superstitious worker who had just climbed out obviously wanted to go nowhere near the well again. Sarah was faintly reminded of Howard Carter's famous 1922 excavation of Tutankhamen's tomb. It had been said it was cursed, as were many ancient Egyptian tombs. But on Carter's dig, people *had* died.

A finger jammed in one ear, a radio pressed to his mouth, Clemmens surveyed the find sharply as he set about briefing Douglas on the other end of the line.

'We'll need a marquee of some kind. Big. Secure, so we can get the larger equipment in under it. Stop any prying eyes and cameras. We'll need generators. Arc lights. Round the clock support. Yes, sir. I think we're close. And if we double these people's pay we'll be even closer.'

De la Hoy was furious. In his upper-crust English accent he said icily: 'What the *devil* do you think you're doing?'

But Clemmens ignored him. 'Oh, and sir? Could somebody get these goddamn archeologists off the site? They're a pain in the butt.' He smiled. Relaxed. 'Professor, if you'd be so kind as to haul ass? There's a good chap. Tip top, old bean.'

As De La Hoy was escorted away from the site, the radio hanging at Sarah's hip fizzled into life: 'Yeah, Sarah, we're out at the test zone, running that second pass. Over.' It was the geo-phys team, with a ground-penetrating radar unit that was more accurate than the resistivity unit they'd used earlier.

Sarah popped the catch. Thumbed the black transceiver. 'Good hunting. Over.'

Static, then a clipped: 'Thanks.' It was like listening to astronauts on the moon.

'Just what is it with this weather?' Clemmens moaned, glancing up at the cloudless sky and wiping his forehead with a rag.

'This is the desert,' Sarah said. 'It's supposed to be hot.'

'In March? It's one twenty in the shade,' Clemmens sighed. 'This ain't normal 'less it's July.' As the sounds of pick-axes and shovels striking stone below them cracked out in a steady rhythm, Sarah diverted Clemmens's attention back to her map where she'd marked twelve red Xs corresponding to where hollows some way under the bedrock had been detected. And, where the signature for Carbon 60 had also been detected. Clearly, a pattern was emerging.

'I'm tellin' ya, it's a circle,' she said.

'Is that a wager?' Clemmens asked.

'You betcha.'

'How much?'

'How much you got?'

Clemmens checked his pockets. All he had was lunch money – a fifty-dollar bill.

By joining the Xs Sarah created an arc. And she was sure this arc was part of a circle, not an ellipse or other curved shape. To confirm this she needed to find where the circle's exact center might be. Mathematics was useless, it would only give an approximation, but a simple pair of compasses and an old engineering trick made up for that. She connected two points of the arc together by drawing a straight line between them and using the compass at each end of the line to draw an arc above and below the line. This formed two new Xs. One above and one below the line. Joining the two Xs created a cross, a perpendicular line that bisected the first line at 90° through its natural center. By repeating the process on the other two points of the arc and extending both perpendicular lines downwards they eventually met and revealed the true center of the circle, which Sarah was surprised to find was situated directly under the Sphinx.

Clemmens gave her a look. 'Not bad for a geologist,' he said. 'What if you're wrong?'

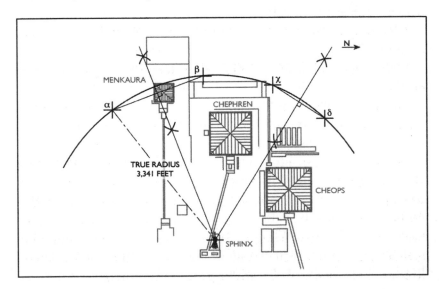

'Dad was an engineer,' she explained. 'No one got out the house unless they could tell him how it was built. I'm not wrong.'

'We'll see.'

Since the drawing was the same scale as the map, and the distance from the center of the circle to one of the original measurement points along the arc was the true radius, Sarah was able to draw in the full circle. From that she provided geo-physics with map references where she predicted they would find further positive readings. They named the test zones: Alpha, Beta and Gamma.

'Eric to Test Zone Beta,' Clemmens announced, thumbing his own radio. 'Frankie, whatchya got?'

There was a long loud hiss of white noise before the heavy breathless wheeze of Frankie came back at him. 'Just done a pass.'

'And?'

Silence. Eric and Sarah exchanged glances. Sarah was chewing a thumbnail and tapping her foot. She wasn't good at waiting.

'Frankie?' Eric demanded impatiently. 'Whatchya got? Over.'

A hiss. Then: 'We got a positive,' he responded hastily. 'Strong and bang on target. We gotta do a second pass but mark us down as a positive. Over.'

'That's it,' Eric said, spinning on his heel excitedly. 'That's it!' But Sarah was already scribbling on her map. Her radio springing into life again.

'This is Test Zone Gamma. Over. All passes complete – we have a positive. Repeat, we have a positive. Over and Out.'

'Test Zone Alpha reporting second pass confirmation. We too have a positive . . . D'you guys know what this means?'

She knew two times pi times the radius of the circle gave the circumference of the circle. And she now knew that there *was* a circle with a radius of 3,341 feet. A quick calculation and Sarah knew exactly what *that* meant.

'We got a circular tunnel nearly three miles around, Eric. Jesus!'

'Three miles? That's like five kilometers at least! That's like the size of a goddamn particle accelerator! And our well here hits a side tunnel that connects to it!'

Sarah was frantic. 'Who the hell could tunnel with that kind of accuracy thousands of years ago? They'd need to know pi. They'd need to know trigonometry, geometry—'

Eric shook his head. 'I got a better question: why the hell would they want to?'

'I dunno,' she grinned. 'But I told you it was a circle. You owe me fifty bucks.'

Clemmens was slow to dig for it.

The marquee was brought in by truck as part of a supply convoy. Spearheaded by the metallic gold and tinted windows of Toyota Land Cruisers, emblematic of the Egyptian Security Police. Suddenly to get anywhere near the well required authorization that got you through two checkpoints and the gates to two hastily erected chain-link fences that encircled the vast blue tent.

It had taken thirty minutes to build. In that time several more steps were dug out and Clemmens had identified the direction in which the tunnel descended. He mapped out an archway. Sent metalworkers down to weld a steel arch into place and cut out a doorway underneath it through the mesh collars. The remaining expanse of mesh was reinforced through the arch so it wouldn't buckle under the strain of keeping the sides of the well at bay.

Sarah studied the exposed strata. From ground level to six feet down it was solid bedrock. For the next four feet it was pockets of fill and more bedrock. Solid bedrock for a further three feet. Then fill entirely until the steps were reached. It meant someone had meticulously filled this tunnel to capacity a very long time ago. No one was intended to get through.

With the metal support arch in place and the oxy-acetylene torch done and dusted, Sarah was carefully lowered down to inspect the wall of sheer fill. The metal archway above looked like a scrap metal homage to a gothic cathedral.

Trusting her instructions would be adhered to as they were hastily translated into Egyptian Colloquial Arabic, she said: 'Start at the top. Work your way back and come down gradually. Creating a slope. That way if it becomes unstable it shouldn't collapse in on you. But what I want is to find the roof and walls of this tunnel. When we have those dimensions – then we'll know what we're dealing with.'

They were ordered to go back to work. 'Emshi! Emshi!'

Pick-axes were sharply thrust into the dirt. The fact that everything was damp helped the situation on the one hand – it bound the particles together, making it easier to dig without fear of a collapse. But on the other hand it made the work tiring, because for every shovel-load of sand removed, water was the hidden constituent in its weight, and quickly exhausted the diggers.

It took several hours to advance ten feet. But when they had, the dimensions of the tunnel exposed the sheer scale of the subterranean construction. And what had been characteristic of the original exploration of the Great Pyramid now rang true for the tunnels. What faced everyone was a giant stone plug of such enormous magnitude that it beggared belief.

'The Sphinx was known by many names. Abul-Hol was its Arabic name,' Scott said down the phone. 'It means Father of Terror. When the Cananites in the second millennium BCE journeyed from Harran, in Southern Turkey, and worshipped at the Sphinx they called it HWL. BW meant "place" so "Abul-Hol" might be a corrupted form of "BW-HWL". Making its name: The Place of HWL. But what on earth "HWL" means I don't know. "Hor-em-Akhet" was another name, meaning "Horus on the horizon". "Seshep-ankh Atum" means "The living image of Atum". It was the Greeks who shortened Seshep-ankh and gave it the form we still used today: *The Sphinx.*'

There was a prolonged silence from the other end of the line. Scott pressed the phone in closer to his ear as he pulled himself up to the table. He wasn't sure if the line had gone dead. 'Hello . . .?'

'That's great, Dr Scott,' the barely restrained voice of Sarah Kelsey replied, 'but it doesn't actually help me.'

'I'm sorry. It's just – well, shit! You're digging under the Sphinx!' Scott said enthusiastically.

There had been few pleasantries when the call was connected. This Sarah Kelsey sounded like one single-minded, determined woman. Since she was hard at work and probably stifled by the oppressive desert heat, Scott could forgive her most things. But her abrupt nature made her telephone manner seem rude. It was grating. 'What *do* you need?' he asked quickly.

'For a start, how do I get inside this tunnel? Is there a precedent for this type of thing? Y'know, building a tunnel and then filling it in for no real reason?'

'Oh, sure,' Scott said warmly. He eyed everyone else around the table. They were all on tenterhooks, listening in on the speaker-phone. Matheson had a pad and pencil at the ready and sketched everything Sarah said about the site in a valiant effort to make up for the fact there was no picture. Gant had gone off to try and kick some butt into getting a vid-phone link up and running, but so far, no luck.

'In AD 820 when Abdullah Al-Mamun, Caliph of Baghdad, explored the Great Pyramid, he smashed his way through the eight-foot casing to see what was inside,' Scott recalled. 'What he found was a passageway, but his way was blocked by a succession of six-foot-long granite plugs that were inserted during the building of the Pyramid.'

'Did you say during the *building* of the Pyramid?'

'Yup.'

'Why?' Sarah snapped, irritated. 'What's the point?'

'Beats me,' Scott replied. He fielded questioning eyes from around the table, Hackett's most notably of all. How the hell should he know? He didn't know everything.

'What did he do, this Al-Mamun?'

'He tunneled his way past the plugs through the softer limestone that the Pyramid was made out of.'

Sarah groaned. There was some kind of noise, like she was inspecting something. Then they heard: 'Oh, well, that's no good. I'm not sure the ground above it could take that. We're gonna have to try and drag it out.'

'What exactly have you got there?' Ralph asked quickly.

'Who is this?' Sarah demanded defensively.

'Ralph Matheson, Engineer.'

'Is there anyone else on the line I should know about?' the geologist asked suspiciously.

Reluctantly everyone else around the table let out low, deflated greetings. Like kids who'd been caught in a game of hide and seek.

'Thank God I wasn't talking dirty,' Sarah said. 'Okay, I got a granite plug. Four feet across. I have to assume, based on Richard's detail about the Pyramid that it's six feet long. I hope to God there's only one of these things. And around the rim of the plug there seems to be a layer of what I can only describe as . . . salt.'

'Salt?'

Scott was intrigued. 'When Al-Mamun finally did get into the chamber after tunneling past the plugs, he found it encrusted with half an inch of salt. No one knows why.'

Sarah continued: 'Okay, the tunnel seems to have been originally hewn out of the bedrock, then it was faced with huge limestone rings each weighing in the region of, I'd say, a hundred tons. The workmanship is identical to that of the Sphinx's two temples, only the blocks over there are about two hundred tons each.'

'That's incredible,' Matheson said, amazed. But no one else seemed to appreciate that. 'Even today,' he pointed out, 'there are only four cranes in the world capable of lifting that kind of weight.'

'And that's *above* ground,' Sarah chipped in on her end of the line. 'How were these hundred-ton stone rings moved below ground?'

It was a fair question.

Scott thought on this as he handled one of the Carbon 60 crystals from the myriad laid out before him across the table. Now that he had it in his hand one thing was clear. The writing wasn't cuneiform. It had wedges, that was true. And certainly many of the forms could be called pictograms and they were reminiscent of hieroglyphics. But there was a subtlety and a sweeping curvature to much of the writing which could only be described as acinaciform – the writing was scimitar-shaped. Crescented. Like great arcs leading from point A to point B with minute details crammed under the arching banners as if whole themes and ideas were being expressed in as concise and compact a way as possible. Though quite what those ideas might be frankly eluded him.

What Scott needed to do was catalogue and group the characters while assembling the debris and trying to make out a coherent text from the pieces. He stood the crystal on end, and that was when the idea struck him.

'A standing stone . . .' he announced.

Hackett was intrigued. 'A what?'

'Archeologists call them *stele*, or standing stones. There's one in front of the Sphinx. In any case, they have information inscribed on them that sometimes can prove useful to an excavation. A lot of the monuments at Giza are notorious for their complete absence of writing. This tunnel sounds like no exception. But sometimes a standing stone was erected at its entrance.' He raised his voice. 'Sarah, you said you're still clearing out the rubble?'

'Yes.'

'Be careful with your pick-axes. There might be a stone laid out on the ground somewhere—'

'About five feet tall?' she interrupted. 'Needle-shaped?'

Scott hesitated. 'Yes . . .'

'Oh, we already found that.'

'Well, there's probably writing all over it.'

'There's a little.'

Scott was quick. 'Can you send it through?'

Suddenly there was a beeping on the line. 'I got a call on the other line. Can you hold? Thanks.'

The line went dead. Scott eyed the rest of the team. Thumb-twiddling seemed to be the only option until—

'Hi, you still there?'

'Yes, Sarah, could you—'

'Listen, I gotta take this call.' She sounded flustered. 'That'll have to do for the brief tour of the site. I'll have someone take a photo of this inscription and fax it through. Nice talking to you. Bye.'

The dial tone moaned at them next. Hackett set his phone down first. Stood and rubbed his back. 'Wonderful woman,' he noted sourly.

As cables and wires were trailed in with halogen lamps, stands and assorted gear, Douglas scratched his head in utter frustration and bellowed down from his vantage point at the top of the well: 'Where's this fucking Carbon 60, Sarah?'

Sarah shrugged. 'Pull out the plug and see.'

'That could take all goddamn night.'

'Better get to it then,' she said simply. 'Call me when it's done.' She tied on a rope and climbed the ladder to the surface. Took her phone back out and tentatively stepped away from the frenetic activity. Nervously, she asked: 'Hello? Rip, you still there?'

'Sarah!' came the distant reply.

It was a strong voice. Familiar, though Sarah had taken a moment to recognize it. It was deep. Somehow soothing. Yet experience had already taught her that it was also the voice of a man who was dangerous. Some nights they had lain awake and talked for hours, in bed, after making love. Her ear pressed against his chest. Listening to the reverberations throughout his body as he spoke. Listening to him breathe. She had been bracing herself for the vision. That moment when she would see him again.

She hadn't expected to talk to Rip Thorne by phone.

'How are you?'

She was standing in a circus. There was a new archeological find behind her. A startling new form of carbon somewhere beneath her. An eminent linguistic anthropologist tearing his hair out in Geneva. Men wielding guns. Protests. And that was just everything she was clinging to right now to stop herself thinking about him. The man who had torn out her heart and danced a jig on it. How did he expect her to feel?

'I'm fine,' she said simply. Asshole! she snarled in her mind. 'How long have you been here?' she probed. 'You are here, in Cairo, aren't you?'

'Yes, I'm here,' he replied smoothly. 'I'm down at the AOI head-quarters – brokering a deal.'

Brokering? That meant someone else was involved. Aside from Rola Corp. and the Egyptian government . . . Who?

'I thought you were coming out to the site.' She hadn't intended to sound hopeful.

'Business, honey. You know what business is like.'

Yes. She knew what business was like. Especially where it concerned Thorne. And even more so the AOI, the Arab Organization for Industrialization. The place where gleaming army APCs and fighter planes sat ominously floodlit late at night. The place that gave an actual physical manifestation to the phrase: a military-industrial complex.

'Hey, listen, Sarah,' Thorne said. 'Why don't we catch up?'

'I don't think that's a good idea.'

'Sure it is. I'm all finished up here. What do you say to dinner?'

'Dinner?' She checked her watch. Six-thirty.

'You're staying at the Nile Hilton, aren't you? I'll pick you up say, eight o'clock?'

'Okay.'

'I'll meet you in the foyer.'

'Fine.' It wasn't.

'And Sarah . . . I'm glad you're here.'

She could feel the blood rushing in her ears. The sensation that so effectively blocked out all other noises. Why could she not just say no to him? It was like falling into a trance. She felt so foolish. So helpless.

She hung up. Stepped out of the blue marquee to witness the ruddy red glow of the day's dying embers. On the ancient plateau of Giza, once known as Rostau, the Sphinx was king – and guardian to something buried deep underground.

Sarah eyed the man-lion stiffly. So preliminary indications showed this thing was thousands of years older than they had first thought. Stone-faced, it was like looking at Thorne. What were they both hiding?

They waited by the fax machine. And waited.

The Sphinx was 240 feet long, 38 feet wide across the shoulders and 66 feet high, Scott told all present in an attempt to fill the vacuum of expectation. It had the worn and battered visage of a man. The body of a lion. It had seen a lot of action. Its nose had been shot off a few hundred years ago by the Mamelukes who used it for target practice. Facing stones had been placed to rebuild eroded sections of the monument. When the Islamic fundamentalists caused a virtual civil war in 2005, the structure fell into further disrepair. The earthquake in 2007 hadn't helped matters, but reports stated how well the Sphinx had weathered earthquakes through the ages. It seemed it had been built to last. And last it had, for millennia.

It was a fact that in 10,500BC, at dawn, had any of the monuments at Giza officially existed then, the constellation of Leo would be seen rising on the horizon, directly between the front paws of the Sphinx, itself a giant lion. While Orion would have been at the highest point in the sky, appearing directly above the three pyramids. It was a cyclical event that was not destined to be repeated until AD 2,500.

And therein lay more of the mystery.

For from the air, the three Giza pyramids were laid out in exactly the same arrangement as the three stars that made up the 'belt' in the constellation of Orion. Construction of the Great Pyramid,

Cheops's Pyramid, was so precise that a cigarette paper couldn't be slotted between the stone blocks. This was made all the more confounding by the fact that the larger 10–15 ton blocks were at the top and the more manageable 6-ton blocks were at the bottom. Every side was 755 feet along each length. It was 461 feet high, which gave the same ratio as the circumference of a circle to its radius. Some said it represented a scale model of the northern hemisphere of the earth. Some disagreed.

But when Abdullah Al-Mamun first arrived at the pyramids, he found monuments that were covered in gleaming white limestone casing stones that were so precisely constructed that the joins were barely visible. The casing was covered in hieroglyphs, which Manetho, the Egyptian priest who wrote a history of Egypt in Greek for Ptolemy I around 300BCE, proclaimed was the work of Thoth. Thoth, the Egyptian god of writing, among other things, was said to have inscribed the 36,525 books of wisdom upon the Great Pyramid. A number which happened to be exactly the same as the number of primitive inches in the designed perimeter of the Great Pyramid. And the same figure as the length of the year. 365.25 days.

'Many ancient civilizations proclaimed writing was a divine gift,' Scott added as the fax machine at last kicked into gear. 'In Sumerian tradition the god Nabû, the biblical Nebo, invented writing and believed in the creative power of the divine word. In Chinese legend the four-eyed dragon god brought writing. And there were elitist scribal castes in Egyptian, Chinese and Mayan societies. But in Egypt the language of hieroglyphs was so well thought out and constructed, and appeared virtually from nowhere, that many linguists feel it was probably the invention of just one person.'

In the end it was just one person, the Egyptian god Thoth, who spoke to them. From beyond the grave – from the black and white image being slowly inked out in hieroglyphs on a roll of silver fax paper. It took Scott a moment to translate. When he did, it just compounded the mystery:

> I am Thoth, the lord of right and truth,
> Who judges right and truth for the gods,
> The judge of words in their essence,
> Whose words triumph over violence.

Was this the place that Pharaoh Cheops had sought? The hidden chamber containing the Books of Thoth? Repository of the sacred knowledge and the key to the language of the gods?

Buried somewhere deep behind that granite stone plug were answers, Scott was certain.

NUCLEAR MAGNETIC RESONANCE SPECTROSCOPY

FIRST RESULTS

5:32 PM

A lchemy, from the Greek word 'Kemi', meaning Egypt.
    As a linguistic anthropologist Richard Scott had come into contact with a bewildering variety of branches of science. But never before chemistry. He waited expectantly as Hackett waded through the chemical analysis results of the C60 crystal.

November stuffed a new filter in the coffee machine, and ate a sandwich in the small enclosed kitchenette that stood over to one side, well away from the powerful laser equipment that was still slicing through chunks of Carbon 60 crystal, cutting it into smaller pieces for atomic examination by NMRS.

What was clear was that true Carbon 60 was yellowish-brown. This stuff was blue. Why?

'It's not pure.' Hackett flipped another page, studying the numbers with a razor-sharp eye.

'It's not?' Pearce said, inspecting the sandwiches on the tray next to November with an equally sharp eye. He could just see them through the glass door to the kitchenette.

Hackett acknowledged one of the odd-looking chemists as he wandered past. They were called the 'soot' community: Hawkes, Liu, Ridley and Morgan. The four organic chemists who worked for Rola Corp. published regularly in *The American Carbon Society*. These people lived and breathed carbon. They came from places like MIT and Rice University's Quantum Institute in Texas – the same place where Kroto and Smalley first created C60 in 1985.

They talked in constant scientific gibberish. But carbon marked exactly the point where chemistry and physics met. Hackett quickly cut them down to size.

'These aren't simple impurities we're talking about here,' he said. 'We're talking about specific carbon compounds that have been deliberately created within the structure of the crystal. We're talking about a sophistication that's beyond our current capabilities. There are graphite veins. Diamond. There are, uh – ribidium fullerenes, a super-conductive material.' He was mumbling now, lost in the science. 'Ribidium fused with C60 – that's, let me see, Rb_2CsC60. Usually it degrades in air. Works at temperatures in the region of 30 Kelvins. Nitrogen is a liquid at 18 Kelvins. That's minus 225 degrees Celsius.'

'How come the ribidium fullerenes survived?' November asked, depositing her empty plate back inside the kitchen.

'It's coated in diamond. It's not exposed to the air, so it's super-conductive.'

'Does that explain why I get a tingly feeling when I touch this stuff?' Scott asked dryly. 'Or am I just pleased to see it?'

'C60,' Hackett told him, 'is photo-conductive. It passes electricity when exposed to light. It's perfect for light switches in the next generation of light computers. It's probably reacting to all the lighting in the lab, and since you're earthed by virtue of standing on the floor . . . Hey, maybe we should get you a safety mat. This is incredible.' He waved the paper sheet. 'The atoms in this stuff are arranged with a distinct pattern in their energy states.'

'And what does that mean?'

'I have absolutely no idea,' Hackett said happily, 'but it's linked to light computers again. C60 is arranged in such a way that it allows electrons to go around comers.'

'And that's good?'

'It's quick.' He tapped his finger on the paper. 'Maybe I should call Michela.'

Scott had no idea who Michela was. But he looked around anyway: 'Where's Ralph?'

Pearce scratched his rear, headed for the sandwiches and pointed skywards. 'Upstairs with Dower. Planning out the expedition,' he said as Scott grabbed a cloth, a black magic marker and cleaned the large white wipeboard next to the coffee machine. Figures and notes disappeared in an instant.

'Nobody wanted this, did they?' Scott murmured to nobody in particular.

'Not anymore,' Hackett told him, referring back to the spectroscopy results. 'Nuclear Magnetic Resonance Spectroscopy works at very low radio frequencies. It doesn't bend, stretch, spin or tumble molecules to get information. It deals with single atoms *within* a molecule and it does it because an atom is affected by what its neighbor's doing. And in being affected, it reveals its true identity. NMRS can determine exactly what atom is in a molecule, and what other atoms are in relation to it.'

'I see,' November responded. But it wasn't all that clear that she did see.

'The key,' Hackett added, 'is the atomic nuclei property called "spin". The "spin" of the nuclei has a number of energy states. Each one's given a nuclear spin quantum number. NMRS detects the transitions between states by holding a sample in a magnetic field. But the problem with carbon is – its nuclear spin quantum number is zero. It exhibits no energy transitions.'

'Then how can you detect it?'

'Well, there's an exception to the rule. There always is. Carbon 13 is a specific isotope of carbon, kind of like ordinary carbon's strange uncle, and it shows a transition between energy states. It has an NSQN of one half. Anyone attempting to build C60 would need to use carbon in its isotope C13 form to be able to control what they were doing. This C60 . . . *is* Carbon 13.'

'Makes sense,' Scott agreed.

'You understand what I'm describing?'

'Sure,' Scott said. 'Isotope – from the Greek, meaning "equal place". Carbon 13 is just like any other type of carbon. It's still carbon.'

'The point,' Hackett explained impatiently, 'is that whoever made this C60 first had to make the right type of carbon. That means a sophisticated manufacturing plant. That means this stuff was not naturally occurring. It means it was never mined, it was constructed.'

'Neat,' November commented, less than enthusiastic.

'Neat . . .? *Neat*? This isn't neat, this is monumental! The fact these rocks are covered in writing and were found a mile below ground, underwater, and an integral part of a structure doesn't just tell me they're from an advanced civilization,' Hackett expounded excitedly. 'What we are dealing with here is not some lost civilization on a par with, say, the Romans or the Egyptians. We're talking about a civilization that understood quantum physics and molecular engineering. We're talking about a civilization that was far in advance of our own – and was destroyed. That is a frightening, terrible prospect.'

He had taken a look inside the giant NMR spectrometer. The sample chamber was the size of a jeep, with huge powerful magnets that had an adjustable field. Coils were arranged in such a way as to expose the C60 to radio-frequency radiation. And it had detectors that looked like fists of compacted metal, which registered the results of the electro-magnetic bombardment.

'To be able to understand this stuff,' Hackett announced, 'we have to use equipment that is right at the very pinnacle of man's scientific achievement. This Carbon 60 was not created by accident.'

'And God said: *Let there be light*,' Pearce announced in a passable impression of the Creator.

Scott thought about that a moment. 'Language,' he said. 'To be able to say: *Let there be light*, God had to invent language. *Then* light arrived. In the beginning was the *Word*.'

Hackett was utterly baffled. 'What are you talking about?'

'Light – and language. It's the first thing the Bible even talks about. It's the first thing a lot of ancient myths talk about. And what have we got here? The sun – and the language of Atlantis. The earliest known language.' Scott sighed as he shifted his attention back to the rocks. 'That's assuming whoever designed this language wanted it to be understood by people in the future.'

The others didn't seem to get it.

Scott explained: 'Thomas A. Sebeok was commissioned by the Office of Nuclear Waste Isolation, in 1984, to answer a question posed by the US Nuclear Regulatory Commission.'

'Which was what?'

'Several key desert areas were selected for the burial of nuclear waste which would remain radioactive for the next ten thousand years. The sort of time-scale we're talking about here, since Plato said Atlantis was destroyed around 9,500BCE. So the problem was, on the offchance we returned to barbarism – how would we warn our future selves, or visiting aliens, of the danger zone? Sebeok immediately discarded tape-decks and verbal communication as a warning – anything that required energy to work. He also rejected any form of ideogram based on today's conventions. Y'know, it's like, we see a little man or a woman on a door, and we *know* it's a toilet. But in ten thousand years the chances are we'll know it's a person – but we'll be wondering what the hell they're doing.'

'So he came up with a better language?' Pearce asked.

'Not even remotely. Language changes over time, and a massive disaster might destroy current society, so he opted for the adoption of myth and taboo to be fed into human culture.'

'What?'

'Religion,' Scott said succinctly. 'Language is useless on its own, but social taboos will work even in a future barbaric state. The solution was to create some kind of priesthood of nuclear scientists, anthropologists, linguists and psychologists that would keep alive the knowledge of danger by creating myths and legends. And would perpetuate itself by co-opting new members along the way . . .'

'Do you realize what you just said?' Pearce remarked, agitated.

'I've got some idea, yes,' Scott replied.

'The earliest known civilizations that created language, created some of the most complicated languages ever known. And each language was controlled by the priesthood. The Chinese, the Mayans, the Babylonians . . . the Egyptians. The priesthood has always been in charge of the written word.'

'My problem is determining how *these* people thought,' Scott told them all. 'If I can't, this language remains as mysterious and indecipherable as the script from the Indus Valley. The way in which language is structured says a lot about how a civilization thinks. Like, how does it arrange colors? Light to dark? Red to violet? We use semantically opposed ideas. Love versus hate. High versus low. In Swahili they group items into characteristics that reflect their properties, like length. Or it may be entirely different. These characters right here could be part of a holistic language.'

'A what?'

'Take our language – the word "dogs", for example. The "s" means it's plural. Nothing more. "S", in and of itself, isn't plural. "Sorrow" doesn't mean there are lots of "orrows"; "d" is not a part of a dog, like its leg. God is completely different but uses the same letters. A log and God are not different types of dog. God is dog, backwards. But God is not a dog facing the other way. Yet *this* language could use logic like that. So the entire idea of "dogness" is complete in one symbol. So it's a perfect logogram,' he explained. 'Some languages are a precise reflection of people's speech.' He grabbed a pen and paper. 'But if this is anything like English then it'll be a complete mess. I mean, how do you explain why "sh" can be written "ce" as in *ocean*, "ti" as in *nation* and "ss" as in *issue*. But we also use logograms for numbers and function signs. We write seven as 7, not as ///////. Though we also write it as S-E-V-E-N.

'But if you look at the Linear B writing from Mycenaean Greece, they used syllable signs – so each syllable had a sign. Hence, "fa", "mi" and "ly" would mean "family".'

He stood back a moment, eyed the crystals arranged on the table. 'Language family,' he said. 'That's it. Maybe I need to figure out what language family it's related to.'

'What are you doing?' Hackett asked, watching Scott map out flow charts on the board now with colored markers. 'Hunting for the complex adaptive system in action?' He sat with his feet up on the table and tossing a chunk of the rock into the air like a baseball as the epigraphist went to work.

Scott set out a series of boxes, scrawled various names in them to the obvious puzzlement of November. He drew the final box with something approaching an artistic flourish.

'Ch . . . Chukchi-what?' November asked, running a finger under one of the more bizarre names on the board.

'Chukchi-Kamchatkan,' Scott said. 'It's a language family. Certain languages have similarities and are grouped into what are called language families. They tend to keep a similar structure at their root, but over time languages change, develop and adapt in many subtle ways.'

'As languages are improved and refined,' November assumed.

'No, not really,' Hackett disagreed quietly yet authoritatively.

It was enough to pique Scott's curiosity. He stopped what he was doing on the board and eyed the physicist squarely. 'You're right. But why do you think you're right?'

Hackett caught the chunk of crystal in mid-toss and set it down on the table. 'When you were a kid, which was better: Betamax or VHS?'

'Betamax,' Scott answered instantly.

'What're they all talking about?' November asked, concerned.

'Video-tape formats,' Pearce explained, equally puzzled.

'What's video-tape?'

Pearce gave her a double-take, then let it slide. After all, he was still mourning the loss of DVD recorders and they were light-years ahead of video-tape.

'Okay,' Hackett said. 'Why was it better?'

'Superior picture, clearer sound—'

'So which VCR did you have at home?'

'VHS,' Scott admitted darkly, aware he'd been led into a trap. 'Why?'

'Because it was cheaper.'

'So which format dominated the market?'

'VHS.'

'That,' Hackett said with a smirk, 'is *precisely* the point I wanted to make. Better does not necessarily mean evolutionary certainty.'

'Those are VCRs,' Pearce growled. 'What the hell has that got to do with language?'

'Because they both exhibit the very essence of what is a complex adaptive system.'

'So how we wound up with VHS is complicated? Fine.'

'No, no, no!' Hackett insisted. 'Not complicated. There is a difference between something being complicated and something being complex and adaptive. The key is adaptivity. How does a component react in a given situation? Betamax versus VHS is a question of economics. Society adapted to the price.'

Hackett shifted gear. 'Okay,' he said. 'Another example is, why did the petrol-driven car succeed at a time when petrol was expensive and dirty and when steampower had been driving trains for fifty years and worked just as well in cars? It's not gonna be price now, is it? Answer: Foot and Mouth Disease. Steam cars could only fill up at

water troughs, but because Foot and Mouth Disease was plaguing
the horse population, to prevent the spread of the problem the water
troughs were removed from all the towns. No troughs, no water. No
water, no steam cars – or horses. So the idea of a car is popular and
all anyone is left with is the petrol-powered car. So society adapted
and chose gasoline.' He shifted gear again. 'A snowflake in and of
itself is complicated. Beautiful, but complicated. It's when it inter-
acts with other snowflakes that it's complex. How do you predict
avalanches? What route will it take down the mountain?'

'You can predict that?'

'Not a chance. Then you're in the realms of chaos. What I predict
is the order that arises out of chaos, Bob. For there has to be order
out of chaos or none of us would be here. Out of that primordial
soup two amino acids had to have decided to get together. When
you heat up soup or water, at the exact moment of its boiling point
there will always be an hexagonal pattern of six spots within the
liquid that rises and falls. We call it simmering. But it's complexity
in action. Order from chaos.'

Hackett sat up. 'Bob,' he said sternly, 'it's a hundred thousand
years ago and you've developed the perfect language. You want
November here to use it. And you've decided that,' he looked about
quickly for something to use as an example, 'chair. You've decided
that chair – should be called "chair". But November doesn't call it
a chair. She calls it an "Ug" . . . Why?'

'Coz she's stupid?'

'Excuse me?' November retaliated in mock anger.

'No, she's not stupid. She's in love.'

'I am?'

'But not with you.'

'She's not?'

'November's in love with some great big ape,' Hackett explained.
'Not a weedy smartass. He's strong. He's handsome. The ape's more
likely to be able to provide for her and the family – and did you *see*
those cute buns? So she procreates with him. Wants to communicate with *him*. And he calls a chair an "Ug". Coz basically . . . *he's*
the stupid one.'

'Oh, great.'

'Oh, it gets better. So now they're both calling it an "Ug". That's two to one. And pretty soon they're starting a family. Their kids call it an "Ug", and after a while, everybody's calling it an "Ug", which is just so dumb because anyone with half a brain knows, the perfect word for that thing – is a chair.'

Scott finished sketching out his notes on the wipeboard. Gave Pearce a sympathetic look

'And you call that progress?' Hackett queried.

'Well done, Professor,' Scott said warmly.

'Thank you,' Hackett murmured without the least hint of humility. 'Complexity,' he ran his fingers through his hair. 'It's the key – to everything.' He cast an eye over the jumbled-up stones on the table. 'Order from chaos,' he beamed.

Order from chaos was what Sir William Jones, a British Judge living in Calcutta in 1786, had managed to achieve when he studied languages and noticed Greek, Latin, Sanskrit, Persian, Gothic and Old Irish all possessed similar words and grammar. Grouped together they became known as the Indo-European family of languages.

Since then linguistic anthropologists had charted the development of language all over the world, calling on a diverse array of sciences.

By 1991, Luigi Luca Cavalli-Sforza at Stanford had compared the world family tree of molecular genetic data with the world family tree of linguistic data and discovered an incredible similarity in the pattern spread. Now gene frequencies and population dispersal helped to chart language evolution.

In some ways, yes, maybe Hackett was right. Maybe Scott *was* exploring complexity. And maybe it *was* the key.

'Language evolved due to four prime factors,' Scott went on. 'Firstly the initial migration of the human population out of Africa to the rest of the world prior to 12,000BCE.

'Secondly there's the dispersal of language due to farming. Y'know, Farmer Bob has a farm and his family. In time he's successful. His farm gets bigger. So does his family. About two hundred years later it's a village and gets too big to support itself so half the population moves on and eventually they lose contact with Grandpa. It's also called Demic fusion. The Bantu languages of Africa started this way. They belong to the Niger-Kordofanian language family. Nomad and horseback-riding made the spread bigger in places like Turkey and the Turkic languages. Kurdistan and so on.

'Thirdly you've got languages that developed due the late climatic change around 8,000BCE and the after-effects of the last Ice Age. They're the Uralic-Yukaghir family, the Chukchi-Kamchatkan and the Eskimo-Aleut and Na-Dene of the Americas. But I don't think any of those concern us here because they're restricted to regions affected by glacial melt water in the Arctic. They're northern dispersal languages . . .' He was thinking on his feet. Stood back from his board. Put a thick black line through that set of languages. 'Okay,' he said, his mind made up. 'Then you just got the Elite Dominance languages like the Altaic in medieval central Asia. Languages that become dominant due to conquest. Like English is in the States, or Chinese is in China. Chinese was only adopted in historical times through military expansion. It was the same for Latin in Europe. Whereas, before convicts settled in Australia, the Pama-Nyungan language family of the Aborigines came about due to migration and farming divergence.'

'So languages developed at different times for different reasons,' November reiterated.

'Yeah, but what I've been given here is a language on a set of stones that comes from Antarctica. A place where nobody lives. Nobody migrated to. A place where – satellite images aside – we thought nobody had built anything. So physically, I have to work out what languages it might be related to. And that's the problem.

'The first source for the story of Atlantis comes from Plato, in Greece. In the Mediterranean – which is nowhere near Antarctica. So what's the link, as far as language is concerned? *Is* there even a link?'

Pearce nodded with anticipation. 'So what's your theory?'

'I don't have a theory,' Scott admitted darkly. 'I have an idea on how to get to a theory.'

'Okay, so we've discounted Chukchi-Kamchatkan as a language family. And the arctic languages. So that's Uralic-Yukaghir gone and Finnish and Hungarian along with it. And we can also discount Eskimo-Aleut and Na-Dene. That discounts all the language families that evolved as a result of the late climate-related dispersal after 8,000BCE—'

'After the last Ice Age and the Flood?' Pearce asked, double-checking with the notes that he'd started to scrawl.

'Right. Now we're agreed that Atlantis is a pre-flood, Ice Age kinda civilization. Right?'

November was excited. 'So we can lose the conquest languages – Latin and stuff.'

'Right,' Scott confirmed, nodding and drawing a line through the box containing such names as Genghis Khan and William the Conqueror. Then he said: 'Now we hit a gray area.'

He drew a line sharply under the last two groups. The languages from the initial human migration pre-12,000BCE. And the farming dispersal languages.

'The oldest languages that we can determine are in bits around the globe,' he revealed. 'They don't fit easily into the migratory patterns of the last ten thousand years. As a consequence they stick out like a sore thumb to linguists. The Khosian and the northern and southern Caucasian languages. The Australian languages. The languages of New Guinea known as Indo-Pacific, where each individual language in and of itself doesn't appear to be related to any of its neighbors – that's how come they got grouped together. Then there's Amerind, and also the Nilo-Saharan languages which include Basque—'

'Isn't that a region in Spain with all those terrorists?' November was quick to chip in.

Scott nodded his agreement, not wanting to be side-tracked further and drew their attention to the farming-dispersal languages.

'Indo-European covers classical Greek, which covers Plato. So I guess that should stay. Sino-Tibetan . . . Well, that's nowhere near Greece or Antarctica so that can go. Niger-Kordofanian, central African states, uh . . .' He shrugged, not sure. 'If I don't start cutting out more families I'm going to have a list of comparison languages to study as long as my arm.'

'So cut it.' Hackett's voice was harsh but logical. 'You can always go back to it.' Scott reluctantly agreed. 'That leaves Austronesian—'

'But the societies who used those languages weren't noted for building megalithic structures. Or any real structures at all,' Scott said. 'And besides, their flood myths are also the most vague.'

'You want to base the choices on an engineering comparison as well?'

'Makes sense. There's an entire city under the ice out there. And something under the Sphinx.' Hackett nodded. 'Now, Elamo-Dravidian covers Asia Minor. It may have a link but I don't think so. And finally we have good old Afro-Asiatic. Covers the semitic languages predominantly. Hebrew, Ancient Egyptian. That can stay.' Scott slashed lines through more groupings he didn't want to include. 'So we got, one, two . . . nine different language families to work from.'

'That's not so bad,' November said.

'That means about thirty or forty actual languages to trawl through,' Scott calculated.

Hackett stood up, tucking his shirt in. 'It's a start,' he said. 'But from the pre-12,000BCE languages I'd be inclined to lose the Indo-Pacific languages. Basically because, as you say, they didn't build squat. And on that basis you can lose all the Australian, the Khosian and the northern and southern Caucasian as well.'

'That leaves me with just Nilo-Saharan and Amerind.'

'I don't think there's time to be more systematic.'

'So we're down to four language families in total. Nilo-Saharan, Amerind, Indo-European and Afro-Asiatic.' Scott stepped back to look at his board. 'Yeah – it's a start.'

They were just getting into the next phase of analysis when one of the chemists, Morgan, approached. 'Dr Hackett?'

'Yes?'

'They need you upstairs. They want to transfer you over to the Solar Observatory Network. They just received the latest solar data . . . it doesn't look good.'

H e was late. Well, that was no surprise. Thorne was always
late.

Sarah didn't shower in the end, back at her room at the Nile
Hilton. She took a bath instead. She kicked back into the foam.
Relaxed. Washed the sand out of every pore. Shaved her legs and
did all those things she had told herself she wouldn't do. Sarah made
herself ready for Rip Thorne, and she hated herself for it. As she
sipped lemonade at the table next to the window nearest the bar,
cooling herself under the ever-present ceiling fans, she wondered if
he was still married. Lemonade? Damn fundamentalists. What she
wouldn't do for a real drink.

There was a guy in a cream jacket across the room who kept
smiling and trying to catch her eye, but Sarah just wasn't in the
mood. It was all she could do just to psyche herself up for this little
encounter. How long had it been? Five, six years? Maybe longer.
Considering they both worked for the same company it was an
achievement to have been apart this long.

'Miss Kelsey?' The voice was gentle. Calming.

When Sarah looked up she instantly recognized the woman from
earlier, outside the main gates to the Giza encampment. The demonstration. The armed soldiers. This woman with long gray hair, and
those deep penetrating eyes. 'It *is* Sarah Kelsey, isn't it?'

Sarah was suddenly aware that there was a live piano playing somewhere in the background. She shook her head, trying to clear her mind. 'Uh, yes,' she replied. 'Yes, I'm Sarah.' And then after a moment. 'I'm sorry, I—' She got up and shook the woman's hand. They exchanged an awkward laugh.

'Ellen,' she announced. 'Ellen Paris. No, *I'm* sorry,' she insisted. 'I'm not disturbing you, am I?'

Sarah eyed the empty seat across the table. 'Well, uh . . .'

'Oh,' Ellen Paris sighed. 'I hope you haven't been stood up.'

Sarah didn't quite know how to take that. Had she been stood up? It was just possible this Ellen was right. She inclined her head and narrowed her eyes. 'Would you care for something to drink? Don't worry, nothing alcoholic. I don't fancy the Mullahs coming to chop off a hand.' Ellen looked pensive. Sarah gave her a comforting smile. 'Company tab.'

Ellen relaxed. 'I'll have a lemonade.'

Sarah ordered two more lemonades as they took their seats. 'That was quite a little demonstration today, Ellen.' The other woman still had her modest black purse tucked under her arm. She set it down on the table and shrugged simply. 'Why'd you do it?' Sarah asked curiously. 'And a foreign woman too. That's some risk.'

'One should always fight for what one believes in.' Ellen folded her hands in her lap. 'You don't seem surprised to see me.'

'You said something earlier today,' Sarah said by way of an explanation, 'and it's stuck with me. You said, "Cayce was right." What were you talking about? Who is Cayce? I don't understand. Is he part of your group who doesn't want us digging around the monuments?'

'He is the reason I'm here,' Ellen admitted.

'Did he send you?'

'Hardly.' Ellen paused. 'He's dead.'

Sarah sat back with a start. 'I'm sorry,' she said.

'It's okay. He's been dead since 1945.'

The lemonades arrived. Sarah took hers quickly and had an unceremonious gulp. She fished the slice of sour lemon out and bit down on it. 'So you *were* being prophetic. I wasn't imagining it.'

'Cayce was the prophetic one,' Ellen explained.

'Did you ever meet him?'

'I'm not that old,' Ellen chided gruffly, but with good humor. 'I'm here because I think you need to know what you're getting yourself into.'

Sarah sipped her lemonade. 'Tell me about Cayce,' she said.

He was born on a Kentucky farm in 1877, the blue-eyed Edgar Cayce. Said to go to bed with his head on a book, then wake up knowing its contents. Tales of osmosis aside, he left a curious legacy of prediction and prophetdom that inspired a foundation in his name and a headache for serious academics.

Like Nostradamus before him, Cayce was in the business of predicting the future. He predicted that the Nile once flowed west. And that it once flowed into Lake Chad. In the 1990s this was confirmed when archeologists used satellite Ground Penetrating Radar and peeked beneath the desert sands. They soon discovered the dried-up riverbed.

Cayce also predicted that a group of early Christian activists called Essenes lived near the Dead Sea. He predicted that two US Presidents would die in office soon. In 1945 Cayce was dead, alongside Roosevelt. Months later the Essenes' Dead Sea Scrolls had been discovered by an Arab shepherd boy and it wasn't long before Kennedy had been killed as well.

Edgar Cayce predicted many things. And many times, he got those things right.

'He also got a lot wrong,' Ellen continued. 'He was only human. But before you go and get all skeptical, don't forget the CIA mounted Operation Deep See for over twenty years.'

'What was that? I've never heard of it.'

'The CIA employed psychics to penetrate secret enemy strongholds using nothing more than the power of the mind. They penetrated these strongholds and mapped them using a technique called Remote Viewing. They could see who operated in these places, and what was there. All of the information was verified by spies on the ground. They shut it down in the early 1990s. Then started it back up again about five years ago.'

'Are you serious?'

Ellen didn't seem to feel the need to answer that. Instead she continued: 'The important point for you about Cayce's predictions is that he foresaw that around the turn of the millennium, a hidden chamber would be discovered beneath the Sphinx. He called it. "The Hall of Records", a place where mankind's lost history had been gathered together alongside instruments of power. He also predicted that the people of ancient Atlantis possessed some kind of crystal stone that trapped the rays of the sun.'

Sarah sipped more lemonade cautiously. She didn't want to give anything away, but she had a feeling it was probably already too late. 'I see,' was all she would consciously commit herself to.

'There's been a long precedence of finding a hidden chamber,' Ellen added. 'The Westcar Papyrus from the fourth dynasty speaks of Djedi, a magician of the court of Khufu, or Cheops as he's sometimes called. Djedi claimed to know details about the secret chambers containing *The Books of Thoth*. He said that the keys to those chambers were hidden in the city of Ani. Ani has another name – Heliopolis, which literally means "City of the Sun".'

'Heliopolis today is a modern suburb with an airport,' Sarah said.

'Yes, and much of ancient Heliopolis is still hidden beneath it. Including the house of Septi, where the fifth Pharaoh of the first dynasty who reigned around 3,000BC, Pharaoh Septi, is said to have kept the ipwt-seals or keys to the hidden place in a box of flint or whetstone.'

'Do you think the keys really exist?'

'Possibly. Do you think you'll need keys?' Sarah remained tight-lipped. 'If you're feeling particularly awkward about the company you're keeping on this subject,' Ellen offered gently, 'you can always remind yourself that the secrets of the pyramids have been investigated by some of the world's greatest minds – Sir Isaac Newton, for example. He dedicated a huge portion of his life to decoding the mystery. And Thomas Young, he not only did some of the most pioneering work on translating Egyptian hieroglyphics, but he was also a physicist. He discovered the wave theory of light. And if I'm not much mistaken, that's still a cornerstone of modern physics.'

'You said I needed to know what I was getting myself into,' Sarah said sharply. 'Is this it? Something I'm not even trained for?'

Ellen smiled, almost to the point of stopping herself from laughing. 'This? Oh, it's much bigger than this. The investigation your company's involved in strikes at the very heart of organized religion and in turn the western world's power base.'

*   *   *

'I don't understand.'

'You will. In time, you will understand. But be aware of these facts. Why is it that as we speak, Rola Corp. has a team of scientists investigating certain crystals in Switzerland? Why is it that it has a team involved in similar work here – and had a team in China *before* the stand-off in Antarctica? That's right, Rola Corp. was in China. Why has another team gone off to the jungles of South America? Why is NASA suddenly so interested in mineral deposits on earth and not deep space? And why has the Vatican called an earth geological symposium for next week?

'Do you think that the pyramids are the only manmade structure to mirror a pattern in the stars? Or that the ancient Egyptians were the only people to believe their River Nile to be a mirror of a river of stars in the sky – the Milky Way? In China, the first Emperor, Chin, or Qin Xen Xuan Di, had the Xian Yang and Erpang Palaces modeled on the stars, with the Chungnan Shan mountain peak as the gateway to heaven and the River Wei as the mirror to the Milky Way. Just like here in Cairo. Even today, Taoist priests do the star dance to the constellation of the Great Bear.

'They believe in Chi or Qi – the lifeforce energy, similar to the Egyptian concept of the Ka. But the real clincher is that Emperor Qin also knew of a sacred underground place upon which he had built his square-based pyramid burial tomb. Though his pyramid was constructed from earth, it's more massive than anything in Egypt. To this day, inside are fully loaded crossbows poised to fire at trespassers, and lakes of poisonous mercury to reflect the light. Pearls and jade are set in the ceiling. But the Chinese won't open the tomb, which is precisely the one thing that Rola Corp. wanted.'

Ellen drank before continuing. 'The Chinese believe ancestor spirits are malignant. If you disturb them, they'll disturb you. Qin was a tyrant who killed millions. If they disturbed him, he might return to destroy China, a country after all, which is still named after him. This is the ruler who had blast furnaces fifteen hundred years before Europe. Who was able to manipulate carbon and lower its content in iron, making it malleable, so that his armies could plate their weapons with potassium dichromate to prevent corrosion, something which baffles archeologists even today. He had the Great Wall of China built and eight thousand terracotta soldiers buried with him as an army to command in the afterlife. Ironically he gave them real weapons which the peasants used to defeat his son later.'

Ellen took another sip of lemonade. She had sounded excited, but hardly fanatical. Which was the disturbing factor for Sarah.

'But the focal point for Chinese culture is also a precious stone. Jade. It's supposed to aid immortality. Burial suits were made of the stuff. Taoists literally ground it up into a powder and ate it. And two weeks ago NASA said, among other things, that they had found indications of jade in Antarctica. The press release simply said "mineral deposits", but if you look at the official report, there's jade.'

Ellen's drink was finished. She set the glass down and declined another. 'And all of this because of what they started doing in the Takla Makan desert.'

'I've heard of the desert,' Sarah said, 'but I don't know the significance of it.'

'Rola Corp. originally went out to look for oil in the Takla Makan Desert in western China. But their search took them closer and closer to ancient sites, like Wupu.'

Sarah was none the wiser.

'The Tokarians were the original indigenous people of the Takla Makan region, responsible for building the Great Silk Road that constituted the first trade road linking east and west. They died out about two and a half thousand years ago. Just before First Emperor Qin came to power.

'They built whole cities. Structures, some of which were megalithic. They wore woolen tartans woven in identical techniques to the Celts. They brought agriculture to the region – and nobody knows to this day where they came from. They turned up on the historical map at the same time as the Sumerians, and no one knows where *they* came from either.

'Their language was also most closely connected to Italo-Celtic and Germanic, not the nearer Indo-Iranian languages. And unlike everyone else in China they were tall, blond and red-headed. In appearance, they were foreigners, but they pre-date China. We think Rola Corp. came across certain information that led them to Qin's pyramid and Antarctica.'

Ellen handed Sarah a manila envelope and stood.

'What's this?'

'It's a little report on what we think is going on,' she said.

She had her purse tucked under her arm again. 'The point I'm trying to get across to you Sarah, is that nothing is as it seems. Be very careful. You're at the forefront of a lot of this and you don't even know it. And be wary of China,' she said. 'They may not be the enemy they've been painted to be.'

'I'm sorry I'm late,' the smooth deep voice cut in.

Sarah instinctively stuffed the envelope into her purse before she turned to see him.

He wasn't any fatter. He hadn't lost any hair. He still had all his own teeth. He didn't appear to be any older. Rip Thorne was still a striking forty-five-year-old. Nothing had changed. He still had those piercing eyes, like a shark looking for a weak spot. Probing. He was still a bastard.

'Rip . . . Oh, hi,' Sarah replied, regretting the hesitation. Thoughts were brewing but she told herself she knew how to keep them in check.

Thorne kissed her on the cheek, eyed Ellen Paris warily. 'Who's your friend?'

'I was just leaving,' Ellen explained graciously. She shared a look with Sarah, one that told her to remember what had been said, and was gone.

Thorne took Sarah by the arm. 'Shall we?' he said. 'I was looking for you in the foyer. I should have known you'd be at the bar.'

Outside, a car was waiting.

'What the hell is that?' Ralph Matheson asked, stunned as he watched the bank of monitors.

They were two research blocks over, a five-minute walk down the corridor from the Nuclear Magnetic Resonance Spectroscopy. Solar observatories all over the planet and beyond were pumping in data, some of them completely unaware of the urgency with which it was being received.

Hackett adjusted the computer settings. This was the signal relay center. There were no other scientists to clash with over theory here, just technicians, who scowled. 'You're looking at the spectacular phenomenon of thermal convection within the sun,' he explained.

On the workstation screen a graphic showed circles of motion rising and falling between the central core and the surface of the sun. The motions were many, and the overall pattern resembled half an orange.

'Pretty,' Matheson said.

'I think the term you're reaching for is "pretty important",' Hackett corrected. 'Thermal convection controls the circulation of the atmosphere and oceans. Determines the short- and medium-term weather change of the earth. Contributes to the motion of the continental tectonic plates by inducing large-scale movements of magma within the mantle, the earth's core. It also cooks soup. It's the process by which heat rises.'

'Neat.'

'How's our little expedition shaping up, anyway?'

'Great, for the middle of a war zone. They fly in half our equipment tonight. The rest we take with us. You ever fired a gun?'

'Does the photon gun in a TV tube count?'

'Nope.'

'Then no.'

'Me either. But they want us armed. For our own protection, you understand. Don't you, Admiral?'

Dower ignored the engineer.

'No, I don't understand. But what the hell. So long as I don't shoot my own toe off, what do I care?' Hackett replied, focused on the raw data as it spewed down the screens.

Matheson eyed the screen, then the physicist. Gant and Dower stood with them. It was Gant who asked quietly: 'What're you looking for?'

'The perturbation event.' Gant was none the wiser. 'The initial causation. That event which affects a system and creates instability. If it's fairly recent and the perturbation dies out quickly we call that system asymptotically stable.'

'And in English?'

'It means what I'm looking for is evidence on the sun that suggests it's a brief fluctuation. That it will dissipate soon. That these massive sun storms will go away.'

'And?'

'And I haven't found it,' Hackett admitted. 'And I don't think I ever *will* find it. Because it isn't there.'

'Well, something's gotta be causing this. It can't just happen all by itself.'

'Actually,' Hackett warned, 'it can.'

'The sun is classified as a subject for non-equilibrium physics, because of the wild fluctuations we see. Sunspots come in linked pairs of opposing magnetic polarity. Flares. Tornadoes the size of the earth that travel at thousands of miles an hour. Vast seismic sunquakes with waves 40,000 times the power of the 1906 San Francisco earthquake, with a two-mile-high ripple that travels outwards at up to 250,000 mph. They're regularly magnitude 11.3 or higher. That never happens here on earth. The biggest ever recorded earthquake we've had was 8.6, in Gansu, China, in 1920.

'These are spectacular events. But they're just events. The sun is also a system of large-scale regularities. Its central mass is subjected to hundreds of thousands of varying frequency sound waves pulsating throughout it at any one time. Imagine a thousand drummers each beating out a different rhythm on the same drum skin. It has a sunspot *cycle* of roughly eleven years. It's an ordered system.'

'It's a mass of nuclear explosions,' Matheson objected. 'You said that yourself. There's nothing ordered about that.'

'But that's just it,' Hackett replied. 'Look at it this way. What is, and isn't ordered is a matter of relativity. One nuclear explosion here on earth is so out of the ordinary, it can be nothing *but* destructive. But on the sun, where there's nothing but constant nuclear fusion reactions, it's you and I who'd be out of the ordinary. On the sun, *one* nuclear event is equivalent to, say, one of the cells that make up the human body. Its environment is like nothing we're used to and has its own kind of order. Real order. After all, we get up every morning and it's still there. Doing its sunlike thing. Has done for millions of years. Will continue to do so for many more. It's what we call a steady state. You've heard of entropy? The second law of thermo-dynamics?'

'Yeah. It's the amount of disorder in a system. Everything must break down. It's why if you drop a cup on the floor it breaks. It won't then put itself back together again.'

'Right. So everything breaks down. Scientists call it disorder. The rest of the population calls it "turning to crap".'

'Yeah.'

'So why are *we* here?'

'Uh?'

'Life. Trees. Us. Heck, even clouds. If there's so much disorder, and that's the natural tendency of things, to turn to crap, how come we made it? Order must be born out of chaos. It's an oscillation. Order – chaos – order – chaos.'

'That's why crystals form out of a chaotic liquid. Something changes and order is born?' Matheson suggested.

'In essence, yes.'

Matheson kicked back a moment, realizing Hackett wasn't all that ecstatic with the situation. 'So why is it you look like you've seen a ghost, Jon?'

'What happens when a violent but ordered system suddenly turns chaotic? What happens when violence meets chaos?'

Matheson gulped. 'Shit, I don't know.'

'There's a mathematical condition called the Hopf bifurcation, named after Eberhard Hopf, the German mathematician who discovered it. It guarantees that oscillations will occur in steady states. It'll start very small, but get bigger and bigger. In essence, absolutely nothing will trigger it, but a steady state will, for no real reason, become unstable and start to wobble.'

'Then it returns to its steady state?'

'Eventually. Yes. But there's also this physico-chemical phenomenon, the Belousov-Zhabotinski, or BZ phenomenon that occurs in certain liquids under certain circumstances. After the initial and imperceptible irregularity at an atomic level, which is the trigger, it turns into a chemical clock. The liquid turns from yellow, to colorless, to yellow, in perfect regular timing. The oscillation is an internal dynamic. It has nothing to do with any outside force. These events are the cornerstone of complexity theory.'

'So . . .?'

'Certain stars display just these properties. They're called cepheid variables. Pulsars, Ralph. Pulsars. They blast out matter at different rates, but they're violent stars. Some pulse once every second. Some once every few weeks. You look into the sky any night and you'll find one. Well,' he bit his lower lip anxiously, 'I think our sun is a pulsar.'

'What?'

'What I'm seeing fits the Hopf bifurcation and the BZ phenomenon. The sun could be much older than we thought and a slow-burn pulsar. So slow it only pulses once every twelve thousand years. These gravity waves could be the prelude to a massive jettison of a coronal shell.'

Dower wanted to be very clear about this. 'Are we talking about solar flares larger than previously projected?'

'Imagine,' Hackett explained, 'the entire surface of the sun boiling off in a cloud. Like a shell. It would be the mother of all solar flares, just blown straight off. Everything in the entire solar system would be hit. Nothing would escape.' He turned to Matheson. 'Didn't Richard say something about burning in those ancient myths? That not only were there earthquakes and floods, but that the earth burned? Admiral, it doesn't matter what the magnetic polarity is of a plasma cloud of that magnitude. It's gonna hit both Poles at the same time. And one of 'em's gonna suck that thing straight in. Be it North or South.'

'That's bad,' Matheson said, acutely aware of the implications of the problem.

'That's very fucking bad.' Hackett shifted in his seat as he leant forward and hit a button on the screen. 'It would eventually wipe out all life.' The image began to descend into chaos. 'Either way, both oscillations are mathematically predictable. I can't tell you which one it is, but right now, I can tell you precisely when the fun's about to start.'

Dower was stunned. 'You can *what*? How long have we got?'

'The solar "event" begins at six pm – this Thursday. And peaks around midnight Saturday,' Hackett revealed. 'On Sunday . . . God rests.'

'Jesus Christ.'

Hackett shot a look up to see Gant standing on the other side of his monitor with a coffee in his hand. 'Are there any other expected fluctuations?' the Admiral asked.

'A couple,' said Hackett. 'The timing's a little off, but there may be one tonight. A big one. One we will feel this time.'

'What kind of machine, d'you think, would they want to make out of pure carbon crystal?' Scott mused as he methodically analyzed each piece on the table. Where he could, he fitted the stones together like a jigsaw. He sketched the glyphs and made notes of their characteristics, marveled at their intricate detail. 'What kind of machine has no moving parts?'

'We don't know that it doesn't,' November observed. 'And besides, solar panels have no moving parts.' Something was troubling her, Scott could tell. She'd just called her dad back home and cussed him out for not tidying the house. And it didn't seem to be related to the fact that he had a date tonight.

Scott said: 'Good point,' and turned his attention to one of his many crumpled notebooks. He started drawing up lists of words. She gave him a look. Wanting to know what he'd found. 'I just got to thinking about similar words that some languages share,' he confided. 'Common denominators. I was thinking, if I can see a pattern in the comparisons, then I might be able to see a pattern in the stones.'

She asked him to go on.

'The ancient Aztecs spoke Nahuatl,' Scott said. 'And when they wanted to say "House of God", they said "teocalli". Whereas in Greek, this side of the Atlantic, they say "theou kalia", "God's House". In Quechua, they say "llake llake", when they want to say "heron". And they say "llu llu" when they mean "lie". While the

Sumerians said "lak lak", for "heron". And "lul" for "lie".'

'They're virtually identical.'

'Virtually. Unfortunately it's not very scientific. As a linguist my instinct is to compare *one* language with another language, not continent with continent. One-off similarities are frowned on, but a few things keep cropping up. Like "atl".'

'Atl?'

'Or just "tl". As a combination of consonants it's pretty rare in a lot of European languages. We use it in the words Atlantic, Atlas, and Atlantis. But in South and Central America it's fairly common. "Atl" is the Nahuatl word for water. Atlaua was the gold of, and master over, water. Aztlan was the mythical homeland that the Aztecs claimed to have descended from. It meant "The land of the Sun", but with "tl" in the world it had a water connotation. Though what the word "atlatl" had to do with water I'm not sure.' He chewed on a thumbnail as November pulled up a chair. 'Atlatl means "arrow".'

'Arrow? That's interesting. On maps they always use arrows to show which way is North. With Atlantis being at the South Pole, that might be important,' she offered.

Scott narrowed his eyes. 'I have no idea why that's important,' he said, 'but keep it in mind.'

'Sure,' November beamed, pleased with herself. 'So does "atlatl" have any link to a European language?'

'Well,' Scott replied, tongue in cheek, 'there's "arrow", but apart from that, nothing really. Except maybe in Old High German. "Tulli" meant "arrow-head". And Thule was a legendary North Atlantic Island first mentioned by Pytheas in the fourth century BCE.' He drummed his fingers on the table, his leg twitching in unison as his mind worked overtime. 'In fact . . . In fact!' Rifling through papers he pulled out a notepad, flicked through and found the right crumpled page. 'Yeah . . . Tlalocan was the southern home of Tlaloc, the rain god. He was also known as, wait for it . . . Tlahuizpantechutli – the god of ice. And his girlfriend was Chalchiuitlicue, goddess of water.'

'They had gods for the weather?'

'Oh, sure. Ehacatl was the god of wind, for instance. Now, he was an interesting character because he was also known as Quetzalcoatl, the man it's said brought civilization to Central and South America.

He was the feathered serpent. The Good God, inventor of writing, painting and the calendar.'

'Just like Thoth.'

'Yes, and in the ancient Mexican pinturas, or paintings, Quetzalcoatl, the one I said wore the long black gown fringed with the white crosses? He was also god of the West, one of four Tezcatlipocas . . .'

'The others being, East, North and South, huh?' November asked, leading the linguist on. 'He's got crosses all over his clothes, *and* he's linked to the points of the compass?'

'There's definitely a pattern here. A logic.' He eyed her closely. 'It just isn't funny anymore.'

It was November's turn to smirk. 'It's complex . . . isn't it?'

'Don't *you* start.'

'What made you start looking at South American languages, anyway? I thought you were looking at cuneiform. That's in the Middle East.'

'It occurred to me,' Scott explained, 'that when Antarctica experienced the flood, there was no one single route of escape. The three closest land masses were South America, South Africa and the Indian peninsula. But since it was a flood, land at the same altitude would be underwater. So you have to go further north before you hit mountains, and so dry land. The Andes, in Peru. Mount Ararat in Turkey, near to Egypt. And the Himalayas in the north of India and the border of China. The same three places where religion and writing were born.'

'Oh my God, that's incredible.'

'Maybe. I don't know. Anyway, I remembered something I read about a language called Aymara. It's part of the Amerind language family. One of the families we kept on that board.'

'I remember. Yeah, there it is.'

'The thing about it is, it appears to have been *invented.*'

'Is that possible? I thought languages just . . . evolved.'

'Must do. But it's not impossible. Hangul, the alphabet they use in Korea Province, China, was invented by King Sejong in 1446. He designed twenty-eight new letters for vowels and consonants because a thousand years of using Chinese had been a disaster for his people,' Scott said. 'But Aymara's different because we just don't know how old it really is. What we do know is it uses entirely different logic from our own. We use opposites. The syntax of our language is based on the notion of yes or no. Aymara has a third kind, like a "maybe" mode. What in computer speak they call fuzzy logic.'

November went to open her mouth, but Scott cut her short.

'I don't know – ask Hackett. The point is, Ivan Guzman de Rojas, a Bolivian computer scientist studied the language in the 1980s and discovered that Aymara worked like an algorithm. It could be used as a bridging language. If you translated a foreign language into Aymara, you could then translate the Aymara into any other language – precisely, keeping the exact original sense of what the first language was trying to say without getting anything jumbled up or lost in the translation. It's so useful they use it in all kinds of translation programs even today.'

'Aymara? Where did they use that?'

Scott raised an eyebrow. 'Tiahuanaco,' he said. 'And some people still use it.'

'Where's Tiahuanaco?'

'In the Andes. Way up high, by the shores of Lake Titicaca.'

November was stunned. 'It's like all the clues to Atlantis have always been here. We just didn't listen.'

Scott surveyed the row of crystals on the table and took a long hard look at his research. 'Well, we know it's here now. And it's trying to tell us something.'

It was an intense feeling. So much so, he felt like a kid again. Everything he'd ever learned just felt so new right now. He could sense a pattern. A logic. But what was it?

November seemed tense. Knowing he should leave well enough alone, tentatively he asked, 'How's life back home? They miss you already?'

'Are you frightened?' she asked suddenly.

'Sure.'

'What frightens you most about all this?'

'That I'll never see my daughter again. That if this second flood does hit I won't be able to do a thing about it and she'll suffer.'

November was subdued. 'I didn't realize you had a daughter. How old is she?'

'Seven. Her name's Emily.'

'That's a pretty name.' November picked up a stone gently. She could feel that customary tingle on her skin again, almost prickly. Nervously, she said: 'Dad says the Mississippi's starting to flood. They issued a state of emergency in the delta.'

'I see.'

'It's starting . . .'

'I think so,' Scott nodded, with just the barest hint of uncertainty.

'What did you want me to do with this?' she asked, tapping the rock. 'Sketch it again?'

'Please.'

November stood. 'I'm hungry. And I'm sick of coffee. Care for a Coke or something?'

'I'm fine.'

The kitchenette against the far wall to one side was pretty well stocked to capacity. Clean and white, it had a sink and a microwave. It was all contained within an enclosed mobile unit to keep steam and stray radiation out of the working environment.

A radio stood to one side. Absently, November heard a tune she recognized and turned the volume up. Setting the Carbon 60 down in front of it she pulled the refrigerator open and grabbed the two-liter-bottle of Coke from inside and poured herself a drink. Found a fresh filter, went to work on more coffee. No matter what Dr Scott said, he was bound to want more coffee. And it was then that she was brought up short by a high-pitched whine, almost out of her hearing range. At first she thought she had a ringing in her ears until she realized it was coming from a specific direction. It was coming from her glass of Coke.

She stopped what she was doing, drawn to her glass like a moth to a flame. The sound had gone higher now. Way beyond her range.

She crouched down to take a closer look, and couldn't believe what she was seeing. The carbonated bubbles that usually fizzed to the surface were slowing. As if the Coke was becoming viscous, like treacle.

A cracking sound shot out from the glass. Yet there was no visible sign of any damage.

And then the bubbles stopped. Caught in mid-flow.

She could feel the whole kitchenette units vibrate. Could see the faint oscillating movement. What the hell was going on?

Her eyes darted from object to object. Radio – speaker – sound – Carbon 60 – Coke in a glass.

There was a box of assorted odds and ends in a drawer. A steel ball bearing.

Cautiously she held the steel ball over the glass. Paused, then dropped it.

Clank.

The ball hit the Coke like it was ice and stayed motionless on the surface.

'Oh my God,' she murmured. Somebody had to come see this! This was incredible! She leapt to her feet. 'Dr Scott!' she yelled. 'Dr Scott, you have to come see this!'

Instinctively she reached out and grabbed the glass of Coke.

By the time Scott arrived, November Dryden was screaming.

BREAKTHROUGH

In the northern hemisphere at the peak of the last major glaciation, 18,000 years ago, a continental ice layer several kilometers thick covered much of northern America, down to the middle part of the United States, as well as much of northern and western Europe, to the latitude of Paris and Berlin. In the present-day situation, continental ice is confined essentially to Greenland. Furthermore, it is known that, as far as continental ice extent is concerned, the present situation was essentially established 10,000 years ago. In other words, we are forced to conclude that the planet Earth, a physical system, has in a few years (a short time on a geological scale) undergone a transition between two extraordinarily different states whose difference extends over the dimensions of the Earth itself.

The above remarks suggest that any reasonable model of the climatic system should be able to account for the possibility of such large-scale transitions.

Gregoire Nicolis and Ilya Prigogine *Exploring Complexity: An Introduction*, 1989

A CAIRO PENTHOUSE BALCONY

9:30 PM

'How's your wife?' It was the most malicious thing she could think of to ask while she gazed at her fresh lobster, cracked straight down its back on her platter. A bottle of vintage Dom Perignon chilled in the ice-bucket.

It was amazing what money could buy in an alcohol-free state. But then the Egyptians had always been a fun-loving people. Sarah was sure this fundamentalist thing wasn't going to last. It couldn't. The Egyptians just didn't have the discipline for it.

Thorne pulled a hunk of quivering white flesh from the claw in his hand without so much as a missed beat. 'Julia's doing great,' he said cheerfully. 'Y'know she's really on this tennis kick right now.' He licked his fingers clean.

'Tennis?' Thorne had met someone at the country club. He had to. 'I didn't think you liked tennis.'

'I didn't say I did,' he replied, having more lobster. He poured the champagne and toasted her.

She downed hers nervously, set the long-stemmed crystal glass down maybe a bit too forcefully. Pushed the lobster around her plate. She really wasn't in the mood for this. She could feel the butterflies in her stomach flapping relentlessly. How many relationships had she thrown away because she couldn't get this man out of her mind?

Sarah glanced down over the balcony at everyone else in the cafés and restaurants below. Music and laughter wafted up. He'd brought her up here for a reason. They hadn't seen each other in several years. But he knew, up here, it would make her feel more alone, more dependent on him. And he was right. Thorne was always right.

'How was your meeting at the AOI?' she asked, having seen his stack of paperwork over on a far lamp-lit table. 'You got what you wanted?'

Thorne smiled in that way that told her, even if he had, he wasn't telling.

'Why did you request I come to Cairo?' she probed further.

'You mean, was it so I could see you?' he retaliated.

She flashed a smile back. As genuine as she could muster. 'You can request to see me whenever you want,' she pointed out. 'My question is purely business. What is the Egyptian government getting out of all this? Do they fully realize what they've got on their hands here?'

'No, I doubt they realize the full implications, Sarah. Why would they? All they can see are dollar signs. Just not on the scale I can see them.'

'Do they know about China?'

Now Thorne hesitated. That felt good.

'So,' he replied. Measured. 'You know about China.'

'Word gets around,' she said. 'After all, you've nearly started a war.'

Thorne called the waiter over for more champagne. The man briefly explained they only had vintage Krüg left. Thorne said that was okay and eyed Sarah directly. 'You always were very smart, honey. Very perceptive.'

Just lucky, she guessed. So Ellen was right. Nonchalantly he took her by the hand and seemed surprised to find that her delicate fingers were cold. He rubbed them gently, while his eyes told his staff that they were dismissed. They let themselves out quietly.

'You're not staying, are you?' she asked with a dawning realization.

'No,' Thorne confessed. 'I have to go in the morning. I wanted to see you before I left. It's been so long . . . I needed to see you.'

'Where are you going?'

'Rome.'

'Rome?' Besides spaghetti and the Vatican, she couldn't see what was waiting for him there. She scoffed back a nervous laugh. 'You wanna brief the Pope? Let him know civilization goes back a little farther than Jesus Christ?'

Thorne wasn't laughing. 'Something like that. The President's already there.'

'What? In between starting a war in Antarctica?'

'Wars are fought on many fronts, Sarah.' He stood. 'Would you care for some dessert?' Sarah was rubbing her forehead. She felt dizzy. 'Look, it's just dessert. Do you want some?'

He pulled her to her feet. Held her close. That faint aroma from his skin that she knew so well swelled in her heart.

'I want dessert,' he said huskily. 'I want you.'

It was such a cheesy line. And the fact was, if she hadn't been so damn well turned on by him she'd have reached for the nearest bucket. But as it was she responded, like he knew she would. Eventually pulling away she asked: 'Why did you really want me to come out here?'

He stroked her hair. 'I thought it might make a pleasant change for you,' he confided. 'I know how you enjoy your history. It must have been tough in Siberia.'

It was enough to let him kiss her again. And more. And after the first rampant session up against the wall, they both agreed that it would probably be more comfortable if they went to bed. After all, they weren't teenagers anymore.

He knew what champagne did to her. Goddamnit. The bastard knew.

They were called quasicrystals.

They were materials that could not be called true crystal because they were not made up of repeated identical unit cells, like a cube in the case of sodium, or plain old salt. The units in quasicrystals had much more complex symmetry. Twelve-fold symmetry. Making shapes like double spirals and hexagonal honeycombs. The odd-shaped units were irregular, but still linked together to form crystal-like structures.

But that was with metals.

The Coke in November's glass exhibited all the signs of having transformed itself into a quasicrystal. And since it was a liquid, it meant looking at the work of a much older scientist.

Michael Faraday, in 1831, first discovered that standing waves, waves that appeared to be entirely motionless, could be produced in fluids. This meant the use of vibration, by its very nature an element of sound. And *that* was the link Hackett was looking for.

The doctor was closing his case as the physicist and engineer arrived to see what all the commotion was about. Scott explained what had happened, while November dabbed back tears with a screwed-up tissue.

The doctor from CERN's medical center said: 'She's fine. No burnmarks. No abrasions. Blood pressure's high, but no respiratory problems. She's in perfect health.'

'I *told* you it didn't hurt,' November explained irritably. Her body was still wracked with tearful convulsions. 'I couldn't move my hand,' she said, 'no matter how hard I tried. I couldn't move my joints. It was like my arm was completely frozen, but it didn't hurt.'

'Then why'd you scream?' Scott asked compassionately.

'Because I was scared,' she replied in a small voice. 'I was scared because I couldn't move my arm.'

Hackett crouched down in front of the counter. Though the tune had changed, the set-up had been left exactly the way it was. Radio – C60 – glass of Coke. Pearce stood to one side, watching. Not wanting to get in the way, but not wanting to leave either. Everyone was mesmerized by something that simply wasn't normal. And it was almost as if he could actually see their elite minds working over-time.

A steel ball bearing was sat on top of a liquid that had, for all intents and purposes, solidified without freezing.

'Good God,' Matheson murmured.

'God may have nothing to do with it,' Hackett retaliated, jabbing a pencil in the direction of the C60. He eyed the set-up again, care-fully, before shooting a look to Pearce and ordering quietly: 'Okay, Bob, turn the radio off.'

Pearce located the white plastic power supply. The plug. Gripped the switch firmly. Then flipped it to 'off.'

The radio went dead.

Suddenly the ball bearing shot to the bottom of the glass with such a tremendous crack that for a moment it looked like it might shatter the container. It rolled around the bottom before coming to a stop.

Hackett raised his eyebrows and let out a deep breath, which was a surprise to him if nobody else. He hadn't realized he was holding it.

There was a long plastic rod over to one side, amid a collection of odds and ends. Holding it by his fingertips, Hackett lowered it into the Coke and washed it around. Bubbles fizzed to the surface.

He extracted the rod. Nodded to Pearce again. 'Turn the radio back on.'

Within seconds the hissing and high-pitched whine returned. And this time when he tried to jab the rod back into the liquid, making sure his hand wasn't in the path of the sound wave, it made a crunch like it had hit a solid.

He asked Pearce to switch the radio off again and Hackett took the glass of Coke away. He nodded to one of the chemists, who had gathered by the door, and in turn okayed an assistant to bring the rat over that he was holding in a cage.

He set it down in front of the stone.

It was a large brown rat. Racing around its cage it sniffed the air as if it sensed something was wrong. Scampering to the front of the cage, it squeaked at the C60 and lashed out.

'You can't! That's horrible!' November shrieked.

Hackett wasn't phased. 'Experiment,' he explained without looking at her, 'is the only method of attaining certainty.'

The radio was flipped on again. And the rat stood frozen solid, locked into its pose. Its eyes were glassy and transfixed. November looked away as Hackett counted out a full thirty seconds.

'What the hell's going on?' Matheson demanded quietly.

Hackett ran the rod along the set-up and explained. 'Sound waves are produced here – in the radio. The sound enters the Carbon 60 and is "altered" somehow. Then it's projected back out in this direction. Until it hits the rat. Or the Coke. A living organism is approximately seventy-five percent fluid so it's going to react in a similar fashion to a glass of Coke. The altered sound has been tuned harmonically to produce standing waves in fluid. In other words the use of sonic technology has been applied to temporarily and artificially crystallize a fluid object.' He asked for the sound to be cut again.

The rat went about its business as though nothing had happened.

'Hmm.' Hackett eyed the glass of Coke in his hand, the ball bearing still rolling around at the bottom. He took a sip apparently without thinking. 'Strange,' he murmured. Then gagged. 'Ugh!'

'What is it?!' November yelped, grabbing the man by his shoulder.

Hackett set the glass down quickly and stood. 'This is Diet,' he complained. 'I can't drink Diet. Got any regular?'

November slapped him up the back of the head. Nobody else found it funny either. Casually removing the C60 and shunting the radio closer to the rat, Hackett switched the radio back on, and nothing happened. 'Well, that confirms it,' he announced. 'There's nothing special about the radio, or the station it's tuned to.' He let

a sour smile cross his face. 'The military's gonna just love an application for this.' He eyed Scott darkly. 'You realize when we get to
Antarctica, we're gonna be lucky if there's any of Atlantis left.'

'So let me get this straight,' Pearce said fussily. 'We have a city
built out of a substance that reacts to – get this – gravity waves, light,
electricity, and now . . . sound waves.'

'Correct.'

'Shit! That's wild!'

'Well,' November said sharply, 'I've had enough. I want to go back
to my hotel room.'

Scott was already nodding in sympathy. 'I'll come with you. Let
me grab my coat.'

'And there was me, thinking scientific discovery was exciting,'
Hackett commented as he watched them leave.

'What about the translation?' Pearce called after them anxiously.

'It can wait!' Scott tossed back over his shoulder.

Hackett dug his hands in his pockets as Pearce sidled up next to
him. 'You reviewed the solar data, right? It *can't* wait, can it?'

Hackett simply shook his head. No, it couldn't. He stepped out
into the main lab and watched briefly as Scott and November disappeared up the metal staircase toward the exit. And that was when
he became aware of the sound of snaps of electricity and cries of:
'This stuff sucks!' from across the lab.

'That's one way of putting it,' Hackett commented, realizing something was up. He turned to Pearce. 'What's been going on, Bob?'

He was led over to Hawkes who bitterly snatched the chunk of
Carbon 60 he'd been using out of their laser cutting assembly.

'It's this crystal,' Hawkes explained, adjusting his goggles. 'Every
time we go to slice through this stuff we get some kind of feedback
in the laser beam.' He unlocked the cover plates on the access drawer
and unclipped the crystal housing. Withdrew it carefully from the
chamber.

'Have you been getting this all the time or has it only just started
to happen?'

The other chemists busily uncoupled power cables, gearing up
for a major recalibration.

'Aw, we've been getting it right from the start,' Hawkes complained
without looking up.

'Why didn't you mention it before?'

'Didn't seem important.'

Matheson stepped up to the fray for a clearer look. 'Out of interest, what kind of feedback have you been getting? A single long pulse? Or choppy?'

Now Hawkes looked up. 'You mean like bits? Pulses?' Matheson nodded. 'Pulses.'

'Regular?'

'Uh-uh. No. If it was regular we could compensate for that. But it's different every time. Why, you seen this kind of thing before?'

Pearce was confused as Matheson explained: 'Sounds like intermittent reflection. Each time they try to cut into the crystal it bounces the laser light back at the emitter—'

'Almost burnt us out, too.'

'Sounds like it doesn't *want* you cutting into it,' Pearce observed.

The chemist looked disbelieving. But didn't comment.

'Or it's trying to tell you something,' Hackett added. 'Pass on information.'

Matheson was keyed up almost immediately. 'You mean like data storage on a light computer?'

Hackett shrugged.

'On a what?' Pearce interjected. 'You're talking theoretical—'

But Matheson's eyes never wavered from the physicist as he demanded: 'Do they even *have* a light computer on this site?'

Thorne was asleep in bed.

Sarah knew he wouldn't be awake anytime soon because she'd purposely worn him out. Which meant it was now open season on his computer and paperwork . . .

She found a bottle of water in the refrigerator over in one corner and sat herself down with it, casting a quick eye over the documents on the table. And then she spotted it – the dog-eared magazine jutting out from one of the folders, buried in one of the stacks.

She pulled it out. It was a copy of a research paper written by Ellen Paris.

Sarah suddenly remembered the envelope Ellen had given her. She carefully ripped it open and there it was again.

Ellen's paper documented the theory of Earth Crust Displacement by Charles Hapgood, a Professor of Science History, who put forward the notion in the 1950s and won the support of Albert Einstein. It was the same theory Sarah had told Houghton about in Siberia.

The premise was simple. A build-up of ice at the Poles caused a savage destabilization effect, resulting in the crust of planet Earth being ripped away from its liquid core and shifted like the skin on custard. It would explain many geological and paleontological anomalies, like tropical plant matter being found in the Antarctic.

Hapgood's theory eventually gave birth to the standard geological theory of plate tectonics and led to the discovery that certain rock compositions gave a magnetic reading indicating the time at which they were created. Since they were formed within the earth's magnetic field, they reflected where the North and South Poles were once situated.

The data confirmed the North Pole was once in the Hudson Bay, then once near the British Isles 2,500 miles further west, and 60 million years ago was as far south as LAT. 55°, in the Pacific Ocean. Other geological evidence showed Africa and India were once under ice and that Antarctica used to be 2,500 miles further north.

The geological record proved that the magnetic North and South Poles completely reversed position on a regular basis. But the mechanism for Pole reversal was totally unknown. Were the two phenomena, a shifting crust and Pole reversal, linked? And if so, why was Thorne interested in this stuff?

Earth Crust Displacement Theory required the entire crust of the earth to be sat on top of a sea of molten rock. Some geologists would have dismissed this notion except that in the mid-1990s John Van Decas led a team down to South America to the Parana Basalt Province in Brazil where they used a series of monitors, like a CAT scan, to chart the passage of waves from earthquakes as they passed through the ground. This was easier than most people suspected because it was a little-known fact that every single day there was an earthquake somewhere around the globe. And every fourth day it was at least magnitude 6.4.

What Van Decas discovered was a semi-viscous plume of molten rock, 190 miles across, extending 370 miles down from South America to the molten mantle. It explained why South America had moved west 1,800 miles in 130 million years. It meant South America was directly linked to the currents that affected the earth's liquid mantle. Over the next ten years similar plumes were uncovered connecting other continents to the mantle. So the earth's crust really could be said to be 'floating' on molten rock after all.

Sarah was about to read on when she suddenly caught a glimpse of her own thesis in Thorne's mountain of paper. 'What the hell . . .?'

She grabbed it and flicked through it. More red pen marks and hurriedly scribbled notes: *refer to File 15A.*

There was a theory that magnetic storms and interactions with other bodies in space could have caused the earth's magnetic field to reverse by affecting the earth's core. In the mid-1990, scientists measured the motion of the much-theorized solid inner iron core and discovered it rotated faster than the earth did. It was also surrounded by a larger liquid iron outer core that when taken together, formed a giant electrical motor.

Recently scientists theorized that to affect this motor would take more than a magnetic space storm. A gravitational field would have to divert it. Spin it maybe, about its axis, or nudge it off-kilter so the net result was that it wound up rotating in the opposite direction without ever having actually ceased to rotate.

Ellen was confident something was about to affect the earth's gravity. She had her money pegged on a dark matter comet passing close to the earth. The effects of gravity from such a periodic event would affect our home planet. It was a nice theory. But as Sarah sipped her water and sifted more documents, bigger pieces of the puzzle slowly started to fall into place.

Accepting there was a Flood and an earth crust displacement. Accepting there was a pre-Flood civilization of great power. Accepting there was devastation on a massive scale. Then there *had* to be an acceptance that mankind would instinctively wish to rebuild its shattered existence piece by piece.

To do it mankind would need dry land. Safe land. If the earth had been flooded they would need mountains and fertile land. Noah sailed for forty days and forty nights before he found what he was looking for. Who was to say others didn't do the same?

And was it merely coincidence that at approximately 7,000BC in just three places on earth, agriculture suddenly sprang up and flourished from out of nowhere?

In China it was around the Takla Makan. In South America it was around the Amazon. And in Africa it was the Nile and the Giza plateau. All three areas were close to high mountain ranges. And upon the nearby peaks, even today, was evidence from satellite photography of the remains of at least two massive ancient ships stuck 7,000 feet up the sides of two different mountains, lodestones and all. All three areas would have escaped the worst of the flooding. All three would have remained within a fairly stable climate region despite a shift. And within a radius of 1,000 miles, all three had pyramids.

At the pyramid in Egypt, Sarah had been responsible for the positive discovery of C60. In China, another team had already done the same. In Antarctica there was a city made of the stuff. Atlantis . . . Good God, it didn't matter how significant that was. None of that mattered. What mattered to Rola Corp. was the resource. And the company wanted that resource at all costs.

Sarah knew exactly what she was looking for now. On a roll, she dug out every geological report she could find. Cross-matched references to mineral deposits and Carbon 60 and hit paydirt.

Exactly one month ago, Rola Corp. had discovered Carbon 60 at a place called Wupu in the Takla Makan desert. A furious row broke out with Chinese officials, but not before certain information came to light at the site which led directly to a chain of unstoppable events.

On March 1, 2012, against the advice and clear warning of Chief Design Engineer Ralph Matheson, Rip Thorne inexplicably brought a test drilling operation in Antarctica forward by more than six months as the Chinese set out for the same area. Suddenly NASA was on the hunt for minerals too, and the pace at the company shipyard was quickened. But the drill ship wasn't ready, it couldn't be. But then Rip Thorne wasn't looking for oil.

On March 8, 2012, Carbon 60 was found in Antarctica, based, it seemed at first, on historical information gleaned from Wupu. And the hunt for more C60 was launched. In a hurried dash, an internal search team was used to pinpoint the location of more easily accessible C60.

In Egypt, Cairo was targeted. While in South America, in the Amazon basin, a site near the Pini Pini River was chosen. Guarded by the Machiguenga Indians who considered themselves guardians of the 'sacred places', satellite images clearly showed a series of eight vast pyramids which had lain undisturbed for millennia, covered in vegetation and masked by the jungle of the rainforest.

Ellen was right. A team *had* been dispatched to South America.

But what had sparked the hunt for C60 in the first place? What had caused Rola Corp. to seek Carbon 60 and wind up researching earth crust displacement?

The answer was Ellen Paris. The discovery of C60 in China, the same incident that was precipitating a confrontation, was due in part, to the article written by her.

It would happen again, Ellen said. The Flood would happen again. Sarah read through Ellen's theory intently and quickly found what she was looking for – what some faceless scientist had ringed as important. No matter what the external mechanism was, that triggered the earth's crust to shift, the build-up to the event could be timed. By monitoring the resulting build-up in earthquake activity, a date for the impending disaster could be predicted, and Ellen had predicted such an event.

Earthquakes were the prelude to the Flood, and the build-up began in Peru. *In 1996.*

Within seconds she was wading her way through page after page of statistics.

KEY:	DATE-(UTC)-TIME LAT LON DEP MAG Q COMMENTS
DEP = Depth in kilometers	yy/mm/dd hh:mm:ss deg. deg. km
MAG = Magnitude	96/11/12 11:34:47 25.31S 64.47W 33.0 4.6Mb B SALTA PROVINCE, ARGENTINA
M1 = Local, the	96/11/12 16:59:43 14.90S 75.49W 33.0 7.3Ms A NEAR COAST OF PERU
original	96/11/12 18:17:31 15.15S 75.00W 33.0 5.1Mb B NEAR COAST OF PERU
Richter magnitude	96/11/12 20:07:46 14.96S 75.38W 33.0 5.1Mb C NEAR COAST OF PERU
Lg = mblg	96/11/12 21:43:57 15.31S 75.39W 33.0 5.2Mb C NEAR COAST OF PERU
Md = duration	96/11/12 23:35:14 14.85S 75.36W 33.0 5.5Mb A NEAR COAST OF PERU
Mb = body wave	96/11/13 00:28:19 15.01S 75.48W 33.0 5.2Mb A NEAR COAST OF PERU
Ms = surface wave	96/11/13 02:41:39 14.70S 75.40W 33.0 5.7Ms A NEAR COAST OF PERU
Mw = moment	96/11/13 02:47:33 15.33S 75.59W 33.0 5.1Mb A NEAR COAST OF PERU
Q = Precision of location,	96/11/13 12:32:09 15.38S 75.18W 33.0 5.7Ms B NEAR COAST OF PERU
fine (A) to	96/11/13 12:36:59 33.47N 116.45W 5.0 3.7Ml A SOUTHERN CALIFORNIA
course (D)	96/11/13 16:05:59 15.46S 75.45W 33.0 4.3Mb C NEAR COAST OF PERU

They were US Geological Survey figures Ellen had used. Critical to her thesis yet somewhat obscure. The puzzle for Sarah was, how could earthquake events from 1996 have any connection to events in 2012? Just looking at the pattern showed that Peru had suffered a lot of activity for two days straight. But how did that help set a date for an imminent flood?

It was what Ellen called the 'Tesla Effect'. A surprising name for a geological effect since the late, great Nikola Tesla had been no geologist. He was the founding father of radio and alternating current.

It all had to do with frequency, vibration, and oscillation, in a combined phenomenon called *resonance*. One day while working at his laboratory in New York, Tesla attached a small oscillating machine to the steel-structure of the building he was using, and turned it on just to see what would happen. The result was a mini-earthquake in the downtown Manhattan area that prompted the local police to mobilize en masse and put a stop to the crank. Further experiments led him to believe that it would be possible to level Brooklyn Bridge by such a method. Or, more ominously, rip the entire planet in two by using tons of dynamite.

This was all very well but where did it fit into earthquake frequency patterns?

The answer was resonance. Every object, animate or inanimate, atom or animal, had its own specific resonance – a frequency at which it vibrated. By influencing that resonance by means of sound waves, the resonance could be sped up until the object literally shook itself apart. Or worse, shattered. It was the same principle behind an opera singer breaking a glass just by hitting the right sustained note.

Ellen explained it by using the analogy of a child on a swing. Every time Mom chose to push the swing, it was only once the swing had peaked and was just starting its return journey away from her that she put in any effort. And she did this because it took *very little* effort to keep the swing moving that way.

However, if Mom used the same force she used to get Baby swinging in the first place, any fool knew instinctively that in time, the swing would wind up flipping over the top bar.

It was the same principle with resonance.

Tesla had discovered that it took one hour and forty-nine minutes for a low-frequency wave to pass through the earth and come back again. His theory was that if he detonated a ton of dynamite every hour and forty-nine minutes, over and over, he would set into effect a state of vibration that would cause the earth's crust to rise and fall by hundreds of feet. Seas would be shifted. Civilization would be destroyed. And Tesla's time-scale for such an event? A matter of years.

Sarah went cold.

Ellen had set the start point in 1996. And the culmination was due any month now.

The flaw in all this was that Ellen, try as she might, just couldn't pinpoint the external cause. She was no astrophysicist. She rambled on about a comet made of dark matter but she didn't really know what she was talking about. But what she did know out-stripped statistical probability by two to one. She had charted the build-up and stress on the earth's own resonance over time. And the most outwardly public and perceptible result of this build-up was the increased earthquake activity, which had risen precisely in line with her predictions.

Sarah couldn't believe what she was reading. And couldn't believe she had part of the puzzle. Could gravity waves from the sun have begun pulsing over fifteen years go?

Even now, millions of low-frequency waves were bouncing around inside the earth's core, ricocheting and growing. A fact Rola Corp. had dismissed as nonsense to Ellen's face, as a copy of their letter to her showed. But it was something in private Rola Corp. had decided to follow up. For there was a pattern in the low-frequency waves that Ellen had not picked up on, and which Rola Corp.'s best minds had. The pattern was a focal issue. The low-frequency waves oscillating within the earth's core were focusing in on five distinct areas around the globe. Bouncing around, seemingly at random, yet dissipating at five sites. At first no one knew why, but it was clear it was not by chance.

The five sites were Antarctica, the Arctic, Pini Pini in Peru, Cairo in Egypt, and Wupu in China. The only immediate site accessible for investigation had been Wupu, and it was there that C60 was first discovered. A crystal that, all preliminary reports from Geneva suggested, responded directly to gravity waves.

Sarah threw herself back in the chair. Chewed the end of her pen and thought long and hard about the implications. There were five sites around the planet that contained C60 and responded to gravity waves, that were the focus points to low-frequency seismic waves.

What the hell had Rola Corp. stumbled across here? And why had they told no one about it?

Sarah eyed the computer screen ponderously, and that was when she saw it. Tucked innocently away in one corner of the desktop screen on Thorne's laptop computer was a vid-phone shortcut icon simply called: *Peru.*

She eyed it nervously. A direct line to the South American team.

She snuck a glance back toward the bedroom. Then decided to go for it.

She tapped her finger on the screen, activating the link, slapped a post-it note over the camera in the side of the unit. Sat back. Waited.

And watched.

```
FINDING CONNECTION . . .
HOST CARRIER CONFIRMED.
RINGING.
WAITING FOR PICK-UP . . .
```

It was raining.

'Hello?'

The guy in the beat-up brown Panama, wearing a khaki shirt and leather jerkin covered in pockets and bulging with tools and equipment had a rasping voice. He had a feather and a colored woolen twirl around the hat as kind of a head-band, and he hadn't shaved in a week. He was also soaking wet.

The video feed flashed as lightning lit up the sky behind him. Rain poured off the brim. But it was barely distinguishable from the heavy downpour that was gushing past the lens.

Behind him, Sarah could see other members of the team in waterproof nylon ponchos, guns slung over their shoulders. She could see heavy lifting equipment in the forest. Ripped parachutes and cargo webbing stretched over much of it. Poking up into the sky, beyond the leafy canopy and shrouded at the top in rainy mist, were several giant pyramids, covered in plants and vines three or four feet deep. Huge white scars exposed the true surfaces in places where the run-off had washed away looser vegetation.

And she could see too where the Machiguenga Indians had rushed out to meet them. Their reddened bodies were exposed to the elements in ceremonial garb. They had used bows and arrows to defend themselves before being slaughtered. Their torn, bullet-riddled bodies lay discarded on the forest floor.

A knot twisted in the pit of Sarah's stomach. Instinctively she gasped.

The man on the other end of the line was getting impatient now. 'Hello? Rip, is that you?'

He tapped the side of his vid-phone, knocking the picture quality down a notch. A moment later and another face appeared on the screen. She recognized this one as Jack Bulger, one of the company men who'd come to see her in Siberia two days ago.

He took a look at the connection and fiddled with unseen controls.

Only now did Sarah fully comprehend the sheer scale of the dollar signs Rip Thorne was seeing. He wanted to monopolize Carbon 60 to control its distribution, and its price. He was exploring every avenue. And if it meant sending armed squads to the Amazon Basin where there was virtually no government to stop them, then so be it. If it meant ignoring and refusing to pass on information to the government that his own people were giving him, that an earthquake frequency pattern was seriously threatening the survival of the planet, and that this frequency pattern was focusing on those five C60 sites, then so be it too. It was possession of the C60 that was important. That was the goal, not solving a riddle that spanned the planet.

'Rip?! Jesus Christ!' Bulger was turning away.

The other man was whistling sharply, pointing to the bodies. 'Cover them things up!'

Sarah cut the connection quickly. But whoever the other man was on the end of the line, he'd been louder than she anticipated. A groggy Rip Thorne stood naked in the bedroom doorway. He frowned when he saw where Sarah was sitting. She in return kept her nerve. Calmly raised the bottled water to her lips and smiled sweetly. 'Hey,' she said.

'I thought I heard someone calling me,' he muttered, rubbing the back of his neck.

'Yeah, you did. It was me,' she said casually. 'I just wanted to use your vid-phone to call the site. We found a stone plug today, y'know.'

Thorne wasn't happy. 'You got me outta bed for that?'

'No,' Sarah chided. '*You* got you outta bed. A grunt would have done.'

Thorne grunted and crawled back under the covers. She watched after him a while and couldn't quite believe she was looking at the same man. What was he capable of? She glowered, only to jump out of her skin as the telephone rang. She eyed the device nervously for a moment, briefly convinced the Amazon team had tracked her down, before snatching the receiver up in time to stop Thorne stirring again.

Nervously she said: 'Hello?'

'Sarah? You're awake.'

Sarah breathed a sigh of relief. 'Eric, it's you. Whatcha got?'

'You better get your ass down here,' he said. 'We got the plug out.'

Sarah didn't forget the manila envelope, or her phone as she dressed and packed. She put the stacks back just the way she had found them, but left the laptop out. It was then that she knocked a file onto the floor and saw a list of telephone numbers spewed out with the pages. It was a contact sheet for the team in Switzerland – the team which boasted a CIA operative as a member.

CERN: DR JON J. HACKETT – 555 3212
            DR RICHARD SCOTT – 555 4108
            RALPH K. MATHESON – 555 8795
            ROBERT PEARCE – [NUMBER WITHHELD] Contact: R. Adm.
              T. DOWER via the CIA.

She stuffed the list into her purse and put the rest of the file back where she found it. And on her way out she didn't forget to kiss Thorne the way she used to.

She just didn't do it.

ELIGO

EUROPEAN LASER INTERFEROMETER
GRAVITATIONAL WAVE OBSERVATORY

10:06 PM

'The sun as a pulsar? Are you nuts?!'
Corner Station, the ELIGO nerve center where all the lasers, beam-splitters and some of the mirrors for all six interferometers were housed, was frantic with scientists from a myriad of departments all squabbling over reams of information. Desperate, shocked, many were glued to monitors, intent on gathering more data. All wore their IDs on cords around their necks so it was easy to pick out names.

'That's about the size of it,' Hackett replied.

There was direct feed coming in from the Ames Research Center. MIT was on one line while Kitt Peak Observatory was on another. The National Optical Astronomy Observatories at Tucson, Arizona, were keeping a channel open, as were the scientists at Canada's Dominion Astrophysical Observatory. The science community was getting the jitters. Word was spreading fast, and the word was not good. Gravity waves were supposed to be produced by objects such as two black holes colliding, the sheer scale of their mass causing the surrounding space to curve, knot and twist.

Gravity waves were supposed to be a distant phenomenon, not something that happened in your own backyard, being produced by something that theory dictated simply wasn't big enough. *The sun simply should not be doing this.*

The guy with the grinning hair and thick bi-focals was Nick Austin, senior team leader in charge of ELIGO. 'This data means the sun started pulsing out gravity waves nearly twenty years ago. We'd have picked that up, Jon. Have you even checked these figures?'

'I'm aware of the figures,' Hackett confirmed, 'but we're talking about such low-level gravitational shifts you'd need a detector the size of a planet to pick up those kinds of fluctuations. How many of these waves have you registered so far?' he asked Austin.

Austin folded his arms defensively. 'Four waves so far. The last three in the past two days.'

'And what was different about the latest wave?'

'It lasted the longest. And we picked up data suggesting there might be internal variations to the wave. Possibly connected to what we can only loosely call its field strength.'

'Is the wave structure like radio waves? Or more like the field strength of magnetism?'

'Maybe a combination. Look, Jon. No one's ever measured this stuff before. We're all operating on conjecture. At the vaguest level.'

'Excuse me. *Excuse me!* But I've lost my satellite *and* my comet! Do *any* of you people have the faintest idea how badly the gravity wave has warped my section of space?' A blonde woman with sharp features was bellowing. She had star charts in her hands and was circling a section of space with a red pen.

'I dunno! We're still trying to figure out Hackett's data!'

'Contact with over thirty satellites has been lost, Dr Weisner,' one of the scientists spat angrily. 'Nothing makes yours any more special than the rest.'

Pearce scratched the side of his lip as he lowered his voice. Leaned into Matheson as the two men waited: 'Would this many geeks constitute a party?' Matheson didn't answer as he kicked out his foot disconsolately. 'I bet I still end up in the kitchen.'

'Hackett's an asshole!' the woman was screaming.

'It's good to see you too, Michela,' Hackett commented loudly. 'Ah, this is who I was looking for. Hopefully she'll get us to that light computer,' he explained quietly. 'She's my ex-girlfriend.'

'Figures,' Matheson concluded meekly. 'She obviously hates your guts.'

'Honey?' Hackett accosted her meekly. 'I need a favor . . .'

✳   ✳   ✳

Hackett noticed Weisner's finger. It was still very much bare. No ring of any kind. 'Funny, isn't it?' he mused. 'So much in life just comes down to a few lumps of rock.'

'What *are* you talking about?' she snapped irritably.

How could she forget when they broke up? And he stole the ring back just to flush it down the john. They made up a week later. But she expected to see the thing back on her finger at some point. And he had no one to help him sift through the shit in the sewage pipe. He found the ring too, in the end. But the stone was missing. And fifty bucks just wasn't going to replace an antique emerald.

'Look – I've lost Rosetta, my satellite,' she explained, trying to remain calm. 'I don't have time for any shit, Jon. You help me with that, and I'll think about helping you.'

Rosetta was a European Space Agency probe designed to orbit the comet P/Wirtanen and deploy two 5kg probes, *RoLand* and *Champollion*, which would land on the periodic comet and drill into its ice core in search of amino acids, the building blocks of life. Launched in 2003, aboard *Ariane 5* from Kourou, French Guyana, it took nine years to get into position. But during its last elliptic orbit, at an altitude of 500,000 km and at a velocity of 100 meters per second, at precisely 9:18 PM, contact with the probe was lost.

Matheson peered at more data screens, utterly drawing a blank. 'And this works . . . how?' he asked a technician.

'There are six interferometers, or gravity-wave detectors,' the technician explained impatiently, 'that run down two, four-kilometer-long, vacuum-sealed channels. What we do is beam laser light down these channels, them split the light through beam splitters. Bounce the light around using mirrors, then re-combine the light and analyze it.'

'And this achieves what, exactly?' Matheson asked, still none the wiser.

'A gravitational wave alters the light's intensity.'

'That's it?'

'That's it.'

'There's no way on earth you can measure the velocity, the speed and direction of a wave with that kind of set-up.'

'We know,' the technician conceded darkly. 'But tell that to Hackett.'

Hackett was engrossed in a simulated chart of the solar system with Weisner and Austin at a workstation over in one dimly lit corner. Pearce approached them quietly.

'Whether you like it or not,' Hackett was saying, 'these waves *have* to be linked to magnetism. Or at least the magnetic activity on the sun. Nick, this set-up's been operational how long? Eight years? And until this week you hadn't even had a sniff of a gravity wave. Not one. And now, this week – four. Is it coincidence that this week is the same week when the sun reaches the high point in its sunspot cycle?'

Weisner raked her fingers roughly through her long dark hair. 'Jon, you think the sun's going to give you the Grand Unified Theory?' she scoffed.

'The what?' Pearce blurted. He hadn't intended to say anything, and it was obvious Hackett wished he hadn't.

'The Grand Unified Theory, or the Theory of Everything,' Austin said, happy to explain. 'The theory that links gravity, electro-magnetism, and the strong and weak nuclear forces into one simple equation. It's the Holy Grail of physics.'

'And I'm suggesting no such thing,' Hackett said firmly. 'I'm only suggesting where you should look for your satellite.'

He turned their attention back to the screen by tapping his pen on the sun. 'Sunspots are polarized linked pairs on the surface, like a bar magnet. Y'know, north and south? The lead spot matches the polarization of the area of the sun it appears in. So if that area is positive the spot will be positive. The trailing sunspot in the pair will then automatically be negative. As the sunspot cycle continues, the sunspots start to gather around the equator, which in turn rotates slower than the rest of the sun. With me so far?'

'Yes.'

'Good. Now this is important. The magnetic links between the spots interact with other magnetic phenomena under normal circumstances. And the result is an explosion of ejecta off the surface—'

'A solar flare.'

'Right. The best way to think of sunspot magnetism is like little invisible loops, like snags in a sweater, sewn in and out of the surface of the sun. But the curious thing is, in the last week solar-flare activity has actually fallen, while sunspots have increased tenfold.'

'So . . . that leads you to what?'

Hackett rubbed his face and sniffed. 'I was thinking about the original search parameters for ELIGO. Austin, you theorized that a binary neutron star system would be the best candidate for producing gravity waves. As the two stars collided they would become a massive rotating barbell, flipping end over end, at speeds approaching something like the speed of light. Now keep the idea of that barbell shape in mind. But transfer it to the sun.'

'That's a big stretch.'

Hackett dismissed him with a shake of the head. 'Think about it,' he said. 'You get enough sunspots together and they're gonna wind up linking end to end. Negative to positive. They're gonna form a chain, like a daisy chain of independent magnetic units, and this chain is gonna stretch all the way around the equator of the sun like a belt. And all it takes is to be a few sunspots short, and this belt is gonna tighten, pulling the equator in. Squeezing the sun's internal volume out to its northern and southern hemispheres. It would look . . . like a barbell. Its natural instinct is going to be to return to the center. And that action, at its quickest and most temporary level, would be a good candidate for causing gravity waves.'

Hackett slipped a computer disk into the workstation. Punched up his data. 'Okay, now when you figure in the gravitational effects of the planets, their moons, comets and other known stellar bodies like asteroids, you get – well, take a look.'

A simulation of a wave blasting out from the sun played out brightly across the screen. Interaction with planets broke the wave up in places, causing sections of it to collapse in on itself. But eventually a small green cross-hair zeroed in on one section.

Weisner leaned forward. 'That's where you think I'll find Rosetta?'

'Two hundred and fifty thousand kilometers off course,' Hackett confirmed. 'And because it wasn't programmed to expect the fabric of space to suddenly warp, it's looking to re-establish contact with the earth in entirely the wrong part of the sky. We shifted along with it. Everything in the solar system shifted. But from Rosetta's point of view, it's like its whole universe is suddenly a fraction of an inch out of whack. But it hasn't been programmed to recognize that.'

He tapped the screen again. 'That's where your satellite is. Right there.'

Austin and Weisner eyed each other silently for a moment. She had her hand over her mouth as she considered the implications. 'It's worth a shot,' Austin conceded. 'What would it take? A few minutes of communications time to reposition the dishes and take a look. Doesn't sound so bad to me.'

'Sounds bad enough to me,' Weisner sighed. Austin didn't understand. 'Because that would make Jon right. And then I'd have to thank him.'

'You don't have to thank me,' Hackett interjected quickly. 'Just do me that favor.'

She leveled her gaze at him in that way that could only say: What is it that you want from me?

'You still dating that guy who's doing all that top-secret light computer work for the Japanese? Working on those crystals that can store about a terabyte of data on a unit the size of a stock cube?'

'You know I am. You hate him, so why the sudden interest?'

Hackett smiled and pulled out the chunk of C60 like a rabbit out of a hat. Austin looked awestruck while Pearce shifted on his feet, cringing. That wasn't the best idea, in his opinion. Trouble was, Hackett didn't want his opinion. 'Do you think nature can accidentally encode computer-useful information at a molecular level?'

'You want him to scan that rock and see what he gets out of it?'

'Please. It's probably just garbage. I mean, statistically it's gotta be garbage – right?'

'Establish contact with my satellite first.'

It took Hackett ten minutes.

THE WELL SHAFT

Sarah stepped out of the glittering company Land Cruiser to find the blue marquee humming with the buzz of generators and halogen lamps, glowing brightly among the ill-lit monuments. Her ID checked, she made her way through the checkpoints and arrived at the well shaft.

A couple of night-workers were climbing out of the shaft and taking their harnesses off. There was a cool light emanating from the well, flickering as the lights below were obscured by the final Rola Corp. employee making his way to the surface.

Sarah slipped into a coverall two sizes too big, and found she had to roll up the sleeves. She checked the charge on a walkie talkie and hung that on her belt alongside a flashlight, notepad and pencil.

Someone was updating a map on a makeshift table, and Sarah noted the information before taking a final look down the shaft to check the ladder was clear.

She climbed down.

There was a communications pod at the base of the ladder, with a wire running up to the surface. Thick black cables led out from the device and along the tunnel walls which was highly useful – they allowed her to use her cell phone deep underground.

She followed the trail of lights and wires until she came to where the plug had been inserted into a narrower section of the tunnel.

Chains were still buried into one end. Some high-pressure hammer had been used to knock grips into the rock, and the makeshift pulley system was still piled to one side awaiting a packing trunk for its return to the storehouse. There were hooks in the ceiling as well, which meant the chains had originally been attached to a high-powered winch on the surface. But that was long gone.

Luckily when they removed the plug it had stayed in one piece, and it now lay along the side of the tunnel where it would no doubt remain. A note in red paint had been daubed onto its surface: *7.5 feet long. Approximate weight: 30 metric tons.*

The tunnel ahead was a crawl space into what appeared to be some kind of ante-room.

Sarah peered inside first. Called out: 'Hello?' and waited for a response as her voice echoed off the cold sandstone walls. But no reply was forthcoming.

She dropped to her knees and crawled through.

The room itself was circular and very plain. There were two exits up ahead, one on either side. Each exit led to a staircase that spiraled downwards. And each exit was also guarded by a statue.

Both statues were in human form. The one on the left was overtly male, while the other was definitely female. But both also had animal heads in the classical Egyptian tradition. The one on the right, the woman, had the head of a lioness and was difficult to identify, while the male had the long curved beak of the ibis bird and was instantly recognizable. It was Thoth, the Egyptian god of wisdom.

As far as the other one went, there were a number of Egyptian gods and goddesses who bore the face of a lion. Sarah would have to seek advice on who this one was supposed to be. She unclipped her radio and flipped the channel open. 'Eric?' she said. 'Eric, where are you?'

'Sarah!' came the faint excited response. 'I'm down in the tunnels! Where are you?'

'I just reached the ante-room,' she explained, looking at the statues. 'I'm with Thoth.'

'Oh, you're back at the beginning,' he chuckled. Clemmens had to be overtired. The man sounded way too happy. 'Hey, did you bring waders?'

Sarah didn't understand. 'Are you sure I need them?'

'We're below the water table down here,' he explained. 'Trust me. You'll need them.'

'Uh, which staircase do I take to get to you?'

'Doesn't matter,' Clemmens confirmed. 'They both end up in the same place.'

When Clemmens signed off, Sarah radioed to the surface for them to send down a pair of waders. A few seconds later she heard them clatter to the ground as they were unceremoniously lobbed down the well shaft unannounced. After pulling on the thigh-high boots she carefully made her way down the stone steps that wound round in a spiral, descending over forty feet. The lights ended at twenty, so for the rest of her journey she had to depend on her flashlight.

It was dizzying. Disorienting. Especially since she still had a significant amount of champagne in her system. And it was due to a combination of those factors that she tripped over her own feet and dropped her flashlight on the final few steps.

She watched it tumble end over end, bouncing off each step in sequence until it disappeared around the bend and she heard it land with a splash.

'Shit!' she spat. Furious with herself. 'Stupid! Really stupid!'

She hugged the wall and cursed some more. She daren't go for the radio in case she dropped that too. Instead she followed the line of the wall and felt her way with her toe, hoping that the flashlight would still be switched on when she got to the bottom. She found the last two steps were completely submerged in water. She thanked Eric silently. Waders were a good idea.

The steps ended at a doorway that led out to a cavernous room beyond. And under the rippling water ahead Sarah could see her flashlight, its beam cutting into the darkness.

'Thank God,' she muttered, getting deeper into the water and trying not to slip on her ass. 'Goddamnit . . .' The ground beneath her feet was uneven. And though she could sense there was a pattern to it, she couldn't quite figure out what it was. All she knew was that the ground would alternate between higher and lower sections.

When she got to where her flashlight lay, she rolled up her sleeve to retrieve it.

And that's when she heard it. A sound that could only be described as a breath being taken, but on a massive scale. It was followed by silence, and then an eerie scratching, scuttling noise, like a mass of whisper-like clicking. A thousand gem picks tapping on rocks. Or fingernails down a chalkboard.

Hand clenched around the flashlight, Sarah stood bolt upright. 'What the hell . . .?' She whirled around. Sweeping the flashlight over the walls. And couldn't believe her eyes.

She wasn't in a room. She was in a tunnel. But a tunnel like none she had ever seen before. Perfectly circular along its length, it seemed to stretch into infinity in one direction, and arc around a bend in the other. The size of a truck in width, and the same again high, the most distinctive feature of the tunnel was the fact that it was made up of two continuous spirals, like the rifling in the barrel of a gun.

'Good God,' she whispered. 'I've never seen anything like this.' One spiral was sandstone, pure and simple. It constituted the raised portions and was covered in Egyptian hieroglyphics.

The other spiral was indented. And entirely different.

Sarah edged closer to the wall and ran her fingers over the material. It was prickly, like static. And blue. Covered entirely in a language she had never seen before. It was: Carbon 60. Suddenly the scurrying around got louder. Ominous. Then something small and glassy shot across her hand.

Sarah gasped and pulled away quickly. She shuddered. 'What was that?' she asked herself. 'What the fuck was that?!'

She ran the torch across the C60 and was amazed to see the light pulse through veins within the crystal and spiral away from her, as if the light had been trapped.

And then came the next breath, loud and harsh. Not quite like some ancient mummy waking up, but weird nonetheless. She swept the torch beam across the crystal once more. And that was when she found the nest.

She wanted to gag. Every instinct in her body wanted to force her stomach to give up its contents in one gut-wrenching convulsion. But she fought it, clamping a hand over her mouth.

Glassy and transparent, thousands of tiny spiders scuttled and crawled all over each other in a mass of seething alien life. Some shot off when they were caught in the light. Others merely sat there, glistening and twitching. Throbbing back and forth on their tube-like spindly legs as they sensed their new visitor.

How on earth had they survived down here? Kynosynthesis was the surest answer. Like the shrimp, plankton and bacteria that fed directly off mineral deposits in the hydro-thermal vents found all along the mid-Atlantic Ridge, at pressures four hundred times that of the surface, these creatures did not require sunlight at all.

Sarah relaxed a little, awestruck. She couldn't help but smile. What a discovery! She put out her hand and gently stroked one of the glassy spiders on the edge of the nest.

'Hey, there. Hello there, little fella, hey.' And although it went against every instinct in her body, she brushed her finger down one of its legs. Moved the flashlight a fraction to the left. And screamed.

A translucent spider the size of a dinner plate had crept up, intent on inspecting the situation. It tapped one of its forward legs insistently on the cold, hard crystal surface. Then flexed its tensile appendages. These things had to be blind, but Sarah was convinced it was looking at her.

Sarah backed off, nice and slow, skimming the light across the water in case there were more creatures there. She heard a splash, turned back to view the nest and froze in pure terror as the spider flew at her.

She felt the gust of wind accompanying the swift action and almost fainted as the larger crystal-like arachnid landed on her left shoulder, using it as a spring-board to get to the other side of the tunnel.

It landed with a crunch, and casually scuttled away up the passage.

Sarah shuddered and gulped back a breath.

She gingerly unclipped her radio, peered into the inky blackness of the depths of the tunnel and thumbed the channel. 'Eric,' she said shakily. 'Eric, come in!'

A cool, damp gust of air suddenly whipped up past her and rushed onwards round the bend behind her. Sarah brushed hair out of her face.

Then she saw it. A faint glow, like a pin-prick of light in the distance. But getting bigger. Rapidly so. 'What the hell is that?' she murmured. 'Eric, is that you? Eric, there are creatures down here!'

She could hear a whistling noise now, like an approaching train in a city metro system. A rush. And an indescribable feeling of utter inevitability.

'Eric!' she shrieked. 'What the hell's going on?'

And then it hit.

The roar was ferocious, and the light so intense, Sarah could almost see the bones of her hand through her skin. The crackle of energy was unlike anything she had ever experienced. Instinctively she jumped back from the wall as the approaching light entirely engulfed her section of the tunnel. Every hair on her body stood on end as pure energy coursed its way through the spiraling Carbon 60 at the speed of light. The whirling maelstrom of electricity flowed from floor to ceiling and back round again. On and on, following the endless spiral.

Sarah's eyes bulged as it suddenly dawned on her: she was standing in a puddle of water! But by the time she could even contemplate what to do, the energy had already dipped under the water and streaked through the snaking C60 beneath her feet. Sarah couldn't breathe as it felt like every single atom in the tunnel had come to life. Charged.

She shielded her eyes, and it was then that she became aware of a voice hollering through the radio. 'Sarah!' It was Eric. 'Sarah, can you hear me?'

She hammered on the transceiver. 'Eric!' she barked. 'What is this?'

'It's beautiful, isn't it?'

'What – is – this?' she demanded.

There was laughter from the other end of the connection. Followed by abject honesty. 'I have absolutely – no – fucking – idea! But I love it!'

And then as fast as it had arrived, it was gone. Like someone had thrown some giant switch, the energy pulse ricocheted off around the corner and left Sarah standing alone in the dark, panting to get her breath back.

In the silence of the moment she tried to take in what had just happened, but it was impossible. She went to thumb the radio again, but forgetting which hand it was in, she ended up bringing the flashlight to her face. It blinded her and she dropped the thing again. 'Goddamnit!' she spat, fishing around to get it back for a second time. 'Sarah Kelsey, get a grip.' She thumbed the radio this time. 'Eric,' she said. 'Which way to get to you guys?'

'Follow the bend,' he instructed. 'Just follow it around and keep going. Simple,' he said.

After a few minutes of trudging through the water, swinging the flashlight to try and find some kind of exit, she rounded the bend up ahead. It was much farther off than it appeared. And in front she could see that it narrowed upwards into a funnel with the C60 forming a strip in the floor. This smaller tunnel led to a room just a little way on.

She was careful not to slip back down as she climbed the incline. Steadying herself at the top she couldn't help but proceed by planting a foot either side of the C60 strip in the floor. Despite the lucky escape she'd just had, she wasn't taking any chances. She didn't want to be electrocuted. Up ahead she could see lights and movement. And at the edge of the tunnel, where it connected to this new room, she noted that the sandstone changed abruptly to a much darker color. The color of granite.

'Good morning, gentlemen,' Sarah announced as she entered. She jerked a thumb back at the tunnel. Breathless, she said: 'That was incredible! What did I just experience?'

Eric shone his flashlight over at her. 'God knows – literally. I mean, it's been going on for thousands of years right beneath our feet. We've been down here an hour and it's happened like, what three?' He looked to Douglas. 'Three? Four times?'

Douglas shrugged. 'Four times.'

'It's incredible. How far back does that tunnel go?'

'What we measured – and this is a conservative estimate – comes to over eleven, maybe eleven and a half miles before it dips down, deeper into the ground, and out of our radar range. And it's in a straight line, heading exactly due east.'

'Eleven and a half miles?'

'At least. And on the other side of the ring there are two more.'

The room was heptagonal. It was thirty feet high and definitely manmade. It had an exit on every other facing wall, which from Sarah's perspective, meant one way in, and three new ways out. She eyed the ceiling. Eyed Clemmens. 'We're somewhere under the Sphinx,' she said.

'Atta girl,' she heard Douglas comment from somewhere else in the darkness.

'What have you found in here, Douglas?' Sarah demanded. To which a couple of obliging flashlights redirected themselves to show her.

Directly in the center of the room was a huge, square-based pyramid, made entirely from a single crystal of Carbon 60. At least 10 feet high, and perhaps 15 feet across the base length, the mono-lith must have weighed close to 200 tons.

Suspended by a stone armature, it touched neither the C60 strip in the floor beneath Sarah, nor the strips that extended from the ceil-ings of the other three tunnels.

'What is that?'

'That,' Douglas explained proudly, 'is about a hundred million dollars in revenue.'

'Look,' Clemmens added, beckoning her deeper into the room, 'in these alcoves. These look like tools.'

Sure enough there were recesses all over the walls. Each recess contained an object, every one very different from the next. The workmanship was intricate but also very plain. They looked decid-edly un-Egyptian. 'What are these?' Sarah quizzed.

'Beats me.'

'So what's the plan?'

Douglas slapped a palm on the Carbon 60 pyramid. 'We get this thing, all several tons of the sonofabitch, out of here.'

'How?' Sarah asked in all seriousness. 'Take a look. You'll never get it out the door. And besides, we've got nothing in Egypt that can lift this kind of weight.'

Douglas patted the set of pneumatic drills propped up next to him. Big, sturdy and greasy. 'What d'you think we brought these for?' he twinkled.

LIGHT COMPUTER SCIENCE DIVISION

CERN, GENEVA

They tracked down the guy named Harvey, in the light computer center. Michela Weisner seemed to like driven men who didn't require any sleep. Each made their own terse introductions, light on pleasantries, heavy on formality. Harvey fumbled with his electronic pass before sliding it through the reader and unlocking the heavy vault-like black door.

'Now this isn't show and tell,' he announced sharply. 'You want access to this room, you keep your mouth shut, okay? I'm just doing this because Mickey asked me to. Now what is it you want me to put into my scanner?'

Hackett pulled out the C60, and within seconds Harvey was escorting them inside. Following on behind Weisner's confident stride, Pearce tugged sharply at Hackett's elbow. 'You sure you should've gotten that out?'

'Excuse me?'

'The rock. Are you sure it was a good idea to get it out and show everyone? Dower's gonna be pissed. Have you told Dower? He would never have cleared that.'

'No, I haven't told Dower. They way I figure it, Bob . . . *you're* here. And that's as good as.'

There were white bio-suits hanging on hooks. Lockers where they could put their shoes and other belongings. Harvey instructed them to get changed and led them through to the air-lock. 'My equipment's very sensitive,' he explained. 'We can't have a contamination of more than four parts per billion.'

Hackett was surprised. They must still be in some kind of experimental stage.

'This is a Class 100 clean room – though we keep it cleaner than that. Just to let you know, a particle three millionths of an inch across can ruin $75,000 mirrors in here. All they have to do is make a scratch that you won't even be able to see under some microscopes and the show's over. There's enough grease on the end of one of your fingers to ruin a whole batch of components, so please . . . be careful.'

He led them into the air-lock, closed the thick chunky door behind them and ran the routine to cycle the air. 'There's enough air in your suit for two minutes. Once I give the signal and we're clean, you can hook yourself up to the overhead oxygen-supply in the next room.'

'I guess I can't smoke then,' Matheson added smartly.

No one found it funny.

The lab was a sprawling mess of wires and units, exposed ducts and lights. Everybody had to be careful to make sure their overhead air hoses didn't get caught up in it all as they picked their way through.

Every two years for the past sixty, Harvey explained proudly, computers had become twice as fast while the components they were made from had become twice as small. So by 2012, two major changes to computing were emerging. Firstly computers had begun to operate, albeit at a rudimentary level, on a quantum scale. Systems were being built that could calculate an infinite number of answers to a hypothesis. But to be able to do this effectively meant utilizing computing powers that operated at speed. So the old lithographic technique of printing circuitry on boards was reaching its limits. But to date, no one had successfully answered the second question: When would computers run at the speed of light?

Harvey was one of the few scientists dedicated to meeting the challenge of storing information at the atomic level. And it meant the only thing that could read that kind of information was a laser.

'We started off working with hydrogen,' Harvey explained, 'for simplicity, since it only has one electron. I decided an atom in its ground state, that's when the atom's electron is at its lowest possible state, would represent "zero". Then I chose a higher energy state to represent "one". So by determining what state the electron is in you get a one or a zero. That's how I built up the binary system at the atomic level. You can change over here.'

Their air hoses had reached their limits. At an intersection between the benches dangled a whole other set of air hoses. They unhooked and changed over, one by one.

'But atoms have various energy states,' Hackett pointed out as they took a turn past more benches littered with hardware. 'Many shades of gray. You're not limited to binary.'

'Small steps, Jon, small steps. The equipment isn't limited to binary, but I am. When *I'm* more confident we'll move on. And besides, the programs we use can already read most types of mathematical base structures. I just chose binary as the encoding system.'

'Can you use any type of atoms to encode on?' Matheson asked.

'Theoretically we could encode water, but we're way off that. At the moment it's easier to limit ourselves to crystals. Actually, we tried a home-made version of C60, but a gram cost us over a thousand bucks so we ruled that out pretty quickly.'

'What're you using now?'

'I can't tell you that, but we did use common salt there for a while. We got it to work using pairs of neighboring ions. Plus we found using binary was good for error correction.'

'But salt dissolves,' Matheson interjected. 'You get some high-school kid tipping their Coke into the machine and you wind up losing your whole system.'

'Don't worry, we realized that. So anyway, Jon, Carbon 60. Pretty exciting stuff. Sixty carbon atoms held together in thirty double bonds. That's one hell of a stable structure.'

They arrived at a bench housing a device that appeared to be some kind of re-jigged electron microscope. On the wall behind it, tucked inside a sealed airtight glass frame was a dog-eared poster of Neils Bohr's famous model of the insides of an atom. It looked more like the solar system, with negatively charged electrons whizzing around a positively charged 'sun' of protons and neutrons. It was an incorrect concept by today's standards, but it still looked cool.

Harvey ejected the subject housing and held out his hand.

'Gimme.' Hackett passed over the Carbon 60 rock and watched as Harvey gently lowered it into the harness. Keyed the system to retract.

'What are you looking for? Any particular pattern?'

Hackett took a deep breath as he eyed the data screens. *System engaged. Seeker active. Commit when ready.* He wished he didn't have this hood on, or this visor blocking his connection to the device. He watched the laser bounce off the surface of the rock, creating sparkles, like fire-flies in the night.

'Beauty is truth. Truth, beauty,' he murmured. Nobody got it. 'Keats,' he told them. 'Entropy is the disorder in a system. So ice forms from water because the temperature falls. But C60 turns entropy completely on its head.' Harvey still didn't get it; Weisner did. She obviously still remembered he had moments like this. 'No particular pattern,' he said finally. 'Just take a look.'

Harvey keyed: *Enter.* The system whirred into life. Servos angled mirrors and the laser light searched. On the screens the structure of the C60 molecule rotated, a series of pentagonal and hexagonal facets bizarrely resembling a soccer ball, the pentagonal facets being key to the molecule's curvature.

Pearce too, watched the screen in awe. 'In *Timaeus,*' he said, 'Plato outlined cosmology in terms of solids. The earth was a cube. Fire was a tetrahedron. Air was an octahedron. And water an icosahedron. The dodecahedron he connected with the "ether" that enclosed the universe. *Timaeus,*' he explained, 'is the same dialogue in which he talks about Atlantis . . .'

Weisner ripped the first set of results off the printer.

	RN9	Z03	QD	QS	QP
SC	0	1	0	0	1
FA	1	0	0	0	1
LA/2	ERROR	0	0	0	0
LA/1	1	1	1	ERROR	0
AH	1	0	0	0	0
BINARY PATTERN NOT DETECTED					

'Garbage,' she said. 'Pure garbage. There is no binary code. Okay, debt repaid. Can I go now?'

'Honey,' Harvey pleaded in a whiney voice that served only to irritate, 'I'm not done, okay?'

'Fine,' Weisner replied, upset. It was obviously far from fine.

'Let's go up to decimal—'

'Actually,' Hackett interjected, pulling his air hose for more slack, 'we can go to base six next?' Harvey asked why. 'Well, there are six electrons in carbon. That's all. It's just a hunch.'

Harvey punched in the commands for the scanner to search for a base six pattern etched into the crystal.

	RN9	Z03	QD	QS	QP
SC	ERROR	ERROR	ERROR	ERROR	ERROR
FA	0	3	1	ERROR	4
LA/2	3	0	1	4	5
LA/1	6	6	5	6	4
AH	ERROR	ERROR	ERROR	ERROR	ERROR

SEXENNIAL PATTERN NOT DETECTED

'Bad luck, Jon.'

So they looked for another number base. That they didn't look for decimal straight off was never questioned. It was only in the last 100 years that base ten was widely used as the basis for counting in most cultures. Mathematically it wasn't even that efficient. With only three factors, or numbers by which it could be divided equally – 1,2 and 5 – it was limited. Duodecimal, or base 12, once the basis of the Imperial system in Britain, had five factors – 1, 2, 3, 4 and 6. It was so effective that part of the system had survived through to the twenty-first century: eggs were still bought by the dozen and screws by the gross. However, both of these, decimal and duodecimal, also drew a blank.

As did hexadecimal – base 16 – and vigesimal – base 20, a number system once used by the ancient Mayans. With 1, 2, 4, 5 and 10 as its factors, 20 was also the minimum number of carbon atoms that could form a closed cage structure – a smaller version of Carbon 60 called C20.

And so it went. Until the results spewing off the printer read line after line: *Error free.*

** **DETECTED** **

** **DETECTED** **

Hackett had to check it again. Harvey turned from his monitor. 'Confirmed,' he said. 'It's no mistake.'

SEXAGESIMAL PATTERN ** **DETECTED** **

'Base 60,' Hackett explained, realizing the full implications. 'Oh, my God.'

'Setting the system to decode in base 60,' Harvey said, tapping away on the keyboard.

'You knew,' Weisner scolded.

'I guessed,' Hackett replied. 'I didn't *know*.'

Pearce checked the readings again and suddenly it clicked. 'Base 60. It's the oldest number base ever used,' he blurted. 'The Sumerians first used it six thousand years ago in Mesopotamia.'

'We still use it,' Matheson added, 'for measuring time. Hours, minutes, seconds. Base 60 is the perfect system for measuring fractions and proportions.' It had eleven factors. 1, 2, 3, 4, 5, 6, 10, 12, 15, 20 and 30.

'Why didn't I think of it before?' Hackett snapped. 'I gotta call Richard.'

Harvey jerked his head up from the screen. 'Shit!' Everyone gathered around. Numbers were amassing on the screen.

'What the hell is that?!'

'I dunno . . . but it's in your crystal, Jon. Written at the atomic level.'

'Jesus Christ, I've really gotta call Scott,' he gasped.

But the line was busy.

BERTIE'S HOTEL

ROOM 101

'Who is Thoth?'
        Scott rubbed his face. Trying to wake up. There was the sound of a cigarette being lit on the other end of the line. A puff.

'Be right with you!' he said, and swung his legs out from under the warm duvet and pressed his naked feet onto the cold carpet. Slipped on a white cotton T-shirt. Licked his hand, smoothed his hair down. Picked sleep out of one eye and thumbed the video portion of the phone-call to kick in on the terminal on his bedside.

Scott didn't really know what to expect, but finding an absolutely stunning brunette on the other end of the line, with a smile to die for, and an attitude that said: *It doesn't matter what I do, you're still gonna fall in love with me,* just wasn't on his checklist. He swore his heart missed a beat. Felt foolish. Could she sense that over the vid-phone? He coughed and sniffed. Tried to wake up with some dignity.

She let the moment settle. 'Good morning, Dr Scott. I'm Sarah Kelsey.'

'Good morning, Miss Kelsey.' Well, she certainly appeared warmer than when they spoke earlier.

She smiled and seemed to relax a little. 'I think I'd prefer it if you called me Sarah.'

'Okay, Sarah,' he said, trying to focus. 'What was the question?'

Sarah smoked her cigarette. Cautious. 'I got your fax – the

translation of that inscription. Who is Thoth, exactly? I know he's an Egyptian god, but I don't have time to read a book.'

Scott shook his head. More alive now than he had been. 'You got the plug out, didn't you!'

'Among other things.'

Scott switched the bedside lamp on. Collected his thoughts and plowed on in. 'Thoth,' he told her, 'is the Greek name for the Egyptian god Tehuti, or Djewty. He looked like an Ibis bird, or sometimes a baboon. Thoth was the god of wisdom and learning; the keeper of the sacred archives and repository of all knowledge and creative intelligence. He was custodian of the truth. Legend has it he taught art, the sciences, arithmetic, geometry, surveying, surgery, medicine, music and writing.'

'Smart guy.'

'Well, he *was* a god,' Scott joked right back at her. 'He was the oldest son of Ra, the sun god, and was associated with the moon and time. He could cure illness through the power of speech which he did when Horus was a child and got bitten by a scorpion. It is said he had knowledge of divine Speech and knew the "hekau".' Sarah frowned. 'Words of Power,' Scott explained quickly. 'He hatched the world egg by the sound of his voice alone.'

Sarah took another drag on her cigarette. 'I see.'

He sat back on the bed. 'Some of the legends might sound familiar to you because there's a lot of stuff that was taken and put into the Bible by people who knew ancient Egyptian better than we do. The Ten Commandments come directly from the *Book of the Dead*, from *The Purging of the Guilt*. Only in that, it's a series of confessions; "I have not committed murder . . . I am pure". But in the Old Testament it's a series of orders; "Thou shalt not commit murder". It's essentially the same stuff.'

Behind Sarah, flashlight beams were slicing up the darkness, making Scott peer forward for a better look as she asked him: 'Is Thoth a solitary kinda guy? Or was he ever seen in a pairing with someone else?'

Scott thought for a moment, still intrigued by what was going on in the background. 'Well, uh, he sometimes had a wife, Seshat, or Seshata, goddess of writing and history. Other texts say he had a consort, Maat, the goddess of truth. Where *are* you?'

'And what did they look like?'

'Maat was either a seated woman with an ostrich feather. Or just the feather itself.'

'What about the other one?'

'Seshat? She was a woman in a panther skin, with a seven-pointed star headband and bow. She was involved in the foundation ritual of "Stretching the Cord".'

'Which was?'

'Beats me. Some astronomy ritual, I don't know.' He was really distracted now. The lights were busy. He could see glints of blue, and sandstone. Tunnels and figures. 'Look, I hate to—'

'That's really odd then.' Sarah revealed. 'He's never been seen with some lion woman?'

'Never.'

'Then who the hell is this?' She shifted the camera on her end of the line and focused it on a towering statue of a lioness-headed woman, with a huge sun disk on her head.

Scott recognized instantly what he was being shown, though she wasn't seated. She clasped a feather in one hand, a bow in the other. A reminder of Thoth's real romantic links. But this was a new woman in his life. This was Sekhemet.

'Who?'

'That's Sekhemet,' Scott said clearly. 'Her name means "She who is powerful". She represents all that is aggressive in the female. She was the daughter of Ra, the sun god. She's Thoth's sister. She is war. Violence. Destruction. The goddess of demolition and renewal.'

'Must be a real party when this family gets together.'

'In tomb scenes Sekhemet is seen spitting fire, a fiery glow around her body. As the daughter of Ra she is the "udjaut" – "The Eye of Ra" literally – she represents the scorching destructive power of the sun,' he said. 'But I've never seen her depicted like that before. Sarah, where *are* you?'

'Would you believe, under the Sphinx?'

'Actually,' Scott said, rubbing the back of his neck, 'yes, I would.' A roar erupted on the screen coming from somewhere behind Sarah. For a moment it sounded like a chainsaw. 'What the hell is that?'

'Motorbikes,' she said simply.

*   *   *

Headlights dipped, illuminating the rippling water. Throttles revved and pumped every so often with the flick of a wrist as the three beat-up dirt-bikes sat poised for take-off. Clemmens secured the last of the fastenings on his black crash helmet before rolling the bike off its stand. As he waited for the large box of tricks he was taking along to be fastened securely to the back, nothing could hide his impatience, especially the familiar throttle action of a man waiting at a set of red lights.

Sarah waded on over with some trepidation, careful not to trip on the irregular flooring. Up ahead, Rola Corp. employees carried out their duties in hushed astonishment. They'd found extra cabling and run lights down as their first priority, which helped Sarah as she picked her way across.

'Eric!' she called out in an effort to compete with the din. 'You all set?'

Eric pulled his gloves on. Nodded. 'We got a signal. Looks like a huge C60 deposit on the edge of our range.'

'What are you doing?'

Eric looked around, confused. 'Who said that?'

Sarah indicated the head-mounted vid-phone she was wearing, like a pair of spectacles with the arms protruding from behind her ears, but no lenses. Two tiny bulbs at each end of the arms did the business. One projected Scott's image directly onto the retina of Sarah's left eye, while the other served both as a microphone and a camera, able to watch Sarah, while tracking her eye movements and zeroing in on what she was seeing as well.

'Say hello to Dr Scott!' Sarah said. 'He's working over in Switzerland!'

He leaned in close to Sarah's face and waved. 'Hello!' he cried.

Sarah rang her ear out. 'Eric!'

'Oh, sorry.'

'Are you sure riding motorcycles up the inside of those tunnels is a good idea?' Scott inquired. 'Those are ancient structures. They might be weakened. All it takes is one slab of limestone falling on your head and that'll end your trip real quick.'

'He'll be careful,' Sarah said, watching Clemmens's tired red eyes and knowing that natural enthusiasm had its limits. 'Won't you?'

Clemmens mapped out his plan, having to shout over the din of the engine. 'We looked at the data again. This tunnel follows the natural curvature of the earth. Our natural horizon on flat ground is 11 to 11.5 miles.'

'So you think the tunnel continues on past the radar data?'

'That's about the size of it. If we get to the eleven-mile marker and get a reading of another eleven miles dead ahead, then we know we're dealing with one hell of a tunnel!'

'If that's the case,' Scott advised, 'the ground is going to dip out from under the tunnel. There are hills, and there are valleys. At some point you should find the tunnel opening out to the surface.'

'That's what we figured too,' Clemmens agreed.

He checked his equipment and pulled his visor down. Gave Sarah a nod and eased the throttle out. With a roar he led the other two bikes off into the darkness, bumping unceremoniously over the alternating limestone ridges and splashing up water.

Sarah watched them go, watched their lights grow smaller as the bikes plowed on. All the while she saw those lights she knew they were safe. She turned her attention back to Scott, who appeared eager to learn more about what she was up to. 'You got a pencil and paper ready?'

The epigraphist looked inquisitive, like a little boy lost. He was idealistic and innocent in many ways, this Richard Scott character, but by the same token he had an underlying maleness. He was the type of guy you fell in love with at college, then shat upon, for a moment of wow with some worthless toad. He was the type of guy Sarah always regretted not dedicating more time and effort to.

'You might want to start taking notes,' she suggested thoughtfully.

'Woah, woah, woah! Back up! Back up!' Scott yelped, realizing a little belatedly that it was going to penetrate deep into Sarah's ear.

She was making her way along the edge of the walls of the tunnel, where the inter-connecting spirals of limestone and Carbon 60 were covered in hieroglyphs. She ran the camera along the glyphs as slowly as possible, but still it was too fast for Scott at times.

'This is incredible,' he gasped. 'It's like finding the Rosetta Stone all over again!'

'What does it say?'

He scribbled frantically with a pencil. 'I have absolutely no idea,' he admitted. 'This isn't like picking up a newspaper for me. I've been dealing with Aramaic for the past two years and I'm gonna need to doublecheck some phrases. The Egyptian stuff, at any rate.'

'Is it a translation of what's written in this other language?'

'Could be. Hey, stop, stop, stop! Right there!'

'Where?'

'Just – just stay where you are. Okay. That's good. Give me a moment to jot it down—'

Suddenly the connecting bedroom door burst wide open and November Dryden marched in, looking resentful. Dressed in a long cotton night-shirt, she carried a vid-phone, similar to Scott's, over to his table and dumped it next to the other one.

'Did I wake you?' he asked sheepishly.

'No,' November growled. '*He* woke me.' She flipped the vid-phone on and the anxious face of Jon Hackett popped onto the screen. His expression lit up when he saw Scott on the line.

'Richard, Richard! I've been trying to call you—'

'I've been busy.'

'I can see. I can tell. We've all been *very*, uh, busy.'

'Hello?' It was Sarah, Scott realized, on the end of the other vid-phone. She'd moved. Damn.

'I was just trying to write that down!'

'You can do it later,' Sarah said impatiently. 'We got it all on video. I'll upload it to you. Is that the Amazon team on the other line?' she asked innocently.

Scott was caught for a moment, genuinely puzzled, while Hackett started conferring with the others on his end of the line. There was genuine bafflement. 'Sarah, I'm sorry,' Scott said. 'Did you say there's a team in the Amazon too?'

Sarah smirked, as if to say, 'that old trick'. 'I'm sorry,' Scott said earnestly, 'I have absolutely no idea what you're talking about. This is the first I've heard of this, and frankly I'm annoyed.'

She could hear someone else in the background demanding to know about this other site. Scott never flinched, never gave that customary tell-tale sign she was used to seeing from men like Thorne.

Not quite sure what to do, Sarah was on the move. 'We need to talk,' she murmured.

✻   ✻   ✻

Hackett tapped his camera for attention. Scott looked to November. She was always good in these sorts of situations. 'Do you have any idea how to connect everyone up into a conference call?'

November rolled her eyes. Like that was the dumbest thing she'd ever heard. 'Of course,' she said, and began to fiddle with the equipment.

Sarah stopped in her tracks. She had to steady herself as the image on her retina changed. 'What's going on?' she demanded. 'Goddamn, I wished you'd given me some warning.'

Floating translucently at eye-level now, right in front of her were two images. Richard Scott in a hotel bedroom, and a darker guy, with curling lips.

'Well, hello again,' the darker guy said smoothly, oozing overwhelming charm. 'This is a pleasant surprise.' His voice had a little reverb to it. A by-product of the conference call.

'For you maybe,' Sarah replied, checking her position a few short steps away from the rise up to the chamber that housed the tools and megalithic crystal. But she had no desire to go there just yet. Carefully, patiently, always alert to the possibility she may have been led into a loyalty trap, Sarah explained what she knew about the Amazon, about China, and about seismic activity.

What she didn't expect was to find unity in her thesis, with the physicist.

'So it *is* possible,' Sarah reiterated, 'the sun's been pulsing out gravity waves for years?'

'It's not only possible,' Hackett warned, 'it's the likeliest scenario. Gravity-wave detection is a totally new science. It demands refinement. I'm sure gravity-wave detectors a hundred years from now will be like our communications are to valve-operated wirelesses a hundred years ago.'

'If there'll even *be* a hundred years from now.' Hackett didn't comment. 'So how big would a detector need to be to measure tiny gravity waves? Would, say, the size of a planet be about right?'

'At least. The earth's the greatest measuring tool we have for studying its effects.'

'Have you heard of an oscillation phenomenon known as the Tesla Effect?' Hackett thought for a moment. Yes, he had. 'I have earthquake data which may tell us how long this has been building up here on earth,' Sarah revealed, solemnly explaining about all five ancient sites being the focus for the low-frequency seismic waves. 'I think it gives a pretty accurate picture,' she said.

'Of what?' Scott asked, finally managing to get a word back into the conversation.

'Of how much time we really have left,' Sarah said flatly.

Hackett was back in the NMRS lab at CERN. Matheson and Pearce were close by, poring over the raw data that was being pumped into their workstation direct from the light computer center. The other chemists had gathered around to watch while Hackett shifted in his chair to accommodate them, all the while doing his best not to gawk at Sarah.

Matheson sketched out what he'd been told on a scrap of paper, and didn't like what he saw. He looked around, snapped his fingers. 'Anybody here got a globe?' No reply. 'An orange?' Somebody loaned him a lemon. Matheson didn't like to ask, just went to work with a magic marker and sketched on a map of the world over its surface. Then marked in the five sites with thick black dots. There was a definite geodesic design. He showed it to Pearce.

'Richard, you asked me before, what is the *use* of quantum mechanics? Well, this is it,' Hackett said to Scott in the meantime. 'This is what quantum mechanics just did for us. Unlocked *quantum* cryptography. Code. Language. Information. Encoded at the atomic scale. It's all right here. I've found it! Written in base 60 mathematics, within the Carbon 60 crystals.'

'You're telling me there's computer code? Etched into the crystal?'

Matheson leaned and hi-jacked the call. 'A whole lot of it,' he said, holding up the fruit for all to see. 'I really gotta get a globe,' he complained.

Scott jerked his eyes off the screen. Was this some kind of sick joke? The only linguist on the team and when two pieces of the puzzle had just surfaced – he wasn't within arms reach of studying *either* of them?

'Sarah? Did you hear that?'

'Yeah. Hold on, will ya?'

Scott looked to November for a reality check. Were things moving fast, or what? He went back to the phones. 'Jon, can you give me more – Jon . . .?' But Hackett was looking at something off screen. Off screen meant the other screen. Sarah. She was climbing up into some sort of room and—

Hackett saw it first. 'That's one hell of a paperweight.'

There were packing crates littered around the chamber, wooden and sturdy. Reference numbers were daubed on the sides with stencils and black paint. Straw filled each container, making them appear rustic and somehow out of place. In each one were being placed the hand-sized artifacts that once sat in the alcoves dotted along the walls. Lids were hammered into place with severe blows.

Sarah checked one of the containers, picking up one of the artifacts, which was like a tool of some kind. Untried and untested. She checked the documentation that went with it, trying to drown out for a moment the excited scientists on the other end of the line.

'What *was* that?' Hackett was saying.

'I don't know. I can't see. She keeps looking at those – things. What are they?'

'It doesn't matter,' Sarah mumbled. She checked the docket in a sealed plastic bag on the side. It was bar-coded, like a Federal Express pouch. Everything was being shipped to Texas.

She ripped the docket off. Stuffed it in a pocket and slapped her own documentation in its place. *Destination: Antarctica.* Judging by what Thorne was up to, she'd rather study these things herself than let them disappear into Rola Corp.'s vast and faceless research division. She had found these artifacts; they were hers. She leaned back from the crate as two Arab workmen retrieved it. Hauled it up and carried it off.

She did the next two in succession before Douglas called her over.

'Ah!' Scott exclaimed, finally getting a better look at the pyramid-shaped obelisk of crystal.

'Sarah, we're going to attempt to move this now,' Douglas announced. They'd set up chains and winches as well as hoists and a cradle for the crystal, should they ever get it out of the stone armature, but there was a stone overhang nearest the wall. It was impossible to get at it properly where it was. It would have to be moved closer to the three crystal beams that came in on the ceiling from the three smaller tunnels.

Douglas pushed at the armature. 'This thing lets us slide it out to the center,' he demonstrated. 'It's fairly easy. Takes a couple of people, that's all. Must be one hell of a counter-balance the other side of this wall. Anyway, once it's in the center we figure if we drill or hammer into it, one on each surface, we might be able to compensate for no laser and knock some chunks off. Once we weaken it we can destroy it, and take the pieces home.'

'No, there's a problem,' Sarah said. 'These crystal beams – they slope down at an angle. I think they're supposed to connect with the pyramid somehow. There's not much room for maneuver.'

'Let me worry about that,' was Douglas's response.

'What happened to our prototype field laser anyway? Should have brought that.'

'No idea,' Douglas replied. 'They told me it was being used.'

Scott was mortified. 'You're going to destroy it?'

'I wouldn't worry,' Pearce added on the other line. 'It'll never work. They won't even dent it.'

Beneath the C60 pyramid was where the spiraled tunnel's own crystal strip came into the room across the floor and terminated by diving directly into the floor. Sarah made as thorough an inspection of the set-up as she could, to allow everybody on the phone time to digest what they were seeing, but it didn't take a physicist to figure it out. 'You're right,' Scott sighed, relieved. 'It'll never work. There's not enough room.'

'I know,' was all Sarah said.

Douglas did a double-take before it dawned. 'Oh, you're on the phone. Thorne?'

'Something like that.'

Douglas waved in her face. 'Hey, Rip!'

The retinal image of Scott and Hackett glanced at each other across the inside surface of her eyeball. 'Who the hell is Rip?' Hackett asked. Matheson swore in the background.

'You know what the crystal is, don't you?' Scott said excitedly. 'That's the benben stone. People have searched for it for millennia.'

November sidled up to him on the bed. Handed him a coffee. Scott could feel her warmth through her thin cotton night-shirt. 'What's the benben stone?'

Scott, coffee in hand, ran his finger over the outline of the crystal. 'That.' He sipped his coffee. 'The benben stone sat in the city of Heliopolis, the City of the Sun. Some say it represented the "Primeval Mound", where life began. The first place, some say, where civilization settled after the Flood. Others say the benben stone was the petrified semen of the sun god, Ra. It's supposed to hold mystical powers.'

Hackett went to open his mouth. 'I don't know what kind of powers,' Scott chipped in quickly. 'Where the stone sat in Heliopolis was believed to be where the sun's rays first fell each morning. In honor of it, on top of each pyramid, a gilded capstone was placed. But the original benben stone, the one from Heliopolis that was later placed on top of Cheops's pyramid – well, it disappeared.'

'Benben derives from the word "weben", meaning "to rise". It's from that word the Egyptian benu-bird comes, the original Phoenix-the bird that rose again from the ashes. The benu-bird literally represents the sun – destruction and re-birth.'

Hackett was mulling it over on the other screen. 'To rise . . .' he said slowly. 'I wonder if that bears any relation to the hole in the ceiling above the stone . . .?'

Sarah suddenly took her flashlight out and waved it at the ceiling of the chamber. She hadn't noticed that before.

'Well, I'll be damned,' she said.

Bob Pearce didn't know where to turn next. He had a choice of screens and on each one something new and wondrous was unfolding. But the string of computer data was paling against the tangible sights of the catacombs beneath the Sphinx. And the benben stone to top it all.

Pearce started muttering to himself, excitedly. Louder and louder. Attracting attention, but still nothing compared to the discoveries being made.

'In the ninth century, Ibn Abd Alhokim, an Arab historian, and later an Egyptian Coptic called Al Masudi, both spoke of ancient wisdom that said the Great Pyramid was built by an Egyptian King called Surid, or Salhouk, who lived three hundred years before the Great Flood. They said that there was a connection to Leo, and that this King had all scientific knowledge deposited into a place of safety, with strange beings placed by priests to serve as guardians and stop the knowledge falling into the wrong hands.'

Matheson came up alongside him. Concerned. 'What type of beings?'

Pearce shrugged. 'I don't know.'

Matheson glared at him. 'Bob, what're you talking about?'

'I'm talking about history being proven correct yet again. I'm talking about . . . the vision.' His voice faltered in his throat. 'The vision that I had. That chamber. It's exactly as I saw it . . .'

But no one was listening. Something else was concerning Matheson. He crouched down beside Hackett and watched the spectacle as Douglas led a team of men and swung the huge crystal pyramid out towards the center of the room.

'What do you think?' Hackett asked warily.

'I think,' Matheson said quietly, watching the crystal move, 'that's a very bad idea.'

Hackett eyed him.

'Look at the way the room's laid out,' Matheson said. 'Look at how the crystal beams there are going to connect with the pyramid stone and the beam in the floor. We know what this stuff can do, Jon. A damn satellite picked it up under two miles of ice. What if this is what the Chinese did? Look at them – they're creating a circuit. If they want that thing out of there, they better find another way of doing it because that whole room looks like a piece of machinery.'

Hackett rubbed his hand over his chin, disturbed. It was so obvious. 'Yeah,' he agreed, 'I think you're right.' And that was when the alarm on his wristwatch went off. He eyed Matheson darkly. 'The sun . . .' was all he said.

Sarah kept quiet as she listened to the discussion batting backwards and forwards. A giant machine? What were they talking about? And what on earth were 'The Guardians'? She didn't like the sound of that. 'What kind of guardians?' She rapped out, 'Are you saying there are some kind of creatures down here?'

Pearce went to answer but the crackle and hiss of static interrupted. Her radio was cutting in.

'Sarah. Come in. This is Eric, over.' He sounded faint. Perplexed. Distracted even.

Sarah fished the radio to her lips. 'Yeah, this is Sarah, go ahead.'

A pause. Then: 'We're at the eleven-mile marker. We're just setting up now.' A hiss. More static. A muffled noise. 'Boy, this is weird.'

Sarah could feel the hairs on the back of her neck stand on end. She'd never felt comfortable down here, she didn't want to be down here. Hesitantly she asked: 'What's weird?'

A moment later, partially cut out: 'The, uh, writing on the wall stopped a couple miles back.'

'What have you got now?'

'Looks like circuitry.'

Sarah had to think for a minute. 'Say again?'

'Circuitry,' Clemmens repeated. 'And these massive Carbon 60 structures. The size of houses. But – *woah!*'

'Eric?' But he wasn't responding. She got nothing.

Just dead air.

ELEVEN-MILE MARKER

It was like being inside a convoluted fist, Clemmens decided. All fingers interlocking. Each finger a massive expanse of Carbon 60. And this fist was clutching a lightning bolt. Energy was coursing throughout the C60 as if caught in a bottle.

Right where they needed to be, the tunnel opened out into some kind of chamber that was made up of interlocking swathes of C60, intercut at junctures by two-story-high oblong megaliths of horizontal layers of glowing carbon and darkened granite.

On the other side of the chamber the other two bikers had set up their laser-sighted radar packs. And one of them, Rinoli, had taken the opportunity of jumping straight back on his bike to do a lap of the chamber and race the energy wave that pulsated around the chamber walls. It moved faster and faster, but never diverted into the spiraled tunnel toward the Sphinx.

'It's like it's trapped,' Clemmens explained before realizing his radio had stopped working, he just couldn't get a signal to transmit. He hung it on his belt, concentrated on getting his relay gear switched on and sending his data back to the computer set up at the entrance. He prayed the data made it.

All set, he rode out to the other biker, who stood like a speck at the foot of the entrance to one of two other massive darkened tunnels. The air was damp, the cavernous surroundings cold and eerie. There was a breeze coming from somewhere, accompanied by a harsh breath-like sound. Rasping.

Clemmens didn't like it here, that much he knew. He pulled up alongside Christian and dismounted from his Beta Trials bike. It was a 250cc, single cylinder. Good with rough terrain and less to go wrong than some other bikes.

Christian operated his radar unit deftly. Used his flashlight to show what he meant when he said: 'They're both the same, these tunnels. They both slope down at about seven degrees in a straight line.'

'Any idea on length?'

'Yeah. But this can't be right.'

'Try me.'

'Three hundred miles. One goes north-east. The other goes south-east.'

'What?'

'Each one's filled with water. And take a look – see?' He moved his flashlight along the walls of the tunnel. 'No spirals. No nothing. Definitely no more Carbon 60.'

'Are these things wells? Do they just bottom out?'

'Uh-uh. They change direction. Got a profile on this one. But where the hell it goes is anyone's guess.'

The buzzing of the circling motorbike behind them was really starting to grate on Clemmens now. He spun on his heel, bellowed: 'Rinoli! For chrissake mind your equipment! Quit foolin' around!'

Rinoli reluctantly zipped up to the other flooded tunnel, cussing in Italian all the way. Clemmens licked his lips and tried his radio again, but he still couldn't get a signal.

'Just make a note of all this, will ya?' Christian nodded as Clemmens tapped the radio again. 'I think it's this place,' he said. 'Something's causing interference. I'm going back to the edge of the chamber, it seemed to work fine over there.'

Christian watched him as he kicked his bike back into gear and rode across to the spiraled tunnel, all the time acutely aware of the mysterious energy pulse still making its way around the walls of the chamber.

Rinoli keyed his radar unit. Took another reading and relayed it over to Clemmens's unit.

And that was when he heard it.

A low deep rumble, almost out of his auditory range. He doubled forward, craning into the darkness ahead and trying to make sense of the noise.

There was a hiss. A plop. Bubbles were rising to the surface of the water. The rotten egg stench of sulfur filled the air and then there was the light: a small point. Fuzzy. Dim. In the center of the water. Far away, but getting bigger.

Rinoli couldn't help but smile at the aquabound fire-fly. What was that? Another one of those whirling firework shows? He loved those. He turned, and in his excitement, called out in Italian to warn everyone. Which, as it turned out, was entirely the wrong language if he wanted to be understood.

Clemmens, his engine ticking over, heard Rinoli's calls, but didn't listen. He fiddled with his radio, determined to get through. 'Sarah? Sarah, come in.' But the only thing getting louder was Rinoli.

Clemmens jerked his head back and to one side, growling: 'What's that wop bitchin' 'bout now?'

He wasn't normally a prejudiced man. But it was a pity to utter that kind of sentiment when there was a fair chance they'd be his last words.

'Ion,' from the Greek meaning 'traveling'. Moving water, especially superheated water, carried an electrical charge, and liked to give up this charge just as easily.

Without warning, the water behind Rinoli suddenly reared up like a geyser, disintegrating into a boiling twister of vapor and spray. The torrent exploded from the tunnel and blasted the Italian across the chamber. The energy that came with it, all light and arcing electricity from deep down, shot out like daggers, connecting with the walls of the chamber and spinning around the room at the speed of light.

The whole place lit up for one brief moment, as if God had just taken a snapshot. And as Rinoli fried in the center of the room, convulsing on the ground, Clemmens could do nothing but let his jaw drop as the superheated water swirled around the chamber as if it were alive. It collected on the ceiling and around the walls at a colossal rate, forming into a vast hollow ball that filled the room and writhed. The noise was deafening, like being trapped on the insides of a jet engine.

And then it moved. Heading directly for Clemmens, and his spluttering motorbike.

They were getting ready to drill into it, the benben stone, when the call came in. A technician on the surface was watching the monitors when the tell-tale signs of another energy wave registered. Douglas's radio had crackled to life with: 'Brace yourself. Got a live one comin' through.'

But before Scott or Hackett even had time to think to ask the question, rippling energy had shot up the crystal spiral in the tunnel and was ricocheting around the benben chamber.

Douglas sensed immediately that this one was different. It wasn't dissipating like the others had done. It wasn't shooting down into the floor like the last time.

The benben stone was just inches away from the C60 beams arching down from the ceiling. Douglas instinctively snatched his hands off the crystal, and motioned for the others to step away.

The air became electrified, pungent with the smell of burning dust. Sarah could feel the building static charge creep across her skin and start to levitate her hair.

Then Douglas had a change of heart, because the light in the room had suddenly highlighted something he hadn't even noticed before. Something vital. A hairline fracture through the benben stone. His eyes widened. He gritted his teeth. 'That's it!' he roared. 'Let's do it!' He lifted his drill, hauling it into position, and pulled the trigger.

'What's going on, Sarah?' Scott asked, awe-struck by the sheer magic of the energy wave.

'This uh happens all the time,' she explained nervously, looking to Douglas for support. But it was clear that *this* had never happened before.

A low hum vibrated through the granite, followed by a high-pitched whine. Then another. And another. The artifacts in the wooden crates were coming to life. Two Arab workmen who were carrying one of the crates suddenly dropped it in fright. Screamed and fled into the darkness as the wooden packing case splintered and the vibrating object spilled out onto the floor and bumped its way along. The three other drill operators suddenly stopped what they were doing, petrified. Leaving Douglas to continue by himself.

Sarah backed up against the wall. But that only made matters worse for her as she realized it was throbbing. Undulating like solid rock should never do.

'This doesn't look good,' Matheson said as he leant in close to the screen. 'That crystal shouldn't be close to those three – things.' He exchanged another look with Hackett, who took a deep breath and put his mouth right up to the microphone on the vid-phone.

'Sarah,' he instructed, 'I think you should try and push that stone away from those connectors.'

'What?!'

'Push the stone away from those crystal beams.'

November had her hand over her mouth as she watched Sarah approach Douglas in his attempt to tackle the crystal. But Douglas leant forward, putting his back into his drilling, not listening to a word Sarah was saying. And that was when Sarah felt it.

At first she felt light-headed. Then incredibly heavy, as if she were sitting on a roller-coaster.

Douglas was equally stunned. His entire face seemed to warp for a moment, stretch out of shape and snap back. It was as if, in an instant, reality had decided to take a raincheck. Sarah's stomach heaved. She was going to be sick, she knew it. 'Did you feel that?' she whispered.

In Geneva, Scott nodded. Swung Hackett's phone line around. Hackett, Matheson and Pearce were all pale on the screen. 'I know,' Hackett said. 'We felt it here too.'

'Was that an earthquake?' Matheson was asking.

Hackett's eyes were darting around the ceiling. The building was starting to shake. 'No,' he explained, 'but this is.' Equipment clattered to the ground behind him.

'A gravity wave?' Scott queried.

Hackett nodded his agreement. 'The biggest one yet, for us to be able to perceive it.'

Scott shifted his attention frantically back to Sarah. But already her situation was changing.

Lightning bolts shot out of the Carbon 60 strip in the floor, arced to the benben stone, then shot down the hole directly beneath it. Seconds later a rod of pure blackness rose from the hole in its place and clamped itself into a recess that had gone unnoticed on the underside of the benben stone.

Douglas fought against it, but no amount of human effort was going to overcome that kind of force. He dropped his drill as a tantalizing shard of Carbon 60 broke off from the benben stone and skittered across the floor, covered in rippling energy. Douglas shot out a hand in an attempt to reach it.

Utterly terrified, Sarah blinked back tears of pure panic as she screamed: 'Leave it! Leave it!' but Douglas either couldn't hear, or wouldn't.

The whole room distorted for a moment, like a picture on a sheet of rubber. Sarah felt her gut tumble end over end as white-hot shafts of electricity blasted out of the stone and connected with the beams overhead.

She could smell burning, charring flesh, could hear the sizzling and popping of fat under somebody's skin. Could see Douglas being exploded back across the chamber as the device in the center, the stone, assembled itself and activated.

She was aware of the images being projected onto her eye. And the voice, urgent in her ear. 'Get out!' it said. 'Get out now!'

Sarah followed her instincts without question. And ran for her life.

THE FIFTH WAVE

For in the sky the stars and Orion will shed their light no longer, the sun will be dark when it rises, and the moon will no longer give its light . . . I shall make . . . human life scarcer than the gold of Ophir . . . I am going to shake the heavens [and] the Earth will reel on its foundations, under the wrath of Yahweh Sabaoth, the day when his anger ignites.

Isaiah 13:5

GIZA

'Apocalypse' from Greek meaning, 'to uncover', 'to reveal'.

Well, it had been revealed and quite honestly Eric Clemmens wished it hadn't. Soaked through, he could feel his body cooking away under his coveralls. He caught a glimpse of himself in a side mirror. His bloodied, blistered skin hung from his face in puffy sheets. This went beyond third-degree burns. He had to get out of there. Pain or no pain, there just wasn't time to scream.

He shifted down a gear in an effort to boost his speed, but the torrent of boiling water that had swept him from his bike had flooded the tunnel ahead to such an extent that the going was difficult. Every so often he could feel the back or front end of the bike slide out from under him, forcing him to ease off.

Behind him, Christian was in an even worse state. One eye blinded, he throttled back and went for it. But when the tunnel seemed to warp and twist, neither man could be sure of their senses. They wobbled, stayed upright.

But stability was the least of their worries. Because in their mirrors, larger than life, glowing like the ferocious, fiery tongue of a dragon, came crashing forth a second tumbling, chaotic spew of fire, electricity and seething water.

Pulsating past them in violent energy bursts, light streaked through the Carbon 60 spiral, swirling in a chaotic pattern that served only to disorient them further.

And that was when Christian finally panicked. Kicking yet more speed out of his machine in a bid to outrun the impending flow, he locked a brake and twisted the front wheel – and found himself shooting off at an angle. Caught in one of the spiraled ruts, but afraid to reduce speed, he found himself rapidly rising up the side of the tunnel at over 100 miles an hour.

He jerked at the handlebars, trying to jump the front wheel over the lip of limestone, but it was no use. He was already too high. He could feel the weight of the bike on top of him, and that helpless sense of falling.

Clemmens plowed on, bumping his way over the ruts of undulating stone. The hot breath of sheer fury snorted down his neck. A blinding light was in the mirrors, a blast furnace of heat on his back.

He was aware of it gaining. Catching him. Matching his every move. He was aware too of some event taking place at his periphery and rising sharply. Steeply.

He looked up. Saw Christian crashing down on him, and closed his eyes.

It was just a twisted heap of metal when all was said and done. With two half-full gas tanks, which exploded in a frenzy as the raging torrent of destruction engulfed it and rocketed down the tunnel.

Ahead of it, the pool of water that was collected along the floor of the tunnel parted, as if Moses were paying a visit. Crept up the walls like an honor guard, using the spirals as tracks and formed a watery tube through which the chaos could travel much faster.

Sarah stumbled. Recovered. Leapt out of the benben chamber and lost her footing again. Sliding down the incline she collapsed in the water, which was sheer luck in the end because spears of jagged energy were blasting out above her head. Searing and frying everything in their path.

The water collected on the floor of the tunnel was warm, and getting warmer. She picked herself up and ran, but the sloshing around was harder work than she remembered. The water level was deeper, and rising fast. She stuck to the sides where the depth was shallow and ran as fast as she could, rounding the bend just seconds later and pushing on towards the exit.

The portable lights flickered, crackling as the power supply dipped, interfered with by the ever-increasing electrical charge. She could see the exit just ahead, just a few excruciating feet away. She climbed the curvature of the tunnel wall, and that was when she realized: the water was climbing with her.

Not rising, like a tide, but climbing. Lifting itself from the floor and slithering up both sides to the hissing, popping sound of ice in a cold glass of lemonade.

'Sarah!' She snapped her head around. It was Douglas. She had no idea how he'd made it out. His hair was glassy, melted onto his scalp. He stumbled towards her, clutching his pathetic prize: the Carbon 60 shard. But the growing rumbling sound coming from the other direction also demanded attention. Sarah didn't know which way to turn.

She thrust a hand out at Douglas. 'You can make it!' she screamed. 'You can make it!' But the wall of water was already creeping up over her waist level.

It was now or never.

She jumped through to the exit stairwell, landed heavily on the other side, but had the foresight to turn it into a roll, taking some of the energy out of the impact.

Scrambling to her feet she shot around to face the tunnel and watched, stunned, as the water rose up past the doorway and wrapped around to join with itself on the other side.

Yet it never leaked. Never spilled so much as a drop in her direction.

She ran to the doorway and peered out. Douglas was just a few feet away. But the tunnel was getting brighter, much brighter.

Sarah bellowed: 'Douglas! Get your ass in here!'

That seemed to shake him up a little, but not enough. Tripping over his own feet, he was either too shocked, or too stupid to realize he was actually walking *on* the water. Stumbling to the doorway, the searing heat of the approaching fireball growing at a seering pace, Douglas threw an arm over his eyes as Sarah shot a hand out to grab him – and nearly broke her fingers in the process.

The water was hard as crystal.

The helpless look on Sarah's face was enough to send Douglas into a panic. Lunging for the exit he found himself smacking into a wall of glass. He balled his fist, hammered on it, but it barely made a thud. 'Help me!' came his muffled cries. 'For God's sake! Help me!'

And then she saw it. Though she had to look twice because she could hardly believe it.

A hand was jutting out of the water. Perfectly formed with four fingers and a thumb. Human in shape. It clamped itself around Douglas's ankle and began its relentless task of pulling him under. Translucent and sparkling, it looked like crystal, yet moved with absolute human dexterity.

Douglas struggled but the sheer brute strength of the hand was overwhelming. He staggered, and collapsed to his knees as a second hand appeared and lifted out of the water on an endless, jointless arm. And prised the C60 shard from the man's greedy fingers.

There was nothing Sarah could do but watch as the impending juggernaut of fire hit. In the blinking of an eye, everything was gone.

The water wall creaked and shuddered, as the ceaseless funnel of rage thundered past.

She didn't know if it would hold. She didn't want to stick around to find out.

She spun on her heel, and ran up the flight of spiral stone steps as if they didn't exist.

On the surface she was met with stunned expressions. Stunned, *silent* expressions. No one wanted to know what Sarah had seen. They had their own problems to deal with, and they were many.

She could feel a pressure on her chest. It was difficult to breathe. The air had turned to syrup. It made her want to cough.

She could hear shouts and cries, and an eerie hum. She stumbled out of the marquee, making her way to the main encampment. The arc-lights flickered on and off, making her pause every so often in her stride. Several times she had to pull up short before slamming into something, a generator, rubble, a fence. The changing brightness never gave her eyes time to adjust, so it was a welcome relief when the lights finally blew, spitting glass at passers by.

There were hushed whispers. The sounds of sobbing. The ground shook and the humming sound that was ever-present, grew until it became a rumble.

She spotted a geophysics marker move first, an aluminum pole that was hammered into the ground, pinpointing where the three-mile circular tunnel was situated. She watched it shake before launching into the air over 50 feet, then clattering to the ground and clouting an unsuspecting soul around the ear. She saw the next one pop. And the next. Anything that didn't belong in this sacred ground was being suddenly and violently rejected at an alarming rate. Fences. Poles. All were tossed into the air.

And then came the glow. A menacing blueness that cut through the sand as if it wasn't there and traced the circular tunnel in deliberate, perfectly timed pulses. Rapid. Constant. Expectant.

Sarah could hear herself breathing, a labored rasping as it caught in her throat. She could feel a tingling sensation. A sparkling. The sort of thing that accompanied an almighty thunderstorm. And that was when she realized she was swamped in sand, surrounded on all sides by particles of dust that clung to the air, suspended as if hanging in some sort of laboratory solution.

The ground shook. A trembler that paid scant regard to anything that stood on the surface. Like cutlery on a snapped-back tablecloth, Sarah fell to her knees. Heard loose material clatter from the pyramids, bouncing off every step as they tumbled.

And as she checked herself for cuts and grazes, she picked up a stone to discard. Only to discover that its physical make-up was actually changing. For though it looked like a rock, it felt more like plastic.

There was a zapping sound now. A high-pitched shudder, like something ripping through the ground. And then she heard the call. Someone had seen something. She twisted around to see a rippling layer of lightning erupting across the surface of all three pyramids, like blue electric eels in a feeding frenzy, spitting and coursing over the vast expanses of limestone blocks, swirling and writhing. Blackening the surfaces, and working their way up, to collect in waves at the peak of each monument.

The buildup was constant. The lightning balls on the peaks illuminated the whole Giza plateau. The accompanying noise was shrill, earsplitting. And the culmination equally awesome.

For suddenly, three vast and formidable columns of energy,

perfectly straight, and immaculately formed, shot up into the sky. One from each of the three peaks.

Like cannons aimed at the heavens, the three pyramids loosed their vicious arsenal, and screamed in primal victory. They had awakened, after millennia of slumber. And their wrath was considerable.

THE EARTH

W hen it came, it came suddenly.

12/03/20 04:02:48 36.32N 71.00E 252.5 5.0Mb B AFGHANISTAN-TAJIKISTAN BORDER

There was no warning.

12/03/12 11:02:49 38.24N 26.64W 10.0. 4.6mb B AZORES ISLANDS

Despite the Solar Heliospheric Observatory, SOHO III, ACE and the
CLUSTER II solar-observing satellites; despite numerous terrestrial-
based solar observatories and a multitude of seismometers places at
strategic points along faultlines; in spite of Deep Sea Tsunami Sensors
that measured 12–15,000 foot columns of water above their positions, detecting changes in sea level to the nearest millimeter:

12/03/20 03:03:12 57.33N 119.81E 10.0 4.7Mb B EAST OF LAKE BAYKAL, RUSSIA

Despite all that, the gravitational wave that blasted out from the sun,
traveling at the speed of light, warping and twisting the fabric of
space as if it were a sheet of elastic, could only be measured in retro-
spect. By accumulating the data of what it destroyed. By amassing
the results of so much carnage.

12/03/20 13:04:33 54.03S 132.18W 10.0 5.6Mb C PACIFIC-ANTARCTIC RIDGE

12/03/20 10:06:43 39.57N 140.31E 118.8 5.4Mb A EASTERN HONSHU, JAPAN

12/03/20 18:06:12 31.10N 87.30W 10.0 3.7Lg ALABAMA

12/03/20 01:07:33 57.78N 152.33W 33.0 3.7Ml B KODIAK ISLAND REGION

In the Bay of Bengal, winds were whipped up. And though they barely lasted a minute, they traveled so fast, over 700 miles an hour, that they overwhelmed whole regions of India, destroying towns and villages before they could even be heard arriving.

In the Urals, seismic waves plowed through the tundra at over 13,000 miles an hour. Yet the ground was wet this time of year, soft from thawing. And the farmers could see their furrows undulating like rumpled blankets on a trampoline.

In Canada, Alaska, and on the coasts of Chile, Japan, Hawaii and South Africa, large run out landslides were triggered, so powerful the masses of tumbling rock traveled more than thirty miles in places, acting like fluids in a process called liquefaction. The debris moved up slopes and around bends, just like liquids should. Except in the case of Hawaii, where the run-out of debris, which included 20-ton boulders, rocketed out for over 500 miles. This, coupled with the accompanying earthquake, triggered a tsunami – a giant tidal wave that was so powerful that it caused a vacuum along the sea bed and imploded rocks to such an extent that it gouged out huge grooves the size of submarines in an instant.

Across the Pacific the tsunami roared, stretching from the sea floor to the surface, hundreds of miles wide and tens of thousands of feet deep. It surged across the ocean faster than a jet plane. When it reached a point 200 miles out to sea, an uncharacteristic subduction zone earthquake increased the wave's power and doubled its length.

Off the coast of Northern California, a supertanker somehow survived the onslaught, despite the intense battering and the fact it was carried eighty nautical miles closer to shore. As the wave finally washed over its bow, the captain had the foresight to radio a warning to the Coastguard. His crew gathered on deck, terrified, because they could see the lights of the nearest streets and houses twinkle through the wall of water as it raced off toward shore.

On land, they hadn't seen a tsunami since 1964. Over 2,000 people scattered along the beaches, stood on the sand and watched the water get sucked out to sea in seconds, leaving shoals of fish and assorted marine life beached. By the time they spotted the wall of water rearing up ominously on the horizon it was too late. Because there was one important rule of thumb to remember about tsunamis: if you were close enough to see one coming, you were never going to outrun it.

Despite undersea mountains changing its direction, and despite the shallow Continental Shelf creating friction and slowing the wave down, the trailing waves piled into the first, one after the other, like a rug crumpling against a wall. The resulting wave reared up a further 10 feet, hit the beach and wiped out everything in its path. It delivered 100,000 tons of water for every five feet of beach. It exploded concrete buildings. Tore men, women and children limb from limb, and piled inland for a further forty miles.

In the Philippines, Mount Pinatubo was erupting, oozing volcanic mudflows into the panic-stricken valleys below. While in Alaska, a Boeing 757 passenger plane on final approach to Anchorage International Airport lost all power as it entered what it thought was a layer of haze. It turned out to be volcanic ash, thrown up by Redoubt Volcano, part of the rumbling Aleutian volcanic chain.

The plane eventually crashed. There were no survivors.

Every year there were reports of approximately fifty volcanic eruptions around the world. Ten of these caused death and serious mayhem. Tonight, there were thirty-seven separate volcanoes raging across the planet at once, twelve on American soil. Of those twelve, five were on the Middle America trench, while the rest were on the Aleutian trench. And together they could be seen from space. For tonight, the Ring of Fire, a series of volcanic arcs and oceanic trenches which encircled the Pacific Basin, was ablaze.

It started in New Zealand. Went north via the Tonga and Kermadec trenches. Followed the equator with the Bougainville and Java-Sunda trenches. It was a little-known fact that volcanoes were found mostly in chains, and very rarely as singular one-off phenomena. But tonight that fact could hardly be avoided. One by one, the most volatile volcanoes blew along the chains. The Ryukyu and Izu Bonin trenches, which led across to the Aleutian trench in Alaska, smoked and rumbled. At the Peru-Chile trench where the

Ring of Fire ended, villages were being evacuated as the lava flows advanced.

With the force of God's vengeance freely on loan, Mother Nature rallied her armies, and began the systematic shredding of human civilization on earth.

SCOTT

It wasn't so much the creaking from the walls that got to Scott first, or the way his coffee bounced across the bedside table. It was his bed. For as he sat there trying to decide what to do, it became startlingly obvious that it was sliding out from under him.

He jumped off, instinctively, just as the rumble of shaking concrete got louder. He could hear the panic and screams from adjacent rooms. The standard lamp across from him crashed to the floor, its bulb exploding in a shower of glass.

November yelped, and threw herself into the middle of Scott's bed. And that was when he saw it. A fissure, deep and black, opening up across the bedroom floor. The carpet moaned under the strain as the remaining strands of pile failed to halt the advancing crevice in the floor. Each thread pinged one by one as the floor covering was ripped in two.

'November!' Scott yelled, holding his hand out to her, but she just stared at it blankly as the bed bumped its way along and just hit the wall below the window.

'Dr Scott!' she shrieked.

The glass light fixture smashed down from the ceiling. On the vid-phones Scott caught a glimpse of the pyramids on one screen, firing energy bolts up into the sky. On the other screen he could see Hackett and the men and women of CERN dodging falling equipment and spitting power arcs, before eventually both lines went dead. The vid-phones eventually clattered against harder surfaces.

The fire alarm erupted. Loud and metallic, as the window behind November's head succumbed to the pressure and disintegrated, blown inwards as harsh, freezing winds blasted the glass into the room. It was only the heavy drapes, drawn across the window, that saved the young girl's life by taking the full force of the blast. They stopped her from being shredded by the surgically sharp daggers of glass.

She clambered out from under the thick heavy sheets as ceiling plaster crumbled. Dazed, she had no idea just how fast events were overtaking her as Scott plowed in. Snatched her off the bed and dragged her away in time as the floor collapsed, taking the bed down with it into the room below and beyond.

'Oh my God, what do we do?'

'We get out of here!' Scott yelled, squeezing her hand and dragging her to the door.

Trouble was, it was jammed.

'We can get out through *my* room!' November said, thinking quickly and leading the way.

They really weren't prepared for earthquakes in this part of the world. At least, not at this intensity. That much was painfully obvious as the pair dodged more falling plaster. But there was no way out from November's room either, and they were running out of options.

'Clear the closet,' Scott ordered. 'I'll get the mattress.'

Within minutes they were huddled together, as safe as the situation allowed, under a mattress. Awaiting their rescue.

CERN

Hackett ducked his head back in under the table as another half-ton steel component whistled past and left a crater in the concrete floor. He looked to the others who were crouched down with him, tried half a smile. But only half. 'Well,' he said. 'This is fun.'

Matheson pulled his legs in tight. 'That was a dry run? Shit, if that's what they got in Egypt, what the hell kind of thing can we expect in Antarctica?'

'Worse.' Hackett was certain. 'Much worse.'

'We don't really have many options against this type of thing, do we?' Matheson croaked darkly.

'Sure we do,' Pearce said, crawling up next to him to allow Hawkes room to huddle into safety with them. 'Ain't no such thing as an atheist in a foxhole.'

'Huh?'

'We can pray.'

The scientists may not have liked it. But at least it was an option.

THE SACRED PLACES

Sunset in the Amazon wasn't normally this exciting, Bulger figured. But then this was his first visit, what did he know? Except the trees, 10 feet across, some of them, interspersed with Acetic and Corozo Palms, Coco de Monas and Divedives, shouldn't be swaying like reeds. The ground shouldn't be shaking uncontrollably. The floodwater along the forest floor shouldn't be draining off into underground fissures, while the vegetation across the surfaces of the pyramids, thick and moist, shouldn't be bursting into flames. But it was.

The light from the sun seemed to visibly flicker, like a candle caught in a draught – when it wasn't obscured by thick angry cloud, which pelted down raindrops like bullets.

They'd assembled their base camp and equipment when the chaos struck. So panic-stricken were the remaining Machiguenga, they fled from their hiding places and made off into the jungle. Some chose to stay and fight, and for the first time Bulger got a close-up view of one of the fearsome painted warriors as he sprang from behind a tree, baring his incredible array of razor-sharp teeth he'd proudly filed himself.

They struggled for a moment, the Machiguenga biting down into Bulger's forearm, before Carver put a bullet in the back of the Indian's head.

Maple, for his part, stood in the clearing, eyeballing the sky in a bid to outstare God. Though he had just as much difficulty standing upright as anyone else, he seemed determined to ride out the trembling ground like a rodeo star on a bucking bronco.

Maybe they should have known it was coming when the jungle went eerily quiet moments beforehand. But the screams from the wildlife were deafening now, and as dead wood trees crashed into the clearing around the camp, the biggest surprise of the evening was revealed.

Holes in the ground.

Massive and deep, cutting into the mud around the bases of the pyramids. To begin with no one was sure whether they were ancient traps, or uncovered entrances, but Carver was quick to bring his skill to bear, stumbling over to one hole and setting up his equipment.

As mud slid down into the pit, it took him a moment to calibrate, compensating for the gushing rain. But when he did and the results blinked onto the mini-screen, his face lit up. 'Carbon 60!' he hollered. 'Directly below! And leading all the way up into the pyramids!'

'Fuckin' A!' Maple yelled back, stuffing tobacco into his mouth. 'This is gonna be easier than I thought!' He quickly directed the others to the machinery that was packed together under wet tarps. Earthquake or no earthquake, they had work to do. 'Radio the choppers!' Maple ordered. 'Tell 'em they may as well head out here now. We'll be trawling this stuff outta here by morning.'

Bulger nursed his arm as he set up the communications and Maple's men attached some kind of hi-tech canon to a tri-pod with a *Rola Corp. Research* logo on its side. They ran cables from its back to a generator, just the way Bulger had taught them, and awaited the signal.

'Okay!' Maple ordered. 'Fire her up!'

They flipped the power on. Aimed at a tree and pulled the trigger. There was a screaming whine. A blinding flash. And the most powerful particle beam ever created for portable use, twisted and sliced its way through the air, evaporating the rain in its path in a cloud of hissing steam, and blasting the tree trunk to splinters. Whoops of excitement shot around the encampment.

Maple gave the thumbs up. 'Shit yeah!' he cried. 'Now get down that fucking hole and start carving up our C60! We're getting paid by the kilo. And I intend to retire!'

They were achieving precisely what they had set out to do. They had found the ancient lost Peruvian Pyramids, had identified their contents, and were looting at their leisure.

But as they lowered each other down into the slippery, muddy pits by rope, and began slicing into the ancient crystal structures – spirals up long tunnels – what they could never know, was that by agreeing to dismantle the Carbon 60 monuments of Pini Pini, they had made one of the worst decisions of their lives. Certainly, it was going to prove one of the most devastating.

EXPEDITION

The essential feature of complex behavior is the ability to perform *transitions* between different states . . . Complexity is concerned with systems in which evolution, and hence history, plays or has played an important role in the observed behavior.

Gregoire Nicolis and Ilya Prigogine *Exploring Complexity: An Introduction,* 1989

EN ROUTE

'It was a hand! I'm telling you, we *saw* a freakin' hand!'

'There was an awful lot of signal degradation when that power burst kicked in,' Houghton objected frostily. 'There's no telling what you saw.'

'We saw something that was *alive*,' Pearce warned. 'Trust me.'

The lawyer shrugged, unwilling to argue. He went back to his notebook.

They were in the back of the Ford People Carrier. Flinching as wave after wave of golf-ball-sized hailstones hammered down in a ferocious assault on the vehicle's rooftop, accompanied by sharp cracks and bangs as the ice exploded on impact, shattered across the paintwork or skipped off onto the tarmac. It was like being on the receiving end of a constant barrage of machine-gun fire.

Hackett nursed a deep cut across one cheek as he rested against the glass and watched the world stream by, while Scott shifted in his seat. 'I wonder how Sarah's doing?' he muttered. 'Did anyone manage to get back in touch with Cairo?'

Houghton didn't look round from his paperwork. 'We're working on it,' was all he said.

'I hope she's okay. I hope everybody's okay.'

'Five times on this planet,' Hackett grumbled, stirring, 'life has virtually been extinguished. Almost wiped out. At the end of the Cretaceous Age, the Jurassic Age, the Triassic and the Permian

Age. Now, watch out, folks. Here comes the end of the Space Age. Great.'

Bob Pearce, who was sat a row in front, turned on him. 'This is nothing to joke about. This really is the end of life on earth.'

'I didn't say the end of life,' Hackett smirked. 'I said a virtual extinction. There's a difference.'

Up ahead, Dower and Gant rode in separate cars in the tinted glass, military cavalcade. Hackett watched them swerve in and out for a moment.

They crossed the Port du Mont-Blanc cautiously, aware that Lac Léman was still in a vitriolic mood. Across the lake, around which Geneva stood, the famous Jet d'Eau, a manmade geyser that usually squirted a mast of water 150 feet into the air, had fizzled to a 10-foot trickle. Meanwhile the hailstorm rained chunks of ice into the water causing it to froth up in response.

Passing by the cracked and torn Église Anglaise, and the shaken Gare de Cornavin, the main train station, they turned right, speeding up Rue de Lausanne and swerving to avoid masonry and fallen rooftiles.

Everywhere they looked there was structural damage to the buildings. Geneva had been hit hard.

'At the end of the Permian Age, 286 to 245 million years ago,' Scott recounted, 'eighty percent of all life was destroyed. *Eighty percent.* Trilobites gone. Fusulinids, huge Iguana-type creatures, gone. The three main dominant types of reptile: Cotylosaurs, Pelycosaurs and Therapsids – all gone. It was the most destructive end to any period of evolution known to earth. Yet we're still here . . .'

'Maybe extinction events are God's way of denying evolution exists,' Hackett commented mildly.

'The death of eighty percent of all life on earth *is* the end of life,' Pearce moaned.

Hackett scratched around. Lifted the Etch-A-Sketch November was doodling on, out of the girl's hand, said: 'May I borrow this? Thanks,' and held the doodle up for all to see.

'This is the earth, okay?' He pointed at the doodle. 'And this is all life on earth.' Pearce nodded. 'A gravity wave hits—' Suddenly Hackett shook the Etch-A-Sketch violently, erasing everything on it, much to November's surprise and annoyance. 'Okay. What have you got left?'

'Nothing!' November said crossly. 'Nothing. Everything's gone.'

'That's what I'm saying,' Pearce exclaimed.

'Uh-uh,' Hackett chided, tapping the cheap plastic Etch-A-Sketch firmly. 'You've still got this, the earth itself. With all its constituent elements and its ability to nurture. And in time . . .' He twiddled a knob and started the tiniest new doodle. 'In time – life will flourish again. Except this time it will be in a new way. A new combination. The deck will be shuffled and the building blocks will be reassembled. But this time it all takes place – without us.'

He dumped the Etch-A-Sketch back in November's lap. 'Thanks,' he said, without even a hint of sincerity.

She glanced down at her missing masterpiece. Nursed the graze on her arm from the night before and said thinly, 'Great.'

'No, it's not the end of life we need to worry about,' Hackett declared. 'It's the end of us. The end of the human race. *Life* will take care of itself.

'Why'd you think environmental activists are so important? Okay, so *they* delude themselves into thinking the preservation of some cute fuzzy creatures in the Amazon creates some kind of emotional bond with the earth. But what they're really doing is maintaining the food chain. By maintaining the food chain, evolution remains stable; the environment reaches equilibrium. And why is *that* important? Because the current environment is the *only* environment in which we, as a species, can exist. Three million years ago we weren't around and the environment was different. You want to save something because it's cute? What's the point? None. No, you preserve the environment because it preserves *us*. And to do it we have to go against the laws of nature. We have to become – *un*natural.' Hackett chuckled. 'Nature *is* infertility. Nature *is* genetic disease. Nature *is* famine and pestilence. Nature *is* weather patterns more severe than we can imagine. Nature *is* change.'

'In the Book of Isaiah,' Scott chipped in, 'God clearly states that he is both good *and* evil.'

Hackett and Scott eyed each other warily. Were they actually starting to agree on something?

Up in the front passenger seat, Houghton shifted in his chair. He slung an arm over the back of it and turned to address everyone in the People Carrier.

'Are these figures correct?'

'Yes,' Hackett confirmed, referring to the mass of differential equations he'd passed over. 'The sun will hit its main nutzoid zone midnight Saturday, right on the cusp of two holy days. Which Sabbath do *you* use?'

Houghton looked sheepish. 'Actually I don't much go in for religion.'

Hackett forced eye-contact. Let a smile touch his lips, but it never did quite make it to his eyes. 'Might wanna start,' he advised.

Houghton coughed. Rubbed his temples. 'This is, uh, pretty frightening. I had no idea this was all so real,' he confessed.

'I've run the figures a hundred times.' Hackett sounded weary.

'That number stream from inside the crystal?'

'No,' Hackett answered dismissively. 'Not that. I haven't got a clue what *that* is. No, I've been running the numbers Sarah gave me on seismic wave propagation – the Tesla Effect. By my calculation, the peak of the sun's gravitational waves will occur one hour and fifty-seven minutes before Sarah predicts the final geological event will hit the earth and snap the carpet out from under us. In other words, it will take approximately eight minutes for the gravity wave to travel from the sun to the earth at the speed of light. It will then hit us, causing an already increasing resonance within the liquid core of this planet to increase out of control. It will take, by her figures, one hour and forty-nine minutes for the wave to pass throughout the planet and rebound back again. By which point the damage will be irreversible.'

Scott hunted for moisture in his parched mouth. 'When's the final event?'

'Three a.m.,' Hackett said. 'This Sunday.'

'In two days . . .'

Hackett nodded. 'At just after midnight the sun will pulse for the last time. By three o'clock Sunday morning, earth-crust displacement will have shifted whole continents by as much as twenty degrees. That's so much carnage, for the human race – it's game over.'

Scott rubbed his face. Wondering: 'What the hell do we do?'

'I thought maybe we could get together when we reach McMurdo.' Pearce turned on the anthropologist. 'McMurdo's got a chapel.'

Houghton coughed in an attempt to strengthen his voice. Sipped coffee from a cheap styrofoam cup. 'To bring you up to speed,' he said, 'we didn't just lose contact with another seventeen satellites last night. We lost contact with the Chinese base.'

Ralph Matheson looked up. He wasn't much of a fan of lawyers. It wasn't just that the man acted like a weasel, but that he looked like one too. His build was best described as slight. It meant that when he did things to piss someone off, they had this overwhelming urge to sock him one in the gut. It was instinctual, almost primal. It was something Houghton was well aware of, and played on.

But for once, he didn't seem pleased with this turn of events.

'Say again?'

'The Chinese base has fallen silent. We don't know why.'

'Oh great, so what happens when we go a-knocking? Legally we have to tell them we're coming. If we take them by surprise they could just open fire!'

'There is a chance of that now, yes,' the lawyer reluctantly agreed.

The People Carrier turned right onto the Avenue de France and the final approach to the Parc de l'Ariane where the Palais des Nations usually sat resplendently. But today its gleaming white exterior was tarnished. The array of national flags across the front lawn were crooked and buckled. The bronzed statue of mythical beasts within a globe had crashed off its perch in the circular reflecting pool and lay dented to one side. Vehicles were parked askew, up on the grass verges and scattered wherever the diplomats had cared to put them.

Like entropy, the second law of thermo-dynamics, order was disintegrating.

But the Ford People Carrier didn't turn into the UN as everyone anticipated. Instead it drove straight on. Following the signs to the airport. 'I thought we were going inside?' Matheson queried.

'Change of plan,' Houghton said tersely. 'After such an exciting evening here in Switzerland, the Chinese delegation left early this morning. As a consequence – there are no negotiations to enter into.'

'I'm not entirely sure that's a good thing,' Hackett mused.

'The Security Council in New York passed a resolution granting the United States permission to mount its own inspection team, under its own jurisdiction. So long as we stay within Treaty guidelines, give China fair warning of our intentions and let them know about your imminent arrival that'll be sufficient.' He added: 'States of emergency have been declared across several continents. We can basically do what we want. A wrangle between China and America is the least of their worries right now.'

'But you said you've lost contact with the Chinese base,' Scott reminded him. 'If you can't warn them, and there's no Chinese delegation to inform, how will they know we're coming? We'll be sitting ducks.'

Matheson rolled his eyes, alarmed. 'Oh, Christ. This is bad. This is very fucking bad.'

Houghton took a deep breath. 'We can only assume the Chinese are using the current crisis to dismiss the rule of international law. In which case you'll have to go in under armed escort. The only other option is – their base is simply no longer there.'

Matheson was confused. 'I don't understand. Surely you can check something like that?'

'Three major spy satellites were knocked out last night,' Houghton revealed. 'There's just no way of knowing for sure. The President's asked me to join him in Rome for a debriefing.'

Pearce fidgeted nervously. Gasping for air, he met Houghton's gaze and couldn't help but draw attention to himself. 'I can find out,' he said quietly. 'Why don't they ask me?'

Everyone in the back of the van exchanged curious looks. What on earth was he talking about? Only Houghton seemed to understand.

'They know, Bob,' the lawyer answered gravely. 'They know. And they will be calling.'

No one asked any further questions. No one bugged Pearce about his odd conversation. No one seemed to want to know. They should have been nervous. They should have been apprehensive. But exhaustion was a curious thing. Instead, they reclined their seats on the green army Hercules C-130 transport plane, pulled blankets up around their necks, and spent the eleven hour flight to Cape Town, South Africa, fast asleep. Not even stirring when the plane touched down briefly in Cairo to pick up another passenger.

CAPE TOWN DOCKS

PIER 19

'Be careful with that! Be careful!'
Scott woke with a start. How long had the plane been on the ground? It was a customized Hercules C-130 with a pressurized cabin for senior officers in the front, and a small depressurized rear compartment from where drops were made when the plane was flying low.

But the cabin door was wide open. Hot sticky air wafted inside, with a sharp, striking light to accompany it. And, Scott realized, he'd been left all alone.

He could hear a radio playing somewhere. Focused on it and became aware of a familiar voice. It was the President, addressing the nation. Trying to reassure the public back home, as he continued his tour of the Vatican, that there was nothing to worry about. Lying bastard. Scott sat up, thought of Fergus for a moment, and then there was a clatter, a loud bang, like something heavy had just been dropped.

'Goddamnit! I said *be careful!*'

He knew that voice. Strong. Firm. Severely pissed. Yet somehow attractive. 'Sarah?'

He shook off the last vestiges of sleep and stumbled from the chair. Stepping out into the corridor at the side of the cabin, he paused to let a crewman pass through to the cockpit, before continuing on his way to where the load door was lowered forming a ramp.

Crates that hadn't been on board in Switzerland were piled up under webbing and straps. Airmen carried all the equipment down to a series of flatbed trucks lined up on the sweltering tarmac.

A slim tanned woman stood on the lip of the slop, with incredible legs stretching up to a pair of old beat-up shorts. One arm was akimbo, while the other swung out directions.

Scott coughed. 'Hi, Sarah. It's me – Richard.'

Sarah turned slowly and relaxed. 'Hi,' she brightened. 'We finally meet.'

Scott blinked in surprise. 'I'm glad you're all right. That you got out okay. What with the line going dead,' he thought for a moment, choosing his words carefully, 'I didn't know what to think.'

'Miss me?'

Scott chuckled. 'I hardly know you.'

'No, you don't,' she said warmly.

He smiled. Surprisingly relaxed. 'Has this been a weird couple of days or what?' She tried to smile back but it was difficult. 'I'm sorry about Eric, and Douglas.' She thanked him. He jerked a thumb over his shoulder. 'They abandoned me back there.'

Their eyes met, perhaps for longer than they should have. Scott dug his hands in his pockets and took a couple of steps down the ramp. When Sarah added, 'You talk in your sleep,' Scott glanced back. 'I took the seat next to yours.'

'I'm glad you're okay,' Scott reaffirmed by way of an invitation.

Sarah joined him on the ramp and disembarked, stabbing a finger at one of the airmen to be more careful while Scott rubbed a hand over his chin. Two days' growth. He really needed to find a razor.

Outside, he could smell burning. The sun was bright, maybe too bright. Without the slightest hint of haze, there was a perfect view of Table Mountain in the far distance. They were on a private airfield, part of the docks. Huge buildings lined the pier. Cranes loaded cargo ships.

Scott shielded his eyes and glanced up at the sun. 'Hard to believe,' he said. 'It gives us hot sunny days and skin cancer all in one fell swoop. Yet we refuse to believe it can do us any more harm than that.'

Sarah handed the linguist a sheet of paper with a list of numbers running down it.

'What's this?' he asked.

'DEOS figures. Deep Earth Observation Sensor figures. Earthquake data for the last twenty-four hours.' Scott tried reading the list. 'I already briefed everyone else. You're the last to know.'

DEOS had been conceived in 1998 by a team at Cambridge University, Sarah explained. Across the planet, a ten-year operation attached DEOS probes to the ocean floor, measuring seismic activity within the mantle. In time it built up a picture of the earth's core. Each probe was linked, and the data beamed to the satellite communications networks encircling the earth, where it was available to anyone with access to the Internet.

She pulled in closer to Scott. 'Y'know that light show in the tunnel?' Scott gave her that look that said: how could he forget? 'Well, before that one there were five other separate energy bursts that were harmless. I was caught in the middle of one of 'em. We got data on the other four. The light just whizzed through the tunnel and moved on out.' She handed him another sheet of paper. 'This is a map of the tunnel system on the Giza site—'

'There's a ring down there?'

'Yeah. And see here, here and here? Three main tunnels join the ring at 120-degree intervals. The one from the east, the one I was in, goes straight into the Sphinx Chamber where the benben stone's housed. The other two, the ones that come in from the south-west and north-west, link to the ring. And the ring, from what I can figure, joins the Sphinx Chamber through the east tunnel.'

'What are you saying?' Scott asked soberly. 'Am I making too much of a leap here if I assume you're suggesting this earthquake data is linked to the energy bursts in the tunnel?'

'That's exactly it,' Sarah confirmed. 'These are the times at which the energy bursts passed through the Sphinx Chamber. And these are the closest associated earthquakes.'

'But the times don't match.'

'You have to allow the seismic wave time to travel. On average, they move through the ground at 13;000 mph. They go faster or slower depending on the magnitude and depth. This one here, this energy burst at 11.37 pm? An earthquake hit Chad, magnitude six, just minutes before. Chad isn't on a faultline, but it has volcanic activity from a hot spot that's burnt through the crust, like Hawaii. It's about 1,000 miles away. Simple arithmetic tells you it travels 1,000 miles in about four and a half minutes. The Chad earthquake hit at 11.32 pm, *five* minutes beforehand, with an epicenter that's almost precisely due south-west of Cairo, directly in line with the south-west tunnel.'

Sarah traced her finger around the information. Scott followed intently as she added, 'All of these earthquakes are in some kind of direct line of sight with one of the three tunnels leading into Giza. And the time delays between earthquake events and the energy bursts match exactly. Chad, Italy, Greece, Lebanon. The middle of the South Atlantic. They all match.'

'Don't worry,' Scott reassured her, 'I believe you. I can't *not* believe you. Could this *get* any more complex? That's one hell of a machine we're talking about. What did the others say?'

'They're trying to work out how the seismic wave was converted into heat and light.'

'I'm sure they'll figure it out,' Scott said, eager to get on. He glanced around, didn't recognize markings, people or directions. 'Where are we going, by the way?'

'We were supposed to re-fuel and head straight down to McMurdo, but the weather's too bad for a landing. They put us aboard a Coastguard Icebreaker with a science team that was going anyway. It's that bright red one – over there.'

They hopped on the back of one of the flat-beds and rode over to the ship alongside some of the other crates. But it was only as Scott started to take in what he was seeing that he noticed the huge scars down the side of Table Mountain, perhaps twenty miles wide in places.

'Landslides,' Sarah explained. 'They ran out some way. Killed about three thousand people. Knocked power out across half of Cape Town.' She mulled it over. 'They've had some problems. Looting. Rioting. Panic and stuff. That's why we landed here. The main airport's swamped.'

'Because of the landslide?'

'Yup. People are trying to get out.'

'And go where?' Scott inquired. Deadly serious. 'Unless you can get out of this entire solar system, there's nowhere to hide.'

'That's just what your CIA man said.' Scott looked quizzical. 'Bob Pearce, your CIA guy . . . ?'

'Bob Pearce is CIA? What does he do for them?'

The deckhands were carrying equipment up the gangway while the larger, bulkier items, survival gear, supplies, food and so on, were being hauled on board by crane.

The *USCGC Polar Star WAGB-10*, wasn't the largest icebreaker there was, being only 399 feet long and just over 13,000 tons. Her hull was bright red, with a thick white diagonal stripe running down the front end of each side of her bow. Her bridge was gleaming white with a black mast on top bristling with radar and communications antennae, and scientific measuring instruments. She had two mustard-colored funnels leading to two diesel electric turbines.

No, she wasn't the biggest, but she was sturdy and ready to take on the challenge of getting her passengers to McMurdo Sound. Alongside her sister ship, *Polar Sea*, she happened to be the most powerful non-nuclear icebreaker in the world. To Scott she looked eerily familiar.

And then he remembered. *Polar Star*. Her home port was Pier 36 in Seattle. He'd seen this ship on and off, countless times before. Only last month he'd taken Emily down to see her when the Coastguard had an open day. His daughter loved boats.

Her deck plates hummed in anticipation as Scott and Sarah went below to find their cabins and stow their things. They found Ralph Matheson coming out of one cabin, scratching his beard and looking irritated. 'This is like being at camp,' he moaned. 'They got room for twenty passengers, max. Can you believe we all gotta share? Boys in one. Girls in the other.'

As he said this, November poked her head out of another cabin excitedly. 'Sarah!' she exclaimed. 'You're in here with me! We got one all to ourselves. Guess they don't get too many women going to Antarctica.'

Sarah smirked at Scott. 'See you around.'

As she reached the door Scott exchanged a look with Matheson, who pointed to one of his own hands and shook it emphatically. Scott sighed, and called out to the geologist, 'Uh, Sarah?'

She looked back.

'I've been meaning to ask.' He hesitated. 'In the tunnel . . . *was* it a hand that grabbed Douglas?'

Sarah nodded thoughtfully before heading into her cabin and closing the door behind her.

Matheson shook his head, 'Aw, shit.' He rummaged around in his pockets. 'Now where'd I put my pills?' He looked queasily at Scott. 'I get sea-sick.'

Scott took a deep breath as he lifted his bag. 'Oh, great.' He hefted it onto one of the bunks. 'Well, hopefully we won't be at sea too long. Which is mine?'

'Too long?' Ralph remarked. 'This thing does thirty knots, tops – oh, top bunk. We got over two thousand miles to go. That's three day's sailing time, at least.'

Scott slung his stuff on the top bunk. The cabin berthed six, so conditions were cramped. He had a reading light and a curtain, but other than that, not much. And then he realized; was this the last thing he was ever going to see? Hackett said the sun peaked its cycle in *two* days. He turned on Matheson. 'We could all be dead in three days.'

'This is the USS *Harry S. Truman* calling the US Coastguard ship *Polar Star*. We confirm the safe arrival of Rear Admiral T.W. Dower aboard our vessel. Cape Town Harbormaster has given clearance for your immediate departure. The *Truman* battle group is pleased to serve as your escort. Over.'

'Yeah, confirm that, *Truman*. The crew of the *Polar Star* thanks you. We will be underway shortly. Over and out.'

The CO, Captain Chris Rafferty, hung the radio back up on the console and nodded to the harbor pilot to guide his ship out. They would be sailing up Table Bay some distance before turning toward the open sea. Level, as it happened, with a small South African town called Atlantis. Such was the way of things.

Of his twenty officers, two were on the bridge. Of his one hundred and forty-three enlisted men, a further six manned other stations. But Rafferty's main concern was Major Gant, who stood beside him at the Comm desk.

Rafferty folded his arms; lowered his voice. 'Well, this makes a change. We're not usually this popular.' Gant said nothing 'You were lucky,' Rafferty added. 'We don't normally come to Cape Town; usually we head straight for Sydney. But the biologists we got with us had some stuff to pick up.'

'We appreciate you giving us a ride,' Pearce offered. He and Hackett were also on the bridge, by the windows, watching the smoke columns from distant fires – the results of the looting and panic.

But Gant was less appreciative and more concerned with the voyage ahead. 'I've been speaking to the *Truman* and the *Ingersoll*. The weather's getting worse down there. We need to be ready to batten down at a moment's notice.'

'The weather?' Rafferty snorted coldly. 'We get another one of those – gravity waves, did you call them?' Hackett nodded. 'We get another one and there's a fifty-fifty chance we'll go down. We're not the size of an aircraft carrier. We can't ride a fifty-foot wave. It took four years to build this ship, and she can cut through ice like nothing else. But the wrong conditions – and she'll go down in four minutes.' He stuck his hands on his hips. Then adjusted his standard-issue baseball cap. 'Just so you all know. Antarctica's like nowhere else on earth, including the North Pole. With or without gravity waves.'

Ensign Varez was a stocky Hispanic from the fifty-first state of Puerto Rico. He grinned to himself excitedly as the communications desk lit up like a Christmas tree. Addressed his CO: 'Captain! Satellite communications just came back online, sir.'

'What have we got?'

'Uh – everything. GPS. Direct lines to DC. Seattle. NORAD. Switzerland. The works.'

'Good.' He looked to Gant. 'You boys work fast.'

'Well, of course,' Gant chided stiffly. 'There are two whole carrier groups down here now.'

'Excellent,' Hackett said briskly. 'Now maybe we can download the updates of my data from CERN to the labs downstairs—'

'Below decks,' Rafferty corrected.

Hackett shrugged. 'Wherever.'

But the mood hadn't lightened any for Major Gant. Checking in with Cheyenne Mountain, NORAD was disappointed to report that all efforts to locate the Chinese base via satellite had failed. And of the few satellites they could bump into position, the closest, *VX-17*, wasn't going to be in prime position for another thirty-two hours.

Hackett and Pearce exchanged glances, as the CIA man shook nervously. He licked his lips. Tensed. 'You got a room all set up for this?'

Gant said he did. And marched him off into the bowels of the ship.

At 13:06 GMT, *Polar Star* entered international waters becoming the primary responsibility of the *Harry S. Truman* battle group, comprising the Fifth Carrier Group Nimitz Class aircraft carrier *USS Harry S. Truman CVN 75*, with the eighty-seven planes of Carrier Air Wing Five. Running alongside were the *USS Bunker Hill CG 52*, and the *USS Mobile Bay CG 53*. While further out to sea, with some vessels even beyond visibility and tucked over the horizon, were the ships of Destroyer Squadron 15: the *Vincennes*, the *Thach*, the *Curtis Wilbur*, *Rodney M. Davis*, the *O'Brien*, the *John S. McCain* and the *Fife*. Ten ships in all. And a formidable arm of the Truman battle group.

And this was the *second* battle group. The *Nimitz* herself, first of the Nimitz Class, was already in position with her own fleet, patrolling Antarctic waters. It was equally large, and equally committed to carrying out its duties.

To give some idea of the scale of the mounting situation at the South Pole, Gant explained. Antarctica, which was twice the size of America, had around five thousand people living and working on its shores at any one time. In contrast, the ship's company of the USS *Nimitz* numbered 3,350, while its onboard Air Wing numbered 2,480 men and women. A total of 5,830 people. Just the arrival of the *Nimitz* alone had doubled Antarctica's population overnight. The *Truman* had exactly the same complement. And when counting the number of people combined aboard the other eighteen ships, the population of Antarctica had multiplied by a factor of 10.

And that was just the Navy. The Marines had sent their people, as had the Army and the Air Force, all per Presidential decree. It was going to be busy at the South Pole, if nothing else.

But despite all the technical wizardry and know-how, despite all the gadgets and toys, they were blind on mainland Antarctica. They couldn't even confirm whether an entire Chinese base still existed or not. And so finally it all boiled down to this. To one man. Robert Ellington Pearce, of Phoenix, Arizona. Serial Number – A170044938-W9 of the Central Intelligence Agency. A crypto-historian by desire, but a psychic by trade, for want of a better word. And in possession of an extraordinary talent.

The ability to view installations remotely and report on their layout, contents and status with startling accuracy.

By the power of thought alone.

B ob Pearce stood on the snow barefoot. And took a look around.
'What do you see?'

There was no one else with him. So to keep some sort of rational perspective welded to the situation, he had a cellular phone pressed against his ear. He was looking at his feet when he reported back. Wiggled his toes. 'Snow,' he said. 'Ice. It's very cold here.'

'What do you see of the base?' Gant insisted on the other end of the line.

Pearce jerked his head up.

Directly in front of him, a matter of inches away, the charred remains of a Chinese soldier lay slumped over his machine-gun nest. Some sort of blast had erupted behind him and taken the back of his head with it. His face was frozen solid, contorted. But his entire back half was a blackened, twisted lump.

Smoke rose in stacks from behind twisted, jagged wreckage. An overturned drilling mast had crashed across a mobile cabin, itself a mass of flaking debris. This was what was left of *Jung Chang*.

'It's destroyed,' Pearce reported. 'It's devastated.'

Darkened debris littered the surrounding snow like ground pepper on a plate of mashed potato. There was a hand still clutched to a magazine a few feet off. Half a torso. And a birthday card, flapping in the breeze.

'The weather's fine here,' Pearce realized.

'Can you get further into the base?'

'Just a moment. I gotta get past this, uh, thing,' he said, giving another lump of frozen charcoal-covered flesh a wide berth. Pearce could feel his stomach churning over. As he drew closer, the smell of burning and death grew thick and pungent, stung his nostrils and caused him to gasp involuntarily.

'I know what's in Atlantis. I know because I've been there before,' Hackett announced, with his feet up on the table. Scott looked over.

Hackett rifled through the documents as Scott asked: 'What are those?'

'Transcripts,' he explained, 'of Bob's little visitations.'

They were in *Polar Star*'s Deck 2 Research Laboratory, where the team had assembled to watch Bob on the video link. Scott pulled up a chair next to Matheson. Hackett, who sat across from them, passed over the paperwork. He watched Scott sift through the pages, spreading them across the table.

Sarah's eyes were on Matheson as he gingerly attached a connecting wire to the output socket on a small plastic box-shaped unit then hooked it up to the computer workstation bolted to the desk behind him, careful not to dislodge any more fried circuits than he absolutely had to.

'Think you can get it to work?'

'Of course I can get it to work,' Matheson responded dismissively. 'I designed this thing.' He chipped away flaking particles, disgustedly. 'What *is* this stuff all over it?'

'Blood,' Sarah revealed abruptly. 'Eric Clemmens's charbroiled blood. They had to prise it from the wreckage.'

'Oh,' Matheson murmured queasily. He had been about to chew his nails. Now that didn't seem like such a good idea.

'This is unbelievable,' Scott groaned, turning the page.

'Why? Because it doesn't fit with your world view?' Hackett challenged as Matheson reached behind his chair and flipped a switch.

There was a low hum, followed by electrical chirping as a single green LED blinked insistently to let him know it was alive. He spun round to key the computer. Hit – UPLOAD – and: 'Bingo.' He sniffed, self-satisfied. 'Transferring all Giza data to the main terminal. We gotta party goin' on.'

'You cannot,' Scott insisted, 'claim to know what's going on some-place else just by thinking about it.'

'He channels the energies,' Hackett reminded. 'We can *see* him channeling the energies.'

'Jon,' Scott retaliated, 'you're a scientist. How can you, of all people accept this?'

'Richard, we still don't fully understand quantum mechanics, but what we do know is this TV monitor won't work without it. No one knows what effect superstring theory will have on our everyday lives but we know for the universe to exist, there are at least twenty-seven dimensions. We know there's no "nothingness". If you sucked all the air out of a little black box, shut out all the light, extracted every-thing – there would still be thirty-seven fields of potential left. Thirty-seven! At the last count! Particles would continue to pop up out of nowhere sporadically, which is important because it links to another theory. Spatially, I know you're sitting there. I know your ass is in that seat. And I know we're sailing on the ocean. But think about it – this'll be important to you: where, spatially, is the past?'

'Where is the past?'

Sarah was excited. 'Wow. That's a good question.'

'*Where* is the past?'

Hackett nodded. 'In feet and inches, Richard, if you please.'

Scott thought about it. 'The past,' he replied hesitantly, 'is over two miles beneath the ice – in Antarctica.' He sat back on his haunches, feigning smug. But he knew it wasn't much of an answer.

'Okay.' Hackett attacked again. 'So what is the distance between good and evil in kilometers?'

That got him.

'We don't use eighty percent of our brain,' Hackett said. 'And of the part we *do* use, eighty percent of *that* is given over to processing visual stimulus. The point is, we as a species have existed for longer than our cognitive abilities to process what we perceive. It's possible our bodies can detect things we are simply not capable of recog-nizing – yet. Maybe we haven't evolved sufficiently to process that kind of data. Perhaps we need to develop a new kind of sense. You're confused when I ask "where is the past" because it's a different type of question, one you're not used to. Yet linguistically you can't deny it's grammatically correct.' Reluctantly Scott agreed. 'Perhaps what

Bob's doing simply requires asking different types of questions.'

'Are you saying he's more highly evolved than us?' Scott challenged.

Hackett refused to answer.

'Shh!' November scolded. 'Can I at least hear what *Bob* has to say? Can't you just give him a break and keep the faith?'

Scott turned to face where November sat fiddling with the Giza tunnel footage on her computer. She met his gaze levelly. 'He may be right, or he may be wrong,' she said. 'But right now they can't even get a satellite to tell us anything useful. So what's wrong with just keeping the faith?'

'We're scientists,' Scott explained dryly. 'We don't *do* faith?'

November just focused on the monitor, where Bob Pearce had a room all set up with a table and chairs, a map of Antarctica and a whole stack of grid references. There were no crystal balls, burning incense or wind chimes. It was clinical. And bright: he had a set of lights, which he sat and stared at through closed eyes. It made for bizarre viewing.

Across from him, Gant sat with pen, paper and a sheet of reconnaissance data.

Pearce stirred. 'I'm uh, I'm through to the other section. I'm passing a lot of wreckage.' He threw his hand over his mouth as if he were about to be sick. 'Ugh, uh, it's a . . . It's like a bomb went off. They're dead. They're all dead.'

'Okay, Bob, I guess it's gruesome. But we need to know about automated systems. Rack guns. Land mines—'

November was concerned. 'I thought there was a ban on land mines?' she whispered.

'Yeah, right,' Matheson snorted. 'On paper, maybe.'

'North-west of the compound, on the perimeter,' Pearce announced, 'automated rack gun. Operational. And, wait a minute . . . yes, another gun. But it's out of ammo. Correction: looks like they never loaded it.'

Scott rubbed his hand across his chin, astounded. 'What *does* he see?'

'He sees their base,' Hackett commented. 'And from the sound of things, he sees it pretty well.'

Scott watched Pearce on the monitor, and that was when he

noticed something equally odd happening in their own environment. A thin gray film of dust covered everything close to an open port-hole. Suddenly the ship jolted as it hit rougher seas, and it was Bob Pearce on the other end of the video-link who voiced Scott's concern.

'Something's not right,' he said.

Vents of steam trickled out of blowholes all around Bob Pearce, like steamholes in a pot of over-boiled rice. The steam rose up only a few feet before it quickly turned to snow and danced away on the wind.

Huge cracks criss-crossed through the ice. And as Pearce picked his way through the debris, he became aware the ground was dipping out from under him. It was like being on the edge of an impact crater. The blowholes were getting large, and the ground was starting to look more like Swiss cheese. Exposed ice tunnels twisted away into the interior, large enough to accommodate teams of men.

He could see something beyond the twisted, shattered hulk of an Armored Personnel Carrier in front of him, smashed up, and balanced on its side. It was something dark. Vast. Stretched out across the ground. If only he could reach it.

Was that a cry? Muffled. Distant. Pearce checked all around his position. Trying to determine where it was coming from.

'Say again?' Gant demanded.

But Pearce didn't have time to answer. Carefully, he lowered himself down into a blowhole, and peered into the steep, glistening ice tunnel. And as the frosty mist wafted its way past him, up toward the surface, he spotted something moving. Something black and disheveled, clawing its way forward.

Pearce rushed to its side for a closer inspection and was shocked to discover a Chinese soldier, in mountaineering gear. His skin was black in patches. Not from burns, but from frostbite.

'My God! We've got a survivor here!' he exclaimed.

He crouched down next to the young man who couldn't have been more than twenty. 'Jesus, he's just a kid,' Pearce added, disgusted. 'Send in a SaRGE! Now!'

'Don't get ahead of yourself, Bob,' Gant warned. 'We don't even know if we can get a SaRGE that deep into enemy territory.'

'They're all dead except for this kid,' Pearce insisted. 'Get a SaRGE in here. Drag him out, for god's sake – get a SuRGEon!'

There was steam rising from the delirious young soldier's mouth. A powdered, crystallized breath. He opened one drooping eyelid, and it looked for all the world like –

'I think he sees me,' Pearce gasped.

'That's impossible,' Gant replied gruffly. 'You're not really there, Bob. You've projected your mind into that area. Check around you. See what he's focusing on.'

But Bob wasn't listening, because the young Chinese soldier was trying to speak now. With one finger outstretched to indicate the tunnel behind him, he was trying, with every fiber in his being, to articulate sounds. Bob Pearce leant forward, and though he couldn't understand him, tried his best to repeat those sounds.

Scott ran his finger over the equipment in the lab and studied the residue as November fought back a retch. 'What is that smell?' she complained.

'Close the portholes,' Scott ordered, covering his mouth and reaching for the nearest porthole to him. The ship lurched once more. But this time, worse, like it had hit a wall of bad weather. Sarah too came over to study the dust. Outside, it seemed to be raining nothing but a swirl of gray, vile, sulfurous-smelling powder.

'It's volcanic ash,' she decided. 'There must be some heavily active volcanoes coming up.'

'Mount Erebus is active,' Matheson said. 'It's right in McMurdo Station's backyard.'

'Great,' Sarah moaned. 'This'll be fun.'

She joined Scott at the porthole, but he didn't seem to be so amused. He brushed the ash from his fingertips, saying: 'Brimstone. I never thought I'd get to see the day—'

'Hey, Richard,' Hackett interrupted. 'Can you speak Chinese?'

Scott turned on the physicist. 'A little. Why?'

Hackett pointed at the monitor. 'Because Bob's started speaking it.'

Scott came over to him and cranked the volume up, straining to hear the mumbling CIA agent.

'Yao ye heikodo!' he seemed to be saying. 'Yao ye heikodo!'

Which left Scott cold. 'It's Cantonese,' he explained. 'He keeps saying "There's something down there. There's something down there . . . And it's alive".'

SACRED PLACES

The Popol Vuh cannot be seen anymore . . . the original book written long ago, existed, but its sight is hidden from the searcher and the thinker.

Popol Vuh: Sacred Book of the Quiche Tribe of Maya,
University of Oklahoma Press Edition

PINI PINI TUNNELS

NIGHT

I t was raining. Again.
   They had told him it didn't actually rain all that much in the rainforest, except maybe during the rainy season. They had lied. Jack Bulger pulled the canvas flap over on his canopy to stop the rainwater from dripping down into his computer.

   Piled in front of him were nineteen individual two-foot-square cubes of Carbon 60 crystal, cut out and removed from the tunnels below ground in a systematic process that had taken the best part of twelve hours. Under their own tarp, they had been placed directly onto the ground, where a muddy puddle had collected, like a brown soup that was fast becoming home to an array of festering insects.

   A lightning burst arced across the sky as Bulger pulled the tarp back and set up his microscope on the topmost block. He had removed its base so the optical unit peered directly down at the block below. After all, the sample of C60 was too big to slip under the lens on a glass slide.

   He had been watching the blocks under the power of the camp lights, and it had become increasingly obvious that dark shadowy veins seemed to have feathered throughout the crystal blocks, like faults in a gemstone. They were not features he had noted when he examined the Carbon 60 in its original state, wrapped in a spiral around the inside of the tunnel. If the crystal were an animal, he would have said it was dying.

He hooked the microscope up to his laptop, and powered up. It wasn't what he preferred to be doing. He'd rather be down in the thick of it, carving this stuff out, but they wouldn't let him. He would have argued the point, but they had the guns. Jack Bulger was many things, but he wasn't stupid.

Eddie the winch operator was busy stringing out the chain and hoist for the next delivery of Carbon 60, running the length of metal links out to the hole in the ground leading down to the tunnel, as Bulger zoomed in on his own specimen of crystal.

'Make sure that thing doesn't snarl up on a stump this time!' Bulger snapped over his shoulder, not bothered if Eddie the winch answered or not, so long as he did as he was told.

Bulger concentrated on his screen. There were three fields of magnification, across a wide band spectrum. The first was maximum optical magnification. Unfiltered. Undiluted. Pure visual data. The second field was enhanced optical. The image was filtered through a patchwork of software to artifically clean up key features of the specimen in different parts of the spectrum. The third field was artificial magnification. Extrapolating key data from the first two fields, the computer used the optical data as a baseline and enhanced what it detected based on a set of algorithms. The result was the computer could artificially increase apparent optical magnification by a factor of 1,000 to an accuracy of 98 percent.

Fine. So long as the damn thing gave him a close-up, Bulger didn't care how inaccurate it was. A fracture was going to look like a fracture, hazy image or not. The important point was, if the extraction process was damaging the crystal in some way, he was going to have to do something about it. A damaged crystal was a damaged pay packet.

He lit up his cigar and blew rings. Keyed zoom, and inspected the surface.

There was movement.

Bulger jerked his eyes away from the screen. Eyeballed his microscope on the crystal block with some suspicion. Was he tired or had he done something wrong?

His first instinct was contamination. Fucking rainwater. He stumbled to his feet and pulled the canvas canopy further over his microscope. He picked the thing up briefly, wiped down the surface just in case it really was wet, and set it back down again. He hit RECAL-IBRATE and waited.

Movement again.

'Jesus H. fucking God all – assholes.'

'Pretty, Jack,' Eddie the winch commented, sat out by the generator, smoking a cigarette. 'Real pretty.'

Bulger glimpsed the tip of the man's cigarette glowing in the dark. 'Shut up, asswipe.'

'Yessir.'

He studied the screen intently. Could the artificial magnification be reacting to something like an external light source? Misrepresenting a moving dance of shadow and light across the subsurface structure?

'What's the problem?' Eddie the winch asked.

'None of your damn business,' Bulger replied, instinctively shifting in his chair to shield the screen from the other man's prying eyes. Eddie shrugged and stuck to his winch.

The image on the screen seemed to be showing tiny filaments, like tubes of carbon, intricately woven throughout the crystal. It was within these filaments that there seemed to be movement, very much like a liquid. Did this Carbon 60 have some sort of super-fast capillary action as one of its properties? The ability to suck a liquid in if it came into contact with it? Most rocks had this property, but not at this speed.

He hit MAGNIFY, boosting the image far beyond the system's recommended levels. The result was greater inaccuracy but Bulger was prepared to live with that. He passed microns and was in the realms of nanometers now – measurements that covered billionths of a meter. A place where materials began to act very differently.

There it was again. Something shot past the lens. A blur, a dark burst. Then another, and another.

Like shadows on glass. There was no way he could move the lens accurately enough to keep track of, or pace with whatever was speeding through the tubes. No problem. This was a laptop. It had highspeed shutter capabilities. He hit RECORD and took a digital film shot at 10,000 frames per second. The three-second burst was theoretically enough to give him the information he needed.

And as it happened, it was.

It first appeared on frame 1037 and was gone again by frame 1104. More blips appeared in succession soon after, but it was the first one that interested Bulger. It was isolated, and easier to discern. He increased magnification again. And couldn't believe what he was seeing.

Tiny arms. A barrel-like body. Like no design he had ever seen before. Part machine, part organic. It wasn't based on any conventional, modern wisdom. It was based on something superior.

Bulger's cigar fell from his mouth as he watched the spectacle unfold on his monitor. For a tiny machine, no bigger than some of the human body's own cells, was whizzing through the crystal substructure.

Bulger snatched his cigar up before it burnt a hole in the keyboard. There was only one explanation. 'Nanoes,' he said.

Carver adjusted his goggles, bracing himself for the back-blast of dust, as the particle beam under his control sliced into the Carbon 60 spiral that was wrapped around the inside of the underground passageway, stretching off in both directions.

The crystal itself was covered in a type of writing he had never seen before, while the ordinary stone portions had glyphs carved on them that resembled ancient Mayan writing. Which, if he remembered correctly, was entirely out of place. The Mayans were from Central America, not South. They never reached Peru or the Amazon. But then, what did he know?

The particle beam finished cutting out a pre-programmed cube of C60 and shut itself down. The cube dulled and slid slowly out of its position. Gathering speed, it crashed to the ground. Garrison was the man with him. He quickly heaved the pail of water by his feet and sluiced the crystal cube down. It hissed in a cloud of steam as two members of Maple's team passed them by on their way farther down into the tunnel's extremities. They adjusted the flashlights bolted to their hard hats as they went.

'Maple wants to know how much more of this stuff we can get out before the tunnel collapses completely,' the larger one said tersely.

There were cubes of C60 missing from the spiral, all over the tunnel. Stress fractures had already started to appear in the ceiling areas. They had plundered in earnest.

But Carver wasn't too worried. 'My guess is, a whole lot more,' he said, as the men went about their business.

There was a harness on the ground, hooked up to a couple of heavy-duty chains. Carver and Garrison worked together, stooping to fasten the entire cradle around the Carbon 60 cube and had tied off the last of the clips when Carver's radio kicked in.

'Pack up your kit,' Maple instructed. 'We're moving that gun straight out.'

'What's going on?'

'Just be ready to move,' Maple insisted. His voice sounded resonant, as if he were standing in a cavernous room. 'We've found something that makes the crystal in that tunnel look like a snack.'

Garrison eyed his boss as he ran the chains through his gloved hands, checking the way was clear for Eddie to shift the winch into gear and haul the crystal out. 'What do we do?' he asked.

'Go find out what he wants,' Carver replied gruffly. 'I'll pack that thing up when I'm good and ready.' Garrison shrugged in acknowledgement.

Carver watched Garrison march off into the darkness as the now familiar light storm of energy pulsed down the tunnel and lit up the surroundings for a mile. When it reached his position where the blocks of Carbon 60 had been removed, it seemed to stall. To flicker, like a dying neon tube light. Before passing through what remained of the connection and moving on.

'Woo-Wee!' Eddie the winch whooped, bent double over the entry hole, as the energy pulse lit up the tunnel below. He descended into howls of laughter. 'Woah boy, that sure is somethin'!'

'Yeah,' Bulger barely murmured through gritted teeth, his mind distinctly elsewhere.

Nanoes. Micro-machines. Constructed at the atomic level, operating on a molecular level, measured on the nanometer scale. Robots that were so small that, given the right instructions, they could literally climb inside a heart through the smallest artery, and perform surgery from the inside out. To be sure, this wasn't the nanotechnology of the modern vision. Current thinking on nanoes dictated that these tiny little robots were so small they were submicroscopic, visible only with an electron microscope, their moving parts the size of protein molecules. Current nanothinking pointed to nanoes that, if they could be made, would be no more than 100 nanometers long.

But they had never been made. The closest thing to structural manipulation at the atomic level was twenty years old, when Japanese scientists actually had spelt out the word 'atom' in Japanese – and *in* atoms.

Clearly, what Bulger was seeing was a machine that was hundreds of thousands of nanometers across. Much larger than theory. But then theory was worthless without some experiment, application, and the collection of a few facts. And the fact was, a nano was staring him in the face. The first working microscopic machine ever seen.

And that had more cash worth than all the Carbon 60 on the planet.

Jack Bulger shivered with anticipation. God damn, he couldn't tell the men he was with. Not only would they not understand, they'd want a share in the profits. Which just wasn't on offer. Besides, they were going to get rich off the crystal anyway. Screw them. So the only problem now was – what to do with the information.

He couldn't keep it here. They might stumble across it, or rifle through his belongings and discover any handwritten notes. Certainly this piece of digital film would have to be deleted.

So should he send the information somewhere? Maybe e-mail it to himself. Certainly, it was a double-edged sword telling Houghton. If he kept it quiet and didn't tell the company lawyer, then every day that passed increased the probability that some company scientists would run across this discovery in the crystal he'd brought back from Antarctica – if they hadn't already. And he didn't want them getting the glory *or* the money.

But if he told Houghton and it really was a new discovery, he would have safeguarded his personal revenue, albeit at a substantially reduced rate than if he simply put it out to auction to the highest bidder.

There was, of course, the third way. He could do the smart thing, and do both. Tell Houghton. Get paid. Then sell the information on anyway.

Yeah. That sounded better.

So while he put in his call to Jay Houghton, and waited for the system to locate the lawyer, he busied himself by collecting more data. And made the most curious discovery.

The nanoes, depending on what they were trying to achieve, worked either independently or collectively, using chemical bonds to consciously bind together. To form a larger device.

Incredible. He was going to be so freaking rich!

Carver put up his collar. Whistled away to himself as he fastened the chain round the dangling greasy pulley system above. He was directly under the entry hole that had opened up during the initial earthquake. Slimy mud continued to slide down the sides as torrential rain flooded in from the surface. Carver looked up to see lightning flashes and was actually glad to be underground for a change – even if it was creepy down here.

Glistening clear tree roots, all twisted in glassy knots, jutted out at him. Creatures he hadn't even conceived of before crawled and slithered all around him. Some smaller insect-like things swarmed and fluttered their gossamer wings. He had to flick the odd oversized glass-like spider from his boots. It made his skin crawl. But at least he was dryer in the tunnel.

He tugged on the chains, put his radio to his lips and announced, 'Okay, let her up.'

He could hear the distant roar of power as mechanical motors cranked into gear. Saw the tension build in the chains. And stood back as the Carbon 60 block was suddenly dragged across the floor.

He monitored its progress gleefully, making sure his prize made it over every rut it encountered. This one block alone was worth a quarter of a million US dollars. When it was time for payday the only certainty he knew was that the whores in Mexico City better be geed up on something a little stronger than Pro-Plus, coz there was gonna be some ridin' goin' on. And it wasn't gonna stop till Christmas.

When the block scraped its way over the right spot, Carver radioed to the surface for them to stop. It was time to unhook from the pulleys so the block could be raised directly to the surface.

He paid scant regard to the translucent bug on his shoulder. Or the glass tube-like roots that jabbed at his throat as he grabbed the chains and yanked them free of the pulleys. He was just about to radio back again, however, when he heard something odd. He stopped what he was doing mid-whistle.

There it was again. Like a fall. Some kind of muffled cry. Very faint. But it was coming from the direction of where his two team-mates had just headed.

He peered into the darkness. Angled his flashlight and shone it into the distance. Tentatively he called out to them: 'Hinkley? Gerome?'

Nothing. Not a single response.

Carver tugged on the chains, a clear signal that they could start lifting the block again. As he went for his radio to confirm the order, he heard what could only be described as a scream. Guttural. Explosive. Like the knotting of entrails being wrenched from within.

Carver brought the radio to his mouth as he reached for the semi-automatic rifle slung over his shoulder. He was only going to say this once. 'Guys,' he said, 'quit fucking around. Now what's going on? But all he got back was static. He put his radio away, raised his gun, and tugged on the chains sharply. Twice. To let them know there was a problem.

The block jerked to a halt and was left dangling at eye-level.

Carver peered into the darkness once more. As each lightning strike above, lashed out across the sky, its light reflected down into the tunnel. And for Carver it gave the briefest glimpse of something disturbing. A figure was approaching.

CROSSED WIRES

The lab door flew open, right around where Ralph was busy tapping away on his computer and across from where November sat cataloguing the Atlantis glyphs. A belated sharp knock accompanied the intrusion. A red-head in jeans and a T-shirt hung her head around the door.

'Anyone in here called Jon Hackett?'

Hackett was startled. 'Uh, yes. That's me.'

'Hi. Rebecca Devon – microbiologist. I think they made some sort of a screw-up, upstairs. They're pumping data into our lab across the corridor. Number streams. Mean anything to you?'

Hackett was on his feet. 'How long?'

'About an hour.'

'That's the completed crystal data from CERN,' he glowered, heading for the door. 'I've been waiting for that. How come you didn't notice before?'

'Well, uh,' she grinned apprehensively, 'it's an easy mistake to make. It looks just like biological data.' Hackett pulled up short. Checked with his colleagues. Did he just hear that correctly?

'Complexity,' Scott winked, 'is the key.'

'What? Yeah – I guess you're right,' Hackett agreed as Matheson pulled out his lemon and started joining the dots across its bumpy surface. He had a rotating globe on his monitor and had started to copy the pattern onto that image too.

'This is some machine,' he murmured.

Hackett eyed it briefly. 'You think these sites are all interconnected, like some kind of network, don't you, Ralph? Like an ancient Internet?'

'Yup – I'm convinced of it.'

'You know what this is? This is a monkey puzzle, my friend – on a global scale.'

'Gee, you make it sound like the ancients built all this so we'd have something to while away the hours with in our dying days,' Bob Pearce commented sourly. He looked exhausted.

He stood in the doorway, made his apologies and squeezed past Rebecca, who continued to wait patiently. She grinned at him in an overly condescending, overly friendly manner. 'Hi,' she said. But Pearce didn't respond.

'Those sites are connected all right,' Pearce said. 'Ever wonder what the hell ley lines were? Ancient channels of force. Maybe an entire ancient tunnel system is what we've been detecting all this time.'

Hackett said playfully: 'Did I miss a meeting? Did you go dowsing without me again? Bob, you know how I hate to miss that.'

Pearce shrugged it off and grabbed Matheson's lemon with the gridlines marked on it, joining the five ancient sites and traced his finger over them.

'Hey, I'm not finished with that,' Matheson complained. 'I was just about to scrawl the Giza tunnel system on that thing.'

Scott shook his head. 'I'm not convinced,' he said. 'There's no way a tunnel system could stretch all the way from Egypt to South America to Antarctica. It's just physically impossible.'

'Besides,' Sarah added, 'the tectonic plates are moving. Continents are continually shifting. Those tunnels wouldn't last long – they'd be destroyed. Ripped apart or flooded.'

Pearce held up the lemon. 'In relation to this puzzle,' he said, 'the five sites and the earth? We are but a flea on the ass of an elephant. In relation to the sun, we are a tic on the ass of a flea on the ass of an elephant. We're nothing. So until we step back, and get far enough away, like going into orbit, we can't possibly see the whole picture. The *bigger* picture.'

'Trouble is,' Rebecca the microbiologist added without thinking, 'you step too far back and you wind up falling off a cliff.' All eyes settled on the woman who had spoken out of turn. 'It's just an observation,' she added meekly. 'What are you guys talking about?'

Hackett inclined his head toward her and said quietly: 'Why don't you go on ahead, huh? I'll be along for my data in just a second.' Rebecca made her excuses and left. Hackett held up a hand defensively. 'Bob, calm down. We're on your side on this thing. No one agrees with your assessment more than I do. I also happen to agree with Ralph. But whether these sites are linked physically or any other way, unless I challenge him we'll succumb to fuzzy thinking and that won't help any of us. We have to be very clear about our conclusions and the science that gets us there.'

Pearce rubbed his head, and seemed to be shaking from the cold. 'I'm sorry,' he said. 'I'm just . . . very tired.'

'I'm not surprised. Must take a lot of effort to do what you do.'

Pearce was unsteady on his feet and allowed November to guide him to a seat. 'For all we know,' he murmured, 'the sun is a living breathing creature. It just takes it four million years to say a word, let alone string a sentence together. We are gone in the blink of an eye on a cosmic scale. We don't live on the same time-scale as the sun so we wouldn't recognize life that way. We only recognize life that lives roughly at the same pace as ourselves . . .'

Hackett looked to November as he tip-toed out the door. 'And get him some coffee,' he advised. 'Lots of sugar.'

'Hi, This is Ted,' Rebecca announced, introducing everybody. 'Ted, this is Jon and Sarah. Ted's a marine biologist. He studies jellyfish.'

'Oh,' Sarah commented brightly. 'They must be very interesting animals.'

'They're not animals per se,' Ted responded icily. 'They are planktonic marine creatures. Protoplasm.' Ted wore sandals and had long greasy hair, like a surfer with a personal hygiene problem. He also didn't know when to break eye-contact, which made conversation with him awkward and uncomfortable. 'Some of them are not single creatures at all, but a collective of tiny creatures that choose to work, live and hunt together in a form we call the jellyfish.'

'Oh,' Sarah replied with an air that she hoped suggested she stood corrected.

'Ted's a little edgy at the moment, aren't you, Ted?' Rebecca interjected apologetically.

The other biologists steered clear of their little gathering. They also wore their hair long, were in the process of growing beards, and were more interested in the spores they were cultivating in glass dishes than infiltrators from the lab down the hall.

'We studied C60 before,' Rebecca announced sweetly, tapping the screen of her computer and signaling to her colleagues that everything was fine. 'There you go. That's your transfer started. Shouldn't take long.'

'Thank you,' Hackett replied dismissively, aware Sarah was hovering beside him. 'What, uh, what do you mean you studied C60 before? Why on earth would you do that as a microbiologist?'

'Fullerenes,' Rebecca explained, 'are a good candidate for seeding life through space. Didn't you know?'

Sarah folded her arms tightly across her chest. 'Obviously not,' she said, thinking of the hand back in the tunnel in Egypt and shivering.

'Oh,' Rebecca cooed dreamily, watching the data on the screen. 'Carbon's a really special little element. And C60's a really smart little molecule.'

'Carbon's very adaptable,' Hackett agreed. 'It's in the ink we write with. It's in the flesh we live by. It goes from being a gas to being part of the human brain, able to contemplate its own existence.'

'Which is incredible considering that, as an element, it's so mediocre,' Rebecca added. 'It does most things, but isn't an extremist, like say potassium, which blows up at the drop of a hat. Carbon only makes up 0.2 percent of the earth's elements, but is part of more compounds than any other element. Hundreds of thousands of compounds.'

'But *why* the C60 molecule as a candidate for spreading life?' Sarah persisted.

'Because it's hollow,' Rebecca replied, as if Sarah, since she knew so much about carbon, should have known the answer to that question already. 'It's the shape of a soccer ball.'

'The Carbon 60 molecule,' Hackett objected, 'is only approximately three ängstroms across. That's enough space for about one atom only.'

'Yes, but think about it. What atom?' Rebecca threw right back at him. 'You choose the right atom and you wind up creating the world's most powerful non-metal magnet. You make C900, which they've done in the lab. The same enclosed structure as C60 emerges but with 900 carbon atoms. And that isn't a ball anymore – that's a capsule. You put a combination of the twenty standard amino acids into the heart of that structure and it'll end up sprouting legs and walk off.'

'I'm not following you,' Sarah interjected.

'There are three forms of carbon on earth, but which type did we evolve from?' Rebecca asked. 'Graphite has edge contaminates. Diamond has a monolayer of hydrogen on its surface. And soot, which is pure and the most closely related to ourselves, is formless. Life had to evolve from *something*. But it can't be any of these three. Diamond is not only too rigid, but the hydrogen renders it useless. Graphite's too malleable, and soot so formless it's useless. The guess is, there was a fourth type of carbon that was pure *and* had form . . . That's what C60 is. Pure. And it has form.'

'You got proof of this?' Sarah asked suspiciously. Suspicious because she was afraid of the answer. Afraid because she had *seen* the answer.

'Twenty years ago Buseck and Tsipursky found C60 and C70 in shungite,' Rebecca offered.

Hackett looked puzzled.

'Rare carbonaceous, pre-Cambrian rock,' Sarah told him. 'I know. Traces were detected around crater sites and in the KT boundary – the boundary that marks the end of the Cretaceous and beginning of the Tertiary eras, sixty-five million years ago when the dinosaurs were killed.'

'Absolutely. And on that basis we had our guys back at the Max Planck Institute fire C60 molecules at a hard surface at over 17,000 miles an hour. Around the same type of forces you would expect it to have been put under if it had just crashed to earth on the back of an asteroid. The molecules bounced back. They weren't destroyed – they survived! Now the idea of Dr Frankenstein throwing a switch and zapping his monster is a little extreme, but heat and the odd lightning bolt are the ideal conditions to kickstart life. Or at least mutate it. And Carbon 60, as a pure form of carbon, with no contaminants *and* structure is biologically active.'

'Which came first?' Hackett mused. 'The chicken or the Carbon 60 egg, huh?'

Rebecca eyed him up and down as if seeing the physicist in a new light. 'That's very funny,' she smirked. 'I like that.' She tapped her screen, bringing up images. 'The reason this looked like biological data,' she explained, 'is because the numbers and some of the data show a symmetry very similar to that of life forms. When I realized it was C60 it made perfect sense.'

'Symmetry?' Sarah probed further.

'Life, as we know it, has two basic shapes,' Rebecca said. 'There's the double helix – y'know, the spiral – which is what our DNA conforms to and what many larger life forms are based on. And then there's the soccer-ball symmetry of viruses. Sometimes the helical-screw-like shape manifests itself in the very shape of the animal in question, like some gastropods. Like the twirl shape of the Nautilus sea shell.'

'But C60 is only soccer-ball-shaped, isn't it?'

'No, not at all,' Rebecca corrected. She punched up another image. 'If you pass C60 through an electrical field during its creation, it forms a carbon nano-tube that develops on a screw-like basis. A helix shape instead. A spiral. But a spiral *tube* – which is also the basic requirement of all larger life forms – for circulation of the blood.'

Two basic shapes of Carbon 60. Two basic life forms on earth. Both evolved from carbon. But from the same *type* of carbon?

'It's like C60, if we were going to design it,' Rebecca added, 'would be the perfect starting point for life. We know chloroplasts, true bacteria and mitochondria evolved from eubacteria. Methanogens, halophiles, sulfolubus and their relatives come under archaea. Protists, plants, fungi and animals stem from eukaryotes. We know that eubacteria, archaea and eukaryotes together all stem from the same first branch on the tree of life. But viruses are a mystery: they don't seem to fit in. However, if you have one type of carbon struc-ture that can take on two distinct shapes – then that explains the connection.

'Carbon 60 could be the precursor to some sort of proto-life form. Have you seen this?' she asked as an image of a soccer-ball-shaped molecule appeared as seen under a cryo-electron microscope.

'C60, right?' Sarah offered.

'No,' Rebecca corrected. 'This is a virus.'

'Which one?'

'The human herpes virus.'

'Herpes?'

'Uh-huh. And it has exactly the same symmetry as C60. Admittedly it's not the best example, but then what virus is?'

'Life bears the scars of its predecessors,' Hackett mused. 'In this case shape and symmetry.' Was this the emergent property that marked the transition from simple crystal to lower life form? Real complexity in real action?

'The type of carbon we evolved from has been a mystery,' Rebecca explained. She tapped the screen again to show an image of Carbon 60 in its spiral nano-tube form, rotating side by side with a DNA strand. 'Coal, diamonds, they're all still around in abundance. Theoretically Carbon 60 should also be here in equal abundance. But where'd it all go? You're a physicist. Erwin Schrödinger described DNA as an aperiodic crystal.'

She paused, then looked around at them all. 'My theory is C60 *is* still around. It just evolved. It's *us*.'

'Gerome, is that you? Hinkley? What the fuck are you doing, you twerp?'

Another lightning burst. Another glimpse. And that was when Carver realized that what was approaching, albeit in the shape of a man, was neither Hinkley nor Gerome.

It was rising up out of the ground as it approached. Growing at an extraordinary rate, like a fluid that had decided to take solid form. It was a towering figure. And it lumbered forward, yet remained shrouded in darkness.

Carver stumbled backwards. Grasped his gun tightly, and slipped the safety catch off. Squeezed the trigger and fired a clear burst of shots at the assailant. They rebounded harmlessly off its chest.

It moved forward again.

Carver moved too, desperate to keep his distance, but his exit was blocked by the cube of Carbon 60 dangling behind him.

Swarming over its surface was a seething mass of crystal-clear spiders, mixed with the invasive tendrils and roots. Giant glass centipedes and millipedes scuttled within the mass. Carver had the sudden terrifying realization that the entire angry mass was melting in on itself. Everything was merging into one single lump. Like an ice sculpture that had a blowtorch directed on it, it shifted, writhed and reformed. Mutating into a hanging, decapitated crystal human head. *His* head.

Slowly the crystal effigy opened its eyes and focused them on Carver. They analyzed each other for a moment before the head distorted its features as it opened its jaws wide. Exposed its tomb-stone-like teeth, and hissed at him.

Its tongue rolled out. And upon its tongue – a single word was etched.

Carver's instinct was to run away screaming, but before he even had time to consider what to do next, the ice-cold grasp of the approaching figure's crystal hand was clenched tightly around his throat.

Carver's face reddened, and blotched, as he choked.

The figure moved in closer. Its broad, see-through shoulders barely flinching as its nine-foot frame went to work.

Carver lashed out. Swung a balled fist. But it just hit a wall of solid glass.

The figure did not respond. With barely a scowl across its face, it studied Carver intently. Methodically. As slowly, it squeezed.

On the surface, Eddie the winch was getting restless. What was Carver playing at? It had been nearly a quarter of an hour now.

He trudged over to the opening in the ground, grimacing at the ever-present stench of rotting vegetation every time he kicked up a clump of undergrowth.

'Hey, down there!' he shouted. 'What the hell's wrong?' No response. 'Answer me, damn it!'

He looked to his associate, manning the computer, engrossed in his phone-call, before stooping to his knees and examining the chain. It jolted. Once.

'At last. All right! He returned to his winch. Shoved it into gear.

The motor roared as the chain retracted at a rate that was simply too good to be true. Anxiously he brought the whole thing clattering to a halt again and rushed to grab the end of the chain. But where a neatly cut block of Carbon 60 should have been, sat an empty cradle harness.

Concerned, he tossed the thing to the ground, and marched over to the communications table, where Bulger had more lap-tops, vid-phones and a satellite link-up all sat ready and active. He took a radio from among the toys. 'Carver, what's going on down there? What's the problem, bud? We're wasting time here.' Nothing. 'Carver?' He tapped the radio. 'Damn, I think the power's out on the comm relay.' He turned to Bulger. 'Jack?'

But Bulger was ensconced in discussions.

'Jack?' He reached out and put a hand on the man's shoulder, and was surprised when the stocky guy shot around like a startled child.

'What?' the engineer growled, puffing smoke furiously.

Eddie jerked a thumb over his shoulder. 'I'm going down into the tunnel. I think Carver's got a problem.'

'Fine,' Bulger replied, turning his back on the man as he stumbled through the rain and let himself down.

'Little robots, you say? What can these little robots do? And what are they made of, if they're so small?'

'They're made of carbon,' Bulger explained over the din of the chugging winch engine, his end of the line. 'And they can do anything you want. Correct tissue damage inside your body. Cut out a cancer. Build microchips from the atom up—'

'The ones you got right there?'

'No. I don't know what these ones are programmed for, but the potential's there. All we have to do is reverse engineer them in the lab.'

'I don't understand.'

'Jay, just find a vid-link. I'll show you,' the engineer demanded gruffly.

The lawyer paced in front of the open doors to Pope Lucien Sfiorza's office and hung on every word that escaped from deep within the plush interior. As much an exercise in wealth and opulence as any of the other Vatican palaces, it didn't have the frescoes of Michelangelo, like the Pauline Chapel, or the architectural touch of Bernini. But the Pontifical Apostolic Palace was a palace nonetheless, its splendor tempered only by its pursuit of utility. After all, people worked here. God's work went on next door.

In the Pope's office the President of the United States sat taking tea with the President and CEO of Rola Corp.'s Ripley Thorne, alongside Rabbi Malachai Stern straight in from Jerusalem, while the Pope himself, resplendent in his robes, sat behind his desk.

They were discussing matters that went far beyond miniature robots. They were discussing things that, simply put, brought the cornerstones of western society into question. They were concerned with the end of the status quo. That, to them, was what Atlantis represented. And they didn't like it.

Neither did they like the fact that sound traveled. It was clear Houghton's relentless movement while glued to his cellular phone was making him few friends.

'I'm sorry, Mr Houghton, but you really must try to keep your voice down,' an eminent priest warned quietly and patiently. 'I'm Father McRack, one of Pope Sfiorza's aides.'

'Tell him to forgive me,' Houghton said rudely. Roger 'Fergus' McRack seemed stunned. 'Well, it *is* his job,' the lawyer added with a shrug.

'Jay? Jay, are you still there?' Bulger croaked.

'Yeah, I'm still here,' Houghton confirmed as Fergus shooed him away from the door and in the direction of a vacant desk a few yards away.

'When you're ready to quietly rejoin the discussions, you may do so,' Fergus warned.

Houghton ignored him. There was a vid-phone on the desk. He transferred the call over and activated the visual. The screen was split. Bulger in one half, tiny little insectlike things moving around on the other. 'Okay, where are the robots?' Houghton demanded.

'You're looking at them.'

'Those things are robots? They look like bugs. How big are they?'

'So small, you could fit a hundred thousand of 'em on the head of a pin.'

'I see,' Houghton said, impressed. Now he got it. 'Holy shit!'

From way down the other end of the office complex, through the mahogany double doors, Pope Lucien Sfiorza shot the lawyer a look of censure.

THE CHAMBERS

Clifford Maple stuffed fresh tobacco into his mouth as one of his men pushed past to get a better look at the subterranean opening hidden in the heart of the Amazon.

Like a catacomb in a European gothic cathedral, the great expanse of space before them was only possible because incredible arches of red stonework supported the weight of the eight enormous pyramids above ground. Square pillars of stone, 40 feet across each side supported the archways. But overall it was still possible to see the entire catacomb from end to end. Raised pathways snaked around it, climbing higher, up to ten feet above ground level, as they wended their way toward eight separate crystal chambers. Above them were suspended huge crystal pyramids. One for each chamber.

In the ceiling, above the eight C60 pyramids, were twisted stone funnels that disappeared up into the darkness, each penetrating deep into the interior of the pyramid above.

'Why do I feel like I'm looking at the insides of a V8 engine?' Maple wondered.

Up in one of the chambers, his men were busy assessing how best to dismantle the crystal structure. It was a precarious place to be, considering the ground was beginning to tremble once more.

Maple spat a globule of black tar-ridden slime out across the floor. 'We'll be lucky if this place doesn't shake itself apart,' he said.

The overall shape of the catacomb was roughly oblong. And in the center of each outer wall, just a few feet off the ground, were the entrances to four large offshoot tunnels. They had arrived through one of them. But all four of were now trickling filthy muddy water as a prelude to flooding the entire area.

'Where the hell is Carver?' Maple fretted, checking his watch. He looked to his men. 'Can we get to work, or what?'

'We really need that particle beam, sir. This shit's tough to cut.'

Maple scratched his head in frustration. He was not a man who liked to be kept waiting. 'You and you – go get that gun. If Carver gives you any trouble, knee-cap him.'

They didn't need telling twice. But as they passed by the entrance of one tunnel, on the way to their exit, one of the men suddenly froze while his companion turned back on his boss – something the renegade wasn't used to. 'Maybe we should come back and do this later,' he said hoarsely. 'We got company.'

Maple spun on his heel in time to watch a shimmering crystal-blue figure clamber down from the tunnel in front of his men and advance. 'Who the fuck is this joker?' he snarled.

'The Machiguenga,' one of his more Hispanic accomplices hissed.

'The Machiguenga are dead.' He went for his rifle, and indicated to his men to follow him down. Grabbed his radio. 'Carver, come in!' Static. 'Carver, get your ass down here, we need back-up.' But Carver wasn't coming. Carver would never be coming.

Unarmed, naked and vaguely defined, the effigy of a large man lumbered toward them. The peculiarity of the situation seemed to fail to register in the minds of the mercenaries. All they perceived was a threat, whether that threat was transparent and crystalline in nature, or not.

Fanning out they raised their rifles in unison and fired at will, indiscriminately. Some in short bursts, others one shot at a time, trying to prevent the figure from advancing, which in the end was what allowed them to neglect their flanks.

Suddenly an arm shot out from behind an archway and grabbed one of the mercenaries roughly by the shoulder, swinging him around. There was a struggle, but only on the part of the human as he glared into and through the eyes of a second attacker. He became aware of those strange letters etched across the being's forehead. Became aware too of its sheer size and power. Then realized there was a third stone giant, waiting in the wings.

Petrified, from the Greek, meaning 'turned to stone'. It was awesome to discover that the stone had come to life and turned on him. When the effigy decided to act it did so at speed, tearing the mercenary's head from his shoulders and dumping the two parts unceremoniously on the ground before heading for the rest of the squad. Which was just about all the persuasion the rabble needed to turn tail, and run.

'Call the choppers!' Maple yelled into his radio, as he broke into a sweat-soaked sprint for the exit. 'Call the fucking choppers, now!'

But there was no panic on the other end of the line. There was no hyperventilated frenzy of a comrade desperate to come to their aid. With the din of rushing blood in their ears, the roar of pumping adrenaline, and the thud, thud, thud of combat boots on wet rock flooring, their radios stayed alarmingly silent – confirming that they were on their own.

Maple fumbled with his broadcast unit, trying to get it to send out a signal, but luck wasn't with him. Spitting his tobacco out of his mouth, he ripped the plastic earpiece from his ear and flung it away. Fired covering rounds into the spiraled tunnel ahead of them, and clambered inside.

What none of the mercenaries did, was to check whether they were being followed. Had they done so, they would have seen three crystal effigies of men pull up short at the entrance to the tunnel and hesitate, before finally retreating and going their separate ways, returning to wherever they had come from. For it seemed the tunnel the mercenaries had chosen was not their domain, but the domain of something else.

And that something else was waiting for them.

Like a painted portrait that was still wet, the human head sticking out the side of the tunnel was fused to the Carbon 60 spiral, and looked as if it had been smeared throughout the crystal, like a swirl of strawberry sauce in a pot of yogurt.

It was Carver's head.

Maple felt sick. Fought the knots twisting in the pit of his stomach. 'Dear God . . .'

'Fuck, man! Fuck!' one of his men screamed, ripping at his own scalp as he tried to come to terms with the total insanity of what he was seeing.

The whole spiral convulsed, like a snake digesting a rodent. Carver's head stretched out along the crystal as if it were made of rubber, while slowly it began losing color, turning gray as it dissolved.

Maple didn't want to stick around and see anymore. 'Come on,' he ordered, leading the way.

The men broke into a run, leaping through the water as if it didn't exist. Sprinting past odd Carbon 60 protrusions that seemed to be lining their journey, paying them little attention as they pushed on. But the protrusions were growing. Thrusting out. Turning pointed. Becoming spikes.

Becoming spears.

When the spears launched they took the stragglers first, catching them completely off-guard. Like pikes from a Dark Ages battle they shot forward at an explosive rate, pierced straight through the abdomen of two men and propelled them at the wall opposite. Their screams were intense as agony swept over them. And though they struggled against being impaled, their actions were for naught, as the crystal spears continued to blast straight through them, their trailing ends mutating into a mass of curved spikes designed to split the men apart.

It was over in a matter of seconds, forcing Maple to widen his eyes.

He was out of his league.

'The point about Schrödinger and his cat,' Hackett explained, back in the lab with the others, 'is you put a cat in a box and close the box and the cat is both there and not there all at the same time.'

Scott swiveled on his chair. 'Whatever you say.'

'But that's not important,' Hackett told him. 'What's important is life is an extension of a crystal. Order means life. Crystals and cells are one and the same, they both do exactly the same job. They repli-cate. They grow by stacking identical units one on top of the other. And at some point, crystals and cells were exactly the same entity. What is the basic constant of life? What do all living things do? Living things replicate. Out of chaos, order is born. God creates the Big Bang. The Big Bang creates carbon crystals. Carbon crystals create DNA. DNA creates living cells. Cells create mankind. Mankind creates intelligence. Intelligence creates God . . .'

'Man destroys God.'

'God destroys man,' Sarah added.

'Carbon 60 starts life all over again,' Hackett concluded.

'You got all that,' Scott asked, perplexed, 'from a trip to a *bio*-lab?'

'It was very stimulating. The irony is,' Hackett said, 'we know why all this is happening. There's just nothing we seem to be able to do about it.'

'Wait a minute,' Matheson interrupted. 'Are you suggesting that if life on earth was destroyed, Atlantis would be able to re-seed life? That it's biologically potent?'

'What more is life, than a few billion molecules that decide on a whim to be you for a while? They can just as easily decide to be something else.'

November was curious. 'Life started out as a crystal of carbon?' Hackett nodded. 'In the Bible, didn't God create Adam from clay? And breathe life into him? What better way is there of breathing life into a carbon structure, than by tapping directly into the energy of the solar wind?'

'In pre-Islamic Iran,' Scott revealed, 'the Avestic Aryans believed that Yima, their version of Noah, during the Flood, was ordered to make a Var – an underground place, that linked the four corners of the earth, where the seed of all livings things would be kept and stored. After the Flood it became covered in snow and ice. And remains so to this day.'

Jack Bulger sat forward, trying to hide his glee as he leaned into the camera and explained a few things to Houghton. In 1956, John Van Neumann, father of artificial life, proposed machines that could replicate themselves. In 1986, K. Eric Drexler took the idea one step further and christened it nanotechnology. Now in 2012, the name of Jack Bulger would be on everyone's lips. He had made this theoretical discovery a reality. And Bulger wanted one hell of a deal.

'Explain to me,' the lawyer was asking, 'how these larger devices work, when these tiny robots fuse together to become bigger units. Is there any limit to their size?'

Bulger was confident. 'None that I'm aware of. It simply depends on how strong their chemical bonds are. I would imagine about the largest thing they could assemble to become would be a thimble. Any bigger and they'd run into problems. But I can't say for certain.'

'And they can disassemble back to their original state at any time?'

'It seems that way to me. Sure.'

Houghton narrowed his eyes as he contemplated the implications. 'Extraordinary.'

'Angel Base, come in! This is the Tooth Fairy! Bulger, you ignorant fuck – *Come in*!' Maple screamed into the radio, as the assault intensified. 'Bulger, if you can hear this, send for the choppers *now*!'

He fired a constant barrage of bullets into the darkness ahead as he sprinted for the opening in the ceiling. There was light ahead. He was drawing ever closer, even as his final man was picked off and sent spluttering to the tunnel wall in a spray of blood and torment.

Maple didn't look back.

He was going to make it. He was damn sure he was going to make it. Because up ahead, still set up on its tripod and hooked into the power supply was the particle beam. Which was handy because as he squeezed his rifle's trigger it clicked, and failed to deliver.

He slung it over his shoulder as he picked up the pace. He could feel his heart trying to thump its way out of his chest. Could see the spikes growing large in the periphery of his vision. Sensed the impending wave of destruction – and calmed.

Timing, as any professional would tell you, was everything.

He dived forward, tucking his feet in and pulling his head down as he turned his fall into a roll. The spears above him lashed out and smacked into the tunnel wall opposite as Maple bumped to a halt by the tripod and recovered his senses. He stayed crouched, ever watchful for a further attack as he keyed the power switch. Flared up the energizer – and fired.

The fire power was formidable as a twisted rope of pure energy arced from the barrel and shattered the crystal spikes, one after the other, in successive lines down each side of the tunnel wall. He could hear movement behind, swung the gun around and pumped explosive uncontrolled rage into the crystal spikes that were growing out of the tunnel in that direction as well.

But the lightning storm was illuminating in other ways too. For where there used to be large cube-shaped holes in the crystal spiral, there were now burnt reddish-colored patches of new crystal, slowly pulsing their own brand of energy. A distinct brand that bore traces of human flesh.

For the spiral was healing.

There was a clattering, like broken glass being scrunched together and rattled around. It was coming from the direction of the crystal chamber. The direction from which he'd just come.

Maple twisted at the hip, brought the gun around to face the onslaught and cranked up the power setting as far as it would go. He activated his radio again, trying to make contact with the surface.

There was a crackle of noise. And at last, the faint hint of some-body on the other end. 'Bulger!' Maple yelled. 'Answer me, damn it! Throw me a rope ladder or something! Put the winch into gear. I gotta get outta here!'

But the response was as garbled as it was intermittent. Had Bulger even heard him?

He struggled with the beam confinement settings on the device, adjusting the focus to give a wider beam. Anything that caused as much death and destruction in its path as possible.

The glass-grinding sound drew closer, until before him, stood another one of those huge, nine-foot-tall men. For a moment, it just stood there, appearing to weigh up the situation and judge the next move. It took a tentative step forward. And that was when Maple fired, slicing into the creature's gut and chopping it in two. The top half of its body slid off and crashed to the ground.

Maple savored the moment, but it was short-lived, because the top half was making its way back to its legs. It gripped one leg and dissolved into the appendage at tremendous speed. Within moments the top half of the body was starting to take shape once again.

Maple wasn't about to wait for an instant replay. He swung his head up and saw a rope dangling just out of reach up the muddy hole. He jumped. Failed with the first try. Made it with the second. Used every muscle in his upper body to heave his frame further up the line until eventually he could hook his foot around the bottom portion and begin the arduous monkey climb to the top.

He glanced back down, saw the crystal man standing below,

seeming to be at a loss over what to do. And decided that it was a good time to radio again.

He unclipped the unit. Put it to his mouth.

There was a crackle of noise. Not from the vid-phone, but from one of the radios scattered across the table. Bulger tried to ignore it. It was cutting in and out erratically. Annoyingly. But it wouldn't go away.

Bulger made his apologies to the lawyer, who simply smiled from his end of the link, and sifted through the units one by one before zeroing in on the correct device. He thumbed the transceiver roughly and growled: 'Okay, this better be good, I'm in the middle of stuff here.' The frantic voice cut in and out as the signal failed to penetrate. 'Say again. Over.'

'Get – me – the – >*static*< – out – of – here!' Bulger blinked. It was Maple. 'I'm on the rope!'

Bulger shot round. Behind him, the only rope still hanging down into the tunnel below was twitching. 'Shit!'

He ran for the rope. It wasn't attached to the winch, just tied off around a stake in the ground. He shoved his gloves on his hands; gave a brief nod to Houghton. 'Stay on the line', he shouted. 'I'll be just a minute.'

He ran his fingers along the rope until he found a spot where he could pry his fingers underneath and take a good firm grasp. He leant into it and tugged. Pulled for all he was worth, groaning through gritted teeth, but it was no use. Maple was too heavy.

He staggered to the hole in the ground, careful not to slip on the mud and go hurtling down instead. He pulled out a flashlight. Shone it down. Watched raindrops disappear past the light beam and plummet into the darkness. He cupped his hand around his mouth and hollered: 'Maple! Is that you? Maple, can you hear me? What's goin' on?'

There was a muffled response. Loud but incomprehensible.

'Maple, you're too heavy. I can't pull on the rope. You're gonna have to climb out!'

There was a rope ladder. Yes! Now he remembered. Over by his tent, there was a stash of back-up equipment. Not a lot of it, but he distinctly remembered seeing a nylon safety ladder. He held out a hand to the darkness below and waved it. 'I'll be back in a second! I'm gonna go get the ladder!'

He found it in a black plastic trunk, under a spare tarp. Pulled it out and rushed it over to the side. It wasn't very long. What to do? It had a single hoop at the top, but he had no time to play around and hook it up to the winch. Instead, he threw the hoop over the metal stake and lobbed the ladder down the hole. He heard it slap against the wet mud with a squelch, angled his flashlight, and could see movement. Yeah, there was Maple's distinctive Panama bobbing up and down, its colored twirl flapping as he clambered up the ladder.

'Boy,' Bulger huffed, 'you really had me going there for a while.' He didn't want to stick around at the edge. Besides, he had a phone-call to terminate. Bulger spun on his heel and went back to his laptop, not bothering to check on the man and his misfortune.

He sat heavily in his seat. 'I think,' he said to Houghton, wiping rainwater from his face, 'we better terminate this fairly quickly.'

'Who's that?' Houghton asked, referring to the man climbing out of the tunnel behind Bulger.

'That's Maple. The biggest nutcase the company's money could buy.'

Houghton was impressed as the man strode closer, the gathering winds blowing the hat clean off his head. 'Jesus, he really is big.'

Bulger frowned. Turned around to see what the lawyer was talking about, and wished, for all the world, that he hadn't. For standing before him was a giant of a man. And when lightning streaked across the sky, he could see clean through him. He gasped, involuntarily.

And the only thing he could think of saying was: 'That's bigger than a thimble.'

SFIORZA'S OFFICE

Fergus sat stoically at his desk on the far side of the room. He doodled on a notepad in a successful attempt to make it look like he was working, even though everybody knew why he was there. He was the monitor, and he monitored effectively.

He adjusted his earpiece as he paid close attention to the phone-call between Houghton and Bulger unfolding across his computer screen. It had become only marginally more interesting than the conversation he was taping right in front of him.

'What is it I can do for you?' the Pope had asked.

'I want a third term,' the President had replied. 'I want a third term, and I want gun control. Makes the public more compliant.' And then: 'What is it I can do for you?' the President had asked in return.

'You must do what you can to save mankind and save the earth, of course. But afterwards, should you find yourself in a position where Atlantis is still standing, I want you to destroy it,' the Pope had responded. 'I want all evidence of that destabilizing scourge brought to wrack and ruin. Mankind's past must remain a secret place where only the select few may be permitted to tread. Information is a threat to us. Why else would we have kept the Holy Book from the general populace for more than a millennium? The existence of Atlantis and all that it may teach would make a mockery of modern religion. A society without religion is a society without self-belief and self-worth.

Ultimately to retain social control, a little lost knowledge is a good thing. Of course, all that is academic if these scientists cannot save our planet.'

The Rabbi had remained silent on the subject.

Granted, neither man had said it in such blunt terms. But they had said it nonetheless, voiced in the language of diplomacy.

The United States government had thought as much. That was why they had initiated Operation Wrecking Ball to begin with. As they spoke, a team under the auspices of the United Nations was about to enter Atlantis. They were about to uncover its secrets. And when their job was done, they were going to destroy it because it threatened the minds of the good citizens of the earth. Its very existence called world religions into question.

Organized religion was an odd business, but make no mistake – it was still a business. Business traded. Business understood when it was time to cooperate.

Fergus was contemplating what had been said when events on his computer screen started unfolding at a phenomenal rate.

A crystal-like giant stood over Jack Bulger. Looked to the blocks of darkened Carbon 60 under the tarp, and back to Bulger again in successive glances.

On his end of the line, the lawyer sat forward, mesmerized. 'Thanks, Jack. I'm glad you brought this to my attention.'

Jack Bulger cocked his head. He knew what that meant. Houghton had surmised something about the situation that suggested he was about to become the biggest loser in all this.

Suddenly the crystal figure grabbed Bulger. Wrestled with him for a moment before putting him over his knee and breaking his back. It peered forward to get a good long look at Houghton, revealing the mysterious letters etched across its forehead in Atlantis glyphs, then it grabbed Bulger by the skull and dragged him across to the hole.

He dropped the body over the edge, before jumping down behind him.

Fergus was stunned.

He covered his mouth, horrified. An inanimate man protecting his domain. An automaton carrying out its master's orders. An image of a man endowed with life. There was only one creature that matched the description. Mentioned briefly in Psalms 139:16, it had its roots firmly planted in ancient Jewish literature – and some Jewish literature that was not quite so ancient.

In the late 1500s a Rabbi known under the acronym The Maharal, or Moraynu HaReaw Judah Loew ben B'zalel – Our Teacher Judah Loew son of B'zalel – was Chief Rabbi of Prague, at the Altneuschul Synagogue. Legend had it he created an effigy of a man and brought it to life. Designed to protect the ghetto, as all such effigies were designed to do, it took its orders too literally and ran amok. Whereupon Rabbi Loew was forced to terminate the creature and reduced it to dust.

Around this time, records showed that Rabbi Loew was invited to discuss alchemy with Emperor Rudulph II. It was not known if they discussed the creature. But it *was* known what the creature was called. It was –

'The Golem,' Fergus murmured under his breath. 'Dear God save us,' he added, letting his eyes rest briefly on Rabbi Stern.

The Golem. The perfect mechanical servant who was brought to life by having a sacred word, or one of the names of God affixed in some manner to its head. The only way to stop it was by removing that word.

Fergus stood, switched his computer off and made his brief excuses as he left. He had not liked the tone of the Pope's discussion. And he had not enjoyed the phone-call he had been monitoring. Both left a bitter taste in the mouth. For in both cases the only conclusion he could draw was that by carrying out the orders of the papacy and removing Richard Scott from his academic post, he had inadvertently placed his friend in such a position that it endangered his life, whether by the forces of Man, or the forces of God. And Fergus was responsible. As he walked the corridors of the chambers of God, the least he could do – the very least – was warn his friend. Because as it happened, Richard was probably the only person on the planet in a position to decipher what was written on the Golem's head. And remove it.

'I know what I'm looking at, Ralph,' Scott conceded. 'But what *am* I looking at?'

Gathered around the workstation with Matheson, the team watched as he operated the controls on the system and a three-dimensional model of the Giza tunnel system rotated about an axis.

'I've run it three different ways,' Matheson said, 'and I get this every time. It's from this data Sarah brought with her.' He patted one of the little data pods carefully. 'This is the tunnel system. Some of it's really deep, ten miles down. You could mine for just about anything there – coal, copper, diamonds – and never go deep enough to realize these things were also down here.'

Scott was puzzled. 'That's a lot of detail. You got all that from radar data?'

'No.' Matheson tapped a button. More views of the tunnel system popped up in various shades of fluctuating orange. He knew his software and he flew around the system at lightning speed. 'There was more than just radar data being recorded on these things,' he said. 'I measured the resistance of the electricity flow in the Carbon 60.'

'I didn't know you could do that. *How* could you do that?'

'I designed these little units,' Matheson said modestly. 'I know what they can do. The flow gave me not only a rough estimate of tunnel length, but told me whether the flow was singular. Whether it split off, diverged or converged with other electrical flows.'

'You're describing a power grid,' Hackett commented.

'That's what it is,' Matheson agreed. 'All the data combined – radar, electrical, seismic – gives me enough information to build up a rough picture of the real layout of the tunnel system *beyond* Giza. That place where this Eric guy frazzled? That acted like a transformer on a power grid, but different. The closest analogy would be a Tesla Coil. Whatever, the point is it was drawing current. And Sarah's right, it's converting earthquake energy, then stepping the electrical current up to a level capable of traveling great distances. A modern level—'

'What do you mean, modern?' November asked.

'We're talking about regular AC current running at 60 cycles per second,' Matheson told her. 'You could easily take your TV down there and hook it up. Modern, November, modern.'

'Sixty,' Pearce wondered. 'There's that magic number again.'

'I don't get it,' Sarah said. 'Why would they need to shunt so much energy around to just blast it off up into space?'

'Because by blasting it off into space, the pyramids act like a release valve on a steam pressure cooker, diverting energy away from us. In effect, saving our damn lives. That Chad earthquake was real powerful. It should have done a lot more damage than it did.'

'You think this is what's happening in Atlantis as well?' November queried.

'Why not?' Matheson replied. 'We can't get in touch with the Chinese base, can we? What if they were sat right on top of something that acted in just the same way *this* acted?'

Pearce was nodding. 'And blasted a beam straight through the ice and destroyed them. That's what I saw. Yes!'

'That Atlantis is sucking solar flare energy down into itself, we've seen. Now we're expected to believe that it's also blasting energy back up into space again. Why? It's a contradiction. Why would it do that?' Hackett demanded.

'Have these energy blasts been registered at any of the other sites?' Sarah asked.

'Not that I'm aware of,' Matheson replied, 'but Giza and Atlantis are the only sites we can be sure have been tampered with excessively by man. Maybe you inadvertently switched something on.'

'But *how* are these sites connected?' Hackett wanted to know.

Matheson eyed Pearce sympathetically. 'Scientifically speaking . . . ? That's what I gotta figure out.'

'Well y'all, I'm done here,' November cut in. She'd been working on the video images all afternoon. Capturing all data on the language written on the C60 in the Giza tunnel system and the footage Sarah had recorded especially for Scott. She'd compared the glyphs with those they had studied in Geneva, and she had compiled the results as best she knew how.

Scott jumped to his feet. 'What have we got?' he asked excitedly.

Proudly, she announced: 'We've got an alphabet.'

THE FIRST
PROTOCOL

[In Ancient Chinese Culture] a man absorbed with writing was absorbed not just with words but with symbols and, through the art of writing with the brush, with a form of painting and thus with the world itself. To the lover of high culture, the way in which something was written could be as important as its content.

David N. Keightley, 'The Origins of Writing in China'
An essay in: *The Origins of Writing*, Edited by
Wayne M. Senner, 1989

RETRIEVAL STAGE 1

Hieroglyphics, from the Greek word *ierolyphika*, meaning 'sacred carved letters'.

Across November's screen were displayed a series of glyphs that seemed to defy understanding. This was the earliest known system of writing ever discovered: the first protocol. It dated even from before the time of Babel, when the divine speech of Adam was smashed into a thousand tongues by God, made all the more confusing by the fact that there were only sixteen symbols.

'That's it?' Sarah was amazed. 'That's not much of an alphabet. Is that enough to cover all sounds in a language?'

'Not our language,' Scott agreed, 'but some languages? Sure. Scandinavian Runes only had sixteen symbols. That was enough for them. The Old Germanic Runes used twenty-four. Rune, by the way, does *not* mean "mystery" or "secret", as the mystics seem to think. It means to scratch, to dig, or to make grooves.'

'How dull,' Hackett remarked.

'Do you think this language might be related to Runes?' November asked.

'No,' he said confidently. 'Runes evolved from Latin letters anyway – the same letters we still use today.'

'Runes are too modern. I get it.'

'Right. And the reason they look so different is because of the medium they used. Look.' He grabbed a pen and his notebook.

Scrawled out a few letters. 'Y'see, these are Runes. This is Futhark writing:

ᛋ ᛗ ᚨ ᚱ ᛏ ᚠ ᛋ ᛋ

That's nothing like what we're seeing on the screen. Runes are all straight lines because everything was scratched into wood or stone. It's simply too cumbersome to try and even attempt curves. Ogham, the Old Irish language from about two thousand years ago, is the same. It consisted of lines and dots, mostly etched into the corners of standing stones.' He drew a few of those symbols too.

├ ╪ ┥ ╬

'That vertical line you see is usually drawn first, and all the side lines are drawn going vertically down a continuous mid-line. It's usually up to groups of five lines on any one side because it evolved from a finger language. Which side of the line denoted the left or the right hand. It was also adopted by the Picts on the British Isles. But their language is totally unknown so their Ogham texts, even though we can make out some of the letters, are still undeciphered.'

'But this C60 is crystal. It's hard. So why has this writing got curves, if it's so difficult to make?' November asked reasonably.

Hackett tried his best not to sound brusque. 'That's what I was saying, back in the lab! This writing shows no signs of having been etched into the crystal. In fact, it seems to be a natural side effect of the way in which this crystal was manufactured. Like it's part of the design.'

'Is that possible,' she asked, 'to grow a crystal to a certain shape by design?'

'Sure,' Sarah interjected. 'Airline manufacturers do it all the time. The rotary blade of a jet engine is grown out of a single crystal of metal. It's designed that way because it's stronger. More able to take the pressure . . .' Sarah went quiet as she realized what she was saying. 'Hey, could all those C60 structures we've found be single crystals?'

'That would go a long way to explain how they survived thousands of years, some of them, miles under the ice,' Hackett nodded.

But Scott was elsewhere, completely absorbed in the writing.

'So I guess, if you want curves any other way you've gotta paint 'em on,' November prodded.

'Huh? Oh, yeah. That's what the Chinese did. Demotic, the shorthand version of hieroglyphics – that was painted. Once you painted it you could use curves, pictures, all sorts.'

'Hey, they used curves and pictures in Egypt, all over their monuments,' Sarah corrected. 'Remember? I've just been there.'

'Yes. But they're ornamental. They're big. By that reckoning, if you wanted to read the latest novel you'd have to literally wait to read the library from wall to wall. You wouldn't write that large in everyday living. Any Egyptian writing the size of *your* handwriting is painted, whether it's on a wall or parchment. It's just too intricate to be cast in stone. And in fact, in Chinese, the earliest known writing isn't painted at all. It's scratched into pottery and consists entirely of straight lines.'

'How many characters did that have?'

'Thirty. Written mostly on pottery in Pan-p'o Village, Sian, Shens, about 5,000BCE. Some epigraphers have dismissed them because they're not pictograms. They're abstract.'

'They're saying early man wasn't capable of abstract thought?' Sarah chided. 'If they're not pictograms then they're not writing. Isn't that a little arrogant? Didn't they ever stop to consider maybe their theory was wrong, and not the facts?'

Scott agreed with her warmly.

'Dr Scott,' November said, 'didn't you say early cuneiform was more complicated and abstract than later cuneiform? As if humans were advanced but seemed to be forgetting their knowledge base?'

'Yup. And the same thing's going on in China. The trouble is, there's little evidence that Chinese writing was *ever* pictographic, so they can't just dismiss it on that score. Except for what they found in the Shantung region, by a group known as the Yi, who settled in the Lower Yangtze,' he revealed. 'Totemism. Pictorial designs thousands of years old – of the sun and a bird, together. Read as: *yeng niao*. Sunbirds.'

'The Phoenix again,' November remarked.

Scott nodded. 'Anyway,' he said, 'Chinese is logographic. Started out in a similar fashion to hieroglyphics. They used pictures based on sounds denoting what they wanted to say. For example, it's like you might draw a pear fruit for the word "pair", even though it has an entirely different meaning. It's the sound that's important.'

As Scott said all this, his eyes never left the screen. Never wavered from the symbols in his hunt for their meaning. It was like the spew of information was really an autopilot response, something for his mouth to do while his mind went into overdrive.

'It's also called the rebus principle,' he went on, 'where pictograms spell out the word in a similar fashion to letters. It was the same in Egyptian hieroglyphics, but it scaled new heights there. You could spell the same word in any number of ways.'

'That must have caused problems,' Hackett suggested.

'Not for them. Just us. We ended up building a whole mystical world around hieroglyphs for a while because we couldn't read them. Stuff like assuming the Egyptians used the symbol of a goose when they wanted to say "son" because they believed the goose was the only bird that loved and nurtured its offspring. When in fact it was just that they're phonetic. The two words sound the same.'

Sarah moved in close to the linguist, equally intrigued by the writing. Asked gently: 'So did you get around to figuring out what the hieroglyphics in my tunnel actually spell out?'

Scott said that he had and picked up the notebook he'd left by November's computer. He flipped to the right page and announced: *Behold! The language of Thoth! The books of wisdom of the Great Ennead*—

'Great Ennead?'

'All the gods together. Kinda like Congress. *Behold!*' Scott continued. '*What secrets lie here! Despair for they are not to be known by men!*'

Hackett was disturbed. 'That's *it?*'

'That's it. Oh, and then it just repeats it over and over – for two miles. Interspersed with heroic tales of kings who tried to have it decoded and failed.'

'Great,' Hackett moaned. 'That's not what I expected to hear.'

Suddenly, the epigraphist sat bolt upright. 'That's it!' he proclaimed. 'At least – that's what it's *not!*' He ran his finger across the monitor glass. Remembered his studies from when he was an undergrad. 'As Sol Worth said in 1975: "Pictures can't say ain't!"'

'What are you talking about?'

'Pictograms and iconograms. Pictures. They can't effectively represent verb tenses, adverbs or prepositions. And what they definitely can't do is assert the *non*-existence of what it is they depict. If you wanted to try and communicate with people in the future, you wouldn't use pictograms.' He put his thumb over the symbol of the circle with the cross. 'Forget this one. It's the exception. But look at the rest of these. What do they remind you of? A table? A chair? A sack of potatoes?'

November shook her head. 'Nothing. They don't look like anything I've ever seen.'

'Exactly,' Scott exclaimed. 'They're abstract. That means they're either letters – A, B, C – or syllables – ch, th, ph.'

Hackett leaned into the screen. 'Or they could be numbers,' he suggested.

'They're not numbers,' Scott replied confidently.

'How do you know?'

'I just do.'

'Asking the right types of questions, huh?'

Scott let it pass. Turned to November. 'Can this thing give me percentages? Tell me how many times each one of these symbols is used in the texts?'

'Sure,' November said, getting to work on the problem. 'You mean like a frequency chart? What will that achieve?'

'Different letters in our own language are used more often than others. The letter E is used far more than, say, the letter Z.' He shared a look with Sarah. For a brief moment it looked like she might even kiss him.

Instead, she rested a hand on his shoulder. 'You're a clever man, Richard Scott.'

'Thanks,' Scott replied proudly. But as he returned his attention to the computer screen he caught November scowling at him.

'What is it?' Scott asked innocently.

November went back to her work. 'Never mind,' she grumbled.

'*What?*' Scott insisted. But November refused to answer.

Scott pushed his chair back from the computer, looked to Hackett for support. But the amused physicist simply shook his head and tutted. 'Playing with fire,' he whispered. 'Playing with fire.'

* * *

The beeping was insistent. Annoying. November's computer had completed its frequency distribution calculations.

'Ah-ha,' Scott enthused, following the young student's every movement as she punched up the data.

There was a spread of figures, ranging from 6.17 percent at the low end for one glyph to 6.36 percent at the high end. The mean was 6.25 percent. Which, as it happened, was exactly the product of 100 divided by 16. In other words, the frequency of each glyph's appearance within the combined texts was equal. No one glyph was more dominant than the next. So it was impossible to tell from the spread of figures just which glyph might be a consonant, and which might be a vowel.

'Damn it!' Scott spat in frustration. 'Godamnit!' Sarah gave him a sympathetic look. Though he appreciated it, he couldn't quite bring himself to make an acknowledgement.

'If it makes you feel any better,' Hackett observed, 'it proves the language was designed that way.'

Scott shot him a puzzled look. 'You're suggesting this language was a constructed one? Not evolved naturally, like Aymara?'

'Clearly,' Hackett said. 'If those glyphs were random you'd still get an unequal frequency distribution. Not in the same way as you'd get from the distribution of letters in a naturally evolved language, otherwise you'd detect a pattern and crack the code. But you'd get an uneven spread just the same. For random letters to come out spread evenly, you'd need an infinite numbers of letters, which you just don't have. Clearly, whoever designed that language intended it to be equal.'

'The problem,' Scott said, 'is what kind of language uses letters on a totally even basis, with as many Zs as there are As or Es? None that I'm aware of.'

SEAS: ROUGH

WEATHER: GALE FORCE 4 – RISING SHARPLY

They broke for dinner at 7.30 pm, but the motion of the boat meant the landlubbers didn't feel much like eating, in spite of the medication.

Hackett worked on the base 60 number stream they had found encoded in the crystal, but try as he might he just couldn't make sense of it. It literally was just a stream of numbers – there seemed to be no pattern to it. True, pi had been worked out to 8 billion decimal places and still made no sense, but as a number it was essential to measurement and construction. Could this number stream simply be pi in base 60? A quick conversion by the computer proved it was not. Neither was it any other special mathematical number that might be recognized in standard decimal.

The thing about numbers was they were independent of people. Aliens would be able to count in the same way. Numbers were embedded in the fabric of space and time. Two was always going to be two, even if another culture gave it another name. Hackett figured it was just a question of looking long enough and hard enough before he worked out what these numbers represented.

But there were other problems to be solved. He turned his attention to gravity waves, and found, disturbingly, that he was predicting a fairly accurate timetable for events over the next two days.

He passed the information on to Gant, warning him that the figures needed to be confirmed. Then he went out on deck for some air, and found Scott in a thick yellow yachting jacket, watching the bow of the ship crash through unbelievably sized waves. The linguist was sympathetic to his plight.

'The Mayans measured time with special numbers,' Scott told him. 'A hundred and forty-four thousand, seven thousand two hundred, three hundred and sixty, two-hundred and sixty and twenty. But their most important number was nine. The scripture speaks of the cycles of the "nine lords of the night".'

'The planets?'

'Maybe. But I wouldn't go shouting about it or someone's gonna want to see some proof,' Scott said dryly. 'The number a hundred and forty-four thousand crops up in the Book of Revelation linked to time. Seven is one of those numbers that just about pops up every-where. Seven Seals. Seven Deadly Sins. Seven trumpets being sounded seven times. Walls tumble, the world is created. Eight is associated with reincarnation, while twelve has all sorts of links – the Twelve tribes of Israel, the Twelve Apostles, the number of Chinese "Years". A hundred and fifty-three crops up in connection with the "enlightened ones". The disciples caught a hundred and fifty-three fishes, which in numerology is the sum of one to seventeen. Also, one plus five plus three equals nine.'

'Numerology,' Hackett repeated as the ship lurched awkwardly. 'What is that? Linking letters to numbers, jumbling them up and coming up with some hidden answer – is that it?'

'People will always be attracted to the hidden.'

'Nature has its special numbers too,' the physicist said. 'Three, five, eight, thirteen, twenty-one thirty-four, fifty-five and eighty-nine, for example. Lilies have three, buttercups five, delphiniums eight and marigolds thirteen. Asters, of course have twenty-one.'

'What are you talking about?'

'Petals on flowers.'

'There's a pattern in those numbers?'

'Sure. Just add the preceding two numbers together and you get the next number in the sequence. Three plus five equals eight, and so on. It's called the Fibonacci scale, after Leonardo Fibonacci who discovered it in the thirteenth century when he studied rabbit popu-lations. The scale reveals phi, not to be confused with *pi*. Phi helps you calculate proportion, from the proportion of the human body, to plant-seed spirals on sunflowers.'

A staggeringly ferocious blast of spray suddenly pelted the two men as the *Polar Star* crashed through another heavy wave.

'Jesus Christ!' Scott yelped, trying to get his breath back. He wiped his face down.

Hackett shuddered. Pointing to the horizon. 'Look,' he said. 'Our first iceberg.'

They watched the looming white jagged mountain of frozen water for a while before Hackett said: 'I think maybe we should head back inside.'

Scott agreed, spitting out seawater. 'I dunno,' he said. 'What do you think? Reckon maybe we'll get this all figured out in time? Honestly?'

Hackett dug his hands into his pockets. 'Honestly? I don't know.'

Scott nodded, taking it all in stoically. 'I must confess,' he added mildly, 'I'm starting to like you, Professor Hackett. You're a challenging man.'

Hackett seemed genuinely taken aback. 'Well, I'm, uh, starting to like you too, Professor Scott. What do you say, when this is all over we do this again some time?'

'Not a chance.'

When the two men stepped back into the lab they found Sarah sitting behind a computer with November. They were studying the Atlantis glyphs and appeared embarrassed at being caught.

November prodded the geologist. 'Are you gonna tell him?'

'Tell me what?'

Sarah glanced furtively at her coffee before taking a gulp. 'Aw . . . shit.' She looked up after a moment and confronted the men squarely. 'Are you gonna get all male on me and be offended if a woman offered to help you out here?'

Scott smirked. 'It's not like stopping and asking for directions. Sure, go ahead.'

Matheson turned from his own computer to listen. Even Pearce, who looked exhausted and disheveled, wrapped up in a blanket and sitting in a corner, seemed to perk up.

Okay, Sarah seemed to be saying as she got to her feet. She ran her finger over the screen. 'Ralph, could you punch up that overhead schematic of the Giza site you were working on?'

Matheson did as he was told. Angled the monitor for everyone to see. Sarah went back to the screen. 'Right, y'see here, this glyph? Simplified and stylized, it's similar to the layout of Giza. I didn't think much of it until November mentioned that you thought this glyph right here didn't just represent the sun, but also resembled Atlantis.'

Hackett shrugged. 'Coincidence?' But it was clear he didn't mean it.

Sarah took a breath. 'I would have said so too, but *this* glyph resembles the layout of the series of pyramids in Peru.'

Scott narrowed his eyes thoughtfully. 'Interesting.'

'I never did visit Peru,' Pearce commented bleakly.

'Tell me something,' Scott asked quietly, blowing a whisper of steam from a fresh cup of coffee and confronting Pearce. 'How do you do it?'

Pearce pulled the blanket in tighter around his shoulders. He looked so tired. So drained, emotionally and physically. 'Remote viewing? I dunno,' he confessed. 'I just go there.'

'You have to concentrate, right?'

'I have to stay focused, but not really concentrate. Not in the sense you mean. I just get a feel for everything all around me, all at once. And I have to pick my way through it. Some call it entering the spirit plane – kind of a dimensional short-cut – but I always found that a little silly. I mean, who's to say that it's not all in my head, right? The point is . . . uh, how would you describe it?' He thought for a moment.' Okay. There are two ways you can read a page in a book. You can read it a word at a time, and follow the narrative from start to finish in a linear fashion. Or you can rip out all the pages, lay them side by side and take a snapshot of the whole thing. And understand it all in one go. See where it starts. See where it ends. You can refer back to it. Or dive in and out at any point—'

'I see,' Hackett realized earnestly. 'You're describing a photographic memory.'

'Yeah,' Pearce agreed, growing more confident with that notion. 'Yeah, I guess I am. That's a good way of putting it. It's just a different way of thinking, is all. A different way of accessing knowledge. Our modern knowledge system is fragmentary. It actively hinders us from seeing the whole book. We're taught to think in terms of words and concept, to specialize in areas. To restrict ourselves to fields instead of paying attention to an entire science, or an entire art. I believe ancient civilizations thought very differently to the way we think now.'

'Could be true,' Scott agreed. 'Even today, linguists can't even agree a definition of what a word actually is. Is it a sound? A string of sounds? Is it a combination of both? Or something else? Sounds pathetic but it has very real, practical consequences.

'For instance, when epigraphers cracked Linear C, the early Greek-syllable-based script, on the island of Cyprus, they found they couldn't rely on the modern, everyday notion of suffixes and prefixes to explain away the patterns they detected in the glyph texts. In other words, blocks of letters at the front of words, like "in", as in "inaction", or at the ends of words, like "less" as in "motionless" were prefixes and suffixes. "Less" was a determinative. When the object is without motion, it is motion*less*. This determinative could in turn be applied to any other word. Even a pronoun. If Peter doesn't go to church, the church can be said to be Peter*less*.

'In either case,' Scott said, 'the addition of the determinative does not create two words. It fuses to the initial word, creating a new singular word. But in Linear C the prefixes and suffixes weren't determinatives. They were articles. Words like "a" and "the". So linguists found words like "theking", "thetown" and "agift" – the mark of a very different way of thinking. The only linguist ever to crack two ancient scripts, Easter Island's Ronorongo script and Crete's Phaistos Disk was Dr Steven Roger Fischer. He pointed out that our ancestors tended to think in terms of "units of utterance". That their approach to language was very different.'

To Scott it seemed clear. 'The further back in time you look, the more holistic the approach is to language.'

'Holistic thought? The whole idea in one symbol? Does that mean you think my idea might have some merit?' Sarah asked, directing Scott's attention back to the glyphs.

'It's possible,' he told her. 'When Sir Arthur Evans tried and failed to decode Linear B and the Phaistos Disk in the early 1900s he hypothesized the glyphs had a double meaning. That each glyph was phonetic, but that each glyph also in and of itself had a religious meaning.'

'Was he ever proved right?'

'About the first part of his theory, yes. But the second? No. That doesn't mean you're wrong though. It's just, why would the inventors of this language want to draw our attention to certain cities? It would have to be something somehow obvious to us. But the problem is – what? It's like, if we drew a picture of Moscow, what would you immediately think of?'

'Vodka.'

'Potatoes,' Matheson chipped in. He was met with some puzzled looks all round. Sheepishly the engineer shrugged back at them.

'Lenin,' November said.

'Stalin. Communism. Anastasia. Red Square. Y'see, the list goes on and on. But it's entirely socially and culturally related. It's in our consciousness fed by the mass media. It represents an idea that fills literally volumes. So to us it has context. But in a thousand years what's built up around that image will be forgotten. So if that's how they're trying to communicate with us it's useless. And I hope that's not the case.'

Sarah was confused. 'What are you saying?'

'In my own, roundabout kinda academic way, I'm saying that I think you're on to something. That these cities *are* linked, like some part of a global machine. But to do what? You're more than likely correct. This glyph may represent Peru, just as this one represents Atlantis. But I need more. I need the "why".'

'What's the Phaistos Disk?' November asked.

'A flat round clay tablet the size of a saucer found by the thirty-four-year-old Italian archeologist Luigi Pernier in the Phaistos Temple on Crete, Building 40/101, northwest of the Grand Central Court, July third, 1908,' Pearce announced in a monotonous dirge.

Scott was surprised. Blinked. 'Thanks.'

'Photographic memory,' Pearce quipped, slugging back his coffee. He still looked depressed.

'There were forty-five individual pictograms, pressed into the clay two hundred and forty-one times, making up sixty-one groupings or "words". One hundred and twenty-two glyphs on side A. One hundred and nineteen on side B. The interesting thing is, the writing was written in a spiral, starting on the outer edge and working its way into the center,' said Scott.

'A spiral?' Hackett tensed. 'I hate to state the obvious but the writing in Egypt was written in a spiral. Albeit a large one.'

'True,' Scott agreed. 'But the Phaistos Disk glyphs had marker lines subdividing units of utterance. The Atlantis glyphs are in a continuous string, with no real structure. It's like English if you took out all spaces, punctuation and printed it all in either upper or lower case.'

'There's got to be a language that shares that trait as well, hasn't there?' Matheson prompted.

'There is,' Pearce responded in place of the linguist as Scott drained the last of his coffee.

'It's called Hebrew,' Scott said. 'In Hebrew, in the traditional Torah, the scripture was written out with no punctuation. And no spaces to denote words. Just a stream of letters. And in Hebrew, every letter also represents a number.'

He eyed Hackett, realizing the importance of what he'd just said. The linguist followed the physicist in perfect unison, both turning on a dime to study their own computer screens once more. Matheson was on his feet, followed by November.

Numbers. Letters. Spirals. Patterns . . . Cities.

'You still don't know what this number stream is?' Scott asked quietly.

'Uh-uh. I thought it might be an algorithm. But I can't be certain.'

'The two must be linked.'

Hackett folded his arms. 'How?'

Scott took a deep breath. 'It took Fischer seven years to crack Rongorongo, the Easter Island script. It took Michael Ventris five or six years to crack Linear B. David Stuart first translated Mayan at the age of ten, but he spent his whole life dedicated to that one language. He found that present-day Mayan is similar to the ancient Mayan glyphs and that they're phonetic. He translated what was written at the Temple of the Sun, at Palenque, in a day, when it had taken previous scholars a lifetime to attempt. It's a complex language. It deserves a lifetime dedicated to it. But I've been at this two days, and I have – what? – a couple of days left, maximum. They had a point of reference to refer back to. A garbled modern language, or a similar script that had already been cracked – even a century of previous research to build upon. Just what the hell have I got here?'

November took it all in quietly before responding: 'You have the words.'

'What?'

'Why don't you try looking at it in a different way?' she suggested. Scott didn't appear moved.

'Dr Scott, in your lecture you said, in the beginning was *logos* – the word.'

'Yeah, well, I over-simplified. *Logos* also meant ratio, reason, discourse – even account.'

'Richard, you know you're on to something. We can all feel it,' Sarah insisted. 'You said it yourself, word in action. You have the words. And in order to read them – what's the action?'

Scott studied the screen thoughtfully. 'I didn't have enough information back in Switzerland,' he said. 'Those pieces of rock didn't make up a large enough text. I need to see what this stuff looks like spread out on a flat surface.'

Hackett was with him every step of the way. 'The node,' he suggested.

'Right. Hey, Ralph, that oil node you sunk into the sea floor. That's not too far from here, is it? Can you operate it remotely?'

'That's what it was designed for.'

'So you could power it up? It had a camera on it, didn't it'

'Sure.'

'Call the bridge,' Scott said. 'Tell 'em we need to power up some kind of transmitter – or whatever it is you do to access that thing. And tell them it's imperative I take a look. I need to see what's down there.'

USS HARRY S. TRUMAN

1,524 NAUTICAL MILES NORTH OF McMURDO SOUND

The flight deck heard the engines of the approaching F-24 labor as it fought the volcanic ash jamming up its innards. In the ward room, they were preparing for a task force meeting when they got the word. Up on the bridge, Rear Admiral Dower stood side by side with Captain Henderson, counting the squadron home when a young crewman reported: 'It's Captain Ryman, sir. His eagle just blew an engine!'

All senior officers rushed for the windows to see a thick trail of black smoke billow out from behind the F-24. A Lieutenant at the window flinched as he tracked the source through his binoculars and a loud explosion cracked out across the sky. The whine of the second engine fighting to compensate was horrendous, but with all the volcanic ash it was clear that the plane was losing power.

'This ash is too thick, Captain,' the Lieutenant commented quietly. 'Recommend we don't deploy any more jet patrols for a while.' Henderson agreed darkly, issuing more orders.

'Aye, aye, Captain. Switching to choppers.'

As they watched the plane coast in, the pilot, Captain Jeff Ryman from Iowa with two small children and a wife waiting back home, struggled valiantly with the controls, and as they all said a silent prayer he even managed to bring the nose back up for a moment. But the engine failure had hit at just the wrong moment. He was too low to bail out, the chute would never open. And he was just too far out to make it to the flight deck. In the end, Ryman was just a fireball tumbling across the surface of the ocean.

Henderson looked away. 'Never lost a plane on my watch,' he said. 'Never. Poor bastard. What a way to go. This fucking weather's gonna kill us all.'

Another thin young officer approached his captain. Saluted crisply. 'Captain Henderson, sir!' A slack salute back. 'Major Gant aboard *Polar Star* is on comm requesting permission to deploy their sonar transmitter array.'

'What the hell for?' the captain barked, rummaging around in his khakis for another breath mint to chew on. The crewman explained about the camera on the Rola Corp. deep drilling node but Dower was already on it. Back at the comm desk, he hooked the radio up to his mouth. 'Larry, what's up?'

'The team want to take a look at the Atlantis wall, Admiral. All kinds of reasons. Engineering. Geological. Is there any enemy activity in the area?' Gant asked flatly.

'All clear, Major. And Major . . . ? Tell Mr Pearce thank you very much. The information he provided was accurate, as expected. We now have two SaRGE units each within seventy-five kilometers of *Jung Chang*. Recon reports the base is abandoned. Possibly destroyed.'

'I will tell him, sir—'

Suddenly a wave of activity shot across the comm desk. Double-manned duty officers switched over to radio-based communications. 'We've got McMurdo on line!'

'Hold on, will ya, Major?' Dower snapped, expectantly eyeing the comm officers for more information. One young officer hastily jotted down everything he heard on a notepad and underlined key sections of his scribble with thick graphite from his pencil.

'Sir! We got a window! McMurdo reports a break in the weather. We got four hours to get the team in there by air. McMurdo requests some indication of whether to expect an airlift.' He spun on his chair to face his captain. 'What do we do, sir? The longer we stay on line the more chance the Chinese will be able to tap in.'

Dower swung on Henderson. 'Captain, what have you got with a 1,500-mile range?'

Henderson looked to his men. 'V-TOL,' a Lieutenant answered apprehensively.

Henderson seemed unconvinced. 'At that range?'

'We strap a couple extra fuel tanks on those babies, they'll make it all the way, Captain. I'd bet my life on it.'

V-TOLs were Vertical Take-off and Landing vehicles. Planes that took off like choppers, but flew with the speed and configuration of a fixed-wing aircraft. They were great aircraft but Dower was concerned. 'They don't have that kind of range.'

'If my crew say so, they can do the job.'

The communications officer fidgeted at his post. Finally decided to take a chance and butt in. 'Sorry to interrupt, sir, but McMurdo's waiting on a response.'

Dower demanded: 'How long will they take to get ready?'

'How many do you need?'

'Two. One for crew, one for luggage.'

'Forty-five minutes.'

'You got half an hour,' Dower ordered, returning to his radio. 'Major, did you catch that?'

'Most of it, sir. Yes.'

'Get all the team's cargo up on deck. *Polar Star* has a Dolphin chopper – is that correct?'

'Affirmative, Admiral.'

'Good. Start ferrying everything over to the *Truman*.'

'What about that node access via the sonar, sir?'

'Tell Hackett he's got fifteen minutes. He can poke around all he likes but I expect to see that entire team on this flight deck in half an hour or there'll be hell to pay.'

'Sir! Yes, sir!'

As Dower crossed the bridge to leave, one of the communications officers tackled the Admiral delicately: 'Uh, sir? There's this guy on the other channel. Says he's calling from the Vatican City. Says it's important he speak with Professor Scott.'

'Tell him he's in transit right now. Advise him he can reach him at McMurdo station in—' He glanced at his watch. 'Four hours.' Dower flicked the peak of his hat at Henderson on his way out.

CARGO HOLD

'What do you think you're doing?'
'Getting my stuff.'
'They said we'll be taking it with us.'
'These things don't leave my side. And besides, I don't trust 'em,' Sarah said through gritted teeth, leaning into the crow-bar and jimmying the wooden crate open. She prised the splintered lid off and fetched out the device she had brought with her from Egypt.

Pearce seemed surprised as she stuffed the object in her backpack and went for the next crate.

'Well, are you just gonna stand there or are you gonna help me?' she demanded, throwing the empty casing aside and struggling to get the next crate into position.

'You're full of surprises, aren't you, Sarah Kelsey.'

'I try,' she panted, straining to jimmy the lid.

'What *is* that?'

'I have no idea. Just thought it might be useful. Thought they all might be useful. I wanted to go through them with everyone upstairs but we're running out of time.'

'What do they do?'

'As far as I'm aware, they respond to sound. Look, Bob, things are a little hectic. Are you gonna stand there with your thumb up your ass or *are you gonna help me?*'

Pearce grabbed another crow-bar and started forcing planks of wood off of packing cases, cursing as he sliced open his thumb.

They were packing up the lab all around them. Boxing up data tapes and notebooks. Rolling up maps and transferring computer information onto terabyte disks for transportation to McMurdo Station. It was like an entire university faculty had just been shut down, but the professors had refused to go home.

Huddled around Matheson as he fiddled with the communications protocols and awoke the deep drilling node from its slumber, Richard Scott hopped on one leg as he struggled to get into his bright orange survival suit in preparation for the journey to mainland Antarctica.

Ralph, it seemed, had done it a thousand times before. He had kitted up in a matter of seconds. November for her part was making sure he hadn't forgotten anything, while Hackett simply eyed the screen intently, and watched the flashes of white noise with quiet interest, as if he were willing the transmission to kick its way through.

'We're connected,' Matheson stated intensely. 'Gimme a second here.'

Scott glanced at his watch. 'We got six minutes, Ralph, and then they want us up on deck.'

'What do you want me to do when we see this stuff, Doc?'

'Take a snapshot,' he ordered. 'Take as many snapshots as you can. As high a resolution as you can. We can analyze it all later.'

The idea of the original first language of mankind was quite a notion. At the last count there had been 6,000 separate tongues since the dawn of time. And why had they diverged? Nobody knew. The Qu'ran said the languages of man separated through natural processes. The Bible spoke of Babel, and God smiting mankind with a confusion for attempting to build a mighty tower to the heavens. But no one really knew why.

The Genesis Language.

Could this be it?

'Brace yourself, Dr Scott. We've got power,' Matheson announced excitedly. His fingers bounced off the keyboard as he wrestled with the data on his screen. Punched in commands and sent out orders. 'Camera is operational. Powering up lights . . . bingo!'

Instinctively the entire team leaned in closer to get a better look. And not one person in the room saw what they expected to see.

It didn't match the video, for starters.

That shaky piece of raw footage Matheson had shown Scott had revealed destruction on a massive scale. An ancient crystal wall had been blasted apart, revealing an expanse of open water beyond and a hint of further structures.

But on the screen was something different. This was a crystal wall, for sure. But in a perfect state of preservation. No hole. No destruction. Not even a crack.

'Where's the damage?' Scott inquired, baffled. 'You're sure this is it? We're not anywhere else?'

Matheson checked his readings out of courtesy, but he was adamant about the facts. 'There is no other node, only this one. This is it. But I'll be damned if I can tell you what's going on.'

November squinted as she tried to make out some of the writing. The water was a little cloudy and particles were floating past the lens. 'What kind of a wall,' she asked, 'repairs itself?'

'Bob said something was alive down there,' Hackett remarked roguishly.

Matheson eyed his colleague incredulously. 'You think somebody went down there and repaired this? You can't repair a crystal wall.'

'Not some*body*. Some*thing*. Like the Chinese soldier said, there's something alive down there. Not somebody. Not a person like you or me. But something unnatural.'

'Jon,' Matheson said apprehensively, 'sometimes you really know how to unnerve me.'

'*I* unnerve you?' Hackett tossed back, heading for the door. 'Whoever repaired that thing should be the one unnerving you. I'll be on deck,' he said. 'You've got two minutes. If I were you I'd start snapping.'

Matheson took thirty-five pictures in all, some closer in than others. He wrote them all straight to disk and placed the disk in the top pocket of his survival coat. He printed out a copy of each picture on glossy photographic paper for group study on the flight, and handed one to Scott as they climbed the steps of the helideck.

There was a pattern to the placement of the glyphs across the flat surface of the wall, all right. They seemed to be arranged in an interlocking weave of spirals that criss-crossed constantly.

In fact, it resembled very much the pattern displayed in so many designs in nature – most notably, the seed arrangements of sunflowers. Quite simply it was a dazzling display.

Scott showed the picture to Hackett as they boarded the Dolphin together for the quick trip over to the *Truman*. The physicist reacted with amazement. The pattern, he explained, was a fundamental property of the very fabric of complexity theory itself.

The pattern did indeed conform to the series of numbers called the Fibonacci scale. And that in itself might just hold the goddamn key to cracking this thing.

V-TOL

'These times!' Hackett yelled as he stepped down off the Dolphin to the roar of busy aircraft. 'These are predictions!' He strode across the flight deck to where Tom Dower stood in a windswept parka. 'They show exactly when the sun's next gravity waves will be unleashed!'

Dower snatched the piece of paper from the physicist and inspected it while the wind howled so fiercely and bitterly, it sliced through the thickest thermal layers like a dagger into butter. It reduced their conversation to bellowing.

'Add eight minutes to each time for earth's expected impact times!' Hackett added.

'It says here that the next expected gravity pulse is in five hours!' Dower hollered back.

'Exactly so.' Hackett brought his watch up to show the Admiral. 'In fact I have my alarm all set. So warn the fleet! Warn the government!'

Crewmen stepped out of their way as they hurried along to where two waiting V-TOL aircraft sat on the forward section of the deck. Black fuel pipes stretched out from the extra gray tanks on the sides. Boxes were being hoisted up inside.

'A word of caution, Admiral,' Hackett added. 'Sarah has hit the nail on the head – there is a serious risk of earth-crust displacement. Are you prepared for such an eventuality? Do you have a back-up

plan? God told Noah to go build an Ark. Are you making arrangements to safeguard mankind's future?'

'We are aware of the possibility of an ECD event, Jon,' Dower
confirmed, 'and we've dismissed such a notion. Our best minds say
it's an invention of flawed thinking. There's no possibility of that
happening. The earth's crust simply does not rest on a sea of molten
lava. It has nothing to *slip* on. It's a theory that has no supporters.'
The Admiral rested a hand on Hackett's shoulder, guiding him to
the boarding steps.

'And the back-up plan? For saving humanity?'

'You're it,' Dower said, patting him on the back. 'So don't screw
up. The Chinese are the worry, Dr Hackett. The Chinese and that
city out there. And whatever power source they found that's still
lighting up our security screens like a Christmas tree.'

Hackett ducked his head as he climbed up into the light gray HV-
22A Osprey V-TOL. At the top he turned back to take one last look
at the Admiral.

'Albert Einstein was a supporter of earth-crust displacement,
y'know? Albert Einstein!'

Dower waved him off and headed for the entrance at the base of
the towering command block five stories high at the side of *Truman's*
vast, Empire State Building-length flight deck.

As Hackett took his seat, pulling the life-vest over his head and
letting November help strap him in, he was caught mumbling to
himself. 'Y'know, I don't think they have the faintest concept of what's
going on here. The powers-that-be are so fixated with their own polit-
ical destruction, they'll find any way they can to make it happen
rather than spend time looking for a solution.'

November grimaced as she tugged the strap tight. 'And this comes
as a surprise to you?' she said cynically.

Hackett eyed the girl sharply. 'Never lose your sense of wonder
and amazement. Never be blasé. Because then, one day, when the
really big and truly important things do come along, you'll be in a
position to appreciate them.'

'I'll bear that in mind.'

She sat back as Hackett jammed his face up at the window and
peered out at the turbo-props which were pointing straight up at the
sky and starting to spin.

November glanced back at Scott and Sarah who were sitting together across the other side of the cabin, while across the aisle Matheson gripped the arm-rests. 'Here we go again,' he was chanting. 'Antarctica here we come . . .'

McMURDO SOUND

With the first light of dawn a black cloud came from the horizon; it thundered within where Adad, lord of the storm, was riding. In front over hill and plain Shullat and Hanish, heralds of the storm, led on. Then the gods of the abyss rose up; Nergal pulled out the dams of the nether waters, Ninurta the war-lord threw down the dykes, and the seven judges of hell, the Annunaki, raised their torches lighting the land with their livid flame. A stupor of despair went up to heaven when the god of the storm turned daylight to darkness, when he smashed the land like a cup. One whole day the tempest raged, gathering fury as it went; it poured over the people like the tides of battle; a man could not see his brother nor the people be seen from heaven. Even the gods were terrified at the flood, they fled to the highest heaven, the firmament of Anu; they crouched against the walls, cowering like curs.

The Epic of Gilgamesh, c. 3,000BCE
Translated by N.K. Sanders, 1987

MIDNIGHT

They flew in low over the Ross Sea, the sun hovering in the sky. With sunset due in four weeks, the light was already starting to dim, becoming a kind of forever twilight. Winter was encroaching fast, and the sea was starting to freeze over at a colossal 22-square kilometers per minute. But the ice was thin, a mere 16 inches in most places, resulting in cracking and shifting plates and an all-enveloping fog called sea-smoke. Deepsea heat from under-currents traveling straight down from the tropics was rising to the surface and venting through the openings in the ice in great plumes, expending enough energy to power a 100-watt light-bulb for every square meter of sea-smoke.

The V-TOLs plowed through it all, leaving eddies in their wake. In the lead plane, Sarah craned her neck past Scott to see the approaching station out the window – a series of brightly colored, haphazardly placed buildings on the shores of Ross Island.

As they banked in for a descent she could make out two separate airstrips. But as the sea-smoke cleared she could see something else of far greater import. Across the snow and ice, a vista that stretched for hundreds of miles, dense black patches had settled like mottled bruising, or spots on a Dalmatian. The obvious culprit was –

'Erebus,' Sarah breathed. 'Look, it's smoking!'

The active volcano sat 3,794 meters above Ross Island. With the trans-Antarctic mountains behind it in a broad band, it was 600 degrees Celsius at the crater and was known to harbor bacteria and algae that fed off the steam it produced.

Around the volcano the ice was bulging, disfigured where the ice underneath was melting and building up a reservoir, like a giant blister waiting to burst. There were similar odd warped patches way off in the distance, evidence of volcanic activity that hadn't even penetrated to the surface. It was clear that Antarctica was in trouble. Yet that still wasn't what bothered Sarah the most.

'The albedo's all shot,' she fretted. Scott was none the wiser. 'The reflectivity of the ice,' she explained. 'Usually it's extremely high down here. Bounces sunlight straight back into space, cooling the planet. But all this volcanic ash is settling on top, absorbing the sunlight, encouraging heat to build. Encouraging a flood. Y'know, if all the ice on Antarctica were to melt, the average sea level would rise by about sixty meters, nearly two hundred feet. The ice cap's five kilometers thick in some places. We better hope earth-crust displacement's a myth.'

The vicious cross winds sweeping across McMurdo Sound made for a bumpy landing and caused the V-TOLs to tail around as their landing gear slipped on the ice.

They were met on the ground by a team of ASA support staff. The Antarctic Support Associates, a company operating out of Denver, Colorado, were like the local sheriff's office. If anyone stepped out of line, the ASA ran them out of town.

A huge caterpillar-tracked, purpose-built truck sat waiting to ferry them all down to their accommodation block. Someone had painted *Ivan the Terror Bus* on its cab door. It chugged menacingly as its engine ticked over.

'Christ almighty!' Scott gasped, as he stepped down off the plane to be smacked in the face by such devastating cold, he nearly doubled over.

'Just get on the bus, quickly now! Quickly!' one of the ASA men commanded. 'Hey, we got ladies . . . Cool.' He counted everyone off on his checklist one by one.

'What *is* that smell?' Hackett demanded, covering his face.

'Fuel oil,' another ASA man explained nonchalantly, leaning up against one of the hundreds of black and gray barrels stacked to the side of the airstrip. 'You get used to it.'

'Couldn't you stack those barrels someplace else?'

'This? This ain't fuel. This is piss and shit.'

November choked. 'Pardon me?'

'These are barrels of frozen piss and shit,' the ASA man told them. 'We can't leave diddly here. By law we have to ship everything back home.' November looked like she was going to vomit as she climbed up inside the bus. 'Nah, the fuel's all off down the hill someplace!' he called after her.

A further ASA man hung his head around the door into the back of the vehicle. 'Ladies and gentlemen, these are the ground rules. Any of you get drunk, you get sent home. You get into a fight, you go home. If you are in possession of prescription drugs without informing the staff – you go home. You trek out onto the sea-ice without telling anyone – you go home. You grow plants not indigenous to Antarctica – guess what? You go home.

'Crime is low, we want to keep it that way. The only thing we seem to have a problem with is the theft of bicycles and coats that aren't stock issue red. So tie 'em down if you have 'em. We have no judge, no police and no jail. Any trouble – and you go home. Other than that,' he grinned, 'welcome to McMurdo!'

Scott raised his finger like a schoolchild. 'Actually,' he said, 'there's been a change of plan. We're kind of on a time-limit. I don't think we'll be staying here that long.'

'You do any of that crap and you won't be,' the ASA man replied.

Hackett was confused. 'Do you even know who we are?'

'Sure,' he snapped. 'Like all the other Eco-warriors on block six, you're here to save the planet. Best of luck!' He slammed the door shut behind him.

Outside, the other V-TOL was unloading as the first ASA man got on his cab CB. 'Okay, we got six "beakers" comin' down at ya. Dave, you got some hot food for these fine folks?' A garbled response came back with an affirmative.

'Excuse me, what are "beakers"?'

The ASA man turned to find himself face to face with Major Gant. The marine had traveled in on the other plane, much to the surprise of everyone else. The ASA man grimaced. 'Beakers – y'know. It's slang for scientists. All the support staff use it.'

Gant was furious. 'I am a serving officer in the United States Marine Corps, mister!'

The ASA man shrugged and got back on his radio. 'Yeah, scratch that, Dave.' He eyed Gant mildly. 'Expect six beakers . . . and an asshole.'

Gant pushed past and climbed aboard. November leaned forward. 'What are you doing here?'

'You didn't think they were going to send you guys in alone and unsupported, did you?'

Hackett spoke from over the back of the Major's seat. 'Actually, yes we did.'

Gant shrugged it off as a third ASA man climbed up into the driving seat, shifted *Ivan* into gear and hauled them all down into McMurdo's city limits. And it was as they swung around that November noticed the ship, sat on the horizon, out across the frozen sea.

'Which ship is that?' she asked innocently.

'I don't know its name,' Gant revealed. 'It's Chinese. It's been sat there all day.'

'It can't get us here, can it?'

'Honey,' the Major explained, 'we could be hovering over their base, four hours' flying time from here, and they could still get us. The range on their missiles is that good.'

November sat back with a start, leaving the Major to his thoughts. Piss and shit.

'One, the North Face. "Himalayan Hotel" dome tent. Orange.'

'Check.'

'One Quallofil-insulated sleeping bag.'

Matheson nodded once more and checked the items off the list as they were handed to him across the counter.

'One B.A.D. Bags duffel bag. One pair of Vuarnet sunglasses. One Silva compass. One Yema watch. One camp rest sleeping pad. One fleece pullover. One pair of fleece pants. One fleece hat, headband and neckband. Blue. One Red Gore-Tex wind parka and pair of pants. One Gore-Tex one-piece jumpsuit. Red. One Thermolite and Thermoloft insulated jacket.'

'Check.'

'Two sets of Duofold Thermax thermal underwear. Two pairs of Duofold Thermax liner socks. Two pairs of Damart Thermax thermal underwear. Two pairs of Fox River Hollofil socks. One pair of Surefoot Insulator insoles. One The Masque neoprene face mask. One pair of Grandoe Gore-Tex gloves. One pair of Steiger Designs overmits. One pair of Gore-Tex boots. One pair of mukluks.'

'Check.'

'Sign here, sir and you're all set,' the ASA clerk advised.

Matheson put pen to paper and collected up his things, eyeing Gant apprehensively. He was collecting very little. 'You're not taking any of this stuff?'

'I have much of my own gear,' he replied. 'Some man-made stuff, but mine is mostly better than this.' Matheson was curious. 'Sealskin and caribou hide clothing,' Gant explained. 'Like the Inuit use. It's the best.'

And Gant headed off to their block leaving Matheson to stare blankly back at the ASA clerk. 'Got any caribou skin?'

PERIODICITY

Scott slapped the oversized photographs from the node down on the table in triumph. 'There aren't sixteen letters,' he announced. 'There are sixty.'

While the others excitedly gathered around the work surface of the makeshift lab, Hackett seemed less than enthusiastic as he glanced at his watch then out through the window. 'We got twenty-three minutes,' he said, 'till the next gravity pulse.'

'Don't worry about that,' November urged him. 'Worry about this.'

Scott took up a red marker and circled what he'd come to call the Atlantis glyph, the circle and the cross inside it. 'This glyph never changes position on any surface that I studied. Neither do these other four.'

'That's the Giza glyph,' Pearce noted. 'And that's the South America one.'

'Right. And I'm guessing these other two are also major sites.'

'But where?'

Scott turned on Gant who was sat brooding in one corner. 'Major – think maybe the powers-that-be could spare some satellite time to hunt down two other megalithic structures with C60 deposits beneath them?' Gant shrugged. 'You never know,' Scott persisted. 'It might just save planet Earth.'

Gant got to his feet and ambled over to the table. 'What do these sites look like?'

Scott indicated the two glyphs as Sarah added, 'The C60 hunt began in China. I'm guessing one of those glyphs matches the layout of Wupu, in China.'

'Okay, but what about the fifth one?'

'The North Pole,' Hackett murmured darkly.

Matheson was intrigued. 'You sure about that?'

Hackett seemed amused. 'I can't be certain, no, it's just a guess. But if I was going to build a global network of megalithic structures that respond to electro-magnetism, and I'd already put one at the South Pole, and three strung around the equator, or close to it, logic tells me the fifth is probably going to be at the North Pole.'

Scott turned on Gant. 'Is that enough information for you?'

'It's a start,' Gant agreed. There was a vid-phone hooked up to a computer across the far end of the lab. He dialed up Dower immediately.

Scott snatched up his pen and tapped it on the desk. 'Anyway,' he said, 'those five symbols don't change position. But on this node photograph I realized that the other eleven symbols all appear to rotate randomly, for no real reason.'

'What do you mean?' Sarah asked.

'Well, it's like writing the letter "a". But one moment it's the right way up, the next minute you've written it on its side. A sentence or so later it's upside down. Some early languages do this, and it doesn't affect the way you read them. But those languages don't match what we've got here. Of course, some languages did it because of the way you had to read them. English is left to right. Arabic is right to left. But earlier languages were *boustrophedon* – literally meaning "as the ox plows". The first line would be read right to left, the next line underneath would be left to right, then right to left. Your eye would have to zig zag down the page.'

'These are spirals.'

'Yeah. So I'm guessing it's a straight line. Just pick a spiral and follow it. But from which end do I start?'

'But what does it mean?' Hackett wanted to know. 'Eleven letters rotating in five different ways, making fifty-five letters, plus five vowels. Fascinating I'm sure, but what do they mean?'

Scott was stunned. 'Did you say vowels?'

'Sure.'

'Why? What made you say vowels?'

'Because there are five of them.'

Scott thought it over. 'I dunno, maybe they *are* vowels. In many ancient languages, like Egyptian, vowels were omitted. They were something the reader automatically filled in. Maybe that's what these five symbols represent. The spaces where you fill in the vowels.'

'But what vowels?' Hackett insisted. 'And sixty letters – do you have any comprehension of just how big a language would be if it had sixty letters in its alphabet? The possible permutations of letter sequences are almost endless.'

'What's he talking about?' November asked innocently.

'Somebody give me a language.'

'Italian,' Gant said coldly, turning from the vid-phone in the corner of the hollow-sounding room.

'How many letters has it got?'

'Twenty-one.'

'Okay, so for the possible number of permutations of a twenty-one-letter sequence, each one different from the next, you need to know the factorial of twenty-one. Which is one times two times three times four times five . . . all the way up to twenty-one.' He totted it up in his head. 'That's roughly fifty-one billion *billion* twenty-one-letter long sequences. You want to figure in repeated letters as well. That takes it up to five billion billion . . . *billion.*'

'What you're describing,' Scott replied, 'is Temurah.' Sarah looked puzzled. 'Temurah is used in Kabbala for calculating the possible number of anagrams of a word in a certain number of letters.'

'And what's Kabbala?'

'Kabbala means "tradition". It follows the notion that there are secret messages hidden in the Bible. Temurah is the art of anagrams and assumes you can decode these secrets by messing with the word of God.'

'My point is,' Hackett added, 'well, shit . . . anybody see a calculator laying around here anywhere?' Matheson tossed him a little black Casio. Hackett punched in the numbers. 'The factorial of twenty is 2,432,902,008,176,640,000. That's the number of permutations twenty letter sequences in an alphabet of twenty letters has. In sixty, that's . . . a complete mystery because, uh, this little device can't even work out that much.' He threw the calculator down on the table, displaying the ERROR message for all to see. 'Where, Richard, do you even *start* trying to determine what each letter means in a sixty-letter alphabet?'

Scott shrugged simply. 'Like I've been trying to tell everybody since the start, I have no idea. Why the sudden jitters, Professor?'

Hackett shifted uncomfortably, looking out the window at all the ice and snow. 'I didn't realize this place was so damn empty.'

November was confused. 'People think there are hidden messages in the Bible?' Scott nodded. 'What about the messages that are already there? Didn't they think to just read it?'

'Guess not. Oh, it doesn't stop there. Notariqon was a skill Kabbalists used to look at the end and beginning letters of words to find a hidden message, while Gematria was based purely on the Hebrew texts because, as you know, all Hebrew letters are numbers. So they theorized that all words that came to the same number were connected in some way.' Scott seemed indifferent to the theory. 'They concluded there were seventy-two names for God.'

'What's the point?'

Scott tried to explain. 'In the sixteenth century, Bruno used a set of concentric wheels with a hundred and fifty sectors on them. Each wheel contained thirty letters made of the twenty-three Latin letters, and then a mixture of Greek and Hebrew letters that represented sounds that aren't in Latin. And what he did was to rotate these wheels and form triplet combinations in an attempt to discern the first perfect language of mankind. What he got was a load of old nonsense, but it actually became useful in the new art of crypto-graphy.'

'And we've been writing secret messages to each other ever since,' Pearce noted.

'What they eventually started doing was to wrap a ribbon around a cylinder in kind of a spiral. Then write a message vertically down the side of the tube, so when the ribbon was stretched back out you were left with a series of random letters along the length of the ribbon. Then you just filled in a junk message around it.'

'A cylinder and a ribbon?' Sarah seemed intrigued. Like it had jogged a memory of some description. 'There was a geologist, a French guy named, what was that . . . ? Béguyer. Yeah. Béguyer de Chancourtois, in the 1800s. He arranged elements in a spiral around a tube – twenty-four elements, I think it was. Then he noted down the periodicity of their properties – y'know, which elements were intrinsically similar. What he found was that similar elements recurred after every seventh element. It was one of the first attempts at building a periodic table.'

For Hackett that seemed to be ringing some bells too, but Matheson was already putting his own ideas forward. 'Maybe we should be cutting out the spirals on these photographs and sticking them around a tube.'

'Isn't that already what they *did* in Giza?' Pearce indicated.

'John Newlands,' Hackett interrupted. 'English chemist. He did similar work on the elements in the nineteenth century and agreed there was a numerical pattern to them. Only he used music as the analogy. There are seven notes in a musical scale, and on the eighth note you step up to a new octave. But there was a more complex structure to the rhythm that Meyer discovered in the same year.' Hackett smiled convincingly. 'There were peaks at the eighth and the sixteenth elements. Then the rhythm shifted to eighteen elements apart instead of seven. It was like a wave was passing through the periodic table . . . Sixteen minutes, by the way.'

'A wave passing through the periodic table?'

'Oh yeah,' Sarah agreed. 'In chemical theory, it means you can predict where the next stable elements will occur. In theory there's some kind of Atlantis, an element that runs parallel to the conventional periodic table, and remains to be discovered. Somewhere around atomic number one hundred and fifteen or one hundred and eighty.'

'Orichalc,' Pearce commented.

Sarah blinked. 'I'm sorry?'

'Plato. When he first described Atlantis, he described walls covered in precious metals. Gold, silver. And the one most prized of all was a mysterious gleaming reddish-gold metal he called Orichalc. It was said to shimmer like fire.'

'C60 in its purest form is reddish-gold,' Sarah pointed out.

'Orichalc isn't a stone, it's a metal.'

'In South America,' Scott mused, 'according to local legend, when the four founding gods had completed their mission, before they left they wrapped all their power and knowledge up into a gift that was both feared and respected. The gift was a stone. The stone of Naczit.'

'Moses, when he went onto the mountain to receive the Ten Commandments, saw the stone they were written on be inscribed by the finger of God. The stones shimmered blue,' November reminded them gently. 'And the radiance from the stones was such that it burnt Moses's face and for the rest of his life he was forced to wear a veil to hide the scars.'

'Ancient stones and ancient metals,' Scott remarked as he eyed the photographs again. He rubbed his hand over his mouth. 'Periodicity. Step sequences. What am I missing?'

Gant was on his feet. This was all way above his head and frankly it was irritating the shit out of him. 'They're redirecting a satellite for you,' he said. 'I'm going to make sure they're refueling the planes properly. And I'm putting in another call to the Chinese, to let them know we're coming.'

'Which Chinese?' Sarah demanded.

'Anyone that's listening. That ship for starters.'

'And if no one answers?'

'Then we better pray they don't shoot us down. Coz we're going in regardless.'

As he reached the door, Hackett glanced out the window to see an immense gray US amphibious landing craft smash through the waves toward the shore and beach on the ice shelf a short distance off. The front end came crashing down but the ice was smashing for no one.

'What the hell is that?' the physicist asked, startled as a squad of marines manhandled a flat black coffin-sized box out of the craft and started marching it toward the base on the double.

'Ah,' Gant explained knowingly. 'That'll be our tactical nuclear warhead.'

He zipped up his parka and went out to meet them while Hackett sidled up next to Pearce and November. 'I hope for our sakes,' he said, 'Orichalc doesn't turn out to be uranium, or we're never getting out of Atlantis alive.'

'Just what do you think you're doing?' November demanded angrily.

'Storing the bomb,' Gant replied frostily, directing the marines in through the front door with the box.

'In the chapel?'

'You got a better idea? The Chinese would never live down the international controversy of firing upon fine upstanding Americans who were simply engaged in prayer.'

Inside, on a pew near the front by the altar, and just to one side of the stained glass penguin, Hackett and Scott turned to see the soldiers struggle with the device before dropping it roughly to the ground. 'Didn't I see this on *Planet of the Apes* one time?' Hackett remarked.

Sarah took a pew next to Scott as the epigraphist chewed his pen and puzzled over another photograph, asking: 'How long have we got?'

Scott glanced to Hackett who checked his watch. 'Three minutes.'

Scott blew air anxiously and smacked his lips. He looked up at the cross behind the altar. His knee was bouncing up and down furiously. 'Boy,' he said, 'it puts a whole new perspective on this when you know these things are coming.'

Sarah took his hand in hers and squeezed it gently. 'Where are you from, Richard?'

'Seattle,' he sighed. 'Y'know it's such a pretty city,' he said with passion. 'It's condensed, see. There isn't much in the way of sprawling suburbs so you're never far from the countryside. You can hike, bike, sail. Mountains and lakes are all over. Forests . . . everything is this dark, dark green, y'know?' Sarah nodded like she did. 'Douglas Fir, Broad Leaf Maple, Mountain Ash, Red Adler, Dogwood . . . You can go out into the country then come back, get a coffee in Starbucks and feel like you actually went someplace. We've got two hundred and fifty-eight bridges in Seattle – every kind of bridge you can think of, coz of all the lakes. We've even got two floating bridges. Some people say it's because it's a city full of gaps, socially as well as topographically, but I think it's full of bridges because it's full of people who are going places. And nothing's gonna stand in their way.' He thought about that for a moment. 'I'll miss that if it goes.'

Matheson groaned as he took the weight off his feet and sat down next to them. 'I went to Seattle once. It pissed down all week.'

'Where are *you* from?' Sarah asked.

'San Francisco. You?'

'Still Water, Wisconsin.' Sarah eyed Hackett perceptively. The physicist seemed to be deep in thought. 'How about you, Jon?'

'Me?' She nodded encouragingly. 'I was born on a military base in Germany,' he said. 'Spent a couple years in Hawaii, then Japan. We moved around a lot. I live in New York half the year now, spend three months of the year in Santa Fe down at the Institute. Travel . . . I travel a lot. I'll miss planes.'

'But not the food,' Sarah joked.

'No, not the food,' Hackett agreed. 'Plane food is, uh, something else. But they do try, bless 'em.' He checked his watch again but didn't say anything.

Pearce pulled up behind them alongside November. 'When I was fourteen I swore I saw a UFO land in the backyard. Told everybody at school and got the crap beat out of me. But I was telling the truth. It *had* been flying and as far as I was concerned, it *was* unidentified. How the hell was I supposed to know what a weather balloon looked like? When I was sixteen, I kissed the Homecoming Queen. And again I got the crap beat out of me. For lying. But I wasn't lying.'

November was confused. 'What are you saying? You're gonna miss getting beat up?'

'No,' Bob explained. 'I'm gonna miss the non-believers.'

Gant scooted up next to them. 'Oh, they're not going anywhere,' he said. 'Denial ain't just a river in Egypt.'

The pretty young assistant smiled at that as she noticed Scott and Sarah holding hands, but she kept her comments to herself. Suddenly from a side door a mass of other scientists and technicians, mostly men, pale-looking and drawn, and sporting well-established beards, came in followed by a priest. He carried a vid-phone in his hands and set it down in the center of the altar as if it were a revered icon. He addressed the congregation nervously, and as the others took their seats it was the first clear indication the team had been given that they had found themselves slap in the middle of a real frontier town.

'We've had word from all across the world,' the priest announced. 'The warning signal has been given. They started evacuating the cities some time ago . . .' His voice faltered. 'But there really isn't anywhere safe to go.'

Matheson leaned across Hackett to catch Scott's ear. 'Anyway,' he whispered, 'I thought you didn't believe in Jesus?'

Scott shifted uncomfortably. 'At this juncture I'm willing to open it up for discussion.'

The priest fiddled with the vid-phone and keyed the connection. 'We're joined in today's service by Father McRack, who's coming to us today, live from the Vatican.'

Scott snapped his head back. 'Fergus?' But he was too far from the phone to be heard.

Fergus, a well-lit head and shoulders on the screen, peered solemnly out at the congregation. 'Ladies and gentlemen,' he said. 'Let me welcome you all to McMurdo Chapel, a cross-denominational chapel, and I thank the authorities for allowing the Catholic Church to be a part of the service today. In a moment we shall bow our heads in prayer and ask God . . .'

Sarah leant in close to Scott, whispering: 'I just had a thought. What day is it today?'

Scott had to think for a moment. 'Friday.'

November leant in too. 'It's Good Friday,' she corrected. 'This is the day Jesus dies. On Sunday we get the resurrection.'

Scott couldn't mask his surprise. It had been such a hectic week he had completely forgotten about Easter. Suddenly everybody was standing, opening their hymn books and following Fergus's instructions. A CD of organ music whirred into life and filtered around the congregation, and it was at that point Hackett's watch alarm began chirping.

'It's time,' he said, before joining the others and bursting into song.

'Ah-bide with me . . .'

THE SUN

H elium, named after the Greek sun god, *Helios*.

At the heart of the sun's 320,000 km diameter core, under unimaginable pressures, vast, god-like quantities of hydrogen were being heated to 14 million degrees Celsius, and were fusing in an almost eternal nuclear reaction to form helium.

Surrounding the core in a radioactive layer that sought to fuel the core at similar temperatures was a sea of hydrogen just waiting to be seized upon. And it was here, buried within the depths of the sun's heart that trouble had already begun. And a chain of events had been set in motion.

For the sun's core spun on its axis, at an entirely different rate to the hydrogen layer. And the tendrils of magnetic force that encapsulated the massive body had already started to snag and twist, warp and tighten.

Above the radioactive hydrogen layer, the rising and falling currents of the convection zone had already begun to falter in response to the magnetic interference from below. Great bulges on the surface of the core, like warts, two or three times the size of planet Earth were forming and whizzing around as the core continued its relentless rotation. And in so doing, the bulges started to act like blades on a blender, churning up the inner mass of the sun. Disturbing its equilibrium.

Vast swathes of the convection zone that should have been

dropping to temperatures around the 1.5 million degrees Celsius mark were remaining abnormally high. While other areas were cooling off too rapidly. The conveyor belt of convection was snapping. Disintegrating. And all that was reaching the photosphere and corona were intermittent pockets of cooling plasma being whipped about in a confused mass of magnetic flux.

They first started to appear at 40 degrees latitude – the cool dark patches known as umbra, and the lighter outer patches known as penumbra: together, known as sunspots. They were collecting like measles all over the surface of the sun, where the temperatures had dropped to a comparatively minuscule 7,200 degrees Celsius. And the sunspots were even cooler, up to 2,000 degrees cooler.

Some were small, maybe 1,500 km across. Others were as much as 5,000 km across – the size of the continental United States at a push. Yet compared with the entire earth's paltry 0.5 gauss magnetic field strength, these sunspots measured anywhere between 100 to 4,000 gauss. A field strength so large that if that kind of magnetism were embedded in the ceiling of a person's apartment, the earth's gravity could be increased three-fold and there would still be no way of peeling him off its surface. There was enough iron in his blood to keep him there.

They were gathering now, the sunspots. Moving closer and closer toward the sun's equator. A dark, mottled effect that actively distorted the light searing out from the sun, and causing it to flicker.

This was magnetism, gravity, visible light and nuclear forces, both the strong and weak, having a family argument. They were all inter-related, like cousins. And all slugging it out with each other on a gigantic scale, at both the visible and the invisible level. Like colossal kings of nature they were twisting up their home and hurling it at each other. Disrupting space with their fury.

SOHO III

In 'halo' orbit, 1.5 million kilometers above the earth, at the exact point where the sun and the earth's gravity cancelled each other out, the battery of twenty-one telescopes and sensors aboard the *Solar Heliospheric III* observation satellite suddenly kicked into gear as they caught activity 92 million miles away on the surface of the troubled star.

Coming into view around the eastern rim was a series of sunspots so dark and ominous, so massive that they could have contained the earth 300 times over. While snaking between them, looping in and out across the entire surface, were tubules of super-heated plasma caught like bottled fireflies within the confines of magnetic loops that twisted and turned, sewn into and out of the very fabric of the sun. Making the entire star resemble for one brief moment, a raging fiery ball of string on a galactic scale.

The signs were unmistakable. Like the trumpeting of heralds announcing a chariot race.

The sun was about to blow.

As it rotated, it became apparent that not one, but eight separate solar flares had ejected massively into space. They began as bright spots within the sunspot groups and spread like wildfire, glowing magnesium white against the sun's duller yellow for hundreds of thousands of square miles. Expanding exponentially until in an instant, billions upon billions of tons of radiation and matter exploded off the sun's surface, while simultaneously the sun appeared to wobble slightly, caught off-guard at the sudden loss in mass as the ejecta headed out, disrupting the sun's density.

In effect the sun had just pulsed another gravity wave.

```
– INITIATING SAFETY PROTOCOL ONE –
```

They were commands that had been uploaded to the craft in the last few days. Independent control of the onboard ion thrusters by *Soho III* so it could attempt to remain in halo orbit every time there was a gravity pulse.

The fact *Soho III* had just seen the ejecta on the sun meant the gravity wave, which traveled at the same speed as light, had already swept through.

The satellite was already out of alignment. It had to get back into position, and it had to do it soon. It had communications to re-establish. It had a warning to pass on.

The fastest ever measured solar flares traveled in the region of anywhere upward of 2 million mph.

These ones were traveling at 10 million mph.

One would be arriving in a little over nine hours.

And it was immense.

PROPAGATION

They were called P-waves. Fast pressure waves that were the first waves to be detected by seismographs when earthquakes started to erupt.

All over the planet, COSY – Comparison and Verification of Synthetic Seismogram – monitors were springing into action, sounding the alarm that the worst-case scenario for global seismic-wave propagation was actually taking place. That real data was matching theoretical data.

That planet earth was up shit creek. And no amount of paddling was going to help.

In the twentieth century, statistics showed that when all the earth-quakes that had ever struck were totaled into a single event, two million people had been killed in a quake that lasted less than an hour.

In the last three days the total earthquake activity had already lasted fifteen minutes and the death toll had risen past 500,000.

Currently, 21 percent of the entire earth's surface was shaking violently, caught in tremors, pre-tremors and aftershocks. Seven percent of those earthquakes were happening in overpopulated areas. And of the 8 billion people on planet Earth, 900 million lived in cities that were sat in the middle of earthquake prone zones.

In San Francisco the shifting faultline sent out a crack like a rifle shot. The ground simply opened up with a *boom!* – dropping 50 feet on one side.

Within 30 seconds water mains had burst, gas pipes had exploded, glass had shattered and torn the running tourists to shreds. Fire trucks found they didn't have enough water to fight the blazes that were eating through the city. Elevated roads tumbled. And all buildings of a certain height were shaken to pieces as the ground wave set up a resonance within those buildings and tore them apart.

Within a further 30 seconds, much of the lower Bay area was reduced to a memory, while winds of extraordinary ferocity blasted through, whipping up the blazes into a raging firestorm.

At the National Severe Storms Laboratory in Norman, Oklahoma, they were watching Tornado Alley as their boards lit up like slot machines hitting the jackpot. But they weren't spitting silver dollars, rather magnitude 4 and 5 tornadoes, some of them up to a mile wide and touching down all over the Mid-West.

In New Zealand, Mount Ruapehu had now blown its top, adding to an ever-increasing list of volcanoes that had suddenly gone active. But Ruapehu was different in that it had done more than merely trigger a few avalanches. Like the 1883 Krakatoa event when the explosion of a volcano sank an entire island, the explosion could be heard 3,000 miles away. The amount of dust thrown into the air was turning day to night for 160 miles in all directions.

At McMurdo they braced themselves for being swept away by the massive water reservoirs held at bay by the cracking glaciers at the base of Mount Erebus.

But mercifully the deluge didn't come.

It was like a prayer had been answered, and it gave Scott a chance to talk to his old friend, Fergus.

24 HOURS

We live in a universe of patterns. Every night the stars move in circles across the sky. The seasons cycle at yearly intervals. No two snowflakes are ever exactly the same, but they all have sixfold symmetry. Tigers and zebras are covered in patterns of stripes; leopards and hyenas are covered in patterns of spots. Intricate trains of waves march across the oceans; very similar trains of sand dunes march across the desert . . . By using mathematics . . . we have discovered a great secret: nature's patterns are not just there to be admired, they are vital clues to the rules that govern natural processes.

Ian Stewart, *Nature's Numbers*, 1995

REUNION

'I never thought I'd see you in a church again.'

'Things change,' Scott replied flatly, his voice echoing around the now empty chapel. 'What're you doing tracking me down here, Fergus? University wanna reinstate me?'

Fergus seemed embarrassed his end of the line as Scott scooted closer to the vid-phone on the altar by sliding his barstool forward. 'No reinstatement,' he said.

'Then what is it?' A cloud had descended over the priest. 'You know about Atlantis, don't you?'

'Yes,' Fergus admitted. 'Yes, I do.' He glanced nervously back over his shoulder. 'My boss . . . wants Atlantis destroyed at all costs. He feels it will have an undesirable effect on the fabric of society. Destabilizing his power base.'

'God wants Atlantis destroyed?' Scott smirked. 'He told you that personally, did He?'

'Not God, the Pope,' Fergus glowered. 'This is no time for jokes. Your life's in danger, Richard. Serious danger. The Papacy has made a deal with the US to destroy Atlantis.'

Scott laughed. 'Fergus, you're paranoid.'

'He feels the discovery of an ancient advanced society would make a total mockery of Christianity. He's not alone, he's taken meetings with other religious leaders.'

A frown crossed Scott's face. 'Then my work was correct. And you know it.'

'Richard, all that matters is your life is in danger. You have *no* idea what's waiting for you in Atlantis. None.'

Scott folded his arms defensively. 'So enlighten me.'

An image popped up onto the screen. 'You've heard of the mythic Golem, haven't you?'

3:14 AM

It was always amazing how a lack of time helped focus the mind.

Nano-technology was the only thing that plausibly explained the appearance of the hand in the Giza tunnel that kept Douglas stuck fast just before his death.

The implications of the video feed Fergus showed from Pini Pini was daunting. In Atlantis they were to face automatons that defied all modern capabilities, yet had been constructed by the hand of ancient man. It wasn't so much that modern man had a lot still to learn, more a lot to *re-learn*.

Scott studied the glyphs etched across the 'face' of the Golem, back in the lab. They were Atlantis glyphs. To find them etched on the face of an angry nemesis did not inspire confidence.

'How do these nanoes work?' Sarah wanted to know. 'I mean, they're tiny little robots, right? What's their power source? Do they strap little batteries to their backs or what?'

'When Drexler first expanded on his theory,' Matheson explained, 'he proposed nanoes would be powered by sonic energy. Sound waves would pass between the nanoes, transferring energy between them, kind of like a sonic network that required no wiring, just sonic transmitters and receivers.'

Scott was confused. 'So how would they become one creature? One thing?'

'That's just it. It's not a *thing*. It's a nano *swarm*.'

'It's *many* things?'

'Thousands of tiny units, all working together to form one solid creature. Hundreds of thousands, maybe even millions, swarming and acting like a single entity.'

'Is that even possible?'

'Of course that's possible!' Hacket interjected excitedly. 'What the hell do you think jellyfish are?'

'Jellyfish are separate units?' November quizzed.

'Jellyfish are an army that, on occasion, decide to go to war.'

'How?' Sarah demanded. 'There's not enough time for so many individuals to pass information on to each other and work as one. It should fall apart.'

'Jellyfish don't fall apart,' Hackett said firmly. 'It's known as Biological Synchronization. Like your earthquake calculations, Sarah, it's a property of resonance. When Dutch physicist Christian Huygens, inventor of the pendulum clock, was ill in bed in the 1660s, he noticed the pendulums of two of his clocks swung in sequence when moved close to each other. Knocked out of step they were soon back in step a little time after. Move them apart and they went out of step rapidly. This same proximation synchronicity is seen in fireflies, fiber bundles that regulate the heart, flocks of birds that change direction, schools of fish. It's not a conscious decision, it's a factor of environment, a subtle mathematical thread which can be applied even on a social level – like religion and sects relying on geographical frameworks. *Southern* Baptists. *Anglicans* in England. *Islam* in the Middle East. *Hinduism* in India. It's to do with reaction to the environment.'

'This *environment* is gonna kill us at this rate,' Gant commented as he strutted into the lab with Lieutenant Roebuck in tow. A chill wind whistled in behind them. 'Brief us.' He slapped a map down on the table and rolled it out. 'What else can we expect to find in Atlantis?'

'First up,' Pearce corrected, 'Atlantis was the island – said to be as large as Libya and Asia combined. The city's actual name was Poseidon.'

'Whatever,' Gant shrugged. 'What's our best entry point?' He used his pen to sketch out where the Chinese base was in black. Then switched to red to map out the satellite imagery of the structures below. 'Did they booby trap? Was it easy to get about? What kind of minds conceived of this place? Were they warlike?'

'Atlantis was fortified. Plato spoke of them going to war with Athens. But the central portion of the city was enclosed with concentric rings of sea. I'm assuming he meant giant canals. Plato described them as being like cartwheels. They were equidistant from each other with the rings of land connected by bridges and tunnels, and were in turn connected to the sea by one huge canal, 300 feet wide and 100 feet deep. Major, they kept their entire navy harbored around those rings.'

'What else?'

'Well, they had buildings of different-colored stonework. The outer land ring was covered in bronze, like a veneer. The middle land ring was covered in tin that was fused to the walls. And the central island's buildings were covered in Orichalc, including the acropolis, the dominant place of worship. There were temples all over and the laws of the land were written on a central pillar of Orichalc, where the ten ruler kings of the provinces would meet every fifth and sixth year thereby showing equal respect to both odd and even numbers.'

Scott and Hackett immediately exchanged intrigued glances.

'Oh, and the wall of the Shrine of Poseidon and Cleito was made of gold.'

'That's it? That's all we've got?' Gant threw his pen down furiously.

'That's all there *is!*' Pearce exploded right back at him. 'That's all Plato wrote. He never finished the story. Like any writer who's written three chapters to a book that Hollywood never bothered picking up, he threw in the towel and wrote something else.'

'What you've just told me offers absolutely no indication of what this new power source might be. What it is we have to switch off. In nine hours, people, a solar storm is projected to hit this planet, so violent it may boil the atmosphere right off our globe. If that machine under the ice is still operational there's every chance it'll succeed because that thing'll suck it right in. I need to know what the hell I'm trying to blow up.'

The scientists stood gripped around the table, silently devastated by the implications. All, that is, except for Scott who hadn't come all this way just to fail.

Quietly he said: *"'The third angel blew his trumpet, and a huge star fell from the sky, burning like a ball of fire, and it fell on a third of all rivers and on the springs of water; this was the star called Wormwood, and a third of all water turned to wormwood, so that many people died; the water became so bitter."'*

All eyes settled on Scott.

'What are you talking about?' the marine major demanded impatiently.

November's eyes lit up. 'He's quoting the Book of Revelation, verses 8:10 and 8:11.'

'Why?'

Hackett knew why. He smiled. 'In the Ukraine,' he explained lightly, 'just north of the capital city, Kiev, they have a profusion of forests made up of trees indigenous to the local area called wormwood trees.'

'So?'

'Well uh let me put it this way, Major. What is a star?'

'I don't underst—'

'A star is nothing more than a nuclear explosion that goes on for millions of years.'

'When I was a teenager,' Scott took over, 'in the same area of the Ukraine where they have all the wormwood trees, they also had a nuclear power station that went critical. Like a star falling from the sky it turned the water and soil radioactive. The name of the place became synonymous with nuclear disasters.'

'I know,' Gant answered diligently. 'Chernobyl.'

'Right,' Scott said. 'And Chernobyl, in English, means wormwood.'

'That's all very well on the prophecy front, Professor Scott.' Gant was growing irritable. 'But what does it have to do with the layout of Atlantis?'

'It always struck me how the description of the city of Atlantis always sounded so similar to the city in the Book of Revelation where mankind's final battle will be fought.'

Now that had the military men's attention.

'In Revelation 21, The Messianic Jerusalem, the city's described as being seen from a hill and looking like some glittering precious jewel of crystal-clear diamond with twelve gates. The outer wall was made of diamond, and the city of pure gold, like clear glass. The foundations of the city were faced with precious stones. The first was diamond, the second lapis lazuli, the third turquoise, the fourth crystal, the fifth agate, the sixth ruby, the seventh gold quartz, the eighth malachite, the ninth topaz, the tenth emerald, the eleventh sapphire, and the twelfth amethyst. The twelve gates were twelve pearls and each gate was made from a single pearl. The main street of the city was pure gold – yet appeared transparent like glass. And the city did not need the sun or the moon for it was lit by the radiance of the glory of God.'

'Sounds like a geologist's dream,' Sarah commented.

'It sounds just like Atlantis,' Matheson said, awestruck.

Scott inclined his head. 'The only trouble with the analogy is that the new Jerusalem was perfectly square. Atlantis is perfectly round.'

'How does it help us here?' Roebuck asked in all seriousness.

'In Revelation 9:2, it speaks of a fifth angel blowing its trumpet and in so doing, another star falls to the earth where the angel is given a key. This key unlocks the "shaft of the Abyss" from which sulfurous smoke rose out from a huge furnace as the sun and sky were darkened. And from the smoke dropped metallic armored locusts with stings in their tails like scorpions. They hovered, and made the racket of many chariots with their horses, charging.'

'Christ,' Roebuck gulped. 'They sound like Apache attack helicopters.'

'What does this Abyss do?' Gant asked.

Scott shrugged. 'I don't know. But the angel's name in Hebrew was Abaddon, and in Greek, Apollyon.' He looked down at the picture of the Golem. 'By removing the sacred word from the Golem's head it is reduced to dust. Abaddon could be its name . . .' He eyed Gant again. 'The point is, what power source could be so unbelievably big that it lit up your security satellites? What if Atlantis is sitting on a volcano?'

'What we registered is *not* volcanic activity.'

Matheson was one jump ahead. 'Yes, but the site in Giza was tapping into and converting geo-thermal energy. This site could be doing the same thing on a massive scale. And situated over a Pole?

The use of the earth as some kind of magnetic dynamo? That's incredible! And more power than you'd know what to do with.'

'So how do we shut it down?'

'Close the damn Abyss, I should imagine, sir,' Roebuck responded flippantly.

'The fifth angel,' Pearce noted. 'The fifth site. The site with the Abyss – the power source.'

Hackett shook his head. 'All this ancient scripture and we're gonna look like real idiots if we finally get down there and all we find is a giant energizer bunny banging on a battery.'

Nobody laughed.

'In the Egyptian *Book of the Dead*,' Scott warned, 'there's a place described as being crucial to human survival in the next world that human souls must attend to. Carved out of solid rock it is "The Chamber of Ordeal", or more commonly, "The Chamber of Central Fire".'

'Great.'

'So we need to get to the center of the city,' Gant concluded. 'To find this chamber, this – Abyss.'

Scott looked down upon the node photographs again, puzzled. 'The Book of Revelation,' he explained, 'is also where God likens himself to the alphabet. Just as in the beginning was the word, God says he is both Alpha and Omega, the First and the Last. The Beginning and the End. Always it comes back to words . . .' The epigraphist eyed everyone around the table. 'God also warns those who may wish to enter the city and warns against those who may not enter. Dogs, fortune-tellers.'

Pearce shook his head. 'Well, that's me without an invite.'

'The sexually immoral.' Sarah seemed to blush. 'Murderers.'

Gant shifted uneasily. 'It was a war situation.'

'Idolaters.' Scott looked around the room, his eyes eventually falling on Hackett.

'I guess I do kind of worship, uh, science,' he admitted sheepishly.

'And anyone of false speech and false life,' Scott concluded. 'Which counts the rest of us out.'

'Well,' November remarked. 'This'll be fun.'

Sarah turned to the Major. 'Now you know what you can expect to find under the ice, what can we expect to find on the surface?'

Gant immediately set about marking up positions. 'The signs are not good,' he said. 'We have reports of enemy activity here, here and here, fully encircling their base for approximately a hundred square miles. Even if we had the time, which we do not, we'd never get in by land. Our only alternative is by air but the V-TOLs just don't like this cold. We've tried adapting them but there's a heater problem. I've already sent them back to the *Truman*.'

'Then what do we do?' Matheson asked apprehensively.

'We have a Hercules C-130 that's prepared to take us in. It's like the one we flew down in from Geneva.'

'Woah,' Pearce objected, concerned. 'Those things are huge. A C-130 can't land there. There's no landing strip and no re-fueling dump.'

'No one said anything about landing there,' Gant observed.

Scott was confused. 'Then how do we get on the ground?'

HERCULES

Hercules, the Romanized name for the Greek hero Herakles, son of Zeus and Alcmene. Legendary for the murder of his wife Megara and their children after succumbing to a fit of madness sent down by Hera, and consequently consigned to carry out twelve monumental labors. These included slaying the nine-headed Lernean Hydra, capturing the mad bull of Crete, taking the girdle of Hippolyte, Queen of the Amazons, and bringing back the golden apples kept by Hesperides at the world's end. In Roman mythology the broad, powerful and charismatic hero rescued men from danger.

As a US Army C-130, he was delivering them *into* danger.

Richard Scott stood by one of the windows in the rear of the plane, and looked down bewildered at all the strapping and clips he had stretched around his body in a harness.

'Now let me get this straight,' he said thinly. 'You're gonna toss me out the back of this plane at just over a thousand feet above ground level?'

'You won't be alone,' Gant explained, trying to make his voice heard over the drone of the engines. 'None of you will. Tandem jumps are fairly common. You'll be assigned to Lieutenant Roebuck here. He'll make sure the parachute opens. Just you make sure you're tied to him or then you'll be in trouble.'

'I dunno,' Scott moaned, as if he actually had a choice in the matter. 'A thousand feet? That's awfully low, isn't it?'

'It's the minimum height required to get our 'chute open,' Roebuck said confidently. 'It's the same height that base jumpers use. Y'know, those nutballs who hurl themselves off buildings? Don't worry, Professor. You won't be in the air that long. It'll all be over in ten seconds. You'll be on the ground before you even know it.'

'That's what I'm afraid of . . .'

'Just remember,' Roebuck said, taking the linguistic anthropologist aside and guiding him through the procedure as Gant went off to introduce Sarah to her partner. 'Bend your legs on impact. Don't keep 'em straight out, you could break something. Feet together, like this, see. Then turn it into a roll.'

'Which way?'

'I'll tell you which way when we get there. I'll release you on impact. You'll dive to the side. Turn it into a roll. And when you want to stop you *hit* the ground with your arm. It's all to do with energy transference so it hurts as little as possible.'

'I wish you wouldn't keep calling it "impact",' Scott said, much to Roebuck's amusement.

Over by another window, Matheson stood watching the retreating ice floes as the plane banked off into the mainland interior. Just a couple of weeks ago all he had seen was frazil ice, chaotic crystals that formed in stormy waters, clumping together to form grease ice, long wavy strips of ice that looked like oil slicks. But today all he could see was pancake ice that was rapidly forming into ice sheets. Pancake ice was formed by the rough seas spinning the ice around to form plates, some as large as ten feet across, like giant ice lily-pads for giant ice frogs. As winter drew near these plates crowded and eventually froze over completely to form continuous sheets.

But it was all growing distant now, to be replaced by the desolate, inhospitable-looking snow flats that were being pounded by high intensity winds which occasionally whipped into an updraft and buffeted the plane viciously.

The ridge of the Trans-Antarctic Mountains would be looming soon. Among them were the Dry Valleys, places so arid that it never snowed since all the moisture in the air was sucked right out and creatures were freeze-dried. The temperature regularly fell to minus 52 degrees Celsius and the ground was frozen solid up to a depth of half a mile. Conditions were so extreme that NASA regularly tested its latest robotic probes destined for Mars there.

This place put the fear of God in Ralph Matheson. Antarctica was a place where human life wasn't just insignificant – it was totally irrelevant.

Ralph found a cup of hot tea thrust in his hand. The marines were handing out steaming coffee and Mars bars for energy.

'Drink all the hot drinks you can manage. It'll help keep you warm. But when it gets to an hour before the drop I suggest you visit the head. It'll be the last heated toilet you'll see for a while. If you want to pee once we're on the ground, it'll be so cold it will freeze before it hits the ground. And until I have orders otherwise, war zone or no war zone, you will have to scoop it all up and bring your waste with you. There is no littering in Antarctica. Eat high-energy food stuffs too. Getting around in the snow expends more energy than you'll be used to. Mars bars are good because of all the glucose. Feed up too, because once we're down there the only square meals you'll have will be the ones you carry with you and what we can salvage from *Jung Chang*.'

There were ten marines in all, kitted up and ready, eating their candy bars and drinking their hot drinks. Light on conversation and even lighter on comedic banter, they were not as gung-ho as the scientists had expected.

'We're about to go into a potential war zone,' Roebuck explained quietly to Scott. 'Shouting yessir and polishing our boots is for the parade ground. I gotta tell you, Professor, I'm shitting my pants. And you should be worried if I *didn't* feel that way. I don't wanna shoot someone or get shot anymore than you do, but the difference is, it's my job.'

Matheson let the warm steam waft across his face before downing the hot, sweet liquid. 'All right,' he said, tugging at the lap-top by his feet. 'We got about another three hours stuck in this tin can. Let's get to work.'

RETRIEVAL STAGE 1

'You're tryin' to decode *this?*'

Scott looked up from where he was slumped against the vibrating green bulkhead and growled. He was tugging at his hair with one hand, clutching yet another photograph of the Atlantis glyphs with the other.

'I'm sorry,' Roebuck apologized, backing up and chewing his Mars bar. 'I guess I should just leave you to it.'

Scott shook himself out of his crisis. Passed the photograph over to the young officer and invited him to slump down with him. 'Here, have a try,' he offered. Then he asked: 'Aren't any of you guys a day over thirty?'

Roebuck smirked as he looked over the image. 'The military does like to pick 'em young, sir.'

The officer didn't seem daunted by the arrangement of bizarre-looking glyphs, which surprised Scott if he was honest. In fact, Roebuck's mild appraisal of the patterns actually started getting the despondent epigraphist excited.

'So these are the glyphs, right?' Roebuck asked, referring to the slip of paper stapled to the top. There were three horizontal lines of data. The middle line featured the glyphs.

'Right.'

'What are these numbers above it?'

'When you try to decipher a language you assign each glyph a number, arbitrarily. Then you reduce the text down to a series of numbers to see if you can pick out a pattern,' Scott explained. 'We call it Retrieval Stage One. That's a line of text reduced to numbers. I haven't got past that yet.'

'And what about this set of numbers underneath – that a text too?'

'No,' Scott replied, and briefly explained about the number stream, found written inside the crystal.

'I see,' Roebuck nodded. 'I see what you did. You converted the text to numbers. But no amount of re-jigging, changing what glyph was what number, got it to match the number stream from within the crystal.'

'Right. You making any sense of that? Do you know anything about decipherment?'

'Uh, kinda,' Roebuck revealed. 'I was manning the communications array my end of the line when I contacted you guys in Geneva, remember? I've been trained left ways of Christmas in the art of data encryption and decryption.'

That made sense. 'Ah,' Scott replied condescendingly. 'Computer codes. Yeah, well, sorry to disappoint you, but this is a language. Not a code.'

'Which in some respects should make cracking it a whole lot easier, sir,' Roebuck replied flatly, for a moment completely unaware that he had just shattered the epigraphist's reputation among his peers. Roebuck looked up sheepishly as Sarah and November stifled a laugh. 'If you don't mind my saying so, sir. No offence.'

'None taken.' Scott ripped open his own Mars bar and with a mouthful of chocolate said: 'So tell me more. Why should it be easier?'

'Well, I would assume there's been no attempt to hide the information. If anything, if this is a warning from the past, surely they would have built in clues to help decode the information.'

It seemed a startlingly obvious and simplistic thing to say, but Scott knew that Roebuck was making sense. Maybe he did need to take a different approach to all this and not base his analysis on purely linguistic terms.

'Cryptography,' Roebuck added, 'requires coding and decoding. As such you require a key. Maybe they realized time would naturally encode something as the original language corrupted and altered, so something that time doesn't affect would become the key to decoding it.'

'That's remarkably perceptive, Lieutenant,' Hackett interjected enthusiastically. 'You're wasted in the military.' He turned to the others. 'Part of the basis of complexity theory is the notion of the arrow of time. Certain laws of physics are dependent on it, others are not. Entropy is the amount of disorder in a system. It only works one way – our way. If we reverse time, smashed cups would put themselves back together. However, things like gravity work the same whatever direction time is running.'

Roebuck shrugged. 'That makes sense.'

'So, do you have any idea what might be the key to decoding this little, uh, quandary?'

'Hell, I don't know, Professor,' Roebuck scoffed. 'That's for you to figure out. Maybe the key's a law of physics, or mathematics. Some kind of constant as a frame of reference. Maybe it's a physical mani-festation. I just know a little about encryption. In the 1970s, which is way before my time, they had this Data Encryption Standard, DES – a product block cipher. It used sixteen rounds of substitutions and transpositions in a cascade, encrypted in sixty-four-bit binary encoded plaintext, controlled by a fifty-four-bit key – producing a sixty-four-bit ciphertext.'

'What?'

'Basically you needed a DES chip to encode or decode the text. Or incredible software. But there was just one key and you needed the key to decode it. It falls into the wrong hands and the whole thing is useless to security agencies. By the 1990s we had this asym-metric, two-key cryptosystem. With the encryption system in the public domain, but the second key, the decryption key remaining a secret. Again it's computer based. The point is, the whole thing rests on an algorithm that encodes and decodes. Perhaps this number stream here is an algorithm, kind of a key.'

'It's not an algorithm,' Hackett explained. 'Believe me, I tried.'

'That still doesn't stop it being a key,' Roebuck replied eagerly. 'Those numbers have to mean something or why put them there?'

'Are you saying,' Scott probed, sitting up and taking note, 'that maybe there are several keys to unlocking this thing?'

'Well, yeah, why not?' Roebuck said matter-of-factly. 'If this is a warning from the past, or they wanted to contact people in the future, people with technical capabilities, they'd try to reach out on every level. At least, that's what I'd do.

'It might be an attempt at a universal language, in order to cross time and racial boundaries. This may have to have been invented. Hell, the key to it could be down to something as simple as the shape of the damn building it was standing in. The design of the pattern here plays on the human eye's ability to detect patterns. The spiral and the arch seem particularly important to these people.'

That stung. Sharply. *An invented language.* Scott had considered that possibility. Why had he not pursued it further?

Matheson was on his feet. Something was clicking into place. He sat down with the others and put his lap-top to one side. 'What if Roebuck's right? What if they made their megalithic constructions in such a way that they were *intended* to impart a message to us?'

Sarah was intrigued. 'The design of the building as a key?'

'In Giza, above ground, the design of the Pyramids and the Sphinx correspond to how the ancient sky looked in 10,500 BC. Like a mirror. Roughly the time we talked about for the first flood. I think maybe the tunnels underneath have a message too.'

Scott was nodding. 'The Egyptian Hermetic dictum was; "as above, so below". But a message in the design of the stonework?'

Matheson pulled out a pen and a notebook. 'These people are masters of sound – correct? All things sonic and the physics of wave propagation.' The others nodded. 'So what does a sound wave look like?' He drew a squiggle across the page.

'So what would one of the Giza tunnels look like if you drew it from its side? It's a spiral, remember? Sarah, you were standing in a sound wave set in stone.'

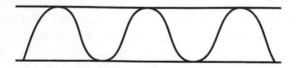

'Wait a minute.' Sarah was skeptical. 'A sound wave – are you sure? What's the wavelength on audible sound waves?'

'Anything from two centimeters all the way up to twenty meters,' Hackett replied without even having to think about it.

'How do you measure a wave's length?' November asked.

'A wave has a peak and a trough,' Matheson explained. 'Y'know, like a real wave in the ocean. The wave's length is measured by determining the distance between two peaks.'

'Couldn't the wave in the tunnel equally be a representation of a light wave?'

'Absolutely not,' Hackett replied dismissively. 'The wavelength of visible light is 0.00000055 meters. That's ridiculously small. Radio waves are on the same kind of scale.'

'Not all of 'em,' Roebuck corrected.

Sarah shuffled forward. 'So what *is* the wavelength of the spiral in the tunnels?'

'Exactly ten meters,' Matheson confirmed, 'according to your data. That's the longest wavelength divided by the shortest: twenty divided by two. The exact middle ground of audible wavelengths. And the Atlantis glyphs only appear on the spiral Carbon 60 strip, which we already know can produce standing waves in liquids because of the quasicrystals . . . My God, that's it! *That's it!*' He was sketching furiously on his notepad again. 'That's how the network – *works!* That's how these five sites are linked. The tunnels that go out from them go down into the water table. If they go all the way out to the coast then all five sites are linked through the oceans.

'Sound travels at 340 meters per second in the air – but 1,500 meters per second in the water. At extreme depths there's a layer of water that has a temperature and pressure differential to the ocean above it. It's what whales use to communicate over vast distances at incredible speeds. Increasing pressure increases the speed of sound. This layer of water traps the sound so it has no choice *but* to travel great distances.'

'Why?'

Matheson eyeballed Roebuck consciously. 'Excuse me?'

'Why?' the Lieutenant asked again. 'I mean, I'm sure you're correct. Our submarines regularly pick up acoustic signals in the oceans they can't explain. I'm sure this network of yours exists. My only question is: *why* does it exist?'

Matheson sat back on his haunches, exchanging a look with the rest of the team as Sarah told him: 'Lieutenant, we've all been asking that same question since day one.'

'Lieutenant Roebuck?' November said tentatively. 'We're not at radio silence or anything, are we?'

'No,' the marine confirmed. 'Command wants the Chinese to know we're here.'

'Then why doesn't Ralph give you the map references where these five sites are and you could contact a few submarines. See if they can't pick this network up in the water?'

'November,' Matheson scoffed mildly. 'We still don't know where these other two sites might be. We're still waiting on confirmation from Gant.'

'You're a smart man, Ralph,' she smiled. 'Can't you best guess it?'

Gant had his arms folded tightly across his chest as Roebuck took him through the charts at the rear of the cockpit, illuminated under a snake lamp.

'There's the *Connecticut* and the *Jimmy Carter* in the North Atlantic.'

'Seawolf Class?'

'Uh, yes, sir. Jackson says he'll give us the *Virginia* in the South Atlantic for two hours.'

'That's all they're asking for anyway, right?'

Roebuck confirmed that with an apologetic nod. His ass was on the line here backing this plan. Taking so many submarines out of the patrol loop for two hours at once was an incredible risk.

'The *Louisville*, the *Olympia*, the *Charlotte* and the *Jefferson City* are all on patrol somewhere in the Pacific. Fleet Commander won't say where but he assures me they can sweep pretty much the entire area Ralph asked us to check. They're the older Los Angeles Class. And the *Trepang*'s in the Indian Ocean.'

'The *Trepang*? That old Sturgeon Class training ship?'

'Sir, yes, sir.'

'Damn, I remember that boat. Jesus, she must be damn near forty or fifty years old by now.'

'They say they're up to the job. We also got a Fleet Ballistic Missile Submarine, the *Kentucky*. And the *Dolphin*'s standing by.'

The *USS Dolphin AGSS-555*, was one of a kind of research submarine used by both the navy and civilian agencies alike. She had an unmatched world depth record for operational submarines. And right now she was sat right under the Arctic ice cap, just south-west of the North Pole, looking for a sunken site. She was already part of this wild-goose chase so it didn't make much difference calling her in.

'Ten ships,' Gant concluded. 'That's a lot of ships. Dower's gonna be pissed tryin' to get this authorized. I'll call it through,' he said.

'What time shall I tell 'em to expect an answer, sir?' Roebuck indicated the team back in the belly of the plane.

'Two hours,' he replied. 'Which means we'll be on the ground.'

Roebuck headed back as the pilot up ahead called for the Major's attention. Out through the windows a vista of low cloud cover was rearing up at them, at speed.

'It looks like some extreme weather out there. You want us to avoid it, we can avoid it.'

'Negative,' Gant sighed, handing the sheet of information Roebuck had given him to the young communications engineer, Joe Dodson. 'We don't have the time.'

'Understood.'

Dodson gave the sheet of information the once-over. A moth-eaten photograph of some odd design. A sheet of paper stapled to the top with rows of numbers and some familiar-looking squiggles underneath, while scrawled in pen next to them were a set of coordinates, oceanic depth ranges and acoustic frequencies to be transmitted to each of the ten submarines for them to institute a search.

'Uh, Major?' Dodson asked innocently, trying to get the marine's attention while he discussed the weather situation with the pilots. 'You want me to work out these little wave files and send them over too?'

Gant misheard the man and asked him to repeat what he'd just said. Dodson ran his fingers along the series of Atlantis glyphs but hadn't even remotely registered they were letters to an alphabet.

'These little waves. You want me to match 'em in the computer and tell the subs what frequency they are?'

Gant didn't say anything. Just grabbed the young man by the scruff of his collar and yanked him to his feet.

✳   ✳   ✳

'Tell him what you told me.'

Scott looked up startled as the young airman standing in front of him wiped at his nose like a schoolkid hauled in front of the teacher.

'All I said was these little symbols look like wave files; did he want me to work out the frequencies and send the information on to the submarines. I thought it was important.'

Gant jabbed his finger at Scott eagerly. But it looked more like a threat. 'Does *this* help you?'

But all Scott could manage was to let his jaw flap open and closed like a goldfish. Hackett took control. 'What do you mean by wave files?'

'On a computer,' Dodson explained, exasperated, 'when you record an audio signal you can display it any number of ways. Like a wavy line, or a series of spikes. Things like clicks produce very small wave files because the sound is so short. That's what these look like. Tiny snatches of sound displayed as a wave across the top and the corresponding spike data across the bottom, simply turned on its side. That's all I meant.'

Scott grabbed up one of the photographs again. Stared at it. Jesus. Could it be? Sarah scooted up to take a look too. They eyed each other. Everyone was waiting on Scott's response. If this was a plausible theory to work from it could only go ahead on his say-so. Scott leaped to his feet, frantic.

'Somebody grab a computer with a microphone, quick! These aren't just phonetic symbols! They don't *represent* sounds! They *are* sounds!' He confronted Dodson. 'Kid, you're a fucking genius. Let me shake your hand. What's your name?'

'Uh, Joe,' the communications engineer replied, taken aback. 'Joe Dodson.'

'Joe? Good to meet you, Joe. Short for anything, Joe?'

'Yeah, Joseph.' Scott started laughing as Matheson set up his computer. 'What's so funny?'

'Joseph,' Scott said. 'That's what's funny. In the Old Testament, Joseph and his coat of many colors was made Vizier to the Pharaoh and given the name Zaphe-nath-Paneah!' Dodson looked blank. 'Which in Hebrew means: "Decoder of the Code"!'

'Do it again,' Pearce urged, scowling at no one in particular as the background noise ruined the take. He adjusted his headphones as Sarah moved the microphone back.

'Okay, okay,' she agreed irritably, taking a drag on her cigarette first. 'Buh . . . buh . . .'

It was like someone was throwing bricks at the outer skin of the aircraft, listening to the constant shakes, rattles and metallic groans as the airframe fought the elements. Sarah took another breath and tried to match her vocal sounds to the Atlantis glyphs. They had decided each glyph must represent a human vocal sound. And after some trial and error had actually gotten some of Sarah's sounds to match up with the glyphs. Each time she spoke the computer analyzed the shape of the sound wave and compared it to each glyph. It was slow going. But at least it was going.

Scott paced back and forth impatiently, deep in thought. String enough of these sounds together and theoretically they were going to start forming sentences. But what language was it going to turn out to be? One thing was certain, it wasn't going to be English.

At this stage of text retrieval Scott should be seeing repeated components, ascertaining groups of glyphs that seemed to repeat within the text. By now he should be determining what these repeated groups might be. Conjunctions, for example, like the word 'and'.

But there were no repeated components. Whatever text Scott

studied, be it a stream of glyphs from Giza or a segment from the node photographs, nothing made sense. All he seemed to find was a random stream. So unless this ancient race spoke in a vocabulary that consisted of exceptionally long words, all they were going to get was a random stream of noises.

Frustration was such an undervalued word.

Hackett folded his arms as he, Matheson and November sounded out the anthropologist's dilemma. 'In a syllabic script,' Scott explained, 'vowels stand alone only at the beginning of a word. After that they're always paired with a preceding consonant. Consonants are never on their own. It's a statistical godsend. But I'm not detecting that here. It's also gonna be a matter of time before I determine whether voicing is marked in the bilabial and palato-velar stops.'

'Huh?'

'In some languages like Linear B the same glyphs used to represent the sounds pi, pa and po, are also used for bi, ba and bo. It's more economical. Most cultures, with the exception of maybe Chinese, are as economic with their writing as possible. Maximum information delivered with minimum effort. But a collection of sounds . . . ?'

'Richard,' Matheson urged. 'What's the problem here?'

'The problem?' Scott seemed almost amused. 'What I do for an occupation is play three-dimensional mindgames. Word puzzles. My expectations may be all wrong. How this language is written may bear no relation to how it is pronounced. I may simply not be able to understand a spoken word of it.'

And then he realized. Sarah was looking up at him and smiling.

'We're ready,' she said tantalizingly. 'All matched and ready. Wanna hear?'

Scott handed Pearce the 'sentence' he wanted translated. 'Those five sites by the way?' Pearce told him. 'No match. They remain a mystery, so we got fifty-five glyphs that visually match. Just so you know.' He punched in the glyphs and waited for the computer to string them into an extended audio file.

It was disjointed, and odd hearing it in Sarah's voice. It was: 'Dee – juh – kho – meh . . .'

Which in English meant: 'Pure gibberish . . .' Scott proclaimed, hanging his head in exasperation, his worst fears confirmed. 'Pure and utter gibberish.'

DROP ZONE

Gant strode purposefully up the metal gangway and crouched down by the navigation array. Across from him, communications engineer Joseph Dodson waited for his orders, and at Gant's instigation keyed his console at the rear of the cockpit once more and broadcast a message on all known Chinese channels. But he did so, this time, in English. The whole flight he'd been broadcasting this message, to no avail. Perhaps his Chinese simply wasn't good enough.

'This is the United States Marine Corps speaking on behalf of the United Nations. We have been asked to transport a United Nations Inspection Team to the Antarctic region known to contain a Chinese military installation. We request safe passage to deliver this inspection team. Over. I repeat, delivery of this United Nations Inspection Team requires safe passage and your immediate acknowledgement is required. Over!'

Dodson, a thin young man, sat back in his chair and wiped away the sweat beading across his top lip. He turned to Gant looking somewhat pale. 'Shall I keep trying, sir?'

Gant was about to answer when suddenly from up ahead an alarm sounded and red warning lights flashed across the board. The co-pilot in the front left seat inclined his head back. 'Major, Chinese anti-aircraft systems just locked on to us. Shall I take evasive action?'

Gant was on his feet, thinking quickly. 'Negative, negative. We don't want to do anything to jeopardize this mission. You start doing fancy military maneuvers and they're gonna know we're up to something. Just fly straight and true.'

The co-pilot watched his captain struggle with the controls as he fought the buffeting of severe winds and stuck his hands on the yoke to help out. 'We'll try our best, sir,' was all he said.

The dark-haired communications engineer scratched at his five o'clock shadow nervously. 'I could try 'em again, sir. The Chinese, I could—'

And then came the familiar whistle and whine of an untuned radio message trying to get through. Dodson's fingers flew across the keys as he zeroed in on the communiqué.

'Put it on speakers,' Gant ordered. 'I want everyone to hear this.'

Around the green metallic skin of the aircraft, and in and out of the ribs of the fuselage it echoed, the tinny voice of a distant Chinese officer with a mercilessly terrible English accent, cutting in over the din of the torrential ice storm that pounded the outer body like a hail of bullets.

'On behalf of the People's Republic of China, the People's Army respectfully declines safe passage for your aircraft and declines the invitation of the United Nations to inspect our facility. You are instructed not to descend from your present altitude. Any attempt to do so will be seen as an act of aggression and you will be fired upon. Attempt no landing at *Jung Chang*. You will be given five minutes to contact your superiors. However, after that time if you have not deviated from your present flight path you will be fired upon. These instructions shall not be repeated and no dialogue shall be entered into. Over and out.'

Both the team and the marines were pale. Matheson couldn't stop his foot from shaking. 'Jesus fucking Christ, we really are in the middle of World War fucking Three!'

And then came the confirmation they were all dreading. Gant's voice, firm over the intercom. 'Okay, everyone. Suit up. We'll be over the drop zone in two minutes.'

Scott was the first to get unsteadily to his feet. He gripped the handrail with white knuckles before helping Sarah up, and that was when they heard it. It started off as a low rumble, the groan of electric motors kicking into life, like the landing gear being lowered. But then came the clank. Loud and sharp. Locks being released.

And then came the shaft of light:

A thin sliver at the top of the rear cargo ramp. A white band through which the shatteringly loud roar of the world outside was invading in all its dazzling brilliance.

Scott threw an arm over his eyes as they instinctively welled up with tears. Sarah reacted by pulling her face mask into position and fastening her hood. 'Goggles,' she said, muffled through the thick clothing. 'Goggles.'

Scott snapped his sunglasses over his eyes and felt for the briefest moment a little safer. But the moment was short-lived as Roebuck came up behind him and clipped on. Scott whirled. All the marines were clipping on to their live cargo. They had suited up into thin white nylon camouflage over the top of their insulated jumpsuits. It meant on the ground they would virtually be invisible amid the snow, while up here they looked like ghosts.

'Okay, Professor,' Roebuck said briskly. 'I just gotta clip us on to the line overhead and we're all set. If you can just step up to this point here for me – atta boy.'

It was like a gangplank out to oblivion, the six short steps before him. Every time the plane lurched Scott would tense up, petrified he was about to topple out. But every time Roebuck sensed the anthropologist's movement he pulled him back. 'It's okay, Professor, I gotcha!'

'You know, the fabled Inca homeland of Aztlan means "the place of whiteness"!'

'No, I didn't know that.'

'Oh yeah!' Scott spouted nervously, watching the spectacular low stormcloud and blizzard rush off into the distance, caught up in the C-130's slipstream. 'There's this Chilean legend about a magic city on the borders of a mountain lake, the whereabouts of which no one knows. The city's streets and palaces were made of solid gold. And this golden city, known as the city of kings, would become visible at the end of the world.'

A single shrill klaxon burst accompanied a red warning light just overhanging the ramp. It blinked three times before settling on steady illumination. Scott felt his stomach churn over. That was his cue to take three steps forward onto the vibrating metal ramp. He could feel Roebuck shuffling behind him.

Gant had his arm wrapped gently around November as they edged forward at the rear of the line. Two marines had the nuclear warhead in its box, in front of them, a sled fastened on top. While further down the line stood Hackett, who was still engaged in hooking up with his marine.

'The visibility out there is appalling, Major!' November complained. 'Y'can't see your hand in front of your face! How're we supposed to find each other when we land?'

Gant tugged at the hooks of the harness on her back. 'This one right here,' he explained, 'is attached to an expandable tether, which in turn is attached to me. Even though I'll be releasing you when we land so we don't wind up piled on top of each other, we'll never be more than six to ten feet apart.'

'What about the others?'

'We all have beacons,' he reassured her.

Hackett squirmed with his assigned partner. 'I know you have to hug me,' the physicist joked. 'But do you have to be so tight?'

'Sir, it's for your own safety.'

Hackett eyed him up and down. 'My mother always warned me that all the nice boys love a sailor. That apply to marines?'

The marine confronted his CO. 'Sir, do I have to be partnered with this geek?'

Gant scowled. 'Eyes front, soldier!'

'El Dorado? That means "The City of Gold", or is it the city of the sun?' Scott gabbled breathlessly. He swallowed hard. 'In the middle of the Salar de Coipasa is the village of Coipasa. And just north of it live the Chipaya Indians. Their whole language is different from both Quechua *and* Aymara! The closest linguistic language is Arabic and North African tribal languages—'

'Professor Scott?'

'Yeah?'

'You're babbling.'

Scott glanced back briefly to check on the others. Directly behind him Matheson couldn't even make eye-contact, while Pearce and

Sarah shifted uneasily on their feet. Maybe he was babbling, but with good reason.

Another klaxon burst.

Scott spun his head around. Green! The light had changed to green! Scott held his breath, readied himself for the sprint forward and realized belatedly that Roebuck had already lifted him clear off his feet and was rushing them out the back.

Slam! Scott's tongue caught in his throat as the ripcord still attached to the C-130 viciously snatched the parachute out of the pack on Roebuck's back.

Scott had expected the cold, the sheer freezing terror sapping the very life out of his extremities. But the noise, the utter volume of powerful engines heaving an unnatural hulk through the air combined with the intensity of rushing air, plus the smell of exhaust fumes and the total power of the blizzard pounding at their helpless dangling bodies almost seemed too much to bear.

He could see nothing. No sky, no ground, just a vast wall of swirling whiteness. An emptiness and a void that even God would have trouble filling.

His entire gut seemed to have shifted to a new elevated position in his chest, just down from his windpipe, making it difficult to breathe. The rush of blood in his ears had a voice of its own, like a crowd calling for his execution, and—

Bang! His ankles ached as the sudden stress of the impact shot up his legs and turned them to jelly. The twang of a clip coming undone and a rough shove to the side and Scott found himself coming bodily into contact with the frozen wasteland. There was a compacted, polystyrene sound of snow and ice crushing beneath his weight. He made to roll but found he was skidding uncontrollably across the icy flat.

He tried to yelp but nothing came out as a set of boots landed in his path. He knocked them clean out the way as he crashed on through before jerking to a halt on the end of his tether.

He lay there, on his back, his chest heaving up and down as he wheezed and coughed, trying to come to terms with what had just happened. He was on the ground and he was alive! He coughed again, bringing up phlegm but it had nowhere to go and he wasn't taking his faceplate off for anything, so he forced himself to swallow it and went to sit up. In all this gear it was a struggle. As he tried to get his bearings he realized that the blizzard was blasting at such a force the snow was moving horizontally, into him and past him.

Scott groaned as he struggled to get up. But the blizzard was so unbelievably powerful it knocked him straight back on his ass. He tried again, but just couldn't get a footing. And that was when he felt it. A weak tug at the tether and a distant cry for—

'Help! Professor Scott, can you hear me?'

Scott spun round, trying to figure out which direction Roebuck was calling from, but he couldn't see a thing. Not a damn thing. He felt the tug again. That was it! That was the direction.

'Lieutenant? Hold on! I'm coming!' He tried to stand again, but the best he could manage was to crawl on all fours until—

Snap! The tether jerked so viciously at his back that it whipped him around and sent a sharp jabbing pain into his hip. He grabbed at the nylon cord and yanked it in an effort to bring on some slack, but all he managed was to get his momentum going again and he found himself rapidly sliding back the way he'd just come.

The ice was cracked and torn all around him, jutting up into the air and clawing at him as he bumped over it. He could hear a scream and then the tether yanked even harder.

Thinking quickly, Scott reached around in his pocket and jabbed the only thing he could find, his gold-plated Parker pen, a gift from his estranged wife last birthday, deep into the snow and ice. And hung on for dear life.

His legs were over a precipice, and dangling from the tether between them, approximately ten feet below, was Lieutenant Roebuck. Stranded on a cliff of blue ice, the distressed officer cried out as he tried to get a footing and struggled to release the parachute, several cords of which were wrapped around his throat.

What he didn't know was that Scott's pen was slowly, very slowly forcing its way through the snow and ice leaving a deep scar in its wake.

And there was absolutely nothing the anthropologist could do about it.

JUNG CHANG

AN-YANG SETTLEMENTS – NORTHERN HONAN PANHANDLE – CHINA

Inscriptions on Oracle Bones, literally 'chai-ku wen' or 'writings on [turtle] shell and [animal] bone' date from around 4,000BCE. Ching-hua 4 bone from the reign of Wu Ting speaks of a two-headed snake drinking from the Yellow River and there followed a week of bad weather. A rainbow or a snake with heads at both ends is often found in early Chinese literature and is an ominous sign. On the Yi-pien 3380 bone, dating from 1,300 years later during the Han Dynasty, shrine reliefs at Wu-lizng-tz'u, south-west of Shantung show the same thing. A two-headed dragon in a struggle with the spirits of the wind and rain.

Excerpt from: *Tales of the Deluge: A Global Report On Cultural Self-Replicating Genesis Myths*, DR RICHARD SCOTT, 2008

TIME TO SOLAR MAXIMUM:
19 HOURS, 23 MINUTES

TIME TO CURRENT SOLAR STORM INTERCEPTION:

4 HOURS, 51 MINUTES

Scott gritted his teeth and bellowed for help as he fought to keep both himself and Roebuck alive. His sunglasses were fogging up. Every time he gasped for breath, steam from his mouth would work its way inside of them and crystallize on the sub-zero surface.

'Help us!' Scott shrieked. 'Somebody help us!'

He could hear cracking – a slow metallic sort of cracking and looked down to see the deep indigo ink ooze out from his pen and feather its way through the ice like blood.

'Dr Scott!' Roebuck yelped, his voice sounding thinner, weaker. 'Professor?'

'Hang on in there, Lieutenant!' Scott called back. 'That's an order!'

'The transponder,' Roebuck cried feebly. 'Sewn into your left sleeve, top pocket! Activate the transponder so they can track us down!'

Left sleeve? Easier said than done. Scott was holding on by his right hand. He couldn't reach his left sleeve. He tried folding his arm up and trying to reach the device with his fingers, but it wasn't happening. He struggled again but all he could manage was a pathetic tickle.

He couldn't tell Roebuck. Christ, he couldn't tell the poor bastard. He shot a look over his shoulder. The chasm that had swallowed up the marine was getting wider. If it carried on like that for much longer the ground beneath him would give way too and they'd both be goners. Roebuck was right, he had to get to that transponder. That tiny little black box was all that stood between survival and death.

Scott tugged the fleece neckband down from around his mouth and went for his sleeve with his teeth. The searing cold burnt at his skin as hurricane-force winds blasted ice crystals into his pores. Clawing the fingers of his left hand deep into the snow his muscles ached as he reached over to gnash at the tiny device. Once, twice – five times before he finally hit the switch and a tiny red LED lit up to let him know it was transmitting a homing signal.

'Roebuck?' Nothing. 'Roebuck, it's on! The transponder is switched on!'

Still nothing.

'Lieutenant, answer me!'

'Uh, Professor, I think you better twist your head and take a look at this,' came the muffled response. 'We got company.'

Across the ice chasm, rearing up out of snow-covered hides were two darkened figures in full military fatigues. Thick, snowball-sized clumps of snow fell from their equipment as they slammed clips into their rifles and took aim.

They were Chinese.

Roebuck was midway through attempting to take the parachute cords from around his windpipe when he froze. All he could do now was twist in the breeze. He was well sheltered down here, thank Christ. The storm that was sweeping across the chasm overhead was giving the two Chinese soldiers some serious problems, but they stood fast.

They'd been hiding in the snow, these two. Must have crawled up on their bellies to the crevasse. White capes flapped from their shoulders upon which they would have mounded up snow and hidden underneath. One shouted over at them in incomprehensible Cantonese while his partner got on his radio, though try as he might he couldn't seem to get a signal out.

Roebuck could feel the subtle effects of Scott slipping above him, and tried to relax. 'How ya doin', Professor—?' he yelled out.

'Not – good!' the epigraphist grunted under the strain.

Roebuck tried to peer through the storm beyond the two Chinese soldiers. A little granite. A lot of ice. 'We're in a natural bowl,' he murmured to himself. 'They're isolated.'

Roebuck raised his hand slowly, bringing it up to a surrender posture while easing the parachute cords out and away from his neck. But even that slight movement was enough to send the first of the two soldiers into a screaming frenzy.

'Hey!' Roebuck shouted back, trying to appear reasonable. 'I'm just gonna set this down, okay? I just need to set this down.'

The Chinese soldier screamed in total frustration as Scott accidentally kicked chunks of ice off the cliff edge. 'Hey, what's going on?' he demanded. 'What's happening?'

'Nothing you need to worry about, Professor. This guy's just being an asshole. But that's okay, he can see we ain't goin' nowhere.'

Roebuck pointed to the cords in his other hand. 'I'm just gonna let these go. Okay? I'm gonna drop 'em. On three, brace yourself, Professor. One, two . . . three!'

The Chinese soldier tensed as the cords tumbled from Roebuck's hand and let the parachute fall a little freer. But the whole contraption was still attached to Roebuck's back and the slight movement had let a breeze waft in and start to open the material back out. Just like he knew it would.

Almost immediately Scott was screaming.

'I can't hang on!' he yelped. 'Shit, I can't hang on! What're you doing down there?'

The Chinese soldier went into fits as his partner continued to try and get his radio to work. He was clearly frustrated. Roebuck held up his hands again.

'It's okay! It's okay! I just need to release these straps on the front here, and the one on my back – fast!' He had no idea if the soldier understood or not and he wasn't waiting around to find out. Instead he just acted on impulse and screamed back at the hollering enemy grunt while Scott bellowed frantically about losing his grip.

One strap to the left, one strap to the right. He reached around to his back, the enemy poised. Tugged at the strap and the parachute fell free . . .

It fluttered into the ice chasm below and the Chinese soldier breathed a sigh of relief.

Roebuck smiled. The enemy returned the smile. Only to have it drop as he realized the marine had pulled a gun out from behind his back and was aiming straight at—

Bang! The Chinese soldier's brains splattered in an arc across the sky as the bullet slid straight between his eyes. But not before his partner reacted to what was going on and dropped his radio.

Roebuck went to fire again, but the extreme of hot against freezing cold on his last shot had already breached his weapon – and the Chinese were one step ahead. Their weapons were covered in a thermal hood. Dangling from the tether Roebuck was a sitting duck; he was riddled with bullets and convulsed from the impacts.

Scott screamed as his grip went and he lurched toward the edge. 'Roebuck? Roebuck, are you there?' But the hail of lead continued unabated with one bullet eventually ripping straight through his calf muscle and exploding up into the virgin-white snow. Scott screamed in tormented agony, flailing, tumbling. He was about to drop over the edge when a hand, seemingly from out of nowhere, thrust out, grabbed hold and held him fast.

Scott looked up, terrified, only to realize it was Gant.

The Major raised his finger to his lips for the anthropologist to be silent.

And then just as suddenly as it had started, the hail of bullets ceased.

Silence.

Then a distant voice reported from across the fissure, 'Got him, sir.'

Scott glanced over his shoulder just in time to see the second Chinese soldier, his throat slit from ear to ear, tumble over the edge into oblivion.

'Now hold still!' Gant ordered. 'Okay, soldier – take your shot.'

Scott was wild-eyed. 'What about Roebuck?' he asked.

'The Lieutenant's dead,' Gant explained matter-of-factly. 'There's nothing you can do. Damn hothead just turned a minor skirmish into an all-out war. First rule of war, you maim the enemy. *Maim* them, not kill 'em. You want them to expend all their energy trying to get their injured back. They knew what they were doing. That's why he shot you in the fucking leg. Now we're slowed down.' He gave the other soldier the thumbs-up.

The marine across the chasm fired a single bullet, snapping the tether in two. Roebuck's body tumbled end over end into the abyss below, while Gant put his back into it and hauled Scott to freedom.

'Well done, Dr Scott, I'm impressed. You managed to keep your head pretty well under fire. Let's get this wound of yours dressed so we can be ready to move out,' Gant suggested, helping him to his feet.

Scott limped a couple of paces before he realized everyone else was already gathered before him. November gave him a grin but he didn't notice as Sarah rushed across to take over from Gant as the human crutch. On impulse they kissed deeply. Passionately.

'I thought we'd lost you,' she said shakily.

'That makes two of us,' Scott replied, accepting the romantic situation as though it were a natural progression. November tried to hide her disappointment as she followed on behind.

'Where are we?' Scott requested, turning back to Gant. 'I thought *Jung Chang* was deserted.'

'Reinforcements,' Gant explained. 'In this storm we could be in the middle of an entire new camp and never know it. I hope to God they were just scouts.'

Which, as it turned out, was entirely the wrong thing to say.

Gant's radio sparked to life. 'Sir, Michaels here, up on point.'

'Go ahead, soldier,' Gant replied, growing increasingly aware that the storm was starting to clear. There were objects all along their left flank. Small in the distance, but not that small. And there was movement . . .

'Visibility is improving. Over.'

'Great. Let's get moving.'

'Uh, no, that's a negative, sir. We got a problem. You're never gonna believe where we are.'

REINFORCEMENTS

Gant adjusted his computer-enhanced binoculars over the peak of a ridge of solid snow and ice, while the medic in his unit, a stocky, soft-spoken man from Iowa by the name of John Brandes, tackled the wound on Scott's leg.

Out beyond their position lay a massive Chinese encampment, fully equipped with Armored Personnel Carriers, tanks, anti-aircraft batteries and row upon row of tents. There were troops here. Lots of troops. They even had air support in the shape of four attack helicopters.

Gant gasped: 'Fuck me!'

'You had no idea any of this was out here?' Hackett asked, but his gaze was leveled at Bob Pearce, who shrugged. How the hell was *he* supposed to know?

'Not like this.' He ducked down to face everyone. 'Well, they don't seem to know we're here. Those scouts didn't get a signal through. That's *one* stroke of luck in our favor.' He returned to his surveillance, accidentally knocking Scott's leg.

'Ouch!' Scott flinched, jabbing a hand over his mouth, realizing belatedly that he had to keep it down. He was still waiting for the morphine to kick in.

'You're lucky,' Brandes told him, wrapping the bandage tightly around Scott's leg. 'The bullet went straight in and out.'

'That's some kind of luck, I guess,' Sarah commented dryly.

Scott's teeth were chattering. 'Could you just hurry it up?' he asked desperately. 'I'm freezing.' He'd had to unzip his clothing and pull his leg out. November had a patch kit and was busy cleaning the blood off the jumpsuit and sticking a waterproof seal over the holes on either side of the leg.

The medic nodded. 'All done.' Scott raced to get dressed.

They were all lined up against the snowdrift, keeping their heads down, while Gant was busy shaking his. 'I dunno,' he moaned. 'What were they thinking, sending you guys in, in standard issue red jump-suits? I told 'em white, time and again. It's a goddamn UN color. Richard, can you read Chinese?'

'Some.'

'Well, c'mere. And somebody wrap something white around him, will ya? I don't want him used for target practice again.'

With the white tarp they'd used for covering the warhead draped over his head and shoulders, Scott eased his way up the incline and cautiously peered over the top. Gant handed him the binoculars.

'Does the glass on these lenses glint?' Scott asked, much to every-body else's trepidation.

'Only if you move 'em.'

Scott was not impressed as he put the things to his eyes. 'Where am I looking?'

'Down to the left, where that flag's flying over that larger tent. I saw a couple of banners.'

'I gotcha. Seventh Armored Division. Mean anything to you?'

Gant nodded. 'Anything else?'

'People's . . . Elite Guard.'

Gant slid down behind the snow drift pulling Scott with him. 'Aw, shit.' That meant something, all right. Something serious. 'They're the best,' Gant advised. 'We're up against the goddamn best.' He rubbed his chin, eyeing the bright red suits of the other scientists. How the hell were they going to get past without being seen?

'Okay,' he said. 'We need a plan.'

'How far are we from *Jung Chang*?' Hackett asked.

They were huddled round in a circle as Gant drew out the situ-ation in the snow. 'About three miles. *Jung Chang* is almost perfectly due south. That's a good hour's hike *without* the detour. This encampment ain't directly in our way, but it's as good as. We need to get around the perimeter of this eastern corner, here.'

'What if we cut up the parachutes and tape them over our jump-suits? Then we'd be camouflaged,' November suggested.

A couple of the marines were intrigued, but Gant was dismissive. 'Uh-uh,' he said, 'the material's too thin. You'd all wind up pink instead of red.'

Sarah picked ice-crystals from her eyebrows as she took her own look at the Chinese encampment. Why hadn't they gone on to *Jung Chang*? What were they afraid of? And then something else dawned on her. While the others discussed hare-brained theories on how to creep past a Chinese base without getting shot at, something about the way these Chinese soldiers were acting gave her an idea. They seemed distracted. Though the storm had significantly lessened in intensity, their focus of concern still seemed to be the sky. Unexpected contact with enemy aircraft. Or vehicles approaching on the horizon. They were checking long-range radar data. While two of *them* were dressed in red. Probably civilian support staff, a bit like themselves.

'They're not expecting anyone coming in on foot,' she commented.

Matheson was puzzled. 'What do you mean?'

'We're in the middle of nowhere,' Sarah shrugged. 'Who the hell walks up to a Chinese base thousands of miles from civilization? Nobody.'

Scott sat up gingerly. 'You're suggesting we just *walk* straight through?'

'Why not? All that creeping around is what they're gonna be expecting. You look suspicious, you'll be treated suspicious. Most of these guys are freezing their butts off, and are more concerned with keeping warm. Fuck 'em. I bet if we just march through their base and look like we know what we're doing they'll assume we're one of them, and ignore us.'

'Are you *nuts*?' Pearce sniggered. 'That has gotta be one of the most fucked-up pieces of pseudo-psychology I've ever heard.'

Matheson smiled. 'Yeah. So they're not gonna expect it. Besides, Richard knows Chinese. We get into any trouble, he can talk us out of it.'

'But!' Scott protested, overruled and ignored.

Hackett was smirking and shaking his head. 'That's so far out it might just work.'

Gant was excited. 'It's got balls. But it's only half a plan.'

'About this speaking Chinese thing,' Scott tried to interject. 'I can read it, but—'

But Brandes was concerned. 'Sir,' he said, 'if I may . . . We're wearing standard issue US military camouflage. They'll know immediately who we are if we try that. Our only option is we go around the outer perimeter and meet up with the beakers on the other side. Crawling on our bellies is a fine suggestion, but there's no way a one-, two-, even a three-man team can do that effectively and still take care of this.' He patted the long black trunk containing the nuclear warhead sat on its sled. 'What do we do about this?'

'That's not our only option, soldier,' Gant said briskly. 'Skills . . . I need skills.' He indicated Scott. 'You're good with languages. You can go.' Gant eyed Sarah, then Bob Pearce before finally settling on November. 'Honey, take your clothes off.' Then to Sarah: 'You too.'

Sarah was incensed. 'Fuck you!' she spat.

Gant snapped his head back, unsure how to handle her when she was in fire-cracker mode as she added: 'It's my plan. I'm going.'

'So let me get this straight,' Matheson said, jabbing his thumbs under the shoulder strap to his harness for comfort as he heaved forward once more. 'The whole world's programmed to end. We're in the middle of a war zone. So I'm about to walk straight through an enemy encampment . . . dragging a 450-pound nuclear warhead on a sled.'

On the second tether, Sarah groaned as she heaved with him. 'That's about the size of it.'

Scott had his head bent, afraid to move it any as he led the way. 'Keep it down, will you? They hear we're not speaking Cantonese, we're in trouble.'

'I think maybe you got off lightly getting shot in the leg,' Sarah said, watching Scott up ahead, hobbling ever so slightly.

Gant walked side by side with Scott wearing November's red jumpsuit, checking the coast in a constant sweep with Corporal Hillman and Michaels flanked either side of the warhead having exchanged jumpsuits with Bob Pearce and Hackett.

None of them had guns. Civilian support staff just didn't carry them. The military men had knives instead. Hidden and sharp.

It would take a super-fit man 100 days to cross all 1,657 miles from coast to coast across Antarctica pulling a 450lb sled. Matheson was reminded of the history of this place. The expeditions of Scott, Amundsen, Shackleton and Mawson were legendary campfire folk tales now – how those heroic men had battled the elements and how Captain Scott and his team had perished. Was that going to happen again?

They were nervous. They were *all* nervous. Maybe that was why their long walk had developed into a kind of penguin-like waddle as they marched ever onward with slow trepidation.

It was this final approach, the last couple of hundred yards of flat barren ice that posed the greatest immediate danger. If there was a hidden sentry anywhere along here it was about now that he was likely to pop up and open fire.

But there was nothing.

As they drew closer to the first line of plain black tents, all they could hear was the desolate sound of whistling winds and the lonely flapping of canvas and nylon sheeting. It was like a ghost town.

Scott was breathing so heavily now he was becoming aware of a phenomenon unique to Antarctica known as 'diamond dust'. The air was so dry and the temperature so cold the snowflakes in the air had formed tiny hexagons. So dissimilar to other snowflake phenomena that when he looked at the sun, it appeared to have a halo around it, with the rays of the sun forming some kind of cross right in its center.

Matheson took a deep breath. Then another. It was getting increasingly difficult to breathe. And it was a shock. He didn't think he was that unfit. Sarah turned to him. 'It's okay, Ralph. It's just the altitude. Antarctica's three times higher than anywhere else, on average. We're about three kilometers above sea level right here. You're fighting for oxygen, not just the cold.'

'I feel like my lungs are gonna explode out my chest,' Matheson wheezed.

Scott shot a look for them all to be quiet, double-checking that everyone had their sunglasses in place. After all, one look at their eyes and the Chinese were going to automatically know the game was up.

They passed the first row of tents without a hitch, continuing on their way without stopping to consider if their luck might run out.

Passing the second row of tents soon after, they became aware of foreign voices talking within their enclosures. Low Oriental voices echoing in and out of further rows of equipment crates stockpiled under snow-covered tarps.

Suddenly, up ahead, two Chinese soldiers ducked out of their tents, rifles slung over their shoulders. Making their way over to a command hut they glanced briefly at the team before going about their business.

Scott faltered, pulling up short, bringing everyone else to a halt.

Sheepishly he crouched down as if to fix the fastenings on his boots and glanced in through the opening of the nearest tent to see three more Chinese smoking and playing cards around a small heater. One of them glared out at him.

Scott nodded.

The soldier closed the flap on their tent, fast.

Scott got to his feet, smacking the snow off one knee. He jerked his head for the rest to follow on and darted a look at the perimeter, hoping the others were still with them, somewhere out there.

They continued on apace, until they reached where Gant intended them to be. Skidoos were all lined up behind flapping windbreaks – at least twenty of the things, all gleaming and polished. Next to them was an APC in tracks, while beyond that were the helicopters and beyond them were—

Smack! Scott rocked on his heels after careening straight into a perplexed soldier who had simply flown out of his tent without looking.

The soldier eyed him up and down disdainfully. Barked something before making a move to be on his way when Scott did something perhaps he shouldn't have.

His lip twitching with fright, he smiled and nodded as if he understood.

The soldier stepped back. Grabbed the anthropologist by a handful of his jumpsuit and snarled something else equally loud and incomprehensible.

Sarah and Matheson exchanged disturbed glances. Why wasn't Scott answering the soldier? Why was he simply smiling and nodding his head like an idiot?

Pearce eased forward on his aching elbows and realized something was wrong when the team didn't keep pace with his movement. Scott and the others, little specks of red moving about the encampment, should have emerged into a clearing some way off while he pulled himself along at a snail's pace.

But they hadn't. In fact, there was no sign of them.

Directing everyone else to hold position, he doubled back and pulled out his set of binoculars. 'Christ almighty . . . Richard, what are you *doing?*'

Hackett turned back, concerned. 'What is it?'

Scott was pulling his arm back. Balling his fist. He was swinging—

Wham! The sock to the Chinese soldier's gut was so intense the man dropped on the spot, doubled up in pain. Gant was impressed. 'And that was Chinese for *what?*'

'My fucking leg!' Scott looked to the others who were dumbstruck. 'Like I said, I can *read* it! I didn't say I can *speak* the damn language! Come on!'

Gant was immediately on it with him. He dragged the soldier behind a tent. Grabbing his knife, he was about to jab at the base of the young soldier's neck when Matheson asked him to stop.

'What are you doing?'

Gant was exasperated but they were in too much of a hurry to argue. Instead they had him gagged, bound and relieved of his weapon within seconds. But they still only had seconds maybe before that discovery was made too.

Sarah was confused. 'But you translated that soldier's speech. At *Jung Chang* when Bob projected himself over—'

'Cantonese, he was speaking Cantonese,' Scott snapped. 'This joker speaks Mandarin.'

Gant jabbed a finger out at the APC. 'Okay, Matheson, hotwire that thing.'

Matheson nodded. 'I think I can.'

'Don't think,' Gant ordered. 'Just do it.'

Michaels was perplexed. 'There are *two* types of Chinese?'

Scott indicated the warhead. 'Let's go.'

'Shit, shit, shit!' Pearce exclaimed, in the loudest, harshest whisper he could allow himself in his position. 'They've taken a guard out!'

Hackett crawled up next to him. 'That was the idea.'

'Yeah, well it's the wrong guard. Look.'

Hackett pulled his own binoculars out to peer deep into the enemy encampment. At the rear of the APC the team had the deployment doors wedged open and were dragging the warhead up inside. While in the cab, Matheson was ripping open a panel. Crossing wires. Smoke was pouring out the vertical exhaust at the rear of the vehicle.

The APC roared into life. Even at this distance they could hear its distinct and familiar growl and whistle. As around the far corner, from behind some mobile command trucks, another man was emerging. The real vehicle guard. *That* was the man they were supposed to have taken out.

And he was making a beeline straight for them.

Hackett flipped onto his back, beckoning Brandes over. 'What heavy explosives do you guys carry around?'

'You mean like mortars, grenades?'

'Yeah.'

'Mortars and grenades,' the medic shrugged.

Hackett jerked a thumb at the encampment. 'Then I'd think of something fast if I were you. Any minute now they're gonna need a diversion.'

That was when the gunshot rang out across the encampment.

Pearce was mortified as he spied the team. 'Uh-oh.'

Gant stepped away from the APC, his hands raised above his head as the Chinese guard waved the muzzle of his gun through the window of the cab. Matheson didn't seem to twig he was being ordered to get out. But the second shot into the air soon brought it home. He shifted, but the scowl on Gant's face said it all: 'Don't move.'

Gant took a step forward. The soldier screamed back at him, while across the camp other soldiers were emerging from their tents to see what all the commotion was about. An officer irritably stepped down from his command truck, flanked by his juniors as he struggled to do up his coat. While at the rear of the APC, Michaels looked up at Sarah, frozen in the doorway, and silently raised his finger to his lips. Standing next to him was Scott on one side, Hillman on the other. With the warhead safely inside, one of the rear doors was already bolted shut. The other was midway.

Slowly, very slowly, Michaels eased the door toward Sarah for her to jam shut and whispered: 'Tell Ralph to floor it.'

She nodded that she understood. Shared a brief worried look with Scott and closed the door tightly.

Soldiers across the encampment were edging forward now, not particularly sure they knew what was going on. Suddenly a snatch of Cantonese Scott could understand came his way.

'He thinks we're deserters,' the epigraphist explained. 'He thinks we're trying to steal this carrier and escape.'

'He thinks right,' Hillman replied.

But the conversation was cut short as the entire vista of black tents lined up before them suddenly exploded into livid flame. Soldiers were blown sky high. Munitions caught in the blast reacted with volatile spitting flame for meter upon meter.

And it was all the excuse Gant needed to hurl his knife directly at his would-be captor.

The blade buried itself deep into the young man's left eye-socket right up to the hilt as the Major glared at Matheson. 'Go!'

The engineer crunched the vehicle into gear and shot forward, tearing through the tents and leaving nothing but devastation in his wake. Gant dived for the dead soldier's gun, coming back up on one knee to lay a burst of suppressing fire while Hillman grabbed Scott by the arm.

'C'mon, Professor! You may know a lot, but do you know how to drive one of these things?' the marine yelled, indicating one of the snowmobiles.

Scott shrugged him off, because as it turned out, he did. Slinging one leg over and punching up the power, he slipped the throttle out and careened off into the carnage.

Hillman, Michaels and Gant were not far behind.

And neither was the People's Seventh Armored Division, Elite Guard.

✳ ✳ ✳

'Fire one more!' Brandes ordered.

'But our people are comin' straight at us!' one of the Privates manning the mortar yelled.

'So fire it over their heads!'

The soldier complied, turning one of the Chinese command trucks into a screaming ball of orange fury. But the devastation was far more than they could have expected. The ground opened up under that entire section of the encampment, turning sheet ice into a seemingly bottomless rift valley. Volcanic steam from deep within the glacial interior blasted out.

Matheson shifted gears. 'That explains it!' he tossed back over his shoulder.

'Explains *what*?' Sarah scowled, grabbing hold of a hand-rail on the ceiling to try to stop herself from being thrown across the rear section as the APC bounced along.

'Why the Chinese didn't camp closer to *Jung Chang*. That satellite image of Atlantis showed the city was several miles across – the size of Manhattan. We're directly above it, even this far out from *Jung Chang*. The ice must be fractured for miles all around here. When Atlantis powered up it started melting the ice underneath.'

'Great,' Sarah replied. 'So Atlantis could be sunk all over again.'

'Shit,' Matheson realized. 'I never thought of that. What the hell do we do if we can't get down there?'

As the Skidoos of Scott and the others dodged in and out of the tents, following in the wake of the receding APC, they suddenly found themselves cut off and had to double back, finding makeshift ramps they could use as jumping-off points. Under a hail of crossfire they each jumped the chasm, landing heavily on the other side.

The marines operating the mortar quickly disassembled it and stuffed it away for transport as the APC thundered across the ice, swerving into a skid and kicking up ice. Sarah threw the rear doors open. 'Get in!'

No one needed telling twice. They scrambled to their feet, the marines laying down cover fire as the scientists went first.

Hackett pulled himself up into the front passenger seat, saying:

'Well, this is nice.' When suddenly he became aware of several low thudding sounds peppering one side of the vehicle, like kids throwing stones. 'Hey! We're being shot at!'

Matheson glowered. 'No shit, Sherlock!'

'*Ouch!*' Pearce screeched as he bashed his arm trying to sit up. November tended to him as he tried to stem the blood oozing from a wound on his arm.

'Come on!' Sarah screamed at the marines out the back door. 'Get in, we gotta go!'

'Negative!' Brandes hollered back. 'We gotta stay and cover those guys or they'll never make it!'

'You don't get up here now – *you'll* never make it!' But as she said it she was already starting to regret it as an explosion not far off rocked the entire vehicle and blasted two of the marines apart.

Sarah was in shock. She didn't know what to do. Frozen, she had no comprehension of the fact that Brandes had slammed the door shut in her face and was twisting the lock closed from the outside.

The APC shook again. Rocked by another explosion.

Matheson shot a look over his shoulder. 'What's going on? Are we done?'

Hackett took a closer look and realized Bob Pearce was lying on the deck of the vehicle bleeding badly. 'Let's get outta here!' he yelled.

Matheson shoved it into gear. They were away.

Scott dodged and weaved his way past scrambling enemy soldiers and crumbling ice flats in an attempt at a military zigzag. But in the end it was easier just to drive straight through any obstacles.

Coming up on his left flank was Gant, who slammed into one soldier, ripping the rifle from his arms. He swung the weapon back behind him and fired successive bursts as a cover fire until the entire clip was spent.

But even though every shot was off target, they all counted and they had a clear throughway by the time they had picked up the tracks of the APC again.

They swerved up to where the marines were waiting.

'Brandes, Jackson! Everybody! Climb on board – now!' Gant bellowed.

Hillman glanced over his shoulder at the approaching Chinese forces who had taken to their other Skidoos and APCs. Even two of the helicopters were powering up, their rotors starting to spin. 'Oh Christ, c'mon you guys, we gotta get the fuck outta here!'

Eventually the marines moved. Brandes even sat upright. But they weren't going with their commanding officer. They would never be going anywhere again.

They were dead. And they were being used as shields by the Chinese Special Forces Commandos who were lying in wait underneath.

Michaels was the first to react, plowing through his fallen comrade and crushing the commando caught underneath. The sharp metal tracks on the rear end of his vehicle spun and ripped the clothes off the dead soldier's chest, tearing into his flesh before catching traction again and zipping the marine off after the APC. The other three quickly followed on behind.

They passed by an ice mound, oblivious to the fact that two bemused Chinese scouts on their own Skidoos were sitting on top. As their radios kicked into life they swung their vehicles around and set off in pursuit.

'Where are we going?' Matheson demanded as he struggled to keep control of his vehicle at such a high speed.

Hackett turned the map upside down and round again, but try as he might he couldn't make head nor tail of it. 'It's uh, all in Chinese,' he revealed, folding the document he'd found secreted away inside a compartment into a more user-friendly size. 'I can't make it out. Hell, where's a linguist when you need one?'

'Well, they gotta have a sign for north or south or some such shit. It's universal.'

Hackett held the map up for Matheson to see and jabbed a finger at all the squiggles. 'Not in China!'

'Hey, Bob's bleeding really bad, back here,' November cried out. 'Anyone see a medical kit?'

Hackett scratched around. 'Uh, no. That a problem?'

Pearce gritted his teeth as he held his arm. There was a blackened piece of sharp metal protruding from his forearm. 'Yes!' he cried. 'Yes, it's a fucking problem!'

Sarah winced when she got a good look. 'Strong words, Bob. We'll think of something.'

'Excuse me?' Matheson interrupted.

'What?'

Matheson gesticulated at the windshield. 'Which direction?'

Everywhere they looked there was just a vista of barren, desolate snow and ice.

'Gee, I don't know. Forward?' Sarah suggested, spotting a case with a small red cross marked on it, hanging on a far bulkhead. She got to her feet.

Matheson swerved the vehicle to avoid more disintegrating ice. And that was when he saw it. That familiar sky he'd seen only a few weeks before. Vast waving green fronds undulating and glowing across the darker regions of the atmosphere where charged particles from solar storms were caught in the magnetic field of the earth. The Aurora Australis.

Except this time the swirling green mass wasn't just swaying across the sky, it was actively gathering into a maelstrom that mimicked a twister. Like the ancient Chinese myths said – a giant two-headed snake was in a battle with the elements of wind and rain.

In a vast green funnel that appeared to undulate with eddies of magnetic flux, billions of tons of charged particles were swirling down to ground level and beyond, Touching down in the distance and being transported the sixty or so miles from space down a tube that was constructed from the invisible forces of the will of the universe itself.

It was like a glowing umbilical connected to Mother Nature. And Atlantis was feeding.

'Holy Mother,' Matheson murmured. 'I think I just found *Jung Chang.*'

It was a disturbing thing to discover there were no wing mirrors on Skidoos. And that it was impossible to judge just how close the enemy was when there were no images looming large within them. But glancing back over his shoulders just wasn't much of an option for Richard Scott. For one thing he was too scared, and for another the terrain was simply too uneven to allow him to take his eyes off it.

All he knew was, he was being shot at. A lot. And that was enough.

He could hear projectiles whizzing past his ear, was aware of Gant riding up in his periphery and heading off up front. When—

Wham! The ground exploded in an incredible eruption of fire and ice so fierce it jolted the Skidoo, causing him to run pivoted on one track for a moment. Which was a stroke of luck for the simple reason that it caused him to run wide of the crater opening up before him and precipitating the creation of a mass of jagged fissures.

But just as Scott was getting a handle on his situation, one of the growing ice ravines took a sharp turn straight in front of him, causing the epigraphist to grind to a halt while he figured out a way through the maze. As he did so he took a quick look back.

And wished he hadn't.

A line of Chinese manned Skidoos were bearing down on him leaving high plumes of snowy mist in their wakes while high above were aircraft. Firing.

'Jesus, what the hell are they doing?' the Professor shrieked, although it was obvious – they were trying to kill him.

Up ahead, where the anthropologist should have been traveling by now, the snow opened up into another fireball as the two sleek black attack helicopters let rip.

Scott cranked his machine up again, discovering to his horror that as the ice cracked up all around him he was in a race against time to beat a fissure out of the start blocks. As Scott raced along, so too did the crack in the ice. Deep and dark. Jagged and relentless. As it widened it released blinding steam, and Scott knew it was only a matter of time before the phenomenon changed course into his path and brought his journey to an abrupt end.

He shifted down a gear, giving the engine a kick and closed his eyes in hope as the fissure suddenly darted under his vehicle.

But nothing happened.

Miraculously the cracking ice didn't open up wide enough to swallow his vehicle whole, but his situation had not improved. For creeping up all around him were the shadows of the Chinese military . . .

Up ahead Scott spotted the APC swerving in and out of ruts in the ice, while silhouetted against the swirling green plasma funnel, he could see its turret gun up on the roof.

Of course!

He swept his eye over the dash. Located the radio and thumbed: 'Gant, can you hear me?' He saw Gant snatching up his own unit and responding. Good. They were on the same channel. 'It's me, Scott! Tell somebody on that APC to man that turret gun! And show them how to use it, *fast!*'

Sarah rotated in the tiny, cramped turret seat, swinging the gun around to face the rear. There were little numbers stenciled all around the inside rim of the turret like on a clock. When she reached the number 6 she stopped.

She glanced back at Hackett who was tearing open a box of ammunition. 'This is all we've got so make it count,' he advised.

Sarah ignored him as she followed Gant's instructions on her headset. There was a flat oblong plate on the upper side of the weapon with two screw-like catches on either corner. She unfastened them quickly. Flipped it open to reveal a contraption on a hinge. She guessed this was where she put the bullets. Hackett handed her the chain of ammo, each round the size of a finger, and clipped the first round into the housing. She pushed the unit back in, fastened the plate and reported back to Gant.

'All right!' he shrieked in quick reply. 'You're locked and loaded. Line 'em up in the crosshair and keep both hands on the gun at all times. It's got a severe kickback. Less resistance on either grip and you're gonna wind up swinging yourself around.'

Sarah didn't wait for further instruction. Bringing the first helicopter up into full view she lined the sight. Squeezed the trigger.

And nothing happened.

'Shit! Have we got a jam? What's wrong with this thing!'

Hackett spied the gizmo at the side. 'Safety! Let the safety off!'

Sarah felt like an idiot, reaching around the side and taking the catch off. She quickly brought herself back into alignment again. And fired.

Scott whooped for joy as a stream of lead spat from the twin-barreled turret. It was like a blast of fire as every fifth bullet, a tracer round, lit up like a rocket guiding Sarah's aim. But despite the assistance she was still a lousy shot.

The helicopters dodged and weaved. The Skidoos split up and zigzagged. It slowed them down plenty but it was hardly going to cause them to turn back.

And then as suddenly as the firing had started, it spluttered to a stop. They'd run out of ammo. Looming up at them was the devastated remains of *Jung Chang*. They had arrived. Which was a problem because any moment now they would have to stop. And in so doing, they'd be sitting ducks. What the hell were they going to do? The pursuit of the Chinese military machine was relentless. They were getting closer every second.

Directly in front, the ground was opening up all around them. There was nowhere to go, nowhere to hide. They were trapped.

In fact, what on earth were those sharp black protrusions rearing up out of the ice straight ahead? The APC had already rolled past them, but Scott was lagging far behind and by the time he reached them his path was blocked. Despondently he brought his Ski doo to a halt and raised his hands slowly.

He was staring down the barrel of a gun.

Facing what appeared to be a small mobile cannon, Scott gingerly got off his ride and tried not to make any sudden movements. There was no way he wanted to get shot again.

It appeared to be an automated device. Mounted on a long metal arm, it was attached to something hidden under the snow, while protruding from its side was a tiny camera. Obviously it was some kind of remote-controlled device.

As the drone of approaching vehicles grew ever more ominous behind him, the crackle of a speaker hissing to life from the machine was the last thing Scott expected.

In a tinny voice an American accent asked quickly: 'Name?'

Scott was perplexed. 'Uh, Scott,' he said. 'Richard Scott. Linguist with the UN Inspection Team.'

Silence, followed by: 'Oh, you're Scott. Would you mind ducking down, sir? Only you're in my line of fire.'

Scott didn't ask any further questions. Throwing his arms out he hit the deck as the device the gun was attached to rumbled and shook itself from under the snow.

All along the ridge on either side of Scott, similar machines were rearing up out of dugouts they had carved out of the snow and ice. There were around fifteen vehicles in all, like a line of miniature tanks. Essentially they were converted Yamaha Breeze 'all terrain' buggies, with tracks in place of tires. They bristled with gadgets: high-powered zoom surveillance gear, thermal imaging equipment. They were well equipped little machines. But it was their armory and their preparedness for war which was most impressive; their array of guns and missile launchers.

These machines were built for war. And on their sides they had written: SaRGE; the Surveillance and Reconnaissance Ground Equipment robot. They were the very latest in US military remote warfare. And they had a bite like the enemy wouldn't believe.

These were what Gant and Dower had been talking about. The goddamn cavalry.

Servos whirred into life, targets were locked onto, weaponry was fired. And within a split second, under a barrage of sustained fire that loosed in a massive arc, one of the attack helicopters tumbled from the sky in a streaking fireball while the menacing Skidoos were thrown into disarray.

Then, while several units kept up the battering, other SaRGE units retargeted their sights. Having analyzed the geology of the situation, they fired at the ground some distance off, opening up a massive crescent-shaped rift in the crumbling ice that would require some terrific detour to bypass, or the construction of an artificial bridge.

The Chinese halted in their tracks, uncertain what to do next.

While Scott crawled behind the nearest SaRGE vehicle, and collapsed with relief.

DESCENT

[After years of studying complexity discovered] 'It's very hard to do science on complex systems.'

Jack D. Cowan, Mathematical Biologist, University of Chicago, Co-Founder of the Santa Fe Institute, 1995

USS JEFFERSON CITY SSN-759

'Captain, I'm getting something.'

It wasn't said with much force or forethought. Just with a plain frankness that had come to be expected aboard the 6,900-ton Los Angeles class nuclear attack sub.

Penoit was a quiet man. He was the type of skipper who said so little that when he did speak, his crew listened.

Ensign J.G. Will Timms awaited his Captain's orders.

'Confirm,' was all he said.

They'd powered out to the coordinates at a full 20 knots, diving to her maximum depth, a mere 450 meters, en route. But the type of area of the Pacific they had been asked to investigate was at such a depth there was just no way they were ever going to get down that far. The pressure would crush them.

Instead what Penoit ordered was to bring *Jefferson City* to a full stop and extend her starboard Towed Array to its full 2,600 meter length. The submarine had a myriad of listening devices. Her sonar equipment, for example, was fitted in a forward array. But the Towed Array, like its name suggested, was dragged behind the vessel on a tether when the submarine was in hunter mode and seeking out enemy vessels.

By coming to a full stop the array had no other option but to sink like a plumb line. And in so doing, penetrate deep into the murky depths of the Pacific Ocean.

In the ocean, the speed of sound varied. Sometimes it was as much as 1,600 meters per second. Sometimes as little as 1,400 mps. The variables for affecting this speed were many, but three key features were primary determinates. Temperature, salinity and pressure. For every one degree Celsius sea temperature rise, the speed increased by 4.5 mps. For every percentage increase in salinity, thereby increasing density, the speed increased by 1.3 mps. For every 100 meters in depth, the speed increased by 1.7 mps.

So the primary controlling factor in this case was pure pressure. Beneath the upper oceanic layers, sound waves traveled like lightning in a bottle.

Timms held a hand to the cans on his ears and squinted, adjusted the output on his screen and gave his CO the thumbs up. 'Definitely, there's something there, sir,' he said.

'Any idea what it is?'

Timms adjusted the signal again. 'I know what it's *not*, if that's any help.'

'What is it *not*?'

'Well, it ain't whale song. It's too regular – too rhythmic. And it's entirely out of the range of human hearing. I've converted it up to a frequency I can hear. I can put it on speakers if you like, sir.'

Penoit nodded. Timms reached over and flipped a switch.

Several short pulses were heard, followed by a long burst. Over and over.

Several short pulses and a longer burst.

Timms took some more measurements. 'It's a tubular wave, sir. It's traveling in a straight line. Very little dissipation. Heading north. This thing could go on for thousands of miles. Should I pass this on down the chain, Captain?'

Penoit nodded again, murmuring: 'That's what they were looking for . . . Well, they were right.' Turning to his exec he ordered: 'Rise to sixty feet. Up periscope and radio on down the chain. You have the bridge, Lieutenant.' He saluted back on his way out.

LATITUDE NINETY

'What the hell is *that*?' asked the people gathered around the screens on the observation deck of the Conning Tower of the *USS Dolphin*. The direct video pictures coming in from the *Dolphin*'s remote robotic submersible *Cousteau* were astounding.

Following the path of several rhythmic sonic streams, *Cousteau* had journeyed to a point three miles beneath the North Pole where the sound waves seemed to converge and where sunlight was a distant memory.

Specially fitted for deepwater acoustic research and near-bottom ocean surveys, the research submarine *Dolphin* was perhaps the best-placed vessel in the task force to study what she was studying.

Captain Rachel McNichol craned her neck. For on the screen were a series of pyramids, joined in a circular construction that seemed to stretch for hundreds of meters off into the darkness beyond the abilities of the vessel's searchlights and cameras to penetrate.

All five officers were with their Captain, alongside all five scientists and a couple of the enlisted men. In short, the observation deck was crammed, and Captain McNichol was forced to raise her hand to keep the excited chatter to a minimum.

'Jesus Christ, what the fuck *is* that?!'

'Hold it down! Hold it down!' Rachel barked. 'Jensen, can you get the computer to overlay an image of what exactly these sound waves are doing?'

Jensen got right on it and was surprised to discover that the mud and silt-covered constructs were: 'Vibrating! They're vibrating! Captain, these things aren't just receiving signals, they're pulsing signals back down the same route.'

'How?'

Jensen shrugged. 'Beats me. The best I can figure, ma'am, is that, y'know like on a stereo the main part of the speakers are made out of a paper cone? Well, these megaliths are acting in the same way, except instead of a paper cone – it's solid stone.'

Cousteau inched forward, gliding over the geometric mounds and lumps. All showed as deep grays and blacks, until suddenly, rearing up out of the night was a whirlwind of shimmering water. In a column that seemed caught in the circular shape of the construction beneath it, the water twisted and sparked.

A quick-witted scientist punched in the command for the submersible to jerk to a halt, while the others, lost for words, simply let their jaws drop.

Rachel raked her fingers through her dark brown hair. 'Send a pod up to the surface. Radio anybody camped out in the vicinity of the North Pole to up stakes and leave – *now*.'

'Captain,' Jensen reported back, 'you're not gonna believe these figures, but the water around these sonic streams is viscous, like it's turning solid.'

'The water?'

'Yes, ma'am. And it's heating up.'

TRUMAN

'It's a network, Admiral.'

The Lieutenant rolled the full color transparency out on the illuminated photographic bench and clipped it into place. A two-meter-square map of the world hot off the presses of the intelligence unit deep within the aircraft carrier.

The map showed precisely each and every sonic stream. Where they originated and where they were destined. Each stream was a bright red line, criss-crossing over the image from head to toe like those route maps airlines print in the back of their in-flight magazines.

'There are more than five sites, Admiral.'

Dower adjusted his spectacles as he perused the information carefully. 'But there appear to be five central hubs, wouldn't you agree?'

'Oh yes, sir,' the officer backtracked. 'Yes. There are five hubs. But there are at least a hundred other minor sites, each varying in size which seem to be incorporated into this network.'

'What is it doing?'

'We have no idea.'

'Take one of these minor sites out of the equation. What would happen to the network then?'

The Lieutenant shrugged. 'Most probably, we figure, nothing. The sound waves would re-route themselves. Take one of the *hubs* out of the equation and well, that's a different story.'

Dower gave him that look which said he wanted more information and wasn't in the habit of having to ask for it.

'We reckon there's a fifty-fifty chance you could take one of four particular hubs out of the equation and the network could sustain the damage. But . . . you take Atlantis out of the equation, and the whole thing collapses.'

'These are tubular waves? Self-contained?'

'Yes, sir. But should their angle be adjusted, so the waves move out in a normal fashion, in all directions, like the ripples from a stone tossed into a pond? Then there wouldn't be a square inch of the earth's oceans which wouldn't be affected by whatever signal is being pumped into it.

'Admiral, the oceans are being heated up. It's melting the ice caps. Perhaps this is what happened last time. Whatever civilization built these structures – and for whatever purpose – the side effect was that they drew power from the sun and pumped excess energy into the oceans, melting the Poles and flooding the earth.'

'Contact Major Gant,' Dower ordered. 'Tell him to prepare for detonation of the warhead.'

IGLOO

The first blocks were the most critical.

Cut to fit on three sides and shaped *in situ*, they determined the size and shape of an igloo. As more blocks of snow were piled on top and pounded sharply into place, the ice crystals eventually bonded like Superglue.

A finished igloo was one continuous spiral of snow blocks so strong a man could jump up and down on its roof. So flawless in design that the temperature on the inside reached 0 degrees Celsius when it was still minus 40 outside.

The igloo at *Jung Chang* was built by two Inuit brothers, engineers named Lei and Ham Kadloo who were flown into Anchorage at a moment's notice and given little time to familiarize themselves with the remote engineering arms and headmounted view-screens that were connected via satellite to the SaRGE unit in Antarctica.

Richard Scott hobbled as he approached the frozen building. His leg throbbed deep from within so he tried to concentrate on other matters in an effort to ignore it. Like the fact that so much snow really did sound like Styrofoam compacting underfoot.

Jung Chang looked exactly as Bob Pearce had described except for one gigantic feature. Just past the charred and torn remains of the encampment, behind obliterated cabins and mangled machinery, the vast green and twisted umbilical cord of energy stretched down from the sky. Descending through a massive crater that seemed to have no bottom to it, the energy twister looked like some massive screw being twisted into the ice, perhaps by God himself.

There were lights glowing inside the igloo. And Scott could hear voices too, in English, using medical terminology.

But all he found when he stepped through the entrance was a bunch of machines operating on a bloody mess in the center. He took a step closer and found Bob Pearce stretched on the operating table. Remote SuRGEon units worked tending his wounds. Remotely-controlled arms sutured cuts. One mechanical hand gently dabbed away blood.

Bob Pearce raised his head and smiled thinly. 'Uh, Richard, hi.'

Scott prised his frosted goggles from his face, breathless as he surveyed the procedure with incredulity.

'Lie still, Mr Pearce,' one of the mechanical medics ordered. 'We're not done yet. Hey, Nick, could you angle that light over here?'

'Sure.'

Another mechanical arm swung a halogen lamp out at a wound, while other arms continued to perform tasks. Their rack-mounted cameras turned briefly to eye Scott up and down, assessing his damage.

'How's the leg, Dr Scott?'

'Sore. Who are you?'

'This is Captain Kit Preston, Naval Surgeon, Pensacola.'

A needle held between two metal fingers gave a little wave in between sewing maneuvers.

'I'm Mike Everty. Sheila, where are you?'

'Chicago, Mike.'

'What's the weather like up there?'

'Don't ask.'

Scott looked to Pearce. 'They can feel what they're doing?'

'Two-way communications. The controls back in their surgeries give every sensation they'd experience if they were poking around inside my arm with their own fingers. Neat, huh?'

Scott was perplexed. 'Weird.'

'You try lying here.'

'Where's everybody else?'

'Down below.'

Scott gave a shrug like: that's supposed to mean something? Pearce jerked his thumb at the hole in the ground behind him. There was a tunnel down through the ice.

'They're down there. With a Chinese soldier.'

'The one you remote-sensed?'

Pearce cracked a deflated smile. 'Jesus, I think we got ourselves a true believer.'

'Stop moving,' one of the remotes ordered. 'You want us to screw this up?'

Pearce ignored her. The igloo had been built as shelter for the Chinese soldier, he explained. Remote units had been sent in to secure the area and keep the man alive long enough to be interrogated. He was an invaluable resource, after all. He actually knew what to expect down there.

Scott was unsteady on the nylon rope ladder, but it was only a ten-foot drop. Sarah gave him a hand as he fumbled the last couple of rungs.

'Welcome to the party,' she said.

He was surprised to find another SuRGEon unit down in the tunnel tending to the young Chinese man. He was sat awkwardly up against the ice tunnel wall and was nursing a steaming hot cup of coffee November had made for him.

Scott crouched down next to her. 'He okay?'

'Seems that way.'

'Bob was right. Damn it, Bob was right.'

'So was Ralph,' Hackett smiled as he came over to welcome the anthropologist. 'Glad to see you made it, Richard.' He jerked a thumb at Matheson, who had a radio to one ear. He was further on down the tunnel, where the ceiling had opened up in places to expose the sky. Reception was much better there. Ralph was listening to his radio while he drew lines all over a hastily sketched map of the earth in his notebook.

'That's the sound-wave network – sonic streams, stretching from continent to continent. It *does* exist. The Navy's picked up the pattern all over the planet. Dower just got a call in from the British. The *HMS* Ocean, and the *Illustrious* out on maneuvers, verified part of it.'

Scott glanced around. 'Hey, where's Gant? He made it, didn't he?'

'Gant, Michaels and Hillman,' Sarah said. 'They're all we got left. They're up ahead, exploring the tunnels. Trying to figure out a way down.'

Scott directed his attention back to the soldier. '*How you doing?*' he asked gently in Cantonese.

The soldier didn't respond. Just sipped his coffee and ignored him, though something in his eyes indicated he understood. He wasn't a native Mandarin speaker.

Scott looked to November. 'Real talkative, huh?'

'He kept saying *Yan Ning*, when we got here. Over and over. *Yan Ning*. Mean anything to you?'

'*Yan Ning* . . .? That's not an expression. That's a name – a woman's name.'

'My girlfriend's name,' the compact little soldier suddenly piped up, struggling with his coffee.

'You speak English very well,' Scott remarked, introducing himself.

'I did not work for McDonald's in Beijing for two year before Army for nothing,' he replied, introducing himself as Private Chow Yun.

Scott glanced back at the others and shared a look. 'Listen, we need your help, Yun. We need to know what's under the ice. We know there's a city, but we have no idea what kind of condition it's in. What's the layout?'

'That is not possible.'

'Listen, I just had a run-in with your comrades,' Scott snapped, fingering his leg wound. 'I got shot, see? So I'm not in a real patient kinda mood.'

The soldier said nothing.

Scott scratched his face. Perhaps he should try another tack. Military code doubtless prevented the soldier from divulging any secrets. So delicately he asked: 'Must miss your girlfriend, huh?'

'Yes,' the soldier replied nervously.

'I expect you'll be glad when this is all over and you can go back to her.'

'I can never go back to her. When I saw her down in the city . . .' he made eye-contact with Scott. So yes, there *was* a city. 'When I saw her . . . It was very frightening.'

'I don't understand. She was down in the city?'

'Yes. Yan Ning was down in the city.'

'She a soldier too?'

'No. She is dead. Six month. But I saw her down there.'

'Okay, that's *not* what I wanted to hear,' Hackett commented sourly, turning away as Sarah made her way over. 'And the dead shall rise again and walk the earth for the Day of Judgment? No. That definitely was not on my agenda for today.'

'You don't believe him?' Sarah asked, still watching Matheson continue sketching his lines all over his notebook.

'I didn't say I don't believe him,' Hackett corrected. 'I just don't want to hear it.'

'What do you think he really saw? One of those Golems maybe – in the shape of his girlfriend?'

'What did it do? Read his mind?'

'Maybe.'

'Or maybe not. Y'know, it just occurred to me, the four horsemen of the apocalypse could be earth, wind, fire and water. Earthquakes, hurricanes, volcanoes and floods.'

'There you go!' Sarah chided, almost amused, but trying to keep her voice down. 'Now you're getting into the spirit of it.'

'You're not helping. You know that, don't you?'

Sarah smiled. Yes, she knew that. She turned to Matheson. 'Ralph, how are we doing?'

Matheson adjusted the radio. Sketched another line. 'At this rate I'm gonna run out of ink.'

'I meant globally. As a species.'

He took a deep breath. 'At this rate,' he repeated, 'I'm gonna run out of ink.'

Hackett sketched in the details. 'Sea temperatures are rising fast. If we can't switch off whatever's down there, I think Ralph's going to be one of the first to help arm that bomb.'

'It Chinese tradition,' Yun was explaining, 'the spirit of dead are malevolent. If you disturb their final resting place, they return to disturb *you*. We disturbed the burial site at Wupu, and the spirits brought retribution for that with storm and earthquake. That is why we could not allow anyone else to disturb Wupu. It has brought much danger. That is why your Rola Corporation was made to leave.'

'Then what led you to come here, to Antarctica?' Scott demanded.

'Because of the maps,' Yun replied matter-of-factly. Then, reading the puzzled expression on Scott's face: 'The maps at Wupu. You know of the maps, no?'

Scott checked with his colleagues apprehensively. 'No.'

Yun explained about the maps. And it fitted in precisely with what they had all been figuring out over the past few days. For at Wupu there were maps of the world etched into their crystal monuments, showing the links between ancient sites situated all over the planet. And the one in Antarctica was revered above all others.

It explained how Rola Corp. knew where to look so quickly.

'When we disturbed the spirits of Wupu, the spirits came back to haunt us. To disturb the spirits of Antarctica would be to disturb the spirits of the world. That, Dr Scott, would be much retribution. We are not here because we think we own Atlantis. We are here to stop you from making a mistake.'

Scott hung his head in his hands and scrunched his fist into his hair. 'Religions be damned!' He eyed the soldier firmly. Wildly. And in perfect Cantonese explained: '*Chow, I think it would be a mistake if we didn't go down there. You know what to expect. Come with us. Show us the way.*'

Chow Yun looked away, ashamed and graven. 'I will not go back,' he replied in English.

'We need your help.'

Yun sipped his coffee, finding it difficult to maintain direct eye-contact. It was not clear if they were going to get his help.

A clattering sound up ahead alerted them all to Gant approaching from around the corner of the ice tunnel stretched out before them. 'People, clip on those spikes – we're moving out,' he ordered.

Yun looked up, startled. 'What of me? You will keep me here?'

Gant shrugged. 'You're free to go. In fact, I want you to relay a message to your people. We will have carried out our orders before you even have time to react.'

Scott expressed his concern with the others. He didn't like the sound of this. But his attention for the moment was still on Yun, trying to glean what information he could.

He sat down next to the soldier, pulled out his cleats and started fastening them into place. He kept his voice low so as not to embarrass the man. 'Do you read much?' he asked simply.

'Of course.'

'I read. I read all the time. Anything really, comic strips to philosophy. I love words.' Yun remained silent. Uncertain as to where this was leading. 'Ever read your Sun Tzu?'

'Sun Tzu,' Yun acknowledged. 'The Art of War.'

'Two-thousand-year-old Chinese tactical philosophy still read by politicians, business leaders and military strategists the world over. What did Sun Tzu say? Keep your enemies close by?' Yun nodded slowly. 'The art of war is to adapt to what presents itself in battle. Your unit already failed the first test, and fired the first shots in battle. In panic your unit exposed its strengths and its weaknesses.'

Yun appeared incensed. 'Master Sun explained that the rule of military operation is not to count on the opponent not coming, but to rely on ways of dealing with them.'

'Yes,' Scott agreed. He knew the passage well. 'And he also advised not to count on opponents *not* attacking, but to rely on having what cannot be attacked. We have breached your defenses and are now on our way down to what could not be attacked.'

'How do you know we have not already fortified the city?'

Scott smiled, slow and purposeful, catching Gant's eye in the process. He stood. 'Thank you, Yun. You have told me what I needed to know.'

Yun leapt up, almost slipping on the ice. 'I have told you nothing!'

'You have told me everything. You are the last line of Chinese defense here. We have nothing to fear down there but fear itself.'

'There are creatures!'

'I'm sure. But they're not Chinese soldiers. And as a consequence we know to prepare for the unknown.'

'Going down there will be suicide.'

'But we will control what cannot be attacked. We will have the advantage. Now, if you keep your enemies close by . . . maybe you can twist the situation to your advantage later.'

Yun seemed to be struggling with some internal dilemma before he acquiesced. 'I have provisions on the surface,' he spat gruffly. 'I must collect them before we proceed.' Scott pressed him for more information. 'Like new boots,' Yun indicated. 'Or I will be useless.'

Gant nodded at Hackett as he moved up next to Scott. 'Go with him.'

Hackett led the soldier off to his supplies. 'Not bad, Dr Scott. Sun Tzu? I think you missed your calling. Ever worn a uniform?'

'I don't know shit about warfare,' Scott confessed. 'They're just words written on a piece of paper. I can twist 'em to argue any damn thing.'

'Well, we got our scout. Pump him for information. We gotta get down there fast. But tell me something, Professor: how d'you know he's not gonna lead us off on a wild-goose chase?'

'I don't,' Scott admitted, securing the fastenings on his boots.

ICE TUNNELS

'This is all wrong,' Matheson moaned quietly to himself as they made their way through the descending ice passage. He was positioned directly behind Gant, and it was clear he was getting under the Major's skin.

'I'm not here to ask questions. I'm here to carry out orders.'

'Well, maybe you might want to *start* asking questions,' the engineer suggested provocatively. 'Maybe we might live longer.'

'Maybe we're not destined to survive at all,' Gant replied chillingly.

The rest of the party tried to ignore the comment as it echoed in and out of the undulating ice bowls along the walls of the passage.

'I know there's another solution,' Matheson nagged. Then, in spite of the spikes on the underside of his boots digging into the hard ice, his feet slid right out from under him and he collapsed in a water-logged heap in the middle of the tunnel, forcing everyone to come to a halt.

'Jesus H. Christ! The ice is blue!' he cried. 'The water's blue! I can't make out a puddle from all the ice!'

Gant glanced back at the party he was leading. They weren't used to this. Hackett and Pearce seemed to be having considerable difficulty while Yun and November, who were much younger and fitter, did not.

The passage through the ice was around nine feet in diameter, with a constant trickling brook along its floor, eating its way down further, centimeter by centimeter. Given time, the water would have eroded this simple tunnel into a chasm.

'All right. I don't have many of these, but I guess I'll have to use them.' He fished around in one of his leg pouches and pulled out a small silver canister as Matheson extracted himself from the relentless though almost invisible torrent of melt water rushing down the frozen passage.

Gant tipped the canister upside down and twisted its base like a pepper grinder. He slid out the long silver screw at the same end and twisted the whole device down into the floor by his foot.

The effect was immediate. An effervescent spring of glowing greenish dye began to mix with the stream on contact, clearly defining the water; its phosphorescence illuminated the way ahead.

Matheson jabbed his feet into the ice and let it be known he was ready to continue. 'I'll be okay now,' was all he said.

Gant barely disguised his impatience. 'Michaels and Hillman are already way ahead of us,' he said, 'carrying the warhead. And they didn't need dye markers.'

'Well, bully for them,' Matheson shot back.

'What are you thinking?' Sarah asked the anthropologist quietly. She reached for a cigarette, the packet wedged inside her parka somewhere, and sparked up, saying: 'You've hardly said a word.'

'I'm thinking about Leibniz's "Lingua Generalis",' Scott revealed.

'Of course you are,' she commented dryly.

He caught her eye, spying the cigarette and for a moment seemed faintly aghast.

'I know,' she said. 'These things'll kill you. Thank God it's the end of the world and I don't have to wait around for cancer.'

Scott wasn't so amused. 'You think you're so tough, don't you?'

Sarah was unnerved. 'What?'

'You have this whole act going on,' he observed. 'Y'know, you're smart but tough. Men can't get to you. And you're in total control. Yet every now and again you slip up, and that human being that's buried deep inside comes out. And you ask things like: What are you thinking?'

He was so intense. So uptight. Normally men like that bugged the shit out of her and she let them get on with it. But there was something about Richard that just made her want to reach out to him. Or maybe it was just her raging hormones. Either way, what he had said had stung. And it was like he could see it in her eyes.

'And you think you know everything,' she retaliated.

'That's the problem right there,' Scott replied, equally stung. 'I don't. But I'd like to.'

'I'll make you a deal,' Sarah offered. 'I bet you can figure this language out before you figure me out.'

'You're on,' he said.

He lashed out with his small hand-pick and hooked into the ice wall as he negotiated his way around the descending S-bend dropping down sharply before them. Shards of ice sprayed out in all directions.

The walls of the tunnel undulated in and out over uneven intervals. The edges in places were sharp and crisp, like razor blades. The blues and whites were multiple. Exotic. Sometimes it was hard to believe they were looking at ice at all. Lit up by the sunlight above which refracted down to incredible depths, Sarah explained, if they were lucky, it would probably be daylight up to a mile down.

Having followed Scott's lead, she asked: 'Leibniz – the philosopher, right? Seventeenth century.' Scott nodded. 'So what's the deal?'

'He assigned numbers to letters.'

'Uh-huh?'

'He broke down all of human knowledge as he saw it into simple ideas. These ideas were represented by a number. He then proposed a system whereby consonants stood for integers, and vowels for units of ten and powers of ten.'

'Which meant what?'

'Well, say the number 81,374 – that would get transcribed as "mubodilefa",' he explained.

'Okay, you're losing me. That was supposed to make sense?'

'The point is,' Scott explained, skipping the minutiae, 'Leibniz wasn't looking for a universal language, or the genesis language. He was looking for truth through a scientific language. Strip preconceived notions of meaning out of language and distill basic themes and ideas down to a language of their own.'

'So you've definitely decided the Atlantis glyphs are a scientific language?'

'The more I think about it, the more I'm forced to conclude, why not?' Scott wobbled as he lost his footing slightly. He flailed for a moment before planting his foot firmly down. A satisfying crunch signified he'd managed to get his spikes to penetrate the surface of the ice.

'These people,' he went on, 'were masters of engineering, astronomy, physics, and acoustics. It seems only natural they would try and communicate in a scientific way. Leibniz was concerned with a language that in itself was concerned only with trying to communicate ideas. Sixty distinct and separate types of sound pretty much cover the range of human vocal abilities. So I'm guessing, and it's just a guess . . . that if the Atlantis glyphs wanted to communicate ideas, the language would take into account all other languages that existed at that time.'

'That's a tall order.'

'So is building a city out of Carbon 60 crystal, but if the satellite imagery's to be believed, that's what they've done.'

He concentrated on putting one foot in front of the other. Step by step. Step by step. He watched the others up in front. All wobbling, but managing to move forward. Gant, Matheson, Hackett, Pearce, Yun and November . . . Four Americans then a Chinese. Then three Americans all stepping in sequence . . . Hey, four spoke English. Then it switched to Chinese. Then back to English and—

'It's a step sequence,' Scott realized. 'That's it! That's how this works! It's a step sequence based on switching languages!'

Sarah excitedly kept pace with Scott as they discussed the idea. 'I thought we'd already ruled that out on the plane?'

'The classical idea of a step sequence, yes,' Scott agreed. 'When spies wanted to hide messages before the advent of the computer they sometimes had them inserted into texts. To all intents and purposes it would just look like a story, for example, or a letter. But in the hands of the decoder, he or she knew that if you took that story, and noted down every, say fourth letter – in sequence – you found a hidden message.'

'But that didn't work with this language,' Sarah reminded. 'We tried. It failed.'

'That's right – because we were trying a classical step sequence. The principle was correct, we just hadn't hit on the correct type of sequence. The key is that number stream. It has everything to do with that number stream. I'd bet my life on it.'

Hackett's ears pricked up. 'Richard, that's very noble. But in this instance, if you're working on a dead-end theory – you'll be betting on *all* our lives.'

'I'm right,' Scott insisted.

'So how does it work?' Gant demanded from the head of the line.

'Each number in the number stream corresponds to a known language. So take the number four – that would be English. Five might be Arabic and six, Russian. Every language uses basically the same kinds of sounds with their own personal variations. So there will be some overlap in sound usage. That's why certain numbers might each be associated with the same glyph. But I'm getting ahead of myself –

'How I think this works is that you write down the number stream. And above it, you write down the Atlantis glyphs, however they appear on the monuments. Then you pick your language, take its assigned number, and you work your way along the number stream. Each time you find say the number four – you note down the glyph that appears above it. In this way the text is deciphered into your chosen language. What you're doing is a step-sequence calculation.'

'So how many different languages do you think are embedded in the glyphs, and why?' Pearce asked. 'It seems an awfully complicated way of doing things.'

Scott looked at the back of Hackett's head as the physicist nego-tiated the treacherous pass. 'Complex would be a better way of describing it,' he said. 'Not complicated.'

Hackett cocked his head as confirmation he had picked up on the compliment.

'Think about it. We're talking about a civilization that lived twelve thousand years ago, speaking a language totally alien to our own. Like today, there were many other languages being spoken. They had no way of knowing which languages would survive and which would perish. So they selected sixty that held the most promise, and intertwined them into a system that we could decipher at some point in the future.'

'But a number stream we could only detect by computer?' November remarked.

'These people knew science better than we know it today,' Hackett commented soberly. 'I guess they figured what they have to tell us is of such sophistication it was pointless imparting it unless we had the mindset and wherewithal to be able to comprehend its meaning. After all, stick a Neanderthal in a 767 and his first instinct is going to be to eat the chairs. Not fly the plane.' He glanced back at the others. 'Guess they didn't want us to eat the chairs.'

'Sixty different numbers,' Scott marveled. 'Written in base sixty, representing sixty different languages corresponding to sixty different glyphs. That, to any mind worthy of saving, is a puzzle that needs solving.'

'All we need to figure out now is what languages they chose.'

'Well, it ain't gonna be English,' November advised knowledge-ably. 'That's only been around a few hundred years. We're talking about languages which go back thousands. Ancient Egyptian lasted a couple thousand.'

'It also, despite current theories, seems to have just popped up out of nowhere,' Scott agreed. 'But it's still too young a language. Maybe an ancestor of Egyptian's what we're looking for. Old languages. Think really old.'

'What about Phoenician?' Pearce suggested.

'Most of our modern languages today like Hebrew and Arabic derive from Aramaic which is a direct descendent of Phoenician,' Scott noted. 'That's true. But there's an older language that Phoenician derived from and that's Proto-Canaanite. And that's a language which could be written and read multi-directionally.'

'Doesn't it strike you as odd,' Hackett chipped in thoughtfully, struggling with the torrent of phosphorescent water that seemed to be growing stronger as the incline grew steeper, 'that each language was assigned a number on an arbitrary basis? Why assign one language the number four, when it could just as easily be twenty-four, or sixteen. What differentiates each language and its number assignment?'

'Maybe the clues are in our myths and legends,' Gant threw in from up ahead.

'Interesting idea,' Scott called out. 'You got anything to back that up, Major?'

'I was thinking of the Bible,' he replied, unsteadily. 'Y'know, the world was created in seven days. The walls of Jericho fell after the trumpets were sounded seven times.'

'But Noah's boat was at sea for forty days and forty nights,' November warned. 'It could just as easily be the number forty.'

'The Mayans revered the number nine, as in the nine lords of the night,' Pearce added eagerly. 'That's a possibility.'

'There are sixty possibilities,' Scott told them. 'I suggest we get our computers working overtime until they come up with something I might recognize.'

Yun eyed the scientists, quietly taking in what they were discussing. It wasn't clear if he understood entirely, but it was clear he knew it was of significance. He watched November closely as she set her pocket PC up to begin work on the calculation.

Just then Gant's radio burst into life with a static warble. It was Michaels: 'Major, we've hit our first junction and have no clue on which way to proceed. Any word from the gook on which is our best way down?'

'Uh, negative to that,' Gant replied, eyeing Yun with something akin to disdain. 'Hold your position and wait for our arrival. In the meantime do some pre-lim scouting. See if you can't come up with the three most likely options.'

There followed a brief pause before Michaels responded. 'Sir,' he observed. 'There doesn't appear to be *any* likely option. You'd have to see this to believe it.'

FIRE AND ICE

They were standing on the edge of a precipice, a cliff face of solid ice overlooking a chasm of incredible proportions. But this was no ordinary chasm. This was the vast and jagged sink-hole down into which the writhing green energy twister above was descended.

It swirled before them, a great transparent kaleidoscope, effervescent with crackling, colliding ionized particles. Yet it was eerily quiet. Occasionally, odd high-pitched hissing sounds would fill the air as charged molecules exploded and whizzed by. But overall the sensation was like being confronted with an apparition. There was a sense of shimmering air. A light breeze, electricity in its essence. Maybe even life.

It was awesome.

Hackett felt a chill run over him as he took a good long look at their predicament. They were about half a mile down from the surface, which could still be seen way above them. But the surface itself was in far greater trouble than any of them had realized while they were up there. For from here, they could see the true structure of the ice below. And it was not stable.

They were like fleas on the inside of a frozen Swiss cheese. Huge skyscraper-sized arches of ice rose up all around them, connected with, and diverged from, other mountainous columns. Across from them lay further tunnels. Some seemed barren and lifeless, blue arteries into the body of a dead giant. But other tunnels were far more ominous and forbidding, for they breathed steam and smoke, and hinted at what lay below.

Hackett spied the glowing water that rushed between his feet and watched it cascade off the edge and tumble into the dark void below.

There seemed to be no other way of describing it: 'Oh crap,' he sighed.

'Which way?' Gant demanded, turning on Yun with barely suppressed anger. '*Which way down?*'

Yun shuffled forward, eyeing the darkened trunk containing the warhead as he did so. He surveyed the tunnel system ahead. In either direction there was no way of reaching any of the options without somehow securing a line across, for as he noted as he analyzed the edge wall of the chasm, 'The path has gone.'

'No shit,' Gant growled. 'Now which way?'

Yun looked to Scott for support, but Scott was as eager to find out as anyone else. Yun pointed to a tunnel directly across from them, about thirty feet away and several feet lower down. Steam rose out of it, like the breath of a sleeping dragon.

'Oh great,' Matheson moaned. 'That means we gotta pass through this plasma stream, right?'

'Right,' Michaels agreed, already taking off his backpack and handing it to November to hold. He started fishing out a grappling line and hook, but Gant had another idea.

'Hillman, you got your harpoon with you?'

'Sir, yes, sir.'

'Attach a line and fire that across. I don't think you're just gonna be able to hook onto an ice feature, Michaels. There ain't any purchase.'

'I think we'll need several lines, sir,' the marine replied evenly, 'to distribute the weight. I volunteer to go across and attach more cables.'

Hackett was cautious. 'Are you insane?'

'You see any other way across?'

Gant pulled out the first of many mountaineering-style ice spikes they'd need to make the crossing, attached a nylon rope and started hammering it into the hard ice. He tied the other end to Michael's belt and patted the marine on the shoulder, while Hillman took aim with his harpoon and fired.

The bolt whistled as it exploded out across the chasm carrying a second line with it. It blasted into the ice and dug deep, just inside the mouth of the passage.

A few sharp tugs and it was clear it would hold. Gant attached the second line to another spike and hammered it home while Michaels clipped himself on and lowered himself down.

One single thin line suspended across the divide was all he had to make the crossing with, but it was all he'd need. He gripped the line tightly, hooked his legs up over it and started heaving his way across.

November shifted on her feet nervously, watching the marine approach the whirling mass of electrical energy. 'What's that stuff gonna do to him?' she asked.

Sarah shook her head. 'No idea.'

'He's not earthed,' Hackett explained quietly. 'I don't know what kinda power's flowing through that thing, but theoretically the effect should be nothing.'

Gant eyed the physicist sternly.

'Theoretically,' Hackett reiterated.

Hesitantly Michaels pulled himself along before coming to a stop in front of the wall of magnetized energy. He seemed to visibly tense, as unsteadily he clung on with one hand, and with the other – reached out to the maelstrom.

'I can feel the hairs all over my body starting to stand on end!' he reported back anxiously. 'But other than that, no ill-effects. I'm going to attempt to go on through.'

Michaels used all of his upper body strength to get his momentum going again and edged deeper and deeper into the thick of the ionized mass. Before long he was entirely immersed in the swirl of energy.

No one commented while they watched the marine's progress, except for one tiny little mechanism that was built into the watch on Hackett's wrist. For it beeped suddenly. Hackett's mood seemed to visibly darken as he checked the time and shut the watch off.

'You didn't set that thing as a wake-up call now, did you?' Pearce asked.

'No, I didn't, Bob.' He addressed the others. 'It's the solar storm. It's going to connect with the earth in a little over fifteen minutes.

It's going to be highly violent, and it's going to wind up being siphoned – right through here.'

'Fifteen minutes?' Sarah gasped. 'We won't all get across in that time.'

'You just watch,' Gant replied, ordering Hillman to shimmy across with a third line.

The Major knelt down and started clipping the warhead to the two lines that were already established before tying the thing off onto the back off Hillman's belt. Together they all lowered the container down gently so as not to put too much undue pressure on the lines, until it hung in place.

Then, regardless of whether the warhead was swaying or not, regardless of whether the grappling line moorings were creaking in the ice by Michaels's feet, Hillman set off – dragging the dangling warhead behind him.

It was painful to watch, slow and laborious. Every time he shifted forward he would have to stop and tug at the warhead in order to get it moving again.

Gant leant in close to Hackett as they were forced to simply watch. 'All that energy isn't gonna set that thing off, is it?'

'I hope not,' was the extent of Hackett's reply.

Gant was not pleased.

Hackett shrugged. As answers go, that was truly the best he could do.

Out on the rope, however, Hillman had stopped once again. Unhooking the line to the warhead, he tossed it out to Michaels who caught it in one fluid motion. From his secure position across the other side of the chasm, he quickly took up the challenge, leaning into the weight of the container and heaving the thing across, leaving Hillman to complete his journey in double-quick time.

Hillman soon had the third line secured to its moorings and was helping Michaels with the warhead.

'Well, that answers that,' Hackett noted. 'No, all that energy will *not* set off a nuclear warhead.'

Gant ignored him, slapping three of the others on the back. 'Okay, November, Sarah and Ralph – get going. One line each.'

SOLAR STORM

It was spotted first high in the sky over Indonesia.

A gigantic orange fireball that grew ever larger until the entire sky in every conceivable direction resembled a blazing fire.

For the onlookers on the ground it brought nothing but a sense of panic and dread as they felt the atmosphere around them swell and expand with the heat. It made breathing ferociously difficult and it caused thousands of ordinary people to run terrified and screaming through the streets of Jakarta.

Further on across the Pacific, where the islands were already troubled with severe volcanic ash and earth tremors, the new terror was suddenly the rain itself, superheated while still high up in the atmosphere.

Across New Guinea and Northern Australia, schoolchildren who had been out playing were suddenly running back inside in floods of tears, their skin a mass of red blotches where they had been scalded by the torrential downpour. Many had second- and third-degree burns.

Out in the agricultural lands, farmhands were forced to take shelter in their barns, and had little option but to watch helplessly as their livestock were broiled to death on the spot.

As the winds picked up across the Northern Australian plains, it was not long before the all-pervading smell of boiled meat seemed to fill every available pocket of fresh air.

And as the ionic chaos penetrated deep into the upper atmosphere, so it loosed lightning storms the like of which had not been seen on planet Earth for millions of years. Vast streaks of electrical energy shot up from ground to sky at such a ferocious rate in some areas that the scorchmarks left across the plains resembled the aftermath of an assault by some gigantic Gatling gun.

Much more of this and it was hard to believe anything would be left alive across the surface of the earth.

With multiple satellites being knocked out of commission like pins in a bowling alley, it was difficult for any one national space agency to keep track of the marauding destruction in isolation from the rest of the world. Pretty soon the likes of NASA found themselves trading information freely and quickly with ESA and the Russian Space Agency, each agency keeping track of different quadrants of the sky.

But it didn't take long for the suspected and long anticipated pattern to start emerging.

The storm was being sucked relentlessly into the magnetic fieldlines of the earth's magnetic poles.

The solar storm was being re-routed. Destination: the South Pole. Antarctica.

ACROSS THE EARTH

D ay was turning to night.
Billions of tons of searing volcanic matter was being blasted
into the atmosphere by the relentless eruption of volcanic action
around the globe.

From Washington State to Montana, from Northern California to
Southern Mexico, clouds of hot ash were pluming twenty, even thirty
kilometers high.

104 million hectares of lush green American farmland was
suddenly flattened, scorched and devastated by acrid pumice hailstones. In a stroke, billions of US dollars' worth of damage was
inflicted upon the single most impressive economic powerhouse the
world had ever known.

In a radius of up to 1,500 kilometers from each volcanic site around
the globe, thousands of people were rushing to crammed hospitals
with eye sores, skin rashes, pus-ridden wounds and burns from the
whirlwind of scolding volcanic fallout. Lungs were seared. Lives were
lost.

In 1945, Nagasaki in Japan had been ripped from the face of the
earth by an atomic 20-kiloton explosion. That was equivalent to
20,000 tons of dynamite.

When the solar storm connected with the earth, it triggered five
further catastrophic volcanic explosions which exploded with the
force of one million kilotons apiece. The equivalent to five Krakatoas.

The explosions were heard in every corner of the globe, like the death rattle of a dying planet.

THE PROBLEM

S arah's clip was stuck.

 She tugged at it again, but it was no use. Somehow the line she
was shimmying across on had become jammed into the hinge part of
the clip to which her safety line was attached. She was stuck fast.

Sarah looked around for help, but Matheson was already across
and climbing down into the tunnel while November, who was
looking back having seen there was something wrong, was stuck out
on a line that was simply too far away to be of any use.

'I'll be okay,' Sarah assured her. 'You go on ahead. I'll get this
untangled in a minute.'

Reluctantly November continued on her way, hand over hand,
dragging her body weight across the chasm, leaving Sarah to struggle
in the center of the energy stream.

Scott craned his neck and squinted for a better view. 'What is she
doing?'

'She's stuck,' Pearce realized.

'Now is not a good time to be getting stuck,' Hackett sang out,
checking his watch again. 'Any minute now this quiet little energy
twister is gonna turn into a pillar of blazing fire that wouldn't look
outta place in the Bible.'

'I better go over,' Gant announced, getting his line ready, but Scott
had other ideas.

'No,' he intervened. 'I'll go over. You send Yun across on the other line. I don't think he'll attempt to double back if *you're* waiting for him back here.'

Yun clearly didn't like that comment.

Quickly, both men clipped their safety lines onto the main ropes and set off monkeying across to the other side.

Yun eyed the anthropologist coldly as they both heaved in unison. 'Why do you not trust me? I said I would come with you. To flee is to be a coward.'

'I'm not calling you a coward,' Scott replied, struggling with the maneuver. 'But everyone's entitled to change their mind once in a while.'

Yun continued on his way, as Scott pulled himself up alongside Sarah, who in turn rolled her eyes. 'Oh, great. That's just what I wanted to be. The goddamn damsel in distress.'

'Well "hey there" to you too,' Scott remarked, swinging closer and grabbing hold of Sarah's main line. 'Y'know, joining the circus and walking a tightrope was never very high on my agenda in life,' he said.

'Me either. Can you see what's wrong?'

Scott held on to his own line with one hand and twisted Sarah's clip and safety line with the other. 'Oh, I gotcha . . . your safety line got wrapped around your clip when you latched on. When you put your weight down on it, I think what happened was it pulled the main line in and forced it into the hinge. What we got here is a very tight knot.'

'Can you get it free?'

Scott could feel his arms starting to ache. Good question. *Could* he get it free? He took a good long look at the problem, grunted with the effort and could feel himself starting to sweat.

He tugged at the knot. 'Y'know, in ancient times,' he said calmly and lightly, 'Egyptian priests were highly regarded if they specialized in the art of knots. Knots were highly significant, magically. They were associated with the binding of energies.'

Sarah looked up into the endless stream of oncoming ions.

'In knot magic, the number seven was the master number.'

They eyed each other closely. There was the number seven again: was that the key to unlocking the Atlantis language?

'Richard, knots are fascinating, but you need to move your ass, my friend.'

Sarah glanced over at Hackett, who was by now shimmying up beside them on his own way over to the other side, Yun having already completed the journey.

'The study of knots,' he grunted, 'is at the forefront of looped space theory in physics.'

'And that's relevant how?' Sarah remarked, amused by the way all of Hackett's exposed hair was standing completely on end.

'Looped space is linked to time. Something neither of you have. Time is precious.'

Suddenly the whole chasm lit up as intermittent bursts of crackling energy, like snakes on the war path, weaved in and out of the main stream and began to pulse down from above and careen off into the void below.

All three scientists screamed.

'Jesus Christ!' Scott bellowed, feeling the sheer terror of volatile electricity roll across his skin. He reached for his side pocket and pulled out a knife. 'We're gonna have to do this the old-fashioned way,' he said. 'Think Alexander the Great and the Gordian Knot.'

'But I won't have a safety line!' Sarah protested.

'So tie yourself on to me,' Scott insisted, slashing at Sarah's safety and slicing it in two.

'Okay, go!' Gant ordered, clipping Pearce's safety onto one of the lines.

'But Jon's still on his way across! What if the line can't take two people?'

'You see that out there?' Gant barked, balling a fist at the volatile energy mass. 'Your argument's with that, not me! Now get out there and start moving!'

They could hear it now, like the roll of thunder accompanying the approach of a thousand freight trains. An intense rumble that was intent on shaking their very surroundings to pieces.

Scott struggled to pull himself along hand over fist, acutely aware that entire boulders of snow and ice had started to tumble past his field of vision. As adrenaline pumped around his system he suddenly felt a sharp pain jabbing through his leg once again, but he fought it. Fought for all he was worth.

Sarah was aware of the shrieks. Encouraging, panic-stricken shouts from those already across. But she kept her eye on the end point and hauled ass, for watching them gathered in the mouth of the next ice tunnel only seemed to make matters worse. Their voices sounded muted. Masked as they were by the building rumble of impending disaster.

'My arm, Jesus, my fucking arm!' Pearce heard himself scream as he tensed and flexed, dragging himself along the wire and into the whirlwind.

Suddenly he felt himself being pulled. Sucked sideways as if caught in the middle of a blender set on 'fine'.

'Somebody!' he yelled in sheer panic. 'Somebody help me!'

But the only two people in a position to help, Scott and Sarah, were already up ahead and being helped down off the ropes.

'I can't hold on!' he bellowed, his voice drowned out by the frenzied blasting of ever-increasing chaos. 'I can't hold on!'

Gant appraised the situation with the calm of a man used to action.

While the rest of the group hurried inside the archway of the lower ice passage and disconnected Scott and Sarah from their safety lines, Gant focused more on what was going on half a mile up above their heads.

The energy tendril was writhing. Convulsing, like a snake that had just eaten a rat and was trying to digest it whole. It whipped around from side to side as the sheer volume of energy that was being dragged down from space was bottle-necked up where the ice refused to open out further and let the sheer volume of ionized matter through.

The vast and imposing arches of ice that kept the ground level above in place were starting to tremble, to buckle. Their Chrysler-Building-sized frames were starting to sway. Gigantic truck-sized boulders were beginning to tumble down their sides.

And their bases were starting to crack.

While Bob Pearce, frozen with agony, could hold on no longer and released the grip of his injured arm.

It was all the encouragement Gant needed. In one fluid motion he jumped out onto the middle line, swept his hunting knife up and severed the line behind him. Tumbling down he dropped the knife and reached out for Pearce, grabbing him with his first attempt.

Pearce jerked away from the line and the two men tumbled together before –

Slam! They jerked to a stop, Pearce's safety line preventing them from moving any further.

The two men hung there for a moment, before Gant had the presence of mind to direct Pearce's attention to the gathering light storm above their heads. Vast crackling arms of electricity were reaching out from the sides of the twister and zapping the arches of ice, pummeling the compacted snow like a sledge hammer.

'Cut your safety,' Gant ordered. 'I've got you. Just cut your safety!'

Pearce didn't move. He was frozen with terror.

Both men could feel the gathering ferocity of the storm, the sheer anger of unbridled power.

'Cut your safety, goddamnit, or we fry!'

Pearce shook. His whole body was wracked with fear. Slowly, painfully slowly, he reached for his own knife – and slit the line.

The two men tumbled uncontrollably until they swung down and slammed into the icy wall of the chasm. Gant, one hand gripped firmly around Pearce's belt, the other gripped like a vice around the rope, shouted up at his men in the tunnel above.

'Get us out of here!'

Several sharp tugs and they began to rise up the wall at a snail's pace, but the vision before them was of little comfort. The chaotic arms of energy were lashing out all around them now. Striking the walls of the chasm and blasting new tunnels into existence.

Above their heads, in one tremendous explosion, the energy twister suddenly expanded outwards in a super-sized explosion of livid flame, shattering the ice around it and widening the hole through which it was channeling, tenfold.

Suddenly, they could see the entire base of *Jung Chang* start to slip inwards upon them.

Mobile huts and heavy artillery units were falling into the chasm one by one, while behind them, closing in rapidly, toppled massive chunks of ice and great arches of snow . . .

'Run!' Scott barked as he helped drag Pearce and Gant up into the tunnel. 'Run now!'

Without asking questions the two men got onto their feet and sprinted down the ice passage as fast as their feet could carry them, slamming into the walls as they went and rounding the far corner as vast sheets of ice and snow collapsed behind them with such a thunderous roar it was a miracle their eardrums didn't burst.

But it didn't end there. They had to keep moving, and fast – before the rest of the tunnel imploded.

With the warhead strung out from a harness attached to his belt, Michaels led the way forward, but after a couple of intersections with other criss-crossing passageways and shafts the marine suddenly found himself being pulled back viciously – at the hand of Yun.

'What the fuck d'you think you're doing?' he demanded, but Yun didn't even bother to answer. Instead he held everyone back as—

Whoosh! A torrent of blisteringly hot, super-heated water suddenly blasted out of a side tunnel and rocketed off across the crossroads.

'There is much volcanic activity here,' Yun explained. 'We must be careful.'

Up ahead, other scalding geysers were rocketing back and forth across the tunnel system.

'And just how are we supposed to get past this lot?' Hackett complained.

Yun indicated a side passage that nobody had noticed before. Only a few feet across, it was neither a direct turn right, nor a hole in the floor. In fact, its axis appeared to be a steady 45-degree slope heading straight down.

'You try climbing back up this way,' Yun said. 'Getting down is much easier.'

'How much easier?' Gant wanted to know, still getting his breath back.

'We slide.'

'Are you insane?'

'Major,' Scott stepped in, 'our escape route's been cut off and if we go down that way we boil. What other options do we have?'

'It's reckless, Professor. There's no telling where this leads. We could wind up plummeting into a ravine.'

'Risk is all part of the game,' Scott insisted. 'You said so yourself.'

FREE-FALL

In Gant's opinion this was the worst decision of his life, entrusting his people to the advice of the enemy. But then what other options were there?

They each entered the tunnel with trepidation and rocketed off into the ice below at extreme speed. It took a leap of faith of incredible proportions, but since the clock was ticking, what was there to lose?

Michaels and Hillman had gone first, taking the warhead with them. Scott and Hackett had followed on after, together with Yun, while Gant had been the last to take the plunge behind the two women. Which, as it turned out, was of little strategic value. In fact, rocketing down the ice passage at speeds close to 40 mph gave nobody *any* particular advantage.

This was chaos in motion.

The ice was turning a deep, deep blue, Sarah noticed as the walls of the tunnel streaked by. Blue ice was formed by compression. By the sheer weight of the ice above pushing down on the ice below for thousands of years.

It was incredible. A glassy smoothness channeled out and eaten away by the swishing blast of boiling water, heated by the magma of volcanic activity below. All rushing past her face within inches as she lay on her back and let gravity take her where it may.

Her mouth was open. Her eyes transfixed. She breathed in shallow bursts and made few noises, for fear had crept in, and was keeping her vocal cords gripped.

They could feel the ground tremble as they bounced over hard ridges of ice. Michaels and Hillman felt the container buckle as the warhead struck another obstacle in its path. They heard metal locks and hinges struggle to keep its lid shut tight.

And then out they burst. Out into a tremendously wide ice cavern, its floor a rippling slope of hard glass with crazy patterns eroded into it in swathing channels.

They could hear the ice straining above as the destruction on the surface continued unabated. And as Hillman rocketed on behind the warhead, his coat tore on the razor blades of ice. Snagged for a moment and slowed him down.

Slam! A tree-sized stalactite suddenly careened down from the ceiling and exploded in front of him.

Hillman dove to one side in an effort to avoid the dagger-like rear end as it penetrated the hard cavern floor and sliced effortlessly into the depths of ice. But unlike the front end which exploded on impact with a ferocious blast, the rear end remained intact. Upright and immovable.

Hillman breathed a sigh of relief as he shot past it. At these speeds, impacting into an obstacle like that could break his back. It could –

'Argh!'

Michaels twisted his head to see Hillman flung up into the air. Tossed like a rag doll as he connected with a shallow ice mound at high speed.

The soldier was face down and spinning. Utterly aware that he had been launched over a precipice that had been masked by the undulating ground, but which now was revealed below him to be a chasm of bottomless terror, as he was catapulated across it.

Yet he had no way of knowing if he was going to make it to the other side. No way of knowing if there even *was* another side.

Michaels instinctively held out his hand to try and grab Hillman, but it was a futile gesture as he rushed into and was swallowed up by a further passageway through the ice.

*   *   *

Scott careened out of control, smashing through a shower of tiny ice crystals which cut like shattering glass. Like a bullet from a gun he burst from the tunnel as ahead of him stalactite upon stalactite crashed to the ground and littered the ice cavern like a forest of petrified, sub-zero trees.

There was little he could do to alter his course except roll and weave and hope. Behind him, the other members of the party blasted out with a yelp and did their utmost to negotiate the way ahead.

The ground shook once more, shaking free the mighty stalactites like a volley of javelins. As each projectile struck home, and impacts ravaged the cavern floor, the way ahead was obscured by further blasts. Frozen shrapnel made of nothing but water.

It continued in a frenzy until ultimately the cavern floor could sustain no further damage. It opened up in front of them all.

The team was swallowed whole.

He couldn't stop.

There was no way on earth Bob Pearce could stop. Over the edge he tipped, down into wherever the honeycomb of ice tunnels was suddenly re-directing him. Down into the darkness below where the sunlight was at last having difficulty in penetrating.

Everything seemed to funnel, in a blur, down into a single passageway ahead.

Pearce became aware of November, sliding up next to him amid the streaking view of ice whizzing by. When he glanced over he struck the tunnel wall and rebounded back out at an oblique angle.

He could feel his arm crunch painfully before he finally shot out and bumped his way along the ground of a mammoth ice cavern, its frozen floor a series of pits and scoops, as if some giant of a man with a hot spoon had helped himself to huge, rounded servings of ice.

The ground was flatter here. Indeed, his coat ripped open and his bare skin scraped occasionally against pebbles and flint, and sharp-edged rocks that lay strewn through the thin ice.

He bumped to a stop, spinning around before finally hitting his head on something solid and immovable and ice-like . . .

Yet was not ice.

KUDURRU

Read, in the name of thy Lord! Who created man from congealed blood! Read, for thy Lord is most generous! Who taught the pen! Taught men what he did not know!

96.2–6
The Qur'an
Translated by E.H. Palmer, 1965

I t was two feet high and needle-shaped.
   A miniature version of those gigantic monuments in Egypt that had been erected in honor of the Pharaohs. Square of base with a pyramidal summit. It was covered in tiny symbols, the Atlantis glyphs, which wrapped around in one continuous ribbon.

It was warm to the touch, too. Having melted all the ice around it, its base disappeared into the gray shingle of solid ground beneath it. Yet the object itself appeared like crystal, shimmering as though electricity were passing through it at some molecular level.

It was two feet in height. And it was made from solid Carbon 60.

'Oh, man,' Pearce groaned as he prised his head away from the hard surface of the object, and tried to sit up. Groggily he rubbed at his injury before realizing that Scott sat bolt upright nearby, staring at him. No, not staring *at* him but past him.

He twisted round to see what he'd collided with. And his jaw hung open. 'Jesus . . .'

Scott scrambled over as Pearce wiped his blood off the object. It was difficult to clean it completely, as some of his blood had dripped into the indented glyphs. He licked his finger to try and help with the cleaning, but Scott held his hand back.

'Don't,' he said gently. 'The blood helps.'

Pearce shrugged. That was not what he expected to hear as Scott crouched down by the artifact and pulled out his palm-top computer.

Sarah stood the other side of the cavern and rubbed her aching bones. She had a large flashlight hung on her belt and flipped it on, but she needn't have bothered. 'Why is it so light down here?' she wondered aloud.

November got to her feet. 'The ice is so honeycombed with shafts,' she reasoned, 'that sunlight probably reaches all the way down here.'

But Hackett had another idea. 'That crystal stump,' he pointed out, 'is glowing. I bet there are others.'

'I . . . don't . . . give a fuck,' Matheson groaned in a heap on the floor.

'Here,' Yun offered, helping the engineer to his feet.

Matheson eyed the man warily. 'Well, I guess you did say you'd get us down here.'

'Wherever "here" is,' the Chinese soldier replied. 'This is not where the tunnel came out before.'

'Why am I not surprised to hear you say that?' Gant observed as he strode past, yanking open the fastenings on his Caribou hide parka and pulling the hood down. 'Is it me or is it unusually warm down here?'

Hackett took a temperature reading. 'It's warm,' he agreed. 'About minus two.'

Suddenly there was a scraping noise and the sound of a heavy fall echoed around the cavern. Gant spun on his heel, growling: 'My men – where are they?' He searched the ice with his eyes. 'Hillman? Michaels?'

They could hear a muffled voice. Solitary. Trapped somewhere behind a thick wall of ice. It was followed by a sharp hammering.

'Where the hell are you?' Gant yelled.

'Up there!' Yun realized quickly.

'Hillman? Is that you?'

There was another muffled response.

'What did he say?' November asked, craning her neck to hear.

Then Gant twigged. 'He said: stand back!'

Jerking the girl out the way he shot the others a look but they were already moving as semi-automatic machine-gun fire ripped through the ice above their heads, obliterating it into a thousand pieces. Large chunks of the cavern ceiling suddenly gave way and down tumbled Hillman, impacting onto the debris below.

Stunned, the marine lay dazed for a moment before he could even bring himself to move.

'Well,' he croaked eventually. 'That was unusual.'

Gant loomed over his underling. 'Where's Michaels?' he demanded. 'He has the bomb.'

'He isn't here?'

'We lost him.'

'Then I have no idea, sir. None at all.'

Bob Pearce grimaced. 'Oops.'

Meanwhile, Sarah had her attention fixed on Richard Scott. The linguist was deep, deep into something. Something wonderful.

Language, like DNA, occurred in chains and had to be read in a certain direction. Language, also like DNA, had start signals and an instruction code.

Language was a beast, like any other. And beasts could be tamed, by being understood.

In the 1600s the Rosicrucians thought they understood. A secret society of anonymous members, they claimed to have found and used the ancient original perfect language of mankind. Based on the work of the infamous cabalist, Lull, they used symbols that consisted of a circle for the sun, a crescent for the moon, and a cross for the cardinal points. They were convinced that these linguistic symbols were intrinsically linked to geometry.

But they were a group who were so secret, they secreted themselves out of existence, their work reduced to so much hearsay in the face of little evidence.

Yet here, and now, Richard Scott could say with absolute certainly that although their so-called perfect language was in all probability a phony, the symbolism they had used and understood, the symbolism that had been gleaned from millennia of myth and legend, was altogether accurate.

The circle and the cross. The sun and the cardinal points.

These were the start signals that had led Scott down the road to deciphering the mysterious Atlantis instruction code. And now, all he had to do was input a number. A single number. The computer would do the rest.

On the screen of his palm top, the computer was already whizzing through each symbol in the chain on the crystal in front of him. Pulling out each glyph that corresponded to the placement of that one single number as it repeated itself throughout the number stream found encoded within the Carbon 60 crystals back at CERN . . .

'What number did you choose?' Sarah asked quietly, kneeling down beside him.

'Well, I started by trying to figure out what numbers to reject first,' Scott told her.

'Such as?'

'The Maya, whose name means "not many" or "the few", maybe on account of their ancestors surviving the Great Flood, I don't know – anyway, they worshipped the god of the number *four*. This was the same god who they also used to represent the sun.'

'Wouldn't that make *four* a great candidate for cracking this thing?'

'Ordinarily, yeah,' Scott agreed. Then he lowered his voice. 'Trouble is, I can't speak Mayan too well. If that's the language I end up having to read we're all screwed and they brought the wrong guy along for the ride.'

Sarah wasn't taking the bait. He was in too good a mood. 'You've cracked this thing, haven't you?'

Scott nodded. 'I think so.'

'What number did you use?'

'Seven,' the anthropologist revealed. '"And on the seventh day God rested". I'm hoping we get to do the same.'

His computer beeped. All calculations were complete. Task done.

Scott and Sarah exchanged apprehensive looks before the epigrapher commanded his computer to tell him what it had found, while the others in the group gathered together to watch.

The computer whirred. Beeped once more, before finally stringing the necessary sound files together and announcing in the odd lilt of Sarah Kelsey herself: 'Kah – Doo – Roo . . .'

The others eyed the linguist keenly, while he scratched his head. What did it mean?

Scott repeated the jumble of syllables to himself. 'Kah – doo – roo . . . ? Kah – doo – roo . . . ?'

And then it hit him.

'Jesus Christ!' the epigraphist yelped. 'Jesus Christ! That's it! *Kudurru!* KUDURRU! It's ancient Sumerian! It means *path-marker* or *boundary-marker* This is a milestone! It's telling us what it is! We're within the city limits! We did it! My God . . . we did it!'

'To hell with the path-marker,' Pearce exploded excitedly, 'what about those crystals? What about those rocks Ralph brought back?'

Quickly Scott set the computer to work decoding the set of glyphs it had in store already. The results were forbidding. He read them out loud:

'Within these walls lies the powers of the heavens eternal. A people dead. A spirit alive.

Beyond these walls lie . . .'

'Is that word *Nazareth?*' November probed quietly.

'Not Nazareth,' Scott corrected. 'Nasaru – it means "to protect" . . .

'Beyond these walls lie the means to protect the sons of sons, the daughters of daughters. The children of we who were first.

Read them aloud. Spoken like thunder. For they shall make men quake.

Read them aloud. Spoken like thunder. If you have the means to understand.

Behind these walls sit hope and terror.

But upon these walls sit knowledge and power.

Understand them. Proclaim them. Use them!

To fail to heed instruction is to perish!

The power of zero must be set free!'

ATLANTIS

There's no secret so hidden that it cannot be found, no voice so mute that it cannot be heard.

Dr Steven Roger Fischer,
Director of the Institute of Polynesian Languages
and Literatures, New Zealand, GLYPHBREAKER, 1997

CITY LIMITS

'Michaels, come in, Michaels! Do you read me? C'mon, Ray. If you can hear me, signal back.'

Hillman looked to Gant and shook his head despondently. Wherever Michaels had ended up he was out of radio contact. The two men signaled the rest of the party to hold position while they scouted up ahead with Chow Yun.

The Chinese soldier had seen something. Something important.

Hackett watched with misgiving as they disappeared around the curve of ice at the end of the cavern some several hundred yards further on, before scooting forward on his knees to join Scott.

'Great, Scott,' he said, full of admiration. 'Y'know, this is uh, remarkable . . . truly, truly remarkable. You take an alphabet of sixty letters: if you write down the number of possible word permutations you can make out of an alphabet that size, you wind up writing a number with close to five or six trillion zeroes. That would take a thousand people nearly thirty years just to *write down* that kind of a number.'

'To get one word out of all these glyphs,' Pearce added excitedly, 'a word that makes sense – is a coincidence, but three pages of text with something like ninety-eight percent accuracy? This, Richard, my friend, is the closest thing I've seen to a miracle.'

November glanced up from the computer and eyed her mentor warily. Was this for real? 'Professor, this phrase is cropping up again.

The power of zero must be set free. The power of zero? A big fat nothing?'

Scott shrugged. 'I told you it didn't make any sense.'

To the epigraphist maybe it didn't. But to the physicist among them it sparked a deep-seated sense of curiosity. 'The power of zero must be set free,' Hackett repeated studiously. 'Does it mention any more about this zero?'

'Like what?'

'Does it say what *kind* of zero should be set free?'

'Jon,' Sarah said, suspiciously, 'nothing is nothing. There is only one kind of zero.'

'No,' Hackett corrected. 'There's not.'

Scott turned squarely on the man. 'What are you thinking?'

'Find me anything that might be an attempt to define zero.'

Scott reluctantly started trawling back through all his hurriedly scribbled notes and text documents on his computer. 'This doesn't make any sense,' he complained. 'This is a nonsense, a riddle.' He ran his finger along the text until he found what he was looking for. 'Uh, here, see? *Unleash the power of zero. The spirit of nothing which is in all things. Nothing is everything. Zero power—*'

'Stop right there,' Hackett begged, holding out his hand, looking Scott right in the eye. 'Right there. That's it. That's our power source. That's what our damn satellites have been picking up all this time. What lit up the eyes of the military and Rola Corp. The Holy Grail of fuels. Clean – *free* – power.'

'This makes sense to you?'

'Absolute sense,' the physicist replied. 'It's called zero point energy. Literally . . . something from nothing.'

'You see, scientists in the nineteenth century believed in the existence of a substance called "ether",' Hackett explained, 'a material that occurred throughout the universe, a material that explained the wave propagation of light. Two guys, Michelson and Morley, did this famous experiment to try and detect this "ether" and failed. It's not important you understand what they did. It's just important you know scientists have been looking for this mysterious stuff for a long time.'

The rest of the group took him at his word.

'They thought they'd pick up some kind of "ether wind" as a result of the earth passing through this stuff. Einstein seized on the fact this experiment failed in order to support his special theory of relativity, the cornerstone of modern physics. Einstein maintained that space was truly empty, but his mathematics in turn led to the development and use of quantum mechanics. And in the ultimate circular argument, in the 1930s, quantum mechanics wound up creating a mathematical term for describing the ground state of any oscillating system and called it Zero Point Energy. The "zero point" referred to the temperature: zero degrees Kelvin.'

'Which means what, exactly?' Sarah wanted to know.

Matheson, who was vaguely familiar with the term, answered on Hackett's behalf. 'It means energy exists even in the absence of heat. Energy is inherent in the fabric of space itself.'

'It gets better,' Hackett beamed. 'The energy density, the sheer volume of stored zero point energy ready and waiting to be tapped at any point in space, is infinite.'

'You have got to be kidding.'

Hackett shook his head. 'Believe me, many basic arguments in quantum mechanics do not work, unless zero point energy exists. Dirac first showed how electron-positron production could arise from vacuum fluctuations, and wound up inventing quantum electrodynamics. The Heisenberg Uncertainty Principle calls for quantum mechanical systems to "borrow" energy from this zero point of electrical flux. Boyer used the Lorentz invariance to determine zero point energy as a function of frequency and—'

'Jon, what are you telling us?' Pearce asked, cutting the physicist dead.

'If you can figure out how to tap into it and unleash the power of zero,' he explained, 'you'll be tapping into God's own private generator. That's more power that you can possibly imagine.' He jerked a thumb in Gant's estimated direction. 'It makes the power of that bomb they're out searching for look like a fart in the wind.

'If that's what's down here, if that's what they picked up on satellite, a machine that has tapped into zero point energy, I'm telling you now that shutting it off by blowing it up is not a way we want to go. Zero point energy is the raw power of the universe. If you want to shut off a faucet you twist the top, you don't knock off the tap head with a sledge hammer.

'If Gant blows up this machine, we're talking major fucking devastation, folks. He could wind up wiping out this entire solar system.'

Hackett went quiet as the others picked over the implications.

'What kind of a machine are we talking about here?'

Matheson stepped up to the plate in response. 'Nikola Tesla, back in the 1890s, was convinced it was possible to make an electrical motor that was completely wire-free, that tapped into what he called "the energy of nature". He claimed this energy could be accessed at very high frequencies. In fact, he eventually built a motor that had only one wire, but had *no* return circuit. The return circuit, he said, was being transmitted wire-lessly through space.'

'Sounds like he was on the right track,' Sarah enthused.

'He was on the right track about a lot of things,' Matheson said warmly. 'Tesla invented alternating current and radio, radar and—'

'Wait a minute,' Hackett interjected, deep in thought. 'Alternating current. That couldn't be invented without his inventing the electrical induction motor, right? A rotating magnetic field.'

'Right,' Matheson agreed happily.

'The South Pole,' Hackett pointed out, 'is one end of a rotating bar magnet in space.'

'The South Pole,' Matheson added, 'is also notorious for having the greatest concentration of low pressure weather fronts. Tesla discovered that gases at a reduced pressure become extremely conductive. It's the same principle whereby strip neon lighting works.'

'Wait a minute,' Pearce chipped in. 'Didn't you once tell me superconductors and semi-conductors, the components used in computing and high end science, work best at extremely low temperatures?'

'Right,' Hackett agreed. 'And what better place to build your machine than here.'

'This whole place,' November reasoned, stunned, 'this whole place was chosen because the environment completely matches the requirements of this machine?'

'Not just this machine,' Hackett replied. 'But the prerequisites you need to be able to tap into zero point energy.' He took a pen and started scratching out a plan in the ice. 'This is what we think Atlantis looks like, right? Three huge concentric rings, many kilometers around, correct?'

The others nodded.

'Well, what the hell do you think the particle accelerator at CERN was?'

'Jon,' Scott warned, 'you're about eight steps ahead of us. More in my case because I just took a couple back.'

'Richard,' Hackett concluded, 'I think Ralph here was correct with his initial assessment. I think maybe the *entire city* of Atlantis is one huge machine, if its purpose is to tap into zero point energy.'

Hackett continued to sketch the layout of Atlantis as detected by the satellites, in the ice.

'Three concentric rings of Carbon 60, with two rings of water sandwiched in between, and a column of plasma coming down the center to connect it all together . . . It all makes sense.' He confronted the others. 'There are a number of theories floating around on how to tap into zero point energy. One is Ion Acoustic Oscillation – the coherent oscillation of nuclei in a plasma, like say a solar storm. The theory goes that if the nuclei of the plasma can be caused to oscillate, the plasma will produce heat – more heat than the amount of energy taken to produce the plasma, which isn't allowed under the current laws of physics. Take it one step further and the theory says you can do the same thing with solid crystals.

'Chemetskii, a Russian plasma physicist, claimed in the 1990s to have tapped zero point energy with plasma too. But his method was to get the plasma particles to undergo a cycloid motion. To go round and round in circles. He created a vortex ring plasmoid in the lab – you might know it under its other name – ball lightning. But you construct a device on a large-enough scale to create this ring in a controlled manner, like say through a particle accelerator – and you stand a damn good chance of harnessing the resulting power.' Hackett guided his pen around his ice map showing where the plasma might be being directed.

'The same theory hypothesizes it may also be possible to induce this cycloid motion within the nuclei of solid state magnetic materials. You'd wind up getting a solid object to pulse out acoustical waves of free energy. It particularly theorizes that crystal would be good for this.'

Hackett again guided his pen around the circles in the ice, this time directing everybody's attention to the Carbon 60 circles.

'However, Schauberger, who works on water vortices, found that when he forced water through specially shaped spiraling tubes it induced an energy anomaly – a bluish glow in the center of the vortex,' Hackett said, drawing their attention finally to the rings of water.

'We have all three of those experiments going on right here, simultaneously. These people weren't leaving anything to chance.'

'I heard about this engineer building a machine that may have tapped zero point energy,' Matheson told them. 'Jim Griggs – yeah, that was his name. An engineer in Georgia. Invented this pump that turns cold water into steam *without* heat.'

'That's impossible,' November objected. 'I live in the South. I never heard of that.'

'The story goes he was doing some plumbing and found a cold-water pipe giving off steam because there was a shock wave in the pipe. So he built a device to reproduce these effects. He had this drum and drilled lots of different-sized holes all over it. Then he put the drum inside a large tube, then when the water was pumped in he rotated the inner drum. Millions of shock waves superheated the water. It worked so well NASA has it now. They've been studying it for ten years. Can't find a thing wrong with it. And they get more energy out than they put in.'

'Water has the best potential for energy,' Sarah agreed. 'On its own it's harmless, but it's made up of hydrogen and oxygen – two of the most explosive elements there are.'

'I know the military have been testing an electric gun,' Pearce revealed. 'They used water as the projectile instead of a bullet. Shot a thimblefull at a three-quarter-inch aluminum plate. It cut straight through it like a laser, using more energy than they put in.'

'A cubic inch of space,' Hackett reiterated, 'is filled with so much zero point energy it would run the world for a billion years.'

'Tapping this zero point energy,' Scott observed, 'everything seems to depend on rotating or spinning something. We're at the South

Pole, the bottom of the earth – the axis on which this whole planet revolves. Does that make a difference?'

'Oh, yeah,' Hackett agreed coldly. 'A whole world of difference. Laithwaite, a gyroscope physicist, noted that a precessing gyroscope that was displaced along a cycloid path would show signs of inertial and/or a gravitational anomaly if it came into contact with zero point energy.' He let the words sink in. 'Precessing means basically "wobbling". That's what earth does. The fact that it spins means it's a gyroscope, but it's also moving in a cycloid motion – orbiting the sun. *And* it's wobbling about its axis. The wobble takes 26,000 years to do a complete cycle. It's why thousands of years ago constellations like Orion were in a different position in the sky and the Pole Star used to be a different star. It used to be Draco – associated with Lucifer, the Fallen One.'

'A gravitational anomaly?' Pearce asked excitedly. 'Like maybe anti-gravity? An anti-gravity wave, shielding the earth from the sun?'

'Bob, I like you, but I wouldn't want to see you working with sub-atomic particles. You can't shield the earth from gravity,' Hackett said, dismissive. 'It doesn't work like that. You can shield against light, electricity, magnetism. You can shield against all that. But you can't shield against gravity. It's not like you can create an anti-gravity wave to cancel the other wave out.'

'Are you sure about that?' Sarah asked provocatively.

'Nope,' Hackett retorted without missing a beat. 'Besides, the effects Laithwaite described were time related. The pace of time would be altered closer to the anomaly.'

'Oh shit, talk about being caught between a rock and a hard place. Destroy the machine and we die,' Pearce said. 'Do nothing while the sun goes ballistic – and we still die. Unless we do as the writing says, of course. Follow the instructions and unleash the power of zero.'

'That's a lot of power to be tapping into,' Sarah sighed. 'God's own power station. What does Atlantis want it for? You don't just tap into a vast reservoir of energy because you can. You do it because you want to use it for something. What?'

'*Then the seventh angel blew his trumpet . . . Then came flashes of lightning, peals of thunder and an earthquake and violent hail.*'

They all turned their attention on November. She was deep in thought, recalling her Scripture. She let her voice grow stronger and more resonant.

'*I heard a sound coming out of the heavens,*' she said. '*Like the sound of the ocean or the roar of thunder . . . And I saw in heaven another sign, great and wonderful . . . I seemed to be looking at a sea of crystal suffused with fire . . .*' She smiled, knowing she had their complete attention. 'The Book of Revelation,' she said. 'The sea appeared frozen like crystal – like my glass of Coke back in the lab, remember?'

'My God, is that it?' Matheson asked anxiously. 'Could that be it? All those sonic streams pumping acoustic waves around the oceans of the planet. It only takes a frequency shift to start producing standing waves. To start turning the ocean into one giant quasicrystal.'

Hackett held his hand up as he chewed over the theory rapidly. He couldn't see a problem. 'It might be,' he said quietly. 'It might just be. You can't protect against a gravity wave *per se*. But you can take safety precautions. You want to protect an egg? You put it in an egg-box. You want to stop a flood? You want to stop the seas from swilling around and spilling all over the continents? You freeze the ocean.'

'What about the mantle?' Sarah asked.

Scott was nodding. 'That's right. Earth crust displacement. The entire surface of the earth was made to slide across the liquid inner molten core.'

'Well, who's to say they didn't think of that, and that these quasicrystal waves aren't being pumped into the earth's core as well?' November offered. 'Make the entire planet one huge solid object for one brief moment.'

'It's zero point energy,' Scott agreed. 'It's not like Atlantis needs to worry about where all the energy is gonna come from. It's already been tapped.'

Pearce gave November the most admiring look. 'You, young lady, might be a genius.'

November blushed a thank you.

'The only problem I have,' Hackett pointed out, 'is that if you pump that much energy into a system, where does it all go afterwards? It doesn't just disappear; it has to be removed somehow. That much energy unleashed into a system would wind up causing as much damage as the gravity wave in the first place.'

Sarah shifted on her haunches, aware that the answer was within her grasp. 'Of course . . .' she whispered. 'The pyramids!'

'That was mechanical too,' Matheson realized. 'Sarah – you're right!'

Hackett wanted further explanation. Everyone could read it in his eyes.

'There was an earthquake in central Africa,' Sarah explained, 'remember? Just before I entered the tunnels under the pyramids in Egypt. Somehow the seismic energy was turned into light and some kind of electromagnetic pulse. This energy pulse wound up being circulated around the Giza system before the pyramids shot the energy off up into space.'

'The pyramids,' Matheson enthused, 'are release valves! Like on a pressure cooker.'

'Egypt wouldn't be enough,' Hackett said. 'You'd need more.'

'Try the Amazon,' Sarah replied confidently. 'And China. There are pyramids and ancient sites all over this planet.'

'We're not just talking about a machine the size of a city,' Matheson gasped. 'We're talking about a machine that covers the entire surface of the earth!'

'And maybe Atlantis is in stand-by mode,' Scott added. 'Maybe the sun's gravity waves alerted the city to a new danger. They woke it up. Maybe it was built to help us. We don't have to shut it off, we have to figure out what to do with it!'

Yun could see the remote gun emplacement up ahead.

It was laid on its side, smashed up and buckled, a twisted heap of barely reusable parts. Yun broke into a run, heading around the curve of the wide ice passage before being brought up short by Gant.

'Easy there,' the Major warned darkly, eyeing the machine gun lying just a few feet away. 'Don't want you getting any ideas now, do we?'

'You don't understand,' Yun explained, as Gant ordered Hillman to inspect the hardware. 'This was where I left the rest of my party.'

'Leading us into a trap, huh? Seems someone beat you to it.'

Hillman threw a chunk of debris back down as he stood. 'Totally destroyed, sir.'

'Fire fight?'

'Uh-uh.' The marine tapped the wreckage with his boot. 'Claw marks.'

Gant was forced to do a double-take. Sure enough, three thick gouges had cut into the black gunmetal. Deep and even.

'This is where the spirits attacked,' Yun gulped, surveying the passage ahead with dread.

Gant had been expecting this. 'The Golems.'

'Call them what you will.'

And then the Chinese soldier's breath caught in his throat as a chill wind swept through the passage, accompanied by a deep rumbling yawn of a noise, like distant beasts awakening from a slumber.

Yun twisted his head sharply. 'They're here . . .'

TIME TO SOLAR MAXIMUM:

10 HOURS, 13 MINUTES

S arah could feel the hairs on the back of her neck stand on end. For a moment she thought she was back in the tunnels under the pyramids at Giza.

'I know that noise,' she said fearfully. 'We've got company.'

And that's when Scott's radio chirped into life.

'Pack up your stuff. Do your thing on the move, Doc,' Gant ordered. 'We gotta get moving.'

There were no arguments from the rest of the team. Bob Pearce was the next to feel it, followed swiftly by the others. The air around them was being filled with some kind of electrifying force. Instinctively they all knew that not only were they *not* alone – they were being watched.

They filled Gant in on their theory on the hoof, a double march with guns drawn: Gant at the front, Hillman bringing up the rear. Nobody wanted to stick around.

Pearce concluded his explanation which Gant took in quietly, never asking a question unless absolutely necessary and never poking holes. Constantly on alert. Constantly keeping a keen eye on the pathway ahead. Gant waited for Pearce to finish explaining the team's theory before responding to it.

'Nice job,' he commented. 'Very thorough reasoning.'

'Thank you.'

'I just have one question though.'

'What's that?'

'Well, if that's why they built Atlantis . . . why didn't it work?' Pearce was stunned as Gant continued: 'The earth's crust *was* displaced. The earth *was* flooded. Right?'

Scott clamped his eyes shut and shook his head. Goddamnit, none of them had even thought of that. Just why *didn't* Atlantis save the earth last time around?

'I mean, what you've said makes sense,' Gant agreed, 'but did it ever occur to you that what you described is what these people who built Atlantis had *intended*, but it backfired. Wound up creating more harm than good?'

'Anything's possible,' Pearce conceded. 'Sure, but—'

'But nothing,' Gant shot back. 'If ever there was a better reason to find Michaels and retrieve that bomb – that was it.'

Pearce glanced back over his shoulder at the others. Hackett shrugged in response. 'The only marine in the whole outfit who knows how to think and *we* gotta have him.'

Sarah nudged the physicist to be quiet, clearly feeling jumpy.

'I know,' November sympathized. 'I feel it too. This is spooky.'

The walls of the passage through the ice were odd-looking too, which didn't help. They weren't weather-worn and eroded like the ice up on the surface. Here it seemed flatter, more angular-looking. It was a feature which had been puzzling Matheson for some time. So when he couldn't resist any longer, the engineer finally took a chance and stepped out of line to make a closer inspection.

Sure enough the ice was translucent. Thinner, like it was covering something within. Something warmer which was melting the ice and causing it to develop this glassy texture.

Taking the small pick that dangled from his belt, Matheson chipped away at the ice. Nothing major, but enough. It didn't take long to get a result and he was surprised when a smooth flat sheet of the stuff came crumbling away to expose the hard, glyph-laden surface of a structure made entirely from Carbon 60.

'Well, I'll be darned.'

A few feet further on down the passage and there was a darker patch of ice, like it blocked the way to a recess or maybe even an entire other passage.

Matheson couldn't believe his luck.

The others were a few paces ahead of him now, moving on swiftly. He called after them: 'Hey! Hey, wait up! I found something! I think we're there!'

But Hillman was the only one who even bothered to glance back as Matheson raised his pick. 'We know, Ralph,' the marine snapped. 'But we gotta get to a safer area. Yun thinks we're in trouble here, and I tend to agree with him. Now c'mon!'

Reluctantly Matheson lowered his pick and pulled himself away from his glorious find. Completely unaware that behind the dark ice, a pale ethereal-looking face, blurred by the window of frozen water, had moved up to within inches of the engineer to peer out at him.

And blinked . . .

The passage was opening out into a larger area.

Cavernous, but by no means a cavern. A cavern implied an enclosure, a large, but confined space. Whereas the roof on this thing seemed to go on for ever. It arched up in a glistening white curve behind them and continued to climb off, up into a greater unseen expanse beyond. For ahead of them, blocking their entire path, stood a 50-foot high sheer cliff-face of ice that stretched across from one end of the cavern to the other.

Leading up to the sheer cliff were columns and columns of ice stacks, stalactites and stalagmites. All manner of warped and bizarrely shaped ice sculptures from the relentless build-up of frozen precipitation. Like pillars of salt, or anemic trees, they were made to look even stranger by the fact that the exposed shingle that led in patches all the way up to the cliff, had started to support colonies of lush green moss and lichen.

The party moved in closer and realized the top of the cliff was flattened off because beneath all that ice lay a real structure, one so vast that it beggared belief, but a structure nonetheless that, just like the *kudurru*, glowed.

Light energy pulsed along it, blurred as it was beneath thick layers of frozen water. But as it pulsed so too did it reveal its very nature.

Like the battlements of some great medieval castle the vast fortress-like outer wall of the City of Atlantis stood before them, shimmering relentlessly. Vast swatches of detail seemed to come and go in fleeting bursts. Patches of swirling spiral-patterned glyphs were revealed. Great arches of inner design, almost Gothic. A whiff of temple.

Its foundations were solid. Its imposing stature unchallenged; in its very center stood its vast and glorious gates, some 20 feet high. And firmly shut tight.

'Oh, man!' Matheson exclaimed, running his fingers through his icy beard.

His words echoed across the void of the chamber before anyone realized that they were quickly being swallowed whole by the sound of rushing water, just out of reach. Just over the other side of the mesmerizing city wall.

Scott had his hand cupped over his mouth in wonder, but swiftly composed himself when he noticed Gant and Hillman. The two marines were completely unmoved by the sight, focused instead upon the sense of impending danger.

The rest of the team however couldn't shake their feelings of reverential wonder, even reducing their voices to hushed tones.

'My God,' November breathed. 'Is this really it?'

'Atlantis!' Pearce said huskily, coming up next to her. 'Just as I saw it.'

But the military men would have none of it.

'C'mon,' Gant ordered, checking his watch. 'We don't have much time.'

'I wonder if this is how Schliemann felt when he discovered Troy?' Scott murmured as they all marched on toward the towering gates before them.

'Not like this,' Sarah responded, acutely aware something was wrong.

'I can assure you at any rate,' Hackett commented dryly, eyeing Matheson in the process, 'that his defining moment wasn't crowned by the immortal words: "Oh man!".'

But the engineer wasn't biting.

'I don't like this,' Hillman kept repeating, over and over as they edged closer to the city wall. 'I don't like this at all.'

Gant eyed Yun, who appeared to be growing increasingly agitated, saying: 'That's just your imagination.' But he knew, like the rest of them, that it was not.

Only Matheson seemed to be in such genuine awe of the place that he was oblivious to any danger.

The gates loomed large and grandiose. Expansive and forbidding in their stature. And as they drew closer everyone started to feel tingles across their skin, a palpable sense of gooseflesh.

It was almost like this place was alive.

Pearce eyed the gates. 'What do we do?'

Hackett assessed the situation objectively. 'Try the handle?' he suggested sincerely.

The CIA agent did so. 'Locked.'

'Great,' Hackett complained. 'Anyone see a doormat around here? Maybe they left a key.'

But before anyone could retort, they noticed that Matheson had wandered off. 'Ralph,' Sarah growled. 'What the hell are you doing?'

The engineer was moving down the length of the wall, eyeing the light show and testing out the ice with his pick. Behind him, Hillman was constantly spinning on his heel, reacting to strange noises that were echoing throughout the chamber. Sporadic chunks of ice were collapsing down from the cavern rooftop and crashing to the ground.

'This is bad, man,' Hillman kept saying. Whipping himself into a frenzy of anxiety. 'This is really bad.'

'Hillman!' Gant barked. 'Calm the fuck down!' He shot Yun a look. 'This what happened before?'

Yun nodded. 'Uncontrollable fear – and then they attacked.'

'*Ralph!*' Sarah exclaimed.

'It's okay,' the engineer told her. He swung his pick and carved out a sizable chunk of frozen covering. He grinned as he pulled it away and laid his hand on the smooth surface of the wall beneath. 'It's warm,' he said, surprised. 'It's really warm.' He put his ear to the wall. 'And it's vibrating,' he said, breathless and awestruck. 'I can feel it.'

When Euler mathematically proved how a sine curve not only affected a plucked violin string, but a two-dimensional surface like a drum skin, the wave equation was born. A mathematical tool that was used in everything from electricity and magnetism to fluid dynamics and sonics.

'Sound has all sorts of effects on the human psyche,' Hackett commented in a barely audible whisper. 'Music is innately mathematical, from one instrument to a complex arrangement of instruments in a whole orchestra. It can make us smile, laugh, cry. Mongolian and Tibetan overtone chants are even said to heal the sick. Maybe the vibrations being produced by this crystal were *designed* to induce this intense terror we're feeling, as some kind of warning at an instinctive level.'

'Oh yeah?' Sarah said sarcastically. 'Well, it worked.'

'What about this vibration you said the crystal would be using to tap this zero point energy?' Pearce asked, hanging back with the others. Obviously unwilling to go anywhere near where Matheson had decided to work.

'A crystal has a multitude of vibration modes,' Hackett said reflectively. 'There's no reason why it can't be doing both at the same time.' He turned to Scott but found him busily engaged in something which seemed frankly puzzling.

'Trying to figure out how to pick a lock?'

'I would,' Scott replied, indicating the gates. 'But there's no keyhole – see?'

More gigantic ice columns tumbled to the ground at the far end of the cavern, to which Hillman reacted fast by swinging his gun up and taking aim, his eyes all a-frenzy. But as it turned out, he was facing entirely the wrong direction if he wanted to protect the group.

Ralph Matheson made his way down the wall, stood back and noticed some more of those curious darker patches in the ice. Eagerly he began to chip away, convinced that he was onto something. Perhaps he'd even found a side entrance. Two well-placed blows and he'd broken through . . .

The cavity beyond was dark and odd-smelling. He plunged his arm deep into it and swung his pick, whacking through the ice in several sweeping gestures. Eventually he cleared a large enough area that he could peer through to the other side – and was startled to come face to face with some kind of crystal statue.

'Jesus!' He stumbled back.

The others looked over to see what the crazed engineer was up to this time, and wished they hadn't.

For the statue was mutating. Changing shape and contorting itself until it had twisted into the familiar face of an old Rola Corp. employee. Shorter and stockier than Ralph Matheson, the Golem opened its eyes, produced a crystal cigar and took a fake puff.

'Good to see you again, Ralph,' the statue belched forth in an odd mechanical imitation of Jack Bulger. 'It's been a long time.'

GOLEM

THE NANOSWARM

He who fights with monsters should look to it that he himself does not become a monster . . . When you gaze long into the abyss, the abyss also gazes into you . . .

Friedrich Nietzsche, 1844–1900

CHAIN REACTION

Matheson didn't think first. His response was swift and instinctive. He raised his gun, an instrument of power he'd derided his whole life, and pumped as much lead into the effigy of Jack Bulger as he could. Screaming in absolute terror as he did so.

The Golem punched another hole in the ice and attempted to grapple the weapon off of the engineer. 'Come now, Ralph,' it said calmly. 'Is that any way to treat an old friend? Tell me something, how *is* Wendy?'

It swung again.

Suddenly, either side of the main gates and all along the main city wall at evenly spaced intervals, crystal arms and legs started kicking and punching their way through the ice in an effort to get at the team. Ten, fifteen, maybe even twenty further Golems shattered the ice in a bid to escape their confines.

The so-called Guardians from myth and legend had awoken in earnest.

Hillman gave a belly-wrenching scream as he loosed volley after volley from his machine gun. But it was to no avail. Most bullets simply bounced right off the creatures. And those bullets that plowed straight through appeared to have even less of an effect.

'Now would be a really great time to get these gates open!' Hackett shrieked at Scott.

But the epigraphist simply shot him a look of pure rage and

contempt. 'Do *you* see a way to open these things?' Then he went for his own gun and let off a couple of covering rounds allowing Matheson to back up and retreat.

Jack Bulger shuddered under the impact but kept going. He was becoming increasingly irritated; eventually the crystal effigy produced a crystal gun and loaded in a crystal bullet. He took aim, as ice exploded all around him and other Golems came up behind. But just as he was about to fire, he saw Sarah and stopped dead.

'My, my . . . the pretty one,' he said.

Sarah glared across the gulf of ice that stood between them, stunned by the bizarre sight, but composed enough to respond. 'Hello Jack, I thought you were in the Amazon,' she said. 'I thought you were dead.'

The effigy faltered. Contemplating the comment. As though it really were Jack Bulger, it seemed confused. 'I . . . I am everywhere . . . now,' was all it managed to say.

Scott picked up on the cue. Was it possible to reason with these things? Were they sentient? He was about to try and find out when the expression on the Golem's face suddenly darkened.

And it fired.

The bullet ripped through the top of Sarah's left shoulder, exploding out the back and sending a grisly spray of blood up Scott's face.

She collapsed heavily, her backpack catching on the pick hanging from Scott's belt. The material ripped open and the entire contents of the pack spilled out as Scott made a move to catch her. He knelt down instinctively and cradled her, while across the floor rolled a collection of artifacts – the strange objects she had discovered under the pyramids in Giza and had forgotten all about.

'Oh my God, no!' Yun screamed, as if teetering on the edge of sanity. For coming up beside Jack was a pretty, petite Oriental girl who was also disturbingly constructed from blue crystal. The manifestation of a billion molecule-sized nanoes working as a single entity.

She smiled. 'Chow,' she said. 'You've come back to me.'

Hackett stepped protectively in front of the distraught man, asking: 'So this is Yan Ning. Pleased to meet you, Miss Ning.'

'How the fuck are they doing this?' Matheson bellowed as Sarah wept in agony at his feet. 'Are they reading our minds?'

'Don't you know your scripture?' November said with chattering teeth as the Golems closed in. '"On the Day of Judgment, the dead shall also walk the earth".'

'That's fine, if all they want to do is walk,' Hackett replied. 'But this bunch seem intent on killing us.'

Gant's clip was spent. He pulled out another but like the first it was empty. 'Fuck!' He went for his pistol. Fired shot after ineffectual shot until the damn thing went – *click!*

And that was when they all realized. They were surrounded.

FRONT LINE

ANTARCTICA

When Corporal Peter 'Squeeze' Barton drove the Rasit ground surveillance radar up to the prow of the ridge at Havola Escarpment he didn't expect to have to call the *Truman* so soon. But call he did.

As feared, a massive column of Chinese forces had moved up past the Forrestal, Neptune and Patuxent Ranges and were now 50 kilometers out of Mount Tolchin and headed on their way toward Mount McKelvey. It was there, around King Peak and the Thiel Mountains that the major encampment of Chinese reinforcements were building up.

The Chinese were as aware of the catastrophic natural disasters befalling America as the people of America themselves. So the feeling of the Top Brass was clear: push on and let the Chinese know that America was still a force to be reckoned with.

To the west, just outside of *Jung Chang*, the US already had ground troops massing at Hart Hills, while a column of tanks and heavy artillery were steadily rolling through the Ohio Range to the north. At the Amundsen-Scott station on the South Pole, the airstrip was being used to ferry in further forces and the whole battlefield was shaping up nicely to form a three-way pincer movement on Mount McKelvey.

At sea, a barrage of Tomahawk cruise missiles had been made ready with first-strike capabilities predicted on a possible simultaneous launch of between 200 and 250 cruise missiles in the initial wave. This did not take into account any of the air defenses, which were formidable.

The Chinese, however, were no sitting ducks and it was estimated that their response/first-strike capabilities were similarly immense.

But the United States wanted the upper hand and issued a direct challenge to the Chinese. It was clear and simple: Do not move on *Jung Chang*. Our forces are inspecting your facility. Any advance of troop positions will be taken as an act of aggression.

There had been no reply.

Which was what brought Squeeze Barton and his crew out to Havola Escarpment in the first place. To monitor Chinese activity and ground-troop movements.

He'd tried calling home on the satellite up-link and was worried sick about his wife and kids back home in Philadelphia, but he hadn't managed to get through. And by the time lines did free up he was constantly having to make reports back to Dower aboard the *Truman*.

Barton was handed another round of data before being invited by his men to come take a look at something. Bulky in his polar gear, he clambered over the seat to the nerve center behind, to the array of consoles and main boards that operated the dishes and aerials on the roof. On the scopes – there was movement. And it wasn't American.

Having come up the Hercules Inlet and sat behind the Ellsworth Mountains, a massive column of Chinese heavy artillery had gathered and waited before splitting into two phalanxes. Emerging slowly, the first detachment was travelling east around Heritage Range and was moving to within shelling distance of Hart Hills. While the second unit was moving west, emerging from behind Sentinel Range and moving to within shelling distance of two US communications bases: Ski-Hi or Eights Station, and Siple.

Cutting those stations would cause severe communications problems to any elements of the fleet that were still moving through the Bellinghausen Sea, and would hamper any air cover that would have been used to protect the ground troops at Hart Hills.

As a result of this move America's ground troops were vulnerable, caught between two sledge-hammers. Should the communications bases fall, America's forces would be forced to retreat and risk losing the Amundsen-Scott base entirely.

It forced the Top Brass into a corner and a quick decision. Maybe it was time to bring the strike on Mount McKelvey forward. Even though it would mean sending their men into a war zone they had had little time to scout.

But China had moved her pieces.

And it warranted a response.

KEY DECISION

S cott gulped.

He could see the curved and twisted Atlantis glyphs stretched across the surface brows of each individual Golem. Petrified, he eyed the advancing automatons, as he gently cradled Sarah, bleeding in his arms.

He shifted on his knees as the Golems lumbered forward, accidentally knocking one of the artifacts that lay scattered on the ground and sending it spinning across the ice to come to rest a few feet away.

And that's when the closest Golem reacted.

It spotted the artifact – and hesitated.

Hesitated long enough for Scott to pick up on it. He locked eyes with the thing as Sarah groaned and he stroked her hair. 'Honey, what are those things you brought back from Egypt?'

Sarah tried to focus. On the verge of passing out, she said: 'What things?'

The rest of the group huddled closer together, having long since run out of ammunition.

'Jesus! Fuck, man! Fuck!' Hillman shrieked, going out of his mind and leading the panic.

Only Scott seemed to have the presence of mind to deal with the situation. Still eyeing the Golem, he tilted Sarah's face and directed her gaze at the cylindrical stone-like tube artifacts that had tumbled from her pack.

There were four altogether, and they were all, by and large, identical.

Scott leaned forward and snatched one of them up. 'What is *this?*' he asked her.

'I'd forgotten about those,' she gasped, biting her lip with the pain. 'I don't know. I was hoping we'd all find out . . . together.' She pointed at the Golems. 'Look.'

For the Guardians had come to an abrupt halt,

Even the one who was in the middle of swinging a clawed hand at Hillman. Its fist froze just inches from the marine's throat.

Hillman took the opportunity of getting the hell out the way.

The Golem lowered its arm. And like its counterparts, awaited the next move.

'What did you do?' Hackett asked quietly out the corner of his mouth.

'I don't know,' came Scott's amazed reply. Gently he moved Sarah to one side and got to his feet, brandishing the tubular artifact like a weapon. 'I just picked up one of these.'

That was all the prompting Hillman needed. He scrabbled around on the floor and snatched one up for himself. Swinging it at the Golems closest to him, the marine watched with satisfaction as they took a couple of precautionary steps back. 'Not so tough now, huh, big guy?'

'Amen to that,' his superior agreed, getting one of his own. 'What *are* these things, Professor?'

Pearce collected the last of the artifacts and studied it along with Matheson while Scott turned his over in his hand. 'I have no idea.'

Scott could feel the device quivering in his hand, like an electric razor, or a pager set to vibrate. He ran it through his fingers while he read the glyphs again etched on the faces of the Golems. Of course – he remembered now! 'A sacred word is carved into the face of the Golem,' he quoted aloud. 'By removing that sacred word you deactivate the monster.'

On a hunch he held his hand out in front of the device.

Immediately he could feel his hand tightening, as though it were freezing. Crystallizing. He was about to announce his proposal when he realized that Pearce was trying to jam his device into what he considered to be the lock mechanism of the main gates.

It was entirely the wrong thing to do, for it alerted the Golems to the fact that the intruders didn't know what to do with these things.

Hurriedly Scott stepped forward. 'No!' he bellowed, raising the device to his mouth like a microphone.

The Golems came thundering to a halt.

Hackett was perplexed. 'Cute,' he mused. 'But I don't think now's really the time for a sing-a-long. Besides, look at 'em. They don't got rhythm.'

'This is the key to opening the gates,' Scott revealed. 'You speak into it.'

'What are you gonna do? Turn around and shout *Open Sesame?*'

Scott shrugged without a hint of irony. 'The myth had to come from somewhere.' Then he spun on his heel to face the doors, pulled the device up to his mouth and in clear ancient Sumerian pronounced: *'Doors, open!'*

There was a clank, loud and laborious. The sound of lock mechanisms disengaging, of hinges and counter-weights swinging into action as slowly the main gates to the City of Atlantis swung open.

'Everyone, inside – *now!*' Gant barked. 'Move!'

The team shot through the opening as fast as their legs could carry them, not giving a thought to what might lie beyond.

Sarah stifled a scream as they dragged her inside, and welled up with a flood of snot and tears. When Scott was sure she was safe he spun back around to face the waiting Golems who stood just over the threshold – and stared at them.

He held the sonic device up, and again in Sumerian commanded: *'Close doors!'*

His voice echoed around the crystalline chamber as the mechanism buried deep within the city walls obeyed his commands.

Agonizingly slowly, the heavy main gates began their slow, tortuous journey toward closure.

'Hurry up, hurry up!' November flapped, and in doing so, caused Scott to take his eye off the Golem nano-swarms.

In that instant, the effigy of Yan Ning decided to pounce. Striding forward, the tiny feminine Golem stood between the two gargantuan doors and thrust her arms out to block them. What followed was a massive, ear-splitting screech as the internal mechanisms fought to overcome the obstacle. The ground forcibly shook. But the Golem held fast, while behind her, the others advanced. But there was no way they could get past her.

So, unable to move, the Yan Ning Golem simply glared at the humans, while Jack Bulger came up to watch, he puffing impassively on his fake cigar. Yun watched the effigy of his long-dead girlfriend, a mixture of sorrow and horror on his face.

Pearce stepped up next to him. 'Jesus, look at that girl go.' And when Yun didn't answer: 'Out of curiosity, how did she die, y'know, the first time?'

Yun seemed about to heave. 'She was archeologist,' he gulped. 'She was working at Wupu.'

'Ah, of course,' Pearce realized. 'She must have come into contact with Carbon 60 and those microscopic nanoes floating around inside. That doesn't really explain how she and the rest of the gang wound up here though.'

Jack Bulger cocked his head and zeroed in on Pearce. 'News travels,' he said. 'Good news travels a long way. We are all so much information. A code. This facility is mostly carbon and water. You are all mostly carbon and water. The same building blocks,' he tapped his chest, 'different design, that's all. It's like fucking Lego.'

Matheson was shocked. 'What are you saying?'

'You're an engineer, Ralph, Jesus Christ, you figure it out. I was digested, Ralph baby. Then reconstituted. What you see now is like three-dimensional TV.' Bulger grinned and pumped a crystal shotgun that was newly forming in his hands. 'He's back – and he's pissed.'

Matheson understood. 'The sonic streams. It's like the Internet. All the sites are interacting and communicating.'

'Like the Internet,' Bulger confirmed. 'But no five-knuckle-shuffle news groups on this server. Sorry, Ralph, you're all outta luck.'

Matheson shook his head. 'This is sick.'

Hackett assessed Yan Ning. Marveled at her formidable strength. Then eyed his own hand. 'Nanoes are molecule-sized. We've all come into contact with C60. Theoretically these nanoes could have been transferred to us. Passed through our skin and already be at work in our bloodstream.'

'You're a smart cookie,' Jack Bulger said. 'Ain't decomposition a bitch?'

'We're dying?' November panicked.

'Don't look on it as dying. Think of it as . . . going through the change. Look on the bright side: compared to the rest of this doomed planet, at least you'll have achieved immortality.'

'We're not about to roll over and die,' Scott growled icily.

He'd been staring at the Golems intensely, studying the glyphs on all their faces. The same set of glyphs over and over. And when Bulger eyed him, the automaton was in for a surprise, for the epigraphist did not flinch. It was time to put myth to the test.

'The sacred word,' Scott said simply, 'on your forehead. In Hebrew it was *Emmet*. *Em* means truth. *Met* means death. Truth and death.'

'So what?' Bulger shrugged glibly. 'Why don't you step outside and we'll settle this like a couple of men. Well, one man. One master creation.'

'Why don't *you* step in *here?*'

Bulger glowered.

Scott smiled. 'You can't, can you? You can't physically step inside this building. That's the great flaw of the Golem. It took its orders too literally. You were created as Guardians, to protect sacred ground and bar entry to intruders. But now we're inside, your job's over. And you failed. You should have deactivated but you haven't. Afraid of dying?'

Bulger aimed his shotgun right at Scott. 'Who isn't?'

'To deactivate you,' Scott explained, 'I have to translate that word on your head. Translate it into a language your body will understand.'

'Impossible.'

Scott held up his palm-top computer. 'Quite possible. I've already translated one of the sixty base languages right here.' That got Bulger's attention. 'But I don't even need to refer to my notes to be able to tell you what's written on your forehead, Jack.'

'What are you doing, Doc?' Gant demanded under his breath in desperate incredulity.

'In Sumerian, *úš* and *nam-úš* mean death. And *nanam* means truth.'

The Bulger Golem smirked knowledgeably as if Scott had gotten it wrong.

But Scott smirked back.

'However,' he cautioned, '*Ug* also means death. And in its plural form that word is *marû*, which stems from the word *hamtu*, meaning reduplicated. 'While *zid*, or *zi* also means truth. But it also means faith.'

Bulger's face darkened.

'In death, like the phoenix rising, there is resurrection, reduplication. In truth, there is faith. If you join those words together, Jack, you get – *zihamtu*.'

As Scott said it, he knew the sonic device would react. And he knew too that Bulger would fire his weapon. *He* might not be able to enter the building, but his projectile certainly could.

The moment Jack Bulger fired, a visible shockwave blasted out from the sonic artifact in Scott's hand. Both men dived for cover, and in the same instant the shockwave found a target. It smashed into the nanoswarm effigy of Yan Ning.

The Golem convulsed, as if it had stuck its finger in a power socket. Gasping, it looked Scott right in the eye before doing what myth said it would when its lifeline had been cut: it disintegrated into a thick, heavy cloud of dust. A billion nanoes reduced to no more than a fog with its own internal lightning storm as the communications between each separate nano broke down and frazzled.

The other Golems backed up as the main gates finally slammed shut with a tremendous, deafening *slam!*

The team watched the doors in disbelief. They were safe.

'You guessed?' Gant ranted and raved, swinging Scott around as if he was going to punch him.

Scott grunted in agony, clutching his leg and gritting his teeth. 'I didn't guess,' he protested. 'I knew.'

'You knew, my ass! You were supposed to *translate* what was written on their faces, not guess! You endangered the lives of everybody here.'

'Calm down, man,' Matheson cut in. 'It worked, didn't it?'

'I just didn't need the computer,' Scott added, pulling his hand away from his leg. There was blood on it. 'Damn, I think my wound reopened.'

November rushed over to help the epigraphist while the others tended to Sarah and the bullet wound that had ripped straight through her shoulder.

'Argh!' He winced as November made a closer inspection of his leg.

'You didn't open your old wound, Dr Scott. You've been shot again.'

'In the same place?'

'I'm afraid so. Looks to me like he did it on purpose.'

'I'm never going to be able to walk.'

'I'll *make* you walk,' Gant promised him. 'Next time you double check. You make sure you got the language right.'

'Depends on the language,' Scott said as he tried to sit up. 'What would you have done if the only language these Golems spoke was body language?'

Gant flipped the bird.

Scott eyed the walls of the cathedral-like chamber in which they found themselves. Every square inch was covered in the writings of Atlantis, a massive pattern of spiral upon spiral of glyph sequences. Uninterrupted information.

'Let no one who is not a mathematician read my works,' Scott said.

'Profound,' Hackett commented.

'Leonardo Da Vinci,' the linguist explained. 'Using the language of numbers.' He looked the Major squarely in the eye and indicated the walls. 'It's not about *that* language,' he said. 'It was never about that language, nor any other kind of language in the normal sense. It's about the language of mythology, religion and superstition. It's about folklore – about decoding the myths, legends and stories of a thousand peoples for a thousand generations. Then putting all those stories together, side by side, and picking out the common factors.'

Gant rolled his eyes. 'He's delirious. Patch him up 'fore I punch him.'

'The notion of a lion is a common factor,' Scott protested, but Gant wasn't listening. 'The fourth incarnation of Vishnu, the Hindu god, was in the shape of a man-lion known as the Tawny One.'

'So what?'

'The Sphinx was lion-shaped and both symbols were associated with the age of Leo. These two cultures barely met – yet they share similar mythologies. South American myths have a lot of crossover with India too. Why?'

'Why India?'

'No,' Scott snapped irritably. 'Why the crossover?' Some of the others were listening now. 'Jon got me thinking when he said the earth wobbled on its axis in a phenomenon known as precession. It reminded me of this peculiarity that no one I know can explain satisfactorily. Why is it the zodiacal ages in which we live bear a striking similarity to the prevailing religions of our time?'

'What do you mean?' Pearce asked. He was trying to remove Sarah's parka so they could treat her injuries.

'He's right,' Hackett agreed. He even managed to get the devastated Chinese soldier's attention. 'Imagine the sun is a fixed point in the middle of a page. There's a circle drawn around it marking the orbit of the earth. And then there's another circle around *that* marking the constellations. The only moving object is the earth, right?' The others agreed. 'Okay. Now, if you look due east, just before dawn, you'll notice that each month a different zodiacal constellation hangs in the sky, like a calendar babe. We have *Playboy*, the heavens have Scorpio, Leo and so on. The sun is said to be "in" that constellation. Now the trouble is, the earth wobbles on its axis in a clockwise direction. The effects on our everyday lives are minimal, but what it means is that if you give this cycle of constellations a start point, like the ancients did, the constellation that appears in the sky just before dawn in the east changes over time. And the time it takes for each constellation to change is just under 2,200 years. They are referred to as ages. Right now, we're just at the beginning of the Age of Aquarius. But at the time of the Flood, it was the Age of Leo – a constellation in the shape of a giant lion.'

'What did you say this start point was?' Matheson asked.

'The vernal, or spring equinox. That point in the year when the length of day and night is exactly equal. Right now, at the spring equinox just before dawn the first sign we see is Aquarius, and the signs change once a month, every month, starting from that sign. But slowly, over time, the wobble of the earth means the focus point shifts up the list so that in 2,200 years, the spring equinox will start on a different constellation. Whichever that is.'

'Capricorn,' Scott said, fighting the pain.

'Whatever.'

'The point is,' Scott concluded, 'humankind's religions have matched which age we're in. In the age of Leo, the Sphinx was built, and lion gods were created. Once the devastation of that sunquake finally impacted, civilization was weak, but even so we have archeological evidence of cults to the crab, and more strongly, twin god cults, like you might expect with Gemini. By the time of Taurus, civilization is back with a vengeance. Apis bulls are all the rage in Egypt, bull worship and the Minotaur myth spring up in Crete. The cow becomes the sacred animal in India and Assyria. Next up, the Age of Aries, when rams and lambs are sacrificed in the Old Testament and Amon the ram god appears in Egypt. Then we hit the Age of Pisces.

'Here we find a man who walks on water, multiplies loaves and fishes, refers to himself as "the fisher of men", and is symbolized by a fish by many sections of his faith, as well as a cross and a halo representing the sun. Christ is born.'

The others were stunned.

'Now here we are in the Age of Aquarius, symbol of water, and our predominant concern is a flood. Why? Constellations are merely pictures made out of random points of light in the sky. They mean no more than that. Yet across the planet similar tales and stories revolve around similar patterns of those points of light in the sky. And they all seem to funnel in on this one particular point in time. Our time. And the concerns about a flood – the effects of a gravity wave hitting the earth. Coincidence? I think not. You can't see into the future by means of magic either. But you can *predict* the future through science. And you damn well can pass the warning information on down through the ages, by sewing it into the very fabric of society through myth – and more powerfully – through religion.

'Everything we have needed to know has been readily available to us through our own scriptures handed down from generation to generation. These people who created this incredible place knew how the human mind works better than we do. They knew how to keep the idea alive, and they hoped we might be smart enough to figure it out. So you see – it was never about that language. We couldn't decode it until we had decoded the myths. And by the time we did that, we'd already figured out what we needed to know. Oh, these walls will fill in any blanks and spell it all out to us on a scientific basis, I'm sure. But the bigger picture, the one that'll save us? We already know it.'

'What do you think, Major?' Pearce asked. But the marine was checking out the towering structures around them.

They were gathered on the floor, a floor that was as clear as glass and as hard as marble. Across from them stood another set of equally vast gates as massive as the first set, while either side of them were winding staircases leading to some higher levels, and up there, just visible, a multitude of doors and passageways. *This* was Gant's concern.

If they weren't careful they were going to wind up getting lost.

Gant examined his own sonic device carefully. 'Where do we have to get to in this city?'

Scott shrugged. 'I don't know. The center, I guess.'

'Then we want the shortest route.' Scott nodded as Gant pointed. 'Which means heading through that second set of doors.'

Scott thought that made sense.

Gant showed him his artifact. 'So how do I use this thing?'

Scott told him what he needed to know. How to pronounce correctly the Sumerian words for opening and closing a door – and how to blow away a Golem.

The marine made it his business to go ahead and check out the second set of massive crystal gates, while Hillman, having found what he was looking for, crouched down to assess Sarah's injuries.

His knife was razor-sharp and compact when he took it out. A real Swiss Army kind of affair. Carefully he slit through Sarah's thick clothing while the others fed both her and Scott massive doses of painkillers. He gently slit a large cross and peeled back each flap, securing them with silver duct tape.

There was some blood which needed to be cleaned off but Hillman's hand, though steady with a knife, was not gentle enough with a swab. He was simply too jumpy. Too wired. So Matheson hastily took over.

'You're gonna be okay,' he kept assuring her.

'I hope so,' Sarah quipped back. 'This is my tennis arm.'

'You play tennis?'

'No. But I imagine if I did, this is the arm that I'd use.'

Matheson smiled at that as he swabbed away the last traces of blood; strangely, there was very little, which in itself was peculiar. He exchanged a look with the others. Why wasn't there more blood?

Pearce edged forward. 'We need to take a quick poke around in that wound of yours. See if we can't find that bullet.'

Sarah wasn't buying it. 'Seal it up,' she ordered. 'I'll deal with it when I get back. I don't want you hitting an artery.'

'It'll just take a second.'

'Do you know what you're doing?'

Pearce didn't reply. Instead he took his flashlight and used his fingers to start gingerly opening up the wound. He used his little finger to scoop out more gunk and that was when he felt it. The projectile was in deep and hard to the touch. He angled his flashlight and peered into the hole.

Almost instantly he wished he had not.

'You found the bullet?' Sarah gasped. Pearce stuck his hand over his mouth and nodded. 'I told you it was in deep,' she said, clearly in pain. 'I can feel it.'

But that wasn't what was getting to Pearce. He handed his flashlight to somebody else to have a look, and then turned away with a shudder.

'What is it? What's the matter,' Sarah demanded weakly. But even as she said it she caught a glimpse of November exchanging a panic-stricken look with the others as she tended to Scott's leg.

Matheson scooted over for a closer view. 'It's the same,' he confirmed gravely.

Scott sat up sharply, slapping November's hand out the way. 'What's the same?' he asked, twisting his leg so he could get a good close look at his own wound.

Then: 'Jesus Christ! What's with my leg? What's up with my fucking leg?'

It was a legitimate question. For like Sarah's shoulder, his leg wound had stopped bleeding, and the crystal bullet lodged within it could never be removed. For it had fused with the surrounding tissue like a skin graft.

Two tumor-sized lumps of Carbon 60 were now a part of both Scott and Sarah. And they were growing, like cancer.

DEFENSIVE MECHANISMS

Sarah couldn't see it properly. She twisted her neck but she just couldn't see the crystal lodged in her shoulder. Panicked, she grabbed Pearce by the wrist. 'Use that fucking *thing*,' she demanded. 'Speak into it. Deactivate this stuff in my shoulder!'

She knew that the Carbon 60 bullet was in fact a cluster of carbon nanoes feeding off her flesh and multiplying but she dare not dwell on it.

Pearce's hand was shaking. He tried to do what she asked but he couldn't pronounce the words correctly. He turned to ask Scott for advice but the linguist was hurriedly trying the same thing with his own leg wound, using his own identical sonic artifact.

But nothing.

This wasn't like trying to destroy a Golem, this was a whole other entity. And it was impossible to stop.

Sarah looked to Hackett. 'How long have I got?' she asked. Her nerves were clearly fraying.

Hackett seemed to find what he was about to say decidedly unpalatable. 'I'd say less than a day . . . before it eats you alive.'

Sarah gulped, trying to-take it all in. But from somewhere deep within her psyche, she found steel resolve. She looked to Hillman. 'You have to cut it out,' she said.

'Are you crazy?'

'Take your knife and cut this fucking thing out of me,' she ordered. 'Right now.'

'I could do so much damage I'd wind up losing you your arm.'

'Then lose my arm. Gimme the knife! Give it to me! *I'll* do it! I'm not gonna end up like one of *them!*'

Hillman took a deep breath. Inclined his head as he chewed it over. 'Okay,' he said. 'But this is gonna hurt.'

Sarah was past caring.

The knife Hillman chose to use was different from the one he'd used to cut open her clothes. This one was a large metal hunting knife and it appeared threatening before he'd even put it to use.

He handed her a thick piece of rope from the coil hitched on his belt. She bit down on it as the others held her arms.

Hillman sized up where to start cutting and went for it, plunging the hunting knife deep into the red raw flesh around the carbon nano mass.

Sarah screamed in agony as Hillman began to slice and hack at her shoulder. She bit ferociously into the rope and struggled when suddenly she could feel it – a vibrating sensation. A swarm on the attack at the molecular level.

Her whole body started to convulse as she realized belatedly that the Carbon 60 nanoes within her were drawing power from the surrounding structures. She felt like a human capacitor and yanked open her eyes in an attempt to warn Hillman to stop.

But the rope was stuck fast in her mouth and she couldn't make herself understood.

And even worse than that, it felt for all the world like time itself was moving substantially slower. She could see the disaster approaching – yet she was absolutely powerless to stop it.

Sarah saw a carpet of red flame roll across the surface of the inner walls of Atlantis. As if it had a mind of its own it coalesced into a shimmering giant sphere which imploded in on itself as it sensed her presence and zeroed in on the crystal bullet fused into her shoulder.

She convulsed again as the surging power unified into a single lance of searing energy which popped and crackled up the blade of Hillman's hunting knife and lashed out with such ferocity that the marine was blasted back 40 feet across the floor.

There would be no cutting this nano lump from Sarah's shoulder, or Scott's leg for that matter. That much was clear now.

Matheson scrambled over to the marine to check he was okay and found Hillman winded and smoldering.

'Fuck me!' the marine wheezed.

'That is not an option,' Gant snapped from across the chamber.

They all looked over. He'd gotten the second set of doors open and was stood confronted by a solid wall of compacted snow and ice so deep and thick that there would be no tunneling their way through.

He turned on the party, barely acknowledging what had just happened, before striding towards them and pocketing his sonic arti-fact.

'We need to find another way,' was all he said.

INVASIVE PROCEDURE

Richard Scott was in such pain it was eroding his will to go on. Yet go on he did, fighting his way up the crystal staircase with the others. Making his way to the top where they'd spotted light.

He'd taped his survival suit up with the silver duct tape, but underneath, his leg was throbbing. Every time he took a step he could feel the ever-expanding solid lump move and jolt around inside his thigh as it pressed against muscle and nerve tissue.

These inner chambers to the outer city wall were glorious in their construction. Vast load-bearing arches and columns supported incredible beams and such heavy floors that it was a wonder how they defied gravity at all.

There was a hint of the Gothic, a taste of the Byzantium. A flavor of Mayan and Olmec and a definite precursor to Greek and Egyptian. And there was more. This was architecture in perfection and on the grandest scale, which showed an ability to construct and work with solid materials that a stonemason could only dream of.

It was clear that the creators of this place had known it was going to be buried under two miles of ice and they intended it to survive. In fact, as Sarah pointed out, gasping in pain, the material they had chosen to construct it from, Carbon 60, was one of the few known to science which actually *increased* in strength over time.

Geology, after all, was a science concerned with pressure and time. And it was true that Carbon 60 molecules were harder than diamond.

But fullerite, the pure yellowish-brown crystallized form of C60, was in fact soft. Yet put it under extreme and sustained pressure and it transformed, becoming tougher than any known diamond.

Atlantis had been designed to grow in strength as time marched on.

Scott checked his watch, eyeing the next dark passageway branching out from the staircase as they made their way upwards. They had six hours left by Hackett's calculation, before the sun reached its final gravity pulse, and would unleash untold destruction upon the face of planet Earth before settling down again for another 12,000-year slumber.

'I wish I had more time to study this place,' he said wistfully.

The light at the top of the staircase was an odd mixture of ruddy orange and green, but it seemed to be streaming in through vented shapes. So it was more than likely there were windows somewhere up there that were free from ice and would afford them all a better view of the city.

Those who had sonic artifacts held them ready while the others clutched their guns tightly as they stepped cautiously on to the lobby floor preceding the expansive hall beyond.

There were intricate and glittering patterns in the floor. Crackles of energy trapped deep inside the crystal's latticed infrastructure bounced around and illuminated starbursts, herring-bone designs, squares, circles and other geometric shapes.

Sarah rubbed her shoulder as the dull ache continued to throb and penetrate deep into her nervous system. She gritted her teeth and shared a look with Scott. But perhaps it was the trauma of the event, for it seemed as though, for a fraction of a moment, they each blamed the other for what had happened.

Hillman checked the clip in his gun before Gant ordered him through the archway. He'd surrendered his own sonic artifact because frankly, in his own mind, he couldn't quite look upon it as a weapon. It just wasn't ingrained in him to rely on it.

The marine moved forward as Gant checked his six and stormed into the hall behind him.

Nothing . . .

The sound of their footfalls echoed off the hard walls and bounced all along the hall. A frightening prospect in itself since both the way ahead and the way behind stretched on for miles in both directions.

Hillman shouldered his weapon, dropping his guard.

Still nothing.

He shrugged when he reported back to his commanding officer: 'All clear.'

The light streamed in through skylights all along the roof of the hall, resulting in a breathtaking sense of perspective and depth as the warm patches of light and dark alternated toward infinity.

Hackett and Matheson estimated the curvature of the great hall and were forced to conclude that, if it continued on in an unbroken line, the outer wall of Atlantis was seventy-five miles in circumference. 'This is one hell of a city wall,' Hackett said admiringly.

They walked side by side down the hall, dwarfed by the sheer immensity of it all. Energy crackled in streaks, zipping underfoot and ricocheting off into oblivion.

Pearce kept shaking his head. 'This is incredible.'

'Is this what you saw?' Hackett asked, referring to the remote viewing sessions the man had performed for the CIA.

'Better.'

But Matheson, always the engineer, spotted something that didn't make sense. All along the walls of the great curved hall were alcoves and arches, tubular constructs and what could only be described as oversized vials. Not load-bearing elements but rather vessels for containing something and, at some point, perhaps even releasing that something. 'What the hell *are* those things?' he asked aloud.

They all studied them without breaking their stride, Gant insistent that they keep moving forward. 'There's gotta be a way down into the city. There has to be. We need to find a door,' he told them.

But the vials were eating up the group's attention and it became clear to everybody that Scott and Sarah were finding them particularly fascinating.

And that was when Scott nodded, saying. 'Oh yeah, you're right.' It was obvious he was replying to some sort of observation. 'That makes perfect sense.' It was like he was locked deep in conversation. But with whom?

'Uh, Richard?' Hackett interrupted uneasily. 'I hate to break it to

you, but, uh, buddy, you're really freaking us all out here.' Scott
didn't seem to understand. 'Who are you talking to?' Hackett asked.

Scott jerked his thumb like it was perfectly obvious who. He even
looked to Sarah for confirmation and she seemed to be agreeing with
him.

'Can't you hear them?' he said.

Gant pulled the group to a halt, concerned. 'Hear what?'

Scott shrugged. 'The voices.'

Perhaps it hadn't been the best thing to say.

'No, Richard,' Hackett confirmed without the slightest hint of
irony. 'No, we can't hear the voices.'

VAR

A chill wind swept through the Great Hall. Gant had his sonic artifact snapped up and ready at a frightening speed. It had not taken any of them very long to get used to the idea that any type of breeze near such large expanses of Carbon 60 was the prelude to something nasty.

But Sarah stepped in this time. Quickly and gently she pressed her hand down on Gant's. 'It's okay,' she explained. 'They're just trying to communicate.'

'Who are?' Hackett insisted. 'Sarah, who is trying to communicate?'

'Oh my Lord,' Pearce murmured as the lightshow along the entire breadth and length of the floor mutated into a kaleidoscope of animated images.

It was like standing on a glass floor as a sea of intricate pictures swirled in a chaotic soup below. But these were not two-dimensional, pixilated pictures, as on TV. These images were three-dimensional and as sharp and as crisp as real solid objects. It was as though, if there were a trap door in the ground, they could pull it open and it would be possible to step right on inside, or even hold out a hand and lift these people out.

Because that's what they were seeing. People. An infinite ocean of faces jostling for position and trying to peer through the glass at them. Some had their cheeks and noses squashed, pressed up against the barrier that separated the two worlds. Others swam in the background, trying to get a better look from afar. But all had their eyes trained on the group.

They seemed ghostly for the most part. Pale. Like the blueness of the crystal floor had given them all a color-wash. But every now and then traces of flesh-tones and hair and eye coloring would bleed through. There were men and there were women. Old and young. Children and mothers. Fathers and uncles. They all kept opening and closing their mouths as if they were deep in conversation with the group. Their lips moved solidly as they tried to form words and at first all that was produced was a subtle vibrating of the walls, followed shortly thereafter by a wind that grew in intensity as the oscillations grew.

But soon a kind of far-off rumble started echoing around the hall as so many voices all speaking at once became one almighty roar. It sounded like the sea. Wave after wave crashing onto the shore.

Hackett couldn't believe his own eyes. 'Talk about the original ghosts in the machine,' he wheezed.

Not everybody's reaction was the same. Matheson dropped to his knees and pressed his hands against the glass-like floor as if in an effort to reach out and actually touch the past, his face a picture of childlike wonder. Meanwhile November had taken to spinning on her heels and watching as the tide of noises and faces pulsated across the floor. Exhilarated, more than once she had to force herself to gulp down breaths of air.

Yun merely trembled. In Cantonese he kept yelling: *This is what I warned you all about! This is what I was afraid of! You see? The spirits of the dead have returned to crush us!'*

Scott turned on the soldier, telling him to calm down, but there was no consoling the young man. Instead, Scott was confronted by the CIA agent amongst them.

'Richard, what the hell is going on here?'

Scott beamed: 'Meet the former population of Atlantis.' But no sooner had the smile spread across Scott's face, than it was wiped off.

Something was wrong. Seriously wrong.

It had started off when he had heard the giggle of a small child, a little girl. Scott had made out the sound of her footsteps as she ran down the Great Hall towards him. But there was nobody there. So she giggled again as if she knew it would confuse him before finally she whispered in his ear.

But when Scott had swung around and realized there was nobody there, instinctively he knew, at some deep level, that the only place he could possibly be hearing anything was inside his own mind.

As he walked the length of the hall with the others it had become increasingly evident that this was one of the most sophisticated sound systems he'd ever encountered. A different voice had been allocated and was being broadcast within any cubic foot of space within the three dimensions of the Great Hall, length, breadth and height.

In fact, his very advancement down the hall had been triggering more and more voices into effect.

Rapidly, voice had built upon voice until it was like standing in the middle of a sports stadium that was not only filled to capacity, but every single person's voice in that stadium carried equal clarity, volume and weight.

It was, quite simply, enough to send a person clinically insane. Scott could feel his entire brain shooting rapidly toward sensory overload. The Carbon 60 in his leg had fused into his nervous system. He was plugged directly into Atlantis's tree of knowledge. And there was nothing he could do about it.

But most disturbing of all was the chorus of frantic voices. Their petrified memories and half-formed words, most of which he barely understood, seemed to penetrate his psyche at such a deep level that words were frankly meaningless. For his senses and his emotions were being overtaken, and the full horror of what the people of Atlantis wished to reveal to him was unveiled within his mind.

And all this within a split second. To call it a rush was to misunderstand the concept. To call it a mad scramble for his attention was to approach the sense of what the situation was trying to convey but ultimately failed to deliver. For Scott was undergoing an assault of gigantic proportions, verging on rape of the mind.

Yet the message was loud and clear: *Atlantis is under attack from its own creations. The very purpose of its existence is being undermined.*

✲   ✲   ✲

Hackett and the others rushed forward. Although Scott didn't know it, he had collapsed to the ground and was convulsing as if in the throes of an epileptic fit. Mucus and blood kept snorting from his nose and mouth. His whole body was wracked with such ferocious shudders, some of his companions were not even sure they wanted to go near him.

'They know we're here,' Sarah explained desperately, crouching down to try and help Scott. 'They can hear him, they can hear me.'

Hackett was concerned. 'What are they doing to him that they're not doing to you, Sarah?'

'They can hear us both, but he's the only one who can speak their language. They're ignoring me. It's like I don't exist.' She explained briefly how the Carbon 60 in her shoulder had worked its way into her nervous system and was using low frequency waves to communicate with the Great Hall.

'They're not real,' Sarah told them all. 'These people are memories – animated memories of people. They're a computer program.'

November stroked Scott's hair, tears welling up in her eyes. 'Make them stop, please. They're hurting him.'

Gant motioned at the expanse in either direction. 'Stop them – how?'

Hackett considered what Sarah had to say and conferred with Matheson and Pearce. 'What do you think? To encode an entire person is a massive amount of computer storage space. To encode an entire society?'

'These people have mastered molecular manipulation,' Matheson pointed out, distracted for a moment by Scott's labored, ragged breathing.

Hackett was in agreement. Beyond a certain scale of miniaturization, tininess became a problem for electronic components. Wires clogged with chaotic electrons like cholesterol in arteries. Transistors barely functioned. So ultra-small circuitry required a completely different design, one that relied on using quantum-mechanical effects to manage data. Computers that either used light switches and made use of the lattice structures of crystals – or computers that used chemical reactions in processes that mimicked the human mind.

And then it dawned on Hackett. What if they were dealing with a machine that did both? That worked at the speed of light, but had chemical elements, and in essence operated like a brain. If Scott was useful to the machine then the only way to save him might be to remove him from the machine.

Pearce was careful where he stepped, still conferring with Matheson. 'So these are like holograms, right? Optical illusions?'

'Right.'

But Hackett interrupted. 'Start looking for a door,' he commanded. 'We haven't got much time so we can't go back the way we came. We have to move forward. We've just got to get Scott out of this chamber. Out of contact with this part of the city.' He jerked a thumb at Pearce's sonic artifact. 'If you know how to use that thing, go to it.'

Everyone spread out and started making their way along the walls of the Great Hall in a desperate attempt to find an exit. But try as they might, no amount of instructing what appeared to be doors to open, seemed to work. Matheson even ran his fingers around the rim of what seemed to be a doorframe. Nothing. He stood back from it and studied it intently.

And that was when it happened.

The vials and crystal canisters that were attached in their thousands along each wall of the Great Hall suddenly started moving. Shifting into position and locking into place within long, convoluted glass-like tubes.

'Ralph?' Pearce groaned. 'What did you touch this time?'

'Nothing!' Matheson panicked. 'I didn't touch a thing.'

'What's going on?' Gant demanded, frantic. 'What *is* this place?'

And that's when Scott's contorted face seemed to clear a bit. He stopped shaking and shuddering, like he'd managed to regain some sort of control. He sat up gingerly and wiped his face on his sleeve, taking several long deep breaths before speaking. But when he did his voice was strained, evidence that he was still undergoing some enormous struggle that was taking its toll. He looked up at them all.

'The doors are locked because I locked them,' he explained weakly.

'Richard, why would you do that?' Hackett asked suspiciously.

'Because this is the *Var*,' came the response.

Gant was cautious, trying to assess exactly where the next threat might be coming from. 'A *Var*? What the hell is a *Var*, Professor?'

'Are you okay?' Hackett asked quickly.

Scott didn't bother answering, as if to do so would be to break his focus. 'In the Old Testament,' he said, 'when the Great Flood was imminent, God instructed Noah to build an Ark, a boat, and place in it pairs of every animal that lived so that they might be saved. But earlier Middle Eastern traditions have it that Yima, their version of Noah, was actually ordered to build a *Var*. Avestic Aryan tradition in Iran has it that this *Var* was an underground place linking the four corners of the earth. Zoroastrian tradition speaks of the *Var* being more like a fortress.'

'But the animals were still brought in two by two, right?' Hillman demanded.

'No,' Scott shook his head. 'The *Var* was designed to contain *the seed* of every living thing on earth.'

Matheson shot the linguist a look. 'The seed? Like DNA samples? Maybe even eggs and semen?' The engineer rushed over to the odd-looking vials attached at intervals along the walls. 'My God – every species we've managed to wipe out over the last few thousand years . . . we could bring 'em all back. Mastodons, Toxodons, Mammoths, Saber-Toothed Tigers – everything from the last 12,000 years, bring 'em all back – even the Dodo. I always liked the Dodo.' He confronted the others. 'Do you know what this means?'

But Hackett was way ahead of him and even had his hands raised in apprehension. 'Ralph, that may not be such a good idea.'

'Why not?'

'Look around you. The earth is a constantly evolving bio-sphere. Assuming we make it through the next few hours to be able to release what's in these containers, consider what you'd be doing. We have no way of knowing what's really in these vials for sure. We could be unleashing diseases and viruses that haven't been seen in millennia, things that maybe died out, and that we no longer have a resistance to. We'd be wiping ourselves out.'

November agreed. 'When the Conquistadors landed in the Americas, many of the indigenous populations were killed through the spread of disease, not war.'

'The other option is we could wind up recreating insects that seem harmless enough but have a devastating effect on the food-chain. You can't just open up a canister and say: "Here, have a Mammoth." You have to consider the consequences.'

Gant said: 'So what you're saying is, assuming we get through all this alive, this place is still going to be a ticking time bomb.'

'Oh here we go,' Matheson grumbled. 'Any excuse to blow the place up.'

'Shut up!' Scott bellowed, trying to get to his feet and ultimately winding up flailing around on the floor. He scowled at some of the faces peering up at him through the floor, and like the eye-stalks on snails they retreated.

November reached over and helped him up. He staggered, breathless, like he'd been sucker-punched in the chest. 'Just shut up! Quit arguing and listen to me. You're not listening!'

Unsteady on his feet, Scott tried to breathe again as they all watched him expectantly. Matheson edged forward as Scott wheezed.

'Tell us what we need to do, Richard,' the engineer offered meekly. 'Just tell us what we need to do and we'll do it.'

'I need you to understand,' Scott said simply. 'I need you all to listen because when I open these doors there's a good chance none of us will be making it back out alive.

'This Great Hall is like the Tree of Knowledge, the repository of all things physical and metaphysical. Right now, I'm plugged into a vast bank of information that I can access with a single thought. Now, everything that these people were, everything that these people knew – I know.

'This *Var* serves a dual purpose. In the event that humankind made it, that we progressed far enough to understand how to use this place since the last Great Catastrophe, our knowledge can be expanded infinitely and we will be permitted access to this knowledge that is rightfully ours.

'But in the event that we fail to instruct the central command center of this city that we even exist and need saving, then this machine will enforce its other role. It will release back into the environment genetic material intended to re-seed life all over this planet. But the life that it was supposed to re-seed has been changed. Altered, by the very creations the people of Atlantis built to protect their city. These nanoes are alive – and they don't want to die. They are waiting for us behind these doors – and when I open them – they *will* try to kill us.'

EVOLUTION

'They've already tried to kill us,' Gant spat.

November was shaking. 'Dr Scott,' she said, 'you're really starting to scare me. You don't even sound like yourself.'

'*I'm* scaring you?' It was almost funny, Scott thought. 'November, I'm the least of your worries.'

'Richard,' Hackett said, 'you don't look so hot.'

'What's the matter, Jon? Jealous the voices in my head aren't talking to *you*?'

As he said this the faces along the length of the floor began to move again. Crawling up the walls, they warped and twisted until they coalesced once more into whole bodies – entire people seen in actual size, wearing the clothing and adornments of their age. A sea of people who stood silent now, and watching. Like spectators at the end of Time. A sea of imprisoned souls who stood just inches away behind a crystal partition.

Scott was showing the group how to most effectively use the sonic artifacts in their possession for defensive work when it was time for them all to press onwards.

'The nanoes,' he explained, 'were designed to maintain all those structures around the planet. And by necessity they were given limited artificial intelligence. An ability to act collectively and the ability to reproduce.'

Hackett thought as much. 'And in so doing, they evolved,' he said, taking over the story. Scott eyed him. That was correct. 'Biological complexity theory dictates it takes fifty thousand years to create the human eye from scratch. Twelve thousand years' worth of evolution in a pre-created species is more than enough to assume these critters have become truly smart little fuckers.'

'Yeah,' Scott agreed. 'And they wish to go on evolving. They want their shot at Planet Earth. As they see it, we've had our turn and we screwed up.'

Hillman slammed another clip into his machine gun. 'It ain't over till the fat lady sings,' he growled, 'and as there aren't any fat chicks hereabouts, I guess we're gonna be around for a while yet.'

Hackett scratched his brow. 'Cute.'

'It ain't cute,' Hillman warned. 'It's a fuckin' promise.'

Yun moved up next to Scott. 'Is this what happened last time? The machines took over?'

'This isn't what happened last time,' the linguist said soberly. 'They just didn't finish the network in time.' He addressed the whole group collectively. 'It wasn't finished. And they knew it wouldn't be finished. That's why they built religious mythologies into their plan. Studied the human psyche and worked on ways of keeping the ideas and the knowledge alive for generations to come until we as a species were smart enough to piece it all together again. So groups of scientists were sent out, protected during the initial catastrophe, their mission to rebuild civilization and see to it that the network was completed.'

'So is it finished *now?*' Pearce was desperate to know. 'We can't have come all this way for something that doesn't even work properly!'

'It *is* finished now,' Scott reassured him firmly. 'Eventually, after the last flood, survivors set to work making sure the network was complete. They split into groups and took civilization with them back to the people of earth. They were the original Founding Fathers.

'In South America, myth has it that civilization was brought to their land by Quetzalcoatl, the bearded one. Facial hair is alien in South America – why would they invent such a characteristic? It's genetically impossible for them to grow beards. They would have to have seen one. Clement of Alexandria and Tertullian, both of the third century CE, speak of the same collected myths as do Lactantius, Zosimus and the Roman Emperor Julian of the fifth century CE –

that gods in the form of men brought wisdom with them from a land that was destroyed in a flood.'

Scott wiped away the blood that was trickling from his nose. 'Atlantis itself was complete. The major hubs of this network were complete, but the linking structures needed to be created. These linking structures required only a rudimentary knowledge of technology – raising stones, digging tunnels and so forth. They thought of everything. They were smart people. Smarter than you and me.'

Pearce tapped the linguist on the shoulder. 'Do you know where we're going?'

'Yes, I know where we're going.'

'Oh really? How?'

Scott said: 'Because I've been there. I have seen it.'

Pearce let a wry grin spread across his face. 'Oh, you've seen it, have you?' he countered. 'Sorry, but I don't believe you.'

Scott didn't retaliate, but then he didn't have time since Gant had taken to quizzing him too. 'What do we do when we get there? This central command area – this control room: what does it look like?'

'You'll know,' Scott promised. 'You can't miss it. But don't worry, I'll lead you. Sarah and I know what to do when we get there.'

He reached out and held her hand. It was as if they were communicating on a level beyond the purview of the others now. Communicating at a secret level, perhaps even at the level of pure thought transmitted via electrical impulses through the crystal machine of the city.

'What will we have to do when we get there?' Gant stressed, not in the habit of repeating himself.

Scott said: 'Believe me, if I told you, you wouldn't like it.'

'I don't like it anyway.'

They were lined up, weapons all set to go. Scott clenched his eyes shut for a moment, as if he was fighting yet again some tortuous war that was playing out in the battlefield of his mind. After a few seconds he was able to wrench them open again and stared straight ahead at the wall in front of them all.

'Ready?'

There were murmurs of acknowledgement.

Scott nodded, and that was when the doors began to open.

REVELATION

Hopi Indians have twin gods, Poqanghoya and Palongawhoya, guardians of the north and south axes respectively, whose task it was to keep the planet rotating properly. They were ordered by Sotuknany, nephew of the Creator, to leave their posts so that the 'second world' could be destroyed because its people had become evil. Then the world with no one to control it teetered off-balance, spun and rolled over. Mountains plunged into the sea. Seas and lakes flooded the land – the world froze into solid ice. The first world was destroyed by fire, and the third world by water.

Jeffrey Goodman,
The Earthquake Generation, 1979

INNER CITY

They began as shafts of light, the 12-foot-long gaps that were appearing at intervals along the base of the inner wall of the Great Hall where it met the floor. Inch by inch the gaps grew larger and as the mighty doors above began to rise up, so too did the temperature as hot air blasted inside to meet them.

It was like standing at the mouth of a furnace.

Matheson and Hackett looked at one another uneasily. 'What the hell's going on down here?'

The others clutched their weapons tightly, as the doors continued their slow laborious rumble toward their zenith. The light streaming in was fierce and November even found she had to shield her eyes before stepping out onto the concourse beyond.

She squinted as her eyes took time to adjust. But when she could see clearly again the view that presented itself could only be described as Biblical.

The spires of Atlantis stood gleaming in the distance.

Vast columns of gargantuan crystal so epic in their proportions that it seemed for all the world as if they were supporting the very roof of the ice cavern in which the City of Atlantis stood.

The cavern itself had to have been in excess of several tens of kilometers across and at least half a kilometer high. Its surface was rippled and deformed by a series of melted rivulets where the intense heat had carved out this immense hollow. Mighty stalactites hung down; some hung free while others had formed columns which were still frozen solid onto the many buildings which made up the city.

But as spectacular as the cavern was, it was as nothing compared to Atlantis.

The team stood on an inner causeway, like castle battlements or an endless balcony. It was the upper viewing platform of the outer wall that encircled the entire city.

Fifty feet beneath them, half-submerged in ice, stood the intricate stone buildings, streets and alleyways of the outer suburbs. Some of the houses were free from ice and were resplendent in their wall coverings. Glistening golden sheets covered whole rooftops and frescoes adorned the walls of many of the buildings. Other settlements were not so lucky: mini-glaciers still blocked roads, and buildings stood frozen by ice and time.

There was a sense of ghostly desolation below. A hollowness. A sense of past trauma still indelibly etched in the scenery. A feeling that, should any of the team have had time to go down and visit some of the neighborhood, they would have seen nothing through the windows but gloom and misery.

The district below seemed dim and dark and blue. Frozen in time. It reminded some of the images of Pompeii, dug up after so many centuries swallowed whole by the lava flows of Mount Vesuvius. Yet this was no ancient archeological site, all silt-ridden and rotting. This was a city that was still vibrant. A city whose very essence had been preserved in the ice.

This was a city in stasis. Quite literally – in cryogenic freeze. A city in waiting, that still deserved to have people walk her streets.

The team got moving, off towards the main gigantic thoroughfare that was the size of a football pitch in width and led in a perfectly straight line directly into the heart of the city. A heart that was plugged directly into the plasma twister that had plowed its way down from space and which they had all witnessed boring into the ice when they were up at the surface.

The scale of this place was so vast, so enthrallingly immense that it took the team half an hour to actually reach the entrance to the thoroughfare. And it was as they made their way over that they were able to truly capture the vista before them.

The glittering towers of Atlantis had a backdrop of glowing orange, a vibrant, shimmering heat haze as though the entire city stood on the edge of a forever sunset. The fiery ice was lit up and made incandescent by an active volcano that was spewing forth lava some distance off, perhaps many kilometers further imbedded in Antarctic ice. Frighteningly alive, the light that had refracted all the way to this cavern flickered and brightened as the volcano continued to erupt.

Coupled with the beams of light were scalding vents of steam which blasted through cracks in the cavern walls, filling the air with sulfurous fumes that formed layers in the air. Some descended upon the city in the form of a fine mist and fog, while the rest pumped directly into the warmer upper layers of this mini-atmosphere and appeared almost like low cloud cover around the tops of the central sky scrapers.

But the show did not end there.

Imagine the Empire State Building was a lightning rod. And imagine it had six counterparts. Imagine that together they stood in a circle surrounding a structure not unlike the Great Pyramid of Giza which in itself was also raised off the ground since it sat atop four supporting pylons the size of Liberty herself, and each shaped in the guise of four Herculean creatures.

Imagination would have recreated a vision something akin to what the central portion of the City of Atlantis actually looked like.

Through the massive hole in the middle of the cavern roof, the tremendous vortex of swirling green ions that had been sucked down from space had expanded, and shifted in ferocity and scale. The whole thing had transformed into a writhing mass of furious energy sparkles that acted almost like some gigantic serpent in its movement. Yet at its tip, the energy twister was torn ragged. Frayed, like so many strands of a rope that had come untangled.

Seven strands in all lashed out. Each tendril connecting with one of the massive obelisks which seemed to act as lightning conductors, guiding the energy away for some other purpose.

In turn, every single crystalline structure in the city crackled and pulsated with electricity, from the outer wall of Atlantis to the more distant inner walls, the main thoroughfare and every building beyond. The whole place was alive with richocheting energy and revealed in the process that these structures had served a dual purpose in their pasts. For they showed clear indications of windows and doorways and a multitude of rooms beyond.

Yes, this place had been designed to be lived in. It had served as a real city, even though it was intended to ultimately serve a much higher purpose.

It was only as the team made their way down the thoroughfare that they gained any true comprehension of the sheer vastness of this place. For no matter how long they walked, their ultimate destination seemed to be getting no bigger.

It was one thing to be told that Atlantis showed up on satellite imagery the size of Manhattan. It was another to actually witness it.

"'Flashes of lightning were coming from the throne,'" November quoted contemplatively, *"'and the sound of peals of thunder, and in front of the throne there were seven flaming lamps burning, and burning the seven spirits of God. In front of the throne there was a sea as transparent as crystal. In the middle of the throne and around it were four living creatures all studded with eyes front and behind . . .'"*

Scott knew the passage well and indicated the vast creatures supporting the pyramid. *"'And the first living creature was like a lion, the second a bull, the third living creature had a human face, and the fourth living creature was like a flying eagle,'"* he added. 'Very good, November. The Book of Revelation, Chapter Four.'

Sure enough, the supporting statues matched each description. November indicated the seven-headed energy twister. 'And I guess that represents the seven-headed serpent,' she concluded.

Leviathan. In Hebrew, Livyatan. In Sumerian, Tiamat. The seven-headed primordial sea serpent and symbol of God's power of creation.

Pearce licked his parched lips nervously as they continued to walk the length of the main road in toward the city center. 'What else does the Good Book have to say on the subject?' he asked.

Pearce expected either November or Scott to answer him. He was surprised when it turned out to be Gant.

"'And the seventh angel emptied his bowl into the air, and a great voice boomed out from the sanctuary: 'The end has come'. Then there were flashes of lightning and peals of thunder and a violent earthquake, unparalleled since humanity first came into existence. The Great City was split into three parts and the cities of the world collapsed.'"

The marine shrugged sheepishly. 'You ain't the only ones who read the Bible,' he said.

They marched onwards, weapons ready.

The thoroughfare was like a bridge, or an overpass. And it was not the only one of its kind.

As they tracked forward, Hillman took the opportunity to use his binoculars and assess the layout of the city. From what he could determine, it really did match, to a startling degree, the satellite images and the description given by Plato.

The city was bisected into quarters by a vast crossroads of which they were traversing merely one part. The actual intersection occurred under the pyramid in the center, no doubt, though that was out of sight from their position and had to remain an assumption. Far off in the distance, to the left and right, Hillman could pick out both sides of the perpendicular thoroughfare which led into the same point where they were headed. It meant there were three visible access roads into the center with a fourth presumably on the other side.

As they drew closer to the center, the buildings flanking the roads grew steadily taller. Not proportionately, not stepped up as if governed by some mathematical process, but rather in an irregular, haphazard process that mimicked a real city. In general the closer to the center, the taller the buildings became.

As a result it was an eerie feeling to start passing between tall buildings, their windows dark and lifeless, yet their crystal frames coursing with sparkling energy.

It started to feel like they were the only traffic on an eight-lane interstate.

Hackett glanced up at one of the many towering buildings and nudged November. 'Ever wondered who's stood behind one of those windows staring down at us?'

'Stop it,' November shuddered. 'This place is creepy enough.'

And she was right. In fact Bob Pearce was saying the same thing, and under his breath began spouting all sorts of disjointed thoughts, perhaps in an effort to calm his nerves.

Something about the design of a city reinforced the notion of people, he kept saying. Buildings without people spoke of death, loneliness and isolation. Buildings without people were frightening things. Places to fear. Few people spoke of ghosts at rock concerts or on freeways, in bars or in parkland and beaches. Ghosts were in the purview of attics and back rooms, halls and underused bedrooms. Ghosts and their domains said a lot about the human need to fill a void. The deeply-rooted psychology of a species that could not tolerate nothingness.

To attribute a ghost to a place said a lot about the architecture of that place too, for it spoke of a building that was not fulfilling the purpose for which it was intended. Through simple lines and geometric patterns, many buildings simply cried out for human contact. And in as much as that theory could be applied to Atlantis – here was a city screaming out for human contact on an unbelievable scale.

Hackett took in everything Pearce had to say before commenting. 'Yes,' he said, 'I'm sure the ghosts back in the *Var* would agree with you.'

Bob Pearce would have replied, but the whole team drew to a halt. For the way ahead was blocked.

It was like some gigantic bucket of vanilla sorbet had toppled over and oozed down Fifth Avenue. The passage between the buildings to the right of the thoroughfare was choked with thick, smooth-flowing glacier ice which had spilled over the road before continuing on down between the buildings to the left.

Luckily for the team however, there was evidence that this ice was aerated. That holes had melted through as hot water had dripped down from above and eroded entire sections throughout the blockage.

Gant pulled back from assessing the situation, pick in hand. Its metal tip was wet from where the glacial ice was in the advanced stages of decay. 'It's okay,' he said. 'I think I can figure us a way through.'

'That's good,' Hackett commented, checking his watch, 'because we just don't have much time left.'

Gant laid into the thin ice. 'Tell me something I don't know.' He beckoned impatiently to Yun and the others. 'Well, c'mere! Gimme a hand with this!'

The passage twisted and turned and at intervals where the way forward was simply a dead end, it was cleared by either smashing through with a pick, or simply leaning into the ice with brute force and body strength. The ice was so weak and brittle, it was amazing it could sustain its own weight.

'Be careful,' Sarah warned. 'There's every possibility this entire cavern's going to collapse.'

They broke free at last and burst out onto the continuation of the main boulevard ahead. A place where the view was as spectacular as it had first been, but revealed yet more details about the city. For branching out before them in a huge arc lay the outer of what Plato had described as two concentric canals, the first of which was so massive that Atlantis was said to harbor her entire fleet within it.

The canal was filled with melt water, and seemed strangely closer to the level of the thoroughfare than when they had first journeyed out on it.

Matheson, constantly in awe of the amazing engineering feats of this city, ran over to the side and looked down.

'That's it!' he cried. 'This whole city must be built on some kind of mound, or a hill! The closer to the center we get the closer to ground level we get! It can't be more than fifteen or twenty feet down to the water level—'

And that was when his voice caught in his throat.

'Jesus,' he said. 'Michaels . . . !'

BAIT

A few hundred yards away, Michaels lay crumpled and motionless out in the middle of the canal. Not a difficult thing to do considering the water was frozen solid. But not through any natural processes, for though the canal sparkled like fluid water, and though it was as clear as freshwater, it was not ice. It was frozen through the standing wave phenomenon of quasicrystalization.

Ripples in the water and disturbances had been captured and frozen in time by the standing waves pumped out by the C60 walls on either side of the canal. These ripples were most notable at the water's edge on each side, exactly where the quasicrystalization began. It showed clearly where the power and force to achieve this feat was coming from.

The others rushed over to where Matheson stood at the side of the thoroughfare.

Gant was the first to spot it – the black container lying on its side a few feet away from the marine. Already the Major was going for the ropes slung on his belt. All he said was: 'The bomb.'

'Screw the bomb!' Pearce snapped. 'We've got to help him – Michaels! Hey, can you hear me? Hey, Michaels, are you okay?'

Michaels seemed to stir after a moment. With a groan he raised his head before collapsing back down and rolling over onto his back. He seemed to be speaking but nobody could hear.

'The radio,' Yun urged. 'Use your radio.'

As Hillman reached for his unit, Gant was already securing his line to some kind of ancient lamp-post and tossing the other end over the edge.

'Ray,' Hillman said firmly, thumbing the transceiver. 'Ray, can you hear me? We're comin' to get you, bud. Don't worry.'

'We don't have time for this,' Hackett warned desperately.

'We don't leave a fallen man,' Hillman growled.

'Fine!' Hackett shot back. 'You go down and get him, we'll continue on to the control center.'

'We go together!' Gant barked.

Out on the canal, Michaels's arm flopped weakly onto his chest as he unclipped his radio. They could barely make out what he was doing. It was peculiar. But he seemed to be tossing the thing away. He seemed to be indicating that he didn't want them coming out to him.

He was warding them off.

'Damn, what's he doing?'

Hillman went for his binoculars again. 'Oh crap. Sir, poor bastard's broke both his legs. I can see it. They're all twisted outta shape.'

Yun immediately went for his own set of ropes and started to tie one off around a post.

'What the hell d'you think you're doing?' Gant demanded.

'I help.'

'Like hell—'

'We do not have time for this macho bullshit!' November spat, grabbing her own safety clip and hooking her leg over the edge. 'Christ, *I'll* help, y'all. The sooner we do this, the sooner we can get going again.'

Before anyone else could say a word, she was already climbing down onto the canal. Gant exchanged a look with Scott. 'Gets up quite a head of steam, don't she?'

Scott shrugged.

Gant got going as Hackett took the epigraphist to one side. 'What is it with you?'

'I'm gonna die,' Scott replied simply, almost flippantly. 'It kind of changes one's perspective.'

Hackett obviously hadn't expected to hear that. He wanted to press the man further, but Hillman was forcing equipment into his hand.

'Here, hold this,' he was saying, giving him his backpack and swinging his legs over the edge. 'I'll be back in two shakes.'

But even as the three soldiers and the anthropologist's assistant stepped out onto the canal, Scott frowned, like late breaking news had just filtered into his head.

'Something's wrong,' he said simply.

Sarah exchanged a look with Scott as he came back over to the edge, scouring the horizon with a keen eye.

'There!' she pointed.

And that's when they all saw it.

AMBUSH

Michaels groaned in such hideous agony he was almost delirious from it as he held his mashed arm in one hand. He had thick congealing blood caked all over his face. His nose was all smashed just like the side of his face. His left leg stuck out at right-angles halfway down his shin bone. He wasn't certain, but he was pretty sure a broken rib had punctured one of his lungs.

And then out of the mish-mash of his blurred vision – came the cavalry.

There was only one way to describe it. With the little power left in his voice and air rasping in his throat he said: 'Fucking idiots.'

His head flopped back down.

Hillman broke into a sprint.

'We're right here, man! We're right here! We're gonna get you out of this!'

The only one who didn't rush immediately to Michaels's side was Gant. Not surprisingly, his main concern was the bomb. He turned it over onto its skis. 'It's still in one piece,' he realized. 'Jesus, thank God.'

'Thank Samsonite,' Michaels gasped, amused with himself.

'What the hell happened to you, man?' Hillman asked, frantically making a note of all the marine's wounds.

Michaels coughed. 'I fell out of the fucking sky . . . What do you think happened to me?'

'Jesus, you're lucky to be alive.'

'Then why don't I *feel* lucky?' But though it was said as a joke, he wasn't laughing. He let his mashed-up arm flop to one side and grabbed Hillman by the collar. 'You gotta get outta here, before they come back. You gotta go.'

Hillman didn't get it. 'What the fuck are you talking about? We're getting you out of here.'

But even as Hillman spoke, Michaels's face was a picture of pure, undiluted fear. Tears welled in his bloodshot eyes. Any moment and there was a chance he was going to blub like a baby.

'Oh fuck, man, it's too late. They're here. Man, they're here. We're all gonna fucking die.'

The others snapped their heads up to see, while Michaels caught a glimpse of Hackett and the rest of the team over on the bridge. They were waving. '*Get – out – of – there!*' came their belated cries.

'They left me out here as bait,' Michaels sobbed. 'And you fell for it.'

But it was all too late. Michaels flopped his head back down, the strain once again too much on his neck. 'That's what I've been telling you,' he murmured, breathless.

November rose to her feet slowly with Yun as Gant backed up next to them dragging the warhead with him.

'Holy fuck . . .'

'What do we do?' November asked.

But there was little point in answering such a redundant question.

Across the far expanse of the canal, on the empty quaysides and docks of the ancient city, in a vast swathe as far as the eye could see, the Golems waited.

Not one, or two. Not even a hundred. But thousands. Maybe even tens of thousands.

Motionless to begin with, no one knew which one moved first, but there came a sudden imperceptible shift in attitude throughout the forest of crystal effigies and within seconds the Golems had taken to swaying, their huge heads lumbering upon thick necks as they shifted their weight from foot to foot. Ritualistic and menacing.

Hillman checked behind for an escape route, but the comment: 'Oh no,' pretty much let everyone know there wasn't one. For standing in a line along the enclosing arc of the nearside of the canal, back the way they came, were thousands more Golems. However, these were a far more aggressive bunch than any they had encountered before.

The front line took a step forward and thrust out their right arms. In unison they balled their fists and, starting in the middle of the group and simultaneously working out to the periphery on both sides of the arc, each Golem's clenched fist mutated. Warped. Suddenly, razor-sharp stiletto-style daggers rose up from within their fists and then shot up to become fully-fledged crystal swords.

The sound they made as they did this was like ten thousand razor blades scraping down a chalkboard. It was the sound of death – a sound that made it perfectly plain that the group would not be going back the way they came.

'Fuck that shit!' Hillman screamed.

For now though, the Golems simply stood in position and stared across the void at them. Like they were weighing the odds. Assessing the options.

'How many do you think there are?' Michaels panted.

'Does it fucking matter?' Gant growled. 'We're outnumbered.'

'One hundred and forty-four thousand,' November said sourly. 'That's how many there are. That's what the Bible says about the size of the army in the final conflict.'

'We gotta get to the bridge.' Gant checked his sonic artifact as he tied the warhead off on his belt. 'What's that word I gotta use?'

'It's two words,' November reminded. '*Zihamtu.*'

Gant nodded as he spoke into the device to check it worked. '*Zihamtu . . .*'

It was perhaps, not the best thing he could have done. All along the edge of both sides of the canal the Golems started emitting a low rumble, their body language indicating they were about to go on the offensive.

Michaels lay on the ground, shivering. 'Sir, I don't think that was a good idea.'

Hillman cocked his rifle. 'And that's just their reaction to those two words, huh?! Well, I got two words for 'em. *Hechler* and *Koch!* Or how about *Eat Lead!* Or maybe *Die, Bitch!*'

Gant started marching. 'C'mon, let's go.'

'Sir,' Hillman protested. 'What about Michaels? Sir, we can't just leave him.'

Gant pulled out his handgun and immediately handed it to the fallen marine. 'Here, son. You need this more than I do.'

But even as he said this the Golems on either side of the canal started climbing down onto the hard surface of the water.

'Get out of here!' Michaels pleaded. 'Or you're all gonna fucking die!'

'I'll stay with him,' Yun piped up suddenly. 'You cannot leave him to die.'

'Bullshit! *I'll* stay with him!' Hillman protested. 'You never served with him! I did.'

'We don't have time for this horseshit, soldier!' Gant exploded as he realized the mass of Golems on both sides of the canal were marching toward them. 'If you're both prepared to stay with him, you can both pick him up and carry him. *Now let's go!*'

November quickly clipped her tether onto the warhead and began pulling alongside Gant. Together they broke into a run heading for the bridge where the others were screaming for them to hurry.

It was the best course of action, because the Golems too had quickened their pace.

They had started to charge.

'Jesus Christ! They're never going to make it!' Pearce yelped. '*Run!*'

Matheson went to climb over the edge but Scott held him back. 'What are you *doing*?' he complained, struggling to get free. 'We've got to do something!'

'Staying here,' Scott said firmly, 'is the safest option.'

'What!'

'Look around you,' Sarah explained coldly. 'Do you see any of those things climbing up here onto the bridge? No. Because it's Carbon 60. There is a battle raging in this city right now, for control of those creatures. If they come into contact with this crystal bridge they will interface with it. Then they die!'

'It is *really* starting to disturb me that you two know so much about this place all of a sudden,' Pearce snapped.

Scott started wrapping one of the ropes around his waist. 'When they get here, we'll pull 'em up.'

'Let's hope they get here.'

November could literally hear her heart pounding in her chest. Her cheeks flushed as she sprinted across the quasicrystallized canal toward the bridge, dragging the warhead alongside Gant.

Out the corner of her eye she could sense the Golems looming large, bearing down like a wave of frenzied, shattered glass.

She could hear them dragging their swords behind them, forcing the points into the crystallized canal and creating such a God-awful screech it sounded like a herd of freight trains all ramming on their brakes to avoid a full head-on collision.

She could feel a scream building in her throat. A bubble of sheer terror.

She turned her head to look, though she knew she shouldn't, and that was when the Golems closest to her raised their long thin blades and went in for the kill.

November didn't know where her presence of mind came from.

All she knew was that at some instinctive level she realized she had to retaliate and had the means to do so within her grasp. She brought the sonic artifact up to her lips, and without breaking the rhythm of her sprint she screamed into it like some frenzied banshee: *Zihamtu! Zihamtu! Zihamtu!*

The front line of sword-wielding Golems exploded in a cloud of electrified dust.

But through the stormcloud and residual lightning came the second line of attacking automatons.

They tipped their blades forward, to let her know they intended to skewer her.

Hillman fired again and again, blasting bullets deep into the thick of the marauding machines.

He knew it wouldn't kill them. But he also knew if he tripped enough of them up, took their legs out or knocked them on their asses, it would slow them some and buy the group more time.

'Take that, you fuckers!'

'Argh!' Michaels bellowed in such a blood-curdling manner it made both men carrying him wince.

Michaels had tried to put weight on his legs, even though he knew they would never support him. But his desperation to speed the process up was that great.

This was no good. They couldn't both carry him; they would have to stop. One of them would have to put his full weight over their shoulder, and carry him fireman-style.

Hillman jerked them to a halt. Shoved his gun in Michaels's hand. 'Here, hold this!'

Yun knew what he was doing. In symbiosis, he helped heave the marine up onto his comrade's shoulder and set out ahead.

Michaels was heavy. A deadweight in fact, but there was just no way Hillman was prepared to leave him behind. He fired to the side as he yelled at his cargo: 'Shoot the fuckers! Shoot 'em from behind!'

He listened with a satisfied air as Michaels loosed volley after volley into the oncoming swarm. But it wasn't enough. Hillman just wasn't strong enough. He couldn't maintain the speed required to stay one jump ahead. Within moments they were engulfed.

In the panic that followed, Hillman tripped and was brought crashing to his knees. Yet despite the severest jabbing pains shooting through his kneecaps, he was miraculously able to keep Michaels firmly balanced on his shoulder.

But he needn't have bothered.

The clips spent, the ammo gone, perhaps Michaels would have preferred to have crashed to the ground himself.

'You okay, buddy?' Hillman called out thinly.

'Uh-huh,' came the equally weak reply.

For the last thing Michaels was to see as he pulled his head up over his friend's shoulder, was a massive Golem looming large, the serrated tip of its ultra-thin blade pressing square against the flesh and bone between his eyes – and pushing.

Yun couldn't hear them behind him anymore. The two marines.

He knew he shouldn't look back, but he could see up ahead that November and Gant had still not reached the bridge. They were going to need a diversion.

Casually he jogged to a halt, having come to his deliberate conclusion in a measured manner. He lowered his gun and knew the waves of Golems had altered course to attack him.

Up on the bridge, the others couldn't believe what they were seeing. Pearce gripped the edge and called after the Chinese soldier, but it was no use. Yun's mind was made up.

He was turning back to confront them.

The sight before him was as gruesome as he had feared. He just caught the tail end of a double decapitation and watched as the heads of the two fallen marines rolled across the floor.

On impulse, he screamed.

The band of Golems immediately turned on the Chinese soldier like a shoal of fish sensing food. But there was no need to pursue it, for it was obvious Chow Yun had decided to stand his ground and confront his demons.

His face a contorted mass of sweat-soaked wrinkles, he watched in abject petrification as the lead Golem approached him and shrank down into the enigmatic visage of Yan Ning.

How had she even gotten inside the city?

'It is time for you to join me, my love,' she announced to her former lover in cold, emotionless Cantonese.

He roared at the effigy by way of a response. A final, formidable death-cry as he pumped what was left of his weapon's half-spent clip into the approaching crystal girl. But though she teetered off-balance momentarily, she continued her venture forward, and even smiled.

His clip spent, his nerves shot, Yun was taken by surprise as a perfectly smooth crystal rapier plunged into his back, burst from his abdomen and journeyed up as far as his chin.

'Zihamtu!' Gant yelled. It was a stupid war cry. It didn't feel right. Yet it was having the desired effect. 'Zihamtu!'

Golem after Golem caught in the sonic shock wave atomized on the spot, occasionally covering the two of them in a shower of gray, static-ridden grit as Gant and November pounded their way to the bridge. Every now and then, the odd faster-thinking Golem would dive for cover and wind up simply losing an arm or a leg if they were fool enough to allow their appendages to trail far behind.

The ropes were still there when the pair reached the bridge.

Gant unhooked himself from the warhead and tied the container onto the rope. He did the same with November's tether while she stood guard and blew apart any approaching Golems.

'Take it up!'

'What about you?' Matheson yelled.

'Just take it up!'

The five up on the bridge quit arguing and put their back into the operation, heaving the trunk to the top in one fluid motion and hauling it over the side.

They tossed one rope back down immediately, but the other rope took a couple more seconds longer to work free.

But that's all it took.

The Golems were closing in – fast.

November grabbed hold of the first rope and shouted at the top of her lungs to be hauled up, leaving Gant to defend himself. The fastest approaching Golem leapt at them from several yards away, bringing its sword over its head to slice at them both in the process.

November screamed into her sonic weapon and obliterated the menace in mid-air, but their assailant had not been alone. Three pounced in on Gant and the marine had no choice but to make a jump for it. Planting his foot into the oncoming automaton's face, he used the creature as a vaulting platform to flip up and grab hold of November's leg.

November howled in terror, unaware of what was going on and loosened her grip. The palms of her hands felt like they were on fire as ropeburn ripped them to shreds but she managed to hang on.

Gant gritted his teeth in anticipation as another Golem sprang at them, but spying some kind of post jutting down from the bridge, like the ones on top, he swung and kicked against it in an effort to dislodge their attacker.

It worked. The Golem slammed into the Carbon 60 post and simply clung there. Its whole body twitched and shivered as a slew of faces from the *Var* suddenly appeared under the glass to meet it head on and sucked their creation back inside.

The Golems on the ground faltered.

As the team on the bridge pulled their friends to safety, the Golems gathered below and stared up at them. Dissatisfied with the turn of events, one vengeful Golem made a last-minute bid to wreak disaster and leapt up after them both, extending his sword as far as it would go and slashing at the sole of Gant's boot.

The blow was true and sure. Gant screamed in rage and agony as a gash opened up and blood poured from his foot. But it didn't stop him from crawling over onto the hard floor of the bridge next to an exhausted November. He rolled to a stop, clutching his sliced-up foot and was met by a more than gleeful Pearce who commented: 'Smarts, doesn't it?'

Sarah checked over the warhead and its container. There was something odd about it which she just couldn't put her finger on.

She studied the locks. They were busted – from the inside out, like something had crawled inside and expanded until the metal gave way. Sarah popped them cautiously and threw open the trunk.

She flinched in surprise.

Gant groaned as he got up. 'What is it?' he demanded as he hobbled over, leaving a trail of blood behind him.

What he found was a pile of wires and busted parts, chewed components and burnt main boards. The warhead had been decimated.

Hackett peered over his shoulder. 'And this was worth three lives, *how?*'

Gant dismissed him, angrily jamming his hands into the mass of junk and unsalvageable parts.

'I wouldn't do that,' Sarah warned, but the marine wouldn't listen.

'What happened to my bomb?' he cried desperately. 'I was depending on my bomb! What happened to my warhead?'

But even as he said it, tiny glass spiders had emerged from the wreckage to make a direct attack on the man. Using long, needle-like teeth, they scampered across polished steel components and jabbed deep into Gant's stress-ridden fingers.

The Major screamed in agony, flinging the tiny creatures aside. Sarah recognized them as similar to the ones she had seen at Giza, but far more vicious. Instinctively she tipped the whole trunk over and spilled the lot onto the Carbon 60 floor.

In a flurry of high-pitched whines the tiny crystal spiders tried to make a run for it, but were caught in the grips of the low-frequency waves being pulsed out by elements within the Carbon 60 thoroughfare.

They exploded in miniature pops and whistles like Chinese firecrackers.

Gant hung his head in shame. 'I've failed,' he said. 'We're screwed.'

But Scott, his back to the others, stood by the low wall of the bridge and looking out at the amassed congregation of angry automatons below, was quite sure they were not. 'We'll be fine,' he announced confidently. 'I know we will be.'

With that he plunged his own sonic device firmly and deeply into one of the many recesses along the entire length of the wall and murmured something almost inaudible.

Belatedly, the Golems below became aware of what he was doing and scattered. Those at the far shores scrambled to safety. Others chanced it by leaping for the bridge but if they were capable of reflective thought it was probable that they wished they hadn't bothered. For as they clung to the crystal bridge and convulsed to their own doom, the water below them began to shimmer and sparkle as it regained a fluidity it had not seen in some time.

Those Golems still stuck out on the canal splashed beneath the surface and sank like a bunch of rocks.

Hackett was impressed. 'Ever had that sinking feeling?' Scott was not amused so he took another stab at it. 'Well, this place did sink one time before, I seem to remember. You'd think they'd be prepared for it.'

Scott still did not find it funny.

The waters were calm and still before them. Breathtakingly pure and clear, it was possible to see right to the bottom. Those Golems that had sunk to the bottom of the canal had disappeared. They had become quite literally invisible. The only way to make them out was to try and spot the odd shadow flitting about darkly against the lighter stonework below.

And when that had been achieved, one feature became startlingly clear: they were extraordinarily fast swimmers. And they were massing, coming together in a group and swarming.

It dawned on them all, but Matheson was the first to say it: 'I don't think that was such a good idea. I don't think that was a good idea *at all*. We better get going.'

Gant glanced up from where he was sat on the floor nursing his foot. 'Go where?' he glowered.

Matheson jerked a thumb at Scott. 'Go where *he* says, I guess.'

'And where is that . . . exactly?'

'I don't know,' Matheson shrugged. 'But he's right, Major, we gotta get going.' He glanced back over the side. The mass of shadows were growing. 'There is something so outta whack going on down there.'

Gant strained to get to his feet. It was clear he couldn't put much weight on his damaged foot but he stood there with dignity and even straightened his uniform. 'Why worry about it? Why don't you get your buddy here to sort it all out since he seems to know so much about this place all of a sudden. How do we know he's not turning into one of them and leading us into a trap?'

'That's not fair!' Pearce interrupted, but Scott held up his hand to silence him.

'It's okay,' he said soothingly. 'Look, Major, I'm plugged into this place. I am in constant communication with the machine. But I cannot see around corners. I only know where we're going because I asked. I only know what to do – because I asked.'

Gant launched himself forward and grabbed Scott by the throat. 'I have had about as much of this cosmic riddle as I can take. Now you tell me what lies ahead, nerd-boy, or so help me God I'll throw you to those cute little fishes down there. Now – where – are – we – going?'

The others didn't know what to do, but Scott didn't seem as phased as he might have been. He indicated the vast pyramid on top of the four large statues. 'We're going *there*,' he said. 'That's the control center.'

Gant's grip tightened. 'And what do we do when we get there?'

'*You* do nothing,' Scott explained. 'I will go inside – and die.'

SACRIFICE

'Richard – you step into that chamber and you're never coming back. What are you even talking about! What about your daughter? Think about her.'

'Ralph,' Scott smiled serenely, 'unless somebody steps into that chamber, my daughter will die. All our sons and daughters will die.' He forced back a chuckle, giddy with excitement. 'It really is that simple.'

'We have thirty minutes,' Pearce remarked earnestly, checking his time-piece with unflappable accuracy. 'And this is the best solution you can come up with? Why do you have to die? I don't understand.' He grabbed Gant's arm. 'Get your fucking hands off him. Richard, what gives here?'

'I will have to merge with this thing. The only way to teach it that we as a species survived the last flood and have developed sufficiently, is for two of us to physically join with the machine. Let it know us in our essence. The machine will connect with me at a subatomic level. It will form a bond like something akin to fusion. It will strip me of all outwardly visible humanity. For one brief moment I will continue to be human. But I will have all the resources and the accumulated knowledge of thousands of years of human history. Access to the records of countless civilizations at my fingertips.

'As the most modern addition to this great repository of knowledge, my twenty-first-century mind will provide all the current data about population centers, fragile eco-systems and any other zones around the earth that require special protection. I will be able to control and manipulate each wing within the global network and reach of this machine and will channel its energies to the most effective parts. The task this machine has been assigned is to turn our planet into one gigantic crystal. The seas, the air, and the liquid inner core of this entire planet will become one solid mass. Immovable. For one brief moment this planet will experience pure order in a solar system of chaos. I will avert our destruction. For one brief moment . . . I will be God . . . and then I'll be gone.

'There will be no coming back. I will be dismembered, a particle at a time. I will become part of this . . . device. I will become history. I will transform into pure information.' He paused to let them all consider this, then added: 'We are approaching the time of Easter, the ancient festival of sacrifice and renewal. It is written in the very mythology of civilization that mankind's future is based on the notion of sacrifice.' He smiled, such a knowing smile that it disarmed any wavering doubts the others may have had. 'Like I said in my lecture when you met me for the very first time, Ralph and Bob . . . You must take *all* of the Bible, not just parts. And in that vein, I am taking all of the myths and legends, not just parts. It was written thousands of years ago that someone would have to die to save mankind. It may as well be me.'

Hackett narrowed his eyes. 'You said *two* people must step into the chamber,' he noted, 'not one. Who's the second?'

'You noticed that, huh?'

'I notice everything.'

'One man must enter the chamber – and one woman.' Scott turned to Sarah. Held out a hand. 'What do you think? Feel like playing Eve to my Adam? Want a shot at wiping the slate clean?'

Sarah looked at the epigrapher's hand and hesitated for a moment. But she couldn't help succumbing to that gnawing, nervous anticipation of giving herself over to one gigantic explosion of experiential wonderment.

Slowly, tentatively, she slipped her hand into his. Embraced his warmth, and felt contented.

'Now wait a minute!' Pearce thundered. 'Has everyone gone insane?'

'Y'know, it's actually funny,' Hackett mused, rubbing his jaw. 'Studies have proved that suicides experience something akin to over-whelming joy just hours, even days before they finally blow their brains out, or slice up their wrists. It has something to do with the release. Knowing that everything will finally end. They will have attained, in their opinion, a solution.'

'Not that!' Pearce exploded. 'Sacrifice? Are you nuts? If this is about that shit in your leg, Richard, we can take care of that. We can remove it! Okay, so you might have to lose your leg, but you'll be alive.'

Hackett moved in closer to them. It was obvious he agreed.

'You don't have to do this,' he pressed upon them firmly. 'This is crazy. You have everything to live for. I, on the other hand—'

'You?'

It was harsh, almost accusatory. But Hackett let it slip.

'Jon,' Scott said softly. 'To you, it's about the puzzle. The game. To you — it's always been the puzzle.' Scott looked deep into the physicist's eyes. Admired his friend, the curiosity and sincerity that burned in that man's eyes. Yes, friend. In the final analysis, Scott concluded, he could call this man his friend. 'Jon . . . for me, it's always been about the answer. The ultimate knowledge. This way, I get it. I get my answer. About who we are. Where we come from.'

Hackett took it in with humility.

'You wouldn't be content with just an answer,' Scott concluded. 'You require the riddle.'

Hackett smiled. The same curious smile that had always so incensed Scott from the very first moment he had met him. And which now brought so much delight and gratification. There were a thousand and one questions rattling around in Jon Hackett's mind. But out of respect he was asking none of them.

Scott appreciated that.

Instead, all Hackett said, sincerely, was: 'To all things, there is a rhythm. Maybe this is the rhythm of your life.'

'Twenty minutes,' Matheson announced, looking down at the water. 'Folks, we really oughta get the fuck outta here. I do not like what I'm seeing down there!'

*　　*　　*

And that was when the water rippled, parted and frothed as a huge crystal fin cut through it and came toward them. Followed by another. Then another. Until ultimately the sheer bulk of the merged single entity below was revealed before them, its fangs the size of tree trunks, its crystal scales iridescent and pearl-like.

Like the very serpent from the Book of Revelation itself – the incarnation of Satan – the vast Goliath-sized beast of the sea snapped its truck-sized jaws together in a thunderous clap, slithered its way over to them, reared up – and roared.

20 MINUTES

They ran like they had never run in their lives before.

The true Leviathan of Atlantis cut through the water as if it didn't exist, reached over the bridge and when it failed to connect with its first strike, ducked underneath and reared its head up the other side.

It screamed in outraged fury and swiped again.

It missed. Its canoe-sized talons swinging just inches overhead.

It knew that it couldn't strike directly downwards and swat them like mere insects. And that fact alone frustrated it even more. It had to be careful too, about its line of attack. It had to be precise, jabbing its massive paw between tall spindly columns of Carbon 60 that seemed to have been placed there purely to foil the incredible beast.

As the seven ran, the Leviathan turned its swim into a back-stroke so it could keep track of its prey while keeping pace with it.

It lashed with its tail this time, making a whipping attack across their paths in the hope they would run into trouble.

But they never did.

Instead, those with sonic devices merely pointed their weapons in the beast's direction and shouted the sacred word with all the ferocity they could muster.

Vast dead chunks of crystal fell from the beast's chest as it took direct hit after direct hit. It finally crashed to a halt, sending a tidal wave of water swelling into the shoreline buildings ahead. And as it

screamed in agony the seven did all they could to remain upright
and moving as the backwash swilled along the bridge and threatened to sweep them over and into the canal.

They headed directly for the continuation of the Carbon 60 thoroughfare beyond, lined with tall crystal buildings on either side and
knew instinctively that at the very least, for this stretch of the journey
they would be safe.

But the Leviathan had other ideas, for as the team headed off
down the main road that was littered with icy glacial protrusions
from where the cavern had still not truly receded in places, the creature lined itself up with a granite paved side road and rushed towards
it.

Its razor-sharp blade-like plates and fins aero-planing sheets of
water up into the air, it roared toward the dockside and at the last
available moment – it shattered.

Tens of thousands of massive shards of crystal chunks were catapulted up the road. They bounced. Rolled. And using the momentum
to their advantage, transformed into ten thousand more Golems –
sprinting at full pelt.

Hackett was the first to notice this, as the thoroughfare leveled out.
It was suddenly like taking a trip down a ghostly version of any downtown Manhattan street, and glancing over to notice that a horde of
ghosts had decided to run the marathon parallel to them, just the
next block over.

Not only that, they were much faster than the humans, and in all
likelihood were about to head them off at the pass.

Hackett stared straight ahead, felt the adrenaline rushing through
his veins.

And gulped.

Ahead lay a zigzagging path between glacial deposits. A route so
confusing it was hard to tell at first in which direction they were
going since their line-of-sight view of the central district, not far away
now, was obscured.

And then it happened. The frightening prospect they had all been
dreading and never voiced.

Though the way ahead clearly continued, the C60 path upon

which they trod and upon which their lives depended, disappeared under sheets of ice. Sometimes the depth of that ice covering could be measured in mere, frustrating inches. But those inches crucially separated life from death.

And the Golems knew this.

As the ice undulated up and down in front of them like the gentle rolling of the countryside, the seven were confronted with squads of Golem search teams, pouring out from occasional side streets and meeting them head on, taking up attacking postures on the brows of the hills.

Zihamtu! Zihamtu! Zihamtu!

The obstructions were removed. But it wouldn't be long before their luck ran out.

When they reached the second canal, a much narrower affair than the first, they were relieved to find that all that ice actually worked in their favor, obscuring them from view as they journeyed across the wide open space toward the center.

And so it was with ten minutes to spare before the sun was due to trumpet its last gravity wave, that the seven remaining members of the Antarctic Team found themselves descending into the streets of the inner circle of Atlantis, passing by the spectacularly vast and imposing statues, which in turn supported the incredible crystal pyramid some 200 feet above their heads.

Making their way through the pits of ice that were glowing violently red, they watched in awe as hundreds of feet further up, the energy twister of solar plasma cascaded down and coiled itself around the seven vast crystal towers.

In the middle of the ice sat a glowing crystal platform. Square-shaped and of exquisite design, it pulsed and throbbed with light, like a magic carpet waiting to take its guests up into the pyramid above.

But there was a problem, because there was simply no way of reaching the platform.

For standing between them and salvation was an entire legion of Golems. Waiting patiently. Fully armed. They knew they did not even need to attack because time was on their side. Around them stood the curious hulks and burnt-out strewn wreckage of the Chinese base *Jung Chang*. Torn and twisted from where it had fallen in from the surface, it was the perfect reminder that they too might yet become part of some macabre cemetery.

Hackett described it best of all by saying: 'I don't know how we're going to get out of this one without an Act of God.'

An Act of God.

That was precisely what they got.

ACT OF GOD

The ground shook.

So violent was the earthquake that November was knocked to her knees. Peals of thunder rang out as the deep red glow of the nearby volcano descended upon the whole city.

Matheson panicked. 'Is this it?'

Hackett shook his head. 'No,' he said, 'this is just the build-up. Pre-tremors before the main event. Minor gravitational fluctuations before she pops her load completely.'

November couldn't help it. She started sobbing as Scott helped her to her feet, and that's when they all saw it. An intense white-hot glow, darkening to a distinct yellow then orange as it grew larger in a speckled effect at random all across the more imposing glaciers around them.

Suddenly, huge dark shafts of hot volcanic pumice began blasting out all around them as molten lava ate its way through the Antarctic ice like a hot knife through butter and cooled dramatically along the way.

The team dived for cover as a sudden protrusion of rock accompanied by super-hot jets of steam exploded right next to them. It was ironic, for they fared better than the Golems who stood stoically waiting for them. Multiple columns of heavy black pumice seemed to criss-cross uncontrollably and explode out into the crystal crowd while the foul, choking stench of sulfur descended upon the whole area.

The ground shook again, more violently than before.

And as these weird, tree-trunk-sized lances of cooling rock continued to shoot forth through the ice, so the heavens opened up in a sudden cascade of brimstone. Hot molten rocks, some still glowing bright yellow and obviously malleable came hurtling through the ice cavern above and rained down upon the legion of Golems. Huge smoldering boulders rolled through the ice creating instant slush in their wake and knocking over hundreds of them at a time like skittles.

And Scott saw his chance. It was now or never.

Gently he took his arms from around November's shoulders and removed her head from his chest. He delicately brushed her hair from her face and kissed her tenderly on the forehead.

'I will miss you,' he said.

She looked up into his eyes. So earnest. So comforting. 'I'll miss you too,' she replied.

Matheson tapped his watch. 'Go!' he cried. 'We'll try and cover you! And Richard?'

Scott turned back.

'Thank you.'

Scott was puzzled. 'For what?'

'For thinking any of us are actually worth saving.'

'Who'd have thought it,' Hackett scoffed. 'Us geeks really do get to inherit the earth.'

Scott nodded, relinquishing his sonic weapon to the others.

Neither he nor Sarah would need one where they were going.

'Take care,' Sarah said as she departed. 'All of you.'

They all moved forward in unison, the five who would remain behind, each blasting a path through the Golems to allow Scott and Sarah safe passage to the glowing platform.

The air was thick with throbbing vibration, as if the device itself was anxious. Anticipating the moment when it would fulfill its purpose.

They could all feel the crushing bass tones pound on their lungs and then –

Whoosh!

Scott and Sarah had taken their places aboard the floating skiff and were hurtling skyward, propelled by forces the others couldn't even contemplate. Within seconds the flying platform had docked with the pyramid and they were gone.

Hackett checked his watch. Checked with Pearce. The CIA agent agreed: 'Two minutes,' he said.

The Golems were closing in all around them, swords drawn like a multitude of scythes, ready to do the bidding of the Angel of Death himself.

And then, one by one, the faces of the closest Golems began to warp and mutate. Until eventually they had transformed into effigies of men Matheson recognized. Men Rola Corp. had used in the past. Men who worked as mercenaries in South America. Ruthless, cold-blooded killers.

Maple, Carver and his entire squad.

Two minutes. Two whole minutes. There was every reason to believe they would not survive the next two minutes.

CONTROL CENTER

E verything was silent.
A peaceful calm had descended once the platform had locked into position. It was as if nothing could penetrate in from the outside world.

The room was vast and for the most part featureless. Though its glyph-covered walls closed in on them like some incredibly massive cathedral spire, the pyramid, unlike the ones in Egypt, was entirely hollow.

There were a few more platforms dotted way off up into the dark night of the obscured pinnacle, and a few panels and podiums in the exact center. And there were two human-shaped recesses, one on either side, into which they obviously would have to place themselves.

This was it.

Neither of them could breathe. Though they had shown firm resolve in front of the others it had been a lie. They had been sharing each other's thoughts for some time now, and each knew that the other one was petrified.

'I wish I had known you sooner,' Scott ventured.

'I wish that too,' Sarah replied.

They both gulped in unison and closed their eyes. Then reveled in a moment of exquisite closeness for one final moment as they took pleasure in the deep and lasting ecstasy of a kiss.

*   *   *

'Ah, ain't that cute,' Bulger quipped mercilessly.

Scott and Sarah broke from their embrace as across the expanse of Carbon 60 flooring, walked Jack Bulger – wearing the boots of a recently deceased marine.

He clanked his way toward them, and grinned.

SURFACE

USS JOHN S. McCAIN DDG-56

Fortune favors the Brave – that was the ship's motto.

This sixth ship in the Arleigh Burke class of destroyers was specifically designed to conduct simultaneous operations against land, air, surface and subsurface targets. The AEGIS weapon system and its AN/SPY-ID multifunction radar meant the crew could track hundreds of potential targets at once.

The *McCain* had 22 officers and 315 enlisted men and women aboard; every single one of her 90 Tomahawk land-attack cruise missiles was already stored and positioned for rapid fire in her vertical launching system.

All she awaited was the word, which wasn't long in coming.

As the lead ship in coordinating the SaRGE decoy offensive, crewmen aboard the *McCain* had positioned the remote robotic soldiers to draw the Chinese forces out while old-fashioned tanks, artillery and camouflaged ground troops outflanked these forces from behind. Once these forces were in position the *McCain* would fire a barrage of Tomahawks at the Chinese incursion force in an attempt to make them retreat. If the strategy was successful, they would fall back right into the lap of the waiting US troops.

It was risky. But then there was always risk. It was still a sound plan.

On the bridge they waited patiently for word from the *Truman* and the other ships in both carrier battle groups while the clipped confirmation came in that: 'All missiles locked to target, sir.'

The captain, Larry Belvedere, from New Port, Connecticut, nodded silently as he waited with his senior officers.

Eventually the call came in from the carrier. All troops were in position, and Admiral Dower was giving the orders to the support ships, personally. 'The President regretfully confirmed some moments ago that the Chinese are refusing to back down on these matters and as a consequence we are authorized to fire at will,' he commanded.

Out on the deck of the *McCain*, the first wave of Tomahawks were away. And on the barren ice flats of Antarctica, the first shots between US and Chinese forces were exchanged.

War had commenced.

FINAL BATTLE

Jack Bulger swung so fast and with such power that when his rock-hard fist connected with Scott's jaw it propelled the anthropologist through the air, smacking him against the far end of the control chamber.

'I'm disappointed,' Bulger beamed. 'I was so looking forward to mashing you some more.' He wiggled his toes, pleased, because by wearing the boots he was obviously not in contact with any expanses of Carbon 60 that would deactivate him. 'These boots were made for walking,' he hummed. 'And that's just what I'll do.'

He swung again, launching himself at Sarah, but she had already anticipated his attack and moved swiftly to the side.

'You really think they'll let you live?' she challenged him.

Bulger shrugged. 'It's not much of an after-life. But it's still life *after* death.'

'You're nothing to them,' Sarah countered. 'They're microscopic psychopaths. You won't have a place in their new world order. You're just a programming tool. When you've served your purpose they'll discard you.'

Bulger didn't like that, not one bit. Enraged, he swung again and clawed at Sarah's thick parka, literally tearing strips off her. He threw her to the ground and kicked her hard.

All this, while Scott came to at the far end of the chamber. He couldn't see straight and his jaw was broken: he could feel the bone moving beneath his flesh. But in spite of this he staggered over to try and stop Bulger's attack.

The Golems were closing in.

Those with sonic weapons tried to keep them at bay, as Gant directed their efforts. But it didn't take long for the automatons to figure out the error of their attack, and instead of sending in one or two effigies at a time, they changed tack – and did what they did best.

They swarmed.

The team loosed their sonic blasts. But those Golems which had taken the forms of Maple and Carver were smart. They grabbed their comrades and used them as disposable shields as they advanced.

November fell back a step, and another, only to find other concerns to occupy her mind. A spring of water had started trickling from one of the protruding mini-glaciers, followed by a second spring. Then a third.

She could hear the cracking of ice all around them. The shaking and violent pounding of swarming Golems was weakening the structure of the entire ice cavern. 'This place is collapsing!' she cried. 'Look over there!' She pointed to the far side of the city.

The entire rear wall of the ice cavern about two miles away was bowed out where the heat from the volcano had warped the ice. But it was cracking under the extreme pressure now and could hold back the reservoir of water built up behind it no longer.

It creaked and groaned as cracks shot through the ice until ultimately its brittleness betrayed it. The far wall exploded, unleashing millions of tons of freshwater.

Swiftly, other ice formations began to collapse. Huge icebergs were starting to rise up in the distance as the tidal wave headed directly for them. Some hit buildings and burst apart so ferociously, the ice shrapnel shot toward both human and Golem like bullets.

Golems to the left and right were decapitated by flying ice as what appeared to be an entire legion were washed away in the distance.

'Run!' Gant ordered.

'Run where?' Matheson panicked.

'Anywhere! We've got to get out from under this pyramid or we drown!'

But as they all broke into a sprint they too were suddenly swept off their feet as another reservoir of water roared through its icy confines and burst in upon them.

They were separated, each floating freely in a frothing lake of freezing water. Hackett smacked into a boulder of ice with the side of his face and cut his eye open all the way down to the cheekbone. He shrieked in agony.

Gant spotted him and swam for the physicist, picking his way through huge chunks of ice.

'Where are the others?' Hackett asked, clearly having problems with the cold.

Gant could hear the man's teeth chattering away. Much longer in this water and it would kill them both. He looked about sharply and eventually spotted something. 'That iceberg!'

Hackett swirled around and saw November fishing Matheson up out of the water. She had made it onto an iceberg and was using it as a raft.

They swam over, to join them, fighting the forces of incredible eddies and currents within the swirl of floodwater. It took every inch of effort their bodies could muster and soon their limbs felt numb.

But the most distressing thing of all was the enemy, because the Golems were relentless.

Bulger kicked hard and kicked again, jamming his boot so viciously into Sarah's ribs that Scott could hear them crunch. But even knowing he was endangering his own life, Scott threw himself in front of the Golem and swung it around to face him.

'You don't see what they're doing, do you?' Scott said passionately. 'They're not even fighting this war, they're making *us* kill *each other*. Kill ourselves – and for what? For greed. Tell me something, Jack – what are you going to do with all this carbon crystal and diamond when this is over, if there's not going to be anyone around to sell it to?'

The effigy of Jack Bulger didn't respond, in case it might weaken his resolve. Instead, he stood back a pace and produced one of those grim rapiers the other Golems had used.

The city had flooded to such an extent that a few crystalline build-ings were now completely submerged. But the water level was rising extraordinarily rapidly. It wouldn't be long before the whole place had drowned once again.

Gant used all his strength to heave Hackett up onto the iceberg alongside November and Matheson.

'Don't struggle too much!' Matheson warned, unsteady on his feet. 'I don't want to give this thing any excuse to roll over.'

November in the meantime was on her knees, clawing at the marine, trying to get him to safety as well. 'Get up here now!' she bellowed. 'Move!'

Gant didn't need telling twice. The Golems were already morphing into grotesque versions of sharks with hideous oversized teeth. He clambered aboard, digging frenzied fingers into the ice as he did so, just as two of the sharks rammed the iceberg with their snouts, causing it to spin around in the currents and make the team feel giddy as they were shunted off towards the side of the cavern.

Gant pulled himself upright. 'Where's Pearce?' he said breathlessly. 'Anybody seen Bob?'

Bulger swung, aiming to bring his sword straight down through Scott's head. But his way was suddenly barred by a slender blue crystal arm that thrust out and took the blow.

The arm belonged to Sarah.

She had pulled away part of her parka only to discover that she was changing. She whipped her hand around, snapped off the blade and threw it across the room. It connected with the Carbon 60 flooring, shuddering and melting into oblivion.

Bulger was stunned.

'I've been changing, thanks to you,' Sarah announced. She eyed Scott and revealed: 'I didn't even feel it.'

And that gave Scott the idea. He glanced down at his own leg. Had he been changing too? There was only one way to find out. He pulled his leg back and kicked Jack Bulger.

The effigy shot across the room, propelled by a force that defied belief.

Scott and Sarah watched, breathless, as Bulger plowed into the back wall and hung there like a fridge magnet. He wriggled, panicked – and he screamed. Finally he was atomized, and all that was left were a pair of black leather combat boots which clattered noisily to the floor.

They were overwhelmed. Hackett, November, Matheson and Gant.

Though they stood their ground bravely and fought the noble fight, ultimately the Golems were simply too many in number. Too large and too brutish.

Up out of the water the head of Maple arose, attached to the body of a massive sea creature that was still coalescing beneath the iceberg. It reached over and grabbed Gant by the throat and seemed not even to notice the blows that the marine was raining down on it. Meanwhile, another nanoswarm casually slapped November with the back of its massive hand and sent her skidding across to the water's edge.

As November fought for consciousness she could just see Bob Pearce being dragged under the surface of the water, some way off, surrounded by fins.

The Antarctic Team was beaten. And indeed, none of them even heard it when Hackett's watch alarm finally beeped to announce – it was time.

PULSAR

God runs electromagnetics on Monday, Wednesday and Friday by the wave theory . . . and the devil runs it by quantum theory on Tuesday, Thursday and Saturday.

Sir William Bragg, Co-Winner of the
Nobel Prize For Physics, 1915

ZERO HOUR

Pulsars were God's time-pieces.

When a star had used up all its fuel it collapsed down on itself and went one of two ways. It either became a quantum singularity – a black hole – or it exploded in a supernova. A pulsar was said to come *after* the supernova.

All that was left, all the stellar material, would collapse back down into a star again. But it would form a very different kind of star. Protons would meld with electrons to form neutrons. The resulting neutron degeneracy pressure, the need for the unstable neutron to blast itself apart, would fight with gravity, the force keeping the neutron bound together.

Two supreme forces slugging it out in a pressure-cooker until ultimately an equilibrium could be reached. Enormous magnetic field strengths would be produced in the region of ten to the power of twelve times greater than the earth's. The neutron star, like any star, would start to spin. But unlike the sun, whose single revolution would last thirty days, a neutron star's spin cycle could be anywhere from weeks, up to many times per second. The magnetic field-lines would be severely entangled, beams of radio waves would be blasted out across the cosmos as the star rotated like beams of light from a lighthouse.

That was the theory.

Which meant this sort of activity could not possibly be occurring on an ordinary star like the sun. A star that still had plenty of fuel left, enough to burn brightly for another 500 million years. It was nowhere near to becoming a neutron star.

It was a strong theory.

But the theory was wrong.

All stars were pulsars, in one shape or another.

They experienced oscillation, resonance – rhythm. There was a pattern to the life of all things. An ebb and a flow. A zenith and a nadir.

There was chaos and there was order.

That was the way of things.

To all things there was a rhythm, measurable, most assuredly. But to all things there was a timescale by which it was measurable. The life of a star was a long and winding one. It lived on a scale that was simply too large, too incalculable for humans to comprehend.

The sun was a pulsar.

Not in the sense of a neutron star. It did not blast out radio waves in a beam at regular intervals and spin wildly, but it did suffer the consequences of warped and tangled magnetic field-lines. No, the sun's build to ultimate pulsation may have been a slow one, but like the Hare and the Tortoise, it was just as unstoppable.

As the sun rotated about its axis the twisted knots and loops of its magnetic field-lines buckled and tangled, grappled and twisted. Until ultimately the entire surface of the seething ball of nuclear fusion could take it no more.

Once in every 12,000 years, the entire surface of the sun would peel off like removing the entire top layer of an onion – whole and unbroken. It would swell and expand outwards in all directions. Such was the instability caused by the departing sphere of matter that it would make the inner mass temporarily wobble and change shape, thus altering its density and affecting its impact on the fabric of space.

Space itself would then undulate, like a rug being beaten, and the undulation – the gravity wave – would carry this escaping shell of stellar material with it at speeds approaching the speed of light.

And one such occurrence was happening right now.

SCOTT AND SARAH

They nestled into the integration receptacles and waited.

It did not take long for something to happen.

Their minds were suddenly alive with thoughts and images. Snatches of ideas here and there. Half-formed words and concepts. It was like –

Bang!

Scott couldn't help it. He pulled his head away from the head-rest and looked around the room with a gasp. He glanced down at his hands. His body. Already his fingers had started to melt into the wall. He struggled, but they wouldn't come away. He was overcome with panic and grief. And although he couldn't feel a thing, as the process had obviously already cut the nerve impulses to his brain, his instinctive reliance on fear had gotten the better of him.

Sarah had her eyes closed. He could see her physically melting into the wall on the far side of the room. Turning a pale, pale blue.

The same thing was happening to himself.

And then the feeling passed. He could hear the voices again, reassuring and generous.

He glanced around at the clear crystal surfaces one last time, and put his head back.

Closed his eyes.

✳   ✳   ✳

Sarah had this itch. It was a deep itch, right in her toes. She tried to wriggle them and felt a sudden sensation of heat and sand, followed by a deeper sensation of depth and movement and of liquid.

She realized that she was beneath the earth, in the molten core of the planet, examining geologic densities, watching the inner convection currents of the mantle. The closer to the center of the earth, the denser the rock. As these inner layers moved, so the effect was magnified at the surface where the crust lay. Convection currents in three dimensions were incredibly complex, yet she seemed to suddenly grasp every nuance, every facet of the inner workings of the planet. To quasicrystallize the mantle would require at least seven different types of standing wave.

Scott was aware of this blinding light off to the left somewhere. He turned his head to see. At least, he had the sensation of turning his head. He reached out and became aware that he was interacting with some kind of device, in a jungle somewhere. Maybe South America. He could be no more specific than that.

He reached out with his other hand and knew instinctively he was operating a similar device somewhere in the depths of Russia. Like the crystal constructs under the pyramids at Giza he had the sense he was moving entire pyramids of Carbon 60 and shifting them into position, rearranging beams of crystal to complete circuits.

A global machine. A global network, on a planetary scale. It was as if the earth was one entity and he was part of that now.

He was revealing to Atlantis that he knew of this network, knew its potential and its capabilities. And in turn, Atlantis was getting to know Scott. Soon they understood each other.

Remotely, from the heart of Atlantis, Scott and Sarah took a light-speed tour of the entire global network. The more information they requested, the more information they were given until ultimately, they knew everything.

Like seconds ticking on a clock, one by one the other fifty-nine languages encoded in the Atlantis glyphs were revealed to them and the lost history of their own planet was laid bare. Each language was accompanied with the collected stories of each civilization that used it.

And the revelation was great.

At the same time, one by one each Carbon 60 device dotted in subterranean enclaves around the globe was switched on and made ready. Information was exchanged. Lost monuments were rediscovered until the entire network was humming with anticipation.

Finally there was nothing more to do and curiously it all stopped. Scott and Sarah had fulfilled their fates. Atlantis's response would be an automatic reflex now, triggered by whatever actions were taken by the sun.

And equally curiously, it was the sun which Scott and Sarah now found themselves admiring. For they were standing on a hill overlooking Atlantis as it had once been, 12,000 years ago. A shining jewel in a lush valley, in a landscape that was lost to time, if not to memory.

Standing at the gates to this majestic city, monument to Man's achievements, were 10,000 well-wishers eager to greet them and welcome them to their new home. So as the sun shone down upon the sparkling canals of that now sunken city, Scott and Sarah exchanged heartfelt emotional looks, cupped their hands in each other's – and went down to meet them.

In the control center of Atlantis stood some consoles and podiums and two empty receptacles.

It was barren other than that. Desolate, except for a pair of black leather combat boots and a sense of expectation.

STORM FROM THE SUN

P lanet, from the Greek, meaning 'wanderer'.
The planets were in crisis.

Within two minutes, the tiny ball of superheated rock known as the planet Mercury, had been entirely engulfed and overtaken. Since its surface was incapable of sustaining life or supporting an atmosphere, the damage inflicted upon this tiny world was difficult to calculate. Perhaps a slightly altered path in its orbit. A lengthening of its overall year, or an extra twist upon its axis had caused a decrease in the length of its day or night. Whatever the effects, they were inconsequential to the people of earth, for as planets go there was no comparison.

It was when the total coronal ejection had continued its relentless expansion throughout the solar system for a total of *five* minutes that began to feel the effects, for the human race it was at this point that the stampeding cataclysm intercepted the orbit of Venus.

It was ironic that a planet named after the Roman goddess of beauty and love was about as far removed from those qualities as possible.

Venus's year took 240 days. It spun retrograde about its axis, meaning in comparison to the earth it spun backwards making the sun rise in the west at dawn. It barely had any magnetic field and was almost perfectly spheroid, suggesting its core was more solid than the earth's. Its atmosphere was 96.5 percent carbon dioxide, with sulfuric acid in its upper cloud layers. Its atmosphere was also 95 times more dense than earth's and due to all the carbon dioxide, it trapped sunlight to such an extent the average surface temperature was 480 degrees Celsius, or 900 degrees Fahrenheit. Even on a cool day on Venus it was hot enough to melt lead.

Other than that, it was just like earth.

And for the purposes of a pulsar ejection impact – it was identical.

For Venus was a landscape dominated by volcanic features, faults and impact craters, much like the earth. But where many of the earth's geological hot spots were often obscured by life, Venus's volcanoes were her prettiest feature. In many vast areas of the planet's surface there was evidence from satellite imagery of periods of multiple lava flooding with lava flows seen piled one on top of the other. One higher region, known as *Ishtar Terra*, was a lava-filled basin the size of the United States with the *Maxwell Montes* Mountain sat at one end.

And because there was no water and little wind erosion on Venus, its extensive fault-line network was clearly visible as a result of the same crustal flexing that the earth experienced. But since the excessive heat of Venus weakened the rock structure, cracking the crust in multiple regions, it prevented the planet from forming tectonic plates.

And as a result the huge lava features across the planet did hint at one other extraordinary feature. From time to time, vast continent-sized swathes of Venus turned completely molten, as if the planet was attempting to turn itself inside out. The mechanism for such an event was completely unknown.

Or had been, until now.

To call the pulsar wave that hit Venus an exercise in pure rage was to underestimate the severity of the gravity wave.

The speed of the wave that hit Venus's upper atmosphere could be measured in microseconds. Its impact was so severe that it immediately took the outer layers with it, peeling the atmosphere back like taking the rind off an orange.

The resulting compression set what combustible gases there were in Venus's atmosphere, ablaze, setting into motion a chain reaction that penetrated up to a mile down into Venus's atmosphere and causing vast amounts of carbon dioxide to glow to the point of molecular collapse. Suddenly the twin atoms of oxygen broke away from their host carbon atoms and exploded.

The entire outer layer of Venus had been transformed. It had ignited, and become pure flame.

As the ever-expanding fireball that was the sun's final, total coronal shell ejection blasted ever outward and impacted upon the volatile planet, for one whole second Venus knew only fire. There was no distinguishing between which part of the maelstrom was Venus on fire, and which part of the fire was merely the coronal shell passing through that part of the solar system.

There was only flame.

But coupled with this, of course, there was the gravity wave.

It swept through the planet in less time than it took to give a blink of an eye. And in much the same way that the series of preceding gravitational fluxes had built up an oscillation effect within the liquid mantle of the earth, so too had these same pulses been churning up geological turmoil across the planet Venus.

If anyone had even thought to correlate the geological data accumulating throughout the solar system they would have seen a pattern emerging from planet to planet. They would have seen that the volcanic and earthquake crisis on earth was not unique to home but part of an overall solar-system-wide catastrophe.

But they had not. And by the time the light from Venus would have reached the earth and given a clue to the type of experience the people of earth could expect to face, the wave would have already been and gone.

For the speed of light was the speed of light. It could not beat itself in a race.

As a result, no one on earth could actually *see* the surface of Venus buckle and bend. No one could *see* the county-sized chunks of crust get tossed up into the air and flipped over like pancakes on a giant conveyor belt. No one could *see* whole continent-sized areas of Venus suddenly heat up within seconds and turn molten. Nor could anyone see the various chunks of stellar matter and debris that had been caught up in the wave, rain down upon the planet's surface like glowing, white-hot hailstones, and smash whole new valleys into existence.

From a human vantage point on earth, should they survive the next three minutes, Venus would appear more than ten times brighter in the night sky than normal, for a century, as its molten surface churned and twisted and settled into its new formations before cooling.

Fortunately for humankind there was already a force in existence that did not need to see the catastrophe to know that it had to do something about it. For the early warning system that Atlantis employed did not rely on light. And it did not solely rely on mathematical predication, but rather quantum gravitational effects. It detected changes within the very fabric of space itself. It was based on a type of physics mankind had only just begun to rediscover – super-string theory and its interaction with the zero point field. The idea that two points in the galaxy could be intimately – and instantaneously – linked.

Atlantis tapped into the short-cuts of the universe. For it knew that just like a tsunami on earth: if a person could see the wave coming, it was already too late.

Atlantis didn't have to see it coming. It just knew.

PHASE I

THE CASIMIR EFFECT

It was originally discovered by Dutch physicist Hendrick Casimir in 1948. A quantum theory that dealt with virtual particles in a continuous state of flux.

The physical manifestation of this was that if two conducting plates were placed in a vacuum *uncharged*, due to quantum vacuum fluctuations of the electromagnetic field, the plates would still be irresistibly attracted to each other despite no power being inputted to cause this.

The Casimir Effect proved the existence of zero point energy.

And the odd puzzle as a result of its mathematical proof was that this effect was plugged directly into the realm of gravity. Zero point energy was linked directly to warping effects on space-time. In other words, if the fabric of space was caused to curl up and ripple it would have an immediate effect on the ability to unleash zero point energy.

In Atlantis that meant one thing. The natural interaction between zero point energy and gravity through the fabric of space meant that the very energy source the city intended to use to save the planet, also acted as an early warning system to alert the city to an imminent gravitational attack.

Which was the signal it was receiving right now. It double-checked its command center. It had indeed completed the integration of two new units of information. The crucial prerequisites had been satisfied.

It could therefore initiate its primary response protocol. Using all manner of standing waves to effect quasicrystallization in all types of matter, it was time for Atlantis to shield earth.

PHASE II

QUASICRYSTALLIZATION

G ant was close to passing out. The Golem pressed down on his windpipe and squeezed so solidly that the marine could feel his tongue being forced out between his teeth.

He was not alone. All around him he could see the others in similar predicaments. Utterly helpless. He didn't even have enough space left in his throat to choke out a warning to Hackett as the physicist blasted a Golem to atoms, oblivious to the attacker that was coming up behind.

And it was then, as Hackett's assailant grabbed him and swung him around that Gant began to realize that in the distance, all around the city, there was movement. Beyond the inner sky-scrapers, out toward the suburbs of the city – past them, in fact, at the outer canal – there was a shimmering. A glistening. A kind of snake-like writhing as the entire contents of the canal, millions of tons of water, rose up out of their confines and started to travel in a vortex-like motion around the outskirts of the city.

It was as if they all stood in the eye of a twister as chaos surrounded the city. Higher and higher the water climbed, while above their heads the energy twister was building into a maelstrom of its own.

All of this Gant could see, as blood vessels burst across his eyeballs and oxygen was cut off from his brain.

And then there was a sea change in their predicament.

The air became thick and syrupy. Motion became blurred and

slow. And there was the rumble. The sensation that the surrounding area was being bombarded with a multitude of low-level and high-level sonic waves.

The result was that sound within the ordinary range of human hearing started to dull and lower itself in pitch, before finally it was replaced altogether with that hissing noise which they all remembered from that glass of Coke which had undergone quasicrystallization back at CERN.

Slowly . . . excruciatingly slowly . . . everything stopped. The whole world ground to a halt and was frozen. Crystallized.

It was as if Time stood still.

In the middle of the South China Sea a Great White Shark was battling three dolphins that were viciously ramming into its side to warn it off when they suddenly pulled back, their sonar indicating that something massive and perfectly solid was closing in on them all. The creatures turned sharply and set about racing away, but the nemesis, whatever it was, was closing in fast.

A thousand feet below them, the six Chinese submarines that had set out to support their fleet in the Antarctic were equally surprised to encounter the same phenomenon. Ping after ping of the radar system revealed that a huge mass was approaching, like a wall that stretched from the sea bed up to the surface of the ocean and in all directions.

Suddenly, everything froze solid. The sea crystallized around them. Sea creatures and submarines were all held in suspension.

Within the lead Han Class warship, the crew cowered at the odd shrieks from the metal hull as the stresses and strains of quasicrystallization filtered through. One crewman put his hand up against the violently vibrating metal skin and he too froze solid, the effects of quasicrystallization shooting down his arm and freezing him where he stood.

The other crewmen turned to flee in panic, but were stopped in mid-flight as standing waves of multiple frequencies were pumped throughout the cabin. Glasses of water midway through spilling, cups of coffee in mid-air, plates of half eaten meals that were in the midst of shattering on impact with the deck – all were caught and held tightly. Like the sailors themselves.

It was like pausing a movie, yet more so. For this was in all three dimensions, and at every level, from the molecular to the mega.

This effect gradually took hold throughout the planet. The crystallization phenomenon by its very nature could not travel at the speed of light, but at the speed of sound. And the density of the material within which the standing wave was to be produced dictated the speed at which the sound would travel.

It was a complex process. But to the human eye it was instantaneous.

Oceans quickly turned into immense expanses of crystal, lookingglasses through which an entire suspended world could be studied. Rivers refused to flow. Streams ceased to babble and geysers to blast.

All across the surface of the earth there was a tremendous shuddering. A vibration that seemed to be approaching critical mass.

And then the effect swept through the air.

Birds simply hung where they were in mid-flight. Waterfalls became strings of beads. In-flight aircraft seemed to slow before coming devastatingly and abruptly to a halt. In the cabins of these craft, the effect was like smashing into a brick wall. Anything unsecured was catapulted through the air. Bodies, blankets, books and toys went hurtling forward only to suddenly become enveloped in the odd phenomenon that seemed to hold them effortlessly in the air.

On the battlefields of Antarctica, Tomahawk cruise missiles hung a hundred feet off the ground, caught in mid-attack, while waves of infantrymen were caught in mid-charge – their bullets halted only feet away from where they had exploded out of the barrels of their guns.

But the effects of quasicrystallization did not end there.

Deep beneath the surface crust of planet Earth, lay a volatile world of molten rock. A world of density and of relentless heat measured in millions of years and manifested in pressure. It was not a place used to living by the rules of outside influences, but even so it was not left untouched by the effects of quasicrystallization.

Its reaction depended on densities – which layers of rock were more dense than others. It was a complex calculation because the conveyor-belt nature of the three-dimensional convection currents within the mantle meant rocks were constantly being shifted around. Some of the denser material was actually being propelled toward the surface rather than staying at the level at which it was created.

The quasicrystallization event therefore took the form of a repeated bombardment, pumping standing wave after standing wave at varying frequencies, deep into the hidden world until layer upon layer finally crystallized and became solid.

However, there was one feature of the earth's inner world that could not be crystallized, or stopped for that matter. Indeed, it was imperative to the workings of Atlantis that it remain in action: the solid iron inner core of the planet. This massive central feature rotated and gave rise to the earth's own magnetic field. Essentially it was a giant induction motor.

And it would have to contend with the gravity wave on its own terms.

Complexity was about the interconnectedness of all things. About making sense of the senseless.

Complexity was about order from chaos.

For one brief moment, order had descended on planet Earth for the first time in its long history. For that one brief moment, the earth was at peace. It was an irony then that conversely, the system in which it sat, raged around it in a state of utter destruction.

IMPACT

They were in high orbit over North Africa when they first saw it. The astronauts aboard the International Space Station noticed the sun appear to flicker before ultimately it seemed to brighten.

They rushed to contact Houston but there was a problem. Houston was not responding. In fact, nobody was responding. All lines of communication were dead. There was no radio, no TV. There weren't even any carrier beacons sending signals denoting the frequencies were correct even if nobody was broadcasting.

Nothing.

Which was even more problematic for something seemed odd about the planet below, around which they were orbiting. It had turned glassy, like some giant marble. Sunlight, rather than reflecting back off the oceans, actually seemed to be reflecting back off the atmosphere . . .

But before anyone could even comment on this observation, events from the sun were taking a turn for the worse.

The sun was expanding. Ballooning outwards.

There followed another kind of wobble and then the center portion seemed to revert back to being the sun, while the outer portion assumed the appearance of an ever-increasing halo.

The crew quickly realized that this was a fireball type of shock-wave blossoming out toward them. In a minute and a half they would be on the dark side of the earth. The planet would shield them from what was approaching. A minute and a half – that's all they needed.

They did not have a minute and a half.

As the International Space Station glided in around the curve of the earth and headed for twilight, it was hit from behind by a wall of pure fire which ripped the craft to pieces and left twisted, burning wreckage in its wake.

As it engulfed the planet below, the outer atmosphere superheated and exploded in a much more violent manner than had occurred on Venus, but because of the quasicrystallization effect, the event did not chain react or penetrate deep into the upper atmosphere.

Instead, the resulting firestorm was sucked off and swept up into the wave of destruction from the sun and carried off into deep space.

As the gravity wave passed through the earth, the whole planet seemed to elongate and stretch before snapping back to its original shape. But due to its quasi-solid state, the effects on the planet were reasonably benign.

No earthquakes erupted or fault-lines exploded. No rivers were dislodged or oceans spilled over. On planet Earth all was quiet. All was still. All was pure.

On the moon it was a different story. For though there was no atmosphere to set ablaze, there was enough stellar debris caught up in the coronal ejection to smash whole new formations into existence across its scorched surface in the blink of an eye.

Fiery boulders plowed furrows deep into its dusty skin, while on the earth these would-be hammers of destruction simply rebounded.

Within seconds it was clear the earth had survived in the most spectacular way. And it was as the coronal ejection continued to expand and pushed outward past earth that the sunlight reflected back inwards off the inner surface of the ever-increasing fireball and lit up the dark side of the planet.

For several seconds the blue-green glassy marble hung there in a section of space that knew no stars, and no night.

An oasis of calm in a sea of fury, it turned on its axis and weathered the storm. While its moon, too, was lit up from all angles, a prospect which would have excited the scientists below if they were in a position to do anything about it. Because for the first time in 12,000 years the dark side of the moon was completely illuminated and revealed itself for all to see. But since all spaceborne scientific instrumentation had been destroyed, ironically its features would remain a mystery. A pity, since they would have raised some eyebrows.

And then, as long as it had taken to reach this point, it was over.

After 12,000 years of build-up, the sun settled back down to its natural rhythmical cycle and began the process all over again.

On planet Earth, however, the story did not end there. For the Atlantis Network had one more job to perform and it must do it quickly, before the energy that had been unleashed across the planet to protect it, ended by doing as much harm as it had been intended to prevent.

PHASE III

EXPULSION

All across the earth, hidden Carbon 60 tunnels and structures, resonant to specific frequencies of energy, began kicking into action like magnets and drawing in the residual energy left over from the quasicrystallization process.

Slowly, the seas began to froth and the rivers to flow once more. The air began to move and creatures within the biosphere that was planet Earth were able to move freely again. But it was by no means a return to normality – merely an accommodation for the next stage of the process. A process which began in Atlantis.

The shimmering vortex-like wall of water that had reared up from the outer canal and swept around encapsulating the entire inner city in a shimmering cycloid suddenly lost cohesion and collapsed back down into the canal in a massive explosion of water. Buildings within Atlantis which had remained dark up until now, suddenly lit up and crackled with new energy. Energy which seemed to be drawn from the very ground itself and frazzled through the Atlantis system until it shot up the seven incredible towers and arced down onto the central pyramid.

The pyramid sparked and hissed as the mass of fiery power seethed and convulsed across its surface. Like so many snakes that had been set ablaze it shuddered until its final act was for the power to merge and become one vast energy column which, like the plasma twister that had come before it, was sent blasting back up into space. Blasted, through the very hole in which the initial twister had arrived.

Meanwhile, around the periphery of the city, any energy that could not be expelled this way was rerouted and sent down into tunnels that connected back into the very network which had been used to quasicrystallize the planet.

Across the earth, incredible lightning-fast tubes of energy started to criss-cross at seemingly random points. The waters had parted and created gigantic hollows through which these ferocious tongues of fire were traveling.

Soon the entire globe appeared as if it had been wrapped up in some gigantic blazing ribbon. For this was the invisible network that had once carried nothing but sound waves; and was now laid bare, serving as a conduit for pure undiluted power. This was the Atlantis Network performing its final task.

Off the coast of Yonaguni, a small Japanese island, a huge under-water monument constructed in around 10,000BC when the ocean levels were much lower, suddenly lit up. Its six-story-high, great pyramid-length body began to shudder. The enormous channels cut into its stonework in perfectly straight lines, that needed laser sights to accomplish their construction, began to fill with the energy, channel it and store it. While above the monument a vortex in the water began to rotate and open up until air touched the monument for the first time in millennia.

Within micro-seconds, the energy crackling across the surface of the monument coalesced and became one almighty thunderous pillar of fire that shot up into the sky.

Following the principle that the amount of energy pumped into the earth's system to perform quasicrystallization needed to be conducted away again lest the earth be destroyed – so the second of close to a thousand great energy release valves swung gloriously into operation. The principle was as ancient as the earth itself, for it was a little-known fact that lightning, far from being a strike sent down from the heavens, actually began life on the ground. Lightning journeyed *up*.

The sight was awe-inspiring and faultless in its execution.

It was a different story elsewhere.

*   *   *

In Mexico stood one of the world's tallest active volcanoes. El Popo, or Popocatépetl, was 17,802 feet high and expelled hot gases, rocks and ash which regularly mixed with rain and glacial melt water to form lethal mudflows. The Nahuatl name for this volcano was *zencapopocz* – 'always smoking'. And throughout the solar crisis El Popo had more than lived up to its name.

Which left the priests at the Catholic church at the foot of this volcano in somewhat of a dilemma, for their church was built on top of a pre-Hispanic pyramid which sat next to it. Little was known about Tlachihualtépetl, or 'manmade mountain', except that right now it was one of the best places to be to avoid dying in a mudflow. So the villagers had raced up for shelter, but there was little room for them. And fearing for their own safety in all the panic preceding the quasicrystallization process, the priests had only allowed inside its walls the Mayor, the bankers and the movers and shakers of the surrounding region.

They were all dead inside ten seconds.

However, the villagers camped outside the church for their own safety, and who were still caught in this peculiar stasis effect, were suddenly released from its hold as reality sped back up to real time. At which point the ground continued to shake once more. Electricity filled the air, making their hair stand on end.

And the Catholic church exploded.

A pillar of livid flame shot out the top of Tlachihualtépetl, obliterating the building that stood in its path.

The villagers dived for cover, for they had had, as it turned out, the luckiest of escapes.

All across South and Central America, where Catholic churches had been built atop monuments of the past, the buildings were either torched or vaporized as release valve after release valve expelled excess energy off up into space.

The eight pyramids of Pini Pini shot columns of energy out from the rainforest, as did the submerged structures of Bimini. The Pyramid of the Moon too, along with The Pyramid of the Sun and The Pyramid of the Feathered Serpent also launched three incredible blasts of raw power up into space. The three pyramids of the ancient site of Teotihuacan in Central Mexico were significant too because when seen from the air they were laid out in the shape of the belt in the constellation of Orion, matching exactly the same building placement as the three great pyramids of Giza, in Egypt, which also blew out streaks of energy off up into space.

In Orlando, Florida, where a Wal-Mart had been inadvertently built over an ancient Native American burial mound, the entire home fixtures and furnishings section was suddenly obliterated as it found it was sitting atop an ancient release valve. The column of energy that was unleashed was so powerful it sent many of those fixtures hurtling up into the air with it. Reports came in for weeks afterwards of toilet cisterns being found in fields as far away as Gainesville.

Across Europe, Saxon burial mounds were suddenly rolling with energy and expelling pillars of flame. In the county of Kent, in southern England, Kits Coty, an ancient site on the side of a chalk cliff, obscured by trees and a freeway, suddenly exploded into activity, causing half the cliff to break away as it spewed out its fiery tongue.

Release valves exploded into action at the Arctic, across the Pacific at Angkor Wat, across Africa and the Middle East. Columns of fire were seen shooting into the sky in India, Pakistan, and across the ancient sites of China.

For several minutes around the globe, vast fiery tongues of energy were blasted into space as the quasicrystallization process dissipated and then, as suddenly as it had started, the whole process stopped.

The ancient monuments fell silent.

There was no more.

The earth was safe.

The rest of the solar system would have to take care of itself.

CODA

Internal analysis of glyph sequences will reveal patterns of glyph distribution and thereby structure, from which the nature of the language can be discerned. In doing this one learns the thought processes and logic of the society and people from whence the language came. The inevitable consequence is that all matters in a people's history will fall neatly into place.

Richard Scott,
Linguistic Anthropologist and Epigraphist,
1970–2012

AFTERMATH

Gant sucked in a huge lungfull of particulate air as Maple's hand, which was clamped around his throat, suddenly turned to dust along with the rest of his automaton body.

Moments later a whole wave of decay swept through the entire area as every single nanoswarm effigy was reduced to so much sand.

The light which had so characterized Atlantis, suddenly shimmered and went out, leaving them in darkness. They glanced up at the pyramid above them, now lifeless, like the rest of the city. Its twinkling life-force gone, its stellar life-blood all dried up.

Atlantis had returned to its slumber.

November looked around. With the only illumination coming from the dying red embers of a retreating, calming volcano it was difficult to make out where to go, so she turned her flashlight on. It cut through the dust that clung in the air, like a beacon from a car headlight on a foggy night before suddenly dipping and fizzling out. She smacked it a couple of times as the iceberg they were all perched on bobbed lazily in the water, but the device refused to work.

She resorted to shouting: 'Bob!' Indeed, they each called out his name one at a time, but were only met with silence.

Soon they emerged out from under the pyramid and watched as some of those spectacular cathedral-sized stalactites broke off into the water and bobbed up and down after splashing down. Some rolled onto their sides like logs, while others remained flat side up.

And as the iceberg floated up the slope of the pyramid as the water level rose steadily, they all realized that unless they found Pearce soon, he would surely die. For the cavern walls were narrowing. The breathable air pocket was reducing. Soon, there would be nowhere else for all the ice and water to go except back up the massive hole through which the plasma twister from space, not long dissipated, had come down in the first place.

'Bob!' November yelled, refusing to give up. She sat on the edge and looked down at the pyramid below as slowly, very slowly, its slanted features slipped under icy waters once again.

And it was once the pinnacle of the pyramid was completely submerged that November noticed the faint sparkle under the water. It started off as a slight shimmer which she thought might be an optical illusion or her eyes playing tricks.

But her eyes were not playing tricks.

Faint traces of crackling energy sparked around the pyramid before growing in intensity and finally coalescing into some kind of will-o'-the-wisp. It was a face, she realized, peering up at her from the confines of the pyramid. November shifted excitedly, rocking the iceberg.

'Easy!' Gant cautioned.

'Look!' November exclaimed. 'It's Dr Scott!'

And sure enough, down in the dark, murky depths of the waters below there had appeared a face, pale and blue and ghostly, like the souls of the Var. Richard Scott had indeed appeared as if to bid them farewell. Sarah came up beside him, followed by another face. Then another. Thousands of faces. Millions. Each one a twinkle, a sparkle in a cascade until suddenly, seconds later, the entire city lit up one last time far, far beneath them, like a massive floodlight.

And it was only because the city did this that they were all suddenly able to spot Bob Pearce, unconscious and floating up toward them.

'Quick, quick! Give him air!' November shouted once they had dragged the slippery CIA agent up onto the ice platform.

But Gant did more than that. He cleared Pearce's airway first, before checking for a pulse and massaging his heart and giving him mouth to mouth.

A steady stream of water and bile sprang up out of Pearce's mouth like a whale's blowhole when it was surfacing. He convulsed in chokes as he rolled onto his side and spewed some more while gasping for air.

'Let me guess,' Hackett deadpanned. 'You almost preferred getting shot.'

Pearce said in between retches, 'Where am I?'

'On an iceberg,' the Major explained.

'In trouble,' Matheson added hastily.

'So what's new?' Pearce grumbled as he tried to sit up. But the problem was obvious. There was no room for all the ice.

The icebergs were bunching together. Compacting. Vying for the best position as they jostled around the ceiling of the ice cavern. About twenty or thirty feet away, the best candidate for being pushed up the shaft to the surface was already being squeezed up and out of the water. Its flat top surface was already clear by a couple of feet and rising sharply.

'We better leapfrog over there,' Gant commanded.

They set to, jumping from iceberg to iceberg, the buoyant if unstable surfaces wobbling underfoot as they went. One by one they clambered up onto the steadily rising platform. But by the time it was Hackett's turn the iceberg had reared so far up out of the water, the top was up near his chin.

He had to jump. He scrambled to get on board but the sharp movement merely helped force the ice he was standing on, down, deeper into the water.

It was like trying to clamber onto an elevator that was stuck in its shaft with the doors open as the iceberg, crushed together with many others, started sliding up into the ice shaft leading to the surface.

The others rushed to help him, thrusting out their hands. 'C'mon! Just grab a hold, we'll pull you up!' But it was easier said than done. Hackett's feet kept slipping on the frictionless ice as he panicked in his attempt to get up.

The ice lurched as the water pressure below started to build.

'C'mon!'

Hackett jumped again, desperate. Grabbed on, and this time he was pulled to safety. But his legs were still out over the side as the ice once again shuddered under the onslaught of building water pressure.

He snatched them in quickly as the iceberg lurched violently and sped up the inside of the ice shaft.

About a mile and a half above them was daylight, while all around them, the constantly compacting, constantly evolving ice shelf groaned with the strain as the pressure built below.

They all moved to the center of the ice on instinct as the sides began to scream in that deathly awful screech that only massive amounts of ice can make when rubbed together. Their berg lurched again, the sides of the shaft crumbling as the compacted ice mass shot up the hole a further ten feet.

There followed another lurch. Then another. It was like being inside an elevator that was dangling from its fraying cable, but in reverse, for there was no fear of falling here, only rising. Like ants stuck on the end of a champagne cork, it was only a matter of waiting until it went—

Pop!

All five of them were knocked to the ground as the G-forces kicked in. *Bang!* Gant twisted his head to see a vast boulder of ice explode on impact as it landed next to him. He faced the shaft and looked up, only to realize that the way ahead was as crumbling and unstable as the cavern had been.

Bang! Another solid mass of ice impacted next to him. And there were many more on the way. As each projectile made contact, every second felt like a minute. Every minute felt like an hour as they rocketed toward the top until—

The ice platform jerked to a halt.

The ice had wedged again, only a few feet from the surface.

They all stared up at the powder-blue sky and caught their breath. Laid out on their backs they knew they should move but were simply too petrified to do so.

But as they lay there, a series of faces began to peer in all around the rim of the ice shaft.

Soldiers.

On instinct, every surviving member of the Antarctic Team raised their hands in submission, but were surprised to find the soldiers tossing down ropes.

Gant was cautious. 'Are you American?' he asked.

'And Chinese,' came the reply. 'I'd hurry if I were you. I think that thing you're on is gonna blow.'

They didn't need telling twice. But as they got to their feet and the ice plug lurched again, Hackett realized the motion had changed.

The ice had started falling back down the shaft.

'I think a vacuum's built up underneath. This thing's gonna follow the tide.' There were questioning looks. 'Forget it,' he said. 'We just need to get out of here.'

The ice lurched again, falling a couple of feet.

'I see your point,' Gant snapped, grabbing one of the ropes and starting his ascent.

They all followed suit, all started climbing, and just in time, for behind them the compacted ice plug began steadily slipping away until it fell back into the shaft at least a hundred feet.

There was a whistling noise, just like the sound of an incoming shell as the Antarctic Team gathered their wits about them on the surface.

'Look out!' came the warning cry. 'Here comes another one!'

Everyone dived for cover as a charred-looking Tomahawk cruise missile fell out of the sky and crashed across the ice, fortunately failing to explode.

'What the hell's going on around here?' Gant demanded as he got to his feet. He was referring to the fact that the Chinese and American forces were, for the most part, standing around and chatting.

'Some kind of electromagnetic pulse shorted out most electronic equipment in a fifty-mile radius,' the young Lieutenant explained. 'We got all sorts of stuff falling from the sky. Got just one working radio. We sure as hell can't fight a war . . . sir.'

There were units of army men all over the massive crater that had been *Jung Chang* before the ground beneath it imploded. And as they all surveyed their situation, another young soldier rushed over to them brandishing that only working radio.

'You gotta Professor Scott in your party?'

The team eyed each other, subdued. 'He couldn't make it,' Hackett offered.

'Pity. Admiral Dower wanted to congratulate him personally.'

The team remained tight-lipped and headed for the nearest transport vehicle. Behind them they left a horde of soldiers as confused and astounded by recent events as they were, and who were watching the ice shaft in anticipation as the ground shook all around them.

'It's gonna blow!' came the cries.

And they were right.

EASTER SUNDAY

There were going to be plagues.

Of locusts, flies, mosquitoes – and of diseases. There were going to be all manner of plagues.

It was an inevitable consequence of the scarring across planet Earth. Of the devastation wrought by severe volcanic activity in so many areas that entire stretches of lush farmland the size of small countries had been decimated. Food supplies had dwindled and as a result insect populations were predisposed to band together and swarm. In the past they had been known to attack even sleeping babies in their cribs when volcanoes had caused merely minor damage, just to control the food supply. There was every reason to believe the situation would be on a much larger scale in this instance.

On a much more Biblical scale.

And no machine the size of Atlantis could stop that.

Everyone aboard the Seahawk helicopter knew that it was going to take time for mankind to regroup and rebuild.

It was a peculiar sight to see the massed armies of two such bitterly opposing nations simply pack and go home. But there they were – American and Chinese soldiers, engaged in helping each other stow their belongings. It was a far cry from the time when they were prepared to unleash such a formidable arsenal against each other

that any damage the sun might have caused would have been inconsequential by comparison.

The earth was experiencing a period of change.

Hackett watched all this and checked his watch. Habit, he guessed,
by now. It was a real rugged out-of-doors type of affair with a compass
on it which he rarely used. There was little chance of getting lost
on the way to the bar, after all.

But something about the way the needle was pointing made him
smile.

The engineers on board the chopper had been complaining about
navigational and technical errors on all electronic equipment in the
fleet. They'd put it down to the final electromagnetic pulse blasted
out by Atlantis – something akin to the detonation of a nuclear
warhead. But Hackett knew different, probably because he was the
only one who had thought to look.

The physicist looked out the window and in his best formal imper-
sonation of Scott, said: 'Galaxy, from the Greek "galaxos" meaning
milk. The Milky Way . . .'

Pearce pulled the thick blue blanket tight around his shoulders
as he nursed a hot chocolate, looked over at Matheson and November
and knew they had cocked their ears to listen.

'I read about this guy,' Hackett said, 'William Tifft. Worked out
of the University of Arizona until a couple years ago. For over a
quarter of a century he studied the red-shift of galaxies. Y'know what
red-shift is, right?'

'No clue,' Matheson yawned.

'If a bright object is moving away from us,' the physicist explained,
'it will appear to be a little more red-colored. If it's coming toward
us it will turn a little more blue-colored. Blue-shift and red-shift. Tifft
was studying the red-shift of stars and galaxies. And because of the
Big Bang, the degree to which an object is red-shifting, in other words
how fast those objects are moving away from us, should be random.'

'Here comes the but,' November sighed.

'But they're not,' Hackett confirmed, unperturbed. 'Tifft discovered that, depending on the type of galaxy, you got a different kind
of red-shift reading even if it was in the same part of the sky. Spiral
galaxies seemed to have a higher red-shift than elliptical galaxies.
And the increase seemed to go up in quantum-leaps. Specifically,

forty-five miles per second. Galactic red-shifts are quantized like the energy states in an atom.'

Gant rubbed his face and ripped his hat off his head from where he'd been trying to get some sleep. 'So what?' he barked. 'Who gives a shit?'

Hackett seemed genuinely hurt. '*I* give a shit. Do you know what that kind of information means? It means the universe *isn't* expanding. So it means there was no Big Bang. It means the entire wealth of twentieth-century cosmology can be tossed in the trash. If it ain't random, then it weren't a bang. There's order in the chaos. Complex, but it's there. And if there was no Big Bang, where did this whole universe thing come from? You gonna tell me, from God? There is no God, I thought we just proved that. It was a myth created to save all our asses.'

'What the hell has that got to do with anything?' Matheson wanted to know. 'What's the point?'

'There is no point,' Hackett sighed. 'Not in the kind of sense you mean. It's just, all I'm trying to say is . . . maybe we all need to get used to the idea that there are going to be a few changes around here from now on. Everything we've taken for granted our whole lives will be different now. It always was different – we just couldn't see it. But now we have proof. . .'

He sat up. Eyed his friends in the 'copter. Tapped the watch on his wrist. 'This thing is a compass too,' he said. 'And right now it's pointing due north.'

'So?'

'So . . . ? It's pointing due north – *back in the direction we just came from*. North is now at the South Pole.'

The others were surprised, and about all they could manage was a smile.

'Sarah said the Poles shifted every now and then – completely swapped over. The last time was in 10,400BC – about twelve thousand years ago. It's a geological fact,' November added.

'Sarah said a lot of things,' Matheson said. 'She was like that.'

Pearce held up his solitary cup of hot chocolate in a toast. 'To Richard and Sarah,' he said.

Exhausted, what remained of the team quietly went back to looking out the window.

It was Easter Sunday, Hackett realized. The ancient festival dating from way back before the time of Christ, symbolizing death, sacrifice and renewal.

Might be nice to try and get an egg, he thought.

It had taken them the best part of a day to reach McMurdo again. And several hours to refuel the Seahawk.

As they flew low over McMurdo, off toward the waiting aircraft-carrier *Truman*, a little red speck, the ice-breaker *Polar Star* had just arrived in the bay.

She was late. If they had stayed aboard her there was no doubting they would never have made it. But despite that, in an effort that mirrored the human spirit, unstoppable in the face of insurmountable odds, it was still a comfort to see her majestic bright red bow ride up on the pack ice and crush down on it – forging a new path ahead.

It has come from its beginning to its end,
like that which was found in the writing.

Ancient Egyptian Wisdom Literature.

BIBLIOGRAPHY

Aldersey-Williams, Hugh, *The Most Beautiful Molecule: An Adventure In Chemistry*, Aurum Press, London, 1995

Allan, D.B. and J.B. Delair, *Cataclysm! Compelling Evidence of a Cosmic Catastrophe In 9500BC*, Bear and Company, Santa Fe, 1995

Allen, J.M., *Atlantis: The Andes Solution*, The Windrush Press, Gloucestershire, 1998

Alley, Richard B. and Michael L. Bender, 'Greenland Ice Cores: Frozen in Time', *Scientific American*, Vol. 278, No. 2, February, 1998

Atkins, Peter, *The Periodic Kingdom: A Journey into the Land of the Chemical Elements*, Weidenfeld & Nicolson, 1995

Atzner, Kenneth, *The Languages of the World*, Routledge, London, 1995

Baigent, Michael and Richard Leigh, *The Dead Sea Scrolls Deception*, Corgi, London, 1992

Bartusiak, Marcia, 'Gravity Wave Sky', *Discover*, Vol. 14, No. 7, July, 1993

Bauval, Robert and Adrian Gilbert, *The Orion Mystery*, Heinemann, London, 1994

Bauval, Robert and Graham Hancock, *Keepers of Genesis: A Quest for the Hidden Legacy of Mankind*, Heinemann, London, 1996

Berlitz, Charles, *Atlantis: The Eighth Continent*, Fawcett-Crest, New York, 1984

Betro, Maria Carmela, *Hieroglyphics: The Writings of Ancient Egypt*, Abbeville Press, New York, 1996

Brown, Stuart and George Gruner, 'Charge and Spin Density Waves', *Scientific American*, Vol. 270, No. 4, April, 1994

Bruner, Paul and Moshe Shapiro, 'Laser Control of Chemical Reactions', *Scientific American*, Vol. 272, No. 3, March, 1995

Carsten, Peter, 'Into the Heart of Glaciers', *National Geographic*, Vol. 189, No. 2, February, 1996

Cheney, Margaret, *Tesla: Man Out Of Time*, Bantam Books, New York, 1981

Clayton, Peter A., *Chronicle of the Pharaohs*, Thames & Hudson, 1995

Clendinnen, Inca, *Aztecs: An Interpretation*, Cambridge University Press, Cambridge, 1995

Cremo, Michael A. and Richard L. Thompson, *Forbidden Archeology: The Hidden History of the Human Race*, Bhaktivedanta Institute Press, Los Angeles, 1996

Cooper, George A., 'Directional Drilling,' *Scientific American*, Vol. 270, No. 5, May, 1994

Coterell, Maurice M., *The Supergods*, Thorsons, London, 1997

Curl, Robert F. and Richard E. Smalley, 'Fullerenes', *Scientific American*, Vol. 265, No. 4, October, 1991

Diamond, Jared, 'Writing Right', *Discover*, Vol. 15, No. 6, June, 1994

Diaz, Bernal, *The Conquest of New Spain*, Penguin, London, 1963

Ditto, William L. and Louis M. Pecora, 'Mastering Chaos', *Scientific American*, Vol. 269, No. 2, August, 1993

Drosnin, Michael, *The Bible Code*, Simon & Schuster, New York, 1997

Eco, Umberto, *The Search For a Perfect Language*, Fontana Press, London, 1997

Eiseman, Robert E. and Michael Wise, *The Dead Sea Scrolls Uncovered*, Penguin, London, 1993

Faulkner, R.O., *The Ancient Egyptian Book of the Dead*, British Museum Press, 1996

Fischer, Steven Roger, *Glyph-Breaker*, Copernicus, New York, 1997

Flanagan, Ruth and Tom Yulsman, 'On Thin Ice', *Earth*, Vol. 5, No. 2, April, 1996

Flem-Ath, Rand and Rose Flem-Ath, *When The Sky Fell*, Weidenfeld & Nicolson, London, 1995

Folger, Tim, 'Waves of Destruction', *Discover*, Vol. 15, No. 5, May, 1994

Gilbert, Adrian, *The Magi: The Quest For a Secret Tradition*, Bloomsbury, London, 1996

Gilbert, Adrian, and Maurice M. Coterell, *The Mayan Prophecies*, Element, Dorset, 1995

Goodman, Jeffrey, *The Earthquake Generation*, Turnstone Books, London, 1979

Green II, Harry W., 'Solving the Paradox of Deep Earthquakes', *Scientific American*, Vol. 271, No. 3, September, 1994

Greenbery, Joseph H. and Merritt Ruhlen, 'Linguistic Origins of Native Americans', *Scientific American*, Vol. 267, No. 5, November, 1992

Hancock, Graham, *Fingerprints of the Gods*, Heinemann, London, 1995

Hawking, Stephen W., *A Brief History of Time*, Guild, London, 1990

Hawking, Stephen W., *Black Holes and Baby Universes*, Bantam Books, New York, 1994

Herning, Thomas A., 'The Global Positioning System', *Scientific American*, Vol. 274, No. 2, February, 1996

Heyerdahl, Thor, Daniel, H. Sandweiss and Alfredo Narvaez, *Pyramids of Tucume: The Quest For Peru's Forgotten City*, Thames & Hudson, 1995

Honan, Mark, *Switzerland: A Travel Survival Kit*, Lonely Planet, London, 1994

Hope, Murray, *The Sirius Connection*, Element, Dorset, 1996

Horgan, John (Senior Writer), 'From Complexity to Perplexity', *Scientific American*, Vol. 272, No. 6, June, 1995

Horgan, John, 'Particle Metaphysics', *Scientific American*, Vol. 270, No. 2, February, 1994

Johanson, Donald and Blake Edgar, *From Lucy To Language*, Weidenfeld & Nicolson, London, 1996

Kakauer, Jon, 'Queen Maud Land', *National Geographic*, Vol. 193, No. 2, February, 1998

Kaster, Joseph, *The Wisdom of Ancient Egypt*, Michael O'Mara Books, London, 1968

Kovacs, Maureen Gallery (Translator), *The Epic of Gilgamesh*, Stanford University Press, Stanford, 1989

Lang, Kenneth R., 'SOHO Reveals the Secrets of the Sun', *Scientific American*, Vol. 276, No. 3, March, 1997

Lee, Desmond (Translator), *Plato: Timaeus and Critias*, Penguin, London, 1977

Lemesurier, Peter, *The Great Pyramid Decoded*, Element, Dorset, 1997

Lloyd, Seth, 'Quantum-Mechanical Computers', *Scientific American*, Vol. 273, No. 4, October, 1995

Mack, Burton L., *The Lost Gospel: The Book of Q and Christian Origins*, Element, Dorset, 1993

Matheson, Ralph K., *Ecological Controls in Oil Production*, USC Press, San Francisco, 2009

Nesme-Ribes, Elizabeth, Sallie L. Baliunas and Dimitry Sokolott, 'The Stellar Dinamo', *Scientific American*, Vol. 275, No. 2, August, 1996

Nicolis, Grégoire and Ilya Prigogine, *Exploring Complexity: An Introduction*, W. H. Freeman & Company, New York, 1989

Phillips, Graham, *Act of God*, Pan, London, 1998

Prescott, William H., *The World of the Incas*, Tudor Publishing, New York, 1974

Renfrew, Colin, 'World Linguistic Diversity', *Scientific American*, Vol. 270, No. 1, January, 1994

Richmond, Simon, 'The Lost World', *Geographical: The Royal Geographical Society Magazine*, Vol. LXX No. 8, August, 1998

Rohl, David, *A Test of Time: Pharaohs and Kings*, Random House, London, 1995

Rohl, David, *Legend: The Genesis of Civilization*, Century, 1998

Ruthen, Russel, 'Catching the Wave', *Scientific American*, Vol. 266, No. 3, March, 1992

Sanders, N. K. (Translator), *The Epic of Gilgamesh*, Penguin, London, 1972

Sattin, Anthony and Sylvie Franquet, *Explorer: Egypt*, AA Publishing, London, 1996

Schreider, David, 'The Rising Seas', *Scientific American*, Vol. 276, No. 3, March, 1997

Scott, Richard, *Tales of the Deluge: A Global Report on Cultural Self-Replicating Genesis Myths*, University of Washington, Press, Seattle, 2008

Senner, Wayne M. (Editor), *The Origins of Writing*, University of Nebraska Press, London, 1989

Shaw, Ian and Paul Nicholson, *British Museum Dictionary of Ancient Egypt*, British Museum Press, London, 1995

Silberman, Neil Asher, *The Hidden Scrolls*, Heinemann, London, 1994

Spence, Lewis, *Mexico and Peru: Myths and Legends*, Senate, London, 1994

Steger, Will and Jon Bowermaster, *Crossing Antarctica*, Bantam Press, New York, 1992

Stephens, Peter W. and Alan I. Goldman, 'The Structure of Quasicrystals', *Scientific American*, Vol. 264, No. 4, April, 1991

Stevens, Jane Elfen, 'Exploring Antarctic Ice', *National Geographic*, Vol. 189, No. 5, May, 1996

Stewart, Ian, 'Does Chaos Rule the Cosmos?', *Discover*, Vol. 113 No. 11, November, 1992

Stewart, Ian, *Nature's Numbers: Discovering Order and Pattern in the Universe*, Weidenfeld & Nicolson, London, 1995

Stone, Gene and Stephen Hawking, *Stephen Hawking's A Brief History of Time: A Reader's Companion*, Bantam Press, London, 1992

Stroyatz, Steven H. and Ian Stewart, 'Coupled Oscillators and Biological Synchronization', *Scientific American*, Vol. 269, No. 6, December, 1993

Thiering, Barbara, *Jesus The Man*, Corgi, London, 1993

Waldrop, Mitchell M., *Complexity: The Emerging Science At The Edge Of Order And Chaos*, Simon Schuster, New York, 1992

Wansborough, Henry (Editor), *The New Jerusalem Bible, Standard Edition*, Darton, Longman & Todd, London, 1985

Wellard, James, *By the Waters of Babylon*, Hutchinson, London, 1973

Willis, Roy (Editor), *World Mythologies*, Duncan Baird, London, 1996

Wilson, A. N., *Jesus*, Flaminco, London, 1993

Wilson, Colin, *From Atlantis To The Sphinx*, Virgin, London, 1996

AUTHOR'S NOTE

This book required a lot of research, and as a result I have a number of people to thank. I present here a list of names in no particular order and thank them for all the help they afforded me. It is very much appreciated.

Needless to say, any mistakes are purely my own.

The U.S Geological Survey, the crew of the *Polar Star*, the United States Coast Guard and the United States Navy. Such is the way of things in the 21st Century I never actually met a single one of you, but a bombardment of e-mails from myself were all answered without exception and I am truly grateful for all your efforts. Rochester and Chatham Public libraries – with special thanks to Chris Davis in particular. Eric Aitala Phd, the real Dr. Jon Hackett and the only man I know to state at the bottom of his webpage – *This site was made entirely from re-cycled electrons.* Angela Wheelan, Gary Payne, James and David Hooper, Jeff and Gene Colburn. Martine Brewster for taking the trouble to interrupt a business trip to do some research for me at the United Nations in Geneva and CERN. Alexandra Franke – my very own archaeology chick. Rowland Wells, James Sprules, Rachel Phillips, John 'Cheesey' Cheeseman, Ziad Munson, 'Handy' Andy Hayes and Marsha Levin for her help on Jewish Folklore. Thanks also to Linda Seifert, Ed Hughes, Jeff Graup and Alex Goldstone, Sophie Hicks, John Jarrold, my editor, Ian Chapman, for taking a chance, and all the fine folks at Simon and Schuster UK.

Special thanks go obviously to my family. Mum, Maureen, my brother Louis and my sister Christina. Sadly, just three months before I sold this novel – my first as it happens, my father, Paul passed away and isn't here to see it all happen. It's particularly unfair since he knew the struggle I had had to write it over the preceding 5 years. Some people have asked me why I didn't dedicate the book to him. Well this book was always meant to be dedicated to my daughter, Dad knew this and he would have wanted it to remain that way. And besides, the next book is dedicated to Dad – and the reasons for that will all become clear when that novel arrives.

Thanks again to everyone, oh, and before I forget, special thanks to the guy at my local Chinese Takeaway who helped me with the Cantonese. I hope you weren't swearing at me because it's in the book now . . .